For Sandy, a shooting star . . .

JOSEPH MARKULIN

MACHIAVELLI

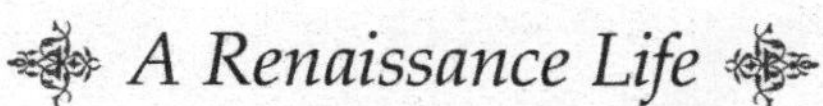

A Renaissance Life

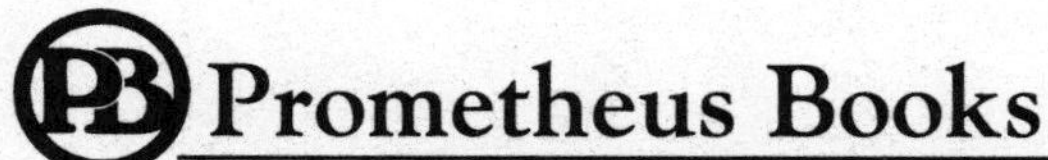

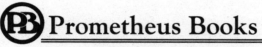

Prometheus Books
59 John Glenn Drive
Amherst, New York 14228–2119

Published 2013 by Prometheus Books

Upper cover image: detail of *Niccolò Machiavelli* or *Portrait of Machiavelli*, by Santi di Tito, oil on canvas dated to the second half of the sixteenth century

Lower cover image: *The Piazza della Signoria in Florence*, by Bernardo Bellotto, ca. 1742, located at Szépmüvészeti Múzeum, Budapest, Hungary

Cover design by Jacqueline Nasso Cooke

Inquiries should be addressed to
Prometheus Books
59 John Glenn Drive
Amherst, New York 14228–2119
VOICE: 716–691–0133
FAX: 716–691–0137
WWW.PROMETHEUSBOOKS.COM

17 16 15 14 13   5 4 3 2 1

Library of Congress Cataloging-in-Publication Data Pending

ISBN 978-1-61614-805-8 (pbk.)
ISBN 978-1-61614-806-5 (ebook)

Printed in the United States of America

CONTENTS

Part 3: The Antichrist and His Extended Family

Part 4: Lessons in Civil Government

PART 5: WHEEL OF FORTUNE

Prologue Ending in an Execution

May 23, 1498

Ercole d'Este was so filled with awe at the sound of his own name that he often choked with emotion when called upon to pronounce it. Not that he was an excessively vain man. Rather, it was an inordinate pride in his ancestry that caused him to treat his name with a respect bordering on veneration.

The Este family had ruled Ferrara for over two centuries, and for the most part, they had ruled it wisely, promoting the general welfare by developing industry and agriculture, building broad roads, and straightening streets. They had supported the fledgling university and had persuaded the eminent Greek scholar Guarino da Verona to come there and lecture. They had built a public park within the narrow confines of the city walls, a thing unheard of at the time. And, of course, most importantly, they had strengthened the city's fortifications.

Ferrara was a small state but a rich one, and like all the other city-states of northern Italy, she was constantly at war. Political turbulence had become a way of life for the dozens of arrogant dukes who were incessantly attacking or being attacked, marching off to battle or waiting out sieges in their impregnable fortresses. Ferrara, by comparison, was at peace more often than many of the others. The Este, through the judicious use of marriage bonds and the skillful weaving of secret alliances, had brought calm and relative stability to the city.

Ercole (Hercules) d'Este managed his affairs well. He had to, for he literally owned the realm, and his prosperity, not to say survival, depended on it. He owned the land and all its bounty; he owned the grain and the vines; he owned the river and the fish in the river; he owned the mines, the mills, and the cattle; and last, he owned the people. He had complete authority to do anything he wished. His power was absolute. He could make laws or dissolve them. He could promote interests friendly to himself and his family, and he could kill his enemies with impunity. He reserved the right to impose taxes, to punish crimes, and to declare war. But as tyrants go, Ercole was one of the less abusive ones, and he retained the love and respect of his subjects.

Attached to the court of the Este family was an illustrious physician by the name of Savonarola. Although originally from Padua, Savonarola had secured his post in Ferrara on the basis of his reputation as a world-famous authority on the curative properties of spas and mineral waters. But more than that, he was a staunch proponent of the beneficial effects of alcohol, which he was always quick to prescribe for any illness. He maintained that it fortified the blood, revived the heart, dissipated superfluous body fluids, prevented fevers, and aided the digestion. If taken in sufficient quantities, it also cured colic, dropsy, paralysis, worms, and scurvy. It calmed toothaches, gave protection against the plague, and drove away wind. In alcohol, the physician Savonarola had found his panacea, and his prescriptions were eagerly received by the Este and their court. His position was secure, and he was much sought out as an eminent man of science. Upon retirement, his duties passed to his son, who faithfully executed, in every detail, the precepts and traditions of the father.

When Girolamo Savonarola was a boy, it was decided that he, too, like his father and his grandfather before him, would study medicine in order to assume his rightful post as third-generation court physician. But the boy was ill-suited to the role. From the way his father talked, young Girolamo had the distinct impression that the court physician had been engaged more as a tavern keeper than as a doctor. Medicine as practiced by the Savonarolas was as much a matter of dispensing cheer and goodwill as anything else.

Unlike his bibulous progenitors, Girolamo was a gloomy, introspective child. Physically, he was small, ugly, and clumsy. He was pale and withdrawn, and he cared little for the company of other children. He preferred to be alone, and the thing that seemed to give him the most pleasure in life was his lute. He would play for hours sad, plaintive melodies that he composed himself. And he would compose verses, too, and set them to music.

Although he showed no particular interest in the study of medicine, he mastered his lessons easily. And, while outwardly he appeared dazed and inattentive, it soon became clear to his teachers that he was possessed of a brilliant mind. Brilliant but restless and nervous. He would dispense with his medical texts and required lessons in short order and then withdraw to the solitude of his room, to his music, to his poetry, and to the one book that brought him solace—the sacred scriptures. He read the prophets avidly—Jeremiah in particular. But the text that he had read and reread perhaps a hundred times and of which he never tired, what sparked his mind and fired his imagination, was the Book of the Apocalypse.

At the age of sixteen, his studies were progressing satisfactorily, and the elder Savonarola decided it was time for his son to be introduced to the court and its pleasures, so that he could begin his practical training for the profitable position that awaited him. The pompous doctor exploded when he saw his son bundled for the august occasion into his usual plain clothes—a simple grey frock with wool stockings.

"You expect to go to court dressed like that! The Duke will laugh at you! They'll mistake you for a lout, for a stable boy! You! A Savonarola! Who would ever believe it?"

He had the boy's mother comb and curl his long black hair. He gave him a velvet cap to wear and insisted that he gird himself with a leather belt from which hung a small, sharp, useless dagger with a jeweled handle. This hastily created courtier, feeling slightly ridiculous, examined himself in the polished tin mirror. He had no choice now but to step out into the cool autumn air, with his new accoutrements, and walk, almost run, through the streets of Ferrara, to keep up with the strides of his energetic father, the great physician swathed in scarlet and silver. Gawky, timid Girolamo Savonarola was on his way to the rich, exciting life that would soon be his.

When they arrived at the ducal palace, the court physician and his young charge were greeted with much merriment, and many cups were raised. Duke Ercole himself, dressed as a soldier, although he seldom ventured forth on any military expedition, welcomed the boy and wished him every success. To say that the young Savonarola was dazzled would be an understatement. Never had he seen such a brightly illuminated hall. In the Savonarolas' modest apartments and in most of the dwellings of Ferrara, evening was a time of soft light, the orange glow of fires and candles. But the Este palace, even at night, was ablaze. The enormous hall was lit by magnificent chandeliers, candles, and lanterns by the thousands, and huge roaring fires to which alum had been added to make them burn a brilliant white. And everywhere the unbelievable shower of light fell, it glanced back, flashing from gold and silver like lightning.

The profusion of silks and furs, lace, leather, and polished armor stupefied the boy. And blonds! He had never seen so many blonds in his life. "Is every woman at the court of Ferrara blond?" he thought. "Is that what separates the nobility from us?" Later he was to learn that these exquisite waves of blond hair were fashioned for the most part, of yellow silk. A few of the billowing coiffures, like that of the duchess, were made of real human hair, brought down from Germany in the north, they say, imported at an extravagant price, or, according to darker rumors, taken in battle.

When the meal was served, the boy's stupor only grew: countless birds and meats that he could not even identify, exotic vegetables that the duke grew on his estates, like the bulbous white eggplant he had had brought from Africa. Others came from the Levant and the Far East, along with spices that overwhelmed the palate.

And what was he to make of this curious pronged instrument set beside this plate? At home they ate with knives, and his mother kept big wooden spoons for soup. But this must be the fork his father had described to them as he grumbled through their evening meals, complaining that all civilized people used a fork and did not spear their meat and toss it at knifepoint into their mouths. Here, fork, knife, and spoon were all of gleaming silver! And the goblets! While Duke Ercole, a profound traditionalist, insisted on taking his wine in a golden cup, not unlike the chalice used by the priests in the cathedral, the other guests were drinking from goblets fashioned of glass, a material so precious and so rare that Girolamo had only heard of it. So exquisite and so fragile.

As the meal turned slowly into a rowdy melee, Girolamo Savonarola drifted unnoticed to a seat against the far wall of the hall, which was now reverberating with the shouts and songs of the drunken court. From this vantage point, he sat in dumbfounded silence and watched the evening unfold without fear of being drawn into its drunken, sinful frenzy.

When the eating was finally over and the tables had been cleared, it was time for entertainment. Every court in Europe has its share of jesters, fools, buffoons, and madmen. Ferrara was no exception. The duke and his family kept a company of assorted dwarves of whom they were exceedingly proud. They even built a special wing onto the palace to house their diminutive entertainers. The dwarves' apartments included a group of tiny, low-ceilinged rooms furnished with miniature beds, tables, and chairs. Small windows placed no more than a foot from the floor opened onto a courtyard where a miniature fountain was surrounded by shrubs and low benches. Whether the Este constructed this tiny world as a convenience for its inhabitants, however, was open to question. Many said it was more of a curiosity—a zoo, really, where the large guests went about bumping their heads comically on the ceilings as they elbowed their way through the narrow corridors. The full-sized visitors would laugh heartily whenever they spotted one of the little inhabitants going about his everyday business. They would gawk and ogle them. Sometimes they made faces.

And so when dinner was finished, nothing was more natural than that the duke summon his troupe of tiny entertainers. The serious, silent boy, sitting apart from the other guests, was staring wide-eyed as twenty little merrymakers literally tumbled into the center of the hall. Never had he imagined that he would see so many dwarves together, all in one place. Few courts kept more than one or two.

They rolled and sweated, turning somersaults, juggling, howling, grunting, and singing in their shrill, unpleasant voices. One crooked gnome danced wildly with a baboon dressed in women's clothing. The cacophony they produced with their toy musical instruments, coupled with the roars of laughter from the court began to mount in intensity. If they tumbled too close to one of the guests in their antics, they were soundly kicked back into the center of the hall. They acted out obscene skits, cackling in their falsetto voices, so that they sounded more like frantic wild animals than humans.

Matello, the leader, was known as the Emperor of Madmen. He appeared in a priest's cassock and began to deliver a sermon to the crowd. At first, he spoke in measured tones, but as he progressed, his harangue reached a hysterical pitch that only caused his congregation to redouble their now-delirious laughter. As he neared the climax of his homily, his voice squeaking up into ever higher and seemingly impossible registers, he invoked the judgment of God, which he proceeded to produce in the form of a huge wooden and papier-mâché phallus that he had concealed beneath his robes. With this unlikely instrument of retribution, which he called the Swift Sword of the Lord, he began to mete out punishments to the band of sinners. He swung his weapon recklessly and energetically and brought it down on the heads of his rollicking flock. In the madness that followed, they pelted him with whatever was at hand—food, plates—until, worn out, the Emperor collapsed and was carried from the hall.

If Matello's comedy brought tears of laughter to the eyes of this sophisticated assembly, there is no way to describe their reaction to Crazy Catherine, the most famous female dwarf in all of Italy. She was an alcoholic, and a bit of a kleptomaniac, hiding the trinkets and treasures she stole in her little room. But Crazy Catherine had one particular talent that made her admirers overlook her defects. In the middle of any show, at any time, she was able to perform her special trick, on command. When one of the Este, or anyone familiar with Catherine's peculiar talent heaved a burning brand onto the floor and shouted, "Water! Catherine!" she would run to the flame, hitch up her long skirts, and, throwing her head back in shameless laughter, proceed to extinguish the blaze with a stream of urine! This trick she could perform a dozen times in one night!

And so the noble company howled ever louder with Catherine scurrying frantically around the hall, putting out fires and farting—that was her other area of expertise—Girolamo Savonarola sat unable to move. Never had he seen such a depraved spectacle. Never had he suspected that the finest and most cultured citizens of his noble city amused themselves in this unseemly manner.

Anyone glancing in the boy's direction would have thought him asleep, overcome by the wine or exhausted by the revels. He was leaning back against the stone wall, head bent forward, with his long dark hair obscuring most of his face. But if someone had managed to look into his eyes, he might have jumped back in terror. For he would have seen burning there a fire that all the water in the river Po might not suffice to extinguish. He would have seen in the green eyes of this skinny, morose boy the holy fire that would one day leap forth to ignite the passions of thousands of sinners.

Later that night, as the young man made his way home through the dark and blissfully quiet streets, he vowed never to return to the court of Ercole d'Este, duke of Ferrara.

If the young Savonarola's first severe disillusionment was the result of his experience at court, the cause of the second was Laodamia Strozzi. Lofty is the word that best describes Laodamia Strozzi. Born of a lofty family, she was tall and statuesque and haughty in her demeanor. Since childhood, she had been imbued with a set of lofty ideas about her origins, her place in the world, and her eventual destiny. Confronted with the spectacle of this irresistible loftiness, the awkward and unattractive Savonarola fell hopelessly in love with Laodamia Strozzi. Despite the revulsion that welled up in him when he thought back on the behavior of Ferrara's enlightened nobility, he had by no means made up his mind to renounce the more discreet pleasures of worldly society, and he was eager to have firsthand experience of the miracles wrought by love. Didn't he know quite a bit about love already? After all, he'd read his Dante and Petrarch. Hadn't he learned from them about the glorious transformations love was capable of effecting, and about how love, in its purity, inspired in men and women alike true nobility of the soul?

What's more, from these two masters, and from many more that he had perused, he learned about the manner in which love takes root and grows. It always starts with a chance encounter, a furtive glance. And wasn't that what had happened when he first saw his chaste Laodamia on the steps of the cathedral in the company of her father? Hadn't she, just like Dante's Beatrice and Petrarch's Laura before her, gazed into his eyes for a brief second? And hadn't that look, fleeting as it was, penetrated to the very bottom of his soul? There was certainly no denying that, by all the standards set by all the great poets of Italy, the lofty Laodamia Strozzi had fallen deeply in love with Girolamo Savonarola. He was convinced of it.

Unfortunately, Laodamia was illiterate and somewhat crude in her tastes, and was therefore unacquainted with the high ideals put forth by Savonarola's poets. So when he began to press his suit in the prescribed manner—admiring his lady from afar and sending her reams of poetry he had written on the uplifting effects of love—she was singularly unmoved. Of course, when she failed to respond to his entreaties in any way whatsoever, he was ecstatic. Everything was going according to plan! Her silence, according to the well-documented procedures he was following, was proof of her love for him. What is more, it was a sign of her unassailable chastity.

When Savonarola judged that the courtship had proceeded to the point where neither of them could contain their passions any longer, he wrote to the girl's father, Roberto Strozzi, with a proposal of marriage. Shortly thereafter, he received a summons to appear before the formidable Strozzi. Obviously, they would begin working out the mundane details of the marriage contract, including the dowry, the wedding date, and the many provisions regarding inheritance of property, titles, and the like. But Girolamo Savonarola was not greedy—he and Laodamia were marrying for love, because of an intense, spiritual bond that had already yoked them together for life, and beyond! He was sure that these practical negotiations would present no obstacle to their union. And furthermore, he knew that, since the Strozzi had been driven ignominiously out of Florence and were exiles in Ferrara, living in poverty, they would certainly have no cause to complain about a match with the son of an eminent man of science. He fully expected to be welcomed into the family.

But what awaited the eager young suitor when he arrived at the palazzo where the Strozzi were temporarily housed was not what he expected. Roberto Strozzi strode pompously up and down as he delivered a vitriolic harangue. Behind him, the lofty Laodamia looked down upon her would-be suitor with undisguised contempt as her father poured abuse on the head of "this pretender, this fool." Shaking his huge face, flushed with anger as much as with cheap wine, the blustering Strozzi enumerated the glories of the Strozzi family. In short order, he declared that his daughter was far too valuable a prize to be wasted on the sniveling son of a physician, and that in fact she had already been promised in marriage to a certain young man, a cousin of the powerful Medici family of Florence. As soon as the wedding ceremony could be arranged, Roberto Strozzi and his splendid family would be returning to Florence to reclaim what was rightfully theirs.

"And to think that this boy," he boomed, "this pigeon-chested, beetle-browed, hawk-nosed cockroach of a boy, this pitiful, untitled, sniveling boy, to think that such a common boy, could aspire to the hand of my Laodamia!" His rage boiled over. His red face turned purple, then almost black. "I am Roberto Strozzi!" He rolled his *r*'s in his rage. He rolled his *z*'s. What followed was an unimaginative catalogue of the usual threats and abuses involving beatings, whippings, dismemberment, the putting out of little swinish eyes, unmanning, the slitting of throats. The collusion of various animals was invoked—dogs, wild horses, buzzards. In the end, what was left of the offender was destined to be dumped unceremoniously into the river Po.

Shaken, Girolamo could find no words to reply. An infinite abyss seemed to open up before him, and he would have stayed rooted to that spot probably forever if the overbearing Strozzi had not commanded his men to throw the limp body out into the street. The scorned suitor was too dazed to hear the suggestion from his beloved that they put the dogs on him to hasten his retreat and provide some amusement.

This rejection in love, so violent and so unexpected, caused young Girolamo to sink deep into despondency. His agony was inexpressible, his despair without end. He spent ever-longer periods of time alone now, contemplating the wickedness and cruelty of the world. Even as a youth, he was already leading the life of rigid austerity that he would observe all his days. His clothes, always plain, were now shabby and patched in places. He ate little, never touched the strong liquors that were so prized by his father and grandfather, and slept on a straw mattress laid on a wooden board. But he did not sleep well, so tormented was he by the pains of love and troubled by the feelings of utter helplessness and uncertainty that overwhelmed him.

One night when he was twenty-two years old, he finally knew what he had to do. It came to him in the first of many, many dreams that Girolamo Savonarola was to have in the course of his tortured life.

In his sleep, he was all afire. His body thrashed as it burned, and the pain was excruciating. Devils taunted him. Suddenly, the sky cracked open, and a torrent of freezing water spilled down upon his head. When he awoke, he felt a tremendous sense of calm, as though the fires of lust that had raged in his body for months, tormenting him day and night, had suddenly been extinguished. Savonarola knew then that he would never marry, that he would never again desire a woman or any other pleasure of the flesh. And so, without telling anyone, on the feast day of St. Joseph in 1475, he rose at dawn and left his father's house. He traveled on foot to Bologna, a day's journey, and there sought admittance to the monastery of San Domenico. Later, writing to his father, it was clear that Savonarola bore him no ill will, nor did he feel any bitterness toward the scornful Laodamia Strozzi. He explained that his decision to enter the novitiate was based on his own weakness and his inability to tolerate the wickedness of the world. For the time being, he explained, he would isolate himself and pray for guidance. "I too am made of flesh," he wrote, "and I must fight with all my strength to keep the devil from jumping on my shoulders and riding me like a mad dog down into hell."

For seven years Savonarola studied and prayed and waited. In 1481, he was summoned by the abbot of San Domenico and told that his period of preparation had come to an end. He was to be sent back out into the world to preach the word of God, to help others fight the devil. The abbot must have chuckled to himself as he ushered his apprentice preacher out through the courtyard and sent him on his way to Brescia, to Genova, and to the villages of Tuscany and Lombardy. The Dominicans were an order of preachers, fierce preachers, aggressive men who knew the world and how wicked it could be. They were not like the orders of humble Benedictines who maintained a rule of silence and withdrew into their isolated monasteries to fast and pray. The Dominicans, proud of their mission, perused it with fervor. It was not for nothing that they were called the Watchdogs of God.

But the incongruous young man who left the abbey that day, Fra Girolamo Savonarola, was a pitiful excuse for a preacher. He was small and thin and ugly, still boyish, and the only part of his body that appeared to have grown and developed into manhood in the past ten years was his nose. His chest was so narrow that it looked hopelessly unsuited to the task of taking in great rushes of air and issuing thunderous and fearsome pronouncements. His gestures were uncouth and graceless, his voice annoying. All of Italy knows that Ferrarrese is one of the most unpleasant dialects on the peninsula, with its high-pitched nasal twang and singsong rhythm. His huge, hooked nose hung mournfully among the folds of his sad face over thick, fleshy lips. But his eyes! That is what the abbot had seen. That is why he sent this unlikely young friar forth to preach the word of the Lord. He had seen the relentless, unquenchable flames that could burn in those green eyes. Beneath eyebrows so heavy they looked like the wings of a blackbird, he had seen the fire of zealotry and conviction. And he knew that when his time came, Fra Girolamo Savonarola would know how to harness that fire and unleash its energy upon the world.

The beginning of Savonarola's career as a preacher was anything but auspicious. Later, in the days when he could boast that all Italy trembled at the sound of his voice, he was to say that in the early days he was scarcely capable of moving a hen. And, in fact, those who turned out to hear him preach in the pitiful villages where he was allowed to do so were scarcely more receptive than hens. They were pious old women more intent on pawing their rosaries and muttering their paternosters than listening to the preacher. It didn't seem to matter that he had studied for years and committed to memory all of the rhetorical teachings and trappings of the ancient Roman and Greek orators. He had learned how to construct his arguments step by step, how to embellish his periods with a high-sounding Latinate vocabulary. He had learned from Cicero and Democritus how to pile up rhetorical effects—*adnominatio, anaphora, enumeratio*. He had learned to manipulate words, arranging them in clever chiastic and tripartite structures, but all this sophisticated, classical learning was lost on the poor farmwomen who sat before him, mumbling their quiet personal prayers and oblivious to the centuries of classical culture that had gone into the sermon of this learned young preacher.

For almost ten years, Fra Girolamo plied the back roads of Tuscany and Lombardy. He preached in the poorer villages neglected by most of his Dominican brothers. He shunned the castles of the nobility and stayed in hostels, and often in the squalid huts of the peasants to whom he brought the word of God. With great humility and devotion, and with infinite patience, he pursued his calling, unaware that he would one day be the greatest preacher in all of Christendom, in all the world perhaps, and unaware too, that on the twenty-third of May, in the year 1498, he would find himself in the Piazza della Signoria of Florence condemned to death as a heretic.

It was just before dawn when a fat little priest, still laughing, made his way down the worn stone steps and let himself out into the courtyard of the hospice. He walked quickly past the enclosure where the chickens were still asleep and stopped momentarily at the well. Grinning and shaking his head, he splashed cold water on his round, red face. He used his chubby hands to wet the ring of thick, dark hair that encircled his tonsured head and plaster it down. His morning ablutions complete, he wiped hands and face on his ample sleeve, saluted the uninterested chickens, and with a ceremonious sweep, turned and was gone.

Hurrying through the stone arch and into the street, he almost fell when his stubby legs got tangled up in the folds of his billowing habit. The stones were still wet from the night's rain, and his leather sandals slipped more than once as he hurried down the Via San Gallo on his way back to the monastery of San Lorenzo. A smile of satisfaction lit up his round face and he beamed like a cherub. "*Ciccio,*" that's what Teresa had called him and, "*Cicciolino*"—my little chubby one. "Ooooo, *Ciccio,* No!" as he wrestled her into the huge, soft bed. He could still smell the thick linen mattress stuffed with straw. Feel the warmth of her body. The warm smell. The straw and Teresa. "Oooooo, *Ciccio,* not that!"

Fra Pagolo Pulci was not a monk who took his vow of chastity all that seriously. Neither was he worrying about eternal damnation that May morning as he hurried, out of breath, through the gate of the cloister of San Lorenzo.

"Lodato sia Gesu Cristo."

"*Sempre sia lodato.*" He exchanged the mumbled formula with the gatekeeper. "Praised be Jesus Christ." "Let Him always be praised." Standard monastic greeting. "Monks," he thought, "why couldn't they settle for '*Buongiorno*' like everyone else?" Fra Pagolo rushed past the chapel where lauds were being conducted. Morning prayers. Only the novices attended them. He wondered why anyone would agree to get up before dawn and kneel, praying in that cold chapel for half an hour. The spiritually intense. Ha! What were they doing in a monastery here in Florence? Better go live as a hermit, out in a cave, out in the country like those crazy, filthy old bastards in the desert. Less distraction there. But here in Florence, oh, there were distractions. Like yesterday morning when he went down to answer the bell and there she was, Teresa Lenzuolo, eldest daughter of Giacomo Lenzuolo, purveyor of altar cloths and bed clothes to the friars of San Lorenzo. Ooooo Teresa! *Lodato sia Gesu Cristo!*

This morning Fra Pagolo ate quickly, not lingering as he usually did over the crusty bread, still warm from the ovens, and the soft, white cheese, creamy and barely salted. Leaving the refectory hastily, he grabbed a generous length of salami, which disappeared into the folds of his habit. It was going to be a long day. He bounded up the stairs to the dormitory where the novices slept. Sure enough, Rinuccio Calvi was still sound asleep in his bed. "Eh! *Dormiglione!* I told you to be ready. Let's go. Hey! Why aren't you down with the rest of the novices, on your knees on the cold marble? Rinuccio! Sometime I question your vocation, you lazy son of a bitch. I worry about the strength of your commitment to the order and the work of St. Francis. Rinuccio!"

The fat priest began to pummel the younger friar, who, suddenly awake, raised his arms to ward off the blows and, with a couple of sleepy, poorly aimed kicks, managed to force his assailant into a retreat. "Hurry, get dressed," said Pagolo, throwing him his coarse brown habit.

As Pagolo pulled him down the corridor, Fra Rinuccio was still cinching himself with the long white rope that was part of the Franciscan habit. The three thick knots reminded the friars of their duty to God the Father, God the Son, and God the Holy Ghost. Yawning and stretching, the lanky novice trailed along behind his rotund companion who had launched into a lecture on the history of public execution in Florence.

Pagolo Pulci was the poor scion of a wealthy family. His father, Ubaldino, had squandered his share of the family fortune as well as the inheritance due his son. And so, as often happens with men of breeding and taste who are reduced to unfortunate circumstances, Pagolo turned to the clerical life. What better place for the noble son of an ignoble wastrel than the monastery? Here he would never have to worry about sustenance, for the friars lived extremely well. Besides, he had a talent that they could put to good use. Educated in the classical tradition, Pagolo could read and write exquisite Latin. And Latin was the language of all official business. The records of the Signoria, Florence's governing body, were kept in Latin. Latin was used for legal transactions, diplomatic correspondence, judicial, medical, and scientific treatises. It was the official language of the church as well. In short, all learning, sacred and profane, was in Latin. And although he was a dissolute scoundrel, Fra Pagolo Pulci was a consummate Latinist. As such, he was of considerable value to his order, and his indiscretions were generally overlooked.

It was Pagolo's eloquence and his scholarship—not his piety—that had earned him the grudging respect of his superiors in the order. And it was the irrepressible desire to exercise that eloquence and display that scholarship that impelled him to launch into a rambling disquisition on the public execution of heretics in his native city. Not that the sleepy young friar with him was listening as the little priest, already winded, explained, between bites of salami, that nobody had been put to death in Florence for heresy in over 110 years:

"Fra Michele da Calci was the last one, a ragged, saintly hermit—you know the type. He went to the stake, charged with the dissemination of inflammatory doctrines. Heresy indeed! His real crime was speaking out a little too enthusiastically against usury, gambling, and fornication. In the Florence of his time, that amounted to heresy.

"As it does today, Rinuccio, as it does today," said Pagolo, wagging an admonitory finger at his younger companion. "Haven't you noticed that the partisans of sin always seem to get their way here, and that excessive saintliness eventually sticks in the craw of most good Florentines?"

Pagolo stopped, pulled himself up to his full height and, with oratorical solemnity, produced the sort of roll call that Italians of all ages have always been fond of producing:

"The city of Florence has given birth to artists and architects by the hundreds—scholars, philosophers, poets, and musicians. More than any other city, we have supplied the world with writers and historians, statesmen, politicians, bankers, merchants, even explorers!

"But," he continued in more studied, weighty tones, "In all of Italy, very few candidates for sainthood have emerged in the past two centuries. Do you know how many? Three, to be exact. The entire peninsula has produced only three saints. And according to our records, Florence, not a single one!

"But I digress," he apologized, and plumbing the depths of his erudition, Pagolo plunged back into the details concerning the execution of the unfortunate Michele, never slackening his pace in the process and all the while tugging the pliant young friar along with him through the streets. Finally, he concluded, "Fra Michele, saint or heretic—whichever you like—was executed in 1389, and Florence has not seen fit to burn another heretic since then." He hesitated, again searching his prodigious memory, then added, "Well . . . with the possible exception of Giovanni Cani—John Dogs."

This latter reflection was enough to prompt a flood of new information from the talkative, rambunctious little priest. "Technically, of course, he was condemned for heresy, but his real crime was sorcery, sorcery being a code word for the concoction of poisons, as you know. The so-called sorcerers are the apothecaries of the dark side, Rinuccio. Only a sorcerer has the courage to collect the ingredients, and they can be very daunting ingredients, necessary for the brewing of certain very effective poisons—disgusting, toxic toads, bugs, snakes, and the unmentionable things they cull from graveyards, battlefields, and hospitals. John Dogs went to the stake for heresy, but his real crime, according to trial testimony, which I have read, was supplying 'hair from a werewolf' to a band of conspirators who tried to poison Cosimo de' Medici. Can you believe it? How do you like that?"

A panting, sweating Fra Pagolo concluded his learned discourse on that note, as the two Franciscan friars hurried toward the center of town. "What do you think, Rinuccio, history today! We're going to see a little history in the making. A remarkable event! A singular event! A momentous occasion! We're going to see the first real heretic to be burned in Florence in over a century. Heresy! I swear you get an eclipse of the sun more often than you get condemned heretics in this city! Hurry, now, or we won't get close enough to see anything."

Dawn was breaking. And around Florence, many people were surprised that a bright May sun was edging up over the horizon. It had rained violently throughout the night. The thunder and lightning had been terrifying, and a sunny day had not seemed likely.

Many others, more fearful, were shocked that almighty God would permit the sun to shine on such a black and evil day. They said there had been signs, evil signs portending terrible calamity. In Via della Croce, only yesterday, a baby had been born with the feet of a goat. In the church of Santa Maria Novella, a statue of the Madonna had begun to weep. Several people had seen it. Real tears had streamed from her eyes down her stone face. A huge, black dog, almost the size of a horse and rabid had been seen prowling through the darkened streets and piazze late at night. What was going to happen? Would the authorities go through with their insane, unholy plans? Would they really try to burn this saintly man? Surely God would not permit it. Surely He would strike these blasphemers in His anger and rescue His beloved from the flames. Yes, some sudden act of God would save him from this abomination. And save our city too, for if we put him to death, the burden of guilt will be with us for all eternity. Marked like Cain, accursed among cities, plagues and famine would be sure to follow. Floods and great destruction.

A palpable fear had settled in the hearts of the citizens of Florence. Fear and trepidation. And many, thinking now about this strange monk who was to be put to death for heresy, remembered only the fire in his eyes when he spoke. A fire that had touched them, seared their souls, a fire of frightening intensity. They asked themselves how this man who was made of fire could ever be consumed in earthly flames. The folly! Light your fires! He will defy them! The fire will not touch him. You cannot harm him!

The authorities charged with the execution, too, were apprehensive. It was not so much the specter of divine intervention that frightened them, but the more down-to-earth possibility of a popular uprising. In order to guard against that eventuality, or to contain it if violence should break out, they had stationed legions of armed guards everywhere throughout the city.

In normal times, a carnival atmosphere reigned in the city on the day marked for an execution. All work was suspended, and by dawn, when the bells pealed and the gates of the city were thrown open, crowds of farmers and other curiosity-seekers from the countryside had already gathered outside. Pushing and shoving their way through the narrow streets, they competed for vantage points that would allow them the best possible view of what was going to take place. The better families had elegant *logge* erected around the piazza, from which they could observe the proceedings in comfort without being rubbed in any unwholesome way by the smelly, unpleasant mob.

Bakers, beer makers, and peddlers of rough wine set up their stands so that by ten o'clock most of the throng was happily reeling in the streets. The bells continued to peal all morning long to add background music to the excited confusion. Crowds gathered around street musicians who sang lewd songs and ballads, much to the onlookers' delight. Jugglers and contortionists plied their trades, as did pickpockets, pimps, and thieves. Dancing dogs entertained groups of fat peasants and drunken, cursing tradesmen. Gypsies told fortunes with their tarot cards and read palms. Just before noon, when the noise and the excitement were reaching a fever pitch, the condemned was brought out of the Bargello and paraded through the streets in a small cart stuffed with straw and drawn by a donkey. Quite often the preparations for these processions were elaborate. As with the great outdoor religious pageants that mark the holy days, craftsmen, carpenters, and theatre people were engaged. Thirteen sets were built at various places around the city, and a comic reenactment of the stations of the cross was staged. Clowns and actors with heavily painted faces or exaggerated masks performed burlesques. The crowds would squeal when an obscene Veronica wiped not the face but the genitals of the condemned and upon examining her famous veil found there the imprint of a huge penis! As the procession wound its way from the Piazza del Podesta to the Piazza della Signoria, it was greeted with shouts of glee and derision. Boys hooted and rained stones down on the unfortunate victim of justice, and buckets of slop were dumped unceremoniously from windows and balconies, accompanied by insults and jeers.

But today was different. The prisoner would not be led disgracefully through the streets and exposed to the mockery of the populace. Instead he would be escorted under heavy guard down a narrow runway built well above street level and running from the Palazzo della Signoria directly to the middle of the square, where the gallows had been constructed. The authorities were taking no chances. And although there were more people that anyone can ever remember jammed into the Piazza della Signoria and spilling into the side streets, there was not a sound. Not a bell pealing or a dog barking. No shouts, no singing, no merchants hawking their wares. The beer and wine sellers were nowhere to be seen. Perhaps miraculously, there were no flies in the great central square that day, and it seemed that even the birds in the countryside had lost their voices. Although it was almost noon and the sun was bright, an unearthly silence hung in the air like the solemn quiet of a great cathedral in the dead of night—a silence so deep and so profound that, when the heavy doors to the Palazzo della Signoria swung reluctantly open on their rusted hinges, they let out a groan that could be heard across the city, as if even the doors were in terror of what was about to take place.

One person who was suffering perhaps less from holy dread than most of the others was Fra Pagolo Pulci. Still lecturing his young charge on the relatively liberal attitudes of the Florentine republic with regard to heretics, he stopped in midsentence when they rounded the corner of the Via Larga and stepped into the broad open space that was the Piazza della Signoria. It was just after dawn, and although the streets leading down here had been fairly empty, the piazza itself was already packed to capacity. Many of the condemned man's followers had been there all night, despite the torrential rains, keeping a silent vigil and praying. All of this devotion and display of piety was too much for Fra Pagolo.

"By the blood of Christ, I don't believe it, Rinuccio. What are they doing? This is a holiday! Where in God's name are the vendors? The vendors are always here when we have an execution. I need a drink. And already I'm famished. I should never have given you any of that salami, my salami. That would have taught you a lesson. Now, by Christ, I'm not going to get anything to eat all day, maybe not until . . ."

But the cynical friar trailed off, and his booming voice became softer and softer, until he was speaking almost in a whisper. It was as if the hushed silence that hung in the air over the piazza were contagious, capable of penetrating for a moment even the heart of this profoundly disrespectful little man.

Presently, Pagolo recovered. "You know what the only good thing about these executions is? I mean now that the vendors and the entertainers aren't here? It's the suspension of that absolutely absurd law that bars prostitutes from coming into this venerable piazza. After all, this is where our serious and incorruptible public officials gather to discuss matters of grave importance. No prostitutes allowed! Not within one hundred feet, that's what the law says. But on days when they choose to make an example of some poor sinner, then they let them in. Bring on the whores! Let them get a good look. Teach them a lesson. Put the fear of the Lord into them."

"Do you think he's guilty, Pagolo?" said Rinuccio.

"Guilty? Hell, yes! Guilty of being a goddamn public nuisance."

"Seriously, Pagolo, what do you think?"

"Seriously, I think he's guilty of being a nuisance, a pain in the ass, and a Dominican. Now tell me Rinuccio, whom do we Franciscans hate more than anybody in the world except for Turks, pagans, and Pisans? Why the Dominicans, of course. Arch-fiends, arch-enemies, and arch-rivals."

"I know all that," said Rinuccio, "But do you think he's really a heretic?"

"It's hard to say in this day and age what a heretic is, my boy. But this man claimed to have visions from God. Directly from God."

"That's just what I mean," said the younger man. "They're going to burn him alive because he claimed he had these visions from God. He predicted that a great flood would sweep through Florence. And it did! Then, he predicted that Lorenzo de' Medici—Lorenzo the Magnificent—would die suddenly. And he did! And finally, he predicted that the king of France would sweep across the Alps into Italy at the head of a savage and invincible army. And, my God, he did! Everything the monk predicted happened just the way he said it would! How can that be heresy?"

Pagolo was about to respond, but it was at that precise moment that the massive wooden doors, ringed and studded with iron, swung open with a mighty groan. It was just as well, because for once, Fra Pagolo did not have an answer.

The use of torture enormously simplifies legal proceedings, and so, just three days after his arrest, Girolamo Savonarola was led out into the sunlight of the Piazza della Signoria, where he was to be hung in chains and burned.

The condemned man's right arm hung useless at his side. With the skill of a perverse surgeon, Gaburra Zolferino, the ex-butcher, for two long days had methodically crushed every one of his bones from shoulder to fingertip. The dispassionate torturer had then resorted to hot iron and molten metal, applied with scientific precision. He went about scorching the already-destroyed limb so that, in the end, it looked more like a charred branch pulled from a fire than a man's arm.

When the tortured man finally agreed to sign the confession they had extracted from him, he had to do it with his left hand, so the signature they obtained was awkward and unsure, like that of a child just learning to write.

For nine years, the preacher had held the city captive with his fiery eloquence. It was he who defied the antichrist Borgia Pope Alexander VI, and he who was idolized by the people. He had saved Florence from the brutal armies of France and had finally driven the corrupt Medici from the city and brought freedom back to the Florentine republic. Today they were going to repay him. But they were afraid.

Nowhere was the fear more apparent than on the faces of the guards closest to him. Despite their heavy armor and the iron and leather gauntlets they wore, they dared not touch him. Savonarola appeared in the darkened doorway of the Signoria, almost naked, with only a filthy cloth wrapped around his waist. He was scarcely able to walk, and yet no one dared help him. They were afraid.

Only Gaburra the torturer did not shrink from the condemned man. He had volunteered to carry out the death sentence two days ago, when the commune's executioner, Giacopo Nero, fearing for his immortal soul, had suddenly disappeared. Gaburra had no illusions as to the destiny of his own soul. And so when he emerged, laden with the heavy chains that he would use to bind the prisoner, he was prepared to go about his business with his usual thoroughness and lack of emotion.

The chains were a new feature. Normally, the condemned was bound with a rope, but there was nothing normal about this execution. The scaffolding and the gallows had to be built by craftsmen brought in from Arezzo. Members of the Florentine carpenters' guild had refused to do the work. The structure they had erected was enormous. The foot of the platform was well above the top of the tallest man's head. Fixed in the middle of the platform was a thick pole twenty feet high. Extending to the top of this grim mast was a ladder, which the executioner would mount when everything else was in place. From this perch far above the crowd, he would be able to hoist Girolamo Savonarola to the very top of the pole, where he would be seen as far away as Fiesole. This is the way they planned it. They wanted everyone to see what happened to heretics.

Burning was the penalty usually prescribed for heresy, and burning at the stake was the almost-universal method of actually administering the punishment. But they had said the stake would not provide a sufficiently edifying spectacle. When the stake is used, the prisoner is lashed to a stout pole, and bundles of faggots are piled high around him. The prisoner is surrounded on all sides by piles of kindling by the time the fire is lit. Often the quantity of wood necessary to accomplish the task is so great that the body of the heretic or witch is completely hidden from view. Furthermore, inside the roaring inferno created by the wall of wood, the victim usually suffocates quickly, and indeed, almost mercifully. And by the time the wall of sticks and flames has burned through enough to get a glimpse of what lies within, the victim is long since dead, the body almost entirely consumed.

Savonarola's enemies wanted to see him squirm and twitch in death. They intended to rob him of every shred of dignity. They wanted to show their power over life and death, and they wanted to do it in dramatic fashion. They wanted to demonstrate to these gullible people that their prophet was, after all, only a man, that he felt pain and fear as they did and that, like them, he was quite capable of dying an ignominious death.

The ingenious scaffolding now towering high above the piazza was designed to demonstrate these simple realities in such a way that no man would ever dare question them again. Instead of suffocating, hidden in a hollow tower of flames, Girolamo Savonarola, the enemy of Florence, was going to be lifted some twenty feet above the base of the gallows, swinging in chains, and slowly roasted to death.

Every eye in the crowded square was riveted now on the pale, helpless figure that stepped, half stumbled, out of the doorway of the Palazzo della Signoria. Even Fra Pagolo had forgotten all about his whores and his appetites and had fixed his attention on the condemned prophet. He had seen him preach many times, but he had never seen him like this before. Had they really defeated him? Broken his spirit? Where was the fire now? The strength? The surging power that drove this man?

Gaburra had set down the heavy chains at the end of the platform and motioned to the guards to bring the condemned man down along the runway. Guards were stationed under the runway at street level, to prevent anyone in the crowd from getting too close. Mothers crowded around, weeping, holding up their babies and imploring the prophet to bless them one last time. The guards had to keep pushing them back with the shafts of their long lances.

Fra Pagolo, who had managed to work his way fairly close to the gallows, was puzzled by what he saw. At first, Savonarola had seemed only a broken, exhausted man. He had been squinting when they brought him out into the bright sunlight and had stumbled once or twice. After a minute, though, he had steadied himself, allowed his eyes to adjust to the light, and was proceeding down the long, narrow walkway to the place appointed for his death.

There was something in his eyes, but what was it? Not the extraordinary fire that would leap out when he preached. Not defiance, but not a look for resignation, either. Fear, it must be fear. "I'd be shitting myself with fear if I were him," thought Pagolo. "But it's not that, either. What you think he'd be doing is staring at those chains, at that pole, frozen with fright. Eyes glazed with terror. But he isn't even paying any attention to those bloodcurdling things.

"He's nervous. That's what it is. Nerves. Anxiety. But not because he's afraid to die. It's something else. Wait, now he's looking around. He's looking for something! Searching the crowd. That's it! He's got his men in place. There's going to be an escape. Oh, this is going to be a glorious day after all!"

Pagolo, too, began scanning the crowd for signs of the armed men who would suddenly reveal themselves, cut valiantly through the troops surrounding the gallows and ride off in triumph with their leader. But nothing happened.

Gaburra began to fasten the chains in place. First, one around the ankles; another around the knees. "If they're going to make their move," thought Pagolo, "they better do it soon." The hangman looped a length of chain under Savonarola's arms and made a kind of harness. Then, by wrapping a long chain around him several times, he bound his arms tightly against his body, behind his back. The clinking of the heavy chains was the only sound that could be heard.

"What the hell are they waiting for?" thought Pagolo. "To the rescue!" Still, nothing happened.

The condemned man scarcely took notice of these preparations, even though the chains must have been cold to the touch, and they were rough and rusty. He was still busy searching the crowd. His agitation had increased visibly, and his eyes were darting about.

Gaburra finally attached the hook at the end of the chain that hung from the top of the pole. This part of his job finished, he turned and climbed the ladder. At the top, he drew a thick leather belt around his torso and clamped himself to the pole for better leverage. Bracing himself with his feet resting on two thick spikes, he began to heave. As he pulled on the chain, hand over hand, with his knotty arms, the prophet began to rise up, up into the air in short, quick jerks.

It took the executioner only a few minutes to get his man to the top. He had to stop once for breath. In that time, Pagolo had concluded that the rescue attempt was not going to be made. What had happened? Did they lack the courage? Had the prophet's supporters underestimated the number of soldiers? Had they been betrayed?

Gaburra secured the chains and descended the ladder. The most difficult part of his job was done. As he stepped back to admire his handiwork, the soldiers brought bundles of wood and piled them high under the friar. Now twenty feet in the air, and tightly bound in chains, Savonarola dangled from the top of the pole, swaying slightly in the warm May breezes. But still his incessant, nervous eyes scanned the swarms of upturned faces that filled the square. And then he froze. He had found what he was looking for.

A hunchback, for there is always a hunchback when grim work needs doing, came out of the Signoria with a torch and handed it to Gaburra. A flame lit in hell. The executioner walked over to the bundled branches, the wood piled now to a height of almost fifteen feet, and thrust the torch into the center, where kindling had been placed to feed the fire. When he was sure that the flames had caught, he turned and walked back into the Signoria, certain of the result of his labors, the quality of his work, and not at all curious to see the grim ending of the spectacle he had created. His job was done.

The fire caught quickly. Although it had rained the night before, Gaburra had had the foresight to insist that the bundles of wood be stored inside and kept dry. In no time, the flames were soaring, almost licking at the heels of the man hanging in chains. But he was oblivious to them and gave no indication of feeling the first bursts of heat that were now rising. All the anxiety that Fra Pagolo had seen on his face was gone. It had been replaced by a look of grim intensity, and the prophet had fixed his gaze on one face in the crowd. The terrible power he had possessed and wielded was there again! It had welled up screaming from the depths behind his fierce green eyes. The cords of his neck were strained. Veins stood out on his forehead.

The flames had reached his feet now, but he did not flinch. The only movement he betrayed was a trembling as his eyes bored into those of an ordinary-looking young man standing in front of the Loggia della Signoria, to one side of the piazza. He was the man Savonarola had been looking for.

The man whose eyes met and held Savonarola's frightening gaze did not turn away. By prearrangement, this young man had agreed to deliver an answer here today. As he looked into the desperate, screaming eyes of the dying prophet, he knew what they were demanding of him. He knew the awful burden they were asking him to assume.

The fire had reached the prophet now, and suddenly his hair burst into flames. He had long, silken hair that would shake in great black waves when he preached. But now, even as that fine hair erupted into a flaming crown, he did not move or avert his eyes.

It took Pagolo several minutes to comprehend. Startled by the prophet's savage single-mindedness, taken aback and confused by the roar of the sacrificial flames, he came to himself only when the acrid smoke filled his nostrils, choking him. Pagolo turned and followed the direction of the holy man's gaze until his eyes too came to rest on the unremarkable young man at the far end of the piazza. And his heart caught in his throat.

He watched in disbelief as the young man returned the prophet's stare. And then he saw him finally, slowly, give a solemn nod of assent.

With that nod, Savonarola knew what he had to know before dying. His work would be carried on. The mission had been accepted. Completely sheathed in flames now, he turned away from the young man. With one last, tremendous effort, he lifted his eyes to heaven. There was a look of triumph on his face as the smoke and flames engulfed him.

As the fire raged, a hymn started, low at first, but soon everyone was singing with so much emotion that the strains of their song could be heard above the roar and crackle of the unholy blaze. They sang of the final days, of last things, of the world dissolving into ashes:

Dies irae, dies illa . . .

Days of anger, days of wrath . . .

What happened after that is unclear. The thick black smoke swallowed up both prophet and scaffold and filled the city. No one could see clearly. When the fire had burned itself out, and the smoke cleared, a set of empty chains was hanging at the top of the gallows.

The hunchback had been instructed to stir up the ashes under the chains to be sure that the body of the dangerous heretic was completely consumed. A relic, no matter how small—a piece of bone—might be enough to fan the flames of insubordination among his followers and keep their hopes alive. And their seditious movement.

The hunchback knew that no matter how tightly binding the chains were, something was likely to slip through as the body disintegrated—an arm, a leg—sometimes the head falls off. He knew because he and Gaburra had experimented the day before with the good brother Domenico and the madman Maruffi, accomplices of this one they burned today. They hadn't hoisted them up quite so high. That wasn't necessary. They just wanted to make sure that the method worked, that nothing went wrong. Gaburra was a professional, and he took pride in his craft.

"Yesterday," the hunchback remembered, "after the fires went out, there were still parts of the bodies hanging in the chains. Stubborn. We had to throw stones up there to knock them down." But today as he searched through the ashes—nothing. "That's odd," he thought, "usually there's bones. Bones are tough. Never burn all the way through. I guess the fire was hotter than we thought."

It was almost dark when the crowds, numbed by the spectacle they had witnessed, finally began to leave the piazza. Gaburra returned to finish the job. With the help of his assistant, he chopped down the post from which the chains had been suspended and laid it on the scaffolding. Huge piles of brush were placed under the platform, and the entire structure burned to the ground. Carters were later called in, and they loaded the ashes into deep, two-wheeled carts. Accompanied by soldiers armed with maces and clubs, they hauled every bit of dust and ash to the Arno, near the Ponte Vecchio, and threw it into the river.

Returning to the convent of San Lorenzo, Fra Pagolo was uncharacteristically thoughtful. People were talking. They had seen things. An old woman swore that when she looked up, she saw not the miserable, naked monk hanging in chains, but a glorious figure clothed in a white robe trimmed with gold. The chains had slipped away. He was free. Through the thick smoke, she swore she saw him rise up, up, transfigured. Angels carried him up to heaven. She swore.

Others had seen things too. Moses and Jesus figured prominently in their excited accounts. The angel Gabriel. Saint Dominic. And no one could deny that, in the stillness that followed the roaring conflagration, a lone white dove had sailed across the wide, open space of the piazza and had come to rest on the windowsill of the Alberghettino, the tiny, isolated prison cell where Savonarola had spent his last night on earth.

But what had Pagolo seen? Angels and a white robed figure? The soul of a sacrificial victim in the form of a dove? "No, none of that," he thought, for his eyes were unworthy. Or at least they were stinging from the smoke. He hadn't see anything out of the ordinary, but something very troubling, nonetheless. Or had he merely imagined it?

No, he had seen what he had seen. He had seen the eyes of one man seek out those of another. At first, he thought of a curse, the curse of a dying monk or something like that—some treachery or betrayal repaid with the undying enmity of a doomed man. But it was something entirely different. A plea? A commission? Had there even been an element of tenderness or pity in that wordless exchange? To Pagolo's way of thinking, it resembled nothing so much as the injunction of a dying father to his only son to honor his last request. But, of course, concluded the befuddled Pagolo, that was impossible, utterly impossible.

No act of intuition on Pagolo's part could have brought him any closer to the truth. There were too many things he had no way of knowing. He could not even have guessed that one man had agreed to become the other's successor and accomplice in an act of terrifying destruction. The terms of that agreement had been spelled out between them in stark and vivid detail, prophetic terms that only thirty years hence would bear fruit. Would Pagolo have even believed that, as a consequence of that agreement, one day a pope would be brought to his knees and the very foundations of Christendom shaken? That the fury of hell would be unleashed on all of Italy? That fire and the sword would come, and in the end, in a last devastating gasp of destruction, Rome, the eternal city, would be overrun by the armies of the new barbarians?

Pagolo had no way of knowing these things. And so, on that balmy spring night he was puzzled. He wondered why this strange monk, this prophet and heretic, had been staring with such grim intensity at that young man. In his last minutes on earth, the fire already ablaze in his hair and giving him the aura of some ancient god, Girolamo Savonarola had inexplicably singled out one man in a crowd of many thousands. And although Pagolo had not seen him in over eight years, he was certain, beyond the shadow of a doubt, that that unremarkable young man was his boyhood friend—Niccolo Machiavelli.

Part 1

SOME THIRTY YEARS EARLIER

A Boyhood at the Summit of Western Civilization

1

Carp, Artichokes, Black Beans, White Beans

Bartolommea was in labor for over twelve hours. The birth had been difficult, but fortunately, without serious complications. She was a frail and pious woman, and it occurred to her more than once in the course of her travails that the pain being visited upon her was just punishment for her having actually enjoyed the embraces of her husband.

The infant, washed and wrapped in swaddling clothes, was nestled comfortably in the arms of its exhausted mother. It was just after dawn, and the two attending midwives had retreated to the kitchen, where they were rewarding themselves with huge plates of fried eggs, swimming in fruity, green oil.

Bernardo, the weary but exuberant father, had climbed up to the wide balcony that spanned the front of his house. He wanted to be alone for a few minutes to take in the cool morning air and to congratulate himself on the birth of his second child.

Even at this early hour, the city below him was already seething with activity. It was 1469, and Florence was one of the world's five largest cities. A haphazard and unsystematic census taken several years earlier recorded the existence of over fifty thousand "mouths of men, women, and children," within her walls. Three other Italian cities—Naples, Venice, and Milan—boasted slightly larger populations. Outside the peninsula, only Paris was larger. London, by comparison, was a squalid provincial town.

Merchants' records of the time indicate that, every day, the 50,000 Florentine mouths consumed 2,300 bushels of grain, 20,000 pounds of cheese, and in excess of 70,000 liters of wine. Each year, 4,000 cattle and over 100,000 assorted sheep, goats, and pigs were slaughtered to supply the hungry city with meat.

From his vantage point, Bernardo looked calmly down at his cluttered and disorderly city. Only two buildings stood out plainly in the general jumble of brick, stone, and stucco—the Signoria and the Duomo, Florence's seat of government and her cathedral, the centers of her political and spiritual lives. All the rest seemed welded together in a solid block of masonry, a tangle of fortresslike palaces, crowded tenements with spiny roofs, churches, abbeys, convents, nunneries, shops, sheds, mills, and manufactories. From this incoherent mass of building material, ancient towers with tiny windows jutted out everywhere, cocked at odd angles.

Irregularity bordering on chaos might be an apt description of Florentine architecture at the time. But there was more to the city than a welter of odd, often ugly shapes. The true measure of her beauty lay in the harmony of her colors—burnt orange and umber, mustard yellow, the bleached red of the terra-cotta roofs. Suffused with the morning sun, Florence was a city of gold.

Despite the cramped character of her urban landscape, Florence was not entirely without breathing room. Empty spaces, gardens, orchards, and vineyards served as a buffer zone between the dense core of the city's center and the massive stone walls that surrounded it. A hundred and twenty years ago, the city had filled these walls near to bursting. But the Black Death that swept through Europe in 1348 and again in 1400 carried off over two-thirds of the Florentine population. The city contracted, pulled in on itself. Tracts of wooden houses on the periphery were burned and were not rebuilt. Now with her diminished population, Florence, although prosperous, floated within the circle of her walls like a small child in the armor of a giant.

Bernardo was roused from his reverie by a terrifying sight. A bright red stain was spreading on the surface of the muddy Arno, as if the blood of an entire army had flowed into the river. "*Sangue di Cristo!* What an omen!" he cried. His right hand moved to make the sign of the cross. And a second later, he burst out laughing at himself. It was only a group of cloth dyers on the northern bank, flushing out their vats to begin the day's work.

Bernardo had already decided that the birth of a child was a momentous occasion and more than enough of an excuse to take a few days off from his work. He went back down the cool stone stairway to the second-floor bedroom where Bartolommea had recently given birth. Both mother and child were sleeping when he looked in—the ruddy, wrinkled face of a newborn baby in the arms of a pale woman. He retreated noiselessly, a broad smile of satisfaction on his face.

It was midmorning, and the sun was already high in the sky when Bernardo stepped out into the Via Romana and darkness. In Florence, even at high noon the street was almost pitch black. Little air and less light filtered down to ground level, due to the *sporti*, the ubiquitous balconies that projected from the facades of the Florentine houses out over the streets. Three stories up, and running the entire length of the house, Bernardo's balcony loomed, reaching out and nearly touching its counterpart across the street. Recently, the city had been waging an aggressive campaign against the *sporti*. Arguing, correctly, that the balconies hampered communication and blocked out air and light, officials banned them and began levying heavy fines on their owners. But this action in no way influenced the thinking of Bernardo, even though he was a jurisconsul and sworn to uphold the law. He preferred to break it and pay the fines. Like many other Florentines, he was not willing to sacrifice the pleasures afforded him and his family by the balcony—dining out in the cool evening breezes, sitting under the stars at night, watching the sunrise. "Besides," he argued, "There's a positive side. So the street's a little dark. At least you don't get wet when it rains."

Bernardo made his way slowly up the clogged and noisy street. Animals were everywhere—barking and grunting and quacking and snorting. Every imaginable variety of dog roamed freely, mangy, starving dogs and pampered, manicured little dogs with silver collars. Tiny mice skipped through the dirty straw and rats lurched into dark drains. Pigs and geese rooted in the doorways. Peasants drove cattle and sheep to the Mercato Vecchio. Oxen drew heavy carts loaded with produce. "Animals and animal shit," thought Bernardo, "Dogshit, horseshit, catshit, and pigshit." He crushed and sniffed the laurel leaf that he always carried with him, perfume to alleviate the stench. Not for the first time, he envied Lorenzo de' Medici his nose. Long and flat and bent in the middle, Lorenzo's nose, although extraordinarily ugly, was the envy of all Florence. It had no sense of smell.

Still, Bernardo reflected, it could be worse. The tanning factories and slaughterhouses, two of the most filthy-smelling industries known to man, had been judiciously outlawed within the city walls. He had been to cities where this was not the case, and the stench was considerably more intense. Then too, Florence had one great advantage over the Tuscan hilltop towns when it came to hygiene—the Arno. Sooner or later, most of the dirt and the shit was pushed into the river and carried off, a gift to the people of Pisa, downstream. Another whiff of laurel.

Bernardo squinted in the bright sun as he emerged on the south bank of the river near the old stone bridge, the Ponte Vecchio. The banks of the river were wide and still grassy in spots, providing a swath of rustic relief in the heart of the clogged city. A merciful breeze blew from the hills in the south, and Bernardo was able to tuck his laurel away for the time being. He made his way across the bridge, the oldest in Florence, oldest because it was the first bridge to be built of stone. The wooden ones had all been burned. The Ponte Vecchio crossed the Arno at its narrowest point, and both sides of the bridge were lined with an odd collection of houses and shops. "Why would anyone want to live on a bridge?" thought Bernardo. In his boyhood, he remembered, the shops were occupied by pursemakers, but now they'd been taken over by butchers. And butcher shops meant one thing—dogs. More dogs here than anyplace else in the city. Bernardo hated dogs. And dogshit.

Bernardo's first stop that day was the Old Market, where, among other things, barbers shaved their customers out in the open air. He sat contentedly, eyes half shut, as the razor did its work. The barber's skilled hands had to stretch the soft, puffy skin of his jowls to shave them cleanly. Ten years ago, that flesh was firm. Still, as a man of forty, a successful man, he was entitled to his indulgences.

A voice more strident than most managed to make itself heard over the general din of the marketplace and attracted Bernardo's attention. It belonged to one of the many professional criers who marched about the town, calling out the news or gossip or whatever. This particular one was enthusiastically touting the virtues and the low prices of some fat, fresh carp caught only moments ago by Nello the fisherman and available, while it lasted, at the far end of the market near the candle makers' houses. Nello paid the crier a penny for each carp he sold. Bernardo, always highly suggestible, made a mental note to inspect the carp. Carp and artichokes would make a splendid dinner to celebrate the arrival of his newborn baby.

The crier continued with the news of the day, and the only news for the past several months had to do with the impending marriage of the city's foremost citizen, Lorenzo de' Medici. Florentines were scandalized when last year it was announced that Lorenzo would wed Clarice Orsini, a non-Florentine, an outsider, and worst of all, a Roman! But the Medici were old hands at influencing public opinion, and in February they hosted a lavish tournament to quell the outraged populace. Heads of state from all over Italy were invited to compete, and 10,000 Medici ducats bought the most splendid spectacle the city had ever seen. Free food and drink for several days and magnificent entertainments ensured the wildly enthusiastic cheers of thousands of supporters. Bread and circuses.

Little was known about the bride-to-be, for she had not yet arrived in Florence. And the air was thick with rumors. She's cross-eyed. She has a moustache! A portrait had been forwarded, as was the custom, but portraits were always flattering. But now, according to the crier, there was news of the girl. Wanting nothing left to chance, Lucrezia de' Medici, Lorenzo's mother, had traveled to Rome, allegedly to visit her brothers. She had actually gone to inspect the girl personally. She had just returned and made her report public. According to the crier, Lucrezia had first caught sight of her future daughter-in-law in the company of her mother on their way to Saint Peter's Basilica. Clarice, after the Roman fashion, was wearing a *lenzuola,* a voluminous gown, that hung loosely and hid the body from head to toe. Lucrezia was furious. All she could determine that day was that the girl was tall.

On her second sighting, she fared little better and cursed the Roman women for covering themselves up so thoroughly. This time, she studied the girl at length, following her from the church all the way back to the Orsini palace. While the girl's figure remained shrouded in mystery, Lucrezia was able to see that she had long and delicate hands, a round face, and a nice complexion. On the negative side, her neck was too thin, and she did not carry her head well, as Florentine girls do, but poked it out in front of her. And, horror of horrors, her hair was red!

The ambiguous report only fueled the fires of speculation, and a whole new round of rumors began to circulate. She's a hunchback! She's incredibly fat! She's already pregnant!

No one was less concerned about the dimensions of Lorenzo's intended than Bernardo. "Who gives a damn? The uglier the better," he thought. In his heart of hearts, Bernardo harbored no love for Lorenzo or any of the Medici. He was glad that he would be taking his family away before the wedding. Before the bread and circuses.

Relying once more on his laurel, a cleanly shaven Bernardo made his way across town, through the usual dark, damp tangle of men and animals, to the Piazza della Signoria. The piazza was the largest single open space in the city and admitted light and air freely. Bernardo's destination was the Signoria, the seat of the Florentine government, at the far eastern end of the square. The building itself was over two hundred years old, finished in the late thirteenth century. It was a massive, austere fortress that reflected the temperament of the men who had built it—hard, assertive, and suspicious. It had been conceived by these builders as a bastion of defense to protect Florence's republican form of government and to preserve her liberty. Over the years, the forbidding palace had been attacked from many quarters, but never destroyed. The Signoria was a monument to the Florentine character, with her brooding facade and high, graceful bell tower, a sign in stone of independence—and defiance.

Adjacent to the palace was the Loggia della Signoria, a collonaded open space, often used as a dignified setting for official ceremonies. But on most days it served as a shaded place where the men of Florence gathered to discuss the two subjects with which they were passionately obsessed—politics and women. Bernardo had spent many hours there himself and had engaged in his share of lively disputes. But today he had no intention of stopping. He had no stomach for what he knew the discussion would surely be about. And indeed, as he hurried by, saluting a few friends and colleagues, his suspicions were confirmed by what he managed to overhear: "I heard she's fat as a house and has a glass eye! She's only seventeen, and her ass has already fallen! She's left-handed!"

He entered the Signoria and tripped lightly up the stairs to the office of the registry. The huge carp that he was carrying weighed over ten pounds, and he was relieved to be able to put it down for a minute. His sleeve smelled like fish.

Bernardo looked around but saw no one. The entire room was

lined with shelves that housed an incredible collection of massive, dusty ledgers—the history of Florence, recorded on a day-to-day basis in a thousand mundane details—taxes, property transfers, deeds, marriages, births, and deaths.

"Folco, Folco, where are you, you ancient bastard?" A wizened, bent, grey man emerged from a door at the back of the room. Folco was as old and as dusty as the books he kept.

"Bernardo! What brings you here?" Without a word, Bernardo reached deep into a pocket in his jacket and extracted two beans, one white, one black. He placed them on the counter.

"Another one, and so soon. Your Totto was born less than a year ago, wasn't he?" queried the old man.

"Yes another one, and not the last, if Bartolommea holds up."

"Well, what is it this time, a boy or a girl?"

"You're a wagering man, you tell me."

"What'll we bet?

Bernardo considered for a minute, "I'll bet this luscious carp, all ten pounds of it, for one of the books you keep back there and never read."

"Which book?"

"*The Caesar*."

"Done! In my expert opinion, I hazard to guess that you have just become the proud father of a baby girl, who will be a burden to you all your days, and who will be so ugly—like her father!—that you'll never be able to raise enough money for a dowry to marry her off."

Bernardo grinned, and played thoughtfully with the white bean, pushing it around with his finger. Then, triumphantly, he snatched the black bean and held it in front of the old man's eyes.

"A son!" crowed Folco.

"Yes, a son. Another son."

"Tell me, is he scrawny like his mother, or fat and ugly like his father?"

"He's red as a beet and wrinkled. But he cries so lustily you know there's spirit in the boy."

"Well, let's get him registered." Folco pulled down a massive tome and opened it to a place marked by a ribbon.

As Bernardo supplied the necessary information, the old man wrote in a cramped but elegant script:

Machiavelli, Niccolo di Bernardo
3 May 1469

When he finished writing, Folco blotted the ink dry and slammed the book shut in a flurry of dust. Bernardo consigned the black bean to the keeper of records and watched as he dropped it into a huge clay jar. The living and the dead of Florence were tallied in that jar. Each bean represented one Florentine citizen, black for boys, white for girls. There were over fifty thousand beans in the jar. Nobody knew precisely how many. Nobody ever counted. Before going home that evening, Folco would drop three more black beans into the jar, and because of a fire that swept through the clothworkers' shacks in the Oltarno section, he would take out a fistful, twenty-four black, seventeen white.

2

The Devil's Ass— and the Angel's Thousand Black Teeth

There was nothing extraordinary about Niccolo Machiavelli's early childhood. As the second son, he deferred in many things to his older brother, Totto. After Niccolo, in short order, Bartolommea gave birth to two daughters, Primerana and Ginevra. The family divided their time between the city and their country house, and Niccolo felt equally at home in each. One of his earliest memories was of the bed where he slept as a child, along with his brother and two sisters. Even by adult standards, the bed was enormous, almost twelve feet across. It stood on a raised wooden platform in the center of the room. The bed was canopied, and heavy drapes hung on all sides. In the eyes of a small child, it was an impregnable fortress, a walled city all to itself.

The four little Machiavellis slept, lined up side by side, under linen sheets. In the winter, *scaldini*, earthenware jars filled with hot charcoal were placed within the confines of their magic kingdom to keep the children warm. As a result of their father's obsession with smells, the air in the room was sweetened by the scent of herbs, burning slowly in pierced globes that hung from the ceiling. Dragoncello and rosmarino were the incense of their childhood.

Bartolommea Machiavelli had always been an extremely devout woman, and as she grew older, her devotion increased. She lived in a world where Madonnas wept and statues of saints moved to signal their approval or displeasure. Not everyone could always see the movement, or the tears, but she could. Every evening, she assembled her children and said the rosary with them. She composed hymns to the Blessed Mother and taught the children to sing them. Niccolo could never carry a tune.

When the boys were old enough to understand these things, she took them to the cathedral to see the blessed relics, purchased at enormous expense by the wool merchants' guild—a piece of the true cross, a fragment of Christ's clothing, and a part of the cane used in the scourging at the pillar.

If Niccolo showed little enthusiasm for the pieties of his mother, he was fascinated by the stories his grandmother would tell him. Once, when she was a girl, her brother Dono had confided to her that a certain woman was a witch. Moreover, he said, every night this witch turned herself into a toad and went about the countryside on her unseemly errands.

"Your Uncle Dono was smart and not afraid of anything, Coluccio, like you. You take after him. One night, he waited outside the witch's house. At midnight, he saw a toad hopping across the field between the house and the barn. And he caught it! He twisted the back leg of the toad and let it go.

"The next day, Coluccio, we saw the witch and she was limping!"

It was not that grandmother Machiavelli was impious or heretical. Hadn't she explained to her grandson that fireflies were the souls of infants who had died without baptism? But she understood that there were things that Christianity did not fully explain. Older, more mysterious things. For her, the night breezes were full of malevolent things. Drafts were dangerous. Phantoms and demons and lost souls roamed the world. They had to be taken into account.

Not all the stories she told Niccolo concerned the sacred and profane mysteries that so fascinated him. Like the stories told to children all over the world, quite a few were intended to curb his rambunctiousness and make him behave and obey. Like the one about the Turk who lived in the attic. The Turk was so depraved and rabid that, on any given day, the only thought in his head was to burst out of the attic and eat little children. Only their good conduct, somehow, mysteriously, kept him at bay. A bird that had gotten trapped in the eaves or a rat scuffling across the attic floor were enough to elicit fearful cries from the children—*Il Turco!* It's the Turk!

After the Turk and next to the danger of being kidnapped by gypsies and being forced to work in the carnival, steal, and drink blood, the worst specter that hung over Niccolo's early life was Agnese. Agnese was a withered old peasant woman, dressed all in black, who lived near the Machiavelli farm in San Casciano. At first Niccolo suspected her of being a witch and transforming herself nightly into a toad. But his grandmother enlightened him. "Never go near Agnese. Hide when you see her. She has a farm and she steals little children, especially bad ones. She makes them work all day, and if they stop, she beats them with big currying combs. At night, they sleep on the floor and get only stale bread and water." To make matters worse, Agnese raised only one crop on her dreaded farm—onions. And the children would weep all day as they worked!

Bernardo Machiavelli was a studious man, and so it was with great pleasure that he undertook the early instruction of his two sons. He taught them their letters and the numbers. Niccolo was an eager pupil and learned effortlessly. Such was not the case with Totto, and Bernardo was grudgingly beginning to admit to himself that there was a certain dullness of intellect in his firstborn son. Ah well, he could always make a banker of him.

But Niccolo, the younger son, showed such promise that, when the boy was seven years old, Bernardo thought it time to hire a professional tutor, and the very best he could afford. Due to his relatively modest means, though, he finished by engaging the services of a certain Master Matteo.

Matteo's credentials were questionable and his past difficult to document. Rumors circulated of a brilliant future at the papal court, of some long-buried scandal, of indiscretions that had put an abrupt end to his career. But there was no question as to his abilities. Bernardo had ascertained that Matteo's command of Latin was masterful, and that several of his ex-pupils were among the most accomplished stylists in Florence. Besides, Bernardo liked the man. There was a fire in his old, crafty eyes that was missing in the young pedants he had interviewed—doe-eyed university graduates. So what if his tastes in literature ran to the lascivious and he preferred Ovid and Catullus to Horace and the moral Seneca?

Matteo provided the boy with sound instruction, even if it was heavily colored by his own irreverence. He often teased his pupil, and like a good teacher, excited his imagination. His pedagogical methods were unorthodox, but they worked. He had a way of presenting a lesson so that it stuck in a student's mind, like the time he taught Niccolo about the devil's ass and the angel's thousand black teeth.

For over a week, he had teased and tormented the boy with that phrase. "No, I don't think you're ready yet to learn about something as frightening as the devil's ass and the angel's thousand black teeth. Not just yet."

Finally, one day he relented. "Open those two books sitting in front of you," Matteo told the boy. "Now what do you see?"

"One is my Latin vocabulary, and the other one is a grammar," replied the boy without hesitation.

"Yes, of course, but they're different, aren't they? Which one is easier to read?"

"The grammar is, the handwriting is so much bigger and it's not as cramped."

"That's right. The grammar was copied only about a year ago. I did it myself, and I used the script we all use now here in Florence, the one developed by that highly revered ass, Coluccio Salutati. The vocabulary, on the other hand, was written in a different script, I would say one that was popular about a hundred years ago. Very difficult to read. And if you ever saw books copied in England or Germany, you'd find them impossible. All the letters look like tiny drawings of those great, pointed church towers they have up there. You might be reading Greek or Arabic, for all the resemblance they have to Latin characters.

"Anyway, you've been writing for a while now, Signor Niccolo. How long does it take to copy a page and do it respectably, so you can read it?"

"It would take me all day, but for a scribe, to do a good job, a few hours, I guess."

"Let's say that four or five pages a day is a decent speed, and that's not counting for illustrations. At that rate, how long would our man require to copy a book of four hundred pages? The arithmetic is simple, come on."

"One hundred days."

"Right. About a hundred days, a little over three months. So you understand why books are so rare, and so expensive. And you understand why so few people can afford to learn to read. But that's all about to change and very soon. And it's going to be because of the angel's thousand black teeth! Here, look at this." He handed Niccolo a small, unpretentious-looking volume, bound in plain, cheap leather. "Open it."

The boy started. Instead of the usual page, crammed with small, characters and tangled ligatures and endless superscriptions and abbreviations, there was a text of startling clarity. The letters were large and regular. They stood, each apart, and not all linked together in longhand. They looked like inscriptions cut boldly and cleanly in stone and not scratched on the page in ink.

"Do you know how long it took to copy that page, Niccolo? About one minute! And in the space of an hour, a hundred more, just like it, were made. In three months, at that speed, you'll have not one book but a thousand books! Think of it, Niccolo!"

The year was 1477, and the first printing press had just been set up in Florence. Master Matteo went on to explain to his young charge the mysteries of movable type. "These thousands of letters cast in lead, then inked, are the teeth of the angel. And they'll bite again and again and again, until the blessings of knowledge are available to all men. It will change the world, Niccolo, make no mistake about it."

The boy examined the book in amazement. So easy to read, so clear, and each page took less than a minute. It was a miracle. Matteo cleared his throat to bring his pupil back to attention.

"And now, young man, let me tell you about something more sinister that they say comes directly from the devil's ass. You've heard of Black Brother Berthold up in Germany, and his diabolical invention?"

Niccolo had not heard of Black Brother Berthold.

"The Black Brother is said to be the man who invented explosive powder, Niccolo. It's black, grainy powder that explodes with tremendous force when you touch a flame to it. If you use enough powder, and pack it tightly, the explosion can shatter the gates of a city and knock down her walls. The walls of Florence, twenty feet high and six feet thick, would not stand long against a blast of flame from the devil's ass!"

Niccolo was both excited and frightened by what he had heard. That night, he slept fitfully; his dreams were full of demons and angels—demons with huge black buttocks and angels with grinning mouths full of rotten black teeth. In the years to come, he would have to carve out for himself a life in the territory defined by these two inventions, between the devil's ass and the angel's thousand black teeth.

While Latin was not the only subject that Niccolo studied, it was the most important. Only Latin could provide access to other areas of inquiry. Everything was written in Latin. It was the gateway to all knowledge. Gradually, as the boy's Latin improved, his tutor would introduce other subjects into the curriculum—history and philosophy and music and arithmetic. But at the beginning, it was only Latin.

After plowing fearlessly through his Latin declensions and conjugations and what seemed at times sadistic grammatical exercises, young Niccolo was ready to read his first book. His tutor had chosen a standard pedagogical text, the *Liber Sanctorum, Book of the Saints*. The book, and others like it, were widely used to teach beginning reading. Its sentences were written in a straightforward, unadorned style, which the older boys scornfully called "baby Latin."

In addition to providing practice in deciphering Latin syntax and building vocabulary, the *Liber Sanctorum* filled another important educational function. It contained the stories of holy men and women whose lives were to serve as outstanding examples of upright Christian behavior for the book's impressionable young readers. Niccolo read it avidly and quickly absorbed all the book had to teach on the ablative absolute and deponent verbs. But the effect of the *Liber Sanctorum*'s moral instruction on the young Machiavelli was more problematic.

When he had finished all the stories, Niccolo made a list:

St. John the Baptist, beheaded
St. Stephen, stoned to death
St. Sebastian, shot full of arrows
St. John the Apostle, boiled in oil
St. Lawrence, grilled
St. Paul, crucified
St. Peter, crucified upside down
Sts. Agatha, Perpetua, Lucy, Agnes, defiled by Romans

Of the thirteen lives contained in the book, Niccolo counted eleven that had ended in violent death. The saints' mysterious desire to fling themselves into the jaws of martyrdom at any cost troubled him, and he was not at all sure he wanted to pursue sainthood as a calling when he grew up.

Puzzled by this spiritual shortcoming, Niccolo confided in his tutor. He did not dare go to his mother with his doubts. She would accuse him of blasphemy, or worse. Matteo, however, laughed heartily when he heard what his young charge had done.

"Signor Niccolo," he said, "it seems that you are not yet ready for sainthood. Read your Augustine again, boy. Don't you see that God is generous, reasonable? And He allows a man to enjoy a long and dissolute youth before calling him to the rigors and sacrifices of the saintly life!" And so it was that Niccolo, under the tutelage of Master Matteo, grew in wisdom and age, if not in grace.

Bernardo, enormously pleased with Niccolo's rapid progress in both reading and composition, decided it was time to give his son the copy of *The Caesar* he had been saving for him. He related how he had won the book from old Folco in the registry on the day of Niccolo's birth.

An avid reader, Niccolo settled down immediately with the prized book and the famous words that generations of students of Latin had read before him. "*Gallia est omnis divisa in partes tres*—All Gaul is divided into three parts . . ." And as he proceeded into Gaul with Caesar and the Roman armies, his admiration for them turned to awe and reverence. Who were these Romans?

They were certainly not the Romans he had been prepared for, the Romans from the saints' stories. Those Romans were awful. They were fat and debauched and gluttonous. They ate and forced themselves to vomit so they could eat more. The greatest pleasure they had in life was defiling Christian virgins. They lived for the day when they had the opportunity to desecrate the holy Eucharist. They reveled in torturing and crucifying converts, in hunting them down like dogs and killing them in their catacombs, in making them fight lions and barbarians in the Coliseum.

Caesar's Romans were different. They were men of iron who could march fifteen leagues in a day across mountains and rough terrain.

They slept in rain and snow, wrapped only in their cloaks, and ate nothing but hard biscuits and dried meat. They swept across Europe, from one end to the other, and nothing could stand in their way. In battle, they were brilliant strategists, always outwitting and outmaneuvering the enemy. And when they had to stand and fight, they fought like men possessed.

Niccolo had made his first real contact with the ancient Romans, and it struck a sympathetic nerve. It kindled in him a passion that he would carry with him to his grave. The Romans! When he finished *The Caesar*, he would read Justin, and move quickly on to Livy's monumental history, *Ab urbe condita*. So dear to him did this book become, that later in life, he would write a thousand-page commentary on it, a meditation on the civilization and the virtues that his Romans bequeathed to the world. But, for the time being, the youngster was fascinated by the battle and the bravery, by the tales of Aeneas and Romulus, by Scipio who destroyed Carthage and Hannibal only to be treacherously poisoned by his own wife. He was mesmerized by Caesar, who became a tyrant—and by Brutus, the tyrannicide.

3

An Ambush and an Apparition

In the shadows just before first light, moving deftly from long practice, the city takes final precautions to conceal her nocturnal secrets. Lovers slip from each other's grasp, and men on more ungodly errands melt away with the fleeing darkness. As Florence stirs to shake off the night's lethargy, all that can be heard are the small, private noises of those who rise before dawn: a cough, a moan, the occasional heaving and sighing of a more determined sort, muttered prayers, and curses.

One by one, the reluctant citizens of the republic drag themselves from their beds. Sluggish feet stumble across cold stone floors; hose are laced; stubborn boots tugged on; shirts are pulled down over tousled heads, here with the whisper of silk, there the rasp of rough wool.

Before long, the shock of ice-cold water will drive off sleep, and a torrent of clanging bells will break the night's hypnotic spell. From outside the city walls will rise a joyous cacophony of mooing and braying and bleating, barking and crowing, the spontaneous chorus that greets the daily miracle of the rising sun.

Under the massive wooden doors of the Porta San Piero Gattolino stood young Niccolo Machiavelli, waiting. The boy was dressed for the country, in woolen hose and a short leather jacket cinched with a wide belt. The quiver and bow slung over his shoulder and the leather game bag that hung at this side were indications that a day of hunting was planned.

As he stood in the dispersing darkness, his eyes darted instantly in the direction of any stray sound that filtered down to him through the maze of towers and twisted streets of the ancient city—the creak of shutters cautiously opened, the scuttling of tiny rats' feet. With his head full of stories, even the innocent click of a latch was a powerful stimulus to his imagination. His thoughts were very much on the night's vanishing denizens, the people with secrets moving quietly in the grey light.

Young Niccolo's Florence was thick with thieves and populated by agile lovers climbing over balconies and down trellises. His enthusiasm for nocturnal complicity knew no bounds. Plots were hatched at night. Transgressions were punished, enemies dispatched, and wrongs avenged. Outside the laws of civilization, justice was administered according to an older code. And in that same darkness, the boy knew, lurked the glories and dangers of love! Ecstatic unions and the fear of discovery. Enraged husbands and resourceful lovers.

As his imagination boiled over with stories of cuckolds and spies, with their assignations and secret signs, Niccolo's curiosity was aroused by a growing clatter in the direction of the Via Chiara. From a distance, it sounded like the approach of a small, noisy army. A scuffle? An arrest? With perhaps exaggerated caution, he went to have a look.

Niccolo was unprepared for the sight that greeted him when he peered around the corner into the Via del Cocomero. He burst into laughter. For, hurtling down the narrow street, off-balance, rattling and scraping against building walls and barely managing to avoid a disastrous fall with every step, was his hunting companion, Pagolo Pulci.

Pagolo's natural lack of grace was aggravated by the heavy leather armor strapped to his shins and thighs. It effectively prevented him from exerting any real control over his legs. To complicate matters, his padded leather casque, too large, had slipped down over his eyes, blinding him, and he had no way of pushing it up again. His hands were fully occupied with juggling the extensive arsenal he seemed to have brought along. Niccolo marveled at the extent of his friend's preparations—a bow and two quivers, a heavy studded club, a spear, a short sword, a hunting knife, several coils of rope, a woodsman's ax, and a horn. He also carried a satchel bulging with bread, cheeses, sausages, and a flask of wine. This tangle of weaponry and baggage might have been manageable, even for the clumsy Pagolo, had it not been for the most extraordinary thing of all. Dragging him along, much against his will, but completely out of his control, at the end of a long leather leash was a small but very exuberant pig!

At the corner of the Via Chiara, the pig lurched sharply to the left, pulling Pagolo completely off-balance. Only Niccolo's quickness saved him from a fall that would have left him at the mercy of his own hardware. Finally, with the help of his friend, Pagolo succeeded in reining in the obstreperous pig. Red-faced and sweaty from his exertions, he plopped down on the pavement and sat cross-legged, catching his breath.

"*Salve,* Pagolo! The great knight has arrived!"

"Shut up."

"I thought we were going hunting today, but I see you've come outfitted for a military campaign. Where do we strike, Pagolo? Pisa? Milano? The king of France? The Mongol hordes?"

"Shut up."

"A Crusade maybe? Against the Turk."

"Don't push me, Nico, you smart-ass bastard."

"Hey, what's that you've got on your leash there, lunch? Or just a midmorning snack?" said Niccolo eyeing the piglet.

"Shut up."

"No, don't tell me. I've heard stories that in India when they hunt tiger, they tie a pig to a tree as bait. Are we after tiger today, Pagolo?"

Pagolo's breathing had returned to normal. As his friend continued to rail at him, he struck out with surprising speed, delivering a blow across the back of Niccolo's legs with the shaft of his spear. Caught unawares, Niccolo's legs buckled, and he collapsed. A playful scuffle ensued. The pig eyed the two boys rolling around in the middle of the Via Chiara with profound skepticism.

A few minutes later, the bells of Florence's fifty-seven churches and hundreds of private chapels clamorously signaled the beginning of the new day. The huge gates were thrown open, and the city sealed in upon itself for the night reestablished contact with the outside world. In no time, the streets would be surging with activity. As the heavy doors of the Porta San Piero swung slowly open, the two boys had to scurry out of the way to avoid the furious rush of a horseman on some urgent mission.

Niccolo helped his heavily laden friend with his gear. "Here, Pagolo, let me give you a hand. You know, I don't understand what you intend to do with all this stuff."

"It'll come in handy, you'll see."

"But armor? Do you think the animals are going to shoot back?"

"Boars. Boars charge. They have tusks."

"Oh, boars. I see. What about the leg pads?"

"Brush. Thorns. Did you know that thorns can be poisonous?"

"Thorns, eh? How come if you're so well protected, you don't have a pair of gauntlets?"

"They're in the satchel."

"What do you intend to do with the ax?"

"Wolves."

"The spear?"

"What if a deer charges us or something? I could take him before he ran us through with his horns."

"And the club?"

"Bears."

"Pagolo, you disappoint me. A club for bears. What kind of strategy is that. We need artillery. Light cannon, at least. We surround the beast in his cave. Throw up a siege. Cut him off. Wait it out. You've got enough food in that bag for a month or two . . ."

"Stop it, Niccolo. You forced me to accompany you on this barbarous expedition for which you know I am completely unsuited. I, Pagolo Pulci, am a scholar and a gentleman. You know I'm no good with a bow. So I thought, with these other things, perhaps I'd have a better chance of not disgracing myself by coming home empty-handed."

Niccolo persuaded Pagolo to leave the better part of his arsenal at the guardhouse, where they could pick it up on the way home. But about the pig, Pagolo was adamant.

"What does he do Pagolo? Track? Retrieve?"

"Better than that. He comes from a long line of swine, bred and trained to one end only."

"What? Bacon? Prosciutto?"

"This pig, with the aid of his highly sensitive snout, is capable of rooting out one of the earth's most exquisite treasures. This evening, Messer Machiavelli, we shall, with any luck, dine on truffles."

The two hunters proceeded through the gates, cleared the crowd of carts and horses that were attempting to jam their way into the city, and set off for the hills to the south. There was a chill in the fall air. A damp mist still clung to the rough hillsides like tufts of cotton and filled the low-lying areas. As the two boys trudged to the top of a steep rise, little puffs of steam betrayed their labored breathing and their conversation.

As boys everywhere are likely to do, they spoke at great length and with exalted authority on subjects about which they knew little or nothing at all—of war and courage, and inevitably, of the mysteries of love. Neither was willing to admit that his "knowledge" of the subject was sketchy, at best, consisting of a few stray facts and some odd misconceptions. Neither would voice his doubts or tip his hand to reveal the countless nagging questions and glaring inconsistencies that troubled him. So they bragged and they swaggered and they exchanged highly colored accounts that were always suitably vague when it came to specifics. The boys' knowledge of the mysteries and mechanics of love had not yet progressed to the point where they saw anything remarkable or mysterious in the story of the virgin birth.

By this time the sun had burned off what remained of the morning mists, and the result was a fall day of stunning clarity. The sky was a fierce, intense blue, and beneath it stood a world of sharp outlines and crisp edges. The two boys reveled in the splendid day, enjoying themselves tremendously, but finding little in the way of game. Niccolo managed a pheasant, but by the looks of it, the bird was old and tough. Roasting it was out of the question. It would have to be stewed or boiled for a long time to break down the hard, stringy meat.

The only real success of the day went to the pig. Rooting around on the damp forest floor, under its cover of dead leaves, he found several troves of the precious black fungus.

By late afternoon, the boys had crossed a considerable expanse of territory and were heading east, where they would pick up the Via Romana, the main highway between Rome and Florence. The road would take them back to town much more quickly than the tortuous paths they had followed up into the hills. Pagolo's limited reserve of energy was all but spent, and he sorely hoped they would be able to hitch a ride on a cart and not have to walk all the way back.

The two flagging hunters were on a trail that wound down, out of the hills. About a hundred yards in front of them they saw light and could make out a break in the trees where the wide road cut through the forest. As they drew nearer, Niccolo thought he heard voices. He warned his companion, this time with a very stern look, to be quiet.

After his friend's repeated admonitions, Pagolo had finally learned his lesson. While he still did not move stealthily through the underbrush, he blundered far less obtrusively.

When the boys managed to get within about twenty yards of the road, they saw that the voices were coming from a roadside clearing, but it was an odd sight that greeted their eyes. Two men and a boy were resting while two donkeys grazed nearby. There would have been nothing unusual about travelers stopping to rest, except that the two men were dressed entirely in black, with huge square yellow hats, almost a foot high on their heads. The boy, too, was in black. Both men wore incredibly long, full, grey beards.

"Strange monks," whispered Pagolo. "Look at those hats, and the beards. They must be from the orient, Syria maybe?"

They boys crept closer. They could hear one of the monks issuing orders to the boy and pointing in the direction of the pack animals. The language he spoke was not Florentine, but a rough tongue full of rasping, coughing sounds.

"The monk's talking to his son," said Pagolo. "Well, what do we do? Go down and introduce ourselves. *Salve*, strange monks. Where is your country? What exotic land across the seas sends you to us here? Do you come in peace?"

"They're not monks, Pagolo," said his companion. "And they're not Syrians. They're Jews."

Pagolo stiffened with terror. Jews! His grandmother had frightened him with stories of godless Jews. They were worse than gypsies. They stole babies and sold them. They especially liked to steal bad, chubby boys. And do you know what they do with these precious, fattened Christian babies in their infernal Jewish kitchens?

Prompted by these memories, Pagolo proposed a plan of action: "Niccolo, let's get out of here."

"No, wait a minute. I want to watch. They look harmless enough." Niccolo too had heard the stories circulated by grandmothers to scare unruly children, but he was dubious.

"Nico, suppose they start doing something. Like some weird sacrifice. Or a black mass. I don't want to be anywhere within a hundred miles of here."

As they watched, one of the elder Jews removed the great yellow box that served him as a hat. Pagolo flinched, half expecting him to have something frightful hidden under the hat. Like horns!

"Jesus Christ, look at that! He's got another hat on under the big one." Pagolo's feverish imagination was working overtime as he tried to divine the sinister implications of this new discovery. Meanwhile, the Jewish boy had retrieved a satchel from one of the donkeys and spread a cloth on the ground. The three sat, obviously preparing to eat. Pagolo cringed at the thought of what unholy victuals they might pull from the bag.

"Nico," he whined, "please, let's go." The young Machiavelli was of the opinion that they should approach the Jews, but in light of his companion's increasing anxiety, he decided, for the time being, to watch. He wanted to see more. His curiosity had been piqued. Niccolo Machiavelli and Pagolo Pulci would not have long to wait. In the next few minutes, they would witness things that would push them forever beyond the bounds of childhood innocence.

The three Jews were finishing their repast, and Pagolo was fidgeting when Niccolo thought he heard something in the distance. From the direction of Florence a group of horsemen was approaching—fast. A minute later, they materialized in a cloud of dust. Upon spotting the three travelers in the roadside clearing, the lead horseman pulled up and came to an abrupt halt. The others did likewise. There were eight in all, dressed like woodsmen. They were heavily armed. The horses had been ridden hard and were lathered.

At the back of the group was a lone monk wearing the black, hooded robe of the Dominican order. The robe's ample cowl completely concealed his face. The monk now nudged his high-spirited mount forward and stopped in front of the three Jews. By this time they had risen to their feet, but showed no signs of alarm.

"*Buona sera, frate*. How may we be of service to you?" said one of the older Jews with a slight bow.

"Service to usssss?" a voice hissed from beneath the cowl. "How may you be of servicccce to usssss? Let's sssssee? I'm sure I can think of something. Why don't you start by handing over your money?" The startling demand was spoken like a casual suggestion. Despite the hiss, the voice was quite pleasant, almost comforting. It spit and sputtered like a kettle on a friendly fire on an old stove.

But at the mention of money, Pagolo froze. "Bandits," he said to Niccolo, squirming, "I'm going to piss myself if we don't get out of here, now!

"Shhhhhshhhh," his companion clapped a hand over Pagolo's mouth.

The Jew, in measured tones and betraying no fear, said, "I'm very sorry, Signore, but we carry nothing. Only our personal belongings and a few religious articles. My brother and I have been in Rome to celebrate the new year with members of our family there."

"Did you hear that? New yearssss in September! How novel! What a rare sense of humor. And thesssse 'few religious articlesssss' that you're carrying, my good man? Gold and sssssilver, neh?"

"Nothing that could be of any value to you, Signore. Prayer scrolls that have been in my family for generations."

"Lies. Jews have always got bags of money with them, great bags of money." This bit of information was offered by one of the monk's company, a small, evil-looking ferret of a man.

"I think you're right Antoniaccio. Let'sssss take a look. Let'ssss see if the gentleman'sssss telling the truth. Have one of the men inspect the bundles on those lovely pack animalsssss."

The oldest of the two Jews, the one who had not yet spoken, protested, offering to open the bundles himself to show there was nothing in them worth stealing. He was standing between the advancing bandit and the animal. The bandit, a dirty, surly, hulking man, with huge red hands like raw beef, grabbed the frail Jew by the beard and, jerking hard, threw him to the ground. His action elicited a storm of laughter from his fellows in arms.

The large bandit then ripped open each of the four bundles, recklessly spilling their contents out onto the grass. As the Jew had said, they contained clothing, food, the scrolls, and a few books. Nothing more. No gold or silver. Incensed at finding nothing, he went back over to the old man whom he had thrown down. The elderly Jew was attempting to regain his feet and had pushed himself up into a kneeling position. The bandit kicked him, hard, in the stomach. Another kick took him under the chin and threw back his head with a sickening snap. The old man sagged a moment, then slumped to the ground, a lifeless heap of black clothing.

It happened so quickly and so casually that the shock of the murder did not sink in immediately. It was not possible. One minute they were eating and talking, the next, a man was dead. Like that. At first it was incomprehensible. Then slowly, disbelief gave way to horror, and horror to panic. The young Jewish boy was the first to make the connection. He screamed and ran.

The monk whipped around. Something flashed in the dying rays of the sun. A whisper, a dull thud. The boy let out a piercing scream and tumbled head over heels. The dagger had entered squarely between his shoulders. Its point had lodged in his spine. His delicate hands clawed wildly at the protruding haft but couldn't reach it. His screams filled the air. Death did not come quickly. His arms had become entangled in his clothing, but still he kicked madly and writhed in the dust. After an interval of infinite horror, the kicking began to subside. One last futile lunge, and he lay still; his small body had come to rest in one of the deep ruts that ran the length of the road.

One of the bandits had seized the boy's father to prevent him from going to the aid of his dying son. As he watched the life drain slowly out of the boy, the Jew ceased to struggle with his captor. His brother and his son were dead, and with that realization, his fear gave way to sadness and resignation. He had only one thing left to lose, and with all his remaining strength, he prayed to his God they would not find it before they killed him.

"Well, sssssir," he seemed to be shaking his head in resignation beneath his hood. "Your people here seem to have met with an unfortunate acccccccident. Thessse banditssss are a wild bunch, energetic boysssss. Sometimes, I have trouble controlling them. Sometimes, they just get out of hand." Then he turned to his henchman, and sighed, "Antoniaccio, finish this distasteful businessssss."

To the remaining Jew, he confided, in almost fatherly tones, "Antoniaccio is going to teach you a lesssssson."

The one called Antoniaccio grinned ghoulishly as he unslung and strung his bow. His lipless mouth was like a wound in the tightly drawn skin that stretched across his skull. His tiny head was bald and pointed. His small, sharp teeth were widely spaced and, like rats' teeth, worn down by incessant gnawing. Whatever eyes he had were lost in the recesses of the two black hollows of flesh that surrounded them.

He led the Jew to a spot between two trees, and with grunts and gestures, indicated that he was to hold up his arms. Higher, higher, he motioned with his bow. For a moment, the ghoul contemplated the tableau he had created—a bearded patriarch, with arms outstretched, holding them up to heaven, pleading.

Then an arrow sang through the air, pinning the man's right hand to the tree. Before he even had time to react, another shot through the left. The Jew winced, and blood squirted from his wounds. Tears streamed down his face into his beard, not just from the pain, but from the enormity of what was happening. Such senselessness, cruelty, madness. "Why," he gasped. "Why?"

"Antoniaccio," opined the leader, "finish him, will you. Put him out of hisssss missssery." Another arrow found its mark in the Jew's chest. It struck him with such force that his right hand tore free, but he was already dead. Two more arrows in quick succession ensured the fact.

The men began to remount, all but Antoniaccio, who, like a pack rat, was going from body to body, searching furtively under the clothes of the dead men. He grinned up at his master with a look of evil pleasure on his face, "Money belts, Excellency. Money belts!"

Niccolo was transfixed, as if the arrows had pierced his body and rooted him to the spot. He had seen dead men before. They were routinely hung from windows and dangled down from walls in the city to demonstrate the fate that awaited the intransigent. But he had never seen anyone die before. He had never imagined that it could be so commonplace and yet, at the same time, so hideous. He had never imagined that killing could be so offhand, so unmotivated—and so irrevocable.

Pagolo had long since begun burrowing in the dead leaves and soft earth so that, by this time, he was almost completely covered. He had curled into a tight ball and was awaiting his destiny. When Niccolo put his hand on his friend's shoulder to rouse him, he screamed.

"Calm down, Pagolo, it's over. It's over. They're gone."

"Are you sure? What if they come back? Maybe they forgot something."

"They've been gone for at least a half hour. I think it's safe now. Let's go down and have a look."

Pagolo and Niccolo, badly shaken, emerged from behind the mossy log that had given them cover. They crept hesitantly toward the clearing, fearful that the evil lurking over the place could still reach out and destroy them.

Nothing moved as they approached the scene, except one of the great boxlike hats, which rolled back and forth without direction, pushed along by the rising evening breezes. Niccolo had no idea what to do next. Should they bury them? Run to the authorities with their story? Or flee, keep quiet about it, and try to drive the memory from their minds forever? He wanted to make a decision, take some action, any action, but the only thing he felt capable of doing at that moment was to sit down on the ground and weep.

Pagolo broke the silence. "Why did they kill them like that?"

"Because they're bloodthirsty bandits. They didn't get what they wanted."

Pagolo had a sudden inspiration, "The Archbishop! That's who it was. It had to be. He's the most vicious outlaw in all of Tuscany."

"Of course," Niccolo agreed, "Michele, the Archbishop of outlaws! That must have been him, the monk!"

Michele was indeed a notorious bandit who operated in the area, terrorizing travelers on the Roman road. He had come to be called the Archbishop because of an incident involving a French cardinal on his way to Rome. The cardinal, the Archbishop of Burgundy, was traveling with all the pomp and lavish spectacle that generally attend the movements of a very wealthy churchman. Michele and his men surrounded the Frenchmen just south of Florence, took everything they had, stripped them of their clothes, beat them, and sent them off to Rome on foot.

Then Michele donned the Archbishop's exquisite robes and rode into Arezzo, where two of his men were about to be hanged. He rode up to the gallows in the main piazza and humbly inquired as to the crimes of the two wretches awaiting execution. He was told that they were highwaymen guilty of robbery and murder. He asked if he could bless the condemned men and absolve them of their sins to ensure the salvation of their immortal souls. When his men recognized the Archbishop as Michele, they fell to their knees, imploring forgiveness and kissing his feet and the hem of his rich, satin cassock.

Michele said, "You see how contrite these men are. How can you hang them? I beg you, give them to me. I will take responsibility for them and see that they amend their ways and that, from this day forward, they walk with the Lord." The people of Arezzo were moved to compassion by the archbishop's plea and agreed to release the two prisoners into his custody. The counterfeit archbishop, laughing to himself, rode serenely and piously out of Arezzo with his men. The fraud was discovered toward nightfall, when the real French cardinal and his entourage arrived, naked, black and blue, and cursing, and told their story.

From that time on, Michele was called the Archbishop. Terrible and bloody crimes were attributed to him. He was said to have the cunning of a fox and the temperament of a rabid dog.

"If we knew who it was at the time, we would have been even more scared, eh, Pagolo?"

Niccolo walked slowly toward the Jew who had been the victim of the bandit's grisly crucifixion. He was hanging grotesquely by his one hand still pinned to the tree. In the boy's mind, time slowed to a crawl, and it seemed as if it took him forever to reach the twisted body. Niccolo was wondering whether he would have the stomach to pull out the arrow when he got there. He swallowed hard, put both hands on the shaft and pulled. It was slippery with blood, and the arrow was lodged too deeply in the wood to come out. He twisted, trying to loosen the point and work it free, but to no avail. He was careful to avoid looking down at the dead man's face, into his bulging, dead eyes. Finally, he snapped the shaft in half, and the torn hand slipped free. "This little bit of peace is all I can offer you," he thought. "At least you can lie and rest now."

Meanwhile, Pagolo bent to examine the dusty, blood-streaked pile in the middle of the road and realized, for the first time, that it contained the crumpled body of the Jewish boy. He vomited. When he stopped retching, Niccolo was at his side with the flask of wine. "Here Pagolo, take a few sips. Slow now. It'll wash that taste out of your mouth." Pagolo raised the flask to his lips and took several long gulps before lowering it again.

Niccolo turned his attention to the pathetic body of the small boy. He wanted to at least move him out of the roadway, so that he would not be further broken and twisted under the wheels of the passing carts and the pounding feet of horses. As he was wrestling with the already-stiffening body, trying to get a grip under the arms, Niccolo saw the dagger. Sticking out of the rumpled, blood-soaked clothing between the boy's shoulders was the instrument of his undoing. The bandit had not retrieved his weapon. Niccolo could see only the handle, since the entire blade had sunk into the boy's back. He reached out and touched the deadly thing. It was sticky. He gripped it, closed his eyes, and pulled.

The knife was a small one, with a sharp, thin point, made for sticking and stabbing—not cutting. The blade was only about four inches long, and the handle was the same length. Niccolo noted that it was well-balanced, good for throwing. He wiped the blood from the stiletto with the tail of his shirt. It was a plain, serious weapon, for killing, not for display. The black, glossy handle was well worn and unadorned except for a simple design cut into its smooth surface:

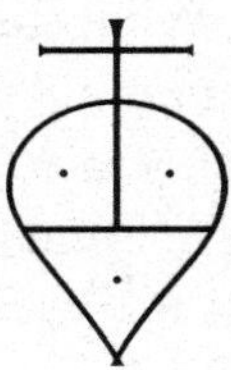

Niccolo continued studying the weapon, turning it over in his hands. This small object—almost a toy—had just inflicted an excruciating death. For no reason. It seemed so easy. Why? Where was its owner now? What was he doing? And—Niccolo tensed—would he be coming back for his weapon? His ruminations were abruptly cut off by a wail of despair from Pagolo's direction. Niccolo jumped. The first thing he saw, not more than ten feet away, was a dozen taut bowstrings and a dozen deadly arrows pointed directly at him. Pagolo wailed again. He was in a similar predicament.

A man stepped out from behind the wall of archers. "Look here. A battle has been fought. Two beasts, really only boys, and three dead men. You, standing over the body with your bloody knife in your hand, are you getting ready to stick him again? He looks dead enough to me.

If you're still angry, why don't you kick him a few times? That should teach him."

The man strolled over to Pagolo. He had an arrogant way of walking. "And you, fat boy, you seem to be enjoying yourself, pouring wine all down the front of your shirt. Celebrating the glorious victory, neh? I suppose the one over there with the arrows in him, Saint Sebastian, was your man. My compliments on your marksmanship. But tell me, how did you kill the third one, the ancient Goliath over there? Slingshots and stones, my little would-be Davids?"

"We . . . we didn't do anything. We were hunting," stammered Pagolo.

"Hunting he calls it! Some game you've brought down. You must tell me then, are old Jews and little boys difficult targets to hit?"

Niccolo spoke, "We didn't kill them. We were hiding over there, behind a log. We saw the whole thing. A band of outlaws did it, bandits."

"Bandits?" the man was suddenly attentive.

"That's right," rejoined Pagolo. "Bandits. It was the Archbishop."

"Ahhhhh, the Archbishop. What did this Archbishop look like?"

"We didn't see. He had on a monk's habit, with the hood pulled up over his head. We couldn't see his face," said Pagolo.

"You couldn't see his face, neh? How do you know who it was then? How do you know it was the Archbishop?"

"Well who else could it be? Who else would do something like this?" pleaded Pagolo.

"I suppose that's what you want people to think, isn't it? A pretty obvious explanation. But you're liars. Liars and murderers! 'We didn't do anything. It was that bandit, the Archbishop. We saw him do it.' But you don't know what he looks like, do you? Let me tell you what he looks like. He's kind of small, about my size. He's got long curly black hair, something like mine. Is that the man you say you saw?" Menace was creeping into his voice now.

"We told you we couldn't see his face. It was hidden in the cowl," protested Pagolo, beginning to whine.

"You couldn't see his face? Then you don't know if he had a long scar down the left side that cut through his eye and a piece of his nostril, just like this scar I've got here. He let that sink in before stating the obvious. Stupid little bunglers, I'm the Archbishop!"

This time, Pagolo's long wail took on a note of desperation. Niccolo gulped. Out of the frying pan . . .

"So you want to cover up this thing by blaming it on me?" He shook his head. "Two old men and a boy—unarmed. Little cowards. Did you show yourselves, or did you hide in the bushes and pick them off? Was it a great battle or an ambush? And what did you find when you tore open their baggage? Jewels?"

"Don't kill us, please," whimpered Pagolo.

"Is that what these poor Jews said before you slaughtered them?" The man paced angrily over to one of his lieutenants and conferred briefly with him.

He announced the results of the conference. "You've just been found guilty. The vengeance of the Lord is swift, and it would appear that, for the time being at least, I am his chosen instrument. When it's over, I'll bury you two and your victims in the same grave. At least they'll have their revenge."

"It's really quite simple out here—an eye for an eye. No time for niceties." Abruptly, he concluded, "Take a minute. Say your prayers." He crossed his arms in a gesture of finality.

Niccolo searched frantically for some detail, some proof, some explanation that would convince the bandit of their innocence. But his mind had raced over everything and come up with nothing. He began to suspect that the only reasonable course open to him was, as the bandit had admonished, to say his prayers.

During the entire exchange, the archers had not lowered their bows or allowed the strings to go slack. When the time came, and the command was given, these men would not hesitate. There was no forgiveness in their eyes.

Pagolo was kneeling now, praying furiously and crossing himself. Niccolo had bowed his head in silent prayer.

"Are you ready?" began the bandit, but he was unable to finish. A clear, commanding voice rang out from behind him, "Let them go. They didn't do anything." The voice was that of a girl.

The bandit whirled. Pagolo collapsed. The archers wavered. Niccolo stared in disbelief. An angel.

From the dense brush on the other side of the road, a woman had emerged and was walking toward them. But not walking. She was drifting, moved by an otherworldly power. To Niccolo, her movements were so graceful and controlled, so fluid, that she could only be an angel.

A few seconds after the initial shock, Niccolo revised his original opinion. This apparition was not an angel, his numbed mind reasoned, for she was not dressed in white and gold, but all in black. He concluded, then, it must be Saint Catherine or Saint Rita.

In the dying light, it was indeed difficult to make out the approaching figure. The Archbishop, a cautious man, had motioned to several of his archers to turn and face her. He did not want any more surprises, especially not from behind his back. The woman stopped in front of the bandit chief. Niccolo strained his eyes, but could see little in the encroaching darkness. The outlines of her black dress were imprecise, and she dissolved into the dark shapes behind her. Her head was sheathed in black—he could not tell at this distance whether it was a veil or long, sleek hair. Only her face shone clearly through the murky shapelessness. Niccolo could have sworn that a single ray of light from heaven illuminated that face.

The girl spoke in a firm but strangely lifeless voice, addressing herself to the puzzled bandit, "You can let the boys go. It happened just as they say it did. Eight men on horseback attacked the three Jews. Their leader was dressed as a monk, and kept his face hidden. I saw it all from across the highway."

"And I suppose you were out hunting too, like our gallant young gentlemen here? Are you with them?" asked Michele.

"No," she replied, "I've never seen them before."

"Who are you then, would you mind telling me? And what are you doing in the country at night, out on the open highway? Did you come here alone?"

"No," she said in her disembodied voice, "I came with them." Lifting her arm, she indicated the three dead bodies on the ground. "The Jew lying dead between those trees is my father."

4

The Archbishop of Outlaws

The odd procession made its way slowly through the Tuscan night. Bathed in the unreal silver light of the full moon, they could be seen on the hilltops, crossing the jagged ridges, silhouetted against the sky. In the lead was an agile man who moved without a sound, bow-legged, round-shouldered, long arms hanging loosely at his sides. Strung out behind the leader were others like him—small, wiry men descended from a race of small, wiry men. They were honest men who worked the land, pruned vines, cut stone, and forged iron; but when pushed, they could be hard men, inflexible men capable of defending and avenging themselves, of arming themselves to steal, and, if need be, to kill.

Following at a slight distance was a small goddess, wrapped in dark cloth, sitting erect on the back of a donkey. The animal was led by a boy whose bent head and listless, trudging steps betrayed his weariness. A latter-day Joseph, leading his child bride to the place where travelers stay. Another donkey carrying another boy, followed. This rider was stout, and he was sleeping fitfully, lulled by the rhythm of his mount. Repeatedly, his somnolent, bobbing head jerked to attention just in time for him to avoid taking a nasty fall. In his hand was a long rope attached to the neck of a strutting, defiant pig.

In the aftermath of the carnage, the Archbishop had taken charge. Issuing orders to his men, he saw to it that the scene was tidied up. A shallow grave was dug in the soft earth behind the log where Niccolo and Pagolo had hidden. The bodies were buried quickly, but not without reverence. Michele had asked the girl if she wanted to say a few words over the graves. She declined.

"You three come with me," he said. It wasn't so much an order as a statement. They complied, for where else could they go? It was now dark, and the city was sealed in upon itself for the night. The gates would not reopen until first light. And so it was that a column of a dozen men and three children wound its way up into the steep back-country hills.

Their progress took them deeper and deeper into the wild countryside. Roads gave way to byroads, byroads to paths, and paths to tortured trails concealed almost entirely by brush. Niccolo could see fireflies, thousands of them. They were everywhere—down in the inky valleys, between the hills. He remembered what his grandmother had said. The souls of unbaptized children. So many lost souls flickering in the Tuscan darkness. Was the soul of the Jewish boy among them?

They passed a quarry. In the moonlight, Niccolo could make out the massive blocks of stone. The scene looked like an abandoned battlefield. The jagged stones were all that was left of some mighty struggle, rocks ripped from the earth by titans and hurled in anger. Broken columns were strewn about like the bodies of defeated giants.

Several times he turned to catch a glimpse of the girl on the donkey. She held her head high, eyes open. Once, the rays of the moon caught her full in the face, and she really did look like a creature from another world. Against the blackness of the night, her pale face seemed to hang suspended in the air, attached to nothing, a floating apparition.

The night air with its heavy burden of fragrances, cypress and pine, was gradually having a soothing effect on Niccolo's inflamed imagination. He began to notice that, occasionally, with some mumbled salutation, one man or two would slip off and be swallowed up in the blackness. The number of outlaws up ahead was dwindling.

The Archbishop forged ahead, picking his way with assurance across the ragged landscape. Where was this bandit with the fearsome scar taking them? What did he have planned? Niccolo didn't know if he was a guest or a prisoner, maybe even a hostage. He was preparing himself for the worst. He could imagine how bandits lived. Lawlessness and disorder, hiding from civilization in the rough hill country. Rowdy, depraved men and lost women living in tents, indulging themselves in Bacchanalian frenzies, sleeping drunk and exhausted on the dirty ground. He would be forced to endure the most depraved sorts of entertainments. Cockfighting.

Niccolo was drawn out of his nightmarish picture of the tawdry pleasures of outlaw life by a long, low howl in the distance up ahead. Michele stopped and, for the first time, turned and spoke to the boy. "*Lupo!* The wolf!" he said, grinning.

What kind of a man broke into a grin at the howl of a wolf? Niccolo wondered, but by this time he was too exhausted to care. Better to be torn apart by a wolf in the open than forced to drink blood, eat dog meat, and swear godless oaths at some barbarous bandit ritual.

The group continued along a trail cut in the living rock of a mountainside. To the left was a deep gorge, and the stones that Niccolo kicked over the side fell a long time before striking anything. The band of outlaws, by now, had disappeared entirely, straggling off one by one. Only Michele was left with his three charges, two boys and a strange girl. Niccolo tensed himself, waiting for the end, for the ferocious beast that would hurl him over the edge and into the void. He heard him coming. Did wolves have red eyes? The scampering feet, the fast breath. He strained to see.

Suddenly, a dark shape lurched into sight, left the ground with a leap, and hurled itself at the bandit chief. Niccolo gasped. Michele was rolling in the dust. He had the animal by the ears. Niccolo couldn't believe his eyes! The bandit was laughing. The animal was licking his face!

Finally, Michele pulled himself to his feet. "My dog, Lupo," he said laughing. "I haven't seen him in a week."

Accompanied by the excited dog, the little band soon rounded the top of a low hill, and in this hostile land of gorges and gullies, they found themselves looking down on a rather large open space. And there was a house. An ordinary farmhouse. Off to one side was a pen with a dozen or so goats.

"We're here," announced Michele.

"We're here?" blurted a surprised Niccolo. "You mean you live in a house?"

"It's nothing extravagant," said the bandit, a note of mock apology in his voice. "I do hope it won't offend the sensibilities of our young gentlemen from the town."

Niccolo, overcome with relief, was stammering, "But I thought bandits lived out in the woods, with, with . . . and . . . Oh, never mind."

Within minutes, the weary group was installed before a bright, roaring fire. Niccolo looked around. A hearth. A table. Benches. Pots.

After the horrors of the day, both real and imagined, he drank in the ordinariness that surrounded him. Real things. Solid things. Warmth and comfort. He sank deeper into his chair. It was padded. It was soft. The tension began to drain out of him. He slept.

The hissing would not stop. He was at the roadside again. The air was full of arrows. Hissing arrows. He was trying to pull the arrow from the dead man's hand. The hissing was becoming louder. The slippery arrow in his hands turned into a snake. It curled tighter and tighter around his hands, hissing and spitting. He tried to run, but his legs were leaden. He couldn't lift them. The snake was writhing and hissing. He struggled to keep it at arm's length, but it was slithering up, up, toward his face, hissing, sucking its forked tongue in and out of its mouth and hissing.

Niccolo bolted in his sleep. His eyes popped open. He was awake, but the hissing would not stop. His heart was galloping in his chest. It was a long, frantic minute before he was able to take in his unfamiliar surroundings and reconstruct the events that had brought him here. Bringing his eyes and his memories into focus, he spotted the cause of the infernal hissing.

Two dozen birds of various sizes and shapes had been spitted and racked over the open hearth and were oozing their juices, drop by drop, into the fire. Niccolo sagged in relief. He let the warmth of the fire and the roasting smells wash over him.

"Hungry?" It was the voice of his host, the most notorious bandit in all of central Italy. The twisted scar on the outlaw's face stood out even more strikingly in the orange firelight, like a fresh wound that refused to close. But the features behind it were kind—a generous mouth that curled into a smile, a strong jaw, a forehead lined with years of concern. There was compassion in his good eye. Niccolo was seeing these details for the first time. Earlier, just after the ambush, he had seen only the scar—and then the reputation.

"Ooo-fa, Michele! Pay attention to the quail! They're burning on that side. Keep turning them." It was another voice, a woman's! So there was a Signora Bandit! A Mrs. Archbishop!

She rushed out of the shadows and swept into Niccolo's line of sight, grabbing the handle of the spit from the Archbishop of outlaws and taking charge of rotating the roasting fowl. Michele's wife or mistress—whatever she was—was a far cry from the diseased, toothless lushes Niccolo had imagined the consorts of outlaws to be.

Pagolo was awake now and squirming, orienting himself mentally, twisting around inside his clothes.

Michele spoke to his wife, "These are my guests, finally awake. Two nameless boys, found, as I told you, under mysterious and dubious circumstances."

"Pulci, Giovanpagolo, at your disposition," declared Pagolo, pompously.

"What an honor! A scion of the famous Pulci family. They used to be somebody in Florence," teased Michele, "but then that was long before your time, eh, Giovanpagolo Pulci?" Pagolo scowled but attempted no defense of his family. Unfortunately, the outlaw was right. The Pulci had seen better days, certainly Pagolo's branch of the family had.

"And our other gentleman," continued Michele, "another illustrious Pulci?"

"No, my name is Niccolo Machiavelli."

"My name, as I've already told you, is Michele, also known as the Archbishop. This is my wife, Cesca."

Cesca looked down at the two boys and smiled. Michele smiled. Niccolo, more and more relaxed, was smiling too. Pagolo was looking suspiciously around. "Where's my pig?" he demanded.

"Oh, that little pig you had with you," said Michele. "That's him on the bottom spit there, next to the duck. He'll be ready to eat soon, though I don't think there's much meat on him."

Pagolo was outraged. He sputtered, unable to mouth a coherent sentence. Instead, it was the bandit's wife who spoke up. "Oh, Michele, stop teasing poor Giovanpagolo Pulci. He's been through enough today." She turned to the boy, "Don't worry about your pig. He's outside in the pen. Nobody's going to eat him."

"What I want to know," continued Michele, "is why a young Florentine gentleman is out in the hill country with a piglet in the first place."

"To find truffles, of course." It was Cesca who answered her husband. "Am I right, Pagolo?"

Pagolo was mollified. She had won him over, and now he, too, was grinning. The easy camaraderie that was developing between them had succeeded in banishing both boys' earlier fears and suspicions.

But suddenly remembering something, Niccolo sat bolt upright and looked frantically around. The Girl! Where was she? Had he imagined the whole thing?

"Don't worry, she's resting." Cesca had immediately sensed his concern. "She wasn't hungry. I gave her some warm bread soaked in almond milk and I made her an infusion. With chamomile. It'll help her sleep."

Michele and Cesca went about removing the spits from the fire and preparing the table for the meal. Niccolo watched, marveling at the absurdity of the situation. He was here at the mercy of the most bloodthirsty bandit of his day. But the bandit had a house, and a wife (and what a wife!). He had a dog. He even had a sense of humor. He had a pleasant smile, and he was about to serve them what looked like a delicious dinner. Nothing made sense anymore. This day had unhinged too many of his assumptions about the order of things. Monks were cold-blooded killers, and the cold blooded-killer was a charming and generous host, with a beautiful wife and a house and a dog . . .

"*A tavola!*" Cesca's voice rang out, interrupting Niccolo's musings and calling everyone to the table. Michele helped her lift a broad wooden trencher and place it in the middle of the table. On the board was a bed of thick slabs of coarse, crusty Tuscan bread. The bread served as the base from which rose a mountain of roasted fowl—the bigger birds were at the bottom—fat ducks from the coastal marshes, game hens, and pheasants. Then came grouse, squab, turtle doves and pigeons, and at the very top, tiny thrushes, roasted whole with their heads still on. Each small bird was garnished with an olive in its beak.

Pagolo's eyes lit up at the sight of this spectacular pile of food. "My father always told me that *contadini* ate awful food. Country people survive on moldy bread and thin gruels, he said, turnips when they can get them."

"And when we're lucky, we get a cup of warm water, to wash it down," said Michele. "But tonight, since we have the honor of the company of Giovanpagolo Pulci, citizen of the republic of Florence, we're making an exception. Go on, Pagolo, eat. Enjoy yourself. If that's not enough food, we'll fix you something else afterward. Maybe something to suit your refined city tastes—delicate peacock tongues sautéed with the livers of little fishes. And you can sprinkle rosewater on it, as they do in France!"

Everybody laughed, and Pagolo took the ribbing in stride. But no sooner had he resolved one problem, than another arose. "Don't I get a knife?" he asked.

"What for?" said Michele. "Use your hands!"

Pagolo thought of protesting, but his resistance was fast disappearing. The lure of the birds, their golden, crispy skin, and the hearty bread soaked in their juices proved too much for him to dally any longer in squeamishness or conversation. Within a minute, he was eating so fast that, several times, he bit into his soft, fat fingers.

Aside from the food, there was nothing else on the table but a wooden cup and a *brocca,* a decorated ceramic pitcher, full of wine. Michele filled the cup, drank deeply, and sighed. He refilled it and passed it on to his wife. She drank, and then it was Niccolo's turn. As they feasted, eating the smaller birds first, and working down the mountain to the larger ones, the single cup went round and round, circling and recircling the table too many times to count.

When all had eaten their fill, there was still a lot of meat on the table. But there was also a considerable pile of bones to indicate just how hungry the company had been. The board was removed, and Cesca brought a salad of fennel bathed in sleek green olive oil. The sweet licorice felt good in Niccolo's mouth. It rinsed his palate and refreshed him. He knew too, from his father, that it should help him digest the heavy meal he had just consumed.

Michele was teasing Pagolo again. "I wanted to apologize for calling you 'fat boy' this afternoon. I should have said, 'plump boy.' Anyway, Pagolo, are you full? Maybe you'd like some zucchini cooked with calf's brains, or little eels fried in butter?"

"You know what they eat almost every day at Pagolo's?" Niccolo volunteered, beaming. "Beans! Florentine broad beans!"

Michele burst into laughter, so Niccolo continued. "Pagolo's father is so stingy that he bought a special table for the kitchen. It's long, but only about a foot wide, so everybody had to eat on the same side, sitting next to each other. In the winter, he moves the table close to the hearth, and everyone eats with their backs to the fire. That way, he can build a small fire instead of a big, roaring one to heat the whole room. He saves money on firewood."

Michele and Cesca were laughing good-naturedly at this revelation of the true state of affairs in Pagolo's family. Pagolo was sated, and he took it philosophically. The wooden cup, stained purple form many years of use, continued to circulate.

Michele turned to Niccolo with a shrewd smile. "And does one eat better at the Machiavelli's?"

"Yes, we eat better. Because my father worries a lot about eating."

Michele was a little puzzled. "Why does he worry about it? If you've got enough to eat, what's there to worry about?"

"Well," Niccolo explained, "he worries about what he eats and when he eats it. He says that eating has to be done in an orderly fashion. Regular meals, regular times of day. We would never have eaten anything this late in the day. It puts a big strain on the digestion, and it gives you nightmares."

"At what time of day are you supposed to eat, then, so you don't overburden the digestion?" asked the bandit.

"We have two meals a day," said Niccolo. "The first is always between nine and ten in the morning and the second is just before dark."

"Hmmmm," said Michele, "I've always heard that the rich man eats when he's hungry, and the poor man whenever he can." But the bandit was amused at the rigor of the Machiavelli household. "Do you eat the same thing every day? Like Pagolo here with his beans? Is that part of the regularity?"

Niccolo answered as if he were giving a prepared speech or reciting exercises memorized from his Latin grammar. It was clearly a lesson in which he had been rehearsed many times: "First we have the antipasto, which can be salad, fruit, little tarts, *salame*. Next is the boiled course, which can be pasta, soup, or poached meat or fish. After that comes the fried or roasted course, and after that, fruit, which is good for the digestion. It's also important never to mix meat and fish in the same meal, so if the boiled course is fish, then the fried course has to be fish too.

"But can I say something?" Niccolo blushed a little. "Despite the fact that you didn't follow the correct order for the meal, and that we ate too late and I'll probably be up all night with indigestion, everything was good, really, really good. My father would kill me, but I loved it."

Michele was pleased with the compliment. He liked this boy, so oddly dogmatic when it came to food, and he liked the boy's chubby companion, who had some time ago fallen asleep in his chair. A little later, feeling comfortable by the fireside, Niccolo confessed to his host his earlier fears—that he had expected outlaws to lead a life of wild and filthy inhibition. "And I can't believe that you live here the way you do. Everything's just so, so . . . normal."

"Except we don't eat our meals in the prescribed order of courses, or at the right time of day," Michele observed.

Niccolo continued, "I'm starting to think you're not really an outlaw at all! You're one of our *contadini grassi,* the fat, happy peasants."

"I may tend vines, keep goats, and trap thrushes, but don't forget that when we met this afternoon, I was at the head of a band of armed men, Machiavelli. When the times call for it, I'm an outlaw."

"Then everything they say about the Archbishop and his bloody deeds is true?'

"There have been—exaggerations," Michele said. "Some of it's true, some not. The part about me holding up the Archbishop of Burgundy is true enough, and that is how I got my name. But since then, a lot of men in these hills and on the roads have done a lot of things, some of them praiseworthy, some very vile indeed, and a lot of these things are attributed to me. So my reputation grows. The people want a legend."

"But you've killed men?" asked Niccolo.

"A few," replied the bandit, "but I'd say they were more animals than men."

"And you rob people?"

"I take things. Let's say that, from time to time, I redistribute things."

"Then you rob from rich and give to the poor!" concluded Niccolo triumphantly.

"Only a stupid man would rob the poor, Machiavelli. They haven't got anything to steal. Now the rich, they're a different story, an altogether more inviting target.

"So, occasionally when I hear of, 'opportunities,' or maybe a problem that needs solving, I put the word out, a few men come together, we do what we have to do, and then we go our separate ways. We vanish. And living a perfectly normal life, like a *contadino grasso,* as you put it, there's very little chance of me being caught. Who would come and arrest a fat, happy peasant? Who would ever suspect?"

"So you can go anywhere you want, and nobody would really recognize you. You could even go into Florence."

"If I wanted to, I suppose I could," said Michele. "But why should I? From what I hear, there are plenty of thieves and cutthroats in the city already. No, there would be too much competition. My reputation would suffer. Besides, there's the small matter of my family being banished from the city for seven generations."

"So your family is from Florence?" Niccolo was surprised, since he assumed Michele was from these craggy hills where he lived and plied his trade.

"Aha! Spoken like a true Florentine!" trumpeted Michele. "Sooner or later they all start asking questions about your family. No other city in Italy is as obsessed with ancestry as Florence. And the big question is always, 'Is your family Florentine?'" Being a Florentine! The ultimate pedigree! Yes, Machiavelli," he conceded, "my family is from Florence."

"You were born in Florence, and now you're banished for being a notorious outlaw?" asked Niccolo. "Officially?" He had never before met anyone who was *officially* banished. "By decree?"

"I am officially banished. By decree. But I wasn't born in Florence. I never had the privilege. It's not that I'm banished for being a bandit. It's the other way around. The reason I'm a bandit is because I was banished in the first place. Because of my grandfather."

Michele stopped for a moment, pensive. Niccolo had been watching his hands. They were big, sinewy hands, far bigger than the hands of most men his size. When Michele spoke, the hands were in constant motion, delivering a running commentary on his account, adding emphasis, expressing anger and then satisfaction.

As he paused for a moment, Michele thoughtfully raised a finger from one of those gnarled hands and stroked at the long scar that trailed across his forehead, down through his dead eye and then down his cheek. It resembled nothing so much as the numeral 7 written boldly on his face in blood.

Niccolo thought the scar the most magnificent thing he had ever seen. Stark, powerful, and evocative. Romantic too. Without being aware of it, the boy had begun to run a thoughtful finger down his own cheek in imitation of the bandit. In the place where the scar should be.

"What did he do? Your grandfather?"

"He led a revolt, a revolution. Did you ever hear of the revolt of the Ciompi?"

"No. Who were the Ciompi?"

"You don't know your history, Machiavelli." chided the outlaw.

"I certainly do," said Niccolo indignantly. "I've studied Livy, and I know all about Romulus and Remus, and the rape of the Sabines, and Marius and Sulla and, and Caesar and the Rubicon, and Brutus and Cassius and Mark Anthony—"

Michele cut him off. "You know all about these things that happened a thousand years ago, God knows where, in some Rome before the priests invaded, but you don't know what happened in your own city a hundred years ago. Some Florentine!"

Niccolo looked embarrassed.

Michele continued, "The Ciompi were the clothworkers, the miserable, despised clothworkers, the salt of the earth. They called them the Ciompi because of the clogs they wore in the washing sheds, those heavy, clomping, clunking wooden clogs. Would you like to hear the story of the day they rose up against their masters? Would you like to hear about their revolution? About the time those clogs marched through the streets of Florence, about how an army in clogs took over the whole city?"

Niccolo nodded his head eagerly, indicating that he would indeed like to hear such a story.

Michele began with a long, thoughtful preamble, "They say that most cities are torn with one great division, but Florence is different, isn't she? She distinguishes herself above all others in being torn constantly with a thousand divisions, great and small. Not content with two warring factions, she's produced hundreds. If any one faction gets the upper hand, why hardly is its triumph complete and its power consolidated, than it splits into two and the fighting begins all over again . . ." The bandit stopped. He laughed to himself. "I should have been less longwinded," he thought, for his guest was already fast asleep.

5

The Jewess

There was a window overhead, and Niccolo raised himself to look out. There were no curtains. Of course not, he was in the country. But his view was blocked by a heavy, oiled piece of cotton stretched over a wooden frame that served to let in the light but keep out the deadly drafts that blew in at night and killed people in their sleep. He pulled it aside and noticed that the sun was already high in the sky. Almost noon. A guilty, involuntary reflex reminded him that lying in bed had caused him to miss the nine o'clock meal. Was that his father's voice?

He sank back down and noticed the deep depression in the mattress where Pagolo had been. It was the kind of day that was bound to present too many problems, too many choices. It was the kind of day you wanted to skip. Drift back to sleep. Yesterday he had been eager for adventure. Today the thought terrified him. Absolutely no more adventures.

Ultimately, it was the burning sensation in his bladder that forced Niccolo from his makeshift bed in the storeroom.

Bootless in his urgency, and already fumbling with the laces of his hose as he ran, he tore around the back of the house, certain that he would never get the knots undone in time. In a final effort of supreme self-control, he succeeded in freeing himself. Then the dam burst. Niccolo propped himself against the side of the house for what he knew would be a protracted watering and watched the puddle form at his feet. It grew in volume and began to trickle downhill. Sighing in blessed relief, his eyes followed the meandering little stream. How far would it go? Niccolo directed his eyes a little ahead to get the lay of the land and to see what obstacles his rivulet might encounter. Nothing in the way for a while, dirt packed by the passage of men and animals, a good hard surface, a shallow rut made by a cartwheel could be a problem, probably slow things up, some grass, a pair of small black boots and the hem of a black dress . . . Niccolo choked.

The Saint! The Angel! The girl was standing there, staring at him, not fifteen feet away!

He gulped. He stuttered. He stammered. He attempted an explanation, but eloquence had deserted him. Finally, giving up on the possibility of oral communication, he shrugged his shoulders, resignedly, and held out both hands, palms up—what can I say?

"Well, go ahead, aren't you at least going to finish what you started?" The curiosity on her face was giving way to amusement at the hapless boy's dilemma. "I suppose I could turn around and let you finish in peace. Shall I?" Niccolo mumbled something as she pivoted and swung gracefully around.

"Jesus Christ," he thought. "Now she's just going to stand there. And wait. I can't do it. Not now. She'll hear it!" He gave up and pulled his laces tight, tighter than usual, as an extra precaution. His ears were burning. "It's alright. I'm done. You can turn around."

The girl's attempts to stifle her amusement were proving unsuccessful. What began as a titter was turning into the kind of lusty laughter that would soon leave her short of breath. The sight of the solemn, frowning Niccolo only served to redouble her mirth. The polite smile that he forced across his face did little to conceal his acute uneasiness.

By degrees, her laughter subsided and she managed to get a hold of herself. She dried her eyes and regained the use of her voice. "I'm sorry. You just seemed so, so—pitiful, so guilty, as though you'd been caught in the act of doing something really dreadful. Come on now; you can relax. I won't tell anybody. Your terrible secret is safe with me." She was giggling again.

Stunned. Devastated. Beyond humiliation. Niccolo was on the point of trudging off in silence to nurse his wounded pride. But his tormentor rescued him by tacitly agreeing to abandon the delicate and painful subject. "Come on, let's go for a walk. My name is Giuditta, and yours?"

"Niccolo," he grunted.

As the two walked, she kept up a steady barrage of questions, inquiring into the minutest details of Niccolo's circumstances—his household, family, likes and dislikes, what he ate and what he didn't. Barely was Niccolo able to satisfy her on one account before she would redirect her probes in another direction. He was getting uncomfortable. This wasn't a conversation, it was an inquisition.

When the assured young woman had gathered enough information to fill an encyclopedia on Niccolo, the Machiavelli, Florence, and the organization of the Christian world in general, she paused for a moment, then, "You're such a quiet boy," she chided. "Are all Christians as stingy with their conversation as you?"

Niccolo was mortified. He had been accused of many things—laziness, arrogance, disrespect—but never of being quiet! Among his companions he enjoyed a reputation for a sharp and relentless tongue. He took great pride in his verbal abilities and had come to regard conversation not so much as an exchange but as a duel. With Pagolo, he was truly merciless, but then Pagolo was so easy to tease, and he took it so well. But this girl had caught him completely off-balance. Like an adroit swordsman, aggressively pursuing some initial advantage, she had charged into this dialogue and would not let up. Groping for an explanation, all the while continuing to fend off the ongoing cross-examination, Niccolo concluded it was the fact that she was a Jewish girl that had thrown him off and tied his tongue in hopeless knots. He had never spoken to a Jewish girl before, never spoken to any Jew before. The explanation satisfied him. But Niccolo was a boy of twelve, and it did not occur to him that his discomfort stemmed not from the fact that she was a Jewish girl, but that she was, quite simply, a girl.

"You know," she was saying, "this is the first time I've ever spoken to a Christian boy. I'm sorry if I've hounded you, but there are so many things I wanted to know." More wounded pride.

By this time the two jousters, one badly beaten down, had circled Michele's properties and come to rest at the goat pen, face-to-face. During the lengthy questioning, Niccolo had not dared to look directly at his assailant. Although painfully aware of the animated presence alongside him, he had chosen instead to concentrate his attention on his own feet and the small stones that he kicked down the dirt path ahead of them.

He was mildly surprised when he saw her face for the first time, close up. She was much darker than he had imagined the night before. The moonlight had played a trick on him, bathing her in its unnatural, white light, hence his first impression that there was something otherworldly about her, something angelic, something saintly. She was no saint today.

She had a wide, full mouth that curled and uncurled into a hundred different smiles. Thick hair, thick eyebrows. Dark, but comely. Niccolo took heart from her appearance. The verbal tidal wave that had overwhelmed him had subsided, at least momentarily, as the Christian boy and the Jewish girl appraised each other in silence.

Niccolo saw an opening. "Can I ask a question, or would that be speaking out of turn?"

"Of course you can ask a question," she feigned surprise. "If you want. You know, I thought you were terribly timid, and so I kept talking to keep you from being embarrassed. But if you want to say something, go right ahead. I don't mind a bit." The girl had been speaking rapidly throughout their colloquy, so fast in fact, that at times Niccolo had trouble keeping up with her. And now, if such a thing were possible, she seemed to be picking up the pace.

"Well, what are you waiting for? I thought you had a question. Aren't you going to ask it?" Her voice was rising in pitch, uneven, swerving from one register to the next, careening a little out of control. "Aren't you? Aren't you?"

Niccolo thought he understood what might be going on in the girl's mind behind the verbal bravado and the gales of laughter. She was making a desperate attempt to stave off the memories and the horrors of the day before by talking, by laughing, by listening, by losing herself in something, anything, by feigning gaiety, by teasing him, by grilling him on countless, meaningless details. But the horror was breaking through the fragile defenses she was constructing and forcing itself upon her again. As Niccolo watched, fascinated but helpless, the bravado dissolved, the mask fell, and her words turned to sobs.

When she had regained some of her composure, the girl wiped her swollen eyes and made a show of courage. "I'm sorry," she stammered.

"I know," was all that Niccolo could say. But he said it with genuine emotion and with an uncommon depth of understanding and sympathy. He had been there too. And out of that dreadful event, a bond was forged. They stood there staring at each other, and there was silence between them and in heaven for the space of about half an hour.

"What's that?" said Niccolo, breaking the trance and indicating a large, mawkish yellow emblem emblazoned on the sleeve of the girl's dress.

It's a badge, a sign," she said noncommittally. The badge in question was about the size of a man's hand. It looked like a wheel with spokes, or a cosmological representation of the sun or a star.

"What does it mean?" asked Niccolo.

"That I'm a Jew," was the response.

"Do all Jews wear them?"

"We're supposed to," she was volunteering nothing.

Niccolo dug deeper, "Is it a religious sign?"

"I imagine it is, although it has no meaning in my religion. I assume it must have some meaning in yours."

The response was less than satisfactory. Niccolo was getting frustrated, and puzzled. "If you don't even know what it means, why do you wear it?"

The girl sighed, and proceeded patiently, as though explaining something simple for the tenth time to an obtuse child, "I wear it because I'm required by law to wear it. Not by my law but by your law, the pope's law. All Jews are required to wear them."

"Why?"

"So everyone can identify us as Jews. That way, they'll have no trouble shunning us or abusing us or harassing us. Or trying to convert us to Christianity. That's the favorite thing, isn't it? Trying to convert the Jew?" An edge of bitterness had crept into her voice.

Niccolo sensed the swing in her mood. And he knew what to do about it. Distract her. Make her think of something else. "What's wrong with conversion? Jews convert to Christianity all the time. Let me tell you about it. There was a merchant in Florence named Gianotto who had a cloth business. And among his business associates was a rich Jew named Ibrahim, who was also a merchant. Gianotto recognized his friend's honesty and his upright character, and began to regret that this good man was destined to be condemned for all eternity and damned to hell because of his lack of faith. So he decided to convert him.

"Gianotto began to lecture his Jewish friend on the error of his ways, and to explain all that was holy and good in the Christian faith. At first, Ibrahim resisted and said, 'I was born a Jew and I'll die one, and nothing will cause me to change.' But Gianotto was insistent. He kept at him and slowly wore down his resistance. In the end, Ibrahim agreed to become a Christian, but on one condition. He said, 'All right, Gianotto, I'm willing to try your religion, but first I want to go to Rome to see the Holy Father and his brothers, the cardinals, and all the Curia. I want to see these great and holy men, so that I can truly understand why your faith is better than mine. Then, I shall allow myself to be baptized.'

"Gianotto was in despair, and tried everything in his power to keep Ibrahim from going to Rome—'It's too far, it's dangerous for a man of your age, it's expensive, the weather is bad.' But Ibrahim was determined, and so he went.

"When he got there, he began to observe the behavior of the pope and the cardinals and the other priests. Ibrahim was astounded. Never had he seen such a filthy, bawdy company in his entire life. He saw every conceivable type of vice, natural and unnatural. He saw that the only way to gain a favor at the papal court was through the intercession of whores and little boys! So Ibrahim, his head hung low in somber thought, returned to Florence."

Niccolo was warming to his tale, and what was best, the girl seemed intrigued. "When Ibrahim got back, Gianotto was ashamed and was even afraid to talk to his Jewish friend, knowing, as any Christian in Italy would know, what he must have seen in the Eternal City. But Ibrahim sent for him, and Gianotto was forced to face him, 'Well, what did you think of the Holy Father?' he asked, cringing.

"'Oh, he was an abomination. And his cardinals and all his priests. I saw no good works there, no holiness, no devotion, no exemplary lives. Instead I saw a frightening display of all the seven deadly sins—I saw lust and anger, gluttony, sloth, fraud, envy and pride. And in such abundance that it's a marvel to me that your God doesn't strike out in His wrath and destroy this pestiferous church.'

"Gianotto was silent, deeply humiliated.

"'But he doesn't!' continued Ibrahim. Despite every effort of the pope and vile court to destroy everything that is good and holy in the world. And this got me to thinking, Gianotto. Any church that is able to withstand that kind of wickedness and corruption must have something powerful going for it. So come now, I've made my choice. What else can I do? Take me to be baptized.'"

At first, Niccolo told his story in a deadly serious tone, but gradually, he began to exaggerate more and more. At the end of Niccolo's tale, the girl was so pleased by the odd twist of events that she clapped her hands in delight. "Beautiful hands," Niccolo thought. "Tiny hands."

He beamed. He seemed to have won her approval. He was happy. She derived some small comfort from his efforts and even had the audacity to plant a small kiss on Niccolo's forehead as a reward.

"If you promise you won't try to convert me, then I think we can be friends," she said.

"I promise," Niccolo vowed.

"Because it gets so tedious," she said, "and they never give up. Did you know that every week they send a preacher down to the borghetto, to preach to the Jews? We all have to go and we all have to sit quietly and listen. It's required by law. And who knows, maybe one of us will convert?"

"We have to go too," said Niccolo, "every Sunday. Miss one Sunday and you go straight to hell. I guess it's the same for everyone."

"It's not the same for everyone." Again, her mood swung, again toward unhappiness. "For us, it's different. We have to wear these badges so you can see us coming. We're not allowed to own land or carry weapons. We're not even allowed out after dark! When something goes wrong, they blame the Jews. When the great plague started, what did they say? That the Jews had poisoned the wells! And on and on." There were tears in her dark eyes.

Neither said anything for a long time. They stared at the bearded goats, impertinent creatures. Niccolo had never thought about Jews at all once he had determined they did not steal away bad little boys. He had always assumed they were content within the closed circle of their bizarre practices and beliefs.

When the girl spoke again, it was not in the agile, lively voice of this afternoon but in the distant, preoccupied monotone of yesterday evening at the roadside. "Do you know how they represent us in their paintings and statues, the Christian masters? How they represent the Jew who refuses to recognize Jesus Christ?"

Niccolo said he didn't.

"As a beautiful woman—with a blindfold."

6

In the Ghetto

The girl stated flatly that she intended to return to the city that afternoon, and Niccolo nearly made a fool of himself in protesting his readiness, his eagerness, his willingness, his insistence, and his boundless enthusiasm for accompanying her. The offer was accepted graciously, if with a certain sly smile, and they made ready to leave in order to get back to Florence before nightfall.

Prior to their departure, there was more eating. Pagolo, with true nobility of spirit, presented almost his entire cache of truffles to Cesca, their hostess, in a gesture of gratitude.

Michele, the archbishop of outlaws, had led the little party through the maze of precarious paths that wound down and out of the hills. Niccolo was careful to memorize the route as they went and promised to return to visit his new friends when he could. Michele left the three wayfarers on a narrow but serviceable road that he said would eventually carry them into Florence at the Porta San Friano.

Niccolo was surprised to discover that they were only about two hours away from the city on foot, less on horseback. In his state of nervous exhaustion, the previous night's journey had taken on fantastic dimensions and seemed much longer than it actually was.

Pagolo was enjoying a postprandial hour of quiet, and Niccolo could have sworn he was asleep as he walked, if such a thing were possible. Niccolo was so absorbed in attending to the young lady in his charge that his chubby companion could have strolled over the edge of a cliff without his absence being remarked.

"Where will you go?" he asked her. Is your mother—"

"Dead," she cut him off. "All dead now. I'll go to Melchisadech, a business partner of my father. He lives in the house next door to us. He'll know what I should do."

"He'll take care of you?" There was a note of disappointment in Niccolo's voice, for he had been evolving an elaborate plan in which the family Machiavelli might be persuaded to shelter this unfortunate orphan, temporarily at least, but perhaps for a long time, perhaps forever.

"Tell me where you live," he said, changing the subject.

Giuditta began to explain, but her task was complicated by a number of factors, foremost among them that Niccolo knew absolutely nothing of the streets of the borghetto, the Jewish quarter, and she knew little else. Furthermore, it was becoming apparent from their attempts to find some common geographical ground that the Jews did not always use the same street names as the Florentines did. A good deal of confusion could have been avoided if, for example, it had been clear from the outset that what Giuditta insisted was the Via dei Macellai, the street of the butcher shops, was in fact what Niccolo referred to as the Via dei Giudei, the street of the Jews. Eventually, however, Giuditta succeeded in bringing Niccolo into the general vicinity of her house.

She was saying, "There is a vacant lot at the corner, full of rubble and stinking garbage. The garbage, they dump there deliberately, all the time, to harass us."

"Who dumps it?" Niccolo interrupted.

"Men with oxcarts. Who do you think dumps it?" she replied. "Now listen. . . . If you continue along the edge of the vacant lot, you'll see a house with a huge mural painted on the side. That house stands at the entrance to the borghetto.

"It's an ugly thing, the mural. A man with wings is standing over a woman who is for some reason down on her hands and knees. I suppose it's a religious subject. The painter they hired was an incompetent, and the thing came out a mess. Did you know the city actually hired a painter to put the clumsy picture there? Someone thought it would be a good idea to put up a religious painting in the borghetto to edify the Jews and bring us one step closer to conversion. So we got a holy Christian painting.

"My father was offended by the subject, and he and my uncle went to complain to the authorities. They said they felt the painting was inappropriate and meant to be an affront to their religion and sensibilities. They asked if they could have it removed. And you know what the reply was? They were beaten and fined!

"But that wasn't the end of it. That night, someone came and did a little extra work on the painting. The next morning, there was a big crowd gathered in front of it crying, 'Sacrilege, sacrilege!'

"The new painting still had the winged man standing upright with the woman on her knees in front of him, but now, now," Giuditta interrupted her narrative and giggled. She blushed and continued, "Now he had the head of a goat. And instead of a sword, he was waving, well, waving something obscene in her face.

"They had to bring the original painter back in immediately to dismember the poor fellow. But the desecration, as they called it, was blamed on my father and uncle. They were arrested and beaten and fined again."

The walls of the city were already in view by the time Giuditta's lesson in the civic use of art had come to an end. Seeing them, she stopped abruptly, and Niccolo stopped too. "I have a favor to ask you," she said.

"Anything," he replied, and he meant it with all his heart—literally anything.

"Yesterday at the roadside, I saw you take something. I want it. I want the dagger that killed my brother." Her gaze was steady, unyielding, emotionless. "So I never forget."

Niccolo turned into the Via Romana and the welcome sight of his father's house. It was still exactly the same as he had left it, solid and reassuring. But everything else had changed. His world had tilted a little, and everything in it was rearranged. The most important things in his life were things that hadn't even existed for him two days ago, when he left this house.

He had little difficulty explaining his absence to his father. Knowing his son Niccolo to be a resourceful and responsible boy, Bernardo Machiavelli was not overly concerned with his comings and goings, and Niccolo was frequently absent for a few days at a time, especially during the hunting season. On the other hand, the absence of his other son, Totto, his firstborn and heir apparent, would have alarmed Bernardo to a considerable extent. Totto was oafish and slow-witted. People could take advantage of him.

However, it might have alarmed even the unflappable Bernardo if he knew that his second son had witnessed three murders, was getting mixed up with bandits, and, worse, was fraternizing with Jews.

"So you were out in the hills and you stayed the night with a *contadino*. Hmpph!" snorted Bernardo over dinner that evening at the prescribed hour. "What did you eat, turnips?"

"Duck, game birds," said Niccolo.

"Heavy meat, greasy. I hope you at least had a salad to put your digestion back into good working order." With these words, Bernardo plowed back into his liver sausages, signaling an end to the conversation. One can only hope that he had the good sense, after such heavy fare, to come to the assistance of his flailing digestion with copious amounts of well-dressed salad.

Niccolo was too excited to eat, and later that night, he was too excited to sleep. He was laying plans for tomorrow, for he had decided that tomorrow he absolutely must visit this strange, strange, beautiful girl.

Their separating had been too hasty, not at all the elaborate leave-taking he had been anticipating, involving, at a minimum, ceremonial hand kissing: *Dusk was already upon the city when they passed through the gates. Suddenly, Giuditta, who was walking a few steps in front of him, turned, whispered, "Thank you and good-bye." And then she was running. Fleeing.*

"Wait!"

"I can't," she called out over her shoulder. "I have to go." And as she and her voice trailed off, "Don't you know, Jews aren't allowed out after dark!"

Niccolo lay awake mulling over the implications of this abrupt separation and planning tomorrow's joyful reunion. Should he take flowers? Should he go on horseback? Should he wear the black-velvet doublet?

These and other considerations occupied him as he tossed in his bed. He made frequent trips to the window to examine the heartless night sky for the slightest hint of dawn's first light. He was feeling a curious combination of extreme agitation and, at the same time, sublime contentment. It was a sensation he was as yet unable to identify, a sensation that Florence's best poet had once described as an "icy fire." In a word, what he was experiencing were the first stirrings and twitchings of love.

Finally, rosy fingers of light began to tickle the eastern sky. Niccolo put on his best white shirt and new white hose and did indeed opt for the new black-velvet doublet. He looked dashing and, he thought, altogether heroic. He made his way downstairs while the rest of the household slept, for his attire would illicit unwanted curiosity, and if the true nature of his errand were somehow divined, insufferable teasing. He saddled one of his father's horses—there were three. He took the black one to match his heroic outfit.

After an hour of aimless equestrian wandering and unbearable anxiety, Niccolo decided that a decent interval had elapsed since sunrise, and it was now an appropriate hour to go calling. In fact, it was a little more than half past seven. He crossed the river and headed north through progressively less familiar territory.

He was thinking now that the girl reminded him of the Madonna. What could be more logical? Giuditta was Jewish and so was Mary. Why shouldn't they look alike? And she was beautiful, but sad. And deep. Like the *Pietà*, with her dead son in her arms, she contained all the sadness in the world. He had seen glimmers of many emotions cross her face—sorrow, rage, grief, even despair—but all were harnessed and brought quickly under control. Not like the Florentine women whose sorrow was a noisy affair, accompanied by extravagant displays of public wailing, breast beating, and, in the more extreme cases, the rending of garments, the pulling of hair, and theatrical swooning. She was passionate, proud, and private. And beautiful. And smart.

He had no trouble locating the pestilential garbage dump and the controversial mural she had described. Even Niccolo, who had little interest in the figurative arts, could see that is was executed by an inexpert and probably shaky hand. The angel Gabriel had a large, square head, with a stupid, blank expression on his face. Mary was hunched over on her knees and looked more like she was scrubbing the floor than receiving the joyous news. Beyond that ham-fisted mural lay the mysterious streets of the ghetto.

Despite the heat of the moment and his desire to present himself in as striking a posture as possible, Niccolo had second thoughts about galloping and clattering full tilt into that unknown Jewish underworld. Discretion prevailed, and he rode on, one street, two streets, until he saw a tavern where it would be safe to leave his horse. Several heavy iron rings had been fixed into the wall of the establishment precisely for that purpose, and other horses idled about, awaiting the return of their riders.

Niccolo jumped down and tethered his mount. He fumbled a little with the reins. He was nervous, and it showed. He was, after all, on the most important quest of his short life. He noticed that the tavern and the houses around it were not of the most genteel aspect, but rather rundown and in need of repair. Trying to appear inconspicuous, he started off down the cluttered, dirty street. He walked stiffly past a group of rough young men several years older than himself who were entertaining what looked like rough and immodest young women. Men in clogs. Women in clogs. He worried about his riding boots, his black-velvet doublet and smart woolen hose. He worried that his finery would give him away in this distinctly unpolished part of town. But he needn't have concerned himself. No one paid him the least bit of attention.

When he returned to the mural where the angel Gabriel had recently confronted the Blessed Virgin Mary with unspeakable rudeness, there was a hubbub at the corner. A crowd had gathered, people of all descriptions, most of them poor. Niccolo mingled, trying to find out what was going on, but the scraps of excited conversation he managed to overhear added up to very little. Only the often-repeated phrase "Jewish witch" emerged with any clarity from the babble around him.

A blustery old man seated on a cistern was pontificating with great conviction in a loud voice. Niccolo recognized him as the kind of man who knows everything before anyone else, who has inside sources, who can put two and two together. "I had it from Simone, the charcoal burner, and Simone's the one who found her," he was saying. "He went to deliver a load, and she was bent over the old man with the knife still in her hand. Cut his throat, she did. And all over the walls, she had drawn ancient Babylonian witch's symbols with his blood."

"Grisly affair," thought Niccolo, "if the old windbag is telling anything even close to the truth, which is highly unlikely."

"And when she turns around, Simone sees she's got the mark of the Jew on her, and being an honest tradesman and a good Christian, he starts backing away from her and makes the sign of the cross.

"But she says, 'Don't go. Come to me.' Oh, and she's such a pretty little thing, black hair, black eyes. Then, in a real low voice like a devil, she says again, 'Come to me.' And she lies down on the floor and pulls up her dress—and she's got a tail between her legs!"

A collective gasp greets this astonishing revelation.

"And because Simone turns to run, she jumps up like a hell cat, and she was on him, scratching at his eyes and screaming curses in some secret Babylonian witch's language. And the next thing Simone knows is she's got her knife and she's slashing at him with it and he can see there's blood all over it already. Dried blood caked all over it.

"Now he is in mortal fear for his life, and he runs screaming out of there." The great bellows of our popular narrator's lungs, the engines that drove his mighty voice, stopped their heaving for a moment, a dramatic pause before delivering the surprise ending.

"And Simone told me"—here he lowered his great voice to a hoarse, confidential whisper—"Simone told me he coulda sworn she flied off, he saw her fly off, right up into the air."

In response to this miraculous piece of news, the teller of tales' curious audience bedeviled him with a hundred questions, hungry for the particulars of his story, and the tale was forced to grow and expand to make room for all the fascinating new details and explanations that this dialogue elicited.

Niccolo shook his head in disbelief and prepared to resume his quest. He entered the borghetto. The streets were narrower here, and it was quiet. He felt as if he had stepped into an underground passage. It was cool and damp.

He followed Giuditta's directions and, with each turn, as he wound his way into the heart of the ghetto, the streets seemed to contract even further and allow even less light to penetrate. What had she called that street, the Via dei Macellai, the street of the butcher shops? Were these the infamous butcher shops that specialized in plump, Christian babies?

In contrast to the bustle of the Christian Florence he had just left behind, there was nobody here. Absolutely nobody. Niccolo began to lose heart. The far-fetched idea that there might even be a witch on the loose added to his discomfort. There were secrets here, and he was not sure he wanted to find out about them. The houses, even the shops, gave nothing away. They had grim, unforgiving aspects and were all shuttered and closed up tight to the outside world. Where was everyone? And on a Saturday?

He was able to locate Melchisadech's house without difficulty. There was the bench covered with green cloth, but no Melchisadech.

No one at all, anywhere! Niccolo was on the verge of abandoning his quest. He could come back tomorrow when there was more light, with some friends. But no. He had to show some resolve. It was for her. He pulled himself up in front of the door and knocked. It was a timid knock. He waited. Nothing happened. He knew he would have to knock much more aggressively if he was to make himself heard within. But did he want to?

While Niccolo was trying to decide, he noticed a small object attached to the doorframe. It looked like a caterpillar. He moved closer to examine it. It was made of metal and covered with symbols he could not decipher. There were indeed secrets here. Unconsciously, he backed away from the mysterious thing.

Abruptly, he banged on the door, not rapping with his knuckles, but beating solidly with the heel of his hand. She would have expected nothing less. To his surprise, the thumping was enough to push the heavy door slightly ajar. He pushed, and the iron hinges rumbled; the door swung open. Inside, it was even cooler and darker. He called out, but there was no answer. He waited, allowing his eyes to adjust to the gloom. Distinctions began to emerge out of the jumble of dark, suspicious shapes.

A table, but it was overturned. Some heavy cabinets, but they seemed to have been pulled down and their contents scattered. Ledgers and account books lay open on the ground in disarray. Niccolo saw a lamp, but he had nothing with which to light it. In the corner to his right was a mountain of rubble. He edged closer. He squinted. Clogs. Hundreds of clogs. There were deeper mysteries here than he had at first imagined. Hadn't Michele said something about clogs? And a revolution? Did it have something to do with the Jews? Another conspiracy?

At the opposite end of the room was another door, another invitation to trouble. Niccolo picked his way toward it, through the junk that lay strewn everywhere—wooden bowls, tin cups and plates, dirty clothes, and always more clogs. Was this Melchisadech a moneylender or a junkman? He looked fearfully behind him as he went, as though he expected the street door to slam shut and some demon to hurl itself across the room and drag him down into hell. He pushed at the door, and a crack of dim light appeared around its edges. It led into a courtyard.

Niccolo could make out a bower covered with vines and a stone bench. He walked over to the bench and plopped down, letting some of the tension drain out of him. Such a pleasant spot, a haven behind the drab, forbidding walls that lined these dark streets.

He stiffened when he heard it. Directly behind him. Something moved. He jumped to his feet and whirled around just as a shriek ripped the air. And another. Fear rooted him to the spot. Then the voice. It was harsh, more like the cackle or croak of an angry bird than a human sound. It was coming from behind the bower, but the boy could not discern its source through the thick tangle of vines and grape leaves. The ghastly voice stopped, then started up again, rasping and wheezing. Niccolo could not understand a word.

He swallowed hard. "Who's there? Show yourself!" he demanded half-heartedly, not really wanting to confront whatever assailant might step out from behind the bower, the owner of that diabolical voice.

"Non mi toccate. Lasciatemi!" "Don't touch me. Leave me alone!" The voice cackled in something that resembled Florentine, before lapsing into its harsh, unintelligible gibberish again. Niccolo waited, but no one emerged.

Reluctantly, he circled the bower, keeping his distance, giving it a wide berth. Niccolo could make out a dark shape, huddled between the vines and the courtyard wall. The shape moved sporadically, and sporadically the harsh voice continued to issue from it. Niccolo moved closer. The shape shifted position. He could see that it was crowned with long white hair. Another shift, and he caught a glimpse of its face. It was an old woman.

"Dai vecchia."

"Come on now, mother, I won't hurt you," Niccolo approached and offered his hand.

She turned her head away. "Leave me alone. Go away." In Florentine, for his benefit.

"I was looking for Melchisadech," Niccolo said, trying to put her at ease and coax her into conversation, but his seemingly innocent query had quite the opposite effect. She screamed and then collapsed in desperate, intense muttering. Was it prayer?

When the torrent of words or imprecations trailed off into silence, Niccolo repeated his request. "Awk," she squawked. But seeing that it was the only way to rid herself of the pest, she nervously complied: "In his study. Through there."

Niccolo made his way across the courtyard in the direction indicated. It was certainly a curious household this Melchisadech kept. After tapping discreetly at a small door and receiving no invitation to advance, Niccolo cautiously let himself in.

Melchisadech was lying on a wooden bench, seemingly asleep. At first, Niccolo could not fully appreciate what he was seeing. Melchisadech was bound tightly to the bench with rope. His eyes were fixed on the ceiling, and there was a gaping wound in his throat. To Niccolo's infinite horror, the walls of Melchisadech's study were covered with bloody scrawl. Secret Babylonian witch's symbols.

7

A Witch Hunt

"Don't know," croaked the old woman. "Don't know anything."

"Did you see who did this to Melchisadech?"

"Awk," she cackled shaking her disheveled head. "Did what? And what am I supposed to see, boy? I'm blind."

"Oh."

Niccolo tried another tack: "They say a witch killed Melchisadech. Did you see a witch? I mean, did you hear a witch? Or feel like there was a witch in the house?"

"What witch? Leave me alone. Or kill me, if you want." She curled up tighter.

"I don't want to hurt you, old woman. I came here looking for someone, for Giuditta. Instead, I found . . ." At the mention of the girl's name, the old woman screamed again.

"What do you know about Giuditta?" she asked, suddenly interested and defensive.

"I was with her yesterday. I met her . . . I . . . We . . . I helped her get back to the city."

The knot the old woman had tied herself into relaxed a little. She poked a sharp face in Niccolo's direction. "You must be the odd boy she told me about. Are you the odd boy?"

Some appraisal. "Yes, I'm the odd boy."

"Then I suppose I can trust you, odd boy." The old woman let out a long, low sigh. Then, surprisingly loquacious, she launched into her tale: "They came early this morning. We were packing to leave, because when Giuditta told Melchisadech what happened to her father and uncle and brother, Melchisadech said there was no time to waste.

Spain, said Melchisadech, Spain, because we have to get far away, because it isn't safe here anymore.

"Too late," she moaned pulling at her disheveled hair. "Too late, because as Melchisadech's servant was packing Melchisadech's bags and putting them on Melchisadech's horse, he came in."

She took a deep breath and continued. "'Taking a little trip?' he says, walking right in, not knocking, the leader. And he says, 'Not leaving town, Melchisadech, are you? Don't we have some businesssss to discusssss?'"

"What!"

"That's how he talked, the leader. Like thisssss. And he says, 'Afraid Melchisadech? Panic Melchisadech?' And he says, 'You know what we did yesterday, Melchisadech? We rode out to meet your businesssss partnerssss to discusssss the successsss of your little venture down in Rome. Unfortunately, Melchisadech, your associatessss were uncooperative. We had to teach them a lesssson.' Then he says, 'Are you in need of instruction, Melchisadech? Shall we teach you a lesson? Same lesssson?'"

"And then Melchisadech was shouting, because they were beating him. Then they dragged him to the study, and he screamed and screamed. I hid. Then everything was quiet."

"And Giuditta?"

"Melchisadech warned her. He tried. While they were beating him, he cried out in our language—'Run, run, the men who killed your father have come for me.'"

"And where was she?"

"Next door. At her own house, getting ready to leave. She was going with us. To Spain."

"And did she hear him? Did she get away?"

"I don't know, because the little black demon understood Melchisadech when he shouted out the warning, and he sent men next door to search."

"The little black demon?"

"The little black demon was with them, with the man who talks like thisssss." By way of further clarification, she added, "The little black demon is a spy."

"And the witch?"

"No witch," she said emphatically. "Just the little black demon."

Although Niccolo continued to pose his questions, the answers he received did little more than further confound him. Melchisadech was dead. Giuditta was missing, or perhaps was taken by the hissing man and his unlikely henchman, the little black demon, who was also a spy. The lone witness to these events was unable to shed any further light on the subject.

"You can't stay here, mother," he said to his informant. "Where will you go?"

"Awk, Spain. Here, help an old woman get up."

He did so, and, at her request, retrieved a bundle and accompanied her out into the street and around a corner. She tapped on a dark door, which swung open only a crack to admit her. Before disappearing inside, she trained her vacant white eyes on him and spoke with intensity. "Find Giuditta, boy. Tell her to go to Pisa. The ship sails in two days' time, at dawn. Tell her not to come back here, ever again." And she was gone.

Despite the uncertainty and misgivings the crone's revelations had engendered in him, one sure thing had emerged: The roadside murders he had witnessed the day before had been deliberate. And Melchisadech's murder had been the last act—so far—in a grisly drama—The Lessssson. The murderer knew his victims' names, he knew their business, and he knew where they lived. There were no bandits or outlaws involved, but people right here in the city, who moved about with apparent impunity.

Now what? Niccolo looked down the street in the direction from which he had come. Nothing. No one. He saw the other bench, the same as Melchisadech's, covered with green cloth. Her father's. The dead man's bench, where he lent his money. So that was Giuditta's house. He appraised it from a distance. It was the same as all the other houses, giving nothing away.

He approached the special house with caution. He noted that a caterpillar, identical to the one he had just seen, adorned its doorframe. A conspiracy? A secret society?

She couldn't possibly be here now, could she? He tried the door, and it opened. The lock had been smashed in and broken. He stepped inside and was greeted by the same rubble and litter he had seen at Melchisadech's, only here an even greater effort had gone into upending tables and chairs, emptying drawers, shredding books and ledgers, eviscerating mattresses, shattering crockery.

He called out feebly, he almost whispered her name, but there was no answer. He crept from room to room, cautiously announcing himself. Nothing, just chaos and disorder and ruination—and clogs, heaps and mountains of clogs. A dead end.

Should he wait? Perhaps she would come back? Then he heard a racket in the street. Someone was indeed coming, and it was not Giuditta, unless she had contrived to arrive in the company of a party of horsemen. He heard men's voices. The door was thrown open, and Niccolo dived into a hiding place behind some broken furniture, afraid to breathe.

"That oaf, Calandrino, where is he now? He's supposed to be on guard duty here."

"Probably asleep, check the garden." After much hallooing, the oaf Calandrino was, in fact, conjured up, and he appeared, rubbing his eyes, from the direction of the courtyard.

"Aaooow, Calandrin', what news?" asked one of the newcomers.

"What news?" he repeated in a dull voice.

"Has anyone been here? Has the witch been back?"

"No, no one. No witch."

"As if you would know. Did you find a nice place to sleep?"

"Bench out back," he confided yawning. "Right in the sun. Nice and warm."

Another man entered the house abruptly. From their respectful salutations, it was clear that he was in charge. "Has the little witch come home to roossssst?" the newcomer hissed. "Has little Giuditta come looking to join her father and brother?"

Niccolo's stomach tightened, and the acid of fear and vomit rose in his throat.

"No one yet, Excellency," volunteered the oaf. "How much longer do you want us to wait?"

"Not much longer. Simone is on hissss way now with the guardssssss. He told that story about the witch to Captain Oca and everybody else he met between here and the Signoria. The whole city is talking about the little Jewissssh witch now. Before you know it, they'll be crying for blood. Witch'sss blood. Jewessss' blood."

"And why not? We produce a mutilated body, signssss of a ritual killing, we produce an unimpeachable witnessss who puts the blame on the Jewish witch, and we have a public outcry on our hands. The good people will demand that steps be taken against the Jewess. Stern measuressss will be called for. A few more of Ibrahim's asssssociatesss might have to be dissssciplined. The smart onessss will leave town, and the onessss who stay will be scared to death, and they'll do as they're told to do. We'll be firmly in control of the money-lending businesssss once more, and it will be a long time before these Jewssss think to defy us again. Business isssss businesssss."

"Ay, but what if the witch isn't produced?" inquired one of the lieutenants.

"She'll be produced. Simone knows what she looks like. He'll go door to door with the guardssss until they find her. We'll offer a reward."

"But if she manages to slip away?"

"That'ssss the beauty of my plan, the witch will be produced. If in a day or so, we haven't found her, the cries for Jewish blood will be so great that some Jewissssh witch or other will be produced. The people are very resourceful on that score. Very capable of locating victimssss. Don't worry. Some Jewissssh witch or other will be brought to public justice. A public burning. Nothing less will do. The people get something to gawk at, and the Jewssss get a lesson—a lessssson in politicsssss.

"And if we ever get word of this particular witch resurfacing, of little Giuditta, why, she will be dealt with precisely as we dealt with her unfortunate family." So saying, the hissing man admonished his underlings to be vigilant, then he turned abruptly and walked out.

"Anything to drink?" the oaf inquired when their leader had gone. And the three guardians of order, business, and politics settled down in the front room, from where Niccolo soon heard, "To your health," "To us," "In a whale's ass," and similar expressions of alcoholic solidarity.

Their drinking proceeded apace, gradually yielding its usual combination of boisterousness and slurred speech. Niccolo saw the possibility of salvation in this development, since, drunk, they would be less likely to detect any movement on his part.

When he judged that an appropriate measure of the inebriant had been consumed, he stole from his hiding place. The front door was out of the question, since the guards were stationed squarely between him and it. The courtyard was his only hope.

As fate would have it, however, one bleary eye was cast in the direction of the garden at precisely the moment Niccolo had chosen for his escape. The alarm was raised.

"What now! Who goes there? Show yisself." All three were struggling to their feet. "Is that our little Jewish witch, come home to roost?'

Niccolo took the only chance he was given. He let out a scream, which froze his opponents for a fraction of a second. Then he turned and made a run at the rear wall. He threw himself as high in the air as he could. He reached and barely managed to grab the top edge. The bricks were rough. His hands held. He pulled himself up and scampered over. Better the uncertainty of whatever was on the other side than what the three brutes might have in store for him.

Niccolo dropped to earth in another world. Everywhere there were rags, heaps of rags, scraps of every description, size, and color, a sea of rags, great swelling waves of rags. And in pockets scattered here and there in the ocean of rags, he saw silent, impassive faces staring up at him. Six harsh faces. Twelve accusing eyes. The steady eyes of old women. The women were seated on the ground among the rags, sorting through them, separating out the good ones. Nobody moved. Nobody spoke.

Meanwhile, his drunken pursuers could be heard launching their assault on the other side of the wall. One had just fallen heavily, but Niccolo knew they would not give up. There was anguish in his face.

One of the ragpickers raised a skinny arm and with a bony finger indicated a small green door to Niccolo's left. He needed no urging. "God bless you!" And he was gone.

A second later, one of the hissing man's henchmen fell to earth among the ragpickers. Then another. Two surly, threatening, armed men. Again nobody moved. Again the women said nothing. Again the skinny arm came up, the shaky finger pointed. Following it, they rushed off, full of bluster, through a blue door, directly opposite the one Niccolo had taken.

8

A Guide for the Perplexed

The escape hatch through which Niccolo plunged led to an alley, the alley to a street, and the street to another, slightly wider, street. In the course of his prodigious, headlong flight, he thought only of getting away, of dodging stationary and slow-moving obstacles and of keeping his footing on the slippery stones. As he neared the square where the ever-vigilant angel Gabriel kept his thankless watch, he was constrained to duck into a side street to make way for a large contingent of uniformed guards on their way into the ghetto. In tow, a small, vociferous mob was chanting anti-Jewish slogans. At the head of the intrepid contingent, he could make out a small, misshapen, blackened imp. The little black demon was gesticulating animatedly with the captain of the guards.

They were going in after her.

The pretty little thing. With the mark of the Jew. The black hair. Black eyes. The knife.

He tried to calm down, by telling himself it was perfectly plausible that some other Jewish girl was the object of their attentions—pretty little thing, black hair, black eyes, a knife, that this ghetto was positively teeming with Jewish girls, pretty little things, hundreds of them, thousands, with black hair and black eyes, and a knife.

Quite by accident, he had stumbled upon hideous, hidden truths, for when things are done clandestinely, there are always clandestine witnesses. Murder and subterfuge were swirling all around him, and at the center of it all was some obscene lesson, but a lesson in what and for whom? And who was the teacher?

Sitting on a patch of damp grass, Niccolo waited hours for the guard contingent to come out of the ghetto. His mission seemed to be over. This grim vigil was the final chapter before his adventure's horrible, foregone conclusion. He didn't notice that moisture from the muddy grass was gradually seeping through his smart white hose, that his hero's doublet was filthy and stained.

Finally, he heard the heavy clatter of iron on iron and iron on stone. They were coming out. He held his breath as they emerged from the dark street. *Deo gratias!* No prisoners taken. No witch.

The praetorians grumbled audibly as they passed him. "We'll get her, don't you worry." It was the captain speaking. "We have men at every gate, we'll search every cart that passes out. We'll seal this city off tighter than a bloated wineskin." The blackened imp seemed to agree, and with that resolution, they passed out of earshot.

In a burst of ecstatic relief, Niccolo sprinted all the way to the tavern where he had left his horse a couple of centuries ago. Retrieving the docile beast, he mounted and rode toward home. His optimism on behalf of his beloved, if he dared call her that, was short-lived, however. As he passed one of the closed city gates, he noted the ominous presence of the guards going about their investigations rudely, but with painstaking attention to detail. Sealed off tighter than a bloated wineskin.

Niccolo rode on in a stupor toward the Via Romana, and then, knowing that the horse could find its own way home, abdicated all authority over it and surrendered himself to his own profound fears and overwhelming anxieties. Eventually, the reliable animal deposited its rider at the door of the Machiavelli household. Mechanically, Niccolo removed saddle and bridle. He went through the motions of watering, feeding, and securing the horse in its stall.

A tremendous amount of saliva had built up in his mouth, and some other bitter taste was mixed in with it. He spit in the straw at his feet. When the blessed portals of home were securely shut and the heavy iron bars rammed to, he opened the tiny wine window and peered out onto the street.

Like many other Florentines who had holdings in the country, his father maintained vineyards and produced wine. It was good, sturdy wine, and when there was enough of it, Bernardo sold off his surplus through the wine window. Nearly every house in the Via Romana had a wine window cut into its heavy door at shoulder height. "A handy device for spies," he thought, the wine window.

His reconnaissance revealed only the usual, unending procession of men and women and beasts in the street outside. What had he hoped to see?

"Psssssssst." He jumped, the reflex reaction of sorely tested and badly frayed nerves. Someone was there behind the barrels of olives and vinegar. But his panic was only momentary. Primerana and Ginevra, his younger sisters, loved to cavort among the stores down here. They built houses, sometimes neighborhoods, even entire kingdoms inside broken barrels. They erected tents of old sackcloth and lavishly entertained imaginary young men in them for hours on end. Niccolo walked wearily over to their hiding place, in no mood for games or tittering or healthy family conviviality of any sort.

"Come on out," he grunted in a dispirited voice, and she did.

Giuditta stepped into the light. "I've been waiting for you," she said, almost matter-of-factly. "Where have you been?"

"Where have I been?" babbled Niccolo. "I've been everywhere—all over the city, up and down, in strange neighborhoods, at your house, at Melchisadech's—where have you been?"

"Here waiting for you," she said a little testily, "What took you so long?"

"Right here," Niccolo stammered incredulously, in my house?" As he said these last words, it dawned on him that of all the places in the city, in the world, where she could have gone, she had come to him. A sense of inordinate pride and satisfaction spread through him.

She interrupted his thoughts: "I had a little trouble."

"A little trouble," he shouted. A company of guards is out looking for you; the whole city will soon be crying for your blood; armed thugs are lying in wait for you at your house, and you call it 'a little trouble.'"

"It's not my fault."

"And who, in God's name, is the little black demon?"

"A spy. And don't swear."

"*Ahime,*" Niccolo groaned in a burst of near-hysterical relief. "Santa Maria, but how could you possibly know where I lived?"

"You told me," she said.

"But only in passing. I just mentioned it once, and you remembered?"

"I remember everything," she said gravely.

When Niccolo had gotten over the shock of finding her, Giuditta explained quickly what had happened. Her account confirmed what

Niccolo had already learned: that the hissing man came for Melchisadech. She heard them arguing over the garden wall. "Then Melchisadech screamed at the top of his lungs for me to run, and I did."

Briefly, breathlessly, Niccolo recounted what he had seen: "They killed Melchisadech. An old woman told me about it."

"Magda, she's Melchisadech's slave."

"He owns slaves?"

"He can't own land," she shrugged. "What else do you know?"

"They made the killing look like a ritual murder, and they're blaming you for it. They even know your name."

"Oh, dear." Was she mocking him and the gravity of the situation?

"They have a witness, a little black imp who's willing to swear he saw a Jewish witch do it. Who is he?"

"A charcoal burner, blackened by his métier. His name's Simone."

"Is he Jewish?"

"Half. He spies on us. He makes deliveries to all the houses, so he has access. He has informants. He pays them."

"Who does he spy for?"

"Interested parties."

"Like the hissing man? Do you know who he is?"

"I've seen him," said Giuditta. "A representative of those interested parties is how he introduces himself. He would occasionally drop by to relay messages to my father, offer him friendly advice."

"About business?" asked Niccolo.

"Mostly. Do you know anything about money lending?"

"Usury?" Niccolo blurted out.

"When your people do it, they call it banking," she shot back. "Anyway, my father and some others lend money to the city at a certain rate of interest, so your leaders can put up more statues of themselves or whatever. Lately, they said the rates were too high, and they wanted us to lower them. That's when the trouble started.

"Especially for my father. He was accused of being the ringleader and a sower of discord. Moneylenders and pawnbrokers were beaten and robbed. Fires broke out in their houses and shops. Many were leaving the city.

"And," she continued, "taking their business elsewhere. My father and Melchisadech found out that the pope was paying a much better rate, and they were pulling out of Florentine business altogether. That's one of the reasons we went to Rome . . ." Her eyes and her attention seemed to drift away as she recalled that journey and its fatal outcome.

"You knew all along your father's murder was deliberate?"

"I was pretty sure."

"Then why did you come back here? Weren't you afraid?"

"We were all going to Spain. We were set to leave in two days' time. I came back to meet up with Melchisadech and the others and to get a few important things. When they came for Melchisadech, I ran. I knew if I hid in the ghetto, they'd find me. So I ran out into great, wide open Christian Florence. I thought I could get to the city gates, and get out. I'm supposed to meet our friends outside the city, at an inn on the road to Pisa."

"And now?"

"You have to help me get out of the city," she said, looking up at him.

"How?" said Niccolo.

Giuditta's reply was almost cavalier, "If I knew how, I wouldn't need your help. You're clever. You'll think of something."

Throughout the course of this interview, Giuditta had remained seated among the casks and barrels that held the stores of the Machiavelli family. Niccolo was standing in front of her the whole time, too amazed to move. As he stood listening, he slowly became aware that his elegant courtier's costume was in shambles. His embarrassment was acute. The fine white hose were muddy and snagged. His velvet jacket was torn, and his soft cotton shirt drenched in sweat. His hair was disheveled, his fingernails were dirty. The hero would need some refurbishing before going back into action.

Before trudging up the stairs to the family apartments, Niccolo helped Giuditta to more comfortable and secure quarters at the back of the courtyard. There was a shed there with rough bunks where peasants and hired workmen slept, and it was empty now. He brought her some food, which she eyed suspiciously, but ate. They agreed that it would be foolish to venture out into the streets in broad daylight, now that the alarm had been raised. They would wait for darkness. But to do what?

To allay the suspicions of his family, Niccolo joined them for dinner. He had managed to wash and change clothes without anyone seeing his tattered knight errant finery. At table, his father was holding forth on the limited availability of fava beans this year. He could not understand it—there had been plenty of rain and plenty of sunshine; it had been a good season. "Greedy farmers," he was grumbling, "they'll hold out for higher prices later."

Niccolo had one enormous problem and a host of smaller, subsidiary ones to occupy his thoughts. How, he kept asking himself, could they get out of the city? The gates were closed at sundown. The walls were too high to climb, and anyway, they were patrolled. The city was sealed. Nothing came in and nothing went out, not without special passes and permission from the highest authorities. When his mind tired of going over the same untenable options and running into the same insurmountable obstacles, he would let it run loose, to the lore of secret passages and clandestine, subterranean escapes. But hard, unforgiving reality would soon steal back. Secret passages, he was forced to conclude, were storybook stuff. Nothing comes in and nothing goes out.

After dinner, Niccolo's mother repaired to her private chapel to fortify herself against the wickedness of the world and the high price of fava beans. His father moved out onto the balcony, where the evening breezes and a flask of hazelnut liqueur would facilitate the arduous but delicate task of digestion that lay ahead of him. Niccolo, feigning indisposition, retired to his bedroom. He knew he couldn't sleep, but he needed time to prepare himself, to compose his thoughts and, he hoped, to find a way out.

He was aware, in a half-conscious sort of way, that he had changed significantly in the past two days, since this morning, even, when he had ridden out in all his finery, on a great steed like someone from the tales of Lancelot and Guinevere, like someone in a storybook. This afternoon, he had huddled, trembling, behind broken furniture; he had heard the machinations of evil discussed openly, plotted and planned in banal detail. Then he had run for his life. Unheroic, to be sure. He had weighed the odds, used his head, and seen that flight was the only practical solution. He had acted quickly, and he was still alive. Yesterday he had seen death, today he had faced it and he was still alive.

His fairytale dreams of the morning seemed far off; bravado and dashing heroism seemed so unreal. The business of heroism was more than mounting a fine horse in fine clothes. It was scrambling in the dirt, slithering over walls. It was knowing when to hide and when to run. It was knowing when to be afraid.

Only last night he had lain on this same bed, his head full of grandiose visions, of escorting his lady to Pisa, of her sitting across his lap while he entertained her with delightful stories and conversation, of her laughing at his wit as they followed the meandering course of the Arno down through the hills to . . .

The river.

Porco Dio! The river. The Goddamn river came and went as it pleased. Day and night. Past the guard towers, under the bridges, through the walls, along the embankments, and out again. Nobody stopped it! Nobody asked to see its papers! Nobody questioned it about its destination! Niccolo had found his solution.

Niccolo dressed, choosing his clothes with an eye to the work at hand—dark clothes for night work. On the way downstairs, he slipped into his sisters' room and rifled through the chest at the foot of their bed until he found what he was looking for.

"Here," he said, stealing into the shed and closing the door behind him, "Put this on."

"What is it?" asked Giuditta, looking up at him.

"It's a Christian frock of good Florentine wool. If we're spotted, they won't see your Jewish sign. That way, at least we stand a chance of talking our way out of it."

Giuditta took the frock and held it up at arm's length for inspection. "It's ugly," she said, "and it's going to be too short in the sleeves. Couldn't you go back and find me something a little more becoming?" Then she laughed. "Alright, I'll put it on," she said, "but can't you turn around? Don't Florentine boys have any sense of decency?"

"All done," she said a minute later, "When do we go?"

"In about half an hour. When the bell sounds, curfew will be in effect and the streets should be empty."

"Except for the guards," said Giuditta.

"Except for the guards," he confirmed. "But don't worry about the guards for now. Can you swim?"

"Of course I can swim," she said defiantly.

"Good," said Niccolo. "Because we're going down the river, right under the noses of the guards where they stand watch on the towers."

"What if they spot us?" asked Giuditta, not a little frightened of the idea of the river.

"They won't," said Niccolo, "Not with one of those." He pointed to a heap of broken and useless barrels piled up in the corner of the shed. "Listen, here's how we're going to do it."

When he had finished explaining, Giuditta seemed profoundly apprehensive but resigned. "Are you sure there's no secret passage?"

Niccolo shook his head, "No secret passage," he said. "Only the river."

They were sitting on one of the hard, dusty beds, at opposite ends. Giuditta's little bundle lay undone, between them. Niccolo was examining the "important things" that had drawn her back into the city. There were coins, what he took for religious objects, some odd iron tools, and a few small books. "What are these," he asked, indicating the tools. "May I?" He picked one up to have a closer look.

"They were my father's," she said. "They're dies for stamping coins. He cut the designs himself." Niccolo squinted in the dim light. The design on the face of the die was of a woman with a balance in her hand. With a blindfold. Justice.

"Look at this," she said, drawing Niccolo out of his reverie. She handed him one of the books. Niccolo could see that it wasn't written in the Latin alphabet, and the characters seemed so fanciful and bizarre, that he doubted it was written in Jewish. Hebrew, he corrected himself. In fact, the characters seemed so fanciful and bizarre that he doubted it was written in any alphabet at all.

"What is it?" he asked, leafing through the pages and remarking symbols that looked like trees and extravagant fish and fish hooks. "A picture book?"

"It's a list of names, of people all over Europe, and even in the East and Africa. These were people my father knew and trusted. They're people I can trust. Don't you think that's a valuable list to have?"

"If you can read it," said Niccolo.

"That's what this is for," said Giuditta brightly, holding up another book. She handed it to Niccolo. This book was filled with page after page of tables, the key to the codes. In addition to many sets of grotesque, imaginative symbols, Niccolo could make out columns of Latin characters, and what he knew to be Greek, and what he supposed to be Hebrew. There were others he could not identify. Sumerian? Egyptian?

"With the codebook, you can decipher the other book," said Giuditta. "Or you can write messages—secret messages."

"You can write as well as read?" Niccolo was amused.

"Hebrew, Latin, and Greek, and, of course, Florentine," she said off-handedly. What about you?"

Niccolo whose command of Greek was nonexistent, to say nothing of Hebrew, fell silent, and the bemused smile vanished from his face.

"I don't know the symbols well enough to use them without the codebook," she was saying. "There are so many, and they can be confusing. Do you want to try one? Look here." She opened the book of the names of the people her father trusted and found the page she wanted. "See, the book is arranged according to city. At the top of the page, it tells you what city."

She took the codebook, opened it to the correct page, and put the two side by side in front of Niccolo. "This is the table to use to read this page. Don't ask me to explain how you know which code to use for which message—that's too complicated. Just trust me. Go ahead, figure it out."

Niccolo was intrigued and set himself to looking up the symbols in the table Giuditta had given him. It took a while to piece the letters together, and the slow going was made worse by the dim light. *L - E - P - O - R - E - S*. Lepores, the Latin word for hare. So what? He was puzzled. "So what does this mean, what does it tell me?"

"You've only done half of the work, so far," she said. "You've decoded each of the letters, but 'lepores' is obviously a code word. You have to look up the code words in another table. Here."

Niccolo ran his finger down the column she had indicated. The words were all names of animals and birds and fish. He found "lepores" and next to it read, "gentes florentinorum." Florentines! This was the page for Florence. He was pleased with his decoding abilities.

"Try one more," she said. "Try this one," she pointed to the bottom of the page. Niccolo began work on the entry she had indicated. He noted that it was written in a different hand from the other entries on the page. The symbols seemed more carefully traced. They were easier to make out. He pronounced the letters out loud—*M - A - C - H*—he stopped abruptly and looked up, knowing what he was going to find.

"Don't stop," she said, softly. "Go on, finish."

When he was done, he had read in the book of the names of people who could be trusted:

Machiavelli, Niccolo, Via Romana.

Giuditta touched his hand gently. "I made that entry," she said, "Just this evening, while I was waiting for you."

Niccolo was moved, and a little embarrassed, too. Luckily, the light was too dull to reveal the deep crimson blush that crossed his face. He put the books down and spoke quickly to hide his discomfort, "What's the last book, more codes?"

"No, that's something else. It was one of my father's favorites," she said. "I took it to remember him by. And because I think I can use it for myself. It's a very old book by Maimonides."

Niccolo turned the little volume over in his hands. "What's it called?"

"*A Guide for the Perplexed.*"

She finished speaking and began to put her things back together, thoughtfully. Niccolo watched the careful hands arrange their few precious belongings on the red cloth in a tidy pile. Before she wrapped and tied the bundle, he spotted one last object that had escaped his previous inventory. It was a small, well-balanced dagger with an unreadable sign carved in its smooth black handle.

A sharp, unpleasant bell, rung at short, quick intervals, warned of the beginning of curfew.

The two of them slipped silently out of the Machiavelli house and headed toward the river along the route that Niccolo had devised. It was a route that steered clear of the well-traveled avenues and the main squares. It was an indirect route through the back streets and dingy alleys of Florence.

Niccolo was an odd sight. He was stooped forward under the weight of a broken barrel that he wore on his back like the shell of a turtle. The barrel was perhaps three-quarters the height of the boy who carried it. Although the bottom end of it chafed against the back of Niccolo's knees with every step, his legs moved swiftly and with assurance.

Several staves had been broken out of this barrel in such a way as to form an open space on one side. Sitting with this open side up, the modified barrel resembled nothing if not a squat, clumsy boat.

Giuditta padded along effortlessly behind him, but Niccolo was breathing hard from his exertions. When he calculated that they were about halfway to the end of their furtive nocturnal excursion, he stopped to rest. As she had done since they left the house, Giuditta continued to look around her in amazement, even awe. The city deserted and suffused in moonlight was an unearthly sight to her, one that she had never seen before, because Jews were not allowed out after dark.

Niccolo, a veteran sneak, had seen the soundless, sleeping city many times before and took little notice of her quiet beauty. Instead, his eyes were fixed on the wonderstruck face of his companion, her features illuminated by the full moon, whose pale light turned earthly women into ghosts and angels.

They kept close to the deep shadows and recessed doorways into which they could dissolve if need be. Niccolo concentrated on his route and his strategy. Everything was working so far, but the hardest part was yet to come. He shuddered when he thought of the river—at night. Things floated down, bloated things, dead dogs and cats. Corpses were not unknown, some of local manufacture, others coming from as far upstream as Bibbiena or Poppi. And beneath the black surface of the water? God only knew. Could rats swim?

They reached the river just to one side of the Ponte all Carraia. Niccolo had chosen this spot for their point of departure because the shore here was crowded with sheds and warehouses right down to the water line. They would not be seen approaching. He put down the barrel and took a deep breath. This was it.

Giuditta looked at him with a deadly serious expression on her face. "I can't swim," she stated flatly.

"God help us," thought Niccolo, but they had come too far to turn back now. "You don't have to swim," he said. "All you have to do is drift. Hang onto the barrel and drift. I won't let you drown. Now get ready. Hitch your skirt up and tie it so your legs won't get caught in all that cloth."

Niccolo went down to the water's edge. He looked out across the river. No floating debris. The river was calm and flat, as if someone had poured an enormous quantity of oil on its surface. He dipped his hand into the black water. Cold, but not too cold. Thank God it was September and not December. He pulled out his shirt and loosened the laces on his hose. With his cupped hand, he splashed water several times on his exposed belly. Giuditta was observing this odd ritual from a few feet away.

"What on earth are you doing," she asked, genuinely puzzled.

"For the digestion," he explained. "If you jump into the water and it's cold, the sudden change in temperature can cause a really violent constriction, total blockage of the digestion. It can kill you. Did you know that most of the people who drown don't drown in the water? They crawl up on the shore and die from the constrictions, strangled."

"Oh, really?" was all she said.

Standing facing each other at opposite ends of the barrel, they lifted it in unison, up over their heads. They eased it down, working their heads into the interior, through the side where the staves were missing. Wearing the barrel like a large, outlandish helmet for two, they walked sideways, one step at a time to the waterline.

The round hole where the tap would go and the spaces between the dried shrunken staves let in enough light for them to make out each other's features, barely, and enough air for them to breathe. They inched into the water. It was cold enough to make them shiver.

Ankle deep, then knee deep. The river bottom was muddy and soft and slippery. Niccolo had warned Giuditta that when the water reached midthigh, the bank dropped off sharply and they would no longer be able to touch bottom.

"Aaaap!" she let out a cry that was cut off as her head went under. Instinctively, Niccolo shot both legs forward and caught her. He heaved. Up came her head, sputtering and coughing. For a moment, Giuditta gasped, unable to catch her breath, then she recovered.

"Are you alright?" said Niccolo in a loud, urgent whisper.

"I think so," she replied, still coughing.

"Did you slip?"

"No, I didn't slip," she said slyly. "It must have been a digestive attack."

Now they were in position to travel. The barrel floated aimlessly, and apparently innocently, on the surface of the Arno. Niccolo had propelled it into the center of the current with a few scissor kicks, and then they were both still, adrift, at the mercy of the river.

Underneath, inside, Niccolo and Giuditta held on for dear life, careful to keep their heads above the water, in the small pocket of air trapped on the river's surface under the barrel. Something long and smooth brushed against Niccolo's thigh. He cringed at the thought of eels.

The inner surface of the barrel was crusty and gave off an overpowering, pungent aroma. It had once been used to store not wine but vinegar. Niccolo recognized the smell. It had nothing to do with the thin, acidic fumes given off by everyday vinegar. This was the deep richness of balsamic vinegar. Aged sometimes as long as twenty years, the acid was mellowed by the oak of the cask, and gradually the liquid became more and more concentrated, the flavor more intense.

With an occasional kick, Niccolo kept the barrel on course, in the center of the current and not too close to either shore, where it might hang up on some obstruction. He was careful not to propel it downstream at a speed any faster than the sluggish current. That would arouse suspicion.

So they drifted. Carrying them and concealing them, the barrel spun in lazy circles, constantly shifting the slanted rays of silver light that the cracks let in. One would fall, for a moment, across Giuditta's right eye, and then slowly rotate across her face to the left. For an instant, her mouth would appear illuminated, then disappear.

Niccolo and Giuditta did not speak. They could hear each other breathing. They were close enough to feel each other's breath, close enough, thought Niccolo, to kiss.

From where they had entered the river, Niccolo calculated that they had to go about a hundred yards to clear the circumference of the city walls. Any minute now, they would be reaching the critical point in their strange and secret nocturnal journey—the point where the walls sloped down to form low ramparts along the banks, the point where two turrets manned by armed guards flanked the river, and the point where, if they were lucky, they would pass out of the city into the open country beyond.

Above the gentle lapping and smacking sounds of the water they could hear voices, at first indistinct, but growing stronger. They were guards' voices—cursing voices, heavy with drink.

"*Cento . . . centocinquanta . . . duecento*—A hundred . . . Hundred and fifty . . . two hundred." They were gambling. "You cheating bastard . . ." The game was interrupted by a voice from the other bank, "*Aaoow, Gianuzzo, Luca, fate attenzione!* Something's coming down the river, closer to your side. Have a look."

Niccolo winced. They had been spotted. But there was nothing to do, no conceivable course of action to take. They hung on and waited, hardly daring to breathe.

"Whasssit?" slurred one of the watchmen. "I can't make it out. Wait . . . it's something fat—and short."

"Maybe a dead priest," offered his companion.

"No, it's a barrel, a barrel, Luca, that could be, just *could* be full of strong drink. Get the pole. We'll pull her in and have a look."

Niccolo kicked his legs, almost imperceptibly, hoping to move them out of reach, in the opposite direction, away from the bank. They were so close, they could hear the guards grunting; they could hear the long wooden pole clatter on the stone wall; they could hear the rasp as it slid out over the rough stone. There was a splash not a foot away from the barrel.

"We almost got it. Here, let me try. Luca, grab me around the waist so I can get farther out." The scene must have been comic, for there was laughter from across the way.

The pole made contact with the barrel, a dull thump, then slipped off. Another bump. "Damn, I can't bring it around. It's getting away. Yo! Over there! I'm going to push it across your way. See if you can get a line on it."

There was a resounding knock on the side of the barrel that sent it spinning off in the direction of the opposite bank. Niccolo almost lost his grip. But he held on and managed to slow their momentum a little. "Come on now, give us a hand and pull it in," urged the voice of Gianuzzo.

"You're both drunk," said the voice on the other bank.

"It's getting away, damn it! That barrel is full of the finest vintage wine from Portugal, I know it! Damn it! Damn it!"

"Why don't you jump in after it, then," taunted the other voice.

"You son of a whore, the least you could have done was . . ." but as the argument began to heat up and the insults to fly, the voices became fainter and receded slowly into distant, indistinguishable snarlings. Then there was only the water, the gentle, reassuring sound of the lazy water carrying them to safety.

"How much farther?" asked Giuditta, "I can't hold on much longer." Both of them were at the end of their strength. Nevertheless, gallant Niccolo encircled her small body with his legs and pulled her to him. His arms and knuckles ached from the effort of holding on, his stomach muscles stiffened as he strained to hold her up and keep her head above water. "It won't be long now," he whispered, their faces almost touching. She was shivering, whether from fear or cold, he didn't know. He drew her even closer in an instinctive gesture of protection and held on.

"I felt it! I touched bottom," said Giuditta in an excited whisper.

Niccolo untangled his legs and planted his feet firmly on the river bottom. They were in about three feet of water. "Can you stand up?" he asked. She did so, so precipitously that she bumped her head on the top of the barrel. Despite the pain, she laughed. They both did. "Keep still a minute," said Niccolo. "Stay under here and don't move. I'll check to make sure we can go ashore." With that, he took a deep breath and was gone, disappearing into the black emptiness of the water, leaving her alone.

A minute or two passed. Giuditta crouched down and waited in her tiny bubble of safety between the night and the blackness of the water. Suddenly the bubble burst.

In a rush of air, the barrel rose, torn from water's surface. Niccolo stood in triumph, waist-deep in the water and only a few feet from the riverbank. "Come on. We made it," he cried, perhaps a little too loudly, but making no attempt to conceal his exhilaration. He grabbed her hand, and they scrambled up the muddy bank. When they reached dry ground, they stopped, breathing hard.

"Just a minute," said Giuditta. "Let me rest. I'm . . . That was . . . I don't believe . . . ," she let out a long sigh and sank, almost collapsed, to the ground, allowing herself to relax for the first time since Niccolo had announced his audacious plan to her over three hours ago. The worst was over.

Niccolo stood, savoring his victory, looking back at the dark walls in the distance. "Formidable, but ineffective," he thought in exaltation. He had done it. He had gotten her out of the city and away. He was exhausted, but he had never felt better in his life.

As he watched their miniature Noah's Ark float downstream, all he could think of was the closeness in there, the intensity of feeling that the closeness brought on, the sense of warmth, even in the cold water, and the sweet smell, and her breath on his face.

Although tired, both Niccolo and Giuditta were too excited to stay still for long, and after only a few minutes' rest, they set off. They easily gained the road and set a brisk pace, to build up body heat and keep warm in their wet clothes. A stiff but not unkind wind was blowing crisp but dry from the south. In no time, they were relatively dry and comfortable in their mud-stiffened clothes.

They kept close to the side of the broad road, ready to throw themselves into the cover of the underbrush and darkness should anyone approach. But no one did. There was a sense of relaxed intimacy between them now, and the sense of shared struggle and victory that unites comrades-in-arms. They had taken risks together, braved dangers and won. Giuditta laughed easily. They joked about bandits. Niccolo wished that the road would go on forever. And that they could laugh and talk together, hurrying down that dark road, all alone, just each other for a thousand, thousand miles. This was the best of all possible worlds.

He had so many questions he wanted to ask her, so many things he wanted to know. Some of the mysteries of the ghetto, she had been able to clear up for him. Like the prodigious number of clogs in her father's pawnshop. Where Niccolo had seen conspiracy and perhaps revolution, there was only kindness. He father often agreed to lend small sums of money to the destitute and took their worn and useless clogs as a sign of good faith. They were poor but too proud to accept charity, no matter how desperate—and from a Jew! The pledge of the clogs kept alive the ritual of exchange and mutual obligation, of equality. And it kept alive in their all-but-crushed spirits some spark of self-respect and dignity. A man could still look his wife and children in the eyes.

Giuditta explained to Niccolo that, while the Jews were always being harassed to some extent or other, during the past year things seemed to have gotten much worse, especially for the moneylenders, and particularly for her father, who was often accused of being a leader and a sower of discord.

"But why Spain?" Niccolo wanted urgently to know.

"Our people are welcome there. And it's one of the few places we can still go. We've been driven out of France and out of England. But in Spain we feel safe. We have communities there. Over 70,000 of us in Toledo alone!"

"Is that where you'll go? Toledo?"

"Yes," she said, sadness and resignation creeping into her voice and replacing the exuberance that had been there until now. "Toledo."

They reached the inn appointed for the rendezvous with no difficulty. It was a little before dawn, but already the small party of Jews could be seen in the courtyard, making their hasty preparations to leave. There were perhaps a dozen men and women, and a few children. Niccolo recognized no one except the ancient blind Hungarian, Magda, who sat stone-faced astride a mule, her head lifted into the wind, her white hair blowing back loose and disheveled.

Giuditta spoke rapidly to the men in Hebrew. They greeted her tale with gravity and concern. Several times in the course of her story, they looked up gravely in Niccolo's direction. They nodded.

Less than a half hour later, the small caravan made its way out of the enclosed courtyard and onto the twisting road that followed the river down to the port. It was taking her away from him, to Pisa and far, far away, to Spain. The odd boy stood and watched it disappear into the distance. He stood there for a long time after it had vanished.

"*Addio*," she had said to him. "Good-bye—forever."

9

The Handkerchief

It rarely snows in Florence, and when it does, it rarely accumulates to any great depth. But Ash Wednesday in 1482 was an exception. Throughout the night, a fierce north wind had driven the wet snow down on the city. Now over a foot of it had been deposited in her streets and on her red roofs. By tomorrow, the unsullied white blanket would be churned to a brownish-yellow slush of straw and mud and animal shit, but for the time being, with a few fat, fluffy flakes still drifting down from the grey clouds, a soft, unnatural beauty had settled on the city. For a child, ensconced in a warm room, by a fire, and looking out over the scene, it would not be difficult to imagine what heaven must be like.

Commerce was disrupted by the unexpected storm, and the usual flood of traffic had slowed to a trickle. Serious business had come to a standstill. The squares were transformed into playgrounds. An old man could be seen flailing at a fruit tree with a long broom, trying to knock the heavy snow off the branches lest they break under the added weight.

One of the few citizens who had braved the weather and wished he hadn't was young Niccolo Machiavelli. It was hard going for him in the snow. It stuck to his feet and impeded his progress. It transformed his usual energetic gait into a less-than-steady plodding. He cursed the cold that had turned his ears and hands beet red. He cursed the icy wetness that had seeped through the leather soles of his boots, through his thick woolen hose, through his skin, to the very bone. He cursed the sharp, tingling pain in his toes that made every step a feat almost beyond human endurance.

But most of all, he cursed his nose. He had felt fine that morning and hadn't even given a second thought to going out in the snow. By midmorning, however, he had succumbed to the most ferocious cold imaginable. His eyes were swollen and watery. From his nose ran a steady stream of fluid that he could not staunch, no matter how hard he tried. His handkerchief had long since been rendered useless.

His nose had been rubbed raw, and he could scarcely bear to touch it. In his desperation, he had recourse to blowing it through his fingers, not into his hand, which would have been unspeakably vulgar, but he did it when no one was looking.

Niccolo shook his head, and through his labored breathing, muttered to himself, "How? How can one man's head be filled with that much fluid?" It was a thought that occurred to him frequently when he suffered from colds. And suffer he did. To make matters worse, his tutor, having perceived the acute discomfort of his pupil, had turned his merciless humor upon him. He tormented him with admonitions not to wipe his nose on his sleeve as loutish boys did. Rising to the full height of his wicked genius, he took down a small and little-used book on manners and gave it to Niccolo for the day's translation exercises.

To his tutor's endless delight, poor, sniffling Niccolo was constrained to translate into Latin sentences that, by alluding to his predicament, made his suffering all the more unbearable. He began with this one from Bonvicino da Riva's *Fifty Table Courtesies*: "When you blow your nose or cough, turn round so that nothing falls on the table."

Other lessons that Niccolo learned that day included valuable wisdom like the following, "A peasant wipes his nose on his cap and coat, a sausage maker on his arm and elbow." The final, ignominious blow was an insulting passage from an anonymous sage on the proper use of handkerchiefs, "You should not offer your handkerchief to anyone unless it has been freshly washed. . . . Nor is it seemly, after wiping your nose, to spread out your handkerchief and to peer into it as if rubies and pearls might have fallen from your head."

"Why didn't I stay home on this dismal, wretched day?" he thought. "Why did I go to all this trouble just to attend my lessons? To learn what? The Latin word for 'snot'?"

Although it was almost midday, it seemed to be getting colder, rather than warming up. Niccolo pulled his cap down farther over his ears and forehead, completely covering the black smudge there that reminded him and everybody else that he was dust and to dust he would return. With his head full of phlegm and the accumulated wisdom of the ages on the various ways of discharging it, Niccolo slogged along numbly through the wet snow, oblivious to everything in the outside world but the biting cold.

A disturbance up ahead attracted his attention. What he saw was a friar who had slipped and fallen in the snow. To make matters worse, the hapless fellow was not only prostrate and apparently incapable of rising, but he was being pelted with snowballs. The source of this barrage was two ragged waifs who seemed to be enjoying themselves immensely at the unfortunate cleric's expense.

Niccolo's sense of justice was outraged. This would never do. "Get off! Leave him alone!" he barked at the youthful offenders. His answer was a cold shot to the left side of the face that took him squarely in the eye. "You little shits!" he hissed, angry now. "I'll kill you." Oblivious to numb feet and hands, Niccolo rushed straight at them, scooping up handfuls of snow, packing it and hurling it in front of him all in one motion. Forgetting the monk they had been gleefully abusing, they turned to face the older boy, but their volleys could not keep him at bay. He was charging them headlong. They fell back, but Niccolo was on them. One, he grabbed by the scruff of the neck. The other managed to escape and stood hooting obscenities from a safe distance.

The anger died in Niccolo as quickly as it had welled up. He could not bring himself to hit his dirty-faced little prisoner. "Go on, get out of here and leave him alone," he said, releasing the smaller boy and giving him a sound kick in the rear to speed him on his way. Niccolo threw a half-hearted snowball at their backs as they beat a quick, disorderly retreat. Then he turned to offer his assistance to the victim of the unprovoked attack.

The friar had struggled into a sitting position, but that was it. He thanked Niccolo for his help in beating off his assailants and gratefully took the hand extended to him by his deliverer. When he had regained his feet, he winced, sucking in sharply. A less holy man might have cursed. "I think I've bruised my hip," he said.

For his part, Niccolo was surprised to find how easily he had been able to lift the fallen holy man—he weighed next to nothing. And he noticed that the friar's hand, which he now held in his own, was small and thin, with long fingernails like a woman's hand.

Yet, despite the slightness of his frame and his apparent fragility, the man was not wearing heavy clothing and, most astonishing, did not seem to be bothered in the least by the penetrating cold. He was clad in the white habit and cowl of the Dominican order, but the cloth was thin and hung loosely on him—and it was soaked through with freezing water! The black mantle he wore over the habit was more of a badge or decoration—the sign of his order—than a proper piece of clothing, and would have as much effect against the cold as his rosary or his scapular.

By contrast, with the heat of battle starting to desert him, Niccolo was shivering again. "You're not cold, *frate*?" he asked incredulously. "You're not freezing?"

"The cold doesn't bother me," said the friar. "There are worse torments than those of the flesh. My small, unworthy sacrifices, I offer up to the glory of God."

"A zealot," thought Niccolo, who had, by now, received a thorough indoctrination in the folly of zealotry from his skeptical and irreverent tutor. And shaking his head, he helped the friar brush off some of the wet, caked snow that still clung to his habit.

"Well," said Niccolo. "What are we standing here for? We should get you somewhere where you can dry off. You're going to catch your death in those wet clothes."

"I was looking for the monastery of San Marco. Is it far from here?"

"No, not far," said Niccolo, and then out of pity and against his better judgment, "I'll take you there if you like. It's up this way."

Niccolo sized up the man he had saved from possible martyrdom. His voice was high-pitched, and distracted, as if it were coming from far away. His face—God, he was ugly! All nose and eyebrows. His long, wet hair hung in scraggly strands and, taken together with the wet clothing on his scrawny frame, made him look like an animal recently saved from drowning.

They set off, the friar walking, or rather hopping, like a bird. Whether it was his hip injury or his habitual way of walking, Niccolo could not tell. To his horror, he discovered further proof of his charge's zealotry. As they made their way up the narrow, snow-covered street, Niccolo discerned the monk's feet occasionally peeping out from under his habit. Sandals! Bare feet in sandals! In the snow! He winced, trying to imagine the unimaginable pain. Better not to even think about it. Offer it up. He shuddered.

"You don't know the city?" asked Niccolo.

"This is my first time in Florence. I was sent by the order to preach the Lenten sermons at San Marco, at the church there," said the man in his reedy, uneven voice. This piece of information was the cause of some chagrin to Niccolo.

That morning, he had faithfully promised his mother that, no matter what, he would accompany her to church in the evening. His father never went. "Church is for women and children," he was fond of saying. Niccolo had already been thinking how miserable the evening was going to be with his runny nose, with his coughing and sneezing. The churches were cold, bone-chillingly cold. That was all bad enough. But now, it seemed that this awkward, drowned rat of a monk was the one his mother had been talking about, the "new priest sent to preach the Lenten sermons at San Marco." He was going to have to stand there and occasionally kneel there on the cold stone floor, to listen to this Saint Stephen of the snowballs preach in his faraway, pious tones—a man who didn't know enough not to go barefoot in the snow! "Oh well," thought Niccolo resignedly, offer this one up too.

"How did you wind up at the mercy of those two little monsters?" asked Niccolo, more for the sake of conversation than out of any real desire to know.

"I'm afraid I lost my way and passed by them several times, first going this way, then that, then back again. I must have seemed a ridiculous figure to them, lost and helpless. They taunted me, and when I slipped and fell, they couldn't resist making fun of me. Then the snowballs. But no harm was done, really, and I hold no grudge against them. It's not their fault."

"Not their fault," cried Niccolo, indignant. "They're little animals! They'll grow up to be criminals!"

"Perhaps," replied the friar, "without benefit of instruction, without moral guidance and direction, without examples of worthy behavior, but they are children of God . . ."

"Children of God?" Niccolo interrupted him. "More like spawn of the devil. Blackguards!"

"And you're thinking you must be better than they?" The friar's eyes turned on Niccolo. There was an unexpected sternness in them. A fierce glare flashed. There was a sudden power in those eyes, just as there must be steel in that slight body and those fragile limbs to be able to withstand the cold without quaking and shivering. Power or madness. Niccolo backed off from the argument.

The monk raised a finger in warning to Niccolo, "Let he who is without fault cast the first stone," he said in tones of dire, priestly reproach. "Or the first snowball, as the case may be," he added, blithely, dissolving the tension between them. "Anyway, I should be thanking you and not preaching to you. So come now, accept my thanks."

"Accepted, Father," said Niccolo, using the honorific "Father," since he realized the friar was also a priest who had received holy orders.

"You needn't call me 'Father,' my son," he corrected. "'Brother' will do. Call me Frate Girolamo."

"Alright, Frate Girolamo," said Niccolo, "Here we are. That's the church of San Marco, at the end of the piazza. The chapter house is just around the corner, in back."

The scrawny friar stopped, staring up in awe at the magnificent church. He had never before preached in a place so sumptuous, so grandiose, so big. "Are you sure this is San Marco?" he asked Niccolo, a little flustered. "I was expecting a more humble parish."

"This isn't Venice, Frate. There's only one San Marco here, and that's it, right in front of you," said Niccolo.

"Why, the order must have made some sort of mistake, sending me here," said the friar with a look of obvious consternation on his face. "I'm not accustomed to anything like this. It's . . . It's . . . so majestic."

"Don't worry, you'll do just fine," said Niccolo, not believing it for a minute. He felt genuinely sorry for the pious, little man. That small, piping voice would never be able to fill the cavernous interior of San Marco.

Niccolo led the dazed friar around to the monastery where the monks lived and showed him the entrance. He left him there, knocking feebly at the door. On his way back across the piazza, Niccolo turned and looked at the poor man, slumped in his humility, waiting patiently for someone to let him in. Then the door opened and the monastery swallowed him up.

As Niccolo left the piazza and turned onto the Via Larga, he was greeted by a snowball that almost knocked his cap off. The two little monsters were blocking his way. That, in itself, would not have been cause for alarm, but with them were three considerably larger monsters, the kind of rough and sullen boys who made Niccolo edgy. Their ragged clothing revealed taut, bulging arms and chests. Their malicious grins showed many missing teeth. There was nothing dubious about their intentions.

"Get him!" squealed one of the little monsters. "Get him! Get him! He kicked me! I want him." Niccolo knew that if they did get him, it would not stop with snowballs.

Seeing that the odds were overwhelmingly against him, Niccolo ran. But with wet boots, aching feet, and the snow, he knew he would not get far. Besides, there was the danger of slipping, and if he fell, they would be on him. He hated to think of the consequences. He was willing to bet those missing teeth were not the result of gum disease or natural causes. These people played rough. They would not listen to reason. "An eye for an eye, and yes, a tooth for a tooth. And then some," he thought.

The church of San Marco was right in front of him. He made directly for it. A vague notion of the ancient right of sanctuary crossed his mind. He would be safe in the church. Nobody could touch you in a church. They wouldn't dare come after him. In a less excited frame of mind, Niccolo might have remembered that some of the most treacherous and grisly murders in recent memory had taken place in the churches of Florence.

He took the steps two at a time and prayed that the smaller door off to the right-hand side would be open. The monsters were closing in on him fast, and he knew he couldn't make the main entrance. He pushed, the door gave, and he was inside. A volley of snowballs slammed into the door just as it closed behind him. *Thump, thump, thump, thwack!* The monsters were the kind of boys who put rocks in snowballs. But Niccolo had guessed right. Whether from piety or superstition, they had not followed him into the church. They had stopped short, at the foot of the steps, and were yelling at him. *Vigliacco! Scoglionato!* Chicken-shit coward! The snowballs, hurled in anger and frustration, continued to fly.

When the noise had died down, Niccolo opened the door a crack and peered out. The monsters were still there, and their jeering began anew. Niccolo, feeling that he was out of danger now, stepped partway outside. Holding the door ajar with one foot, he made a fist with his right hand and brought it up sharply and defiantly, slapping his left hand into the crook of the arm. Up your ass! That was the only language they understood. A furious barrage of snowballs forced him back into the vestibule of the church.

He kept watch through the crack for a few minutes, but the little monsters and their escort of thugs showed no sign of leaving. He would have to wait them out. Damn! He was tired. He was hungry. And he was freezing. His nose was running again. He looked at the boys outside who were effectively holding him prisoner, and he cursed them. Ragged animals—they probably wiped their noses on their sleeves—even worse, on the tablecloth.

Niccolo resigned himself to his captivity. He would have to spend some time in the church, maybe all afternoon. He thought, idly, he would go light a candle and at least warm his hands a little. Backing away from the door, where the occasional thump of a snowball reminded him he was still a captive, he turned to go into the sanctuary. But before he had taken a step, he saw something that made his hair stand on end. His breath caught in his throat.

From the far end of the vestibule, a man had been watching him without saying a word. And in that man's hand, pointed directly at Niccolo, was a short sword, stained with blood.

Nobody moved. The man was smiling. Or leering. His mouth was pulled into a grin so wide it was almost unnatural. And he had all his teeth. Glistening, white teeth. He said nothing. He stood staring at Niccolo with ferocious, bulging eyes. He held the sword at arm's length, without a tremor, perfectly motionless.

His skin was a deadly shade, the color of ashes and cold marble. His head was bandaged. His left arm was in a sling. There was a gaping wound in his throat and blood down the front of his shirt.

"Exc-c-use me," Niccolo stammered. No response. Nothing. Just the unflinching glare of that awful, grinning death mask of a face. And the sword.

Niccolo took a step backward and bumped up against the closed doors. Nowhere to go. He looked down. Those dreadful, menacing eyes were boring into him. He couldn't bear it anymore. The grinning and the eerie silence. He edged sideways, one step, two steps. Maybe he could circle around the wraith. "With all due respect . . ." he began. But when he looked up, the huge eyes were no longer upon him. They were still staring at the spot where he had been standing. He took another cautious step, then two in quick succession. Incredible. The man had not moved an inch. Not followed him with his gaze—or sword! "Oh my God," thought Niccolo. "He's dead. Frozen!"

Niccolo looked the man up and down. Whoever he was and whatever had happened to him, he was a rich man. His short cape was red scarlet silk, trimmed around the bottom in white fur. His black boots were slit up the sides to reveal a second, rakish layer of red leather underneath. Only wealth and power wore boots like that. Summoning up his resolve, Niccolo approached for a closer look.

He couldn't believe it. The man who had held him at sword point, who had had him trembling in mortal terror, was a statue made of wax! The clothes were real, all right. So was the sword. The cold wax fingers wore real gold rings with real jewels in them (real, if not genuine).

Niccolo chided himself for his own stupidity, telling himself that it must have been the light. He was glad no one had been a witness to the embarrassing scene between him and the deadly statue. He was making excuses for himself: You never found statues like this in churches. Wax, not stone. And with real clothes. Real silk and fur. It did look real, damn it, especially in this light.

Niccolo spotted a small, framed document, affixed to the wall behind the statue. It had been written in an elaborate hand and decorated around the edges with scrollwork and golden miniature. It read:

> In thanksgiving for delivering him from the hands of his enemies, and in grateful recognition of God's mercy, we offer this image of our beloved Lorenzo de' Medici to the people of Florence.

So this was him—Lorenzo the Magnificent. Niccolo had seen him before, but only from a distance at public functions and spectacles. He considered the statue with a cold eye: He may be magnificent, but he's not handsome, if he looks anything like this. Big, flat nose, amazing mouth. Jesus, they used real hair!

Niccolo was absorbed in his inspection of the wax figure, when a clipped, nasal voice interrupted him from behind, "Well, what do you think of it? Isn't it lifelike?"

"It's really is quite . . ." he broke off in midsentence and his jaw dropped. It was the mouth! And the nose! The complexion was better, but it was him! The statue! Lorenzo the Magnificent!

Niccolo looked back and forth in disbelief, at the statue and at the man, at the real thing and at the representation He saw the same thick, black hair, the same broken nose, the long, twisting mouth, the same square, jutting lower jaw. Only in height did they differ. The original was much shorter.

And the original didn't have the ghastly pallor of death on his face or a bloody sword in his hand. Amused, and smiling, he repeated his question, "Isn't it lifelike?"

"Yes, it is. It's remarkable," said Niccolo, still looking back and forth.

"So you've never seen him before, our friend here?" asked Lorenzo.

Little by little, Niccolo overcame his amazement and turned his full attention to the living Lorenzo de' Medici. "It really took me by surprise. I thought for a minute it was a real person. You know, with this light in here, you can make a mistake."

"Some of the most skilled craftsmen in the city worked on that wax effigy. I sat for hours while they modeled the face. Even with the hands they insisted on copying every detail. Verrocchio oversaw the entire project. He's a miracle worker. You've heard of my wonderful sculptor, Verrocchio?"

Niccolo hadn't. In fact, when it came to things Medicean, Niccolo knew almost nothing. His father bore the Medici family a grudge and their name was invoked in the Machiavelli household only as the object of scorn and vituperation. To cover his ignorance, Niccolo said, "I thought they only put statues of saints in the churches."

The most powerful man in Florence laughed heartily at the boy's observation. "So you don't think I'm a saint? Well, I suppose I'm not, not in the traditional sense anyway, of fasting and mortifying the flesh," he gave a mock shudder. "I love the flesh too much to give it up. The flesh is dear to me! I celebrate the flesh!

"And yet I am a saint of sorts," he continued. "My Marsilio says I'm the patron saint of poetry and music, of sculpture, painting, and philosophy!"

Niccolo was not sure how to respond to this claim, delivered, he thought, a little rhapsodically. A sneeze saved him from having to say something stupid.

But Lorenzo the Magnificent was off and running now. His eyes gleamed. "The arts," he gushed, "they're what separate us from the beasts. Without music, without literature, what would we be? Brutes! Nothing but brutes! Without the Muses whispering in our ears, guiding our hands and our tongues and our pens, what would man be but another beast of burden? All dross. But beauty has freed our spirits to sing and to dance! That is the only task worthy of a man—the pursuit of beauty! Don't you agree?"

"Oh, absolutely," said Niccolo politely.

The great man continued: "I dabble in poetry, some of it quite shameless, I'm afraid. In fact, this morning I composed some verses that I'm quite pleased with. They're delightful and frivolous. I wanted to escape this dreadful, dismal weather, to think of spring!

Would you like to hear the song?" He did not wait for an affirmative reply.

He began, hands clasped fervently to his chest:

> Quant'è bella giovinezza
> che si fugge tuttavia!
>
> Oh, how lovely is youth,
> though she flees so soon . . .

In a voice that was nasal and high-pitched, he went on to celebrate, as he had previously said he was fond of doing, the flesh. His movements were studied and histrionic, and anything but graceful, his flapping arms and bobbing head were reminiscent of puppet theatre.

Niccolo squirmed. He was still cold. Nevertheless he smiled politely as the performance unrolled and as the performer warmed to it. He followed the sense of the thing—such as it was—easily enough. It was about Bacchus and love and the woods and the wood nymphs dancing and leaping for joy. It was, in a word, everything he had always thought of, not without some disdain, as "poetry."

While Lorenzo recited his verses, Niccolo was locked in a fierce inner struggle. The agonizing tickle in his nose would begin, then gradually become more intense, irresistible, almost unbearable. He did not want to ruin the lovely recitation with a sneeze.

"Di doman, non c'è certezza!—for nothing is certain about the future!" Lorenzo concluded ecstatically and a little out of breath. "Well, what did you think?" He seemed eager for the boy's approval.

"It was . . . lovely," said Niccolo.

"I'm glad you enjoyed it," said the exultant poet. "But as I told you, I'm really just an amateur, a dabbler. Now Angelo! My Angelo, my divine Angelo! He is a poet! He has no equal in the Italian language today, nor in Latin. He will be considered with Dante and Petrarch among the greatest poets of all time. His fame will last a hundred centuries! Longer! Through his art, he will achieve—immortality!" He pronounced this last word with almost religious rapture.

Niccolo wanted to go home, but his companion had no intention of letting him off so easily. "You've read Angelo's divine, divine *Stanze*?"

A violent fit of sneezing drowned out Niccolo's admission that he had not read the divine Angelo's divine *Stanze*, and, in fact, that he had never even heard of either the poet or the poem. Seeing the boy's distress, Lorenzo reached into his sleeve and pulled out a voluminous handkerchief. It was as big as a blanket. "Here," he said, handing it to Niccolo, "I think you can put one of these to good use."

When his wet, raw nose touched the soft cloth, Niccolo was in heaven. Never had it touched anything so exquisite, so luxurious before. For this favor he was grateful. If this man wanted to stand here all day and talk to him about poetry, so be it. He thanked him profusely, and then, once again, plunged his face into that glorious handkerchief.

"But come tell me," Lorenzo pressed him, "what poets do you most enjoy?"

Niccolo had to think hard since he did not, at all, enjoy poetry. "Ah . . . Virgil," he finally said.

"The divine Virgil! Yes, the Virgil of the *Ecologues*! Those wonderful celebrations of the simple life! Good wine, good food, clean air! Limpid streams! Birds singing in the trees! You know, Angelo has studied the *Ecologues*, exhaustively. He knows them by heart, from start to finish. He says they are a source of constant inspiration to him."

"I wasn't talking about the *Ecologues*," said Niccolo almost apologetically. "When I said Virgil, I meant the Virgil of the *Aeneid*, the story of the founding of Rome."

"That long and ghastly thing, full of violence and bloodshed and wars and battles. Whatever could a sensitive young man find to interest him in that?" Lorenzo seemed surprised. "Surely, you read other, more pleasant things?"

"Of course I do," replied Niccolo enthusiastically, thankful to be on more familiar territory, "I read Caesar and Livy, and I've started Tacitus, *The Germanic Wars* . . ."

"Such warlike reading in one so young," mused Lorenzo. "Is that what you're interested in, war? You want to be a soldier?"

"It's not just war, so much," Niccolo explained. "I'm interested in history . . . and . . . well . . . politics."

"How very original! Interested in politics. Now on that score, I can offer you some advice. Stay clear of politics. That is my advice to you. Flee it! Embrace poetry and music. Politics is a painful business. There is no beauty in it, no charm, no joy. It's treachery and scheming and flirting with the devil. I should know. Look there," he pointed to his wax double. "That was the result of politics, that wound in my neck. And worse than that, my brother, dead, murdered." Sadness crept into his voice, the poetic frenzy at an end now.

Niccolo was burning with curiosity. He thought he was never going to get an explanation as to why the statue of this apparently harmless and poetic soul wore a gaping wound in its neck and brandished a bloody sword. "What happened?"

"A conspiracy," he sighed. "The Pazzi, more mad and rabid than even their name implies. They planned to assassinate my brother Giuliano and me. They were jealous. The pope was involved too. 'Liberate Florence from the Medici,' said His Holiness. 'Here, I give you my blessing.'

"They planned to do it at a banquet, with poison, the coward's tool. But my brother was ill for several days and confined to his bed. They grew impatient and, in their anger, seized upon the first available opportunity to assassinate us. They would do it while we attended mass, in the cathedral. Sacrilege of sacrileges!" Here, he made the sign of the cross.

"Francesco de' Pazzi was the leader. Right up to the end, he pretended friendship with us. Franceschino we still called him, out of friendship. Outside the church he put his arms around my brother. He joked with him about his illness, said he had grown soft and fat. He squeezed him with seeming affection. He was squeezing him to see if he had a weapon, to see if he wore armor, and to feel for the soft, unprotected spot where he would plunge his assassin's dagger.

"They threw themselves upon us during holy mass, when the bell sounded for the priest's communion. Two disaffected priests lunged at me, but they were weak and slow. I drew my sword and beat them back. Giuliano was not so lucky. Francesco hit him from behind with a blow that would have felled an ox. His hatred was so great that he continued to plunge his dagger again and again into the soft, dead flesh of my fallen brother. Consumed by his madness and blood lust, he would not stop. When they tried to drag him off, he continued hacking and drove the point of his bloody dagger into his own thigh!

"I got away, and my people rallied. The coup was unsuccessful. I appeared at the windows of the palace like that," he pointed to the wax statue, "shaken, in despair, but not badly injured. I pleaded with my people to contain their anger and their lust for revenge. But it was no use.

"Before it was over, some eighty people were dead, some guilty, some innocent. Bodies were mutilated and dragged through the streets. Even the archbishop was among the conspirators. He and the Pazzi, naked with ropes around their necks, were hurled from the windows of the Signoria. Angelo saw them. I didn't. He said that they kicked and screamed as they dangled, choking, above the cheering mob. The archbishop, the life almost strangled out of him, in a final burst of blind, gruesome rage, sunk his teeth into the dead flesh of Franceschino's leg. They died as they lived—like rabid dogs.

"The two renegade priests who attacked me were castrated and hanged. Jacopo da' Pazzi, the head of the family, escaped, but was found and brought back. He was tortured and hanged when they grew tired of tormenting him. Although he was granted Christian burial—unlike the others—a mob later dug up his body and paraded it through the streets. They said his evil spirit was responsible for the heavy rains and floods that followed the coup attempt. Eventually, he was brought home, to the Pazzi Palace. They propped him up against the door and used his decomposing head for a knocker. They smashed it against the heavy oak slabs, crying, 'Open up in there, it's your master come home. He wishes to enter.' That grisly sport went on until there was nothing left of his skull. His brains and blood and hair were left spattered across the door as a reminder and a warning."

Lorenzo's eyes were almost closed when he finished his story. His long mouth was twisted tightly in a brooding expression of infinite sadness. Then he looked up at Niccolo. "You see why I warn you away from politics?"

The short winter day had nearly come to an end when Niccolo finally left the church of San Marco. As he had expected, his enemies in the snowball wars had long since given up their siege and gone off to other scurrilous pursuits.

"Wood nymphs," thought Niccolo, making his way home. "Poetry." He shook his head. Maybe he would like that sort of thing when he grew up. Maybe it was an acquired taste, like the strong, throat-searing liquors his father drank. He assured Niccolo that he too, one day, would drink and enjoy them. A fleeting vision of adulthood passed through his mind—dozing in a chair, a cup of grappa, and a book of pastoral poetry at his side. He blew his nose mightily into his newly acquired handkerchief. Lorenzo had insisted he keep it.

What a strange man. One minute he was chirping like a cricket about wood nymphs, the next he was lost in a harrowing tale of political assassination. Niccolo was trying to sort things out. True, his father maintained that Lorenzo de' Medici was a fool, and when Niccolo had stood listening to his high, piping voice chanting the glories of wood nymphs, he had been inclined to agree.

He had never seen anything sillier and had to keep reminding himself that this man in front of him, putting on this show, was the virtual ruler, the first citizen, of Florence. Niccolo could only speculate what the divine Angelo must be like, if he was the one who was the real poet.

And then the story of the attempted assassination. It had made Niccolo feel sorry for Lorenzo. He had lost his brother. That, he supposed, was what had led him to despise politics, and throw himself into the pursuit of beauty—and the flesh. Niccolo could understand that.

In the end, Niccolo decided he liked him. So what if his father had said Lorenzo was driving the city to ruin? Niccolo's father had always spoken of Lorenzo as a calculating, moral monster of a man. Niccolo had seen him as just a man, and a rather silly and lighthearted man at that. He was kind and generous—he had even offered to take him into the academy he had established to learn painting and music. Niccolo had said he would have to think about that, but he had already decided against it, knowing his father would be furious if he even mentioned the possibility. Besides, he had little desire to pursue painting and music. Music he had already tried with dismal results. The strings of the lute and the rebec had eluded his stiff, awkward fingers, just as the holes of the flute had done. He was utterly incapable of carrying a tune or hearing the difference between two tones. He liked Lorenzo, but not enough to try to be a musician for him.

Niccolo reached into his pocket and pulled out his great, magnificent handkerchief, already his most prized possession. As he unfolded it, he saw something he had not noticed before, a small sign embroidered in the corner. "Of course," he thought, "it would be Lorenzo's family emblem." The rich and powerful were fond of emblazoning their every possession with their family emblems and coats of arms. He squinted to make out the design in the pale winter-evening light. Niccolo stiffened. A sense of helplessness and confusion swept over him. He had seen this design before. His mind went back six months, back to a simple design he had seen etched in the handle of a dagger he had pulled from the back of a murdered boy.

Part 2

The Prophet

10

BALLS! BALLS! BALLS!

Palle! Palle! Palle! The chant rang up from the streets below.

Balls! Balls! Balls! It was the chant that had greeted Lorenzo de' Medici for over twenty-three years as the Florentine head of state. It was the same chant that had echoed in the ears of his father and his grandfather before him.

Balls! Balls! Balls! heralding his victories; *Balls! Balls! Balls!* rallying in support of his policies when they were not so successful. Even when his actions were downright foolish and their consequences disastrous, there was no shortage of enthusiastic supporters, ever ready with their lusty cry of *Balls! Balls! Balls!* When enthusiasm was wanting, or support difficult to come by, it was simply purchased outright, so that the steady, pounding, intimidating cadence of *Balls! Balls! Balls!* was always there to drown out the objections and remonstrance's of his enemies.

How the balls came to represent the Medici family is a story shrouded in the mists of the Dark Ages. It involves a knight errant named Averardo, attached to the court of Charlemagne, and a wicked giant who was terrorizing the countryside around Florence. A ferocious battle ensued between these two, and notwithstanding the giant's diabolical fury and superior strength, Averardo prevailed. During the fight, his shield had absorbed blow after vicious blow from the giant's iron-studded club. The dents on that shield came to be represented as red balls on a field of gold.

In recognition of the undying gratitude of the people, Averardo cheerfully agreed to remain with them always and to protect them against the depredations of future giants lurking in the neighborhood, intent on terror and exploitation. And so the brave knight settled in the district known as the Mugello and sired the noble race that would someday be known as the Medici and that would adopt as their insignia the famous red balls.

Such at least was the account pieced together by an historian "of considerable accomplishment," hired by the Medici, using, as he claimed, both Latin and French sources of great antiquity. The degree to which his scholarship was colored by a desire to please his patrons can only be guessed.

Those disinclined to credit tales of giants and savage blows heroically incurred offered explanations of their own: It was said that the balls were originally pills, and that the Medici, as their name implies, were the descendants of medical doctors. It was maintained in other quarters, less friendly to Medici interests, that the balls were nothing but coins, the age-old emblem of pawnbrokers and usurers.

Further complicating the matter of the balls was the problem of their exact number. Originally thought to be twelve, we nevertheless find the Medici emblem here with ten, there with seven. Tombs and some buildings sport five balls, but others have six. This confusion in time gave rise to the unkind observation that the Medici didn't know how many balls they had. In a language where courage is measured out in balls, so that the phrase, "He has seven balls," accompanied by appropriate gestures, is meant to convey that he has three and a half times the courage normally allotted to one man, in such a language, this uncertainty about the number of one's balls is no laughing matter.

Balls! Balls! Balls! the chant below continued, and Lorenzo smiled as much as a man in his condition could. The gout had swollen his feet and ankles to grotesque dimensions and turned the skin on them purple and shiny. He had not walked or put on shoes in over two months. The pain had crept up his legs, joint by joint, to his hips, his elbows, his shoulders, even down to his fingertips.

The fever had been raging in him constantly for over a week and showed no sign of breaking. It was consuming him, growing in strength as he weakened. He felt it in his blood and his veins, in his bones and his guts. Poking and palpitating doctors had assured him that his liver was hideously swollen. His nerves were shattered. His strength had deserted him almost completely, so that he could no longer even hold a pen to write. His eyes were failing. At the age of only forty-three, the man who had so often celebrated the glories of youth in his poetry was dying.

For this particular appearance, he had been propped up and tied into a straight-back chair and carried to a window where he was exhibited to the people. He was not an imposing sight, but the distance at which the crowd was held would protect him from careful scrutiny. He was dressed in the simple *lucco*, the citizen's gown worn by the sober and respectable men of Florence. It was a generous garment that could easily conceal the unkindnesses of nature and age. It gave little or no clue that what had once been firm had turned flaccid or that what was then full and robust was now shrunken and shriveled. Wrapped in the ample scarlet cloth, the evidence of his wasting illness would remain hidden from the world—the emaciated arms and legs, the sagging belly, the sunken chest.

He had been shaved and heavily made up for the occasion, mostly to cover the deep, dark circles under his eyes. They had considered washing his hair, which now hung in thick, oily black clumps, but the risk of the cold to his frail hold on life had outweighed cosmetic considerations. Instead, he was saddled with a hat.

His appearance at the balcony was brief. No speech was required of him. An announcement was made dismissing the rumors of his ill health as a cold complicated by nothing more than a case of laryngitis. To the chant of *Balls! Balls! Balls!* it was further explained that a curative visit to the baths at Vigone had been arranged, and that the great man's departure was imminent.

Presently, Lorenzo was bundled back into the room, strapped to a litter, and carried to the courtyard where a carriage waited. Was it his imagination, or was the crowd smaller? Were their lusty shouts of *Balls! Balls! Balls!* a little less lusty? Where was the roar, the staccato rhythm, the fists jabbing in the air to punctuate their chant? Were even they turning away from him now? Would they abandon him in his final hours? Had the friar gotten to them? The pain was too intense for Lorenzo to think clearly about all this now. Secured in his carriage and overcome with exhaustion, he drifted off into an uneasy sleep. It was in this pitiful condition, assailed by doubts and surrounded by sycophants and hangers-on, that Lorenzo de' Medici, called Lorenzo the Magnificent, left Florence in early March 1492. He would never return.

Lorenzo's father, whose chronic afflictions had earned him the ignominious nickname of Piero the Gouty, had died at forty-eight. This painful disease, engendered by indulgence and excess, was Lorenzo's birthright, then. Unable to flex his thin, arthritic fingers, he thought back to how these same fingers could once dance across the strings of a lyre or trace the most delicate and elegant characters that a pen was capable of committing to paper. His now bloated and useless feet had once carried him swiftly and surely across the football field in his youth, and the dance floor as he grew older. They had carried him and many a conquest to the bedroom as well. He had lived well, if not temperately, and the memory of it soothed him now in his agony.

With a sigh, he temporarily lost himself in the past, in the litany of his accomplishments, from the encouragement of learning and scholarship to the sponsorship of painters, sculptors, poets, and musicians. He had designed buildings and had them built. He had assembled the most complete library of classical books and manuscripts in existence. He had made Florence respected everywhere in the world for her brilliance and her preeminence in the cultural sphere.

He had been a good father to his children and affectionate with his wife, a dull matron, a dour Roman, but his wife nonetheless. He had tried to be friendly and helpful to everyone. He loved animals, he bred racehorses, milk cows, pheasants, pigs, and rabbits. He had been a keeper of bees, a cultivator of gardens, and a maker of cheeses. He had done, by his own evaluation, virtually everything fine and praiseworthy that was worth doing in the world.

So what did this friar want of him? Why had he taken the pulpit and denounced him so vociferously? Pursued him with all the fury of a hellhound unleashed? Why was he tormenting him, turning the people against him? Lorenzo did not understand.

For a month he languished, not so much struggling against the disease as surrendering to it and, perhaps because of that surrender, being occasionally granted a day of remission. One such day, a bright day in early April, found Lorenzo in good spirits and even up to talking with the serving woman who had come to change his bedclothes. Deeming her intellect too dull and full of dross to engage in a discussion of the beautiful frescos that lined the walls of the villa, he was telling her about something more suited to her station and limited imagination—the collection of exotic animals that he kept at Poggio a Caiano.

"Imagine an enormous horse, covered with brown and yellow spots," Lorenzo began.

"Sounds like your horse has the plague or a touch of the malaria to me," the maid responded skeptically.

"Now imagine that his neck is so long, he can easily peer over the city walls of Florence! That's what my giraffe is like."

"*Che diavolo d'animale,*" she exclaimed, making the sign of the cross. "God protect us from such monsters! And where did you get such a beast as that?" she asked warily.

"It was a present from my friend, the Sultan of Babylon," he said.

"Babylon, indeed," she snorted. "There's nothing ever come out of Babylon but sin and destruction and whores!" Secure in her biblical knowledge of that city, she considered the matter of the giraffe's demonic origins irrefutably settled.

"Of course, good woman, I have other animals too. Bears! Tigers! Bulls from Spain! Boars! Buffalo! What would you like?"

"Have you got any lions about?"

"Why yes, of course. Why do you ask?"

"It seems the city will be needing lions."

"How so?" Lorenzo was aware of the two lions, proudly exhibited in a cage in the appropriately named Via del Leone—Lion Street. He had, in fact, donated them to the city. As official lions of the commune, they were occasionally used in public spectacles. Once, at Lorenzo's instigation, the Piazza della Signoria had been turned into a giant hunting field, and wild animals of every description were set loose and hunted down there by dashing young men. It was a stirring entertainment. The climax of the spectacle was to be a battle between the lions and a pack of wild dogs. But both dogs and lions were leery of the engagement and scrupulously avoided one another. After much futile coaxing and goading, the idea was abandoned and the entertainment declared a failure. But the lions had been majestic in appearance that day. Frightening! Regal! The embodiment of nobility itself!

"I said, they're dead," she enunciated firmly, drawing Lorenzo out of his reverie.

"What? Dead? How?" what little color he had left his face.

"They killed each other in their cage. In a fight, tore each other apart," she said.

"My God," gasped Lorenzo. "It's a sign!"

"They say, it's a sign of death," she confirmed.

"Whose death?"

"Why, the lion being the king of beasts, they say it must be a sign of the king's death." Her logic was surprisingly sound for one of so little formal education.

This last, terrifying, inevitable conclusion had already forced itself upon Lorenzo. The death of the king was being presaged. But Florence had no king. Florence was a republic. Florence was ruled by the people. Except . . .

Except that the friar had called him, Lorenzo, a king in everything but name. Except that the friar had denounced him, Lorenzo, from the pulpit in the cathedral. Hair shaking in great waves as he preached, arms upraised, he had spoken bitterly to the people of Florence: "You have sold your ancient birthright, your cherished liberty! And what have you gotten in return? What bargain have you struck with your precious liberty in the balance? You have bartered it away, squandered it for lewd entertainments, squandered it for bread and circuses, squandered it for spectacles staged for you by a tyrant!" Yes, the friar had denounced him, Lorenzo, as a king, a usurper, and a tyrant.

"That's not the only sign. They say there've been others," the old servant was going on. "She-wolves howling. They say you can hear them in the hills, and there are lights in the sky at night . . ."

"Stop it! That's enough! What are you trying to do? Frighten him to death?" A handsome, effeminate man of about forty had entered the room. "Madame, you are dismissed!"

Terror had drawn Lorenzo up into a sitting position, and his bony fingers were constricted around the fur-lined edge of his satin coverlet. He was bathed in an acrid, sour-smelling sweat. The new arrival and his dearest friend, Angelo Poliziano, hastened to his side.

The solicitous Poliziano lowered Lorenzo the Magnificent back into the nest of pillows upon which he rested. He gently pried open the quaking, skeletal fists and tucked them safely back under the covers. His movements were busy, fussy even. He made cooing, comforting sounds as he hovered over his master. "Tales, fantastications, inventions. They're just tales told by old women—and old men. It's nonsense, all nonsense. Don't listen to a word."

"Angelo, Angelo, where have you been? What have you been up to?" croaked the dying man in a rasping voice.

"Putting my faith in science and not in the rantings of superstitious old fools. I've sent for help. Look here. *Avanti, Signori!*" He summoned two gentlemen who were waiting respectfully just outside the door. As they approached, Lorenzo recognized Piero Leoni, his personal physician, in the company of a bespectacled stranger.

"Dottor Lazaro di Pavia, physician attached to the court of Lodovico il Moro in Milan," Angelo made the introduction. "They say he has performed wonders."

The new physician pointed his pinched face in Lorenzo's direction and nodded curtly.

"Well, begin your examination," Angelo invited. Lorenzo smiled weakly. The doctor dropped a large and heavy-looking cloth bag. It clanged to the stone floor as if it were full of mason's tools instead of the delicate instruments of surgery. He approached his prostrate subject. He peered into orifices; he lifted the covers; he poked, nodding gravely the entire time. He requested a stool sample, and Angelo informed him that there had been none for over a fortnight. The jealous Dottor Leoni eyed his rival with suspicion.

His examination complete, the new doctor proceeded to cross the room to an alcove where there was a heavy oak table. He heaved the bag up onto the table and sent its contents clamoring unceremoniously out. Angelo hurried to his side, followed by Lorenzo's physician, Piero. "Well?" he demanded, "Can you do anything for him?"

"Of course I can do something for him," he said abruptly as if there were never any doubt. "However, his condition is well advanced. I should have been called in earlier." Turning to Leoni, he said haughtily, "And what treatment, dear doctor, have you been prescribing for your patient?"

Dottor Leoni replied rather pompously and defensively, "Being a physician and not a student of witchcraft, I have avoided the potions and concoctions often favored by 'certain members'"—he spoke with disdain—"of our profession. I have ordered him to be kept warm and dry, to be kept out of the night air so that his system might purge itself.

I have further specified that he refrain from the eating of pears and that he take care to swallow no grape pips . . ."

"Grape pips!" sputtered the Milanese physician. And, as competitive medical men are wont to do, they fell to squabbling, then hurling accusations. The offended Dottor Leoni, after a great show of indignation and with much huffing and puffing, finally left the room.

With a pleased smile, the conquering physician turned to Angelo, "Now that we've rid ourselves of that fool, shall we begin?" He reached deep into the recesses of his black physician's gown and extracted a tiny velvet pouch. Untying the string, he shook a handful of large, milky-white pearls out into a cup. Angelo watched in amazement as he transferred the contents of the cup to a heavy marble mortar and, with a pestle of similar material, began to crush the soft, beautiful stones. He ground them to a fine powder. He repeated this procedure with a variety of precious stones, using a heavier, iron-tipped pestle and more violent blows as the obduracy of his ingredients increased. The sound of iron and stone hammering on stone filled the air and rang from the walls.

Angelo felt more as if he were in a quarry than in a sickroom. He grew perplexed and increasingly skeptical as he watched this madman pounding furiously, smashing precious stones to powder with diabolical glee. He was also concerned that the racket might disturb his master and shatter the fitful sleep into which he had fallen with the help of a bountiful tranquilizing draft.

"Are you there, Angelo?" Lorenzo's faint voice drifted over to the breaker's yard where the good doctor was noisily at work. Instantly, Angelo was at his side. "What is he doing over there, the noise?" he said weakly.

Angelo explained the physician's bizarre procedures and his exotic remedies. A ray of hope crossed Lorenzo's face. He took Angelo's hands into his own and questioned him eagerly. He squeezed hard in his excitement. "It's going to work, isn't it? I feel it. It's just crazy and wonderful and marvelous enough that it's going to work; isn't it Angelo? Isn't it?" Lorenzo was breathless.

Angelo looked away. "Yes," he muttered in assent, "of course it's going to work." Taking his leave hurriedly and returning to his own room, he burst into tears.

Sometime later, Lorenzo was aware that the dreadful din in the alcove had stopped. Opening his eyes and bringing them into focus, he saw the Lombard physician standing over him, his thin lips curled in a gloating grin. In his hands he held up two transparent crystalline vials. "Here," he said, extending his twin treasures to the sick man, "See what I have for you—a remedy fit for a king!"

11

At the Tyrant's Deathbed

Lorenzo coughed and sputtered as the chalky draft was poured a little at a time down his parched throat. The irony of the situation was not lost on him. He had put together a collection of gems, the finest of its kind in all Christendom, painstakingly assembled over a lifetime. And in the past week, he had ingested a good part of that priceless, incomparable collection. Lazaro di Pavia, the Milanese charlatan, had wheedled from him, for medicinal purposes, not just rubies, zircons, emeralds, and a sizable quantity of gold and silver, but over two cups of pearls.

It soon became clear to everyone around him that, despite the extravagant measures being taken, Lorenzo's high hopes for recovery were unfounded. His condition deteriorated. Rapidly. The pulverized precious stones had settled like lead in his guts, clogging already-constricted passageways and further challenging a failing digestive and circulatory apparatus. Then it was discovered that not all of the precious ingredients were making their way into Lorenzo's medication, but rather into the bottomless pockets of the attending physician. Justice was summarily administered. Without ceremony, Lazaro had managed to get his throat slit and his body thrown down a well.

There was no need to inform Lorenzo of the exact circumstances of that disappearance, just as, over the years, so many of the more unseemly and grisly details in the day-to-day running of his administration had been kept from him.

As a ruler, Lorenzo had proven himself no better or worse than other men of his time. In fact, as head of state, he had been more pleasant and congenial than most and altogether more tolerable as a tyrant than, say, Fillipo Maria Visconti, the duke of Milan, or one of his successors, Galeazzo Maria Sforza. The former, a fat, filthy man whose weak, deformed legs were altogether incapable of sustaining his inordinate bulk, took no greater pleasure on hot summer days than stripping the clothes from his hideous body and rolling naked, howling, in the dirt in his garden. He was so ugly that he refused to let his portrait be painted. The sight of a naked sword so shattered his composure that it would send him into a screaming nervous fit. He had a special soundproof room constructed in his palace because he was afraid of thunder. He delighted in nothing so much as a practical joke, his favorite being to produce from his sleeve a live snake, even during interviews of the utmost seriousness where business of state was being conducted. And after his death, things in Milan went from bad to worse.

Milan's Galeazzo Maria Sforza was noted for his instability and his bizarre, sadistic fascination with the disarticulation of the human body. With singular intensity, he personally designed, supervised, and participated in the torture and systematic dismemberment of his real and imagined enemies, who were, of course, legion. The moans of the dying were music to his ears; corpses were his special obsession. When it was a question of tyrants then, Florence was certainly more fortunate than Milan.

Lorenzo's sins as a ruler were more of omission than commission. Under his stewardship, the Florentine government functioned much as the governments of the other city-states of the Italian peninsula did. Espionage, bribery, torture, and murder were the preferred instruments of both domestic and foreign policy. Secrecy, distrust, and treachery were the only constants in the ever-changing equation by which power was defined and calculated.

Lorenzo's place in this government, along with his responsibility for its misdeeds, however, was more ambiguous than in most other states. For himself, he claimed no official title, not king or even duke. He was referred to, simply and informally, as the first citizen, a fiction as transparent as that promulgated by Augustus Caesar, who at the time when he ruled the entire world, styled himself only *primus inter pares*—first among equals. Like Caesar, Lorenzo's authority, when he chose to exercise it, was absolute.

What set him apart from the other tyrants of his day was that he seldom chose to exercise that power directly. His interest in government and public life rarely extended beyond ostentatious display: the lavish spectacle, the parade, the progress, the tournament, the pomp and extravagance of the official state visit. Lorenzo left the serious work of government to his subordinates. And those sometimes-unworthy lieutenants went about their business with bold resolve.

Lorenzo's laissez-faire attitude was doubly destructive, for not only was he the uncrowned head of state, but, more important, he was the head of the largest family-owned commercial enterprise in the world—the Medici bank. The failure of Lorenzo's leadership at the bank was just as egregious as his failure at statesmanship.

He had given far too much latitude to his branch managers and leaned too heavily on the advice of the unscrupulous and the incompetent. The results were not long in manifesting themselves. Because of excessive and ill-conceived loans, the London branch folded. In short order, Bruges, Milan, Rome, Naples, and Lyon followed. The entire organization and the family whose wealth and power it sustained were on the verge of collapse.

On his deathbed, Lorenzo was not unaware of his shortcomings as a banker and statesman, yet he had hoped to make amends before being reduced to his present condition. A little over two years ago, at the peak of his powers, he would have scoffed at the notion of his own mortality. That was when the friar had come to town and begun preaching. At first, the friar spoke out against him almost hesitantly, reproaching him for his lack of vigilance, criticizing his style of living. At Lorenzo's instigation, some of his men promised to look into the matter and suggest to the friar that he find another topic for his sermons. They were sent back to Lorenzo with an impertinent admonishment—Repent or the wrath of God will surely descend upon you!

After that, the denunciation of Lorenzo from the pulpit became the theme most frequently treated in the friar's sermonizing. Lorenzo paid little attention to it and went about his business, or rather his pleasure, in the usual manner, until the friar's preaching took a singular and arresting turn. One fateful Sunday, he went beyond excoriation, calls for repentance, and vague threats of divine retribution. Saying that God had revealed it to him, he went on to predict the date of Lorenzo's death.

"Nonsense!" had been the amused reaction in cultivated Medicean circles, and even Lorenzo, never before in better health or spirits, had laughed at the idea and dismissed the friar as a crank. Now, two years later, Lorenzo was no longer laughing at the credulity and naiveté of those who credited prophecy. The week fixed by the friar for his death had arrived—and he was dying. Notwithstanding the unmitigated worldliness of his life, Lorenzo's concerns now were for the fate of his immortal soul. Panic gripped him when he considered the possibility of its everlasting damnation.

Making up his mind, he spoke to Angelo Poliziano, who was in almost constant attendance upon him. His voice was faint. "Angelo, call him, call the friar," he wheezed. "I must have his blessing before I die."

Angelo tried to discourage him. "Why don't I call Fra Mariano instead. You can confess to him and set your mind at rest."

"Oh, Angelo, Angelo," he moaned in his agony. There can be no rest for me. Don't you understand? Not without his blessing."

So Angelo called them both.

The two friars were a study in contrast. Fra Mariano, the Medicean chaplain, was stately, plump, officious, clean-shaven, manicured, and powdered. He radiated conviviality and generosity of spirit. His attitude toward Lorenzo was affectionate, even fawning.

The other friar, who so terrified the most powerful man in Florence, was diminutive by comparison. He hung back, an almost invisible witness to the bustling ministrations of Mariano. But Lorenzo felt his presence as he felt the steady, blinding pain that knifed through his feverish and tortured body.

Angelo brought Fra Mariano, who removed a fine silk stole from a velvet-lined case that also contained the blessed sacrament. He sat at the dying man's bedside, composed himself, made the sign of the cross, and indicated that he was ready to begin. "Bless me, Father, for I have sinned . . ." Lorenzo uttered the formula in a voice that was all but inaudible. The priest had to bend so close that, along with the words, Lorenzo's uneven breath reached him, reeking of decay.

The deathbed confession that issued from his cracked lips was not a recital of heinous crimes and monstrous evil deeds. It was an enumeration of overindulgences and lapses, of petty jealousies and infidelities. Dissolute, and at times foolish, he had never been wantonly cruel. He had taken money and used it freely for his own pleasures, but he had not done so maliciously. He had stolen, if *stolen* was the word, since he had always intended to pay it back, from the public treasury. He had "appropriated" money from the bank. He had squandered the patrimony left in his trust for two younger cousins, leaving them penniless. He had even dipped heavily into the inheritance of his own son. But he had never meant to harm anybody by these actions.

As Lorenzo counted out his sins, he stole many an anxious glance over the head of his chubby, ingratiating confessor and his eyes found the wraithlike figure of the other friar—the unforgiving, immovable judge, the silent, accusatory presence waiting calmly, waiting, he thought, to snatch his soul.

When Lorenzo had finished recounting his sins and had sincerely begged that they be forgiven, Fra Mariano granted him absolution. The priest then removed the sacred host from an exquisite gold box and administered Holy Communion. The communicant, unable to chew and barely able to swallow on account of his inflamed throat, allowed the sacred wafer to dissolve slowly in his mouth. Exhausted by his efforts, but deriving some small consolation from having received the sacraments, he eased back into his bed. His breathing seemed less labored as Fra Mariano respectfully withdrew, leaving Lorenzo de' Medici alone in the room with Savonarola.

Lorenzo looked up, his large brown eyes wide-open, imploring forgiveness. But he saw no mercy in the face standing over him. The jaw was set, teeth clenched, stern and unforgiving, and the friar's green eyes burned with the cold-blooded fury of an Old Testament prophet. Lorenzo the Magnificent felt small and mean and broken and ashamed. He looked away.

"I'm dying," he stammered, hoping that the extremity of his condition might inspire some pity in this severe man. Savonarola made no reply.

"I called you here to ask your blessing."

"To ask it or to command it, Lord Medici?" snapped the friar.

"To beg for it, if need be," said the dying man.

"What hath the Lord wrought?" replied the friar. "Behold His power! The exalted have been humbled, and the mighty have been laid low!" He spoke softly, but with intensity.

"Your blessing, Father. Can you deny the last request of a dying man?"

"You've made your confession and been absolved. What further need have you? Of what value is my blessing to you?" said the friar.

"I wish to reconcile myself to you, to set things right so that I can die at peace with you, with my city, with the world."

"It seems that you have more than reconciled yourself with the world, since you have spent your entire life pursuing her vanities and sinful pleasures. The city, you have made your personal harlot, and as for me, I am unimportant. It is not with me that you should seek to reconcile yourself, but with Almighty God. It is not I who stand in judgment, but He!"

The friar continued, addressing Lorenzo caustically, "Why not call on your pagan sages, your Greeks? Why do you not turn now to your Plato and Aristotle for help? Implore their blessings? Have them accompany you into the afterlife?"

Lorenzo bowed to these reproaches, but the anger and righteous indignation of the preacher had been aroused: "Your belly has been filled with wine, and your kidneys have rotted with excess. Your hands are stained with the blood of the poor. The nameless poor! Are you even aware of the barbarities inflicted upon them in your name? Do you know about Martuccio, the hermit who died in the hospice of Santa Maria Nuova, torn to pieces by your torturers? They stripped the soles from his feet and held them over the fire until he screamed and the fat ran. They forced him to walk on a bed of salt so that the coarse, crusted stuff burned into his open wounds. And what were his crimes? No real charges were ever brought against him. And it was too late to clear the matter up or question him because he was already dead! These are the fruits by which you are known outside of the charmed circles of your palace and your gardens. These are the deeds credited to your account.

"And you seek my blessing? You want to place your body and soul in my hands. Then do so! Your body you have already destroyed, scourged it with lust and drunkenness, and, as I foretold, it is failing you now. Your soul in my keeping will also get its just rewards—I will hand it over to eternal fire." He spoke with an eerie detachment.

"And what of Christ's mercy, can there be none for me? Is there no recourse?" asked Lorenzo urgently.

"Christ's mercy is extended to those who repent, and to those who believe," said the friar firmly. "Have you repented, Lord Medici? And do you believe?"

"Yes, yes, yes," said Lorenzo racked with sobs. He would have wept, had there been enough moisture in his shriveled glands to produce the salty tears.

The friar's voice turned icy cold, like that of a judge passing sentence or a merchant proposing a dangerous but profitable exchange. "Three conditions," he said.

"Yes, anything," Lorenzo grasped desperately, eagerly at the friar's hand, the hand that might save him. Savonarola withdrew it and stepped back.

"First, will you renounce the error of your worldly wisdom? Will you throw yourself upon God's mercy and acknowledge your faith in his compassion?"

Lorenzo indicated that he would.

"Will you promise to restore everything that you have unjustly taken from others, through subterfuge, deceit, and fraud?"

Again, Lorenzo gave his consent.

"Finally, will you renounce your tyranny and that of your family, and restore to Florence her liberty?"

Lorenzo sat bolt upright. His eyes flashed. "I've made Florence the greatest city in the world! I've made her the envy of all Christendom! Under me, she has flourished and grown rich. She is a new city! Under me! Can I renounce that? Can I renounce the city I have created?"

"You have built, Lord Medici, indeed. But what have you built? Monuments to your own greed! You have built so that your name might become immortal. When Christ comes again in his glory to judge the living and the dead, what will He say of your building then? Will He count the number of fine villas and palaces, the number of frescos, the number of chapels you put up to assuage your guilt?

"Is He concerned that in a thousand years men will speak kindly of the Medici, of their bounty and good taste? Of their buildings and monuments? Will He be impressed? Moved? Or will He ask how those monuments were constructed? With what materials? With the blood and bones of the poor! On their broken backs! And why? So that the high and mighty Medici name might survive in men's memories! That is your immortality! The immortality of a pagan and a blasphemer! That is what you have sought, a thousand years of earthly glory. And that is what you have been granted—that and a thousand thousand years of the fires of eternal damnation!" The friar did not look at

Lorenzo as he delivered his indictment, but seemed to be addressing a larger, phantom audience. When he finished, he stood as still as a bronze statue.

Lorenzo's eyes bulged. There was abject terror in them, but mixed with a deep-seated, uncontrollable anger and pride. He was shaking. His mouth moved, but no sounds came out. In the poorly lit regions of his soul, in the inner reaches of his being, something stopped him. He could not bring himself to renounce his life as he had lived it and his accomplishments. He had striven. He had reached. Would he be damned for that? He could not accept the friar's arguments, could not accept his terms. Sick with fear over the possible consequences of this realization, Lorenzo de' Medici slowly turned his face to the cold, unanswering stone wall.

Lorenzo's final hours were not peaceful or blessed ones. For the rest of that day, he thrashed deliriously, gnawed by doubt and fear, by anxiety over the fate of his immortal soul. Would God forgive him? Or was he damned for all eternity, as Savonarola had resoundingly declared? Did this holy man, this strange, intense, merciless man speak for God Himself, as so many maintained? Was he indeed the prophet, the scourge of the Lord?

This single, agonizing question fed on what little strength was left in Lorenzo. In the end, he was all but oblivious to the excruciating physical pain in his limbs. Finally, worn out, he slipped into a coma. By midnight, precisely as Savonarola had predicted, he was dead.

Lorenzo de' Medici went to his grave unable to resolve a dilemma that would convulse Florence for years to come. Was this Savonarola a saint or a madman?

12

Tavern Talk, Then Church and an Arresting Sermon

After his meeting with Lorenzo, Savonarola was driven back to Florence in a Medici carriage, emblazoned everywhere, inside and out, with the Medici balls. The stony silence with which he had ultimately confronted the unrepentant Lorenzo and in which he now sat did little to betray the turmoil inside him. He too was trembling and on fire, for in his mind, frightful images were beginning to take shape, crowding in upon him—images of disaster, of catastrophic change, of upheaval, and streets running with blood.

In this rush of apocalyptic images, one stood out more clearly than all the others; one demanded his attention. He saw a hand, and in that hand, a mighty, flaming sword, poised in the stormy sky over Florence. On the sword was the inscription, *Gladius Domini super terram cito et velociter*. Already the sermon he would preach was beginning to crystallize and to organize itself around that vision and that inscription—The sword of the Lord over the earth—swiftly and soon!

A storm was raging that night, not only in the tortured visions of Savonarola, but in the world at large, blowing great gusts of wind and rain against the shuttered windows of Florence. It was past midnight when the friar, returning to his modest cell and study in the convent of San Marco, knelt to pray on the cold tile floor. It was dark, but he lit no lamp or candle. That night, he knew, his illumination would come from within.

In another part of town, across the river and nestled among the shabbier dwellings, was a house or an establishment whose inhabitants were not praying in silence and who did not appear to be asleep. Light leaked out from around the shutters, as did noise—drunken singing and shouting and cursing and boasting, the unmistakable sounds of a tavern.

The nightly curfew was in effect, and as was often the case, the patrons of this tavern, rather than risk arrest on charges of disorderly conduct and disturbing the peace, and rather than pay the fines associated with these charges, had elected to stay the night in the tavern. The inclement weather further swelled the numbers of the late-night crowd.

The tavern itself was unremarkable and no different from countless similar establishments throughout Florence, Italy, and the world. It was furnished with stout tables, stout benches, and stout barmaids. Drink and talk flowed freely. The sights and sounds, as familiar then as they are now, were universal in their appeal.

Tobacco smoke was, of course, absent, since the rolling, burning and inhalation of that broad-leaf plant would not achieve any significant popularity for at least another hundred years. While the tavern air was free of the acrid smell of burning tobacco, it was no clearer or less suffocating because of it. Smoke there was in abundance from the greasy, yellow tallow burning in the lamps, and it had imparted its greasy, yellow luster to the walls and fixtures of the place. But since the eyes of the patrons were generally glazed and unfocused and the lamps were dim, and since the harsh light of day rarely entered here, no one ever noticed.

Among the customers oblivious to the sticky, unsanitary surroundings on this particular night, was a boisterous, inebriated Niccolo Machiavelli. In a month, he would attain the age of twenty-three. Eleven years had passed since the traumatic events of his childhood already recorded. In that time he assiduously cultivated his education by day and, as soon as he was old enough, his restless, bawdy pleasures by night. Although interested in women, he had not yet, at this point in his life, seriously entertained thoughts of marriage, preferring instead to pass his time in the company of women to be found in places like this tavern, where embraces were firm and commitments fleeting.

At present he was seated on a low bench and slouched back against the wall for support, but when he stood up, he was tall enough. He was thin, but not gangly or awkward. His nose was long and straight, his brown eyes, alive. While his head was rather on the small side, he carried it well on his shoulders and wore his dark hair long. Had it been shorter, as it was to be in later life, it would have been obvious that there was a certain asymmetry in the size and placement of his ears.

His most salient feature, however, the one that most struck people upon meeting him for the first time, and the one that stayed in their minds afterward as characteristic of him, the one that a skilled caricaturist would have chosen to exaggerate, was the expression on his face. He could not easily rid himself of a sarcastic twist that played continually about his mouth, curling and uncurling his lips. The same sardonic signals flashed from his eyes, and it gave him the air of an extremely astute observer—and a very skeptical one as well. Even drunk, his powers of observation were constantly engaged, and little escaped his detection, just as now he was aware of the fumbling hand of his companion, Biagio Buonacorsi, reaching out under the table to explore the plump and waiting thighs of this Beatrice. Biagio called them all Beatrice, out of profound respect for the chastity of the poet Dante's exalted lover.

When he talked, Niccolo Machiavelli talked too fast—not a nervous or unsure kind of fast, but a breathless, excited fast. It was as if the rushing words were trying in vain to keep pace with the thoughts that were flying, one after another, through his head at tremendous speed. He was rarely at a loss for words, and even when he had been drinking, his eloquence did not desert him.

Niccolo's companions for the evening included a relatively recent acquaintance, Biagio Buonacorsi, and a very old friend, Pagolo Pulci, as well as "Beatrice" and her sisters, daughters of unemployed wool workers and girls from the country whose time and favors the gallant young gentlemen were able to acquire on a cash-and-carry basis.

The ostensible cause for this evening's merrymaking was the imminent departure of Pagolo for Rome, a city whose population of fifty thousand contained at least ten thousand who made their living, with varying degrees of success, by some form of prostitution or other. It was this remarkable fact (established by a recent census) and its implications for Pagolo that were under discussion in the tavern at the table that night.

"They have names like Stella and Fiammetta—Star and Little Flame! And Flora!" Biagio was saying. "My uncle was attached to our embassy in Rome for years, and he says they can sing and dance and even compose Latin poetry if you want. Cultured women! Sonorous names!" Here Biagio pounded his fist on the table and proposed a toast to Fiammetta and Stella and Flora and, of course, to "Beatrice." Dented tin cups were raised, and the sour red wine drawn off.

Niccolo picked up where Biagio had left off, "Indeed, Pagolo, women of high spirits, witty, educated, classically trained! What more could you want? Some of them are more famous than the saints! Did you know that? The stuff of legends, Pagolo, the courtesans of Rome! Take "La Grechetta"—the Little Greek. She conceived and bore a child. Now who was the father? Much speculation on that score. Some said the cardinal of Lyon, others the Spanish ambassador. Fingers were even pointed in the direction of the vicar of Christ himself!

"She wouldn't tell. They pressed her. Finally La Grechetta gave her answer. The wily Greek traced the name of the child's father in the sand, four letters traced in the sand—SPQR, The Senate and People of Rome!"

"Hear! Hear! To all things Greek!" Biagio clamored for another toast. "To wit and classical learning!"

"The problem, Pagolo, dear Pagolo," Biagio continued, "and it is a terrible shame, is that you won't be able to afford them! However, don't despair. There's something for everybody in Rome. My uncle says that there are plenty of girls who operate out of the back of candle makers' shops, hence the charming, delicate, evocative name—*di candela*! A rougher class of girl, Pagolo, to be sure, like Beatrice here, but a simple diet is nothing to be ashamed of. It'll make a man live longer. To longevity!" Once again he lifted his cup.

"Don't you think we're missing the point here, Biagio?" said Niccolo. "All this talk of whores, when, after all, our Pagolo is going to Rome as a man of the cloth! As a freshly minted Franciscan, to pursue a career in the service of Holy Mother Church."

In fact, Pagolo's impecunious father had delivered his only son over to the Franciscan order, and, after several years of apprenticeship in Florence, the order was sending Pagolo to Rome to take his final vows. Pagolo's mere presence in the tavern spoke volumes as to the sincerity of his vocation. He beamed like a cherub. From a plump boy, he had developed into a plump young man. His round face was ringed with brown, curly hair. Soon, that luscious mop would be lying on the floor in some Roman monastery, the victim of some Roman abbot's scissors, and a newly tonsured Pagolo would be committing himself to a life of poverty, chastity, and obedience. He took another drink to put the thought out of his head.

"When you get to Rome, Pagolo, you must give our regards to the pope," Biagio was saying.

"I understand the pope is not well," said Niccolo with mock gravity. "Perhaps Pagolo, with his newfound sanctity, can intercede on his behalf, or maybe effect a miracle?"

"*Caccasangue!*" boomed Biagio. "Did you hear? Do you know what they're doing now to poor Pope Innocent, Innocent VIII? Did you hear of the remedies they're inflicting on the poor, poor man—and this I submit as solid evidence of the absolute fraudulence and chicanery of the medical profession. The pope for some time now has been taking only milk from nursing mothers! And that he is not permitted to drink at the source, I'm sure." Biagio was more informed than most of matters in Rome, due to his family's close connections with that city. His information was accurate.

"At any rate," he continued, "the pope's condition is cause for alarm, so what do they do—aside from the milk? They bring in a Jewish physician. He says that the old, broken-down pope can be reinvigorated by pouring young blood into his ancient body! Three ten-year-old boys are purchased for the medical miracle and bled to death! What a charlatan! What a scoundrel! Down with physicians! To the pope's health!" And he banged and banged on the table.

But Niccolo wasn't listening. At the mention of the Jewish physician, his mind went back, as it always did at the mention of a Jew, went back eleven years, to his mad encounter with a strange girl. From that encounter, mysteries had arisen and desires had been awakened, and for eleven long years, Niccolo had pondered those mysteries and very slowly become aware of those desires. He had also become aware of his own helplessness in the face of them both.

"To the pope's health! To the pope's health!" Biagio had succeeded in arousing the entire clientele of the tavern, and even though Florence had little sympathy for the pope and papal politics, the walls were ringing with drunken good wishes for the health of the supreme pontiff. Eventually Niccolo could no longer ignore the urgent clamor and joined in. When the riotous toasting had died down, he wryly observed, "Good show, Biagio, you've put a brave face on it. But your toast is wasted. Savonarola says the pope will die in July."

"Savonarola says so many things," countered Biagio. "Savonarola says that gambling and card games should be abolished and lewd entertainments outlawed. He says that carnivals and even the palio should be discontinued. And that women should cover up their tits and stop wearing fine clothes and give up scent and powder and paint. I'm sick of all the things Savonarola says. I wish to God he would go somewhere else and say them and leave us alone."

"Then you and our great leader, Lorenzo, are of the same opinion," offered Niccolo. "Savonarola really has it in for him, calling him a Nebuchadnezzar who would send the sons of Israel—by which I assume he means the fair youth of our city—into the flaming furnace. And he's denounced him as Nero, a debauched glutton who eats and drinks and sings while the city burns."

"He has been rather adamant on the subject of poor Lorenzo, hasn't he? But look, for two years now he's been predicting Lorenzo's death, actually saying it was going to happen the first week in April—this week! And what do we have? Is he dead? He's as healthy as a horse. He's appeared in public. Now, he's resting at Careggi, and all the reports are that he's stronger every day and very much in charge. They've even announced that, in a few weeks, he's going to Pisa to personally review the troops. There's no sign that the Medici grip . . ."

"Stranglehold," corrected Niccolo.

"There's no sign that the Medici stranglehold is in danger of weakening. Lorenzo will outlive the friar and probably have his head if he doesn't start keeping a civil tongue in it."

Niccolo smirked, "Savonarola is a great and holy man, Biagio. Don't you have any respect?"

"He's not much of a seer though, Niccolo. Besides, he wants to abolish prostitution and take Beatrice here away from me! That's going too far!"

"*Ahime*, Beatrice," mused Niccolo, turning to the girl. "It's a sad thing that Savonarola has no respect for you or your chosen profession, a sad thing indeed. Do you know what he calls you? Pieces of meat with eyes! With eyes, indeed! He does you no justice! With eyes and lips and tongues! And enchanted fingers! With silky, scented hair and soft skin!"

Biagio picked up Niccolo's train of thought: "Sweetmeats with inviting smiles and long legs, with soft, perfumed breasts and dark, swollen nipples! Down with Savonarola, I say!" And once again he beat on the table, demanding a toast. This time his proposal was greeted with silence and suspicious stares and little enthusiasm from the crowd. Even Beatrice demurred, reproaching him gently, "You shouldn't joke about such a holy man, Biagio."

"Hmmmph," Biagio sulked. "Well, let's get something to eat." Pagolo enthusiastically seconded the motion. Niccolo declined. The thought of the tavern's rough, greasy fare made him shudder. He always ate at home.

While they waited for the joint they had ordered, Niccolo had an idea, "Have you ever seen the friar preach, Biagio?"

"What for? You know I'm opposed to priestcraft in all its manifestations."

"Pagolo?"

"Never."

"I have," volunteered Beatrice. They all stared at her. "He's . . . he's . . . It's hard to describe. When you look at him, you can't look away. Everything else fades away when he speaks. There's only you and him in the whole world. You hear him, but not with your ears. You hear him in your heart. It's wonderful, and it's scary."

Weighing Beatrice's evaluation, Niccolo spoke thoughtfully, "What I would like to propose is this: Let's go see him. Let's judge for ourselves. What do you say, Pagolo?"

"If Biagio goes along, I will."

"I don't see any point in it," said Biagio, "but alright. It might be amusing to see the great preacher who communicates directly with God."

"Decided, then," said Niccolo. "And why lose any time? We can go tomorrow morning—today, rather, since it's almost light. Agreed?"

"Drink up," said Biagio. "I haven't darkened the door of a church since my confirmation. I need courage to face it. I've got to fortify my weak and fallen soul. To Savonarola!" Once again, the mention of the friar's name brought glares of reproach from the other patrons, but Biagio was too drunk to notice.

The little party's conversation had degenerated into a series of slurred assertions, followed by long-delayed grunts of assent. This communal stupor was suddenly shattered, however, by a formidable pounding on the door. "The Guards!" was everyone's first thought.

The alarmed tavern keeper hurried to the door. "Who's there?" he bellowed.

"It's me," came the reply. "Open up."

The tavern keeper obviously recognized the voice, for he immediately began fumbling with the heavy bolts that closed the door on the outside world. The messenger burst into the room—"He's dead," he gasped, "Lorenzo de' Medici is dead."

Shortly after dawn, the smoky tavern disgorged its contents into the streets of Florence. It was a raw, rainy spring day, and the only people Niccolo's party encountered were other denizens of the taverns and gaming houses like themselves.

Bells were ringing, as they did every morning and in particular on Sunday mornings, when they called the faithful to worship. Although Niccolo was not a pious youth and was infected with a rather virulent strain of anticlericism, common in Italy then as now, he had recently taken to attending mass on Sunday mornings—much to the puzzlement of his mother. For years she had coaxed him to accompany her to church, but he had refused. Now suddenly, he was acquiescing graciously. Bartolommea Machiavelli attributed his change of heart to the direct intervention of the Holy Spirit. But the source of Niccolo's "conversion" was infinitely more mundane. Surprisingly, his father, the irreverent Bernardo, who himself never attended mass except on Easter Sunday, was the cause of his son's sudden embrace of the church.

After overhearing another one of the arguments between his wife and son, in which the latter had invoked in his defense, by way of example, the father's failure to attend weekly mass, Bernardo took Niccolo aside. "When I was your age, I never missed a Sunday mass, never," he said.

Niccolo regarded his father with suspicion. "Men don't go to mass," he grunted diffidently.

"That's precisely my point, Niccolo. And if men don't go to mass, who does? Women, of course! And what women? Why, the finest women in the city, Niccolo! Young women! The closely guarded treasures of the best families! Kept under lock and key all week long; it's practically the only place their jealous, tyrannical fathers will let them go. In church, Niccolo, you will find tender, blushing virgins, ripe young widows, and in their most exquisite clothing!" From that day on, Niccolo made it a practice to attend mass.

Since his mother chose to worship at the recently completed Santo Spirito, which was not far from the Machiavelli home, that was where he went for his impious surveillances, and he was not disappointed. He had found an abundance of haughty merchants' daughters whose vulgarity appealed to him more than the aristocratic disdain of the offspring of the "better families." But since Niccolo had limited his church attendance to Santo Spirito, he had never heard the friar speak.

When the three young Florentines reached the church of San Marco, there were already knots of the whispering faithful gathered outside. Our three cavaliers lolled around the piazza, not conspicuously drunk, but still far from sober. The fruits of their drinking, the inevitable headaches and the nausea, were still hours away when a monk issued from the church, made a brief announcement, and went back inside. Almost immediately, the crowds began to disperse.

"Oh no," whined Biagio, "after I've come this far and sacrificed the warm bed of Beatrice, they're going to say that God gave the friar a sore throat and today's performance is cancelled." Niccolo stopped an older couple, busily scuffling past them. "What seems to be the problem?" he asked, managing not to slur his words.

"New revelations!" said the old man, shaking a finger. "The friar has important things to say today, startling things! For everyone to hear and take heed! This church is too small, he says. Today he'll preach in the Duomo! He wants the whole city to come and hear his message!"

Biagio regarded Niccolo imperiously. "It seems we could not have chosen a better day to hear the friar, had we consulted an astrologer."

Santa Maria del Fiore, the Cathedral of Florence, was the most imposing man-made structure in the world. So ambitious was her design, that for a hundred years she stood open, without a roof, since no architect or engineer was able to construct a dome large enough to cover her and not collapse under its own enormous weight. It was in this church, the largest in Christendom, that the words of the prophet were to be delivered unto the people.

There were no pews in the church that day. The temporary benches sometimes used to accommodate parishioners had all been removed to allow the greatest possible number of people to be admitted. And into the vast open space thus created they poured, thousands of people, intent on hearing the word of God.

The friar had chosen not to celebrate the mass, so it began without him. He remained secluded in a small chamber behind the sacristy, the greatest orator in all of history, since Cicero himself. But unlike the latter, who freely admitted to severe crises of nerves and even bouts of vomiting before he spoke, Savonarola was utterly calm. He waited for his moment—and prayed.

By virtue of their early arrival, Niccolo, Biagio, and Pagolo had secured places with a good view of the pulpit from which the sermon would be delivered. After the gospel was read, the friar was summoned. There was a hush in the church. You could have heard a lone fly buzzing high up in the dome, but there were no flies. The friar was preceded across the sanctuary by a deacon bearing a single, lighted candle. He mounted the pulpit with head bowed and stood for a moment in silent prayer. Slowly he made the sign of the cross, slowly he lifted his head and filled his lungs with air. Slowly he raised both arms, and intoned, "Oh, Egypt!" in a trembling voice that unnerved even the most stalwart members of the congregation.

In no one was the consternation greater than it was in Niccolo Machiavelli, in whom the fear of dreaded pronouncements and calamitous events foretold was mixed with the shock of recognition. The great, fiery preacher was the puny monk he had saved from certain death by snowballs over ten years ago! The formidable Savonarola was only the pitiful, defenseless Fra Girolamo!

Shocked as he was by this discovery, Niccolo had little time to consider what it might mean, for he, like everyone else present, was being sucked into the vortex created by the friar's thundering voice and his riveting, hypnotic eyes.

Here he spoke of pestilence and famine, of plagues more severe than those God had inflicted upon the Egyptians, of a great hammer smashing the city of Babylon. The exact words were sometimes difficult to discern, but there was no mistaking the sense of them. His threats and calls for repentance fell like thunderclaps shaking even the relics of the true cross and the bones of Saint Reparata that lay buried beneath the main altar.

Niccolo Machiavelli, more perspicacious than the average Florentine and more inclined to doubt and cynicism when it came to modern-day prophets, began to recover his wits. The force of the friar's onslaught had initially drawn him in, but now, with an effort of the will, he succeeded in resisting the magnetism—in detaching himself a little from the rising tide of prophetic fury.

What, after all, is he saying? Niccolo found himself thinking. Nothing that you couldn't read in Jeremiah, or Isaiah—Egypt and Babylon, wars and rumors of wars, cleansing fire and great destruction. Repent while there is still time! Niccolo was on the verge of dismissing the preacher as a fanatic, a genius, but still, at bottom, just another religious fanatic, when the friar's sermon suddenly took a decidedly modern and quite specific turn. While his rhetoric remained firmly entrenched in the Old Testament prophets, his message became quite pointedly anchored in the history and politics of contemporary Florence.

"I predicted the time appointed for the death of Lorenzo de' Medici. I stood before you and spoke of a flaming tower crashing to the ground. It has come to pass. The tower of vanity has been pulled down, and the soul of the tyrant consigned to hell."

Here Savonarola's tone changed abruptly, became soothing, almost fatherly. He spoke of Florence and her history, of her ancient love of liberty and her recent degradation and subjection to tyranny. It was this attachment to liberty, to civil government, he argued, that set Florence apart, made her constitutionally incapable of submitting to a tyrant for any length of time.

He then called for throwing off the yoke of slavery and reestablishing popular rule. He was no longer dawdling with the prophets on the banks of the Nile and the Jordan. He had come home to the banks of the Arno, and he was calling for nothing short of a revolution. He had taken a decisive step beyond the pulpit, beyond the harmless clamoring of the fire-and-brimstone preacher.

"The Lord's anger has been unleashed upon the world. His thirst for vengeance is not easily slaked. And He has chosen me, unworthy and useless among all His servants, to bring you a warning of His terrible wrath.

"It is for this, to warn you of His coming scourge, that God has sent me here to Florence, for Florence lies in the center of Italy, like the heart in the center of a man. God deigned to choose her for the task of making His proclamation. From here, his message will be spread abroad to all parts of Italy and the world.

"And this is the message—Repent and cleanse your hearts, reclaim your liberty, and make yourselves strong to resist the coming flood." Here the preacher reverted to a harrowing description of the flood, frightening, not in its imagery, but in the unprecedented specificity of its historical content: He claimed that the pope would be dead within three months and even fixed the exact date in late July. And he warned that, in his place, the Antichrist would then ascend the throne of Saint Peter, that a black cross would rise from Rome, stinking and filthy with corruption, and reach out to embrace the whole world, that it would engender storms and tempests and great confusion wherever it touched.

And then he spoke of the vision that had come to him the night before, of the sword of the Lord, poised and ready to strike, of a great voice issuing from three faces, but surrounded by a single light that called upon him to convert the sinners before the coming of divine punishment. He saw a multitude of angels arrayed in white descending from heaven to earth, offering men red crosses with white mantles, which some accepted and some rejected. "Then, slowly, the hand brandishing the sword began to stir, filling the air with dense clouds of hail and thunder, and then with a rain of swords and arrows and fire!"

The people of Florence were spellbound, frightened to death, but Savonarola did not leave them with mere apocalyptic horrors and graphic threats of unspecified future retribution. He went on to interpret the vision for them. Today, as had been announced, he had important news to communicate. What he announced with ruthless specificity and to the utter dismay of his stunned congregation was that in two years' time, Charles VIII of France would storm across the Alps at the head of an invincible army and lay waste to Italy.

In the course of his sermon, the friar's voice had, at times, pounded like mighty waves upon the shore, while at other times it had drawn itself up into placid, shimmering pools among the rocks. Now, for a moment he remained silent, surveying his reeling flock, and then, with otherworldly calm, he delivered the final, devastating blow: "Today, O Florence, you have heard with your ears not the voice of a humble friar, but the voice of God Almighty himself. Amen."

The friar climbed down from the pulpit and disappeared. The mass continued as if a dream, bells were rung on cue, responses mechanically chanted. A few souls even staggered to the communion rail, but no one could put out of his mind for long the message of impending doom, or the fact that he had just heard pronounced before them the judgment of Almighty God.

Even Niccolo left the church deep in thought and feeling drained, as though in the aftermath of some blinding, sexual explosion—or a brush with death.

Meanwhile, the external world was quietly organizing itself for the timely fulfillment of Savonarola's prophecies. Florence tottered on the verge of revolution. Charles VIII, newly ascended to the throne of France, was already twitching with the anxiety of conquest. Pope Innocent was duly expiring, and behind the scenes in Rome, a Spaniard, the most nefarious, abominable man ever to occupy the throne of Saint Peter, was deftly maneuvering to buy the Papacy. All these things would come to pass in the fullness of time. And their effect on the course of Niccolo Machiavelli's future would be convulsive.

And in faraway Spain, too, events little remarked by Savonarola were conspiring to convulse Niccolo's life. The year was 1492, and as is well known, the king and queen of Spain were about to sponsor an expedition to the Indies that would change the face of the globe for centuries to come. Less remarked by history, but infinitely more important for the upheavals it would eventually introduce into the life of Niccolo Machiavelli, the Most Catholic Monarchs, Ferdinand and Isabella, had just decreed the expulsion of the Jews from Spain.

13

Revolution in the Streets, Politics in the Monastery

In the weeks and months that followed the death of Lorenzo, the fortunes of the Medici party rapidly deteriorated, due in no small part to the incompetence and insensitivity of Lorenzo's son and heir, the twenty-two-year-old Piero. Such was his unpopularity that when he was obliged to leave the sumptuous Medici palace, he was generally preceded through the streets by a "penny man." It was his job to fling handfuls of coins at the restive crowds who, in scrambling after them, left a path clear for the haughty Piero to proceed unmolested.

If Piero's sphere of misbehavior was secular government, Lorenzo's second son, Giovanni, chose the church. He had been elevated to the cardinalate just three weeks after his father's death. One of the last acts of Lorenzo's life had been the transfer of astronomical sums into the papal treasury to ensure the ecclesiastical career of his second son.

Unlike Piero, who was handsome and athletic, Giovanni Cardinal de' Medici was flaccid and flabby. Folds of fat already hung about his face and neck. His body was a puddle of soft, pasty flesh. Although intelligent, his habit of holding his mouth wide-open, gaping at all times, gave him an air of moonstruck imbecility. Since infancy, he suffered from an anal fistula that produced a condition of chronic flatulence. Throughout his life as a prelate, wherever he went, he was accompanied by an odor, not of sanctity, but of decay, by the fetid seepage of his own digestion and the smell of rich food rotting away. An abbot at the age of eight, on the day he received the red hat, the badge of the cardinalate, he was only sixteen years old. Already, his eyesight was failing him.

If the Medici grip on the hearts and minds of the Florentine people was indeed growing weaker every day, that of Savonarola was waxing in strength. His uncanny, but accurate, prediction of the death of Lorenzo had once and for all allowed him to lay claim to the mantle of the prophet. The death of the pope three months later and the accession of an insidious Spaniard to the papacy were enough to wipe out any lingering doubts as to his credibility. As his following grew, the friar became more vehement in his denunciation of the Medicean tyranny. He reiterated his call for repentance and urged his followers to array themselves in "the white garments of purification." Above all, he continued to emphasize the perils of the coming French invasion, saying that the king of the Gauls and his armies would come like barbers with gigantic razors to shave Italy down to the skin, clearing the land of everything in their path. At other times, he drew upon the imagery of the great flood and urged Florence to build what he called an Ark of Repentance against the coming inundation.

Apocalyptic excitement was mounting in the city, but it was as yet unfocused. Occasional riots broke out. It was in order to quell one of these that Piero grudgingly assented to address the restless crowds. He did so at one o'clock (an hour deemed propitious by his astrologers) from the same balcony where four generations of Medici leaders had stood and spoken to the people of Florence. Upon showing himself, he was greeted, as were his predecessors, with the shouts of *Balls! Balls! Balls!* But the acclaimants this time were a mangy lot, obviously drunk. As Piero spoke in his thin, unconcerned voice, a new cry was raised from the crowd, something spontaneous and uncoached, passionate and not bought by Medici money. It grew in strength, quickly overwhelming the anemic, singsong *Balls! Balls! Balls!* that issued from the coterie of paid supporters. Piero was forced to abandon his efforts to make himself heard above the roar, and he retreated with what amounted to his death knell ringing in his ears—*Popolo e libertá! Popolo e libertá! Popolo e libertá!*

In the crowd that day were anti-Medici forces from across the spectrum of political postures as well as many of the disaffected—workers locked out of factories, victims of the failing economy. Among them were Niccolo Machiavelli and Biagio Buonacorsi, scions of slightly better families, but for all that, no less enthusiastic supporters of the causes of the people and freedom—*Popolo e libertá*. Young and optimistic, they were swept up in the swell of sentiment that animated this crowd. These were heady times. Revolution was in the air, and for weeks now, the two high-spirited young men had been feeding off of the excitement of popular ferment.

Both were hoarse from the political exertions of the day by the time they left the piazza. "How long can he last, Biagio?" said Niccolo referring to the apparently imminent demise of Piero de' Medici.

"You know as well as I do that he can last a long time if he pays off the right people and hires enough mercenaries."

"But he won't. He's too stupid or arrogant, and besides, this time things are different," said Niccolo. "This time there's Savonarola to be reckoned with, and he's not likely to switch allegiance or let the people forget his distaste—excuse me, God's distaste—for Medici rule."

"You have a point," conceded Biagio. "Maybe they will throw him out. But then what? Do you think the friar is going to run the city? That would be something. Government by paternosters! You go to the friar with a problem, a complaint? Excuse me while I consult God on the matter, he says. It won't take a minute. Someone's convicted of a crime? Seven Our Fathers and seven Hail Marys, my son, now go forth and sin no more!"

"I don't think he's all that naive," said Niccolo. "I think he's up to something concrete. I think he has a plan."

"Oh, sure, he has a plan. He's just waiting for the burning crosses to fall from the sky and the great white flood to sweep across the mountains and a giant scorpion to sting Piero."

"You're not separating the images from the substance," argued Niccolo. "Oh, I don't mean the prophecies—your guess is as good as mine as to what they're supposed to mean. But in every sermon lately, behind the fireworks, he's been talking about tyranny and civil government. I think he's serious. I think he really wants to see the establishment of some sort of representative council to replace the tyrant."

"Maybe," countered Biagio, "and maybe he just wants to be the new tyrant."

"I'm going to ask him," Niccolo declared calmly. "I know him."

"Sure you do," jeered his companion.

"I'm serious," and Niccolo quickly recounted the incident of the snowball attack that had attended the monk's Florentine opening.

"And you're sure it was the same man?" Biagio still seemed doubtful.

"Positive," affirmed Niccolo. "Later that day, in the evening I went to hear him preach. My mother made me accompany her. He was pathetic. I felt sorry for him. A little man in that big, cold church. And his voice—he brayed like a jackass. Jumped around in the pulpit."

"Hmmph! I don't see how it could be the same man, if he was that sorry a preacher," said Biagio.

"Trust me, Biagio. It's him. You want to come along?"

"No, not I," replied Biagio, "I'm going to the tavern. I thirst."

"Assignation with Beatrice?" said Niccolo with a knowing smirk.

"*Ahime,* Beatrice!" groaned Biagio. "You haven't heard then? Beatrice has left me for another."

"And who might that be?"

"Our Lord Jesus Christ!" sighed Biagio, slumping forward on the table. "Beatrice has been touched, yes, touched is the word she used, touched by the friar's preaching. She's repented, Niccolo. Renounced sin and me. She's one of his followers now. Wears the white robe of repentance and spends all day in church praying for poor, lost souls like us."

As the two separated, Biagio called out after his companion. "Tell him to send Beatrice back to me, Niccolo. He owes you one."

Niccolo sauntered out into the midday sun and all the details of life being acted out around him. Two cats were copulating. An old man, absorbed in the low spectacle stood over them, cackling and occasionally poking at them with a stick.

There was a self-conscious spring in Niccolo's step as he made his way toward the church and convent of San Marco. He held his head high, back erect, and hands clasped together behind him as he walked. No more or less dandified than other young men his age, he wore a short, pleated jacket, laced up the front and cinched at the waist. The deep-blue sleeveless jacket was set off smartly by a red shirt and tight red hose, which he judged showed his legs and buttocks to good advantage. Although it was cold and a stiff wind occasionally blew up, Niccolo let his blue cloak hang rakishly open. He was young and hatless.

With respect to dress, Florence was a town of relative sobriety, especially when compared to the extravagance of cities like Rome or Venice. So it was with some amusement that Niccolo turned to stare at a couple he spotted while crossing the Piazza Santa Croce. She was wrapped in at least twenty-five yards of bright green taffeta, crimped and gathered in endless tiers. Rotund of figure, she resembled nothing so much as a walking head of lettuce, if the word *walking* could be used to describe her fitful progress across the icy stones. Leaning heavily on her escort, she tottered on an outrageously high pair of *zoccoli*, a Venetian affectation in which the sole and the heel of the shoe were built up with wood to give the impression of height to those not naturally endowed with it. In the case of the lettuce, the shoes added almost a full eighteen inches to her stature.

But he, oh he, was even more magnificent to behold! All pink and black and shot through with gold and silver. Such was the dazzle of his appearance in the bright sun that it was at first difficult to break it up into its component parts. Gradually the details emerged—the outer cape of shiny silk, pink and black checks, each rectangle outlined with thick braided strands of silver and the whole trimmed in white fur. Hose—pink with fanciful designs woven through them in red and black. The hat, pink and fur-lined as well, its glorious brim wide enough to shelter a family of four from the rain, was surmounted by a curled feather, the length of a man's arm. Intent upon his discourse with the lettuce, the owner of this finery occasionally flung an arm into the air for emphasis. When he did so, other treasures, hidden beneath the shocking cape stood revealed—chains and bejeweled weapons, and what looked like a flowered jacket.

Shaking his head at the folly of humanity, Niccolo watched this monstrous twin-apparition disappear. Even the terrible visions of Savonarola didn't often reach such nightmarish intensity. What could it possibly portend? He snickered to himself. The French are coming?

Niccolo stepped crisply over a pile of still-steaming horse dung that lay in his path. In an hour it would be frozen. In that respect, winter was the most merciful of seasons. "Frozen shit doesn't smell," was one of the maxims of Bernardo Machiavelli, a man more sorely afflicted by unpleasant odors than others of his time.

As Niccolo approached the monastery, he began to have second thoughts. He might not be granted admission. After all, he reasoned, the friar is sure to be surrounded by a flock of nervous, protective monks. They have to be on the lookout for overzealous admirers crawling all over each other to touch the hem of his cloak. And assassins too. And then the friar didn't know his name and wouldn't recognize it if he were announced as Niccolo Machiavelli. Then Niccolo had a thought, and he stooped to scoop up a handful of week-old, dirty snow.

He knocked and a timid young brother poked a tonsured head out from behind the door. His shaved, monkish head reminded Niccolo briefly of Pagolo and the ordeals he must be suffering. "*Laudato sia Gesu Cristo*," the standard monastic salute. Niccolo gave the standard reply and received an inquiry as to his business.

When he asked to see Fra Savonarola, the young monk clucked officiously, "Everyone wants to see Fra Girolamo. Everyone. We can't just go letting anyone in. What do you want with him?" This last sentence was thrown down almost as a challenge.

"It's personal," said Niccolo. "I'm an old friend. Would you ask him if he'd see me?"

"Oh, indeed," said the monklet, eyeing Niccolo with more than a little suspicion. Finally satisfying himself that Niccolo was neither some seeker of a miracle cure for leprosy nor a hired assassin, he relented. "And whom shall I say is calling?"

"Here, give him this." Niccolo thrust the dirty snowball into the gatekeeper's fluttering hands. The nervous little monk jumped back in surprise and dropped the snowball as if it were a coal from the fires of hell. Niccolo patiently bent and retrieved it. He handed it over to the monk, gently this time: "Give him the snowball. He'll understand." . . . "Maybe," he thought to himself.

Satisfying himself that the visitor was unarmed, the monk allowed Niccolo inside to await the outcome of his suit. He left him in a colonnaded corridor that led to the refectory. Niccolo could appreciate the clean lines and the simplicity of the place. The noisy confusion that accompanies most human endeavor was effectively excluded from these cool, quiet corridors. When the doorman monk finally returned, the only thing he said was a curt, "Follow me."

He led Niccolo through the refectory where the monks took their plain meals and listened to the gospels as they ate. He led him through the washing room where they doused their bodies with cold, bracing water and where they meditated together each morning in a long row, perched atop the series of communal privies. He led him through a courtyard and up a set of stairs past a painting of the Annunciation, past paintings of Christ in various situations, past crucifixes and statues, past rows of doors that opened into tiny, austere cells, around a corner and past more cells. At the very end of the corridor was a wooden door like all the others. The monk indicated it with a reverential nod, and then stepped aside to let Niccolo pass.

Niccolo wasn't sure what to expect. He rapped once on the cold, varnished wood, and a small voice bade him enter. The friar was seated on a high-backed bench behind a writing table. A smile played over his lips as he looked from Niccolo to the lump of grey snow he had placed in front of him on the desk. Niccolo relaxed. He was in the presence of the Fra Girolamo of ten years ago, the small friar once laid low by snowballs—of all missiles, the lowliest and most humble. For the time being, at least, the mighty Savonarola, God's personal scourge and the hellion of the pulpit, was safely contained somewhere inside this kindly, smiling presence.

Savonarola spoke first: "I had hoped you were the one who rescued me and not the ones who launched the attack."

"Then you remember," said Niccolo.

"Oh, yes, quite well. How could I ever forget the first time I came to Florence—and the sort of reception she arranged for me? But that was a long time ago, and I bear her no grudge. Besides, there are citizens here like yourself, brave defenders of the weak." He spoke in a sweet, low voice.

Niccolo, at ease, recounted to the friar how afterward, the surly attackers had pursued him until he had to seek sanctuary in the church and remain there for some time to avoid their vengeance. Amused, the friar thanked him again for his troubles, then asked, "What is your name, my son?"

"Niccolo Machiavelli."

"Perhaps I can someday return the service you did me, young Machiavelli?" And then, like a distracted man who had forgotten something and then suddenly, embarrassed, remembered it, he said, "Of course, did you come to ask some favor of me now?"

"No, Father."

"Then why did you come?" He examined Niccolo as he awaited his response, fixing him with his green eyes, the same eyes that his more fanatical followers swore emitted little bursts of flame when he spoke. Niccolo looked into those eyes but felt no discomfort. They were opaque, almost blank. The huge orbs looked like two powerful lamps in which the wicks had been trimmed back and the flames turned down low, nearly extinguished—temporarily.

"I came for no other reason, Father, than to satisfy my own curiosity," he said abruptly. Then apologetically, "If you're busy, I can leave. I don't want to waste your time."

"Not at all, not at all. Now tell me, just what is it that has aroused your curiosity?"

"The first time we met, Father, I went to see you later that evening in the church here, to hear you preach. You'll excuse me for saying so—I don't know how to put it—but you were not then the preacher you've become today. In fact, the difference is so extraordinary that I wasn't sure . . . I had trouble convincing myself . . ."

Niccolo's attempts at tact and circumspection brought a knowing smile to the friar's face. He nodded in agreement and relieved Niccolo of the burden of further explanation. "And now that we've spoken, you're satisfied that the two preachers were indeed the same person, correct?"

"Yes."

"But you still can't believe the difference, right?"

"There is that lingering element of disbelief, Father."

"When I was a child, Niccolo, I spoke as a child . . ." he trailed off and did not finish the quotation. Instead, he explained, "When I began preaching, I simply had nothing to say. I half-copied the sermons of others, I relied on my own weak inventions. But I had no message, nothing of substance to communicate. That was the preacher you saw so long ago, timid and unconvincing.

"Then, three years ago, everything changed. I came back to Florence after an absence of many years. I was drawn here, Niccolo, compelled to come here by a will stronger than my own. In August of that year, I began to expound the Book of the Apocalypse. My message was simple and threefold: first, that the renovation of the church would come about in our time; second, that Italy would be punished by God for her iniquity; and third, that these things would happen soon. Anyone listening to me then would have noticed little change in my delivery. I still labored to get my conclusions across with logical arguments, appealing to men's reason.

"So for a while I proceeded in this way, for I didn't dare reveal the truth. The truth was that these things had been revealed to me by God." He said it as matter-of-factly as another man might say, "It's raining."

As he spoke, his eyes frequently left Niccolo and came to rest on his crucifix. Firmly fixed in the center of the writing table, facing him, it was an imposing presence, half the height of a man. On it hung the naked, twisted, thorn-crowned body of Christ.

"Concern and anger were growing in me. In a fever, one night, I composed a sermon—one revealing the true source of my knowledge and the urgency of my warning. I spared no detail, neither with regard to my frightening visions nor to their significance. But the next morning, reading what I had written, I felt I should suppress the sermon. As the sun was breaking and as I was praying, wearied from lack of sleep, a voice came to me: 'Fool!' it said. 'Do you not see that I want you to announce these things, precisely in this way?' That morning, I delivered a terrifying sermon. And since that time, I have not flinched. I have made myself an instrument of His will."

All this Savonarola recounted with the utmost serenity, never raising or inflecting his voice. Niccolo was dazed. He had never been in the presence of a spokesman for God before. He shivered involuntarily, both at the power of what he had just heard and at the cold that pervaded this bare monastic cell. Wholly absorbed in the friar's tale, he had not noticed the chill before. But now he was becoming painfully aware of it, certain that it was colder in here than outside. There was a fireplace, but no fire. When Savonarola talked, the words left his thick lips in little clouds of steam. The snowball Niccolo had brought with him as a calling card was still there on the writing table. It had not even begun to melt.

Changing the subject effortlessly, the friar asked Niccolo several questions about himself and his family. "And in what sort of business are you engaged now, my son?"

"I have no business at present, Father," said Niccolo haltingly. "I . . . study. I'm a student."

"And what is it you study? Medicine? The Law?"

"I study history."

"As a student of history, are you interested in the political situation here in Florence?"

"Oh, keenly, Father! Dreadfully! Passionately!" he said with all the exuberance of youth.

"And have you chosen sides in the current . . . disputes?"

On more familiar ground now, Niccolo did not hesitate to speak up: "Doesn't the Book of Revelations admonish us in no uncertain terms to be either hot or cold, for the lukewarm He will spew out of His mouth?"

Savonarola seemed impressed with the young man's response, and indicated the paper laid out on his writing table. "This may be of interest to you, then. Come here, have a look at the title."

When Niccolo saw what Savonarola was working on, he could scarcely contain his excitement. He read, "*Del reggimento del governo della cittá di Firenze*." It was a treatise on the way in which the city of Florence was to be governed! The monk did have a plan.

"I've only just begun," he said, "but the argument is already clearly laid out in my mind."

"*Stretto or largo*?" said Niccolo eagerly, going straight to the heart of the matter. He was referring to the difference of opinion on the question of representation in the city government: *Governo stretto*, or narrow, was advocated by the aristocrats, who favored a small ruling elite—themselves, of course—with a firm grip on the reins of power. A *governo largo*, or broad, would allow representation to be distributed more evenly throughout the body politic.

"Not only, *largo*," said Savonarola, aware of the young man's enthusiasm, "*larghissimo!* As broad as possible! Impossibly broad, even!"

And in the same measured tones he had used to relate his experiences with the sparks of divine inspiration, he lucidly explained his plan for broad-based representative government to replace the current tyranny in Florence. He envisioned a grand council, like that of Venice, but much larger, embracing all the people, even the most humble. Briefly, he sketched in the details—who would be represented, in what proportions, how the elections would be held, how often, and so on. Whether this too had been revealed to him directly by God, Niccolo did not dare ask.

When he was finished, Niccolo had a question. "If the council is to be modeled on the one in Venice, then you've left something important out, haven't you? The doge. Who will sit at the head of your grand council? Who will occupy the supreme seat?"

"God will," said Savonarola.

Upon leaving the friar's cell, Niccolo was in a state of profound perplexity. While he had managed to satisfy his curiosity about Savonarola on a number of counts, his interview with the enigmatic preacher had led to hopeless new dilemmas and contradictions. On the one hand, the friar had clear and exciting ideas, concrete ideas for real reform, a plan for a revolutionary kind of government. On the other, he proposed what amounted to a vacancy at the very top, where a strong leader had always been needed.

And when Niccolo had questioned him as to the specifics of the transfer of power, just how to get Piero de' Medici out and the new government of the people in, Savonarola had reverted to his visionary jargon of divine intervention and the coming scourge from across the Alps.

To Niccolo's consternation, Savonarola's political thinking and his visions were inseparable; they formed a seamless whole. Everything fit together. He seemed to move effortlessly between heaven and earth. His speech was marked not by hope or confidence, but by absolute certainty. It was maddening.

Niccolo would have preferred to find the friar a demagogue or a hypocrite, and indeed he had half expected that, too. He had long entertained the notion that the friar's piety and preaching were the mere props behind an outright grab for power. That would have been easier to deal with. That would have been a man whose interests were clear, a man you could understand and negotiate with, a man whose moves you could anticipate. But Savonarola was not such a man.

❧ 14 ❧

A Mysterious Frenchman and a Dental Procedure

Savonarola was not the only preacher in town. Florence was a city in which trade had always flourished and the idea of competition, derived from commerce, had embedded itself deep in the Florentine character. So it comes as no surprise that even the friar had his competitors.

Other preachers there had always been, and they had always arrayed themselves against the whole gamut of sinful behavior from loan sharking to what they charged was a peculiarly "Florentine vice"—sodomy. But Savonarola had changed the narrative. From whatever pulpit or street corner it came, the message now was generally the same: the coming scourge and repentance and warnings of imminent disaster were the order of the day, and those who were content to serve up milder fare in their sermons soon lost their audiences. The field quickly narrowed.

Seeking to take advantage of the mounting popular hysteria and to redirect, if possible, the resultant outbreaks of religious zeal, Piero de' Medici decided to fight fire with fire. He enlisted two proven rabble-rousers in his cause—Domenico da Ponzo and Bernardino da Feltre. The latter, Bernardino, specialized in one particular brand of invective: inciting the populace against the Jews. Although he succeeded at first in drawing large-enough crowds, he could not hold them. Frequently, he came to the pulpit drunk, and there was no urgency in his message. Like the poor, the Jews were always there, useful for stirring up a little resentment, convenient for averting a small-scale financial crisis, but not a real threat, not the sort of problem that demanded the divine physic with which Savonarola was threatening to purge the Italian peninsula.

Out of curiosity, Niccolo had gone to see Fra Bernardino preach. Over the years, he had paid close attention to the conduct of Medici policy toward the Jews and was especially interested in anyone who might be involved in the execution of that policy. He was, in fact, on the trail of crimes committed over a decade ago. It was a cold trail now, but those crimes still burned in his memory, along with the image of their architect and perpetrator—the mysterious man who hissed like a serpent instead of talking and who went about his business so brutally, the business of administering lessssons in politicsssss.

Fra Bernardino took the pulpit and obliged his audience to endure a long, rhetorical pause while he glared at them. He was a gaunt, hateful-looking man with small eyes. Eyes glued to the pulpit. Niccolo waited for the only detail that could give the murderer away—the sound of his voice.

The first word of Fra Bernardino's sermon was *salvation*. He pronounced it "Sssssssalvation!" The thrill of discovery ran through Niccolo.

"Ssssssalvation, O Sssssinners!" he intoned. Niccolo was beside himself. "Vengeance," he thought. "Somehow, someway, the sword of the Lord, swift if not soon!"

But a dawning realization brought an end to Niccolo's triumph.

Not only did Fra Bernardino hiss the *s*'s; he slurred the *r*'s and *l*'s, stumbled on the *p*'s and *b*'s, and swallowed all the vowels. The man was blind drunk.

Disappointed, but with a quiet resolve, Niccolo left the church. He would continue his quest, he supposed, not actively, but not idly; not obsessively, but steadily—steadily, and perhaps someday . . . he would strike a blow for justice, a small gesture for a girl he would never see again.

Drained, he turned his steps toward a familiar place, a place where energy and courage could be purchased by the pint—or the quart if need be. Business at the tavern lately had been off. Following the lead of Beatrice, many of the other prostitutes had forsaken their vocations and turned to more pious pursuits. It was uncanny. Savonarola's calls for moral regeneration were actually being heeded.

Since his initial discussion with Savonarola, Niccolo had become an intimate of the friar's, if anybody could lay claim to intimacy with the strange, indecipherable monk. The friendship that sprung up between them was an odd one, but it gave Niccolo something in which he delighted beyond measure—the opportunity to talk politics. There were only two things worth talking about for a young man his age, and he and Savonarola had little to say to one another on the subject of women. In fact, in many things, in most things, they remained far apart. Savonarola was certainly aware of the distance separating them, but it was at the friar's knee that Niccolo had his second lesson in politics.

At their first meeting, Niccolo had represented himself to Savonarola as "passionately" interested in politics, but that passion was a youthful one, and more a delight in gamesmanship than anything else. It was the easy sophistry of the student who reveled in argument for its own sake—the more subtle, the better. As a result of his education, which placed a tremendous emphasis on rhetoric, the art of argumentation, Niccolo had become overly enamored of the thrill of verbal jousting. To present a devastating argument was the height of accomplishment. And what greater triumph of rhetoric was there than to then be able to turn the tables on that argument by successfully arguing the other side? *Nec christianus, sed ciceronianus!* Not a Christian but a Ciceronian is what he had been trained to be.

From Savonarola, Niccolo began to understand that the current political turmoil was more than just an exchange of rhetorical thunderbolts, that the struggle between the Medici and the people was more significant than that. Niccolo saw that the merits of one side were not always the same as those of the other, that, ultimately, one had to make a choice, and that this game of politics was not a superficial thing, but a matter of life and death. From Savonarola, Niccolo Machiavelli learned about something that had been hitherto lacking in his political education—fervor and commitment.

But notwithstanding his respect for the friar's passionate defense of liberty, there were contradictions inherent in Savonarola's approach to the present situation that continued to plague Niccolo. True, he had worked out a plan for the government of the city, a marvelous plan, detailed, well thought out, incorporating many bold and progressive measures. But what was he doing to bring that plan to fruition, to make it a reality? Was he lining up support, meeting with powerful and interested parties, attempting to piece together some sort of post-Medicean coalition? No! He was waiting!

The friar was preaching almost daily now in the cathedral to huge, frightened crowds. And every day, he hammered home the same message, simple, elegant, and final—"It is coming." The many practical and strategic questions that Niccolo pressed upon him, urgent questions, he met with the same assurance, pronounced with the same eerie finality—"It is coming."

Ruminating on these things, Niccolo entered the almost-deserted tavern, called for wine, and sat back, letting his eyes adjust to the blessed dimness of the place. He was tense. He had a toothache.

Gradually the wine did its work, relaxing him and dulling the throb in his jaw. Now, he felt like talking, like losing himself in distracting, irreverent conversation, but none of his regular companions seemed to be about. In fact, there were only two other patrons present besides himself, and he did not recognize either. Unless . . . unless . . . ? He had to squint to be sure, but it was him alright. Bedraggled, his feathers ruffled, his finery besmirched, besmeared, and befouled, there was still no mistaking that tasteless, unforgettable attire. It was the pink cavalier.

Since first seeing him in the company of the redoubtable walking lettuce, Niccolo had spotted this gaudy figure a number of times and had always been curious as to who he could be and what he was about. Judging from the condition of his clothing, he was having a run of bad luck. Judging from the bruises on his face and around his eyes, he had taken a beating. Niccolo approached him: "You're not drinking?"

"*Caccasangue!*" he spit out in anger. "Shit and blood! The bastards took my money, and this sodden tavern keeper refuses to extend me credit!" Niccolo noted with surprise that he swore like a Florentine, but spoke with an obvious French accent.

"Don't I look a gentleman?" he continued. "Don't I look like a man of parts, capable of discharging my debts honestly? *Caccasangue!*"

Mud-stained and bloody as he was, he emphatically did not look like one who settled his debts in a timely and orderly fashion. Niccolo stifled a comment to that effect and sought to calm him. "The tavern keeper is suspicious by nature, and business is bad for him now. He's adverse to taking risks. Besides, he doesn't know you . . . But, if you will allow me to join you, I believe I can offer you something in the way of a restorative."

"I would be eternally in your debt," the cavalier replied in an oily, polite voice, his indignation vanishing as quickly as it had arisen.

Niccolo introduced himself, "And your name?" he inquired.

"Callimaque," announced the other man with a flourish.

"Ah, then you are French as I suspected," said Niccolo. "From what city, may I ask?"

My dear man, as you and all the world knows, there is only one city in France. Need I elaborate?"

"Petulant," thought Niccolo, "and as pompous as his pink sartorial splendor would lead you to believe." But he saw the hole in the Frenchman's armor: "Tell me now, in Paris is it the fashion to curse in Florentine when one is aroused? Have the French, in fits of anger, taken to hurling violent, bloody imprecations like ours, '*Caccasangue!*' for example?"

Monsieur Callimaque, the rose-colored "Frenchman," eyed Niccolo warily, sizing him up as an opponent. Then his face broke into a broad grin. He shook his head and lifted his cup to Niccolo, acknowledging that he had been bested and his charade discovered.

"One always curses in one's native language," said Niccolo firmly. "Shall we make the toast to Signor Callimaco, then?"

"Done! To Callimaco Guadagni, Florentine! And to Signor Niccolo," added the other, dropping the French accent. "A man who is no fool and apparently does not suffer fools gladly." They both drank.

"Why the French accent, then?" Niccolo wanted to know. "And the . . ." he made a sweeping gesture with his hand, "the regalia?"

"Business purposes," declared Callimaco.

"And, Lord, what a business it must be," thought Niccolo, eyeing the stained pink silk mantle embroidered with flowers. Niccolo also recalled that nearly every time he had seen the mysterious Callimaco, the latter had been in the company of a well-to-do, if less than handsome lady.

"May I inquire as to the nature of that business?" said Niccolo. "I surmise that you provide certain 'services' for ladies of distinction."

"Services indeed! I know what you're implying! That I'm a hired man, a paid performer, a gigolo! Or worse, a ruffian! A procurer! Oh, Niccolo, no! This time you've guessed wrong." He crossed his arms and acted offended. "I'm a professional man," he huffed.

"Alright, I'm sorry. So what profession do you exercise?"

"If you had not jumped to your vile, unforgivable conclusions, I would have already told you. I am, in the most general sense, a man of science, a medical man."

"Then you'll pardon my observing that you are not exactly dressed like a medical man—sober black gown, square hat?"

"For the present, my practice has, shall we say, gone off in bold new directions. For example, I have been able to concoct certain medicinal preparations much prized by the good ladies of this city."

"And what sort of medicinal preparations are these?" asked Niccolo.

"My most popular item has been a solution for bleaching the hair blond. It seems to sell very well here in this city of raven-haired beauties."

"Cosmetics," said Niccolo, obviously amused. "That's what you do, sell cosmetics? You dress like that and purse your lips like a Frenchman to sell cosmetics?"

"You scoff, but it's very effective, this attire," Callimaco explained, "Women here are willing to pay twice as much for exotic French preparations. Blond hair from a French jar, to them, is more shimmering, more luxurious, more beautiful, and more enviable. I give them the opportunity to indulge themselves."

"And you profit accordingly," Niccolo pointed out. "So you're not really a medical man, then, in the generally accepted sense of the word?"

"I beg your pardon!" the indignation was back. "I've studied at the University in Paris and am a doctor of medicine!

"You did? You are?" Niccolo was genuinely surprised.

"Indeed. As you so deftly pointed out, my native tongue is Florentine. I was born here, but my family removed to Paris when I was two or three years old. Political problems, like everyone else. I was raised in Paris, and, eventually, took a baccalaureate in medicine at the Sorbonne. That is the truth."

"Why come back here, then, *Dottore*? Aren't there any sick people in Paris?"

"Oh, more and sicker than you can ever imagine. Foul air and dirty water see to that. But with my studies complete, and my parents dead, there was nothing to hold me in France. I wanted to see the world and what better place to start than the land of my birth?"

"So here you are in the land of your birth, an accomplished man, a doctor of medicine. Then why in heaven's name are you peddling hair coloring?"

"Bad luck and hard necessity. I applied for a license to practice medicine and membership in the guild. But with no one to sponsor me and not enough money to ease my petition along, there were delays. In the meantime, I had to eat. I treated a few patients—and did a superb job, I'm no charlatan—but the guild found out. There were heavy fines and a lot of righteous posturing by greedy old men! Pompous assholes! This would not look good, not at all, this would not advance my cause, this was a matter of grave concern.

"So here I am, reduced by circumstances to a cruel fate, mixing cosmetics and hawking my concoctions to the vainglorious and usually ugly daughters of Florence."

"It could be worse," said Niccolo philosophically.

"It is worse," he indicated his torn clothing and his bruises.

"You do seem to have been badly used. What happened?"

"A misunderstanding, that's all," It was clear that Callimaco did not want to discuss it, and Niccolo probed no further. They drank for a while in silence, Niccolo idly running his tongue back and forth over the tooth that was giving him trouble.

"Hey, medical man," he said suddenly, "what do you know about toothaches?"

"The tooth?" said Callimaco coming alive. "I know everything there is to know about the tooth, the jaw, the mouth, the tongue! You have a toothache?"

"For days now, it won't go away."

"Then I shall treat it. You have nothing to worry about. But first my fee, another round of this bracing red!"

Callimaco was brimming with goodwill and excitement. "In an hour's time," he said, "You will forget that tooth ever existed."

A horrifying thought struck Niccolo. He was almost afraid to ask. "You're not talking about an extraction, are you?" he said hesitantly.

"Of course not! That procedure we use for only the most dire sort of emergency. No, I have a salve of my own invention that works miracles! Draws out the pain, no matter how severe, no matter how rotted the tooth."

Here, he drew Niccolo close to him and in confidential tones whispered, "Do you know what the active ingredient is? The secret ingredient? Come now, you're an enlightened soul, you understand these sorts of things. Let me tell you. A white dog turd—dried and crushed!"

A wave of revulsion crossed Niccolo's face. "You intend to put that in my mouth!"

"If I hadn't told you, you would never have known. Be brave now. And don't worry, you won't taste anything. I assure you. There's oil and mint mixed in to make it pleasant-tasting, like a confection or a digestive pastille."

With Callimaco's coaxing, Niccolo gradually submitted to the idea. And while he didn't really want to dwell on it, he was curious about one detail. "Why a white dog's turd?"

"You're not listening," said the medical man. "I didn't say a white dog's turd, but a white dog turd. You, as a grammarian should be more sensitive to the nuances of your native tongue." He obviously enjoyed needling his new patient.

"In other words," the doctor continued, "it is a question not of the turd of a white dog, which in most cases would be brown, but of a dog turd that is white in color, regardless of the color of the dog. And do you know how to produce a white dog turd?"

Niccolo pleaded blissful ignorance as to this esoteric procedure.

"It's all in the diet," said Callimaco, eager to display the extent of his scientific knowledge. "If you feed a dog nothing but bones, after a few weeks, voila—white turds. Dry, chalky, and for some reason, supremely efficacious against maladies of the tooth and gums." He clapped Niccolo on the back. "Let's go then. And don't worry. You can trust me!" Niccolo took a few more gulps to steel himself for the coming ordeal.

As they passed out into the street, Niccolo noted that a diminutive hunchback had fallen asleep on the pavement, propped against the tavern wall. Callimaco too, spotted the small sleeping form. With a few quick steps, the eminent man of modern science stole over to his side. He brushed his fingertips back and forth carefully across the hump and looked up tremendously pleased with himself. Beaming, he mouthed the words to Niccolo—"*Porta fortuna!* It brings good luck!"

"Oh, God," thought Niccolo, "what have I gotten myself into?"

They did not have far to go to Callimaco's bottega, which was in the same neighborhood as the tavern. This location did not inspire confidence. "Down here," said Callimaco, eager and solicitous. He led the way into a dark, narrow street that was more a tunnel than a public thoroughfare. Niccolo knew this was not the quarter where doctors maintained their studios and apothecaries. Murkier trades were plied here. Zodiacal signs adorned many of the doorways—astrologers! Acrid smoke and strange odors announced the presence of alchemists.

Callimaco sensed his apprehension. "Oh, don't worry about the surroundings," he said brightly. "I told you I was short on funds when I set up shop." They passed through a doorway, down several steps, and into a dank corridor. There was a musty, rotten smell in the air. At the end of the long hallway, across a littered courtyard, they began their climb. They were both a little winded when they finally reached the landing where the staircase ended, six stories above street level. "My study," announced Callimaco proudly from behind Niccolo, who had preceded him up the stairs.

Since Niccolo was the first to obtain the landing, he was the first to see it. "It seems someone has returned your hat," he said.

"Thank God," said Callimaco, bounding up the last few steps, but his mouth dropped open when he saw his once-glorious headgear fastened to the door with three heavy, iron nails and a dagger in the center.

"I wonder, is somebody trying to tell you something?" said Niccolo.

"A practical joke," said Callimaco with a sheepish smile. "They do things like this all the time around here." Ignoring his crucified hat, Callimaco pushed the door open and ushered Niccolo into his chambers. After their labors in the damp, gloomy stairway, Niccolo was surprised to find the room flooded with light. They were just under the roof, where a high, gabled ceiling sloped down on all sides. Motes of dust danced in the shafts of sunlight that poured down through large windows cut high up in the walls. Niccolo heard his friend barring the door behind them.

When his attention settled to ground level, he saw everywhere an unlimited profusion of junk, a welter of tools and instruments, flasks, coils, and distillation apparatus. The walls were lined with row upon row of shelves packed with multicolored vials and jars and earthenware containers and pots and cauldrons. There was a huge fireplace crowded with more equipment. There were tables piled high with books and littered with charts and drawings. Niccolo noticed bones that appeared to be human. It looked like a sorcerer's workshop from the dark ages. It looked like the laboratory where Doctor Faustus would one day sell his soul to the devil.

Callimaco had gone over to a corner where several low pens were built against the wall. The yapping of small dogs could be heard from that direction. Niccolo eventually followed. Peering down, he saw a lively black terrier springing up and down into the air and against the side of his enclosure on stiff little legs. Man's best friend and, no doubt, Callimaco's fantastic machine for the production of dental remedies.

"See," said the physician, pointing to the evidence, "didn't I tell you?" On the floor of the pen, under the excited, jumping animal were scattered the raw material—mostly chicken bones—and the end product—the desiccated, chalky little balls of "secret ingredient."

Mercifully for Niccolo, who had a weak stomach, Callimaco had already prepared a sufficient quantity of the balm in advance, and so his patient was spared the ordeal of its step-by-step concoction. The doctor rummaged through his collection of dusty, unlabeled jars, muttering to himself until he found the right one. He opened it and sniffed to make sure.

"Here it is, Niccolo. Now, please be seated," he said dragging a chair into the sunlight. "Right here," he said positioning his patient so that the direct rays fell upon his upraised head. "Now open your mouth, and let me have a look."

Niccolo opened hesitantly and the doctor peered in. As he proceeded with his examination, Niccolo began to feel more confident. There was something reassuring about the way this man's quick but firm fingers moved about his mouth.

While the doctor was thus absorbed in Niccolo's teeth, Niccolo studied his new friend's face. It was rare that a face came this close to his own without the express intention of kissing or being kissed. It was rare to see this close up a face that needed shaving. And, Niccolo noted, Callimaco's stringy brown hair needed combing. But the blackened, puffy left eye, the broken lip, and the bruises across his cheek and chin did not altogether hide a handsome and well-proportioned set of features. There was intelligence in his dark eyes, and, for the moment, a look of considered concentration that betokened professional understanding and concern. "Maybe he does know what he's doing," thought Niccolo.

When Callimaco swabbed the offending tooth with his miracle salve, Niccolo became aware of an intense, tingling alcohol-and-mint taste spreading throughout his mouth, not at all unpleasant. He made no effort to distinguish the secret ingredient in the balm.

"There," concluded the doctor, "In less than a minute, you'll be fine. No trace of a toothache."

When the dental man pulled his head away, and Niccolo looked up, something untoward swung into his line of vision. A robe, topped by a grotesque mask was suspended from the rafters, a carnival costume, hung in effigy.

The mask, which could be pulled down to cover the entire head and shoulders, had two eyeholes closed with what appeared to be crystal lenses and a large yellow horn protruding like a beak from the front. It looked like some oversized, mawkish bird, eyes bulging with surprise and fear. Both mask and robe were made of fine, supple leather. In a room full of strange and remarkable things, this was one of the strangest.

"That's a rather extravagant costume, isn't it?" asked Niccolo, thinking to himself that it was ultimately no more gaudy or attention-getting than what passed for everyday street clothes with his new friend.

"Costume, indeed!" retorted Callimaco. "That is professional garb."

"Oh, really, what do you peddle when you're dressed up in that? Fresh eggs?"

Callimaco let his friend laugh as he got down the costume. He showed Niccolo how the neck and sleeves could be strapped tightly to the body with leather thongs. At the bottom, the robe had been sewn shut, sealed off except for two openings for the feet, which likewise fastened snugly around the ankles. There were gloves that covered the hands, also made of soft, black leather.

He let Niccolo try on the mask. There was an intense, aromatic odor inside the hood. The beak was hollow and had been filled with herbal gums. Niccolo was surprised at how clearly he could see through the eye lenses. Removing the thing, and handing it back to his friend, he said, "So, what is it for?"

"You notice that with the mask and gloves in place, you are completely cut off from contact with the outside world?" said Callimaco in a serious tone that Niccolo had not heard him use before. "Sealed in this leather sheath, the animalcules that cause diseases cannot touch you. This 'costume,' as you call it, is what I use to go among victims of the plague."

Niccolo shuddered at the images of death and devastation that the word *plague* always invoked. The Black Death. And now, for a fleeting moment, he saw this black leather bird with its grotesque yellow bill treading quietly through the houses and streets of the dead and dying.

"You've lived through the plague? You've seen it?"

"On more than one occasion," said Callimaco.

Niccolo was eyeing his new friend with curiosity. He said, "There's only been one outbreak in Florence, that I remember, and it was a minor outbreak. But my father took no chances. He brought the whole family out of the infected city, immediately. The country is the only place to be when the plague rages."

"Perhaps," said Callimaco, "but not for a physician."

Niccolo said nothing, but he was thinking that there was more to his new friend than he had originally anticipated. He had pegged him for a dandy, a confidence man, probably a charlatan, and a scurrilous, flippant profiteer. But now . . .

As Callimaco was slowly rising in Niccolo's esteem, there was a violent pounding at the door. It was the hard sound made, not by fists, but by the hilts of drawn swords. Niccolo sprang to his feet. Callimaco reacted even more quickly. He bounded to a table placed under one of the windows. "This way," he hissed. "Hurry."

They both scrambled out the window and dropped to the sloping, red-clay roof. With Callimaco in the lead, they clattered across the tiles. "Where in the hell is he going?" thought Niccolo as they headed precipitously toward the end of the roof. Are we going to throw ourselves down into the street?

When they reached the end of the roof, Callimaco pulled up short and fell to his knees. Stretching himself out on his belly, he shinnied as close to the edge as he dared. He reached out and under with one arm and pulled hard on something. A rope, about fifteen feet in length, uncoiled itself. Slipping over the edge and finding the rope with his feet, he smiled apologetically at Niccolo. "This kind of thing happens all the time around here."

The alacrity and the surety with which Callimaco had extricated himself was proof to Niccolo that his friend had indeed availed himself of this avenue of escape before. The rope enabled them to climb down and swing through a window in a staircase at the opposite end of the courtyard. In no time they were rushing out into the street.

But they rushed headlong into an agitated group of men, a small mob moving with determination down the street, some brandishing weapons. Before the two escapees could turn and flee, or even think of doing so, the mob was on them. But the excited men showed no interest whatsoever in Callimaco and Niccolo and swept right past. Out of breath, the two young men stood looking at each other in amazement.

Recovering their senses and their better judgment, they made off quickly, hoping to put some distance between themselves and the assailants at Callimaco's door. But as they went, they saw other groups of angry men shouting, "*In piazza! Tutti in piazza!* Everybody to the main square!"

Something was up. "More rioting," thought Niccolo. And indeed he could hear other shouts rising up from the streets—among them, "*Popolo e libertá!*"

"Come on," he said, tugging at Callimaco's soiled, pink doublet. "I want to see what's going on at the Signoria. Nobody will spot you there in the confusion. We'll be safe in the crowd."

As they pressed toward the heart of the city, there were more and more people in the streets. Frantic activity was everywhere. Niccolo managed to grab hold of one of the less hysterical members of the mob around him. "What's going on? What happened?" he demanded, almost shaking the man and having to shout to make himself heard.

The man looked at Niccolo as if he thought he had just fallen to earth from the moon. "You don't know?" he said wide-eyed. "The French army has just crossed the Alps into Italy!"

"Oh God," thought Niccolo, relinquishing his grip on his informant. "It is coming."

15

Son of the Spider

Louis XI of France came to be known as the Spider King. Through a skillful combination of diplomacy, intrigue, treachery, and naked force of arms, he had succeeded in forging a great, united kingdom that stretched from the Mediterranean to the North Sea. From his seat in Paris, the Spider had spun his web, gradually encircling the feuding duchies of Burgundy, Artois, Picardy, Anjou, Orleans, Franche-Comte, and Provence. One by one, he subdued these independent kingdoms. One by one, with insidious threads of steel, he bound them fast to himself and his authority. What had been a collection of small realms, endlessly warring among themselves, was now a powerful and consolidated kingdom with a central administration. As a result of the Spider's efforts, at the close of the fifteenth century, France was a united country, a nation-state at peace with itself—one people, one government.

When Charles VIII succeeded his father, he did so as undisputed monarch of all France. He inherited a secure throne, a full treasury, a strong army, and an economically prosperous nation. Charles could have lived out his days serenely, content with the bounty that had been bestowed upon him. But he was young and twitching with ambition. He dreamed large dreams. He listened to voices that whispered in his ear, whispered of conquest, of greatness, and of empire. And so it was that the Son of the Spider, burning with a desire for glory, turned his gaze south, to Italy.

In looking across the Alps, he saw the splendor of a bright sun, warm breezes, blue skies, and the smell of pine and cedar in the air. But he also saw that all was not well in this earthly paradise. He saw cruelty and unbridled ambition. He saw atrocity and calamity at every turn—betrayal, bad judgment, all-consuming greed. In short, he saw utter disarray, vulnerability—and opportunity.

On the ninth day of September 1494, the Son of the Spider, at the head of an army of over thirty thousand men, took the decisive step. At Monginevra, he crossed the Alps and entered the northern Italian province of Asti.

The fateful passage of Charles into Italy was accompanied by the usual ominous signs and wonders. In Puglia, three suns appeared in the night sky, flashing with thunder and lightning. Men and beasts gave birth to monstrous offspring. The ghost of Ferrante, recently deceased king of Naples, was said to wander in his garden repeating obsessively to his son, Alfonso, one word and one word only—France.

More than anyone else in Italy, Alfonso, indeed, had cause for alarm, for it was Naples that was the announced object of Charles's Italian expedition. That a foreigner should aspire to the throne of an Italian kingdom was nothing unusual. Divided and lacerated, Italy had for centuries been the battleground where conflicts of European dimensions were fought out. Naples, in particular, had been under almost-continual foreign domination since the fall of the Roman Empire. Over the centuries, even the Moors had managed to gain a foothold in this lush southern Italian kingdom.

Unlike France, Italy was not a nation. She was a hydra-headed geographical entity cut off from the rest of Europe by a mountain range. Although she had attained some degree of cultural and linguistic homogeneity, politically, she was a house divided and subdivided against herself. Confusion reigned. Alliances between the city-states were made and dissolved from month to month, and even week to week. The duplicity inherent in the Italian states' dealings with one another conspired to produce a can, not of worms, but of snakes.

For the Son of the Spider to reach Naples, then, at the very southern end of Italy, he had first to traverse the entire length of the peninsula. In the north, he found no resistance. Milan welcomed him, and Venice chose to ignore him. In the south, the pope was already scrambling to come to terms, no matter how ignominious, with the invading Frenchman.

Everywhere, tributes were being paid, treaties concluded, safe-passages arranged. Italy cowered before Charles. His path to the coveted plum of Naples was being smoothed for him as he went. There was only one obstacle, one unresolved problem. That path led directly through Florence.

Debate raged in the city. Traditionally friendly to French interests, Florence had in a large measure depended on outside support from France to maintain her independence in the perilous Italian political climate. But now things were different. Charles was demanding from the Florentines, not only passage through Tuscany, but major territorial concessions with rights to income and huge contributions to finance his war on Naples. It was the arrogance of Charles's demands that inflamed many Florentine tempers. He was coming, not as an ally, but as a conqueror.

Florence was torn between accommodation or resistance. Piero de' Medici, after voicing vague sentiments in favor of an alliance with Naples, betook himself to his new passion, tilting matches.

The voice of Savonarola certainly made itself heard, and with even more power and conviction than before. After all, another of his prophecies was being fulfilled. The scourge was coming. But absent from the preacher's homilies were any prescriptions as to how to meet that scourge. If he had told the people to arm themselves, they would have done so. If he had told them to hurl themselves from the walls on the backs of the enemies with nothing but their teeth and nails for weapons, they would have obliged him. But he did nothing of the kind. In the face of a very real, earthly threat, Savonarola exhorted his flock to lift their eyes to heaven. "It is coming," he assured his flock. "And there is nothing you can do about it. In vain do men seek to guard a city not guarded by God." He was waiting for a miracle.

Other citizens, less likely to rely on divine intervention, were growing more and more alarmed at Piero de' Medici's lack of leadership in the crisis. Piero Capponi and Francesco Valori were two such concerned citizens, frantically trying to do everything in their power to ready the city for the onslaught of the advancing hordes.

It was an uphill struggle. The best citizens looked only to their own interests, secreting away valuable possessions and planning how best to survive the inevitable sack of the city. Florence had no standing army. If she were to be defended, it would be necessary to hire one, and money was in short supply.

In their desperation, Capponi and Valori implored Savonarola to use his tremendous influence to help them. But the friar was adamant. It was at their second meeting with him that one of the friar's protégées came to their attention, an eager young man who followed their arguments with keen interest, and whose consternation at the friar's obstinacy was scarcely concealed. The day after that meeting, Niccolo Machiavelli presented himself to Francesco Capponi, offering his services to the cause of the republic and volunteering to do what he could to save her from destruction. It was selfishness and the abandonment of the public good on the part of far more capable men that explains why young Niccolo was subsequently entrusted with an important mission. At twenty-five years of age, he was living out one of his childhood fantasies. He had become a spy.

In making its way into Italy, the French army had taken the mountain pass at Monginevra. It was not the most direct route, but it was the widest and the easiest to negotiate. This was why Hannibal had chosen the route over a thousand years ago—so that his elephants, those mighty, lumbering engines of war, might pass easily and quickly through the steep, treacherous mountains. It was generally assumed that Charles had followed the same route so that his lumbering engines of war—unwieldy iron cannons—could likewise pass through the mountains with a minimum of difficulty and loss.

But now a rumor was spreading through Italy like wildfire and had reached Florence. Charles had no cannons! So certain was he of the capitulation of the Italian states that he had not even bothered to provide himself with artillery. If this were true, the defense of Florence would not be an impossible undertaking. There was hope. If it were true. . . . In the confusion that reigned, with few willing to take responsibility and even fewer willing to take action, it was given to Niccolo Machiavelli to ascertain the veracity of this rumor.

Niccolo took with him only one companion—his new friend Callimaco Guadagni, whose superb command of the French language he thought might prove a valuable asset in his intelligence-gathering operation. Callimaco, for his part, was more than willing to go. In fact, he judged it the prudent course. At the moment, it was probably more dangerous for him to remain in the city than to take his chances against the French.

They traveled on horseback, north through the Apennines. Niccolo had seen to it that his friend was more soberly and inconspicuously attired than usual. Despite the gravity of their mission and the precarious situation in which they were about to place themselves, the two were in high spirits. Callimaco talked freely about his past and the rather startling circumstances that had led to his unfortunate persecution in Florence. As Niccolo had suspected, dalliance with a client and a jealous husband were at the root of his friend's problems.

The French host moved slowly. Charles seemed to be in no hurry and was taking time to enjoy himself in this exotic, lovely land. Rumors of his addiction to sensual pleasures preceded the army, and strange tales followed in its wake. Niccolo and Callimaco had no trouble making rendezvous with the advancing army. Its leisurely pace allowed them to track it, at a distance, with surprising ease. What they wanted to know became quickly apparent. Although neither was an expert in military affairs, the situation would have been obvious to a child. The huge, conspicuous carts and the teams of enormous oxen needed to transport heavy artillery were entirely absent from the French ranks.

Having determined this to their satisfaction and great relief, Niccolo and Callimaco felt free to return to Florence, but they decided to follow in the French train for a few days, hoping to learn anything that might be potentially useful. They even discussed the possibility of going down into the French camp for a closer look at the enemy. Nor was this a particularly bold proposition, since Charles made little secret of his doings and security was notoriously lax. By design, of course. Italians were graciously admitted to the French encampments. Peddlers, merchants, peasants, tradesmen, and of course, women. Let them come and see for themselves the spectacle of thirty thousand warriors, thought the king of France—hardened, professional soldiers, grisly and well-armed. Let them come and look. And let them tremble!

Observed from the hilltops, the discipline of the army was impressive, the Swiss, especially, in their patterned red-and-yellow uniforms. They marched in blocks, walls of men in tight formations. Niccolo marveled and wondered idly to himself, did they sleep in those formations?

Once Niccolo and Callimaco had gotten a good look at the entire length of the column, they made it their practice to shadow the army, staying behind it, and lingering in the towns after the French left. Thus, they were free to ask questions and gather information from their fellow Italians without risk. This procedure also allowed them to seek comfortable lodgings and spare themselves the ordeal of sleeping on the damp ground.

They learned that the French soldiery was arrogant and uncouth in their dealings with the "conquered people." Charles himself kept out of sight and treated only with the leaders and the most prominent citizens. Needless to say, they went to him; he did not come to them. But in every town, every night, Charles demanded the company of a young and fair Italian woman. And it was rumored that he had an artist, brought down with him from Paris, sketch a portrait of each and every one. He was going to put them in a book, to help him remember his passage, his lovely, uncontested passage through this docile, gentle land.

The army continued through Imola and Faenza and entered the province of Forli. They set up camp on a broad plain before the fortress of Mordano. The two young Florentines, competent spies now, remained a step behind, in Faenza, drinking in taverns whose customers were their primary sources of intelligence on the habits of the French. Machiavelli and Guadagni were relaxed. Their fears had subsided, and both had come to believe that the danger to Florence was now minimal. The French king had demanded a huge sum of money. Florence would swallow her pride, offer half what he wanted, and they would come to terms. What choice would Charles have? His soldiers could sack the countryside, and their mere appearance terrify a small castle, but a fortified city, well provided, could hold out for months, even years before an army with no artillery. A lengthy siege of Florence was unlikely, especially given that the king's real target was Naples.

Callimaco and Niccolo were discussing possible disguises they might use to infiltrate the French camp. Niccolo thought they could pose as peddlers of relics, which could be fabricated cheaply and readily enough, but Callimaco objected, pointing out that soldiers were fiercely impious men, but superstitious. He proposed selling some kind of elixir, a protection against wounds maybe, which could be concocted just as cheaply. It was during this playful and desultory conversation that the word reached them. Caterina Sforza, mistress of Forli, had denied the French army passage through her territory. She was prepared to resist them, to the death if need be.

The announcement sent shock waves through Romagna. Until now, no one had dared engage the French. Wherever they went, they were bought off, and so, as conquerors, they had been relatively well behaved, limiting their pillage to smaller, unprotected villages. They were in no need of taking what they wanted by force since the servile Italians were gladly handing it over to them voluntarily.

It was the spectacle of this servility that had finally driven Caterina to act. Watching the men of her country eagerly prostrate themselves before the foreign invader, her outrage grew. "If this barbarian king wants Italy as his own," she thought, "then he will have to fight for her."

Caterina was not a woman to be taken lightly. Fierce, iron-willed, Amazonian, she was the widow of Girolamo Riario, Lord of Forli, assassinated by the pope almost ten years before. After his treachery, the pope hastily sent troops against Forli, hoping thus to easily take the leaderless city. But Caterina personally assumed command of the defense and repelled the attack.

Tested in battle and fearless as she was, Caterina was not a reckless individual. For the past ten years, she had ruled Forli with the strength of a lion and the cunning of a fox. She knew when to bend and when to stand firm. She was respected and feared by every ruler in Italy.

Her decision to stand firm against the French king was not foolish, but calculated. She hoped thereby, not only to enhance her own position in Romagna, but to rally the fainthearted around her to a spirited defense of their land and rights. She further reasoned that the French king would not wish to delay his advance with a long, exhausting siege at Forli, but would prefer to proceed southward in a timely manner, especially with winter coming on. He would, no doubt, leave a small force behind to enforce the siege, but, without artillery, there was little they could do but wait. Not only was she confident of outlasting and eventually defeating any such force, her strategy would also have the effect of splitting the French army up into more manageable units. If other cities would follow her lead, and Charles were forced to throw up siege after siege, the army might soon be too fragmented to present a serious threat.

For his part, Charles was growing weary of the never-ending cycle of hedonistic indulgence into which his campaign had degenerated. He longed for battle, and so he accepted the challenge thrown down by Caterina Sforza. Lines were drawn, and in the early part of October, under heavy rains, the French army arrayed itself against the almost-impregnable walls of the fortress of Mordano.

In order to understand how Charles VIII of France revolutionized the conduct of war, it is necessary to grasp the fundamentals of military engagement as they were then practiced on the Italian peninsula.

When a city went to war, she contracted for the services of a *condottiere,* a hired captain. If the condottiere supplied his own soldiers as part of the contract, fine. If not, it was necessary to hire them as well. These mercenaries were recruited from the ranks of the dispossessed, the petty criminals, the runaway slaves, and deserters from abroad.

The condottieri were professionals, and as such, war was waged on a strictly business, cash-and-carry basis. Their interest was not so much in victory as in prolonging the war for as long as possible. They were paid for their time, so the longer the war, the more they were paid. Long campaigns also offered more opportunities for plunder.

The rules of engagement governing the actual conduct of battle were equally businesslike. When armies fought, they fought not to kill but to take prisoners who could later be redeemed for ransom. They never fought at night. If the weather were inclement, they remained in camp. When winter set in, they withdrew to the safety and comfort of towns and barracks.

The battles themselves were masterful spectacles, and looked for all the world as if they had been plotted not so much by a strategist as by a choreographer. Opposing armies danced around each other, feinting and then retreating, carefully avoiding confrontation. The Battle of Anghirai was not atypical. A conflict in which thousands of men participated ended without a single casualty.

When armies marched, it was usually because they had exhausted the surrounding countryside and were moving on to plunder further afield. It is said that most soldiers were more adept at using their lances to herd cattle than to impale the enemy.

Conflicts were generally resolved when one side agreed to pay the other side a suitable sum of money, or to cede the disputed properties or territories. Surprisingly, violence and assassination, so much a part of the political process as to be ranked as civic virtues, were entirely absent from the martial sphere. War was simply business, and business was conducted in a civilized way. Indeed, the Italians prided themselves on their attainments in the area of civilization. In this they were faithful to the example of their ancestors, the imperial Romans. What they did not suspect, as the cultivated Romans before them also failed to do, was that their civilization was about to be assaulted by implacable enemies from the north.

The Battle of Mordano would forever change the way war was fought on the continent of Europe. Technological advances in weaponry were about to be demonstrated in all their terrible finality and splendor. In military terms, the modern era was about to dawn.

16

Amazon on the Ramparts

The Amazons were a nation of women-warriors supposed to have lived in ancient times. In that murky world, before the dawn of recorded history, when giants and gods still walked the earth, they fought on the side of Troy against the Argives in the Trojan War. Their queen, Penthesilea, was slain there by Achilles. Whatever their status in the annals of history—or legend—there can be no doubt that their commitment to war was total and complete. Their name, *Amazon*, means "breastless," for it was said that each of these fierce women, upon coming of age, removed her right breast in order to better handle the bow in battle.

Caterina Sforza, Countess of Forli, was in no way their inferior. Like the Amazons, she was bellicose, and like them, she was willing to sacrifice. Surrounded by an army over thirty thousand strong, she stood on the ramparts of the fortress of Mordano and made what is perhaps the single most defiant gesture in Italian history.

The siege was in its second week, and the son of the Spider had not attacked, nor had he begun preparations to move the bulk of his army south and leave a contingent behind for protracted dealings with Caterina. The Italians were puzzled. Why did he seem to be spending so much time on what, after all, was not an important or even very attractive prize from the point of view of plunder? Far richer targets lay to the south, among them Florence.

In spite of this seeming inactivity, Charles had not been idle. Through the use of spies, he had learned that Caterina had two sons whom she had secreted off in a remote villa near the sea. He had quietly dispatched a small force under the French general Louis d'Armagnac to take the boys. No blood was shed in the operation, since d'Armagnac had decided to use "diplomatic" means. He bribed the boys' guardians. It was very neatly done. It was very Italian.

When the word spread, the entire countryside turned out to witness the confrontation that everyone knew would eventuate in Caterina's surrender. Beneath the walls at the moat's edge stood d'Armagnac, clothed in the blue mantle of a French general. In his hand he held a white silk banner unfurled in the stiff October wind. On it were embroidered the arms of France and the words *Voluntas Dei*—"It is the will of God." Behind d'Armagnac, frightened and looking very small, were Caterina's boys. They seemed like delicately fashioned toys compared to the rude, gigantic men with spears who flanked them on all sides.

Atop the battlements, Caterina Sforza prowled with all the pent-up rage of a caged lioness. She was furious with herself for not having foreseen this treachery. She had offered to ransom the boys, promising huge sums she knew would be difficult, if not impossible, to raise. But d'Armagnac stood his ground. Now there was only one exchange possible—her surrender for the boys' lives.

Caterina drew herself up to her full, majestic height, long blond hair swirling around the concentrated ferocity in her face and eyes. Forehead, jaw, chin, and breasts formed an unbroken line of furious defiance. Legs apart, sword in hand, she weighed her response.

"Well, what it is to be?" said the French general in heavily accented Italian. "Your sword or the lives of your sons?"

She looked down at the sword in her hand as though calculating its value against the worth of her sons. Head bowed, she slid the naked blade quietly back into its sheath. Cold hatred seethed in her expression. Leaning into the wind, she gathered up the billowing folds of her long skirts. For a moment she hesitated, as though undecided. Then, slowly and deliberately, like someone revealing a long-kept secret, she drew the garments up around her waist.

You could see the strength in her long, muscular thighs and a dark blaze of pubic hair where they converged. "Look here, Frenchman!" she cried with an insolent thrust of her hips, "You see for yourself I have what I need to produce more sons. They can be replaced, these sons, but my liberty, never."

From a distance, the city of gaily colored tents and pavilions that had sprung up in a circle around the isolated fortress resembled nothing so much as an enormous, traveling circus. From a distance, there was no hint of the lethal nature of the preparations being made in this seemingly enchanted city.

By the time of Caterina's dramatic refusal, Niccolo and Callimaco had managed to successfully infiltrate the camp of the invaders. Not that much skill had been required to effect this act of espionage. With thirty thousand men at arms and thousands more in attendance upon them, the French camp could be considered the third or fourth largest city in Italy. Local bakers, brewers, and vintners by the dozens had set up shop within its confines. Business was good. The French had money, and inflation was rampant. Prostitutes were reported charging three and four times their normal rates.

Callimaco, too, was exercising his medical skills to advantage and turning a handsome profit lancing boils, cutting off bunions, and treating the endless varieties of venereal disease that raged in the tights and trousers of the invading army. Niccolo posed as his assistant and, when necessary, did in fact lend a hand. But mostly he observed, his greedy eyes drinking in all the details of an army in camp.

The variety of uniforms astounded him. Each company of German mercenaries sported smart jerkins of different colors and hose with different patterns. The Swiss wore shiny steel helmets with flowing, crimson plumes. Every French count and baron insisted on his own colors and designs. Infantry, pikemen, and archers were all marked with something distinctive. The Gascons, smaller and meaner-looking than the average Frenchman, and with a reputation for tenacity in battle, wore bright-blue one-piece uniforms. Niccolo recalled the days of his youth when he thought that uniforms were the essence of soldiery and the only purpose of an army was to play music and march in parades.

But here, he was seeing the truth. Beneath the gaudy surface, it was a rough, man's world. Cursing was the lingua franca and oaths filled the air from morning to night in every dialect imaginable of French, German, and even English. All the gaiety of the tents and the banners and the uniforms did little to conceal the look in these men's eyes. They were men of violent disposition, trained to kill. They had nothing in common with the soldiers he remembered, the gay blades who marched through the streets of Florence with fife and drum, behind Lorenzo de' Medici in his black velvet, pearl-encrusted mantle. Those beautiful pearls would not even stand up to the savagery that flashed from these men's eyes, much less their weapons. And everywhere, sparks flew from grinding wheels at which these instruments of death were being honed. The edges of pikes and swords, axes, halberds, and lances were being ground to sharp and fatal perfection.

Everything was being made ready—armor polished, saddles oiled, weapons checked and rechecked. In taking all this in, Niccolo felt a sense of impending doom. But in the back of his mind was the nagging question—What good were short swords and long bows against a six-foot-thickness of solid stone? And against the resolve of a woman like Caterina Sforza?

The most frightening men Niccolo had ever seen were the great, shaggy-bearded, red-haired wild men from Scotland, said to be the best archers on the face of the earth. He was fascinated by them—their height, their coloring, the skins and pelts with which they adorned themselves. Frequently, when Callimaco was otherwise occupied, Niccolo would find himself strolling in the direction of the Scottish camp to marvel at these bizarre and splendid creatures.

It was on one of these strolls that he became aware of an incongruity. The French knights and captains who formed the core of the king's most trusted advisers were treated, as was the monarch himself, royally. No expense was spared. Rank had its privileges, and Charles had brought down with him from France an extraordinary collection of his own personal and highly skilled serving people—cooks, sommeliers, doctors, musicians, entertainers, and even prostitutes, or rather, ladies of sufficient attainment to be regarded as courtesans. Naturally these people and the amenities they provided were reserved for the exclusive use of Charles and his inner circle. The beady-eyed Gascon infantryman in his little blue uniform was assuredly not the object of their attentions.

Now the gruff Scotsmen who so captivated Niccolo's imagination were near the edge of the camp, far from the king's quarters. As such, they were a relatively unimportant part of the army and were left to fend for themselves when it came to bodily comforts and female companionship. Even more removed from the center of command was a compound consisting of about half a dozen unadorned tents, drawn up closely. They were the type of rough tents used to house the grooms, muleteers, carpenters, and wheelwrights who kept the huge army on the move. And indeed, the men inhabiting this particular compound appeared to be of that rude class. They were, for the most part, dirty, unkempt, and ill clad. There were hundreds like them in the camp, and Niccolo scarcely paid them any mind. Until he began to notice little things.

One evening, he saw two women quite openly enter the compound. He could have sworn they were richly dressed and lavishly coiffed and perfumed in the French manner. What were they doing here? He put it out of his mind. The next day while spying on his enigmatic Scotsmen at mealtime—he wanted to see what they ate—he saw a small train of liveried servants carrying heavily laden platters into the remote compound. The plate was silver, and quite remarkably, the livery was that of the royal house of France! Sauntering over and attempting to appear inconspicuous, Niccolo hoped to stroll inside, but he was stopped by a short, greasy fellow at the entrance to the compound. Niccolo knew enough French to know he was being told to leave and not in a very nice way.

Later, he told Callimaco about his discovery. "I tell you, there's something odd down there. It doesn't make sense."

Callimaco concurred. "Look," he said, "maybe I can get in and have a look around. I'll say I'm the doctor sent down by Duke Somebody-or-Other with the delousing lotion. My French is perfect, no accent—not like some people," he chided his companion. "That should work. *Allons, donc, mon ami!*"

But when they reached the mysterious group of tents, much to their chagrin, they saw they were too late. A thin man in the long black gown of a physician was making his way out of the compound and up the rutted path. The doctor had already made his visit for that evening.

"*Caccasangue*!" swore Callimaco. "We'll have to wait until tomorrow."

Niccolo shook his head. Music was now coming from the camp of the highlanders, and to make up for their disappointment, he suggested they have a look in there. But just as they turned in the direction of the odd, reedy strains, a sharp voice stopped them dead in their tracks. "Callimaque!"

Startled, Callimaco whirled around. It was the black-gowned doctor who had spoken. Pushing his pinched face in the direction of the young men, he repeated, "Callimaque? Callimaque Guadagne? *C'est vous?*"

"Maître Albert? *Mon Dieu!*" And before Niccolo could understand what was happening, his friend was locked in a hearty embrace with the physician. Floods of French were pouring out of the both of them, too rapid for Niccolo to understand. When the preliminary effusions ended, Callimaco turned to Niccolo and explained, "This is Master Albert! I studied medicine with him in Paris!"

The next few hours were dismal ones for Niccolo, who was invited along with "Callimaque" to sup with the French physician in his tent. The patter was rapid and nonstop as teacher and student sought to catch up with one another. Niccolo was effectively excluded from their society. Callimaco promised to fill him in later and then forgot all about him. The hours dragged on. "Nothing is worse than a conversation in a language you don't understand," thought Niccolo. He swore to himself to improve his French.

Finally the incomprehensible evening seemed to be coming to an end. Niccolo whispered to Callimaco, urging him to inquire about the strange, isolated compound from which they had seen the doctor emerge. "Don't be blatant," he said. "Use some tact."

Callimaco indicated that he would, and, after about ten more excruciating minutes of French, they left. "Well," said Niccolo, "did you find anything out?"

Callimaco nodded his head yes. "He says they're . . ."

He groped for the correct word. It was not one that he ever remembered using in Italian before, but, he concluded, it must be pretty much the same as in French. "He says they're—bombadiers."

Within twenty-four hours Niccolo would understand the significance of the presence of the sinister, pampered bombadiers, but before that, he and his friend Callimaco were presented with a unique and extraordinary opportunity—nothing less than a chance to be admitted to the presence of the French king himself.

This came about when Maître Albert sought Callimaco's assistance in a professional matter—the king was suffering from an abscessed tooth. The royal French physician, Jean Michel, had been able to do nothing. Albert, his assistant, was also unskilled in oral and dental work, but knowing that Callimaco had been interested in this particular branch of surgery in Paris, and had even pursued it against his advice, the professor was now forced to call in the younger man, his former student, for a consultation.

Accompanied by his "servant," Niccolo Machiavelli, the dental surgeon was introduced into the royal pavilion by Master Albert. The tent in which the king was lodged was a huge, blue-and-white, cone-shaped structure, as high as the mast of an ocean-going ship. It was surrounded by smaller tents, and guards were everywhere.

The center of the French camp was a beehive of activity. Heralds, ushers, pageboys, and valets rushed off urgently in all directions. The smugness in their faces announced the obvious importance of the errands upon which they had been dispatched.

Once inside, Niccolo marveled that the royal tent seemed a million miles away from the rough world of the military camp outside. Sumptuousness and luxury abounded in the accoutrements and appointments. The furniture was not of the flimsy, portable variety one would expect to find in an army on the march. There were rows of ornate, lacquered cabinets, inlaid with designs in gold and silver. Niccolo could make out the spires of a massive bed, canopied and draped. There were heavy, cushioned chairs and thick carpets. Everywhere, everything was covered with the device of the white lily, the symbol of the kingdom of France.

There was a hush and a subdued quality about the place, despite the presence of a large number of people. Tapestries and curtains hanging from on high muffled the sounds and divided the large open area into a mazelike succession of smaller semienclosed spaces where the various activities required for the maintenance of the royal person were being carried out. Chamberlains and wardrobe keepers went about their business. Bedclothes and tablecloths were being changed and aired, some being taken out, others put away. Cooks and servants were huddled with wary food tasters, who nibbled thoughtfully and methodically at the royal lunch. Concealed harps and oboes produced a soothing, almost-inaudible, background music that hovered in the air above the abundantly displayed richness of satin and soft velvet and fur.

Callimaco, and, by extension, his servant, were first introduced to Jean Michel, the royal physician. He was a man whose face and manner betrayed a wide range of emotions—false modesty, insincere solicitude, exaggerated concern, hypocritical intensity, and a posturing, affected, air of ethereal spirituality. Niccolo saw him immediately for what he was—a creature of the court—and turning away, half-disgusted, half-amused, he left the three physicians embroiled in their technical discussions.

He gave himself over to leisurely observation. It was difficult to believe that he was at the vortex of a military campaign. He felt more like he was in the tent of some pampered sultan, while all about him rustled the sultan's harem, voluptuous ladies-in-waiting, richly, but scantily, clad. There was no evidence of generals or preparations for war. Then he saw a group of men poring over maps that had been spread out on a large table. As casually as possible, he edged over in their direction, hoping to catch a glimpse of what they were planning, perhaps the disposition of troops for the assault on Mordano, or the progress of the army down through Italy. Keeping his back to them, he drifted over toward the makeshift war room. They paid no attention to him. When he managed to get close enough, he stole a quick, furtive glance over his shoulder. "Unbelievable!" he thought. Is this what Charles means by strategy? The men were engrossed in the study of astrological charts.

By now the medical conference had adjourned, and the three doctors, Niccolo trailing behind, were ushered into the presence of the son of the Spider. The king had his back turned when they approached, and Niccolo's first impression of him consisted of two details—the bald spot and . . . the hump.

Eventually Niccolo would notice the white hat, gold-crowned, and the shocking-blue cloak, picked out in gold and trimmed with fur. Eventually he would also notice the absurd shoes. But initially, he was struck dumb, almost paralyzed by the profound, distressing, overwhelming ugliness of the man. Wheeling around on his spindly legs, Charles came at them with the bent limp that served him as a walk. He squinted distractingly from large, pale, watery eyes. He had a great, bloated nose, a yellow complexion, and thick, slack lips that hung open moronically and did nothing to hide a mouth full of black and rotting teeth.

When he moved, he moved nervously. When he talked, he stuttered. His head was too small to house much of a brain. There was a tangled growth of red curly hair at his chin that gave him an undeniably goatlike appearance. At all this Niccolo could not help but marvel. Was this the Sword of the Lord? God's chosen instrument? Was this the man before whom all Italy cringed, this nervous little monster?

Niccolo watched while his friend set to work on the royal abscess. The dwarf-king was placed in a chair, and Callimaco and the fawning Jean Michel exchanged opinions and information in hurried whispers. Niccolo noticed that, in conducting his examination, Callimaco had frequent recourse to supporting the king's head with his left hand while probing the black hole of his mouth with his right. In turning the royal head toward the light, adjusting the angle, pulling it back, more than once the enterprising dentist allowed his hand to brush casually across the surface of the royal hump. Royal good luck!

Visually dissecting the occupant of the lofty throne of France, Niccolo's attention fell to the monarch's footgear. He wore, not boots, but black velvet pumps with a soft sole and low heel. Most remarkable of all was the shape of these shoes. Although narrow at the heel, they splayed out at the toe in a wide, flat arc. Thus shod, the ducklike royal foot seemed more suited to swimming than walking. Who understands French fashion?

It was clear from the gravity of Callimaco's expression that an extraction, or something worse, was warranted. "We're going to be here for a while," thought Niccolo. He let his eyes wander, taking in with the dreamy delight of the pleasure den the never-ending procession of quiet, sensual women, who came and went and laughed softly in the corners. The luxury and the carnality of it lulled him, and he found himself suddenly resenting the intrusion of a figure who clearly did not belong in this harem of soft, buxom women. Standing a few feet from him, and anxiously inquiring as to the king's condition, was a scraggly, barefoot man in long-unwashed sackcloth. He looked and smelled like he had just crawled in from twenty years fasting in the desert. Indeed, as Niccolo was soon to discover, he was, in fact, a hermit.

Perhaps ex-hermit would be a more precise designation for the man who, fretting and mumbling to himself, scuttled out of the king's presence past Niccolo. The reason Niccolo followed him and then stopped him was that the man was fretting and mumbling in Italian, not French. The young Florentine, remembering now that he was a spy, was curious to know what an Italian was doing here on such intimate terms with the king of France.

"Is there any problem with the king?" asked Niccolo, breaking in on the other's sotto voce monologue.

Flustered, the little hermit regarded Niccolo for a moment before answering. Then, recovering his balance, he said, "Problem, with the king?" He chuckled. "What problem can there possibly be for the second Charlemagne? For a man destined to conquer the Infidel and reduce the world to a single sheepfold under a single shepherd? No. No. No problem." He laughed the knowing laugh of the true believer.

"Another prophet," thought Niccolo, rolling his eyes. And more Sword of the Lord talk! But, concealing his skepticism, Niccolo encouraged the little man to elaborate. Putting questions to him, he learned that Charles was considered by many in France—and, indeed, had come to consider himself—the second Charlemagne, destined to rule over a united, worldwide Christian empire. After conquering Italy and restoring French rule in Naples, he would reestablish the true religion in Rome by driving out the corrupt, bestial, antichrist who called himself pope. From there, he would cross over into the east, like the Crusaders before him, and crush the Turk. Finally, he would bring the Infidel dogs into the one, true church.

"How do you know these things?" asked Niccolo, eyeing the scruffy, bearded man.

"God tells me!" he said.

Niccolo took his leave of the hermit and returned to the area where the dental surgery was being performed. Callimaco had apparently administered some sort of sedative, as the formerly wriggling, squirming monarch was now lying quite still. The operation appeared to have been successful, judging from the expressions on the faces of the medical men. Callimaco was washing a bit of royal blood from his hands.

Two chamberlains carried the prostrate King Charles to his imposing bed and with infinite care laid the small, twisted body among the soft cushions. They deftly removed his cloak, hat, jacket, and shoes. Before they pulled the thick goose-down covers over his sleeping form, Niccolo had time to make one ghastly observation. The splayed-toe shoes were no caprice of fashion. They were meant to conceal the fact that Charles VIII, king of France, had six toes on each foot.

Callimaco left the king's tent with assurances of reward for having so adeptly extracted the offending tooth. Beaming with satisfaction, he clapped Niccolo on the back and recounted the particulars of what he called the epoch-making operation. Whatever the operation had been in medical and dental terms, Callimaco was certain of one thing. It would make him rich.

Grinning at his companion, he reached into a pouch on his belt and produced a small, green-black nub.

"You didn't," groaned Niccolo.

"The royal tooth!" said Callimaco triumphantly.

"Maybe we can grind it up and make an aphrodisiac? Eh?" Niccolo speculated.

"Or a potion that will turn a man into a king!" said Callimaco with a wicked gleam in his eyes.

"Or a little twelve-toed hunchback Frenchman!" concluded Niccolo. They both laughed as Callimaco carefully wrapped his treasure in a soft cloth and put it away. He was sure it would come in handy someday, somehow.

Niccolo questioned him as to what the royal personage was like, what he had said.

"He's a mess of a man," reported the dental surgeon. "When he tries to talk, it's like his lips and his tongue conspire to prevent him. The tongue stutters, the flabby lips get in the way, and what comes out is a babble. He was half-delirious, he was mumbling over and over about the second Charlemagne and reforming the Church and liberating Constantinople from the Turks. He believes it, Niccolo. He really does."

Callimaco thus confirmed what Niccolo had surmised from his talk with the hermit-prophet. Monsters and beasts from the Apocalypse were swirling around inside the king's head, and the people close to him were egging him on. He had more prophets than the Old Testament and, apparently, a council of astrologers planning his military moves. But while Niccolo was considering the implications of these discoveries, Callimaco offered him another piece of information.

"And, get this, in his blabbering about his divinely ordained mission and his destiny, he kept saying that the prophet had foretold it and that he had to talk to the prophet, to get his advice."

"I know," said Niccolo. "I met the prophet. He's a scroungy little Italian fellow, from the south to judge by his accent. I think he was sent up from certain parties in Naples to fill the king's head with nonsense and talk him into this invasion."

Callimaco furrowed his brow and regarded his friend with something approaching consternation. "That's not at all who the king has in mind," he said. "The prophet Charles seems so terribly anxious to consult is—in his own halting words—Sav-vo-vo-vo-vonarol-l-l-la!"

"Caccasangue!"

The two spies had succeeded in uncovering what could well prove to be a critical piece of information and resolved to depart for Florence within the hour. But their plans were put on hold when a tremendous uproar erupted in the camp. Tracing the excitement to its source, they saw that much was being made of a convoy that was entering camp at breakneck speed. Niccolo counted thirty-six light wagons thundering past, each in the tow of two hard-galloping, overworked, and clearly exhausted horses.

They had made the trip from Genoa in less than three days' time, it was being said. Good time. Great time. They had crossed the fertile central plain of northern Italy on the wide Via Emilia, built by the Romans in ancient times. They had sacrificed everything to speed and scarcely stopped to eat or water the horses along the way.

"So what?" thought Niccolo. "So the French have just set a speed record for crossing the peninsula. What could be in those wagons that was so important? New clothes for the king's whores? Claret for the king's table?" He had already dismissed the hubbub in his mind and was tugging on Callimaco's cloak to go when a shock ran through him. The convoy of lathered horses, without breaking stride, without even slackening speed, was plunging headlong into the mysterious compound reserved for the bombadiers.

17

The Bombadiers

The use of artillery as a siege weapon was already common practice throughout Europe, North Africa, and the East. The value of cannons in an attack on a walled city or garrison was well established.

One of the most powerful concentrations of artillery the world had ever seen was deployed at the siege of Constantinople in 1453, about forty years before Charles VIII invaded Italy. The Turkish sultan Mohammed II turned a total of sixty-eight pieces against the ancient walls. The biggest of these was nicknamed "Basilica." It was cast for the sultan by the Hungarian founder, Urban, and was universally acknowledged to be the most devastating war machine of its time. It had a range of close to a mile, it had a bore of thirty inches, and it could shoot a stone ball weighing 1,600 pounds.

Notwithstanding the awe such a weapon was capable of inspiring in the defenders of a fortification, the great cannon was not without disadvantages. Sixty oxen and over two hundred men were required to move it. There were no carriages or supports capable of sustaining a behemoth of the Basilica's weight and dimensions. Once the sultan's mighty cannon was hauled up before the walls of the besieged city, it was planted in a mound of earth and pointed in the general direction of the enemy. It was extraordinarily difficult to aim. After being fired, it took over two hours to reload.

Because of its size, a cannon like the sultan's had to be cast very near the site where it was to be used. While there was little the French could do to improve on the firepower of such a weapon, they were responsible for introducing an important new element into the use of artillery—mobility. The light, horse-drawn carts that thundered into the camp at Mordano were the proof of it.

Knowing they would not need their artillery in the north where the Milanese had welcomed them with open arms, the French had secretly sent it on by ship to Genoa. There, the cannons were loaded onto horse carts and speedily transported to the front. It was the quickness of the move that took the enemy by surprise. A train of heavy carts laboriously drawn by oxen might have aroused the suspicions of the Italians and even come under attack. But who would ever have suspected these light, seemingly harmless vehicles racing across the plains? Who would have dreamed what lethal cargo they carried?

Niccolo did not sleep that night, nor did he return to Florence. He had no way of gaining entry into the bombadiers' compound, but from the sounds that issued forth, he knew what was happening. The incessant hammering could mean only one thing—that nails were being driven and that engines of war were being constructed. In his mind, Niccolo pictured the fabrication of siege machinery for scaling the walls or putting archers in an elevated position from where they could shoot down into the fortress. Little did he imagine what was actually being built.

When dawn broke, it was clear that the army was being readied for battle. Shouted orders filled the air. Everyone was on the move, and yet there was no sign of frenzy or excitement. Rather, it was with a slow and deadly deliberation that the men began to draw themselves up into fighting units. Charles himself appeared, a suit of gleaming armor visible beneath his royal cloak, a stout, plumed helmet on his small head. Surrounded by his generals and peers of the realm, he nodded gravely as they indicated, with sweeping gestures, the disposition of the troops and the order of battle. When he seemed satisfied, they were dismissed to go about their business, and the king summoned a half dozen other men from a nearby tent. Niccolo recognized them as the grimy bombadiers. Dressed in the nondescript, greasy clothes of mechanics and tradesmen, they seemed out of place in the sea of magnificent color and heraldry and shiny weaponry that was rising and falling in all directions. However, Charles listened intently as they spoke. When they were done, the king of France solemnly embraced each of them. Niccolo remarked that embrace and was shocked that a king, even a mad one, would have publicly done such a thing.

Niccolo and Callimaco, like many of their countrymen, had turned out to watch the battle. Warfare, after all, was a spectator sport in Italy and on a scale much grander than the palio or the tournament. The music was stirring, the uniforms splendid, and the entire production well worth missing a day's work.

Perched on a low hill well out of harm's way, but close enough to observe what was going on, the two Florentine spies were making themselves comfortable. They were supplied with more than enough food to last the day and copious quantities of wine. Enjoying the panorama that was spread out before them, they discussed, at their leisure, the movement of the troops. The red-and-yellow Swiss and the powder-blue Gascons seemed to be taking up forward positions. The Scotch and English bowmen were also in the vanguard.

Amid much fanfare, a line of small guns was trundled out in front of the troops and began moving into position. So light was the artillery that each cannon had been mounted on a movable carriage that required only one horse to be drawn into position. Niccolo surmised that those carriages, with their spoked, iron-rimmed wheels, were the result of the night's construction activity.

"Would you look at that," he said to Callimaco. "Oh, the French are too much, and their king is utterly mad! I've seen fireworks displays in Florence that had more firepower than those toy guns. I've seen muskets and arquebuses with bigger bores!"

Callimaco agreed, observing that the stone balls fired from these weapons could scarcely be larger than his fist or the French king's tiny, brainless, pointed head. Like everyone else, however, they had underestimated the son of the Spider. He was mad, certainly, but madmen, in the thoroughness with which they pursue their obsessions, can be very, very dangerous.

When the horses were unhitched, two men sufficed to maneuver the guns into their firing positions. Each cannon, with carriage, was only ten or twelve feet long. The barrel itself was the height of a man. In all, only ten guns were arrayed against the fortress of Mordano that day, each manned by a team of four or five bombadiers. When they stood at the ready, the volume of trumpets and drums increased to a deafening roar, until King Charles appeared on horseback. With a solemn gesture and surprising dignity, he raised his sword high in the air and brought it down smartly to signal the beginning of the assault. The music stopped abruptly.

Niccolo and Callimaco watched as the first fuse was lit. They were far enough away that they saw the puff of smoke a split second before the sound reached them. The sharp crack of the explosion was followed by a dull thud as the shot fell short of the walls, and the ball ploughed harmlessly into the mud.

One of the gunners immediately leapt to the spent gun and busied himself with something Niccolo could not make out. He was using a rule and weighted plumb lines to sight down the muzzle of the gun. A series of pins in the carriage mechanism allowed him to change the angle of fire effortlessly and almost instantaneously. The next shot would not fall short.

As the process of reloading began, a second gun fired with similar results. Another gnomelike bombadier was on it, making his adjustments, correcting the trajectory, bearing down on the target. And so in turn, all ten guns test-fired. Niccolo and Callimaco were amused. They greeted the spectacle with derision—the puffs of smoke, the far-off popping noises, the little tufts of dirt kicked up by the misdirected shots.

Caterina Sforza appeared on the ramparts of the fortress, waving her sword and taunting the enemy as they reloaded. Ignoring her insinuations, the bombadiers conferred briefly among themselves and then returned grimly to work at their individual guns. Caterina called up a squadron of archers and ordered them to commence firing on the gunners. Before they had time to reload, she was confident her men could pick off a good number of them.

But her confidence was misplaced. Even as she was rallying the archers, one of the guns fired. There was the puff of smoke, the explosion, and then the ball hit—not with the soft crack of stone ball disintegrating against stone wall, but with a hard metallic sound, a ping. A large piece of the defending stone wall fell away.

Before anyone had time to understand what had happened, there was another report, then another, and another after that. The cannons' aim was deadly accurate. Each one drove its ball into the same spot on the wall, and chunk after chunk of stone leapt out with the frightening impact of each new blow.

The walls trembled under the percussive blows, and Caterina was forced to retreat inside and regroup. The unrelenting volley continued as the fiendish bombadiers, jumping like mad devils around their guns, reloading and sighting and firing, hurled their diabolical missiles of destruction against the rapidly disintegrating wall.

The rest of the French army, including the king, looked on with calm detachment, as though they were viewing a spectacle about whose ending there was no doubt whatsoever. They waited. There was only inevitability. For his part, Niccolo understood some but not all of what was going on. He knew that, somehow, the French had accelerated the reloading process. He had heard stories of sieges where the defending forces came out from behind their walls to slaughter undefended gun crews after they had loosed a volley and before they had time to reload. He had even heard of cases in which so much time was necessary to reload that masons and carpenters could actually repair the damage done to the walls between shots.

Now, reloading was being accomplished in minutes. The rapidity with which ball after implacable ball was hurled against the defender's stronghold was astounding. And even more astounding was the damage done by each and every ball. Again, Niccolo correctly guessed that these were not ordinary gunstones being fired, but iron balls. The ringing sound they made on impact and the appalling rate at which the stone was being blown away was proof enough of that.

What he did not know, but what professionals would be able to tease out of his account later, was that Charles was using a new type of gunpowder, more powerful by a magnitude of ten than what was then common in Italy. And the guns that contained and directed that powerful explosive blast, and yet were so light and manageable, were cast not of iron, but solid bronze.

What could not be deduced from observation, but what would make its way down to Italian ears eventually through the agency of spies and informers, was that Charles had set up a school for gunners, and lavished upon it all the money and attention of a man possessed. In addition to the care and training of his gunners, he had encouraged his engineers and his founders to experiment and innovate. All of these technicians he had taken under his wing, personally monitoring their progress. Now his efforts were being rewarded.

His bombadiers were dancing around their diabolical machines, conjuring up the wind that blows from the devil's ass, harnessing it and directing it in violent blasts of evil and destruction with each round fired. Their hands were black with powder, their faces streaked with grime and sweat and smoke. Not a few were suffering severe burns, yet they went about their mad task with furious energy, like small, deformed Vulcans, hopping and leaping in exaltation at the forge. The son of the Spider had created a living, breathing, bellowing monster, a many-headed, fire-breathing monster of war.

From Niccolo's vantage point, the unrestrained exertions of the bombadiers were not apparent. What he saw in his detachment was the methodical, scientific, almost-surgical dissection of the fortress wall. It seemed that warfare had been sanitized and reduced to geometry, that technical innovation had eliminated the blood and sweat and valor of combat.

In a little over an hour and a half, the wall had been breached. What used to take days, even weeks, to accomplish, had become scarcely a morning's work. The guns were silent. Niccolo expected that, at this point, Charles, having demonstrated his clear superiority, would send emissaries to Caterina to conclude a truce. Instead, harsh martial music blared and troops began to move. The Scottish bowmen advanced on both flanks to provide cover for the infantry. To the thrill of drums and trumpets, walls of pikemen, lances lowered, marched into the opening created by the bombadiers. Solid blue walls of Gascons first, then red-and-gold walls of Swiss. They had no trouble negotiating the moat, since the systematically shattered wall had fallen piece by piece into it, filling it up and creating a bridge. Only a few hundred men were needed to subdue the garrison, although Charles was prepared to send thirty thousand men through that narrow breach to make his point.

Again, to Niccolo, the movement of the troops seemed like another exercise in geometry, like boldly colored blocks of men being moved around on a chessboard. From his perch he could not divine the true horror of it all. He could not hear the strangled screams of the dying. He had no idea what a four-pronged war-fork could do with its four sharp tines barbed like giant fishhooks. Plunged into soft flesh, wrenched and twisted and withdrawn, it tore a man to pieces, tore the heart from his chest and the guts from his belly. Over and over, the war forks rose and fell, hundreds of times within those walls, and in their wake, the lifeless, blood-soaked bodies of the vanquished were thrown into piles like refuse and garbage. The French troops had not entered the fortress to demand surrender and secure advantageous terms. They were under orders to kill everyone in the garrison.

Not three hours after it began, the Battle of Mordano was history. The defenders were slaughtered, what little they had of value was removed from their persons, and their houses and the fortress were set afire. The engineers and bombadiers were called in to render one last service. Charges were planted under what remained of the massive stone walls, and they were blown to pieces. Charles VIII could now proceed across the broad plain of Mordano. Nothing stood in his way.

Notwithstanding the distance that separated them from the carnage, Niccolo and Callimaco sensed that the gay carnival afternoon had taken a sinister turn. It was becoming clear that the victory of the French was to be total and without mercy, a ruthless, uncivilized act of barbarism. Wanting to believe otherwise, however, they hurried down from their lofty lookout point to get a better idea of what was happening. They arrived in time to see the blood-spattered victors straggling back into camp. The parti-colored uniforms did not seem so grand then. Thick smoke filled the air, the billowing black smoke that rises from the sacrificial altar, heavy with the smell of burning flesh.

Numbed by the terrible finality of it all, the two young Florentines watched as the screaming wounded were dragged and carried past them. Suddenly Niccolo came to his senses, the strident call of duty welling up inside him. In a panic, he shook his companion, "We have to get back," he said. "Nobody ever expected anything like this. We have to get back and warn them what they're up against."

Callimaco, mesmerized by the grim scene before them, was scarcely aware of his friend's entreaties. It was Niccolo's insistent tugging on his sleeve that brought him out of his dazed incomprehension. "You go, Niccolo," he said in a weak voice. "My place is here—among the dying." Without even taking his leave, the young physician trudged off to where his duty directed him, to that part of the field where the wounded were being laid out in orderly, geometrical fashion, row upon neat row of groaning men—the cut and the sliced, the hammered and pole-axed, the eviscerated, dismembered, pricked, stabbed, and torn open, heroes and cowards indistinguishable from one another, the victims of one man's dreams of glory.

Niccolo hastened to put some distance between himself and the gory, hellish unreality of the aftermath of battle. Nauseating sensations clogged his senses as he stumbled and choked his way through the heart-rending sounds, the revolting sights and smells. The last thing he saw was the badly wounded body of Caterina Sforza, defiant Mistress of Forli. She was being carried unconscious into the French camp. There was blood in her long blond hair. Her bare white arm had slipped out of the litter and was dangling loose at her side. Her broken sword trailed along on the ground behind her, lashed to her wrist.

Niccolo rode all night to reach Florence. He rode with demons buzzing at his heels and in his head. It rained steadily along the route, so that he was sopping wet and mud-spattered when he dismounted in the courtyard of Piero Capponi's house. He gave his name and was shown inside. Although it was just after dawn, the house was full of people, for the most part important people—wealthy merchants and government officials. Capponi was at the center of an attempt to orchestrate the anti-Medicean sentiment that was by now sweeping the city. His problem, however, was not only to oust the Medici, but to do so without a bloody popular uprising. His chances for success were not viewed as good.

Niccolo in his wet riding clothes cut quite a figure among the well-bred, well-dressed, whispering citizens, whose heads turned and whose eyebrows rose as he was whisked past them. He knew they were staring. His heavy boots, his determined stride, and his mud-caked legs marked him as a person on an errand of some importance. Ushered into Capponi's study, Niccolo found the little man dozing at his writing table, pen still in hand. The normally impeccable Capponi looked disheveled, his thin, grey hair uncombed, his bangs plastered to his ample forehead. It was obvious that he had not slept that night, but when Niccolo made a coughing sound to attract his attention, he was instantly alert, instantly bright-eyed. "Well, young man, you have a report to make?"

Niccolo, who had spent most of the long night's ride going over what he had seen and practicing how best to communicate it, delivered a succinct account of the battle. It made a visible impression on Capponi. The blood seemed to drain out of his jovial face, leaving only the pale furrows of fatigue and age and worry. So absorbed was he in his spy's report that he did not even think to invite him to remove his cloak or to take a seat. A puddle of dirty water was forming at Niccolo's feet.

Capponi considered this new information thoughtfully. His bony hand played nervously over his unshaven jaw and chin. "What you're telling me, then," he concluded, "is that Charles is perfectly capable, from a technical point of view at least, is perfectly capable of destroying this city."

"Or any other city in the world," observed Niccolo. "Why? Were you planning a defense, a military solution?"

"Yes and no," said Capponi. "That is, we were planning one, but in a wretched and half-hearted way. You see, I can't get anyone to agree on anything here or to take any decisive action. The city is in utter chaos. We've managed to bring soldiers in, five or six thousand from the surrounding towns and our allies in Tuscany. But it's not nearly enough if Charles has upwards of thirty thousand." The old man sighed in frustration, then went on.

"We've managed to bring in a good quantity of weapons, with the idea of arming the people, but popular sentiment is so volatile right now that we don't dare distribute them. The people are on the verge of a bloody revolution—and half of them want to throw open the gates and welcome Charles as a savior! If weapons came into their hands, there's no telling whom they'd use them on."

"What about Piero?" asked Niccolo.

"Ah, the latest and least capable of the Medici! Piero is a lost cause. He's waffling again. First he supported Naples, now he's declared neutrality."

"Does he have any support?"

"Only among some of the most highly paid bodyguards in Europe. Everyone else has deserted him. So what we're left with is a city with no leader, half an army, and a brewing popular revolt. The largest and most lethal army ever assembled is less than two days' march from here, and now you tell me that even our walls won't stand up for us," Capponi sounded a note of hopelessness.

He coughed curtly, "So it would appear that the only prudent course of action lies in concluding some sort of mutually advantageous arrangement, and that for us, among ourselves, it would be necessary to agree on some form or other of accommodation." Piero Capponi spoke with the tact and circumspection of the lifelong diplomat that he was.

"You mean capitulation—or surrender?" said Niccolo bluntly.

"Well, not to put too fine a point on it," admitted the wily diplomat, appraising the young man who stood before him. "I don't suppose you have any better ideas?"

"Maybe," said Niccolo. The words came in a rush as he described the astrologers and self-proclaimed prophets with whom Charles surrounded himself. "And of all these fortune tellers and holy men," he said breathlessly, "there's one whom he honors and reveres above all others. In fact, I think he might even be afraid of him."

"Which one," asked Capponi, losing interest but feigning it nonetheless, "the one from Naples?"

"No," said Niccolo, "The one from Florence, Savonarola."

Capponi jumped in his chair. "What!" He saw what Niccolo was getting at. They had a secret weapon—if they could manage to wield it.

The two—the grizzled ambassador and the bright young man—talked rapidly for over an hour, and from their discussion the outlines of a plan arose. It would be tricky and dangerous. The risks would be substantial and the price of failure unthinkable. To Capponi would fall the greater share of the plan's execution, but Niccolo would be entrusted with the single most delicate phase of the entire operation—securing the cooperation of the fiery preacher, Girolamo Savonarola.

Capponi sat back with a look of satisfaction on his face. Renewed vigor seemed to flow into his tired body. For the first time, he suddenly noticed that his spy and coconspirator was soaking wet. "Jesus Christ, Machiavelli, go downstairs and dry off by the fire before you catch your death. And get something to eat! And send Valori and the others in on your way out. Now get out of here, there's work to be done!"

"One more thing," said Niccolo before leaving. "Charles is grossly lecherous. He demands a different woman every night, an Italian woman. You might think about that. You might be able to use it."

Then, trailing water on the marble behind him with every step, he made his way to the door and out.

In the days that followed, Niccolo met several times with the friar to sound him out. He realized he could not ask him, as one might ask a politician, to go to Charles and lie outright. Nor could he make "suggestions" that a more ambitious man would eagerly seize upon. Duping him was out of the question. What then? Niccolo felt certain that Savonarola was incapable of treachery and that personal ambition was alien to him. Of all the things the prophet might or might not do for or to Florence, he would never hand her over to her enemies. He would never betray her.

The same could not be said for Piero de' Medici, the ostensible ruler of the Florentine republic. During the first week in November, the French army attacked the fortress of Fivizzano on the Tuscan border, at the outer rim of the Florentine defensive network. As he had done at Mordano, Charles made another example. Piero's declared neutrality quickly turned to a fervent embrace of the French cause in Italy, and without bothering to tell the Signoria or consult with anyone, he made a beeline for the French camp.

For weeks Charles had been sending emissaries to Florence with a series of demands, which most Florentines considered inconsistent with their independence and their basic human dignity. Florence was critical to Charles's designs because of her strategic location. He was sure that none of the states to the north represented a danger to him. They were his allies, but Florence, in the center of Italy, was a question mark. It was vital for Charles to secure her cooperation, one way or another, to protect his rear flank as he marched south to Naples. He could not allow Florence to remain neutral. Either she was with him or against him, either she cooperated or she would be destroyed. Many of Charles's advisers, well aware of the magnificent riches the city harbored, were actively urging the latter course.

Piero de' Medici met Charles at the fort of Sarzana, just seven miles north of the city walls. The French sneered openly at his cowardice and the absurd eagerness with which he hastily gave in to Charles on every point. He ceded the two Tuscan ports of Pisa and Livorno, the mighty trading city's only outlets to the sea. He ceded the entire peripheral ring of Tuscan fortresses, to be occupied by Charles until his "little enterprise" was complete. He agreed to pay the enormous sum of 200,000 ducats to help finance the invasion of Naples. In short, he gave the city away. All he got in return was a lukewarm endorsement from Charles, a noncommittal recognition that he, Piero, was the legitimate ruler of the city.

In Piero's absence, Capponi moved quickly. He assembled a council of all those who had recently held the highest public offices and of those who had been nominated to do so. It was a coming together of Florence's political elite. This Council of One Hundred unanimously passed a motion to end the Medici tyranny and return to a popular, republican form of government. It was at this time, too, that Capponi began the clandestine distribution of arms to the populace at large. When the Medici prince returned to Florence, they would be ready for him.

News of Piero's abject betrayal preceded him into the city. Indignation rose in the throats of French and anti-French factions alike. Again, and louder and more insistent than ever, shouts of "*Popolo e libertá!*" filled the air.

Niccolo had little time for participation in the sporadic street violence that was breaking out with increasing frequency, because now things were coming to a head. Piero had returned to Florence the night before and was due at the Signoria to make his report. Niccolo had deliberately gone out of his way to station himself at a corner along the route between the Via Larga, where the Medici palace stood, and the Signoria. He wanted to see the coward in what could well be his final hour.

A small contingent of guards in a phalanx proceeded on foot through the Piazza del Duomo with the usual display of pomp and circumstance. It was greeted with shouts of scorn and derision. Piero, looking splendid at the center of the wedge, was oblivious to the cries of the vulgar mob and responded with only a disdainful sneer. He was above it all. He had just averted disaster by concluding an honorable treaty with the barbarian invaders, and he fully expected the city to prostrate itself before him on that account. As his father, Lorenzo the Magnificent, had done so many times, he had saved the city of Florence. Almond-eyed, long-haired Piero had selected a most spectacular outfit for this day; it too was calculated to remind the city of her debt to his father, Lorenzo. It was Lorenzo's "tournament dress," consisting of a white silk cape bordered in scarlet. Under the cape, he wore a magnificent black velvet surcoat, heavily encrusted with pearls. His hat, too, was worked in pearls, although Piero seemed to remember that the pearls looked bigger and were more thickly encrusted when his father wore the thing.

As the Medici party passed, Niccolo fell into step behind them.

He could not stifle his laughter when his eyes chanced on the motto emblazoned on the back of Piero's cape. The hedonistic watchword of Lorenzo the Magnificent seemed oddly out of place on the shoulders of his son, given the circumstances, even if they were done in rubies and gold thread—*Le temps Revient*—"Good times are here again."

Piero's arrogance seemed to swell visibly when he and his group of bodyguards entered the Piazza della Signoria. The formidable building itself loomed dark and unforgiving against the grey sky. As they approached, the dense wedge of soldiers divided to allow Piero to enter the building first. As his foot touched the bottom step, bells suddenly began to ring. A cacophony was unleashed. Tiny clinking bells and pealing bells and the huge, ancient groaning bells of the cathedral all exploded together in sound much to Piero's amazement, while simultaneously, from within, the gates of the communal palace were slammed in his face.

Piero gallantly drew his sword and then just stood there, dumbfounded. From the windows of the Signoria, they hissed insults down at him. They insulted his manhood. They insulted his mother. The first stone took his hat off, and a hail of others quickly followed. The guards made an attempt to shield Piero as best they could while a steady, drumming chorus of "*Popolo e libertá!*" was rising all around them. Under a rain of abusive language and hostile missiles, they pulled back, but they were confronted by an angry mob behind them. They fought their way to the church of Orsanmichele, where they found shelter for a few minutes, until reinforcements could be sent for. It was only with great difficulty that Piero, baffled by the ingratitude of his people, made his way back to the Medici palace relatively unscathed.

In later years, when drunk, Niccolo was not above boasting that he had thrown the first stone, the one that took the tyrant's hat off. But just as the melee was getting underway, he was forced to cease and desist. Duty called, and he remembered that he had an important message for Capponi. Making his way around the communal palace, he was admitted by a side door.

As he expected it would be, the Council of One Hundred was in session, and Niccolo waited patiently in Capponi's chambers. He could hear the noisy proceedings through the walls. Voices were being raised, not in heated debate, but in unanimous proclamation. Capponi was carrying the day.

Upon being made aware of Niccolo's arrival, the nimble little man absented himself from the council for a few brief minutes. He conferred with his young protégée only long enough to learn what he had to know and instantly returned inside. A motion was set forth to send an embassy to the French king to make clear the position of the city of Florence and to repudiate the promises of the cowardly Piero de' Medici. At Capponi's insistence, with his assurances, and over the profound misgivings of many dissenters, it was finally agreed that that embassy should be headed by Girolamo Savonarola.

In a flurry of excitement and emotion, many other decrees were issued that day, including the banishment of Piero de' Medici, who, along with his family, was forbidden ever to approach within a hundred miles of Florence, upon pain of death. To make matters perfectly clear, a reward of four thousand florins was posted for his head.

At nightfall, like thieves or common criminals, Piero and his family fled the city. His brother Giovanni, the flatulent cardinal, remained behind for that night only. Disguised as a monk, Giovanni worked feverishly to squirrel away whatever he could of his father's priceless treasures, his works of art and his library. He hid them in churches and in the houses of friends. Satisfied that he had salvaged what he could, Giovanni too fled, to join his brother in Bologna.

For the first time in over sixty years, Florence was out from under the yoke of Medici rule. The two cousins of Piero, defrauded of their inheritance by Lorenzo the Magnificent, however, remained in Florence. They tore the Medici balls from the walls of their houses and changed their last name to Popolano—"of the People."

18

A Miraculous Delivery

It is one of the great ironies of history that Florence prided herself, above all other cities, on the attainments of her humanistic culture and learning. Yet, in a century when that culture was at its peak, Florence, the very seat of humanistic endeavor, chose as her representative, not a man of learning, not a scholar or a philosopher, but a prophet. Like the saintly Pope Leo who, a thousand years before, stood alone between Attila the Hun and the annihilation of Christendom, Girolamo Savonarola went forth on behalf of his city to meet the new scourge of God. The phantasmagoric quality of the Tuscan countryside where the meeting was to take place—its ragged hills shrouded in the mists and drizzle of early November—did little to dispel the anxiety and mystery that hung in the air.

Both sides had cause for concern, for what was about to take place was in a realm beyond the merely rational, beyond the size of armies and the comparative weight of firepower. The Italians had little idea what their inscrutable ambassador would actually say and do. For their part, many of the French felt the same way about their voluble king.

A wide circle had been cleared in front of the royal tents, and when the Florentine embassy arrived, Savonarola dismounted and stood in its center. Like a lightning rod, he attracted the tension and the emotion of the crowd. All eyes were on him as he stood ramrod stiff and awaited the pleasure of the son of the Spider. Soon, the twisted Charles scuttled out of his tent and stood before the preacher. For a moment, neither spoke. Then Savonarola lifted his hands, and, in a sacerdotal voice, intoned the words, "And so at last, O King, thou hast come!"

Charles burst into tears. He fell to his knees in the mud and kissed the hem of the holy man's garment. The first round went to the Florentines.

Savonarola raised the groveling king to his feet and addressed him. The voice and the power to cow an audience of thousands was directed entirely at one man, and at extremely close range. "You have come as a minister of God, the minister of justice. We receive you with joyful hearts and a glad countenance. We know that through you, Jehovah will abase the pride of the proud, that He will exalt the humility of the humble, that He will crush vice and exalt virtue, make straight all that is crooked, renew the old, and reform what has become deformed. Come then, glad, secure, triumphant! We welcome you in the name of He who died on the Cross!"

Charles was ecstatic, and he wept copiously at the words he heard. Savonarola had just confirmed the divine nature of his mission. The most holy of prophets had approved and welcomed him with open arms.

Savonarola continued in a voice that was not plaintive, but hortatory. He was as much as issuing instructions when he told the French king that Florence had entrusted herself to the mercy of God and that Charles, as God's chosen instrument, could do little but accept that sacred trust and agree to extend that mercy. Savonarola apologized for those who had resisted the mighty king's advance, saying that they were the black of heart, who did not realize Charles was sent by God to do His work.

When the interview concluded, Charles, still weeping, withdrew to the solitude of his tent to contemplate, once again, the miracle of his own divine election, now verified by the most holy of men on earth.

It was then that the bickering over details fell to the more mortal and hardheaded ambassadors. The French generals were furious as their dreams of plunder evaporated before their eyes. Hoping to salvage something of their greedy plans, they insisted, quite correctly, that it was and had always been Charles's intention to march into Florence with the entire army. As strange as it may seem, that was exactly what the Florentines wanted, and they quickly conceded. The details—including the exact cost of Charles's "mercy"—were to be worked out later, after the triumphant entry into the city.

The king had trembled before Savonarola! Capponi, who was in the embassy sent to Charles, was elated and returned to Florence anxious, but confident. To finalize plans for the grand march into the city and to coordinate the Florentine end of the reception with the French arrival, he left one of his assistants behind, the only one with any direct knowledge of the composition of the French army—Niccolo Machiavelli.

Niccolo's duties consisted in working closely with a bizarre coterie of individuals, not soldiers or ambassadors, but designers, choreographers, and directors, whose sole charge it was to arrange the parades, triumphs, and other spectacles that serve to dramatize the power of a huge invading army under a divinely anointed king. As he had suspected, everything was being arranged for effect. But he and Capponi had reasoned that the way that military might is displayed on parade is far different from the way it is deployed on the field of battle. The king's costume designers and theatrical men, with their flair for the dramatic, had indeed concocted an edifying spectacle, one guaranteed to strike terror in the hearts of the average Florentine citizen. But a military planner would have done things very differently.

Before hastening back to Florence with assurances for Capponi that all was proceeding according to plan, Niccolo was conducted on a grand tour of the French army, and details of costuming and formation were pointed out to him. The theatre men were proud of what they had accomplished, the parade to end all parades. Niccolo made only one suggestion which they embraced eagerly, immediately seeing the wisdom of it.

"Those grimy men with the cannons, can't you get them dressed up in something more respectable?"

"Oh, the bombadiers," gushed one of his escorts, "Oh, they are dreadful, they are surly, mean men. They absolutely refuse, and in the most vulgar way, to do anything even marginally respectable. Yet, Charles cherishes them, and they do as they please."

Niccolo shook his head. "The way I see it, they're a black spot in the parade. I mean, you look at them and you think you've got an army of beggars and ruffians. They're greasy, they're uncouth. Suppose some fetching Florentine concludes they are the flower of French manhood? Just suppose. And how do you think they're going to conduct themselves in the city, in a manner consistent with inspiring fear and respect in the Italians?" He made little clicking sounds with his mouth, indicating his sad disapproval.

The heads of the French theatre men bobbed in agreement. "Yes,

yes, something had to be done about them." They commended Niccolo on his taste and discrimination. They murmured: "There's a future for you in the theatre, young man, there is, oh, yes, there is."

Charles's entry into Florence on November 17 was more spectacular and frightening than even Niccolo had cared to imagine. For one thing, the consummate showmen of the French king had decided to stage the triumphal march at night, by torchlight. The effect was eerie. The gleaming surfaces of innumerable blades and armor everywhere caught the glint of red-orange torchlight and flashed like phantom daggers in the blackness. The wet, sweaty faces of the enemy too, glowed with the same satanic light. They looked like legions of ruddy demons marching straight from the jaws of hell.

They entered at the Porta San Frediano and marched down the Via Larga to the Piazza del Duomo, where Charles was scheduled to hear mass at the conclusion of the spectacle. Infantrymen with their heralds passed, six thousand Swiss, six thousand French. Columns of French cavalry and light horse followed. The manes and ears of the huge warhorses were cropped short, so they looked like monsters—hideous, diabolical, and unnatural. When their strutting, iron-shod hooves struck the paving stones, sparks flew out.

Companies of German pikemen passed with their erect lances as tall as trees. Then came Niccolo's favorites, the Scots and the English and Breton bowmen. After that, the royal bodyguard, whose shiny silk capes seemed wrapped around them like sheets of fire in the torchlight. They threw off fantastic shadows that loomed and cavorted off the walls over their heads.

Finally came King Charles, under a canopy of white and blue silk. He wore gilded armor, a cloak of cloth-of-gold, and a magnificent crown on his head. So bedecked with burnished gold was he, so swathed in its fiery glow, that his diminutive stature and his monstrosity were not even detectable to the untrained eye. One detail was not lost on the Florentines, however, despite the distortions of the torchlight and the phantasms it conjured in the night. Charles carried his lance upraised, at rest. It was the traditional pose of a conqueror entering a defeated city.

While the sounds of company upon company of horses and men marching in lockstep were intimidating indeed, the noise that brought up the rear of the procession was even more frightening. To put fear into the hearts of the Florentines, Charles, the conqueror, had brought his artillery with him. Thirty-nine bronze cannons rattled past with a horrible din. The gun carriages upon which they were mounted had wheels rimmed with iron hoops and studded with iron spikes for traction in soft ground. On the irregular, polished stones of a city street, those wheels found little purchase, and so the carriages jumped and skidded, kicking up showers of sparks. The carriages were drawn by huge, high-strung black chargers, who were almost invisible against the darkness. What the frightened onlookers saw then were ghostly gleaming cylinders of bright metal, careening through the night, seemingly propelled by some demonic force, threatening death and destruction from their wild, lurching muzzles.

While most of Florence was awed by the sight of these fearsome, shining weapons and by the deafening roar as they clattered past, Niccolo Machiavelli was grinning broadly. He had stationed himself on a low wall, where a number of bright torches had been placed. They threw a small pool of light onto the street in which the phantom army enjoyed a moment of illumination before plunging again into darkness. The horses drawing the gun carriages moved at a good clip, so that those attending them and manning the guns had to jog alongside to keep up the pace. As they passed rapidly in review through Niccolo's spotlight, he noted how exquisitely costumed they were—velvet and fur, plumes and braids. He could see their faces plainly. They were not the grizzled, unshaven faces of the veteran bombadiers, but the downy cheeks of young boys. They cut fine figures, loping gracefully along. The theatre men had done their jobs well.

Jumping down from his perch, and dusting off his clothes, Niccolo hustled into a deserted side street and headed for the cathedral. He was humming to himself and thinking how perfectly it had gone. Cannons inside. Bombadiers outside. And he had banked on the fact that no one would want hulking, clumsy supply wagons and lumbering oxcarts in a parade. The result: Cannons inside. Ball and powder outside. The advanced technology of death at Charles's disposal had been effectively neutralized. These solid walls of Florence were safe, at least for a while. Rubbing his hands together, Niccolo savored the victory. He was nearly dancing in the street when a loud blast put an abrupt end to his little private celebration. He stiffened. There was another blast, and a fierce light broke in the sky overhead. Then the tension drained out of him and he laughed out loud at his own stupidity. Of course, the fireworks!

As he approached the Duomo, Niccolo began to observe isolated groups of French soldiers being directed to their billetings by obliging, even ingratiating Florentine citizens. They were herded into taverns, shepherded into quiet streets where temporary wine shops had been set up and willing women gathered. They were being courted, caressed, soothed by these most gracious, most hospitable citizens.

This had been Capponi's idea. The main square before the cathedral, while spacious, could not even begin to accommodate all of Charles's enormous army, not to mention the numerous Florentines who turned out to gawk. So, as the invincible army poured into the square at one end, they were siphoned off at the other, and diverted into the complicated maze of narrow, nameless streets, a few in this direction, a few in that. Captains and lieutenants were separated from their companies. Of course, they would require more sumptuous lodgings than ordinary soldiers, something befitting their rank and dignity. Fighting units were split up. The walls of men Niccolo had seen advancing on Mordano were being taken apart, brick by brick, and scattered throughout the city.

Niccolo ran into a company of befuddled German *landsknechts* being tugged along by two urchins making lewd promises with winks and sign language. The lances the Germans carried were over twelve feet long and designed to be planted in the earth to unseat a charging horseman in the open field. In a street less than eight feet wide, these formidable weapons were a useless impediment. In the narrow, cramped streets with their overhanging balconies, it was difficult to hold the lance aloft and impossible to lower it. Niccolo was amused at their plight, and he knew things would only get worse when the Germans were drunk.

By the time the end of the long parade drew up at the cathedral, the bulk of the vast French army was already dispersed throughout the city. The mighty flood had been diverted into a hundred meandering streams and a thousand rivulets. The rush of its destructive power had been reduced to a million trickles that seeped into the farthest and darkest corners of the tangled network of Florence's streets and alleys.

Niccolo reached the Piazza del Duomo just as Charles was making his entrance. The people were cheering wildly, not because they liked Charles, but because they liked a good show. It was a lesson the Medici had taught them. But the cheers turned to gasps and murmurs when the French king dismounted. Under the bright white light from the fireworks display, his defects were manifest for all to see. He could not hide the crumpled body or his crooked, crablike walk. As he hopped up the stairs to the cathedral, his flat feet flopping on the pavement, many saw him for the poisonous toad that he was.

Niccolo scrutinized the buildings surrounding the square. There was not a sign that every rooftop was a garrison, every window a lookout post or an archer's perch. And he knew it was the same throughout the city: every blunt tower and jutting balcony was manned, some by professional soldiers, many by armed citizens, all ready to fight to the death if the need arose. As long as Charles remained in Florence, they would be at their posts. The trap was set. Whether it would be sprung or not was still a matter to be decided.

With Charles safely deposited in the cathedral, where he was to hear a mass of thanksgiving, the long evening was almost over. After the ceremony, he would be conducted to the Medici Palace, which, being now bereft of inhabitants, had been reserved for the accommodation of the French royal party. Niccolo hurried to the Signoria for a final word with Capponi. The entire building was ablaze with light. People were running everywhere, bringing news, carrying messages. The makeshift government was working overtime.

Capponi actually jumped up and embraced his de facto secretary when Niccolo let himself into his study. They congratulated each other, and the old diplomat reported that the plan to disperse the army was proceeding splendidly. In triumph, he declared, "The mighty beast that threatened us, Machiavelli, is now a squirming, formless body without a head."

"We did it," said Niccolo.

"Half of it, anyway," sighed Capponi. "It depends on what Charles says tomorrow. What demands he decides to press. That will spell the difference between peace and bloodshed."

"And the men are in position?"

"As many as we could muster. Close to ten thousand, all told. But half of them are untrained. Still, shooting down on them from the walls in our narrow streets, we stand a chance. In the field, we'd be slaughtered outright."

"The walls are safe too," added Niccolo. "I saw the 'bombadiers.' They're mostly pages and cup bearers, pretty young pups, but they wouldn't know the first thing about firing a cannon. Besides, they have nothing to fire, no powder and no balls!"

"No balls, indeed," seconded Capponi. "No balls whatsoever! No French balls! No Medici balls!" And they clapped each other in another embrace.

Coming to himself and wiping the tears of laughter from his eyes, Capponi said, "Machiavelli, do me one more favor tonight before you go home."

"At your disposal," said Niccolo with a curt bow.

"Her," said Capponi, jerking his head and indicating the recess at the far end of the study.

In his excitement, Niccolo had not noticed "her" before, but now he saw that she was exquisite. She was not so much seated upon as draped across a cushioned bench in an insolent slouch. When she stood up, there was an incredible languor in her movements. "Cleopatra," thought Niccolo, "or Jezebel."

"What do you want me to do with the lady?" asked the young Florentine.

"Escort her," was Capponi's reply.

"The honor is all mine," said Niccolo beaming, bowing again.

"The honor is not all yours," corrected Capponi. "This honor belongs to the king of France."

Niccolo was taken by surprise, and his mouth dropped open for a second. Then he recovered. Understanding dawned. This was the woman, the sacrificial lamb to be impaled on the altar of Charles's lust for the good of the fatherland. A quick inspection, however, sufficed to assure him that the lamb was anything but innocent and docile.

Her hair had been shaved back a few inches or so to raise the hair line and add hauteur and authority to the forehead. It was a good job, noted Niccolo, and done very recently. No stubble. The hair itself was pulled back severely, almost painfully and constructed into a magnificent edifice intertwined with jewels and ribbons. Against the prevailing fashion, she had not stiffened the headdress with gum, but allowed her inky black curls to tumble down, loose and lush about her shoulders.

She had full, sensuous features and green, unnerving eyes. Her mouth looked inviting, but it was easy to see that the invitation was mixed with scorn. Her complexion was white, but not a deadly white, not the washed-out white obtained with "beautifying water," but a bright white, an eerie, glowing white that Niccolo concluded was natural—unless of course she had also bleached and treated her exposed neck, shoulders, and hands. The oversized pearls that graced her bosom and disappeared in the soft fold between her breasts were scarcely discernible against her skin.

Niccolo's greedy eyes followed the plunge of the pearls to where the extreme décolletage revealed the tops of dark nipples. He wondered if they were rouged like her lips. The deep, rich color stood out intensely against the pallor of her skin, as if all the blood in her body was concentrated in her lips and nipples and in her glossy fingernails.

Niccolo remarked her small, even infinitesimal, waist but below that, he could only speculate as to what pleasures lurked. Nevertheless, her dress was cut and she moved in such a way as to invite that speculation. When she approached, Niccolo was enveloped in a cloud of intoxicating perfume.

"Faustina," Capponi was saying. "This is Monna Faustina." Niccolo accepted the hand she gracefully offered. It was cold. Before they left, he helped her with her long, shimmering cape. It was made from the shiny fur of a black wolf.

Out in the street, Niccolo offered her his arm. She gave him a disparaging glance, but then accepted. He made several attempts at conversation, but she did not respond. He was in a hurry, but she tarried, strolling and refusing to keep up the pace he was trying to set. Several times, he had to stop and wait for her. She greeted his huffing and impatience with a look of sly, arrogant bemusement.

She was being impossible, and he suspected she was doing it deliberately, to tease him. Wanting to make a speedy end to the evening, he decided to puncture her bubble of disdain and superiority. "How long have you been in this line of work?" he asked.

"Is it work?" she shot back.

"Do you get paid?"

"Do you?"

And so it went. Maddening. "You're a friend of Capponi? How long have you known him?"

Suddenly her expression changed to one of bewilderment. She bit her lip and looked him in the eyes. In a low, strangled voice, she said, "Piero Capponi is my father."

Niccolo was stunned into silence. How could he! His own daughter! He had to look away. When his eyes found the girl again though, there was laughter and mockery in her face. "You believed it!" she said. "Are you always so gullible?"

Niccolo was furious. But she was smiling at him now. Having demonstrated that she had the upper hand, she was willing to engage him. They talked as they went along, although their discussion was more of a sparring match than a friendly exchange of ideas.

"He's got six toes!" exclaimed Niccolo, proudly producing his piece of inside information.

"I've got ten."

"On each foot! You're going to sleep with a monster," he taunted. "Hunchbacked, deformed."

"I've done worse things," she said nonchalantly. He believed her. It was with a sense of relief that Niccolo finally left her at the gates of the Medici palace. The entire building was festooned with the blue-and-white banners of France. She was admitted by French guards and, with no apparent concern or trepidation, she went calmly to meet the French king. Despite her allure and her lascivious sensuality, Niccolo did not envy Charles this night. She was a wolf in wolf's clothing. He made a mental note to ask Capponi where he had ever found such a woman.

Charles VIII of France did not put in an appearance the next day at the Signoria to negotiate a settlement with the Florentines. Nor the day after, nor the day after that. He was busy enjoying himself in the Medici apartments. He had already located jewels, vases, and priceless paintings that were being crated for shipment back to France. Among other things, he found a whole unicorn's horn and parts of two others. These he kept with him for emergencies. When ground, the horn made a powerful aphrodisiac. If kept intact, it could be used to detect the presence of poison.

As the days stretched into a week, then two weeks, the tensions in the city were palpable. There were scuffles and sporadic outbreaks of violence between soldiers and citizenry, but still, Charles dismissed all invitations to meet with officials and did not seem even to be entertaining the thought of leaving. It was at this time that, in a burst of erudition and cleverness, Charles took to punning on the famous three-word message that Julius Caesar sent back to the Roman Senate from Gaul—*Veni. Vidi. Vici.* "I came. I saw. I conquered." Charles insisted that he had reversed the terms of Caesar's procedure. He was fond of saying he came, he conquered, but so effortless and swift had that conquest been, that he had not had time to see. Now he wanted to look around. "*Veni. Vici. Vidi.*" became a capital joke in French circles.

Finally, with the weather getting worse every day, Charles decided it was time to forge on to the sunny climes, sea breezes, and orange blossoms of Naples. Capponi called the Council of One Hundred into session, and Charles appeared before them, but it was not the Charles who had only days earlier had prostrated himself at the feet of the great prophet. This Charles was testy and petulant. He was not thinking of the global and apocalyptic repercussions of his descent into Italy, but of the practical problems. He was making unreasonable demands again.

In front of Capponi and the others, he had a herald read the treaty he had drawn up. It was in most respects the same treaty Piero de' Medici had agreed to sign, with the same humiliating conditions—surrender of the fortresses and ports and payment of the enormous sum of 200,000 ducats. But going beyond that, Charles claimed overlordship of the city and, as a condition of his overlordship, he demanded the restoration of Piero de' Medici!

Having discussed this with his advisers, the French were in unanimous agreement that a fawning Piero, dependent on French power to maintain his position, was infinitely preferable to a volatile and unpredictable republic. Besides which, the new Charlemagne, with dreams of extending his empire to the ends of the earth, had little sympathy for sniveling, small-minded republics. Emperors and republics did not mix well.

As his conditions were being read, Charles played nervously with the many rings on his twisted fingers. Cries of outrage began to rise from the Florentine assembly. The normally unflappable Capponi was red with rage. In a single tremendous movement, he leapt over the huge conference table, bounded to the speaker's platform, and seized the offensive treaty from the hands of the herald. Holding it aloft for all his compatriots to see, he defiantly tore it to pieces.

Charles gasped. Then, like a wounded animal, he shrieked something in French. His translator addressed Capponi: "He says the treaty must be signed, or he will order his trumpeters to call out the troops and they will sack the city without mercy."

Quivering with agitation, Capponi shouted back, "If you sound your trumpets, we will ring our bells!" There was a roar of approval from the assembly.

Breathing hard, Capponi glared at Charles. In an even, but menacing, voice he said, "Every able-bodied man in Tuscany is armed, is within the city walls, and is willing to shed his blood. All I have to do is raise the alarm. If the bells ring, they will respond as one.

"And where is your army, mighty King? Where are your commanders? Your men? Have you seen them? Sound your trumpets! I dare you. Your soldiers are too scattered and too drunk to hear them. And I have fifty thousand men ready to descend upon them as they lie sleeping and cut their throats!" He bluffed.

The king hesitated. He faltered. Then Savonarola stood up. The friar drew a silver crucifix from his bosom and held it high in the air. Charles cringed and fell back like a vampire trying to ward off the power of the sacred object.

Like a volcanic eruption, the preacher exploded: "God has chosen you, O King, to do great deeds, to reform the church and forge the Christian republic. Why then, do you linger here?

"Your work here is done. You have liberated this great city from the grasp of a tyrant. Go forth now, to Rome, and Naples. Be about your Father's business."

Charles was dazed, stupefied by this injunction. His eyes were fixed in awe on the trembling figure of the prophet. His mouth hung open, far more so than usual. Tears streamed down his cheeks. Muttering something to his advisers, the mighty king hurriedly fled the room and the terrible, accusatory gaze of God's personal spokesman.

Within hours, the task of assembling the dispersed, dissipated army began. Soldiers straggled toward the city gates. Many had lost their weapons and uniforms gambling, or had been deprived of them in a drunken stupor. After eleven days of occupation, the ferocious army was leaving with no more than the loss of ten lives on both sides. In order to save face, Charles had instructed his advisers to stand firm on a demand of 120,000 ducats from the Florentine treasury to cover his expenses. Of course, the Florentines graciously acquiesced, and, of course, the sum was never paid.

19

The City of God on Earth

Si stava meglio quando si stava peggio.

"We were better off when we were worse off."
—Tuscan proverb

There were angels in the street. Again. Niccolo didn't care for the angels. When the angels appeared, that usually meant trouble was brewing, and this morning there was a veritable flurry of angelic activity. Unable to concentrate on his studies, Niccolo looked idly out the window at them. What he was reading, Roman history, seemed meaningless with the angels in the streets. Once he had thought that Roman history could help him understand Florence. Now he wasn't so sure. Once he could think of Florence as the Roman republic, reincarnated. Now she was more like Israel under the judges.

And severe judges they were. A friend of his had been imprisoned and tortured—for gambling! For betting on a cockfight! A woman in the neighborhood had been accused of blasphemy and had her tongue slit open. Astrologers had been burned at the stake. Well, he had to admit, a case could be made for that. Arguably, they deserved it. But last week, the ax had fallen closer to home, and he was still infuriated by the incident. He himself had been fined, heavily fined, for eating meat on Friday.

He had no money, no job, no prospects of employment. He was almost thirty years old. His mother had died recently, and his father had gone into a deep depression. In fact, the entire family was in a kind of stupor. Everyone around him was morose. To make matters worse, most of his friends were gone. Pagolo was in Rome. Callimaco had trailed off after the French army, doing what he could to patch up the torn and broken bodies left in its wake. Biagio had gotten married. And

Niccolo Machiavelli was here, sad, bitter, and alone, unable to concentrate, watching the angels.

Where had things gone wrong? Less than two years ago, they all had been so full of high hopes. The winds of change had scoured the city. It was intoxicating. The son of the Spider scuttled out of Florence, leaving her virtually untouched. The hateful, craven Piero was banished forever, and the city was free—free from foreign domination, free from tyranny. Niccolo never tired of reliving those heady, exhausting days. And how many times had he charted and reconstructed the fateful chain of events that led from those moments of optimism and exhilaration to the present impasse?

He doodled now, as he went over it all once again in his mind. He had written out the names of the most important players, arranged in chronological order—Medici, Charles, Capponi, Soderini, Valori. Over them all, in a thick, angry hand, he had scrawled, SAVONAROLA.

It was all his fault. And it wasn't. As events had unrolled, the friar had become more and more mysterious, and more and more dangerous. On the eve of the French departure, he was acclaimed the miracle-working savior of Florence. Although Niccolo knew that the miracle was not as outright and effortless as it seemed to the popular imagination, Savonarola was nonetheless held solely responsible for saving the city from the French scourge. The people accepted the friar as their undisputed leader. He took the pulpit in all his glory. Niccolo still remembered his joyous declaration. "I announce this good news to the city, that Florence will be more splendid, richer, more powerful than she has ever been. Glorious in the sight of men and of God! From you, O Florence, renewal will begin and rebirth will spread everywhere, because you are the navel and the womb of Italy!"

Everyone believed him. Anything seemed possible. He could have made himself king if he had wanted to. But he didn't. He brought forth his treatise on the governing of Florence. He worked hand in hand with hardheaded, practical men, with politicians like Pagol' Antonio Soderini. And the Consiglio Maggiore was finally established—the Great Council. It was the pride of Florence, the largest body of elected officials in history—over three thousand representatives from every quarter and every walk of life.

Niccolo could still remember the ringing of hammers the day they tore the old Council Chamber apart. People cheered in the streets as saws chewed through the timbers and massive blows knocked out stone walls and splintered wooden partitions. In the days of the Medici, the chamber held only three hundred handpicked representatives. It had gradually evolved into a Byzantine labyrinth of rooms and antechambers clustered around a central common area. Business was conducted and policy made in the privacy of these screened off, partitioned, and closetlike confession booths where sins and abominations were whispered. Bodyguards were kept close at hand, behind the scenes, and assassins lurked in the recesses. Then, reform swept away the architecture of secrecy. A vast, lighted space was created for free and open discussion.

New blood flowed into the sclerotic governing bodies. The old names were still there, of course. The interests of the primati, Florence's finest and oldest families, were well represented. And the men they sent to the council had experience, for better or worse, of politics. But new men also sat beside them now, representing new and broader interests.

Reforms followed. Men known to be in debt were excluded from public office. A new system of taxation went into effect, based on wealth and property. All of this with no bloodshed, no call to arms, no rioting in the streets. All because of the friar. He had acted as the peacekeeper. He had forced the lion to lie down with the lamb. He had established a truly representative assembly, an enormous council, the only one of its kind in all the world. He had set up the vast and complicated machinery of government—and then, quite inexplicably, he had walked away from it. He had given Florence a government worthy of her. He had created it. He saw that it was good. And confident of having created a new order that would endure with the help of the Lord, the friar turned his attentions once again to his real mission—moral reform.

Ruefully, Niccolo remembered how the friar had gradually distanced himself from the day-to-day workings of the council. When two years of bad harvests produced widespread starvation and demanded immediate action, he preached exclusively a doctrine of trust in the Lord. When unemployment stirred up discontent in the working classes, the friar was preaching against sodomy. When the revenue system faltered and Florence was being threatened from without by earthly enemies, Savonarola turned his eyes heavenward.

From his knowledge of history and a close observation of the doings in his own city, Niccolo concluded that the friar's greatest strength, his faith, was also his greatest weakness. It prevented him from doing practical things like controlling elections and packing the council. Savonarola was convinced that moral reform was sweeping the land, making men righteous, and that righteous men would act and govern righteously. He pushed that moral reform. He preached it fervently and from the heart. He exhorted men daily to righteous behavior. He believed they were listening to him and following his advice. He thought a new age of justice and holiness was being born. But he gave the Florentines more credit than they deserved.

Left to its own devices, without strong leadership and direction, the Great Council had degenerated into a hundred bitter, bickering factions. In the face of mounting problems at home and abroad, the legislative process was stalled. The golden age was put on hold.

Savonarola still exerted tremendous moral authority, and he still held the populace in thrall, most of it anyway. But the results of his two years of leadership were not what he or anybody had expected. Despite popular support, the friar was no longer able to bring any significant pressure to bear on the badly fractured council. At the same time, he had mobilized a whole set of forces over which no one had any real control, so that now the streets were full of angels.

Niccolo's candle sputtered and went out. Lethargically, he poked his finger in the puddle of hot wax on the writing table. The day was gloomy. He was cold and stiff, and his back and shoulders ached from bending over his books too long. Grudgingly, he decided to take some air. A walk would do him good, even if it meant wrestling with the angels.

In his general state of misery, Niccolo had been neglecting his appearance. He wore the same pair of red hose for the fifth day in a row, so that they were stretched out and baggy at the knee. He was unshaven and uncombed, and he was too dispirited to care. He tucked his straggling, unwashed hair behind his ears and up under a cloth cap. He covered his lack of sartorial splendor with an old cloak and drew it tightly around himself. Pulling on the boots that he left by the door, he stepped out into the joyless streets of a city he scarcely recognized.

Noise and spectacle and celebration had always animated these streets. Now these had been banished. The entire city was like a monastery, blanketed with silence. Fasting had replaced eating as the preferred form of entertainment. And everywhere there was the incessant, low rumbling of prayer. Niccolo thought of the name he had heard given to the friar's followers. It was so apt—*masticapaternostri*, prayer chewers.

They were also called *piagnoni*, snivelers, but the fact was that, like it or not, the snivelers were having their way in the city. Niccolo once again had the sad proof of this when he passed through the Orsanmichele quarter. He loitered here a while, for old times' sake. In the area of a few square blocks there had been fifty-six taverns. It was the only neighborhood in the city where the taverns had outnumbered the churches. Now they were all closed, every single one. Niccolo had read enough Aristotle to know that this did not qualify as a bona fide "tragic" occurrence. Still, to his way of thinking, it was very, very sad.

He moped around, recalling the rowdy pleasures of yesteryear and thought about how things could have turned out differently. Two years ago, the world was at his feet. He was a trusted confidant of Capponi and was on his way up. But Capponi had not played his cards right with the new regime. His fortunes quickly waned, and with them, the hopes of his protégé. In frustration, Capponi had gone off to fight in the troublesome little war against Pisa. At his age! Now he was dead, and there was not an open tavern in the city where you could drink to his memory.

Lost in mournful self-pity, Niccolo was wandering aimlessly toward the river when he was brushed by an angel, then another. There was a whole line of them, filing out of a wealthy palazzo. They moved in step, at a jog, singing joyfully in their little, piping angelic voices. They had close-cropped hair and wore red crosses on the shoulders of their immaculate white robes. Watching them scamper past, Niccolo remembered the last time he had had the stomach to go and hear the friar preach. As powerful and as beatific as ever, he had said, "The church will be so full of love that angels will converse with men. You cannot believe how much charity and love the angels have for men. They never grow angry with us. And when they see us purged of our sins, they rejoice, and promise to remain with us always." So here they were, like the poor, always with us, Savonarola's legions of angels.

The idea of the angels had begun with the "bands of blessed boys," choristers who dressed as angles and sang Te Deums in the churches and in the increasingly frequent religious processions. But under the tutelage of Pietro Bernardino, a sniveler's sniveler, the bands of holy innocents had gradually evolved into something resembling an unofficial police force. Their jurisdiction was entirely in the area of faith and morals, and they energetically set out to track down and eradicate impiety, wherever they might find it. From singing hymns and collecting alms for the poor, they moved into espionage, reporting on their elders, and in many cases on their own parents, for gambling, for ostentatious dress, and for lascivious behavior. The angels had become notorious as guardians and enforcers of the new moral order.

The band of angels that Niccolo had just encountered seemed to have expanded their range of pious activities to include what looked suspiciously like common looting. Dancing and singing the praises of the Lord, they were carting off paintings and statues, collections of gems and silver table service as well as books, clothing, and a variety of valuable-looking things. Niccolo quickened his step and followed them. As he went along, he encountered other bands of angels, similarly laden with all manner of interesting and expensive objects. He noticed that many of the "angels" were neither young nor particularly blessed of countenance. They had mean faces, set jaws, and hard little eyes. Without the white robes, Niccolo would have taken them for hoodlums. Recent recruits, no doubt, to the angelic ranks.

They seemed to be converging on the Piazza della Signoria, the main square opposite the Communal Hall where the Great Council sat. Another public display of their frenzy for the love of Christ, thought Niccolo. "No!" he groaned out loud, unable at first to comprehend exactly what he was seeing. This was no routine display of religious frenzy. It was an execution. Of sorts.

In the center of the square, a tremendous scaffold had been erected. It was higher than most of the surrounding buildings and shaped like a pyramid. Stairs ran along its sides, up to the top and these were filled with the scurrying ranks of what looked like senior angels, archangels, Niccolo supposed, supervising the ongoing construction. Their building materials were not ordinary timber but the countless precious objects that the jubilant worker angels were hauling into the piazza.

The sight was too mawkish, too unexpected, too endlessly complicated with visual detail to be taken in at a glance. Niccolo prowled around the pyramid, letting his eyes slowly dissect the infinite, jumbled variety of the structure, detail by detail. At the base was a tangle of wigs and false beards, hairpieces, carnival masks, and gaudy costumes and disguises. Above that came the books. Moving closer, Niccolo identified Boccaccio and Petrarch and hundreds of volumes of the Latin poets. He saw a leather-and-gilt-bound edition of the works of Lorenzo de' Medici. There was Livy's *History of Rome,* a complete one tied in a bundle with twine. Niccolo wanted that book badly, and he found himself staring at it, his hand involuntarily reaching for it. The stern, unforgiving glare of an angel warned him off.

Circling slowly, Niccolo continued his inspection. He saw reams and piles of illuminated manuscripts and parchments. As a lover of antiquity, he knew that many were irreplaceable, probably the last remaining copies of important works. Many were already ruined, torn or soaking through with the perfumes, unguents, and cosmetics that were seeping down on them from above. The next layer was composed of rouge pots and pomade jars and scent bottles, along with all the toilet articles women used to apply them. There was a proliferation of combs, brushes, mirrors, veils, headdresses, and the like. Above that, lutes and harps, then chess boards, playing cards, dice, and other accoutrements of gambling.

All the while, angels continued to pour into the square, adding to the pyre as the archangels shouted orders, directing the flow of incoming merchandise. The very top had been reserved for paintings, especially paintings of female beauties in poses that seemed lewd or provocative. Niccolo shook his head in disbelief and backed off from the pile to contemplate it in its dizzying, eclectic entirety.

Someone near him was weeping, "It's such a shame; It's a sin," over and over. Without even turning to look, Niccolo identified the harsh rush of an accent as Venetian. He caught the man's eye and communicated his sympathy with a sad nod. The Venetian approached with dismay written all over his face. "Can you tell me what's happened to Florence," he begged, "Can you explain what's going on here?"

"No, I can't," was all Niccolo said.

"They call it the bonfire of the vanities," sobbed the Venetian. "At sundown they're going to light it and burn everything. It's madness! Madness! Madness!" Before Niccolo could reply and before he could restrain him, the Venetian was pushing his way through the angels, shouting, "Who's in charge here? I must speak to the man in charge."

A particularly surly archangel collared him, and with angelic menace, sneered, "Whaddaya want?"

"I'll buy it," babbled the Venetian. "I'll buy everything!" I've got 22,000 florins. I'll give it all to you. Enough to build a chapel, a whole church if you want!"

In response, one of the angels tore off the poor man's truly incredible fur hat and sailed it into the funeral pyre of the vanities. The last Niccolo saw of the well-intentioned Venetian, he had been strapped into a chair where an artist was sketching his likeness. They told him that it would be burned along with the other effigies of whores and lechers.

Distraught, Niccolo sat on a low stone bench, mesmerized by the never-ending flow of his fellow Florentines filling up the piazza, eagerly throwing the tools and devices of pleasure and beauty on their magnificent, preposterous sacrificial altar. The processions started filing in, more angels and monks crowned with olive branches. Hymns of rejoicing sounded, and bells pealed. He made himself leave before they lit the thing, too embarrassed, too bewildered, and too humiliated to see the ludicrous spectacle through to its fiery climax.

Niccolo trudged back across the river to his own neighborhood. He had to fight the crowds pushing toward the piazza, eager to get a look at the glorious bonfire. Half-consciously, he made his way toward the Piazza Santo Spirto, knowing that in these days of increasing furor and frenzy, it would be a quiet spot. The events and zeal of recent weeks had been orchestrated primarily by the monks of the Dominican order, of which Savonarola was Prior and prime mover. The Franciscans, the traditional rivals of the Dominicans in everything from the purity of dogma to the collection plate, had fallen on hard times. They were out of favor with the volatile populace and with the political leaders who thought it prudent not to oppose Savonarola and his followers too vocally. Santo Spirito, being a Franciscan church, would be exempt from the day's celebrations. It would be a haven of peace and inactivity. Or so Niccolo thought. To his chagrin, he saw the piazza buzzing with people hurrying into the church. "Not here too," he thought. "Isn't there any place where you can get away from it?"

At first he thought they might be angels intent on looting the church. But then he saw these were ordinary citizens and some friars—Franciscans. There were armed guards at the door. Caught up in the rush, Niccolo whisked past them without arousing any suspicions. People were crowding around the pulpit, but no one appeared to be preaching from there. They were pushing and shoving, craning their necks. Occasional gasps of disbelief issued from the tight knot of those closest to the speaker's platform. Shaky hands made the sign of the cross. Niccolo wormed his way through the press of bodies. He got close enough to see that a document of some sort had been nailed to the front of the pulpit. It was flanked by two brightly burning torches. Edging still closer and consumed with curiosity, he was able to make out that it was no ordinary announcement or denunciation. The abundant seals and ribbons, the profusion of red and gold and white, could mean only one thing—a papal bull.

Trying not to be overly rude, Niccolo pushed on toward the front. A papal bull was the most official of official documents, the last, dreaded word of the church, from which there was no appeal on earth, nor, according to many, in heaven. The trepidation of those milling around him was contagious. Finally, from between the rows of bobbing heads, he was able to make sense out of the dancing, flickering script. In the glowering torchlight, Niccolo read, to his amazement, that Savonarola had been excommunicated.

20

The Prophet Dishonored and a Final Interview

When word of the excommunication spread, all hell broke loose in the city. The friar's supporters were incensed, and their frenzied devotion reached frantic new heights. On the other side, with the weight of papal authority now behind them, Savonarola's enemies, so long cowed and cowering, were emboldened. The balance of power began to shift in their favor. To counteract the influence of the notorious bands of angels, squads of young men calling themselves *compagnacci*—bad boys—sprang to life. Made up mostly of the spoiled sons of wealthy families, the compagnacci waged open war in the streets against the forces of piety.

This was not the first time that trouble had arisen between Savonarola and Pope Alexander VI. From the pulpit, the friar gradually stepped up his attacks on what he saw as corruption in Rome, denouncing the church there as a disfigured harlot, worse than a beast, a sink of iniquity, and the new Babylon. Annoyed, but not exactly innocent of these charges, the pope quickly offered Savonarola a cardinal's hat to stop preaching.

The offer only fanned the flames of the friar's moral indignation, and his denunciations became more vociferous than ever. Finally, the pope was left with no choice but to issue the bull of excommunication. Implicit in the sentence of excommunication was a prohibition against Savonarola celebrating mass, administering the sacraments, and, of course, preaching.

For six months, Savonarola all but disappeared, giving rise to many rumors—he was a drunkard, he was keeping a boy, he had knuckled under to the pope, he had accepted bribes in exchange for his silence. In reality, he secluded himself to fast and pray for guidance. Suddenly, on Christmas Day 1497, he gave the pope his answer. Defying papal strictures, he celebrated mass and gave communion to the monks. In the sermon he preached that day, he left little doubt where he stood. "The thunderbolts of the church cannot strike me," he said. "I am an instrument of God, and I fear only God. Those who criticize me would do well to look at the life of their pope! Lift up this excommunication on a lance and deliver it to him in Rome, to the antichrist, Alexander. It is he, not I, who lives outside the laws of God!" Invoking a higher authority, Savonarola had, in effect, excommunicated the pope.

Sensing the danger that could come from the friar's rebelliousness if it were allowed to continue, Pope Alexander moved quickly on a number of fronts. He authorized the Franciscans in Florence to attack Savonarola from their pulpits. To the Signoria, the Great Council, he delivered an ultimatum: Either send the "earthworm" friar to Rome under guard, or have him locked up as a criminal. If these conditions were not met, and soon, the pope threatened to place all Florence under interdict.

At the mention of the word *interdict*, the Florentines trembled. They knew what it meant: no mass, no sacraments. If invoked, all offices of the church would be prohibited for the entire city. Children's souls would be denied baptism; the dying would be sent to their graves without confession and last rights, and they would risk eternal damnation. The interdict was a spiritual death warrant.

But there was another side to interdiction that was potentially even more troubling, especially to the city's temporal powers. No Christian city was permitted to engage in trade or commerce with a city under interdict. In a Christian world, this amounted to throwing up a state of economic siege. Mercantile Florence, commercial Florence, the Florence of money and bankers would be utterly ruined.

The Signoria vacillated. The compagnacci stepped up their anti-Savonarolan activities. On a Sunday when the friar was to preach in the cathedral, they smeared the pulpit with stinking, rancid grease and hung the skin of an ass around it. To buy time, the council reported to the pope that Savonarola had ceased preaching. The pope's spies told him otherwise. This state of indecision could have ended in civil war had not the pope forced the Florentine hand. In March, he ordered the arrest of Florentine merchants and bankers residing in Rome and confiscated their property. More than any threat to their spiritual well-being, this step finally goaded the reluctant Florentines into action.

Oddly enough, it was not the Signoria, but the Franciscans who took the initiative, and it was a bizarre initiative indeed. Many times, Savonarola had claimed that his words were substantiated by supernatural signs and wonders. The Franciscans called on him to prove this assertion and challenged the friar to an ordeal by fire! In a city with the most sophisticated and advanced constitution of its day, the most important legal question of the century was about to be settled by two men walking into a fire. Whoever emerged, if anybody, would be vindicated. This extraordinary turn of events had the blessing of the Great Council, who, deeply divided and with their backs against the wall, saw in it a convenient way of getting rid of Savonarola without their having to intervene and take sides. If he goes into the fire, he'll be burned. If he does not, he'll lose his support and tensions can be eased. So went the prevailing wisdom.

Niccolo saw his city convulsed and deeply divided, without effective leadership and with gangs of competing thugs running out of control. He rarely went out. When he did, everything he saw confirmed his dismal analysis—theocracy running amok and challenged only by the forces of anarchy. Reason seemed to have been banished from the republic. This was not the Earthly Paradise. This was not the New Jerusalem.

Niccolo was toying with the idea of going abroad, to Venice perhaps, or France. He could not bear to see the city he loved thus served, in the sway of maniacs and fools. The final insult was this ordeal by fire! It was insane! A barbarism from the Dark Ages! But despite his abhorrence, the tug of curiosity drew him to the event.

He had not been in the Piazza della Signoria since the night of the ignoble bonfire. The great public square of the New Athens seemed suited to only one type of activity these days—burning things. The first thing Niccolo saw was great piles of wood. He could smell the pitch and resin in which they had been soaked to make them burn more surely and furiously. Between the two rows of sticks piled ten feet high ran a gangway about thirty yards long. It was wide enough for two men to pass through, side by side.

The debates in which the "rules" for the ordeal had been fixed were, to Niccolo, an exercise in absurdity. They had taken a ludicrous idea and made it even more trivial and ridiculous. When things were at an impasse, someone actually proposed that walking across the Arno without getting wet would be just as good a miracle. Finally, both sides agreed that not Savonarola and his challenger, the Franciscan Francesco di Puglia, but two surrogates would actually undergo the ordeal. As these champions along with their supporters were preparing themselves, Savonarola seemed oddly out of touch with the proceedings. Niccolo had never seen the friar so detached and unemotional.

Meanwhile, enthusiastic last-minute challenges were being mounted. The lunatic Silvestro Maruffi, one of the friar's most rabid adherents, had taken it upon himself to argue about the details—he insisted that both men be stripped naked, as their clothes might be enchanted. Howls of indignation were raised on the Franciscan side. After considerable argument, a compromise was reached. Both men removed their clothes, and submitted them to inspection by a neutral prelate. When they were found to be free of enchantment, the monks were allowed to redress.

As the fires were about to be lit, the friar's champion picked up a crucifix and clutched it to his breast. "Profanation!" shrieked his adversaries. "The crucifix will protect him!" More debate followed. It was decided that the crucifix was out of bounds and the Dominican had to capitulate. But just as things seemed ready, he declared that he would not go into the fires unless he were allowed to take the Holy Eucharist with him! "More profanation still!" The cries were raised again and yet another round of forensic activity ensued. Hours passed in dickering. Through it all, the friar stood stock-still, the only one of those involved who seemed to maintain any dignity during the proceedings. Niccolo was watching him and thought he saw sadness in his face, a sense of infinite sadness as these lesser men quibbled like angry dogs in front of him. When the fires blazed up, Niccolo could see that Savonarola's lips were moving in the silent, barely perceptible movements of prayer.

When the flames were deemed to have attained a sufficient degree of destructive force, the champions were led to the starting line. The crowds cheered. The presiding officials looked anxious and a little embarrassed. Niccolo was turning to go, having little desire to see two men roasted alive or smell their burning flesh. Suddenly, Savonarola's head jerked to attention. He looked up at the sky. Then Niccolo felt it too. First one drop, then another. Within a minute, a cruel, drenching rain was falling. And shouts of "*Miracolo!*" filled the air.

On the day of the great ordeal, another event took place that would have an impact on all of Italy, although news of it would not reach the preoccupied Florence for a few days yet. Charles VIII of France, the new Charlemagne, the would-be emperor of all the Christians and all the Turks as well, died suddenly. His quest for glory and dominion was brought to an abrupt and ignominious end when his small head collided with a door during a fit of apoplexy.

Of the hundreds, perhaps thousands of women who had yielded to his ragged lust over the years, not a single one had conceived a child. Charles was sterile, and his royal bloodline, like his vain dreams of world domination, was without issue.

Meanwhile, back in Florence, the effect of the miracle was short-lived, in as much as its significance was open to dispute. Both sides claimed victory; both sides claimed that the rain had saved their champion. Instead of dissolving tensions in the strife-torn city, the aborted trial by ordeal only exacerbated them. Angels ransacked the palaces of the impious wealthy and the compagnacci looted convents and monasteries.

Savonarola had not proven the divine nature of his mission, and many of his supporters wavered. On Palm Sunday, again defying the ban, he celebrated mass and preached. His sermon was directed against corruption in the church, as usual, but the fire was gone from it. Niccolo attended the mass and heard the tired, lackluster sermon. The man he saw in the pulpit was a defeated man, a man waiting for the end. Out of pity and fear and friendship, he decided to go to him, perhaps for the last time.

Niccolo waited in the corridor that led from the chapel to the rectory, along the way the friar would have to pass to return to his cell. Savonarola came out of the church surrounded by a coterie of imploring, angry monks, all pushing themselves and their counsels upon him. For his part, he remained aloof, the undisturbed eye of the storm.

When Niccolo stepped forward to greet the friar, two of the young monks threw themselves on the would-be intruder. Apparently, they were expecting danger. Flustered, Niccolo wrestled with his assailants for a moment before the friar intervened on his behalf. The pugnacious young monks withdrew, and Savonarola spoke to Niccolo in a voice that was almost a whisper. "Why have you come?" he asked simply.

"To see you. To talk." Niccolo replied.

"There is nothing anyone can do," said the friar resignedly. "And this morning I don't want to talk to you. Please don't be offended. I only want to go to my cell and play the madman, the fool. I want to pray. I want to be drunk with a holy drunkenness! With frenzy for the love of Christ." His eyes shone as he talked. In a gesture of affection, he put his hand on Niccolo's and squeezed. "Now let me rest a little," he said and was gone.

Dumbfounded, Niccolo left the Priory and made his way out into the streets to await the end. He did not have long to wait. That day the rioting intensified, and among others, Francesco Valori was killed. Valori, the old compatriot of Piero Capponi, had obtained a leadership position on the Great Council through working closely with Savonarola. He was the friar's staunchest defender in the Signoria, and with his removal the last obstacle to the official censure and arrest of Girolamo Savonarola vanished.

He was prostrate before the altar with the last of his disciples, singing psalms, when they came for him. He was allowed to take his leave of his brothers and receive communion. As the *sbirri,* the rough police officers, led him through the streets, one of the men struck him from behind. "Who hit you, Prophet?" snarled the officer with blasphemous satisfaction.

Representatives of the pope were present at the trial, or the travesty of justice that passed for a trial. Using a combination of perjured witnesses and confessions elicited by torture, Savonarola and several of his followers were condemned to death for heresy. The man who had not confessed a mortal sin in over twenty years was declared guilty of a panoply of crimes that included even the spurious charge of giving communion with unconsecrated wafers.

The indictment that was being drawn up in Niccolo's mind in these days, however, was not against the friar, but against the city and the institutions and the process that had condemned him. In the end, they had acted only out of naked self-interest. The very body that this man had helped create, the Great Council, had arrested and tried him. There was no loyalty in them, only betrayal and treachery.

Niccolo's bitterness had effectively incapacitated him. Gone were his ambitions and his interests in history and politics. He had seen how it worked, once too often, and he wanted no part in this business of robbers and devils. He would take a long trip, see the world. Maybe things were better someplace else, better than in Florence, so full of promise, so hopeful, and in the end, so squalid.

There was a knock at his door and someone came in. In his lethargy, Niccolo did not even turn to see who it was. Then, he heard the sweet voice of his sister, Primerana. "There's a man downstairs asking for you, Niccolo. He seems agitated, in a hurry."

"Who is it?"

"I don't know him. But he looks too old and ugly to be one of your dear drinking companions."

"Alright," said an unwilling Niccolo, "Tell whoever it is I'm coming down."

Standing in the kitchen was a tiny, nervous man whom Niccolo had seen before. Even without his angelic robes, Niccolo recognized Pietro Bernardino, the indoctrinator of angels and the unofficial chief of the child police. Niccolo loathed him and stood there, saying nothing, eyeing Bernardino with undisguised contempt.

In a hoarse voice, the little fanatic said, "Are you Niccolo Machiavelli?"

Niccolo did not deign to answer the obvious question.

"Then please come with me. Come quickly. Everything's been arranged."

Niccolo balked at the man's presumption and his impatience. "Where do you think you're taking me?"

"Why to the friar, of course. To Savonarola. He wants to see you."

Niccolo's shock and disbelief had still not worn off when they reached the Signoria. They were admitted after an exchange of whispers, and he began the long climb to the Alberghettino, the little chamber that served as an accommodation for prisoners of distinction. Guards at the doors let him pass upon a sign from Bernardino, and Niccolo was suddenly alone with Savonarola on the eve of his execution.

The prophet was not kneeling or sitting, but huddled on a hard bench, his head resting on his knees. The great preacher who had rattled the rafters of the cathedral and made the ground tremble under a corrupt papacy was a small, harmless man again, much as he was on the first day Niccolo had met him.

Niccolo touched his shoulder, and the friar lifted his head. He was smiling. "Now we will talk," he said gently.

And he talked, for over an hour, in a fluid, lucid voice. There was no wildness or raving in him, only the calm voice of the seer, of one who has seen much and has at last determined the significance of what he has seen.

Exhausted, he asked Niccolo if he could rest, and his head sank once again to his knees. When Niccolo left him, full of the most profound misgivings, his head seething with doubts and contradictions, Savonarola was talking softly and laughing in his sleep.

Part 3

The Antichrist and His Extended Family

21

The New Pope Enjoys Bullfights

Three days after the execution, women could still be seen kneeling in silent prayer on the spot where he had been burned. They kept a constant vigil, this circle of bent, motionless guardians, clad in mourning and brooding over the blackened stones. In time, the spring rains would cleanse the spot of its stain and the tread of busy, indifferent feet would polish the stones to a tawny luster, so that they would be indistinguishable from those around them. But still, even many years later, there were those who dared not walk across the accursed, holy spot, and whether from superstition or respect, they gravely directed their steps around it, as if some reproachful specter stood barring their way.

For the third time that morning, Niccolo found himself crossing the piazza and staring at the keepers of that mournful vigil. They were, he knew, the exceptions. The rest of the city was clamoring for entertainment. The pent-up demand for drunken public celebration had exploded, and signs of high revelry were everywhere. The gates had been kept open throughout the night while a steady stream of oxcarts laden with barrels of wine and beer rumbled into the city to supply the miraculously reopened taverns.

"How soon they forget," thought Niccolo as he identified a gang of the friar's recent and most staunch supporters—now leering ex-angels in the company of ex-reformed prostitutes who had fallen happily again by the wayside. Niccolo did not consider himself an enemy of fun and high-times, quite the contrary. It was just that the present orgiastic excesses seemed to him, well, ill timed.

More than anything else, he thought the graffiti that had cropped up everywhere on the walls and houses served as a sign of the times. One could read numerous, strident injunctions to fornicate and blaspheme, and even one joyful encouragement to practice that peculiarly "Florentine" vice: Let sodomy flourish again! The reign of the prophet, in spirit as well as in fact, had truly come to an end.

While Niccolo could not exactly condemn the merry rabble, neither could he join them. His present disposition and his memories prevented him from doing so. Oppressive thoughts weighed heavily on him, and difficult decisions demanded his attention. But most of all, still ringing in his ears were the last words of a condemned man. He did not want to think about them—not now, not yet—and still, he could not put them out of his mind. In a not entirely successful effort to do so, he had filled the last three days with a careful attention to the mundane details of life, the distracting, time-consuming mechanical details with which he had somehow managed to fill the hours between his morning headaches and his lapsing into an uneasy, sodden slumber.

Now he was on just such a fool's errand, to keep busy and avoid thinking. But this afternoon, he had solemnly to promised himself. He would reserve the afternoon, the entire afternoon, for thinking. At present, he was concentrating intently on crossing the Piazza Maggiore with an armful of books, books on history and government that for months now had lain unopened and unread.

That morning, he was jolted out of his despondency by a message from the Priory of San Marco demanding his immediate attendance on a matter of considerable importance. San Marco! Savonarola's monastery! Feverish excitement and dread had animated his footsteps. What could they possibly want with him? Was there a message? A legacy?

He had bristled with indignation, all the more so to hide his disappointment, when he discovered that the important matter he had been called upon to settle was a question of library fines! He was being assessed fines amounting to the preposterous sum of 25 florins for failing to return, in a timely fashion, books borrowed from the Laurentian library, now under the custodianship of the unflinching monks of San Marco.

The books had been lent to him by Fra Girolamo himself in better days, and Niccolo was unaware that somewhere, some meticulous scrivener in the bowels of the library had made a record of the transaction. In doggedly crossing and recrossing the city to fetch and return the borrowed volumes, he entertained himself with the thought that in the course of life's vicissitudes and upheavals, it was a comfort to know that precise records were being kept. Violence and bloodshed might engulf great men, convulse cities, shake the very foundations of Christendom! Civilization as we know it might come to an end! And still, bookkeeping goes on.

With the books duly returned and the fines begrudgingly paid, Niccolo chose a quiet establishment that he had never before frequented and where he was unlikely to encounter any of the companions or accomplices of his more boisterous pursuits. Here he would do his thinking over a flask of rough local wine. He would have treated himself to better fare for the occasion, but the library fines had stretched his meager resources almost to exhaustion. He played with his cap, cleaned his fingernails, deciphered some scatological inscriptions, complete with illustrations, cut into the scarred wood of the table at which he was seated. He called for another pint of wine to ease the drumbeat inside his head.

Niccolo had attended the prophet on the last night of his life, but there had been no terrifying revelations from him, no final, fateful pronouncements. Only ambiguity, doubt, and an injunction. "Carry on my work," was all he really said. That was the essence of it. The friar had spoken softly, almost crooning, rarely looking at Niccolo.

He acknowledged that he had failed, failed in his attempts to build the City of God on Earth. "Perhaps the City of God is best left in heaven," he smiled. "Perhaps men are not ready for it here. But we must strive to give them something better than a government of robbers and devils, men like you and I."

Niccolo protested, "Like me? Why me ?"

"Who else? The simple souls who followed me, the ardent ones? Their faith is great, but they have no ability to understand, to work in the world."

The prophet continued, "You see, I remember the day you first came to see me at San Marco. I remember the way your eyes lit up when I spoke of my plan for governing the city. Your excitement, the passion with which you put forth your own ideas, the conviction in your voice—these are rare qualities, Niccolo Machiavelli, all too rare, especially in those who seek to direct the course of men and cities. Believe me, I know," he said sadly.

He went on, "Of all those who came to me, and they were many, you stood out in my mind, because you asked for nothing. Everyone wanted something from me—power, wealth, revenge, even salvation. Everyone but you. You were content to talk and to work and to dream. A city could do worse than to be served by such a man.

"There is a selflessness in you Niccolo, and despite the sins into which I'm sure you have fallen, a certain purity, a purity of purpose. You will laugh when I say it, but you are like me. And, eventually, you will try to do what I tried and failed to do. It can be no other way with you. Perhaps you will be wiser. Perhaps your efforts will be blessed with more success than mine."

Niccolo remembered he had objected and voiced his intention to leave Florence, to go to a foreign place where he could observe the follies and cruelties of men without having to participate in them.

The friar chuckled knowingly, almost to himself, "I, also, thought to withdraw from the world when I entered the monastery, but the hand of God nudged me back into it, sent me back out to preach."

"And God let you down, didn't he?" Niccolo had said, not without bitterness in his voice.

"God did not let me down," Savonarola had replied. "It is I who have let Him down. I have failed to accomplish His work here, but I have tried, in my own way. Perhaps it was the wrong way? Perhaps you will discover a different way? A better way?"

Again Niccolo had objected vehemently to the mantle the prophet was trying to lay on his shoulders and to the vocation he was trying to pass on to him. But undeterred by his obstinacy, Savonarola had continued, "Your struggle will be a long and a difficult one. And in the end, you can do no worse than I did. At least you have my mistakes to guide you."

Looking up at him, directly then, the friar had abandoned briefly his desultory, lilting tone. A stern, frightening certainty had crept across his face. "You will come to think of yourself as the savior of your city, a secular savior, but a savior nonetheless. You will not shrink from the duties laid upon you, from the responsibility, and yes, even the guilt. You may do far worse things than I have done. If the barbarians are at the gates, you too will not hesitate to welcome them, if it suits your purpose, if there is no other way. These things I know!" He was shaking slightly from the effort his words had cost him.

Niccolo felt uneasy. "You've seen things?" he asked, rattled.

"I know them," replied the prophet, wearily. "It's not for you to ask how I know them."

Sitting in the darkened tavern, now with his third pint of wine and looking back over the scene, Niccolo realized that he had actually wanted to be convinced, that he had almost begged the friar to convince him. He wanted to shrink before those blazing eyes, cower before the fierce, absolute certainty he had so often seen in them. But that night, as he looked one last time into Savonarola's smoky green eyes, just before sleep closed them, he saw only doubt and fear. The prophet's final words still haunted him, still rang in his ears: "You will continue my work, Niccolo, what I've tried to do? Won't you? Won't you?"

"Well, won't you!" Niccolo suddenly became aware that somebody was talking to him, a real voice from the present, from the outside world. Lifting his eyes, he found his vision blocked by the ample girth of a brown-clad Franciscan friar.

"I said, you will invite an old friend to share a cup with you, won't you, man? Won't you?"

"Pagolo!" There was no mistaking him—older now, and a little fatter, but it was Pagolo. The two friends embraced joyfully, kissing each other on the cheeks, slapping each other on the back.

"Pagolo, Pagolo, when did you get back? How long have you been in Florence? Why didn't you come see me?"

"First wine, then talk," said the stout friar, thumping on the table to attract the attention of the reticent tavern owner. When he had gulped a long draft to slake his thirst, he upbraided his friend: "I've been looking for you for three days. You're never home. In the usual haunts, nobody's seen you. And now I find you in this dusty, morose hideaway, looking thin and drawn, looking unhealthy. Niccolo, what have you been up to?"

"I've been busy, little things," said Niccolo, volunteering nothing. Undeterred, Pagolo began to pepper his friend with questions. It was nearly eight years since the two had last seen each other, and Pagolo, having spent most of that time in Rome, was eager for news or gossip.

Niccolo sought to satisfy his friend's curiosity on any number of points touching on marriages, pregnancies, infidelities, kidnappings, brawls, arrests, and imprisonments. Talking about these things, he slowly emerged from the morbid self-absorption that had plagued him for the last several days. Pagolo's warmth and good humor were contagious. Niccolo actually felt good again, less alone.

The conversation ranged freely, irreverently over countless scandalous topics, until Pagolo brought it to a grinding halt. Leaning toward his old friend and lowering his voice, he probed cautiously, "The other day . . . at the execution of the Holy Man, you were there weren't you?"

Neither spoke.

Pagolo continued, in a confidential, discreet tone, "I seem to have observed some sort of, and this may be entirely in my imagination, but there was some sort of communication. Am I right or wrong? Why on earth was the prophet staring at you, of all people? You—the king of impiety? The crown prince of cynical disbelief?"

Niccolo mumbled something about it not being important, but Pagolo pressed for an explanation.

"Alright," said Niccolo curtly, "if you must know, I'm his illegitimate son!"

Pagolo burst into laughter. "You're not going to tell me anything, you bastard. And here I am ablaze with curiosity, consumed by curiosity."

"Pagolo, Pagolo, believe me, if I could tell anyone, it would be you." He spoke in deadly earnest. "Think of it as a secret, a confidence I can't betray."

Pagolo harrumphed, pulled at the stubble on his chin, and sat looking profoundly disappointed. Then sensing that he had hit a nerve, like a true friend, he diplomatically backed away, calling for more wine and changing the subject. "Shall I tell you about Rome then? Shall I entertain you with lurid reports of the Eternal City?

Niccolo gladly acquiesced, but before delivering himself over to the enjoyment of Pagolo's uninhibited tales, for a brief moment, he wondered why he had blurted out the line about being the friar's illegitimate son. It made him uneasy. A joke, yes, and an obvious one at that. But it crossed his mind that, in some very real respect, he may have spoken the truth.

"This pope," said Pagolo. "This pope, Alexander, is most definitely and most assuredly, the antichrist. Fra Girolamo of blessed and recent memory, was entirely correct on that point."

"Worse than usual?" asked Niccolo.

"Much worse," confirmed Pagolo. "It's the very excess of his indulgences that distinguishes him from his predecessors. Nobody minds if the pope has a mistress. It's established practice, but this pope has several. Children? No problem, but this pope has too many."

"How many?" interrupted Niccolo.

"Seven, whom he acknowledges and adores, and whom he pushes into the public eye every chance he gets."

"Wouldn't any good father do the same?" asked Niccolo.

Pagolo laughed. "Papa Alexander, in his affection for his children, goes far beyond the bounds of what any good father would do. So rumor has it." His eyes gleamed in wicked insinuation.

"And has rumor got it right?" said Niccolo eagerly.

"Perhaps," said Pagolo judiciously, raising his eyebrows and playing the informed insider. He paused briefly for dramatic effect, then continued. "The death of the pope's favorite son, Juan, did give rise to speculation. He was only twenty-one when they dragged his body out of the Tiber last year with nine stab wounds in it. They said that the pope, the successor of Saint Peter, the fisher of men, had been obliged to fish his own son out of the river!"

"Who killed him?" Niccolo interrupted Pagolo's self-satisfied amusement.

"Juan of Gandia was a dissolute scoundrel, and half the population of Rome could have killed him, or at least would have been justified in doing so. He drank and gambled and whored, he ignored his wife, wasted money. At night, and this is God's own truth, he roamed the city killing dogs and cats."

"Charming habit."

"He was a charming fellow. So sensitive. They say he never went out without gloves for fear that his fine hands might be spoiled by the unhealthy Roman air. He had high regard for his hands.

"One night, after a dinner at his mother's villa, Gandia disappeared. He left with a single squire and in the company of a masked man. There has been much talk about the masked man. He was at the dinner, and was supposed to have visited Gandia every day for the previous month.

"The next morning, they found the squire dead and Gandia's riderless horse, whose saddle and accoutrements showed signs of violence, but no Gandia. The pope was distraught. Six days later, a woodcutter, a Dalmatian, came forward and said that he had been keeping an eye on his woodpile behind the Church of San Girolamo of the Slavs, near the Tiber on the night of Gandia's disappearance. At about three in the morning, he saw two men approach on foot in the company of a man on horseback with a golden sword. Across the rear end of his white horse, a body was slung. At a sign from the horseman, the two men on foot took the body down and flung it into the river. The dead man's cloak was floating on the water's surface, and they had to throw stones to sink it.

"Just downstream from the spot the woodcutter indicated, hung up on a culvert where a sewer emptied into the river, they found Gandia's bloated body. He still had his gloves on, but his hands were tied. His dagger was still in its sheath, and his purse was untouched, over thirty ducats in it.

"They say the pope, mad with grief, grabbed the woodcutter and shook him, as though he were to blame for the tragedy. 'Why didn't you come forward sooner?' he wailed.

"The woodcutter shrugged, 'I've seen over a hundred corpses dumped into the river at that spot, and nobody ever seemed to mind much.'"

"So who was the masked man?"

"That's what I was coming to," said Pagolo. There are several candidates. The most obvious choice is Ascanio Sforza, the pope's son-in-law."

"Why him?"

"I should say ex-son-in-law, since he was recently divorced from the pope's daughter. Not divorced, you understand. The marriage was annulled."

"It must be easy—and much cheaper and quicker—to get an annulment when your father is the pope," observed Niccolo sarcastically.

Pagolo did not stop to argue the observation. "They say Gandia was murdered because he was conducting an incestuous relationship with his sister!"

"What!" said Niccolo. "Let me see if I have this straight. The pope's daughter's husband, the pope's son-in-law, killed the pope's son, because the pope's son was sleeping with the pope's daughter?"

"Precisely, but that's only the beginning. There is also talk that the pope's other son killed his own brother because he was jealous that Gandia was sleeping with their sister.

"Both brothers sleeping with the sister!"

"It gets even better than that. They say the pope had his own son killed when he found out about the incestuous relationship."

"Well, you can't say he isn't showing a little probity there," said Niccolo wryly.

"Far from it!" declared Pagolo. "They say he did it out of jealousy! The pope was angry with his son for sleeping with his daughter because he, the pope, was also sleeping with the daughter!"

"*Ahi serva Italia!*" wailed Niccolo in mock desperation. "Then it's true what I've been hearing—that one woman is the pope's daughter, wife, and daughter-in-law! She must be the biggest whore in Rome! And Fra Girolamo was right—the pope is the antichrist, and the church has become a disfigured harlot in his hands."

"Most assuredly a disfigured harlot," said Pagolo. "Most assuredly."

"So what's the truth, Pagolo? Was it the enraged husband, the enraged brother, or the enraged father?"

"The truth? Who can say what it is?" Pagolo shrugged. "Tongues will wag. The pope has enemies, many enemies. The Romans hate him, and any one of a number of powerful Roman families could be behind the rumors. *Sangue di Cristo!* They could even be behind the assassination. Who knows?"

"So the pope does not enjoy the support of his Roman constituency?" asked Niccolo.

"Not by a long shot. They all hate him. When the announcement of his election was made, a mob promptly sacked his new mansion to show their displeasure."

"Do they hate him because he killed his son, or because he's sleeping with his daughter?" taunted Niccolo facetiously.

"Oh, nothing as elevated as that. The Roman capacity for moral indignation is abysmally low. He could be sleeping with his sons as well as his daughter, he could be sleeping with his dead son and they would hardly bat an eye. They hate him because he's a Spaniard and because he's rich."

Pagolo elaborated in accents and tones approaching the pontifical, "The wealthy and the powerful hate him because he's used the church as an instrument to usurp what they feel is rightfully theirs—the wealth and power of Rome. He's stolen their thunder, and he's been enormously successful at it. The poor and the weak, on the other hand, just hate him because he's a Spaniard. Not capable of understanding the mysteries of Vatican high finance, government, and religion, they fall back—or are pushed back—on their fear of outsiders, simple bigotry, and crude formulations of patriotism."

"Wounded national pride!" crowed Niccolo.

"And, don't forget, wounded national pocketbooks," added Pagolo. "Ever since he bought the papacy, they've resented him."

"I don't understand. Everybody buys the papacy," said Niccolo. "Innocent bought it before Alexander, Sixtus before him."

"Of course everybody buys the papacy. That's not at issue," explained Pagolo. "What they object to is that he was able to pay so much for it. He outbid them, priced them right out of the market—over two hundred thousand ducats!"

Niccolo let out a low whistle of admiration at the mention of such a princely, or, in this case, pontifical sum.

"And since his election, he's appointed forty-three new cardinals. Do you have any idea the kind of revenues that brings in—over twenty-five thousand ducats for each appointment! And to make matters worse, almost every cardinal whom Alexander has elevated to the College is a Spaniard. He even conferred the red hat on his own son!"

"The one who got killed?"

"No, the other one. He's still alive."

"And may or may not be sleeping with his sister?"

"Exactly, said Pagolo. "But it's not just the sale of cardinals' hats that's bringing in the gold. The pope has really turned the Vatican into a money machine. He had a lot of practice when he was vice chancellor. He ran the chancery like a brokerage house for pardons, indulgences, absolutions, you name it. You could get remission for the death penalty for a couple thousand ducats. Everything was up for sale—offices—even the Vatican librarian had to pay up to hold on to his post, and that's not the most lucrative job in town."

"Maybe not," thought Niccolo, "but I bet he does alright." He was thinking ruefully of the 25 florins in library fines he had disgorged that morning.

"In the last analysis," said Pagolo, pontificating, "the Roman nobility is distraught with Alexander, because he pays far too little time rendering unto God the things that are God's and far too much of his energies superintending the things that are caesar's. The fact that he's a Spaniard and an outsider makes it all the more galling."

"He doesn't have the bad taste to flaunt it, does he?" asked Niccolo.

"Flaunt it? Does he flaunt it? Rome is seething with dark eyed, bearded Spaniards—Catalans, Aragonese, Moorish-looking ladies and gentlemen. They all flaunt it. Spanish pomp and Spanish circumstance. When Alexander was elected pope, he staged a procession like Rome had never seen before. All the attendants were dressed in Turkish regalia. Negroes and negresses carried garlands and sang. There were carts with living statues, naked boys and girls, gilded from head to foot. And where did this preposterous extravaganza wend its way? To Saint Peter's? Of course, but not to the church to celebrate a mass and sing the Te Deum, as is customary. In the square, Alexander had arranged to stage a curious and typically Spanish form of entertainment—a bullfight!"

"Bravo," cheered Niccolo. "It sounds more exciting than a cockfight or a dogfight. More thunder! Bravo! Hail Caesar!"

"It's not like a dogfight or a cockfight," explained Pagolo. "The bulls don't fight each other, imbecile. Men fight with the bulls."

"Barehanded?"

"No, they're armed with little swords and some are on horseback. There are usually several men against one bull."

Niccolo looked disappointed. "Not very heroic," he said. "No, I don't see it catching on here in Florence. Besides the guilds would never stand for it. Nonmembers butchering beef in a public place. Never."

Although he considered the bullfight a doubtful extravagance, at best, Niccolo was nevertheless intrigued by the Spanish conception of entertainment. "What else do they do to amuse themselves, these Spaniards, I mean, besides bull-butchery and sexual adventurism with their progeny and siblings?"

Pagolo thought for a minute. "Once they did stage a rather odd event in the Vatican courtyard. They filled it with horses—stallions and mares in heat. The pope and his family, along with his redoubtable mistress, the blond Vanozza, watched from a balcony cheering lustily at the—how shall I put this?—at the frenzy of equine coupling that was taking place below."

Niccolo collapsed in laughter, and, still sobbing, submitted that haughty Rome might finally have gotten the kind of pontiff she so richly deserved.

"By the way, do you know what his arms are? It's too apt—a red bull rampant on a field of gold!"

"*Viva il bue! Viva il Papa!* Long live the Bull! Long live the Pope!" cried Niccolo, lifting his cup. Pagolo and many others joined him.

After a round of refreshment, Niccolo said, "Pagolo, listen, we've heard here that the pope, and this might be nothing more than Florentine gossip, Florentine calumny, but we've heard that he killed a man, with his own hands."

The sagacious Pagolo considered a moment before answering. "Yes and no," he said finally. "It's not entirely true that the pope killed a man. That is to say, he didn't kill anyone as Pope Alexander VI. However, there was an incident, back before his election.

"Nobody holds it against him now—the heat of youth, the fiery Spanish temperament, all that. Besides, it's said that the man he stabbed was of 'inferior condition.' In answer to your question, then, yes, I think he did kill someone back when he was still just a young man from Valencia, when he was still just Roderigo Borgia."

Once he had begun his scurrilous recitations, Pagolo could not be denied. A small crowd had gathered around the animated little priest, and they kept his cup filled. They were all eager to hear the latest news from the seat of Christendom and the throne of Saint Peter. Pagolo spoke with such ease and obvious authority, he larded his accounts with such scrupulous detail, that his veracity was never called into question. One of his auditors, more scandalized than amused at the reports of flagrant misbehavior in the Holy City, roundly denounced the perpetrators of such sin and evil as unchristian dogs.

"Unchristian?" said Pagolo, indignantly. "Unchristian, you say? Quite the contrary! Never has the defense of Christianity been more stiff-necked and unrelenting than it is today in Rome. Only last week I saw a stunning display of Christianity, a heroic defense of Christian virtue.

"A courtesan had been arrested—La Cursetta. She was a respectable courtesan, but had apparently fallen behind in her bribery payments. And she was arrested for living with a Moor, who in order to conceal his identity went about her house disguised as a woman." Pagolo paused for breath.

"Oh, the things you see in Rome these days! La Cursetta was led through the streets, along with her Moor in a stunning black velvet gown, his hands tied behind his back. His flowing skirts were pulled up to his navel, and, since he was shamelessly ungirdled, you could see his powerful Moorish organs.

"When they had made a circuit of the entire city, La Cursetta, in proper Christian fashion, was released, absolved, and admonished to go and sin no more. The Moor, blackguard of a blackguard race, was not so lucky. He was dragged to the Campo de' Fiori by an executioner riding an ass and holding aloft for all to see, on the end of his lance, the balls of a Jew who was said to have copulated with a Christian woman. The Moor was strangled and burned. The defenders of our faith triumphed. Believe me, a smashing blow was struck for Christianity!"

Not sensing the irony in Pagolo's pronouncement, most of his auditors shook their heads knowingly, grumbling their approval at the fate of the unfortunate Moor. Pagolo, by now exhausted, and not a little drunk from the ministrations of his grateful audience, had lapsed into a beaming, contented silence. He and Niccolo were alone when the shadow of a darker, more troubling thought crossed his placid face.

Shifting his bulk and leaning over the table in the direction of his companion, Pagolo motioned for him to come nearer. "Niccolo," he began hesitantly, "do you remember that day, that day in the country when we were hunting and we saw . . . the Jews and . . . what happened to them?"

The sudden mention of "that day" went through Niccolo like a bolt. In all the years, since "that day," in over seventeen years, he and Pagolo had never spoken of what they had seen. By tacit agreement, it was a subject that they never brought up in each other's company, no matter how drunk, no matter how sober. Now Pagolo had inexplicably broken their silent agreement.

The little priest continued, embarrassed, "You remember the girl? Well, I can't be entirely certain. It's been a long time. But, in Rome. I'm pretty sure. I think, I saw her. In Rome."

He stopped and stammered apologetically, almost under his breath, "In a brothel."

22

An Embassy to the Amazon Queen

Niccolo did not set out immediately for Rome, although he was sorely tempted to do so, nor did he embark upon a life of wandering vagabondage as he had also considered doing. Two months, two turbulent months after his conversation with Pagolo, he found himself pushing through the cluttered streets and the smells of a sweltering July morning toward the Piazza della Signoria. He was clean-shaven, his hair was cropped close to his skull, and he was immaculately attired. Gone were the tight hose and gay doublet of youth. In their place, he wore the *lucco*, the Florentine citizen's gown, the very badge of sobriety, honesty, and respectability. That morning, he had dressed with exaggerated care, meticulously smoothing the long folds of the gown, caressing the soft, almost-diaphanous black wool until the garment hung just right. He had tied and retied the laces that closed it around his neck, making sure that his snow-white linen shirt was just barely visible above the line of the dark wool.

Making his way across the piazza, toward the massive building that housed the governing bodies of Florence, Niccolo stopped, as he always did, before the statue. The polished bronze gleamed in the morning sun. The statue, by Donatello, had once been part of Lorenzo de' Medici's private collection, but when the Medici were driven from power and expelled, the people had dragged it here, to the very heart of the city, to serve as an example. It was a statue of the biblical Judith. In one upraised hand she brandished a curved sword, in the other, the severed head of the tyrant Holofernes. So that the meaning of the statue would not be lost on any who might, in the future, contemplate a return to the tyrannical ways of the past, the revolutionaries had added an inscription to the base, "Erected by the citizens as an exemplum of the public salvation, 1495."

Niccolo had always taken heart at the sight of the statue. It brought a smile to his lips to think how far it had come from the voluptuous surroundings of the Medici courtyard, how much its meaning had changed since it was commissioned by the tyrants themselves. They had never even dreamed of its implications, never for a minute seen themselves in Holofernes. Even in the blackest days of Savonarola's mystical republic, Niccolo had seen the statue as a symbol of inevitable resurgence, of the indomitable, if sometimes grim, will of the people.

But it also meant something much more to him—the Old Testament heroine, Judith—Giuditta! Giuditta, the girl who had come to assume such a strange and cryptic place in Niccolo's imagination, if not his life. Over the years, he had begun to regard her as an alternative to the rather squalid series of affairs that constituted his relationships with women. She was distant, aloof, dark, mysterious, different from all the others and linked indissolubly to him by the sacredness of life and death itself—his great, mystical love! So he would dream before mercilessly dragging himself back to the reality of the situation—that the whole thing was based on a childish infatuation, that it was buried in the past, and that his longings were due almost entirely to his own restless dissatisfaction with the present. The mechanisms of fantasy and escape, he understood only too well. Still . . .

Niccolo sighed. The statue of Judith regarded him with silent reproach. For all he knew, she was rotting away in a Roman whorehouse, prey to the appetites of fat cardinals and lean, lecherous northern bishops. . . . Again, his imagination was getting the better of him. With an effort, he shook the image from his mind. Duty called. He walked stiffly past the statue and up the stairs of the Signoria to assume his rightful place in the government of robbers and devils.

He was doing it, he told himself, to keep a promise, to honor a commitment to a dying man. But he was also doing it because he knew in his heart that what Savonarola had told him was true—that he would not be able to do otherwise.

Once Niccolo had made his decision, and he kept reminding himself that it was a provisional decision, he went to his father, who was elated that his lazy, overeducated son had finally decided on a career. Through Bernardo's efforts and family connections, and through the good offices of his friend, Biagio Buonacorsi, Niccolo succeeded in having his name put forward for a position as secretary in the Second Chancery. He was then selected from a slate of candidates and eventually approved by the Signoria. Modest but appropriate sums of money changed hands.

Niccolo Machiavelli was thirty years old the day he first mounted the steps of the Signoria to begin work there. His last thought—and it made him smile—as he disappeared into the stern, forbidding building was that Jesus Christ, too, had waited until after his thirtieth birthday to begin His work.

The Second Chancery, where Niccolo worked, was the administrative arm of the Ten, who were charged primarily with the conduct of foreign affairs and the prosecution of war. The First Chancery, at the disposition of the Signoria itself, had broader powers, but in practice the two worked together, and the lines between their spheres of activity were often blurred. Niccolo's initial duties consisted almost exclusively of writing letters. He wrote letters to ambassadors, commercial representatives, delegates, generals, merchants, and spies. He wrote in Latin, in Florentine, and, later, when he needed to, in cipher.

The room where he worked was large and airy. Floor-to-ceiling windows flooded the interior with light, so that the small army of scribblers could go about their business with a minimum of eyestrain and lamp oil, which was expensive. On his first day, Niccolo was given several dispatches and told briefly how to answer each one. He was then left to his own devices. When he had penned his first official document, he signed it, with a flourish, in Latin:

Nicholaus Maclavellus,
Segretarius

That made it sound more official.

The Second Chancery was a hub of activity, for nearly all the business that the city of Florence transacted with the outside world passed through here. The pace was frantic, and Niccolo was soon caught up in it. He brought zeal and dedication to his work. Occasionally, pangs of conscience forced him to reflect on the nature of the government he was serving. He could not be altogether satisfied with it, but it was a republican government. There were no Medicis and no tyrants. And, he consoled himself, it would get better, things would improve, through his efforts and those of others like him. It was inevitable at this point that Niccolo, giving free reign to his powerful imagination, would conjure up visions in which he saw himself as the stalwart, incorruptible servant of the republic, a republic destined to repeat the glories of the ancient Roman republic! And so, inspired by these visions, he applied himself to his work with all the ardor of an ancient Roman republican. Yes, things were going well for Niccolo, and he would have been perfectly happy in the Second Chancery, had it not been for Marcello Virgilio Adriani.

In addition to being head of the Second Chancery, Marcello Virgilio was a professor of letters. He boasted oratorical gifts. He was a self-declared member of the old school. Although the pompous Marcello Virgilio was only five years older than Niccolo, a gap of over a century separated them. Marcello Virgilio had no cause for concern over the quality of Niccolo's work but was intent on impressing upon him, as he had impressed upon the others, his utter superiority in matters of learning and scholarship.

"This is your work, Machiavelli, am I correct?" Absorbed in thought, Niccolo had not even seen him coming. Marcello Virgilio loomed over his writing table, a tall man, with a letter in his hand. Niccolo acknowledged authorship of the document in question, and asked, "Why, is there something wrong?"

"No, not wrong," said Marcello Virgilio, pursing his lips. "Not exactly wrong. *Inelegant* might be a better word for it. I wouldn't go so far as to say clumsy, but inelegant." The professor of rhetoric weighed his words carefully. Wrinkles appeared on his spacious forehead, indicating deep thought.

"This line," he said with all the petulance of a schoolmaster. "Read it out loud." Niccolo did so. It was the initial line addressed to the most revered, most honorable, most etc., etc. There were two kinds of letters written in the chancery—important ones with specific instructions that were usually in Italian, and then there were the Latin letters. Written, as often as not, to flatter some head of state or prince of commerce, they were nearly entirely devoid of content and were mere exercises in stringing together euphonic, laudatory words and phrases. The letter that had attracted the notice of the meticulous Marcello Virgilio was of the latter variety.

"Now what's wrong with that sentence?" Niccolo waited for the master to answer his own question, which he did presently with much furrowing of the brow. "It doesn't move quickly enough, the phrases don't trip off the end of your tongue. Do you get my meaning?"

Niccolo said he did.

"Here," suggested the venerable chancellor, waxing enthusiastic, "try the same sentence in Greek. You'll see what I mean. It doesn't translate well into Greek at all, but by attempting the exercise, you'll discover exactly where the weakness of your Latin lies."

"Now the bastard has what he wants," thought Niccolo. "I'm sorry, Maestro, but I don't have Greek."

Marcello Virgilio looked shocked, disgusted, and a little embarrassed—like someone whose dog has just vomited in the lap of an esteemed guest. "You have no Greek, Machiavelli? I never knew. No Greek, and to think, you're one of our brightest boys, one of the most promising ones here. You should have studied at the academy, where I studied. You would have gotten your Greek there. By the way, where did you study?"

"With Master Matteo."

"Matteo?" said the scholar, affecting to search the vast vaults of his memory for the name, "Matteo? Wasn't he driven out of town? Blasphemy or something like that?" An almost-imperceptible shudder accompanied this observation. "No wonder you have no Greek, Machiavelli. Well, never mind." And whisking the offending letter away, Marcello Virgilio sailed off with a look of infinite, puzzled sadness playing about his noble features. He had achieved his objective.

"*Stronzo*," grunted Niccolo under his breath. "Turd."

Notwithstanding his lack of preparation in Greek, in the months ahead Niccolo wrote literally thousands of letters, many of which dealt with the sempiternal waging of Florence's half-hearted war with Pisa. When the city was not being threatened by the larger Italian states surrounding her—Rome or Milan or Venice, when the barbarians stayed on their own side of the Alps, and most important, when Florence was not at war with herself, then she inevitably directed all her bellicose energies and martial prowess against the neighboring city of Pisa.

The Florentine economy was based on trade, and her business interests spanned the globe, but Florence herself was an inland city on a river. Where that river, the Arno, flowed into the sea, there was a deep-water port, suitable for large-scale commercial shipping. Unfortunately for Florence, that was the precise site on which the city of Pisa stood. The Pisans, for their part, were as stubborn as the Florentines in their own defense. They tore up treaties, abrogated rites of passage, nullified agreements, demanded ever-escalating sums of money, and in countless ways contrived to control, limit, and frustrate Florentine access to the shipping lanes.

At the time Niccolo began his work at the chancery, the war against Pisa was once again in full swing, and the bulk of the correspondence that passed through his hands had to do with the "*Cose di Pisa*"—Pisan affairs. Arrayed against Pisa, on behalf of the Florentine republic, was a mercenary army composed of the military flotsam and jetsam that drifted ceaselessly across the Italian peninsula—deserters from other armies, Spanish, French, German, and Swiss, dispossessed and exiled Italian nobles with no place to go and no other skill but war, Albanian Stradiots, known for their ferocity in battle and their addiction to looting, the occasional Moor, and, of course, common criminals, who represented the bulk of the foot soldiery. In such an army, the maintenance of discipline was a gargantuan undertaking, made all the more difficult by the intense competition and jealousy that was rife among the commanders and captains of the various units. Given the order of the army, or rather the disorder, it should come as no surprise that concrete military gains were few and far between in the present campaign against Pisa. To Niccolo Machiavelli, secretary in the Second Chancery, fell the unenviable task of sorting through the mounting chaos of the Pisan campaign and doing what he could to keep supply lines open, keep troops in the field, keep tempers in check, and keep the officers from slitting one another's throats. In Pisan affairs, Niccolo was rapidly becoming an expert.

It was Biagio Buonacorsi who brought Niccolo the news of his first important commission. Biagio worked alongside Niccolo in the chancery, and although he had been there a full two years longer than his friend, he had not succeeded in impressing his superiors. Biagio freely admitted that he did mediocre work, not because he lacked talent or ability, but because he lacked motivation.

"Niccolo! You're getting out of this abominable letter factory," boomed Biagio, rushing into the chancery. Niccolo scarcely looked up from the tangled mess of Pisan affairs over which he was pouring. Biagio clapped him on the back, "Did you hear me?"

"I can't go anywhere with you right now, Biagio," sighed Niccolo wearily. "Don't even ask. Maybe later, when I finish all this about Vitelli taking over the command."

"Niccolo, you're not listening! They're sending you out. The Ten! You've got a diplomatic assignment!"

Niccolo looked up in disbelief. He had been at his job now for a year and had incurred the displeasure of his immediate superior, Marcello Virgilio, more often than his favor.

Biagio continued, "Marcello Virgilio is stewing. It's beautiful! He had no say in the decision. It came down from the Ten! From the Ten! They've been reading your dispatches and they were impressed! They're sending you to Forli!"

In celebration of the good news, Biagio finally prevailed upon the tireless Niccolo, the indefatigable letter writer, to take the rest of the day off. Observing that Niccolo could stand some scrubbing up, shaving, and trimming before reporting to the Ten for assignment, Biagio dragged his friend to the public baths. The baths of Florence were spartan affairs, not like the lavish pleasure palaces rumored to be the rage in Rome. In Florence, men and women were admitted to the baths on alternate days of the week.

Relaxing in a shallow pool of warm water, Niccolo was using a rough pumice stone in an effort to remove the ink stains from his writing hand. "You work too hard, Niccolo! Look at these hands—unsullied, unblemished!" Biagio held his two lily-white hands in the air. "You work all day in that chancery, splashing ink all over yourself, and what do you do at night? I never see you. You don't go out. You don't enjoy yourself."

"I do enjoy myself, Biagio, in the quiet pursuits of the mind."

Biagio burst into laughter. "In the quiet pursuits of the mind! You? Whatever happened to the noisy pursuits of the flesh?"

"In due time," said Niccolo with exaggerated detachment. "I'm working on something at home, and I have to finish it."

"Working at home! You don't get enough work at the letter factory during the day?"

"I've got a copy of Livy. A printed edition, the first ever printed in Florence."

"Surely you're not going to read it?"

"I'm making an index of all the place names in it."

"Fascinating!" said Biagio, barely concealing his mirth. "Latium, Tusculum, Lavinium, Ostia . . . Fascinating! You have to be sure to give me a copy when you're done. I can hardly wait."

Niccolo threw the pumice at his friend's head, but missed. He explained, "My father got it from the printer for me. In return for making the index, I get to keep the book."

"And then what?"

"By studying Livy's history of Rome, I'll be able to learn how a real republic was built and what can be done to save the shabby, tattered republic we serve."

"You and Livy and the ancient Romans, Niccolo. It's a sad thing when a young man prefers the company of dead men to the living."

Niccolo Machiavelli disagreed, "You have to admit that a dialogue with the dead men of the past is much easier than a conversation with many of our living contemporaries."

After the baths, after a sumptuous meal at which Niccolo proved himself no enemy of good living, the two young men retreated to the chancery. From the windows there, they had an ideal vantage point from which to view the ceremonies that were taking place in the piazza below. In an attempt to bring some order to the chaotic Pisan campaign, the Signoria had contracted for the services of the renowned condottiere, Paolo Vitelli. Vitelli, along with his brother Vitellozzo, was to be given overall command of the Florentine troops at Pisa. The negotiations were protracted, and Niccolo had handled the burden of the correspondence. Today, in a public ceremony, the formidable Vitelli and his brother were to be sworn in as captains in the employ of the Florentine republic.

Niccolo had never seen the condottiere, although he had addressed scores of letters to him over the past several months. Nevertheless, looking down on the platform, it was easy enough to pick out the famous military commander. He stood out in his armor and in his martial bearing among the crowd of mild-mannered government officials with whom he shared the stage.

"What the hell is that pompous ass, Marcello Virgilio, doing down there?" asked Biagio.

"Don't you know?" replied Niccolo. "Our eminent chancellor has been chosen to give the oration in honor of Vitelli's arrival. He has oratorical gifts." Despite the contempt he had for the man, Niccolo had to admit he cut a splendid figure on the speaker's platform, with his flinty, sculpted features. Standing next to Vitelli, the picture of military glory, Marcello Virgilio could easily have been taken for a stern senator of the Roman republic. The two formed a living allegory, a diptych of ideal military and civil virtue. At least in appearance.

Marcello Virgilio's voice boomed across the piazza. It was striking in its strength and resonance. Niccolo and Biagio had no trouble hearing him through the unshuttered windows, high up in the Signoria. And since they had both received a solid classical education, they had no trouble understanding him. Not so the unwashed populace crowded into the square below. They didn't get a word. Marcello Virgilio was delivering his oration in Latin!

Biagio guffawed. "Only the noble Marcello would address that crowd in Latin. What a fool."

Niccolo listened as the great orator lauded the prowess and excellence of Vitelli. After about twenty minutes, he launched into an exhaustive catalogue of the great generals of antiquity, comparing their strength and accomplishments to those of Vitelli, whom he labeled the modern Horatius, the modern Scipio, the modern Camillus, and on and on . . .

"Niccolo, come over here, there's something interesting going on," said Biagio. Bored with the oratory, Biagio had idly drifted across the long room to the opposite wall, where a row of windows gave on the inner courtyard of the Signoria. In the closed courtyard, several members of the ruling council, dignified and grave in their bearing, were conversing with an eccentric-looking man in rich but outlandish clothing. The man was fluttering solicitously around a table, constantly making minute adjustments to a number of instruments that were set up there. He appeared to be taking sightings on the position of the sun and measuring the angles of the shadows it cast.

"What do you make of that witchcraft?" asked Biagio.

Niccolo was quick to grasp the import of the bizarre scene. "That must be him, he's always mentioned in the letters. That must be Vitelli's astrologer!" As the two watched with amusement, "Vitelli's astrologer" became more and more excited, his sightings and adjustments more frequent and frantic. Suddenly, he threw both arms in the air, "Now! Now! Now!" he screeched, bolting for the courtyard door. The grave parliamentarians filed quickly out after him.

Niccolo and Biagio were obliged to recross the room to the windows with a view of the piazza, and they arrived in time to see the lunatic astrologer burst into the square, waving his arms wildly in the air. He immediately caught Vitelli's attention, and the general raised his arm, giving the agreed upon signal. Trumpets blared. The propitious moment had arrived—the exact moment. Not a second could be lost. The gonfaloniere, the council's representative, hastened to thrust the baton of command into Vitelli's hands. And the ceremony was abruptly over.

Unfortunately, the propitious moment had arrived right in the middle of Marcello Virgilio's exquisitely crafted oration. He was furious.

"It was tragic," he later sobbed to himself, "tragic." He had been preempted, cut off, and there was so much more, the best parts were yet to come, he had still to expound upon the glories of Curtius, of Marcus Attilius Regulus, of Torquatus . . .

The next day, Niccolo was on the road to Forli, only slightly disappointed that the prestige of being a Florentine diplomat did not seem to carry any concomitant monetary rewards. He was told to use his own horse and to cover his expenses with money from his own pocket, from his yearly salary of a scant 192 florins. He would later be reimbursed from the treasury.

He had received his credentials directly from the Ten and was entrusted with a letter written by their chancellor, Marcello Virgilio, he of the wounded pride. Niccolo had not been able to suppress a smirk of satisfaction in the presence of the great orator.

At any rate, his instructions were to deliver the letter and clarify any remaining problems verbally. He was to write back daily to the Signoria, keeping them advised of his progress.

Niccolo's mission entailed a delicate balancing act. He had been authorized to purchase from Forli all the powder, saltpeter, and ammunition she could spare, but he had been told that, in all likelihood, she would be able to spare none whatsoever. He was authorized to arrange a *condotta,* a commission, for Count Ottaviano of Forli to fight with the Florentine troops at Pisa with as many men as he could muster. But he was not to offer the command for a ducat over 10,000, a price so low that the count's refusal was a foregone conclusion. He was permitted to discuss the idea of Florentine support for Forli in the event of an attack upon that city by the Papal States, but the Ten had expressly told Niccolo that such support was definitely out of the question. Mulling it over, he realized that he was embarked on an exercise in pure diplomacy. As Niccolo understood it, the real object of his mission was to win the friendship and goodwill of strategically located Forli without making any concessions, without making any firm commitments, and, above all, without spending any money. The task, in itself, was a difficult one, made all the more so by Niccolo's lack of experience in face-to-face negotiations. What made it truly formidable, however, was that Niccolo's adversary in this, his first diplomatic encounter, was none other than Caterina Sforza, the Amazon of Forli, she who had made a bold stand atop the ramparts of Mordano.

Caterina Sforza had been the wife of a pope's son, and while seven months pregnant, had ridden into battle on his behalf. She had survived his assassination, as well as that of her second husband. She had been defeated by the French, taken prisoner, and held for ransom. She had married a third time, only to lose that husband, too, a year later. Caterina was, at the age of thirty-six, a widow for the third time, the mother of innumerable children, and the absolute ruler of her small state.

It was to this intrepid woman that Niccolo presented his credentials directly upon reaching Forli. He was received in a tent, set up on a hill to catch the few merciful breezes that occasionally stirred in the cruel July heat. He was inordinately pleased to hear himself announced as the emissary from the republic of Florence.

Caterina Sforza greeted the emissary with an easy smile and a graceful inclination of the head. "And what news have we from sister Florence?" she asked in a slightly hoarse but not unpleasant voice.

Niccolo bowed curtly, nervously, reeled off his formulaic introductory remarks, and presented her with the letter from the Great Council written by Marcello Virgilio. He watched as her swift, sure fingers undid the seals and ribbons. There were scars on the backs of her hands.

"Please, be seated," she said. "Ottaviano, bring the Florentine ambassador some refreshment, quick, can't you see the poor man is wilting in this heat?" Niccolo was indeed suffering from the heat, not from nervousness or apprehension, he told himself. All the same, he could feel the sweat trickling down his back, tickling him.

Seated in a comfortable chair with a high back and luxurious cushions, he strove to maintain a nonchalant, dignified posture. He tried not to fidget, not to move his nervous hands in his lap. Within a few seconds, a flagon of white wine and an exquisite silver cup were placed on a small side table at his disposal. Cup and flask gave him something to occupy the uneasy hands while the Amazon perused the letter. The first taste of the wine startled him. It was a delicious, extraordinarily dry white wine, and it was freezing cold on his pallet. He wondered how she kept it so cold in this thick, stifling heat.

Niccolo studied the redoubtable virago as she scrutinized the letter from the Florentine chancery. Her blond hair was tied up loosely on her head, a few fugitive locks dangling down. Artfully applied cosmetics added a discreet blush to her white cheeks and softened the impact of her hard, implacable eyes. But where the layer of powder trailed off, down her neck, Niccolo could see the small imperfections, the thin, snaky red scars.

She was poised without being haughty or threatening. Seated in repose, she was not the terror of the battlements who had thrust her pudenda in the face of Charles VIII of France only five years ago. Like any good general, she was able to put aside the rough ways of the camp and battlefield in favor of a charming, courtly civility. And today, her skirts were down around her ankles.

Niccolo was beginning to relax in her presence, when she suddenly turned a merciless stare upon him. "Did you write this?" she demanded in a decidedly unfeminine voice.

"No," he gulped.

"Thank God," she said smiling, "I'm relieved. I would hate to have to deal with the man who wrote this stilted, stupid letter. Only a man suffering from chronic constipation could have contrived to write such a thing." After a moment's reflection, she added, "Only a man could have written such a letter." Disdainfully, she let it fall to her feet. They both laughed, and Niccolo, eager to pursue the advantage, began to entertain her with tales of the loathsome Marcello Virgilio.

When they had both enjoyed several rather unkind jokes at the expense of the poor chancellor, Caterina sat back in her chair, crossed her arms on her breast, and signaled an end to the merriment. With a shrewd narrowing of the eyes, she brought the conversation down to the business at hand: "Now, tell me briefly, Florence, what do you want?"

Niccolo, having rehearsed most of this material all the way from Florence, made a credible presentation, outlining the Florentine proposals to buy munitions, engage soldiers, and remain on friendly terms with Forli. Caterina listened attentively. When he had finished, she praised the laudable intentions of the Florentines. "The words of the Florentines have always satisfied me," she said, nodding agreeably. "But," she added caustically, "their deeds have almost always displeased me."

"I'll need some time for reflection," she said. "Tomorrow, then?" Niccolo was dismissed.

For several days thereafter, they dickered. She had no ammunition for sale, but she had soldiers. She might be willing to send them to Florence, but 10,000 ducats was entirely too low. Could he go to 12,000? Niccolo consulted with his superiors and was authorized to up the offer. She could have them ready to go under the command of her eldest son by the beginning of September. Florence needed them now, by the end of July at the latest. Mid-August? When they were about to conclude an agreement, Caterina informed Niccolo that Milan had just offered her 15,000 ducats, and a whole new round of negotiations began. Would Florence pledge to help Forli if she were attacked by the pope? Would Forli pledge to assist Florence if the pope sends troops to Pisa? And so it went. After almost two weeks, little had been accomplished other than the sharpening of Niccolo's diplomatic skills and the forging of a tenuous friendship between himself and the iron mistress of Forli.

When he finally received the order from the Signoria to return to Florence, Caterina was disappointed. She was beginning to enjoy his company. On the night before Niccolo's departure, she invited him to join her in an intimate dinner. The two dined out of doors in the dying light and the evening breezes. Caterina Sforza wore a strange gown of oriental inspiration. It consisted of a layer of thin, transparent black gauze, under which was another sheer, provocative layer of the same material, and under that, nothing at all. Her body was discernible through the flimsy, clinging cloth, but just barely, revealed and tantalizingly concealed at the same time. The hem and sleeves were embroidered with fantastic designs in gaudy colors. Niccolo could not help staring, and she was aware of his attentions.

The meal was exquisite—chilled shrimp in a piquant sauce, followed by succulent trout and tiny crisp-fried squid. When the latter were served, Caterina informed her guest that it was a local specialty, known thereabouts as *scherzo alla pescatore*, "the fisherman's joke."

"I personally see nothing funny about them," said Niccolo, crunching a mouthful of the dainty, crispy sea creatures. "Who knows where these names come from? How a legend gets started?" He stopped to squeeze more lemon on the squid, then resumed eating. He was about to comment on the extraordinary tenderness of the small, delicate tentacles when something exploded in his mouth. A blast of fire seared his tongue and throat before he succeeded in quenching it, at least partially, with a deep draught of the cool white wine. His face was flushed, his ears burned and his hair stood on end. His eyes were watering. His nose was running. His scalp was tingling.

"That's the joke," said Caterina laughing heartily at his distress. "One of them has a hot pepper hidden inside."

When they were finished eating, the table was cleared and lanterns were brought out. A sweet, nutty liquor was served to stimulate the conversation and, of course, the digestion. Easy talk flowed between the Florentine ambassador and the Lady of Forli. Niccolo confessed his boundless admiration for the latter in the wake of her remarkable, stunning gesture on the ramparts before the assembled French army.

"You saw that?" He thought she blushed. "It was reckless of me, wasn't it? But it worked. And I told the truth. I have had more children since then, four more in all." Here, a shadow of concern crossed

Caterina's face. "They're all very young yet and . . ." She hesitated. "I'm not sure they're safe in Forli."

Niccolo balked, "Why all of a sudden are you afraid for your children? You didn't seem too concerned when Charles had them."

"Charles was a weakling," she said dismissively. "I bluffed him, and he never called me on it. Besides, I knew he'd never kill them. He was perfectly willing to slaughter common soldiers in the field by the thousands, but he never killed anyone who could be held for ransom. In fact, he went out of his way to save their lives and barter for them afterward." Here, she turned somber. "But now we have a different enemy, don't we? And Valentino doesn't take any prisoners, does he?"

At the mention of the name of Valentino, they both fell silent. Caterina finally spoke again. "So, I was thinking of sending them away for a while, the children. To . . . Florence?" Her voice trailed off. She left it hanging in the air, a question.

Niccolo immediately grasped the significance of her remark. With Caterina's children in Florence, an unofficial pact of friendship with Forli was virtually sealed and his mission would be a resounding success. "I'll need some time for reflection," he said wryly. "Tomorrow, then?"

He was not sure at what point their after-dinner conversation had passed from political trysting into romantic dalliance. In the last two weeks, he had seen Caterina Sforza as an absolute sovereign, and although his republican sensibilities bridled a bit at the thought, he had to give her credit for astuteness, for fairness, and for making her way so intrepidly in a man's world. He had seen her as many things—an adversary, a canny negotiator, a potential ally. He thought of her as the mocking Amazon on the walls of Mordano, as a fearless fiend in battle, and even as someone with a place in history, but in all that time, he had never thought of her simply as a woman. Certainly he had never allowed himself to think, even for a minute, of seducing this larger-than-life warrior-queen.

Yet now, by mutual consent, an easy rapprochement was growing between the two of them. Lubricated by the thick, nutty liquor, their talk took a salacious turn. They exchanged stories of licit and illicit love. They exchanged knowing smiles. She liked the way his smile seemed always on the verge of curling into a sneer. He liked the way her body shifted languorously under the sheer, mysterious, exotic dress. Their verbal exchanges gave way to touching, and then their hands began to linger, slowly being drawn into caresses. Holding Niccolo's ink-stained hand up to the light, and gently tracing the outlines of his long fingers with her own, she cooed at him, "Don't the Florentine boys wash their hands before they eat?"

"Ink," he said. "It never comes out."

"Doesn't it? Come with me," she whispered, rising, not relinquishing his hand. She took a lamp and led him through the quiet corridors of the Palace of Forli.

From an alcove off her bedroom, Caterina retrieved a small jar. It contained a colorless unguent that she applied with great solicitude to Niccolo's blackened fingertips. She rubbed the gel thoroughly into his warm hand, perhaps longer than was necessary. They were both trembling only slightly when their lips met in the first tentative kiss. A second followed, more sensuous, more assured, more hungry. The countess pushed the willing secretary back into the profusion of pillows and cushions that littered her ample bed. She lowered herself onto him, drawing him up into her heavy, perfumed breasts and a night of languid delirium.

When Niccolo awoke, he was alone. The sun was up but not yet high in the sky. He lay back, reliving the night's sweet, urgent pleasures. He rubbed his eyes and was somewhat startled to see the ink stains on his right hand had entirely disappeared. He was staring at the immaculate hand and putting off the decision to rise and dress when Caterina strode into the room. She was dressed in light armor and flushed from some form or other of physical exertion.

"What have you been up to so early?" he said yawning.

"Riding. A turn on horseback, a vigorous turn, the morning after will keep a woman from getting pregnant."

Niccolo was dubious. This information was coming from a mother of six. "Anyway," he said, changing the subject, "You've worked a miracle with my hand. Look."

"Don't thank me," she said taking the hand in question and planting a small kiss on it. "I got that cream from a friend of mine, an associate really. It's extraordinary stuff. She says it will even remove freckles."

As Niccolo dressed, Caterina talked aimlessly about her creams, preparations, and elaborately compounded mixtures, and some of the remarkable things they were capable of doing. "I've always been interested in those things and do you know why? To be frank, it began with poisons. I have quite a collection of them," she said grinning. "Politics being what it is, you never know when you'll need them.

"And then, there's the more mysterious side—the enchantments. I have my philters and elixirs too." Teasing him, she said, "For all you know, I may have put something in your drink last night."

"That would have hardly been necessary," said Niccolo, "between the wine and that dress you were wearing, I was quite sufficiently bewitched as it was, and quite prepared to surrender my virtue without a struggle."

"Ah, you prefer the dress to my martial garb," she said, sweeping the lifeless garment up from the floor where it lay discarded and holding it provocatively in front of her. "How do you know the dress wasn't enchanted too? In fact, the dress was given to me by the same friend who concocted the cream I put on your fingers. And she was no stranger to sorcery."

Niccolo had finished dressing, and they left the bedroom together. As they walked downstairs, Caterina continued, "My family, my first husband's family, owns part-interest in a bathing establishment in Rome. You know what that means. A laboratory is a necessity in that sort of place. There are diseases to be treated, wounds to be staunched, pregnancies to be avoided or terminated. The men want potions to excite them; the women demand compounds for the preservation of their beauty and even their virginity.

"I had working for me several years ago, a quite extraordinary young woman who was versed in the Moorish arts. I used to spend hours in the laboratory with her. She taught me quite a few things. And she gave me that dress—that Moorish dress—which you yourself suspect of being enchanted.

"*A proposito,*" said Caterina suddenly. "She used to tell a most remarkable story about your wonderful republic of Florence, but I wouldn't want to offend you by repeating it here. I'm afraid it doesn't redound to the glory of the republic where there are no tyrants and where everyone lives in absolute peace and freedom." Caterina's dig was more than justified, for many times during their negotiations Niccolo's republican sympathies had gotten the better of him and issued forth in caustic observations about the way Forli was governed. His sarcastic comments had not gone unobserved by the astute countess.

"It seems that as a young girl she was in Florence, this friend of mine, and got into some sort of trouble with the authorities. They wanted to hang her and would have done so if she hadn't managed to escape, which she did in extraordinary fashion by floating down the river one night, her head stuck under a barrel . . ."

23

ALL HAIL CAESAR!

When Niccolo left Forli, he took with him more than just the goodwill of the Countess Caterina Sforza. He took with him her four youngest children, a confidential agent sent to continue negotiations with Florence, and the name and address of a certain "bathing establishment" in Rome.

He had managed to cement relations with Caterina without making a single, real promise or spending a single ducat. Biagio, with whom he corresponded daily during the time he was in Forli, assured him that his letters were highly praised by all and that his reputation in the chancery was secure. In fact, his prospects there were very, very good. But Niccolo was not thinking of his career the first night he returned to Florence. Since the news he carried from Forli was not particularly urgent, he did not even bother to report to the Signoria until the next morning. Instead, he ate an early supper that night and went to bed, where he began to rehearse to himself, the first lines of an important letter he was composing to send to Rome . . .

While Niccolo was away, pleasantly occupied with the affairs of Forli, Pisan affairs had gotten completely out of control. The war was going badly. The new commander, Paolo Vitelli, while unable to show any concrete military gains, continued to ask for astounding sums of money. The treasury was exhausted, and the people groaned under the burden of new and ever more innovative taxes.

In the stormy months that followed, Bartolommeo Scala, the First Chancellor to the Signoria died. He was replaced by the venerable ass, Marcello Virgilio Adriani, whose promotion left vacant the post at the head of the Second Chancery. On the basis of his recently demonstrated diplomatic abilities, Niccolo Machiavelli was named to the position. His salary of 192 florins a year was raised to 200. Because the government was in financial trouble, however, he never received reimbursement for the money he spent during his mission to Forli.

As head of the chancery, Niccolo was inundated with work. He often spent fifteen to sixteen hours a day on chancery business, which meant he often spent fifteen to sixteen hours a day on the disastrous war with Pisa. The Florentines were exasperated, and their patience all but exhausted when Paolo Vitelli captured the defensive emplacement of Stampace and managed to make a wide breach in the walls of Pisa. The fall of Pisa was imminent as several detachments of youthful Florentine volunteers surged onto the field, carrying all before them and making ready to enter the city. At the decisive moment, however, Vitelli inexplicably ordered them to retreat.

Only confused reports from the camp filtered back to Florence. It was impossible to get accurate information. Nobody could be trusted. Niccolo sent Biagio to Pisa in order to discover what exactly was happening there. Biagio had no trouble ascertaining that Vitelli had indeed stalled the attack to prolong the war and thus stretch out his commission as commander of the Florentine troops. Moreover, it was discovered he was taking money from Pisa to do nothing! As Vitelli's treachery became more and more apparent, and Niccolo began to assemble a case against him for presentation to the Signoria, a dispatch was thrust into his hands, marked,

Cito!
Cito!
Cito!

Urgent!
Urgent!
Urgent!

It was written in code, using a simple cipher that Niccolo and Biagio had devised. There was only one sentence in Biagio's hand. In a matter of seconds, Niccolo was able to read that Piero de' Medici and his cousin Giuliano had been seen in the Florentine camp, talking with Vitelli!

It was all done very neatly, very quickly so as not to arouse suspicions. New commissioners were sent to Pisa to look into the state of the army. Vitelli was invited to dine with them, and after dinner, he was shown into a closed room and held fast until he could be transported under heavy and secure guard to Florence. He was examined by the magistrates. The indictment, on behalf of the Signoria, was prepared and written by Niccolo Machiavelli. On the basis of the evidence presented, Vitelli was found guilty and convicted of treason. Within twenty-four hours, he had been beheaded.

Vitelli's disgrace was not the end of Niccolo's problems, but only the beginning. Florence then struck a contract with France to send troops on her behalf and bring the lamentable Pisan affair to a swift and satisfactory conclusion. With the entry of the French, the sad cycle of lethargy and extortion that is mercenary warfare began anew.

The troops mutinied, demanded more money, and even held their own officers hostage until they got it. Niccolo made several trips to the camp at Pisa. France was disgruntled and expressed disappointment with the way her "Florentine allies" were mismanaging things. The Florentines, in their turn, blamed the French, and so a delegation was sent to France to straighten things out.

While Niccolo was dispatched to Paris, he was not the head of the delegation, of course. It would have been a breach of protocol, an insult even, to send a thirty-year-old secretary, no matter how talented, to treat with a crowned head of state. What was needed was a man of experience, a full-blown ambassador, a gentleman with rank and the authority to conclude treaties and undertake serious obligations. The republic of Florence found such a representative in the weighty person of Francesco della Casa. For his expenses, della Casa was allotted the princely sum of eight lire per day. His humble secretary, on the other hand, received only half that—a measure of his relative importance.

News from the delegation trickled back into Florence, most of it taken from the official, secret dispatches received by the Signoria, for in the chanceries, leaks abounded. No one was more avid for this news than Bernardo Machiavelli. After all, these were events in which a member of his family had direct personal involvement. One November morning, as Bernardo rushed into the Mercato Vecchio, he was just in time to hear the tail end of a report on the progress of the embassy to France. The crier was laughing so hard that there were tears in his eyes as he spoke, and he had to stop to catch his breath. Finally, with the encouragement of his audience, he was able to pick up where he had left off: "And the king of France says, 'Why, it's obvious to Us, from the mess you've made of this whole thing, that the Italians know nothing about war.'"

"And he says, right in his majesty's face, 'And the French know nothing about politics!'" The small crowd of Florentines around the crier cheered to see the French crown so royally and soundly rebuffed, and no one cheered more lustily than Bernardo, with his shouts of, "*Viva Italia! Viva della Casa!*"

The crier fixed him with a puzzled look. "You didn't hear me right then, old man? Della Casa, that honorable, fat fart, between his dropsy and his gout and his dyspepsia, he's been in bed for the last two weeks. It was his secretary trimmed the beard of the king of France! It was young Machiavelli!"

As only a father can, Bernardo wept. In the next few weeks, he would continue to receive reports from France, glowing reports of his son's astuteness. Playing off the French king's fear of the German emperor on one hand and his suspicions regarding the pope's intentions on the other, Niccolo, his Niccolo, had managed to preserve intact, the Florentine alliance with France. In the confrontations that were shaping up and threatening to rock the fragile stability of the Italian peninsula once more, the isolated republic of Florence could not afford to lose the support of a powerful ally like France. Bernardo could not even describe the feelings that stirred in him when he heard his son's name proclaimed in the market place or when his sage colleagues at the courts nodded gravely and pronounced Niccolo to be a "true Florentine"—the ultimate accolade of approval. But Niccolo would never know the pride that swelled in his father's chest. By the time he returned from France, Bernardo Machiavelli would be dead.

Exhausted by his travels and exertions on behalf of the republic and stunned by his father's premature death, Niccolo finally agreed to take some time off from his duties at the chancery. Notwithstanding his intentions to get away from it all and simply relax, he packed two heavy crates full of books, letters, and correspondence and had them transported to his family's villa in San Casciano. Among the miscellaneous papers he threw into the boxes was a letter he wrote over two years ago with great expectations and sent to Rome, to a certain bathing establishment there. It had been returned unopened and unread. The envoy who carried it said that the baths no longer existed. They had been burned to the ground.

For several days, Niccolo did little more than go over the family accounts. So zealous had he been in the service of the republic that he was entirely ignorant of the finances of the Machiavelli family of whom he suddenly found himself head. For the first time, he came to realize just how slender the Machiavelli patrimony actually was. When he factored in allowances for two dowries for his sisters and regular disbursements for the good-natured but impossible Totto, who had thus far proven utterly incapable of earning a living, there was barely enough left over to maintain the house in Florence and the tiny villa in the country.

Niccolo's income from the chancery was not even sufficient to cover his own expenses. While not a spendthrift, he had no talent for economy, and the money allotted him for his mission to France had been hopelessly inadequate. As a result, the long delegation had brought him to the brink of financial disaster.

The longer Niccolo pored over his accounts, the more disillusioned he became. No matter how many times he calculated and recalculated, the expense column always added up to a figure slightly greater than the sum of the income column. Dogged in the pursuit of familial duty, he persevered in spite of his frustration, but the numbers were giving him a headache.

He had all but resolved to tear the offending ledgers to shreds, when he heard a horse approaching. Eagerly snatching at any excuse to leave the accursed account books for a few minutes, Niccolo rose to investigate. He recognized the rider as one of the countless boys who loitered around the chanceries, hoping to pick up a few lire making deliveries or doing odd jobs. For his part, the boy recognized Niccolo and, without saying a word, handed him a letter.

Within the hour, Niccolo was in the saddle and urging his mount toward Florence. His account books were still open on his writing table. The cold dinner prepared for him by a local woman remained on the sideboard, uneaten. The letter had been brief and to the point—Valentino had struck!

The Italians called him Valentino because his official title, among others, was Duc de Valentinois. He had received the French duchy of Valentinois from the hands of King Louis XII, the same king who had been bluntly informed by Niccolo Machiavelli that he knew nothing of politics. Although this Valentino enjoyed a claim to a French duchy with the title and the income that went along with it, he was anything but French. In fact, he was of mixed Italian and Spanish blood.

A consummate military commander, Valentino had also procured a *condotta*, a military command, from the pope and been named vicar general of the Pontifical Armies. It was in this latter capacity as commander of the Papal Armies that he was waging his present campaign against the Romagna, the province to the north and east of Florence. Traditionally, the papacy claimed these territories as her own, and they were often designated as part of the loosely affiliated Papal States. But as the poet Dante said of the Romagnouli, they were a vicious race of men with tainted blood, a race of bastards and tyrants whose hearts were never without war. As might be expected from the denizens of such an unruly race, they did not accept lightly the yoke of Rome's authority, and so it was not for the first time in history that a pope was obliged to send an army against them to assert his claims. Valentino, with his reputation for ruthlessness and cruelty, was ideally suited to lead that army.

But Valentino's brilliance on the battlefield along with his reputed physical strength were not the only things that qualified him to lead the Papal Armies. He could, in fact, boast a unique and singular relationship with the papacy, having been a cardinal in the church before consecrating himself to the military life. Before laying aside the purple, Valentino was the only cardinal in the collegium said to have attained his position without having had to purchase it. This rare and coveted sacred honor, a position as one of the princes of the church, had been granted him freely, not because of his predisposition to sanctity, but because he was the bastard son of Pope Alexander VI. He was Caesar Borgia.

The pope was now called simply "Borgia," both as a derogatory reference to his Spanish origins and because he had long since forfeited any claim to the title, "Your Holiness," Of course that was not the only name by which he was known—there were those who insisted on the more precise designations of "antichrist" and "Beast of the Apocalypse." Caring little for public opinion, Borgia had gone about his business and with the aid of his son Caesar had evolved a plan that was simple and elegant in conception, if somewhat startling in scope. Caesar, with his armies, would conquer and unite all of Italy under the auspices of the papacy. The pope would then be, in effect, the absolute ruler of the peninsula—an earthly as well as a spiritual monarch.

The church had weathered storms in the past, suffered through the depravities and excesses and scandals and indignities inflicted upon her by dozens of unworthy popes. But as an institution, she had survived. Now what Borgia had in mind was something new, something shocking, even to the jaded inhabitants of Rome. For the first time in history, a pope intended nothing less audacious than to pass the triple crown of the church, the papal tiara, on to his son! The papacy would become hereditary.

As Niccolo galloped toward Florence, the first steps toward the establishment of that dynasty had already been taken. Caesar had invaded the Romagna. And the ambition and the wrath of the Borgias was first directed, not against one of the wicked sons of that race of bastards and tyrants, but against one of her daughters—Caterina Sforza of Forli.

He covered the seven miles from San Casciano to Florence in less than an hour. Now a familiar and respected figure in the Signoria, Niccolo did not have to wait to be shown into the Great Council Room, but was allowed to make his own, hurried way there. The council was not in session when he arrived, but small knots of worried men were scattered around the immense chamber. Glancing quickly around, Niccolo noted that many of the dignitaries present were, like himself, dressed in riding clothes, a sign of the haste with which they had been assembled.

"Ah, the worthy secretary has arrived. Over here, Machiavelli. Your counsels are sorely needed." It was Bishop Soderini who first spied Niccolo.

"Your Excellency," Niccolo acknowledged his greeting with a curt bow and was instantly at his side. "What's happened?"

"Your friend, the Countess of Forli, has been taken prisoner." As usual, the bishop demonstrated the unruffled aplomb of the clergy in a crisis. He spoke with the measured gravity and concern of a confessor who turns calmly to the murderer and says, "Yes, my son, what is it?"

"Not killed?" asked Niccolo, surprised, but relieved too.

"Not yet," said the unflappable bishop.

"She seems to be in the habit of making herself an obstacle in the path of advancing armies." It was the bishop's brother, Piero Soderini, who turned and spoke. Niccolo had always been intimidated by the majestic Soderini, whose stature and magnificent blond hair gave him the appearance of God the Father as a young man.

Soderini was a friend of the Machiavelli family and had often done business with Bernardo Machiavelli. As a boy, Niccolo had frequently been introduced to him, and the statuesque blond made a permanent impression on the boy. To this day, Niccolo could not entirely shake from his mind the sense of awe that Piero Soderini never failed to inspire in him at an early age. Now in his fifties, Soderini's majesty was undiminished, although a wiser Niccolo allowed himself to wonder, looking at the man's splendid blond locks, whether he tinted them.

Piero Soderini continued, "When Imola surrendered to Caesar, Caterina flew into a rage. 'Rabbits!' she pronounced them and prepared for her own defense. She cut down all the trees around the castle and flooded the surrounding countryside in an effort to slow Caesar's advance. She said she was resolved to show the Spanish bastard that a woman was capable of firing cannon!"

Niccolo grinned to himself. He could imagine the indomitable Amazon once again on the ramparts, where she belonged.

"The siege lasted a fortnight and was beginning to be an embarrassment to the mighty Caesar, stopped in his tracks at a small castle defended by a woman. But Borgia's firepower was second to none, and eventually a section of the walls collapsed into the moat. When the defenses were breached, she fell back to the keep. At this point there could not have been more than thirty men left alive with her, but they flung back every attack." Here Soderini paused and fixed Niccolo with a curious look in his eye. "They say she cast a spell over them, to make them fight like that."

"In a last desperate attempt, she set fire to the magazine and had it blown up in the face of the army that was pouring through the ruptured walls. Eventually they took her."

"But Caesar Borgia doesn't take prisoners," said Niccolo, "and when he does, it's only to play with them for a while, as a cat plays with a mouse before eating it."

Here Soderini smiled, "She outsmarted him. When she saw that all was lost, apparently she was infuriated by the idea of dying at the hands of the Borgia. She swore she wouldn't give Caesar the satisfaction of killing her and so, at the last minute, she surrendered to the French troops that were fighting with him! In doing so, she made it absolutely clear that she yielded not to Borgia, but to France, and that she was placing her life and her honor under the protection of King Louis!"

"Bravo," said Niccolo. "The tigress is safe."

"Not exactly," was Soderini's reply. "She's been 'deposited' in Rome under the joint supervision of the French and the pope. For now, Borgia won't dare touch her. He can't risk incurring the wrath of the French. But things could change."

"And Caesar?" asked Niccolo, suddenly concerned, not about the fate of a friend, but about that of the republic.

"That's the problem," said Soderini. "Caesar."

After his victory at Forli, Caesar quickly consolidated his gains in the Romagna, easily procuring the surrender of the other city-states there. His bold advance and his startling success began to worry the French, who could ill afford a united Italy, armed and dangerous, at their southern flank. Louis XII recalled the contingent of French troops serving under Caesar's banner and temporarily put his conquests on hold. For Caesar Borgia, however, this was only a lull in the action, and he used the time to return to Rome, where he was greeted by his father, the pope, as a conquering hero.

A tremendous welcoming procession was arranged. When it came to making his children happy, the pope spared no expense. Hundreds of retainers marched through the streets with Caesar's name emblazoned in silver on their black, ruffled, Spanish-style doublets. There was the usual multicolored display of civilian pomposity, religious extravagance, and military might. It is said that the horses had shoes of silver, which were fixed to their hooves with one nail only, permitting them to come loose and fall off, so that they might later to be retrieved by the grateful and adoring mobs.

On eleven pageant wagons, the triumphs of Caesar—the first Caesar, this one's namesake, Julius Caesar—were represented, everything from the crossing of the Rubicon to the crowning with laurels on the Capitoline hill. The pope found the procession so moving and so beautiful that he demanded to see it twice. In one of the pageant wagons, was a scene depicting Caesar's conquest and humiliation of Egypt. When he had subdued that nation and brought it to its knees under Rome's dominion, Caesar then crowned his triumph by taking to his bed the Egyptian Queen, Cleopatra. In the Borgia reenactment of this event, in the place of the queen Cleopatra, rode Caterina Sforza. Despite their agreement with the French, the Borgia could not resist this piece of delicious irony. She appeared on a mighty white horse, clad in a black gown "in the Turkish style." Her hands were bound with shackles of gold. Under her wood and papier-mâché horse, her feet had been chained together to prevent escape.

At the end of the procession, there was a solemn ceremony in which Caesar was invested as standard-bearer of the church. He knelt before his father, the supreme pontiff and successor of Saint Peter, and received from his consecrated hands the pennant and insignia of his sacred office. The standard-bearer's biretta was placed on his head and the mantle wrapped around his shoulders. Through a thick cloud of incense, the pope was heard to utter in an emotional voice, "This is my beloved son in whom I am well pleased."

Caesar did not rest on his laurels in Rome for long. He had soon assembled a new army and was pressing north to complete his conquest of the Romagna, where the largest city, Bologna, still held out against him. In the course of that march, Caesar Borgia stopped at Urbino and sent a brief message to Florence. He demanded that the republic dispatch an envoy to confer with him on matters of the utmost importance. Immediately! It was this arrogant and abrupt summons that occasioned the hasty convocation of Florentine leaders and diplomats to which Niccolo had been called. Before the conference broke up late that night, two legations were dispatched, and they left the city at once, not even waiting for the light of day. Piero Soderini set out for Milan, which had been recently conquered by the French and where King Louis himself was now in residence. His brother Francesco, the bishop, was on his way to Urbino to answer the demands of the haughty Borgia. With him was the trusted secretary and selfless servant of the republic, Niccolo Machiavelli.

Niccolo and the bishop took two days to reach Urbino, since the prelate was unaccustomed to travel on horseback and insisted on setting what he called a "civilized" pace. Niccolo, eager to meet the son of the antichrist face-to-face, would unconsciously urge his mount on and then be forced to rein the horse in to await the pleasure of the good bishop.

Everything depended on France and the success of Piero's suit to the French King. As Niccolo had explained to the Soderinis, the French had not taken the Borgia seriously. In fact, it was this lapse in judgment on their part that had occasioned Niccolo's now-famous remark to King Louis that he knew nothing about politics.

As the Florentine representative, Niccolo had explained time and again to the monarch, that Florence posed no threat to anyone, certainly not to France. She asked only to be left alone to govern herself independently and enjoy the fruits of her success. She had no territorial ambitions beyond securing a deep-water harbor through which her commerce could pass unmolested. Pisa was the only object of her attentions.

The Borgias, on the other hand, were dangerous and could pose a threat to the interests of France. If they succeeded in bringing Italy or a good part of Italy under their rule, they could easily challenge their northern neighbor. What, then, would become of France's designs on Milan? Of her hereditary claims to Naples? Of her very security against the threat of invasion from the south?

The Florentine position was simple. If the French would agree to support Florence against the Borgias, their conquest of the peninsula could not be completed, since Florence stood in the middle of Italy, like the heart in the center of a man, like a navel, like a womb.

Arguing the possible responses of King Louis to the Florentine petition, Bishop Soderini and Niccolo rode into the picturesque hilltop town of Urbino on a late summer afternoon. Winding their way through the steep streets of the mountain town on horseback was no mean feat, since at several junctures the horses were actually obliged to ascend stone staircases cut in the side of the mountain. As they made their approach to the Ducal Palace, the two Florentine envoys passed through a dusty little square in an unsavory part of town where an arresting spectacle was taking place.

The square was dominated by a smithy, and the scene was dominated by one who, judging from the size of his arms, was the blacksmith. The big, greasy smith had just succeeded in throwing on his back in the dirt an equally big, greasy opponent unlucky enough to have challenged him in a contest of strength. His rowdy companions were clapping him on his immense shoulders, congratulating him in having thus successfully concluded the brawl, when someone in the small crowd came forward and demanded the smith's attention.

"Ho, smith," he said in a clear voice, "have you got a horseshoe?"

The smith grunted and with a jerk of his head indicated a pile of recently forged shoes alongside a heavy anvil that stood in the doorway of his shop. The man ambled over to the pile and picked a horseshoe off the top, weighing it in his hand, turning it over and inspecting the workmanship. After a moment's silent concentration, he looked up at the smith. "Shoddy work," he said matter-of-factly.

The offended smith clenched his fists and glared at the other man. "I said shoddy work and I'll prove it." With those words, he gripped the horseshoe with both hands, held it across his chest, took a deep breath, and with little apparent effort, bent the curved iron shoe inward until the two ends touched.

There was an audible gasp from several members of the blacksmith's entourage. From the two mounted Florentine diplomats observing the scene, there were whispers of admiration. Then, with as little effort as it had taken him to bend it in, the village Hercules pulled the ends of the shoe back apart again until he held in his hands a broadly curved arc, scarcely recognizable as a proper horseshoe. Laughing, he threw it to the ground and spit. "Shoddy work," he repeated. The blood was rising visibly in the enraged smith's face, and bellowing something incoherent, he hurled himself at his challenger.

The other man stepped nimbly aside and avoided the headlong rush of the bullish smith. Twice he charged, twice the other man stepped out of his path. The animated crowd of onlookers was quick to take sides, shouting encouragement, jeering, making wagers, as the fighters danced and feinted, closing with each other. The smith lunged at his antagonist, throwing a punch that would have felled an ox, but the other man ducked, stepped inside, and drove a fist up into the blacksmith's belly. The force of the blow lifted the burly smith off the ground for a second and sent him crashing into a courtyard wall. There was a cheer from the crowd, but the upstart Hercules had not finished with his opponent yet. Pursuing his advantage, he was on the dazed man in a second. He spun him around, face to the wall, and with staccato regularity, began administering a series of sharp, painful punches to the kidneys. The smith squealed with each new blow. The crowd howled for blood, not forgetting for a minute that the smith was a bully and had given as much, if not more, to many a man. Even the two educated Florentines seemed to be enjoying the rude sport.

He of the horseshoe had already been declared winner, and money was already changing hands to settle bets when the vanquished smith finally sagged to the ground with a groan. But the victor did not back off. He continued to punish the unfortunate smith with the same short, quick, cruel jabs, only this time his target was the blacksmith's face. He pummeled mercilessly, the hammerblows breaking the smith's nose in a burst of blood, cracking his jaw, sending his teeth flying, blackening his eyes, splitting his lips.

There were groans of disapproval from the onlookers now. Things were getting out of hand. The man was going too far. Even in these rough contests among the lowest classes of men, there were limits. Ugly viciousness was not part of the bargain. But who was going to stop such a man? Slowly the disgusted crowd began to disperse. It was Bishop Soderini who finally intervened on the beaten smith's behalf. "You, fellow there," he called. "Don't you think you've had the better of him? Don't you think you can let him go now?"

The victorious strongman turned on the two travelers with a whirl and fixed them with his narrow, intense eyes. Then, his face breaking into a broad, mocking grin, he said, "Of course, Excellency. Anything the gentleman says." There was menace and derision in his voice.

Riding off, the bishop shook his head. "Where do you think they breed devils like that, Machiavelli? If we had a hundred who fought like that, we could take Pisa in a week. We could throw Borgia out of Italy in two!"

Niccolo did not agree. "If we had a hundred like that, we would do better to fear for our own lives."

It was about six in the evening when the two Florentine envoys finally reached the castle. They told the guards at the gate that they had been sent from the Florentine republic on an embassy to Caesar Borgia. They were shown inside, where they dismounted and turned their horses over to the offices of a groom. They were told that the duc de Valentinois would receive them presently. In the meantime, a light repast was laid out for them on a terrace overlooking the courtyard. They were to feel free to refresh themselves after their journey.

After a long, hot, day's ride, both enjoyed the light supper of cold, thinly sliced meats and fruit and the generous quantities of wine. Duly refreshed, they sat sipping the cool wine and awaiting the pleasure of the pope's son. They waited for quite some time. Nobody paid the Florentines the least bit of attention.

Niccolo had always been a minor diplomat, an ambassador without portfolio, and was accustomed to these sorts of delays when seeking audience with self-declared "important men." Bishop Soderini, however, was unused to being kept waiting and was losing his patience. He finally accosted the only person who seemed even remotely aware of their presence, the ancient waiter who periodically brought them a new jar of wine.

"We've been waiting for quite some time now. Would you please go and see what the matter is?"

"I've been instructed that the gentlemen will be received presently. In the meantime, if there's anything I can bring you . . ."

Bishop Soderini cut him off. "You can bring me an explanation for this unconscionable delay, that's what you can bring me," he huffed. "And you can tell me why, if the august Caesar, who is, like us, only a guest in this castle, isn't ready to receive us, the duke, your master, has not seen fit to pay his respects. Surely he's been informed that we're here. He's not so old and decrepit that he can't come down and greet an old friend."

The waiter gave him a wary look. "Caesar Borgia is my master, Excellency," he said with overdue caution.

"Oh, so you're one of his men? Well surely you know where Duke Guidobaldo is. This is his castle and his city, after all. Could you inform him that Bishop Soderini is here and would like to speak to him? And you might remind him that, even if he is an ally of your master Borgia these days, he is and always has been a friend of mine and my family."

The waiter hesitated, then drew closer to the bishop. "You say you're a friend of Duke Guidobaldo?"

"Of course!" mumbled the Bishop, irritably.

"Then you should know that Duke Guidobaldo is no longer lord of Urbino. He has . . . abdicated."

"What!" sputtered the Bishop, releasing a mouthful of wine in the process and losing a little of his unflappable clerical dignity.

"What do you mean, he's abdicated?"

"He's been accused of ingratitude and treachery toward the supreme pontiff. It was only by luck that he managed to flee before being murdered. Now, there's a price on his head and Caesar Borgia is lord of Urbino."

The bishop muttered an imprecation. "Fled? Price on his head? What are you talking about? When did this happen?"

"It would be imprudent of me to talk about it, Excellency. If you'll excuse me . . ."

"I'll not excuse you," said the bishop, "Tell me what happened, man, or I'll see to it that your master learns of this insubordinate behavior."

Drawing even closer so that his voice was almost a whisper in the bishop's ear, the waiter sketched the situation in short, nervous phrases. "Duke Guidobaldo made a treaty of friendship with the Borgia. He sent Caesar artillery. For the siege of Camerino. But Caesar turned and marched on Urbino instead. Marched on the duke with his own guns. The duke was dining outside the city, at the monastery of Zoccolante, when he heard the news about the approaching army. He barely escaped with his life. Where he is, I don't know, but I do know that here, now, we're all servants of Caesar Borgia, Lord of Urbino."

The bishop was dumbfounded and suddenly more than a little apprehensive about the impending meeting with Caesar Borgia. Niccolo, who had been listening intently the whole time, summed up the situation, "If that's how he treats his allies, what can we, his enemies, expect from him?"

They did not have long to ponder the question, for they were soon called to their audience with Caesar Borgia. It was well after midnight when they were led through a series of arched doorways, each guarded by heavily armed men. When Borgia was formally announced, the recitation of the titles that had accrued to his name took almost two minutes. The Spanish stood very much on ceremony.

As he swept into the room, it was not his ornate, foreign-looking clothing that startled and unsettled the two Florentine ambassadors. The lush, black-velvet doublet decorated with pearls the size of walnuts and the shimmering satin and the starched Spanish ruffles were remarkable in their own right, but the bishop and even Niccolo were experienced enough in diplomacy and the extravagances of royal courts so that they no longer balked at mere exotic dress and behavior. But balk they did, for neither was able to conceal his shock and consternation upon discovering that Caesar Borgia, the pope's son, was the ruthless village strongman.

24

The Subtleties of Spanish Hospitality

Borgia said nothing, but it was apparent from his sly smile that he was enjoying the surprise he had sprung on the two Florentine envoys. They were taken off guard. He had put them at an initial disadvantage. He had gained the upper hand. All this, he gave them to understand without saying a word. He was the sort of man who communicated with a nod, a look, a frown, or the pointing of a finger. He was a man to whom actions came more readily than words.

He sat and indicated that they should do likewise. With his hands folded in his lap, Borgia sat absolutely still. There was something uncanny in that stillness that announced the total self-control of the man, the utter calm and assurance. He did not address them. Only the attentive expression on his face told the emissaries that he was listening, that he was ready to do business and was waiting for them to speak.

Still flustered, Bishop Soderini began his formal protestations of friendship and goodwill on the part of the republic of Florence. Niccolo, ever the astute observer, scrutinized their opponent.

The Spanish cut of his clothes, with their suggestions of decadence and foppery would have been ludicrous, even effeminate on most men, but not so on Caesar Borgia. The easy grace with which he moved and the extraordinary muscular control he exerted to maintain himself erect and motionless made the clothing seem superfluous and unimportant. Niccolo also knew that under the capricious clothing were hard muscles capable of bending an iron horseshoe as easily as he himself might bend a soft wax candle on a hot summer day.

When they first encountered him that afternoon, as the village

Atlas, Borgia was wearing a cheap workman's cloth cap. Hatless now, his shiny black hair fell in ringlets down around his shoulders. His impeccably trimmed and tightly curled black beard came to a point on his chin. In an Italy where beards had long been out of fashion for men, this beard gave him an exotic, almost-Moorish air. His swarthy complexion and his deep, dark almond eyes, drooping slightly at the corners with a hint of Spanish sadness added to the impression of vague, oriental menace. In fact, once, in his native Spain, someone had called Caesar a *marrano,* a white Moor. The insult, considered one of the most grave that could be hurled in the face of a proper Spaniard, was avenged with typical Caesarian swiftness. He cut the offender's tongue out with his own hands and had it nailed to a pillory to serve as an example.

Caesar Borgia allowed Soderini to talk on, to ramble. When the bishop would finish a sentence and receive no reply, he would hastily add a qualification, an amendment, some further explanation. He would make point after point, anticipating Borgia's objections and then answering them. He was engaged in a conversation with himself.

His nervousness at eliciting no response whatsoever from Borgia was becoming apparent. The latter betrayed no emotion as the bishop, with less and less confidence, expounded and proposed. Finally, Soderini concluded, his voice trailing off weakly at the end. It was as if Caesar Borgia had just won an argument without even saying a single word.

He studied the Florentine bishop in silence. He brought his folded hands up to his chin, hands that looked oddly refined for bludgeons that had recently beaten a bull of a man senseless. When Caesar spoke, he came directly to the point. He eschewed the long-winded, verbal fencing that was the professional diplomat's stock in trade. His voice was deep, rich, mellifluous.

"I wish to be on a clear footing with the Florentines. If you accept my friendship, we shall be allies in a united Italy. If you decline it, then I have every right before God and man to defend my own interests. If you don't want me as a friend, then you will have me as an implacable enemy. What will it be?"

Soderini faltered. He was unprepared to address such a simple, blunt proposal. His was the art of temporizing, of insinuations and vague promises. "Well, I would need some time, I would have to consult my government . . ."

Borgia interrupted, almost gently. "This government of yours, this republican government, I don't like it. You should change it. If you don't, perhaps I will." His voice was as soft and dark as the velvet cloak he wore.

Bishop Soderini was speechless at the audacity of Borgia's ultimatum. He sputtered, but no reply was forthcoming. Instead, it was Niccolo who answered the Spaniard. "We Florentines have the government we desire. It may, as you put it, displease you, but that scarcely concerns us. We're prepared to deal with you either as a friend or as an enemy. The choice is as much yours as ours."

Borgia regarded the secretary who had spoken, not rashly or impetuously, but firmly and defiantly. There was a hint of admiration in his silent appraisal. "My sources tell me you're the young Florentine who spoke so boldly before the king of France?"

"I felt I was only doing my duty in correcting his majesty on certain points of fact that he had somehow failed to grasp."

"And are there certain points of fact that I've failed to grasp?"

"Most assuredly," said Niccolo without hesitation. "You confess yourself a friend of Florence, yet you send your dog, Vitellozzo, to yap at our heels, to harass Tuscany, and attack us at Arezzo. We don't consider that an act of friendship."

Borgia smiled and answered the accusation, all the while speaking smoothly, melodiously. "Vitellozzo acts on his own. I have no part in his adventures. You know he hates your city. You cheated him out of his command and his money at Pisa. You killed his brother Paolo. Is it any wonder he wages war on you?"

"Vitellozzo is incapable of initiative, incapable of doing anything on his own, without direction, without permission."

"I agree with you," said Borgia. "Vitellozzo is a cur, good for nothing but ravishing the countryside, pillaging, stealing, and burning. He's a howling animal. They say he's mad, you know, and he excuses his hasty and brutal actions by claiming he suffers from the French disease."

"We call it the Spanish disease," observed Niccolo.

"Touché," acknowledged the Spaniard, amused now by the impertinence of the young secretary. "But I swear I know nothing of Vitellozzo and this unfortunate business at Arezzo. Whatever he's doing there, he's doing on his own."

"Perhaps," said Niccolo, knowing that Vitellozzo was in the employ of Borgia and didn't make a move without his knowledge. "And perhaps if you had a word with him, he might desist."

"And if he doesn't?"

"Then it would be extremely difficult for the republic of Florence to offer you its friendship."

"I may speak to Vitellozzo. He may choose to withdraw. Whatever the outcome, though, you must decide quickly. I'll give you until tomorrow. And I warn you, there can be no half measures between us, between Florence and me. If you are not with me, then you are against me."

"Perhaps," said Niccolo wryly. Who'd said that before?

On that ambiguous note, much to the relief of Bishop Soderini, the colloquium ended. That night, both Niccolo and the bishop were up late writing urgent dispatches to their government. They related the reason why Caesar had sent for them and passed on his ultimatum. Without the support of France, Florence had nothing with which to bargain. She had no troops for her own defense, and Borgia was just over a day's march from her walls and gates. He was already within striking distance, with an army that grew in strength every day, and he was famous for acting with blinding speed, without revealing his plans to anybody in advance. His sudden, bold stroke at Urbino was proof enough of that.

Niccolo had profoundly mixed feelings about the man. He was straightforward and blunt in a milieu where no one ever said what he was thinking. He showed resolve and determination where indecision and cowardice were the rule. And his talk of a united Italy intrigued the young secretary.

But this man was the enemy of Florence, and there was treachery in his heart. Despite his admiration for Borgia's single-mindedness, Niccolo concluded his dispatch that night by pleading with the Signoria to come to a swift decision. "The duke professes good faith," he wrote, "and yet his mode of action is to sneak into other people's houses before they are aware of it. Here in Urbino he came like a swift, subtle, fatal disease that caused death before the illness was even discovered." As Niccolo drifted into an uneasy sleep that night, he was haunted by that charming voice, those subdued tones—I don't like your government. You should change it . . . Change it . . . Change it . . .

The next day, the time for the meeting was fixed at two hours after sunset, about ten o'clock in the evening. After discussions that Caesar said would be most brief, the Florentine envoys were invited to dine with him and a few friends. Niccolo had misgivings about the lateness of the hour. He hoped the food would not be unnecessarily spicy, since the violence wrought in his bowels at that late hour would be enough to keep him up all night with nightmares. Perhaps that's why the Spanish appear to be such an exotic race, he thought, they eat too late and spend their nights tormented by fantastic visions.

In the course of the day, the two Florentines kept mostly to themselves, worried, and wrote more dispatches. When they left the rooms assigned to them, they noticed that everywhere there were armed guards. Every door in the palace was guarded—and locked. Caesar Borgia was a cautious man.

Midmorning they received a document from Borgia. It was a contract he had drawn up in which he stipulated his intentions to conclude a perpetual alliance with the republic of Florence who, in turn, agreed to engage him as *condottiere,* or military commander, for the sum of 36,000 florins a year for a period of three years. According to the terms of the contract, Borgia was under no obligation to provide active service, but was simply required to maintain in a state of readiness three-hundred men at arms to be put at the disposition of the republic in case of an emergency. It was a simple, outright bribe. Caesar was obviously aware that the Florentines, in times of trouble, were willing to pay for the public safety.

Niccolo was not surprised at the terms, and indeed he and Soderini were prepared for just such an offer. But 36,000 florins a year! To do absolutely nothing! His own annual salary, as a result of his recent diplomatic triumphs in France, had risen to the princely sum of 210 florins. And he had to work seven days a week to draw it!

Late in the afternoon, the envoy from Florence arrived with the good news. Already a column of French horse, foot, and artillery was making its way toward Florence from Milan. Piero Soderini's mission to Louis

XII had been a success. Furthermore, the French king had also seen the wisdom of curtailing Borgia's empire-building activities in central Italy and had dispatched a special envoy to confer with his "friend and trusted ally, the duc de Valentinois." The substance of the message he sent Caesar was that it was not his majesty's will that his ally, the Valentinois, should proceed against his other staunch ally, the republic of Florence. For the time being, Florence was safe, and Borgia's ambitions in her direction would be checked. For the time being. The dispatch also authorized Bishop Soderini to accept any terms Borgia might offer, knowing all the while that they would never be honored by either side.

The diplomatic colloquy that evening was concluded without any delays or arguments. Caesar was delighted with his new commission from Florence and was assured that his 36,000 florins were already on their way. For the time being, an uneasy truce had been arranged. Both parties were appeased—Caesar with a worthless contract, the Florentines with worthless assurances. All were united, allies, under the wise and happy stewardship of the king of France. The first round ended in a draw.

Dinner was better than Niccolo had expected, and Caesar Borgia proved to be a gracious and charming host. Although he himself took Spanish wine, he realized that it was not to the liking of most Italians, and he thoughtfully supplied the best of what the vineyards in his new lands in Urbino were capable of producing. The food too was excellent and of local provenance. While Niccolo had half expected such barbaric fare as concoctions of oysters and pork, or even worse, eggs and dried codfish, he was treated to thick slabs of duck liver pâté, followed by roasted pigeons and doves. Vegetables were plentiful, including crisp fennel and tiny, tasty cabbages, fried whole. The only curious thing about the food, which was otherwise delicious and perfectly cooked, was the total lack of seasoning. The uniform blandness, even to the absence of salt, puzzled Niccolo, who also noticed that Borgia had at his elbow, a small pot of sauce with which he occasionally seasoned his own food, but nobody else's.

"It's not a culinary preference, but a political necessity," said the host who was aware of Niccolo's interest in his sauce pot. "Did you know that I can detect the taste of poison in unseasoned food?"

"And what does it taste like?"

"Sometimes bitter, sometimes acidic, sometimes very subtle. But almost any poison, even in enormous quantities, can be concealed with pungent spices—pepper and ginger, cinnamon. This sauce, I make myself. It's no secret recipe—garlic, parsley, a little white wine, some herbs. But I make it myself and I keep it in my possession. No other human hand touches it. If I'm satisfied after tasting the unseasoned food, I sauce it myself. Would you like to try some?"

Niccolo said he would and extended his hand to take the sauce pot. His host only smiled. "Pass your plate over here," he said. He was indeed a cautious man.

The dinner was attended by a number of Borgia intimates, mostly Spaniards who kept to themselves, speaking Spanish. There was only one glaring problem with the guest list—Vitellozzo Vitelli.

From the point of view of etiquette, Vitellozzo left much to be desired. From his end of the table came a constant barrage of crunching, slurping, and sucking sounds. Vitellozzo had little to add to the conversation at the beginning of the meal, totally preoccupied as he was with his feeding frenzy, gnawing on the bones and sloshing, rather than quaffing, his wine. In a capricious gesture, Borgia had seated the uncouth glutton next to the refined Bishop Soderini, who was most annoyed at the elbowing and splashing he had to endure at the hands of his dinner companion. It was obvious that Borgia enjoyed his little jest.

"Tell me, Vitellozzo," said Borgia. "How is the campaign against Arezzo going?"

"Not making much headway there, sir," he said between belches. "We're meeting a lot of resistance in the countryside. Treacherous peasants there hiding their corn, their money. They don't want to help us. We have to persuade them." He grinned.

Niccolo could not bear to look at Vitellozzo when he talked. With the yellow pustules all around his mouth, he would have made a repulsive sight anywhere. At table, the impression he made was even more nauseating.

"Vitellozzo has had quite a lot of success in subduing the countryside, though. Haven't you, Vitellozzo?" Borgia smiled. "They say women prefer to throw themselves and their daughters into the rivers rather than be captured by his troops." Vitellozzo cackled in acknowledgement.

"And now, they tell me you have a new ally, Vitellozzo. Don't you? Tell these Florentine gentlemen who it is."

His pockmarked face broke into a broad grin. Vitellozzo smiled at his own cleverness. "Piero de' Medici."

Once again, Borgia had caught the Florentine envoys unawares, and he was savoring his victory. Vitellozzo too seemed to be enjoying himself, and, as the subtle game of glances and gestures played itself out among the cognoscenti, he launched into a bawdy description of his latest enterprise, which consisted of carrying off women and girls on packhorses, like so much merchandise, to Rome. "And there," he said, "if you have the right contacts, if you can find the Turkish merchants who are willing to trade, you can get up to one thousand ducats for one of them. If you can get your hands on a blond, a real blond, they'll . . ."

Borgia did not allow Vitellozzo to finish. He shot him a glance, then jerked his head in the direction of the door. In a matter of seconds, the loathsome lieutenant had obsequiously withdrawn. If there was ever any doubt as to who was giving Vitellozzo his orders, that look cleared them all away. Vitellozzo had already played his part in the little comedy Caesar Borgia had arranged, and he was quickly written out of the play.

"Disgusting man," said Borgia disdainfully, "but useful. Don't be concerned, though. I've spoken to him and he's agreed to withdraw from Arezzo. For the time being. Besides I need him elsewhere."

"Still," he added as an afterthought, "I wonder what sort of mischief he could be cooking up with Piero? It would be worth keeping an eye on those two, wouldn't it?"

Both Niccolo and the bishop understood the veiled threat. Borgia had already said he did not like the government of Florence. Maybe he was contemplating changing it. Maybe he had found a suitable candidate to head a new regime in Piero de' Medici. And maybe he was only bluffing. Maybe.

A master of manipulation, Borgia quickly changed the subject. Having planted the seeds of doubt in the minds of his two Florentine guests, he left them with something to think about and turned to other topics. He spoke knowledgably of poetry and music, both Spanish and Italian. He spoke of art, although his interest in it seemed to focus more on market value than beauty. The wine had loosened his tongue a little, and he spoke of his campaigns in the Romagna. It was here that Niccolo could not resist taunting him.

"I understand you had some trouble with the good lady of Forli?"

"Trouble," said Borgia, feigning surprise. "She gave me no trouble. In fact she was quite compliant."

"How so?" asked Niccolo.

"For all her daring, we must admit that Caterina's defense of her castle was an abysmal failure. Let me suggest, among gentlemen, with the utmost delicacy of course, that once she fell into my hands, her defense of her own virtue was considerably less spirited and considerably less successful." Borgia smiled the knowing smile of the conqueror.

He went on, "She's quite an extraordinary woman, you know, a powerful woman, but after all, only a woman." He seemed to lose himself in his memories for a moment, trying to recall the fond details of his conquest. "It was a tremendous sensation and a unique one, for me. To hold a woman like that in my arms—a battle-scarred Amazon. Do you know how exciting it can be to run your fingers up and down a deep scar on a woman's back while you're making love to her? Up and down the length of her spine?"

The bishop freely admitted that he had never thought about it before. Niccolo said nothing.

"Not only was it an exquisite thrill for me, it drove her into a frenzy, an ecstasy." He sighed, running his fingers under his nose, as if the perfume of that sweet encounter still lingered on them. "Spanish women, I have always found to be superior to Italians," he said. "The blood runs hotter in their veins. But this Caterina Sforza . . ." he trailed off again, leaving the rest to the imagination of his knowing male companions.

It was as the great lover and conqueror that Caesar chose to end that evening. His Spanish compatriots dutifully disappeared while he accompanied his honored Florentine guests to the door. As the bishop tottered off down the guarded corridor toward his rooms, Niccolo hung back a second. "Ever since I saw Caterina Sforza for the first time, on the walls at Mordano, I've always wondered what it would be like to possess a woman like that." He put special emphasis on the word possess. "I envy you."

Borgia accepted the compliment graciously as he always accepted the admiration of lesser men. "But it bothers me," said the secretary. "It bothers me to think that someone as ferocious and fearless as the countess should have a scar on her back, of all places. It's as though she'd been wounded running away."

"In the heat of battle, these things happen. Blows arrive from every quarter," said Borgia dismissively.

"I suppose so," said Niccolo, now eyeing the duke with the sly self-assurance of someone about to spring a trap. "Still . . . I'm surprised that such a wound wouldn't have torn open with all the exertions and vigors of lovemaking, especially with such a lover as yourself."

"Oh, it was an old wound," said Borgia, "completely closed, healed over."

"That's strange then," said the secretary thinking about it, apparently puzzled. "It wasn't there a few months ago."

Niccolo did not wait for a reply. Abruptly, he took his leave, but not before noticing that, this time, it was the duke who was caught off his guard. There was a look of astonishment on his face, followed by the embarrassment of one who has been caught in a lie. Niccolo had opened up a tiny crack in the duke's armor, a small chink in his defenses.

"Fio de putta bastardo." A low, whistled Spanish curse followed the retreating Florentine secretary down the darkened corridor.

The daily policy of petty subterfuge that characterized, of necessity, the conduct of Florentine foreign affairs was extremely difficult to control in all its complicated and interlocking detail. Many things had to be taken into account—the explosive and unpredictable Borgia on the loose with a huge army, the waffling of the king of France, the rapidly shifting alliances among Venice, Milan, Spain, Germany, and the pope, and, of course, the never-ending war with Pisa. Managing a policy to deal effectively with this heaving, swirling sea of states and alliances would have been challenge enough for any government. In Florence, the situation was exacerbated by precisely the quality that the city believed set her apart from her neighbors—the love of liberty.

So fearful was she of a tyrant reestablishing himself or of power being concentrated in the hands of a small group of men, that her constitution mandated what amounted to a state permanently and continuously in the throes of electioneering. Florence's primary legislative and executive bodies, the Great Council of Twelve Hundred, the smaller council of The Eighty, and the gonfaloniere or standard-bearer, were all elected to office for terms of only two months.

Continuity in government was impossible, everything moved slowly and uncertainly, money was wasted, and decisions were postponed and ultimately never made. When mistakes were made, nobody could be found responsible, since magistrates came and went more quickly than the torrential spring rains and the swollen waters of the Arno.

At this juncture, many ideas for radical reform were put forward and debated. All agreed that some sort of change in the government was necessary. What was finally agreed upon was to make the elective position of gonfaloniere—the standard-bearer of the Signoria—permanent. The position was then legally defined, safeguards were imposed, procedures for removal established, and qualifications for office stipulated. In order to carefully limit and circumscribe the power of the new gonfaloniere, the Signoria insisted that he could hold no other office, that his sons, brothers, and nephews were excluded from the council, and that the entire family was forbidden to engage in trade and commerce. When elections were finally held in 1502, the bishop's brother, Piero Soderini, was elected by a large majority, the first gonfaloniere for life.

Although wealthy, Soderini was always considered a good friend of the people and an advocate of liberal government. If he was not a brilliant leader or an extraordinarily gifted politician, he was a competent administrator. Many claimed that it was precisely his lack of exceptional gifts that made him acceptable to the largest segment of the population. He did not excite the passions of his fellow citizens, neither excessive hatred nor excessive devotion, nor was he filled with an overweening ambition to enlarge and extend his power.

If Soderini lacked brilliance, this is not to say that he was stupid or that he exhibited bad judgment. Quite the contrary, for he was fully aware of his own limitations and quick to seek the advice and counsel of those who knew and understood more than he. He had a knack for recognizing talent in others and putting it to good use. And it was certainly no accident that he quickly came to depend on the extraordinary mind and abilities of his secretary, Niccolo Machiavelli. So when, just a few months after Soderini's election, Borgia began to threaten Florence anew and demand the money she had promised him for the *condotta*, and it was decided that an envoy should be sent to him in all haste to clarify the situation, the choice naturally fell on Niccolo.

Caesar was wreaking his own special brand of havoc in central Italy, striking without warning, capturing cities, deposing tyrants and installing himself in their place. Like his namesake, Julius Caesar, he was a brilliant military strategist, and, like the Caesar of old, Borgia yearned to create an empire, although he showed none of his predecessor's hesitation or indecision about assuming the title of emperor. Although he often said that he came to Italy, not to play the tyrant but to do away with tyrants, his recently adopted motto, *Aut Caesar, Aut Nihil*—"Either Caesar or Nothing"—seemed to sum up his views on the immediate future of the Italian peninsula.

This time, Niccolo received his commission directly from Piero Soderini, the gonfaloniere for life and the god-like idol of his childhood. Despite this new proximity to power and the privileges such a position of favor might be expected to carry with it, Niccolo received only half the money he requested from the parsimonious republic, and once again, found himself obliged to use his own horse. So it was with a certain weariness that he rode out of Florence, alone, reviewing what had now become the depressingly familiar instructions—make no promises, spend no money, offer nothing concrete, buy time, try to get information, and report back daily. The only twist, the only area in which he was authorized to come to terms immediately, since it was a matter of the utmost urgency, was in the arrangement of a safe conduct for the Florentine merchants through the territories controlled by Borgia. Trade must go on.

Whether it was the increasingly insubstantial nature of his diplomatic efforts or just overwork, Niccolo had accepted this mission with the greatest reluctance. Then, too, he had little desire to lock horns again with the formidable Borgia, a man who could leap into the saddle with one hand, bend iron, and sever the thick neck of a Spanish bull with a single stroke. Borgia, too, played the diplomatic game, and he played it well, but he did much more than just temporize and stall for time. He acted. He struck. He took the initiative. Where others proceeded with extreme caution, he launched himself with all the impetus and directed destructive energy of a cannon shot.

Borgia's physical prowess made Niccolo vaguely uncomfortable. He sensed a tremendous violence in the man, although it was always under control. But he could not help thinking, what would happen if that control slipped, even for a minute, and the pent-up, black rage that was seething inside him, just below the surface, were unleashed? What could he, the modest diplomat, the man of many words and frail reason, do to withstand the onslaught of such a fury? Niccolo's feelings toward Borgia were a source of growing consternation to him. He hovered between disdain for the man and admiration, between awe and loathing.

The qualities Niccolo most admired in Borgia were the ones that prevented him from actually gaining an audience with the duke for well over a week. Borgia's boldness, his unpredictability, the swiftness with which he struck made it difficult for Niccolo to track him down. When the itinerant Florentine envoy finally reached Camerino, the duke had moved on to Urbino. Upon obtaining Urbino, Niccolo discovered that Borgia had set out for Cesena. Having no other choice, the weary ambassador-without-portfolio dragged himself along in the impetuous conqueror's footsteps, on through Forli and Faenza. At Imola, Niccolo finally caught up with him.

The days on horseback, far from refreshing Niccolo, had only added to the weight of worry that was pressing down on him. The pace he was required to maintain in his pursuit of the precipitous duke aggravated the pain in his back, too long curved over a writing table, and now too long punished in the saddle. What is more, the irregular eating and sleeping habits he had adopted in order to continue on his forced march were creating a terrible confusion in his stomach and bowels. The rain and occasional sleet and snow tended to make matters even worse from both a digestive and a rheumatic point of view.

For fear of losing his quarry yet another time, Niccolo presented himself at Borgia's headquarters *cavalchereccio*, horseman that he was, without even changing clothes. He was ushered almost immediately into the presence of the daunting warrior.

When he realized that it was Niccolo who had been sent to him again on behalf of Florence, Borgia's thin lips curled into a smile. "The impertinent secretary," he announced, seeming to derive a great deal of satisfaction from the situation. "Well?" Laconic and unnerving as usual, Borgia left it to his interlocutor to begin the dialogue.

In rather ornate and formal language, the language of diplomacy, which says much and nothing at the same time, Niccolo reiterated Florence's desire to be on friendly terms with the duke, just as Bishop Soderini had done in their last encounter. Again, Borgia listened without reply or interruption.

"Sit down, secretary," he said pointing to a lavishly upholstered chair. Niccolo hesitated on account of the mud caked on his boots and cloak. Borgia needed no words, only a sneer to indicate his contempt for the fate of the furniture, and Niccolo gratefully sank back into it. The duke remained standing as he spoke, once again exhibiting the same eerie motionlessness, the same supreme muscular control.

"I'm going to tell you things that I've told to few other living men." He put an ominous accent on the word, living. "You spoke freely to me the last time we met. Freely, if deviously. That was admirable, especially from a Florentine, especially from one like yourself. It must have taken courage, since you know I could bend you in half more easily than a horseshoe." Niccolo winced inwardly at the thought, and Borgia continued.

"So let me speak freely to you. Vitellozzo, Paolo Orsini—my captains, my trustworthy captains—long for the destruction of Florence. They lust for it. They are mad for it, and they've pleaded with me, on their knees like beggars in a church, they've asked me time and again to proceed against you. They want me to put Piero de' Medici back in Florence. And what have I done?

"Nothing. I've shown forbearance. I've kept my faith with you. Can the Florentines say as much?" He paused. Niccolo, taking a lesson from the master, kept his silence and made no reply.

"When you asked me to speak to Vitellozzo about his misbehavior at Arezzo, I called him off. I've honored my promises. Have the Florentines honored theirs?" Niccolo was about to repeat his bland assurances that all was in order and that Florence was on the verge of fulfilling her part of the bargain, but Borgia had something more in mind.

"Now the situation is changing—rapidly. Vitellozzo is angry with me for interfering with his fun at Arezzo. He conspires against me, him and the others. They play at rebellion, and they think I don't know." The news of this dissent in the ranks of Borgia's army brought Niccolo to attention.

The duke continued, "Right now they're meeting at La Magione, holding their diet of bankrupts, this league of petty princes and would-be tyrants. You see, I'm completely informed of their every move.

"Now, if I patch things up with these unruly confederates of mine, the old difficulties and recriminations will all come back. They'll be howling for Florentine blood again, wanting to reinstate the Medici again, and I may not be as successful at reigning them in. I may have to make concessions to keep them in line. I may have to let them attack Florence." Borgia's threat was not lost on Niccolo.

"Now is the time for you to conclude this alliance with me, a real alliance. Now is the time to join me. Together, Italy is ours. This is the moment for Florence to act."

But instead of actions, Niccolo offered only words. "I will have to advise my superiors first of these developments, which they will assuredly take into consideration. After deliberations, they will forward their decision—" Borgia cut him off.

"Consideration, deliberations! Is it ever possible to settle anything with these Florentines! With this government of old women and merchants!" Abruptly, he left the room.

Either Borgia's anger was short-lived, or he simply concealed it, for the next day he summoned Niccolo again, and the verbal fencing began anew. In the days and weeks that followed, the two men met almost daily, and a guarded but mutual admiration grew up between them. When pressed, Niccolo would beg off and protest that he was not empowered to make any commitments, but that he would write at once to the Signoria. Borgia, for his part, was likewise suitably vague. When the Florentines demanded to know more about his plans in order to conclude an alliance with him, he would steer the conversation in another direction. Niccolo could not even guess what his real objective was. Was he preparing to strike? And if so, where?

Meanwhile, Niccolo's efforts to gather useful intelligence were meeting with little success. Troops came and went, but there was an air of mystery about their movements. An atmosphere of secrecy prevailed. Niccolo could obtain no estimate of how many troops Borgia had in the field, of where they were, or of what he intended to do with them. Perhaps the only area in which real progress was made was in negotiating the agreement to let Florentine merchants trade in Borgia's territory. Naturally, a tariff was imposed on these transactions, and a decent percentage of the profits went to the duke.

For weeks, Niccolo had been writing to the Signoria, begging to be recalled. He saw his mission as an endless and essentially useless one and implored them to send another ambassador, someone with more authority who could negotiate a deal with Borgia. The Signoria, however, refused. He was doing exactly what they wanted him to do—nothing. In a dangerous and potentially explosive situation where any firm policy was likely to backfire, Niccolo was doing all that could be done. He was buying time.

To sooth their disgruntled envoy, the Signoria kept up a steady stream of letters, lavishly praising his efforts. Even the gonfaloniere, Soderini himself, wrote regularly. And when the letters of praise were no longer enough to revive Niccolo's flagging spirits, they took an unprecedented step. They sent him money.

Niccolo had been with Borgia's retinue for months now, and little had happened. In particular, the issue of the rebellious generals seemed to have almost entirely disappeared. There were scattered reports of skirmishes, but that was all. If most of Borgia's moves were shrouded in secrecy, his plans for dealing with the rebels were the most secret of all. And even though the Signoria pressed him for information on the subject, Niccolo could find out nothing, try as he might. Then, one morning in late November, he saw something that gave him cause for speculation and concern. A liveried messenger hurried past him on his way out of the duke's apartments, which in itself was nothing unusual. The duke was in constant communication with Rome, with France, with his troops, and with the small army of mistresses who followed him from town to town. But this was no ordinary messenger. Although his cap was pulled down over his eyes, and his collar up around his chin, there was no mistaking the poxy features of Vitellozzo Vitelli.

Niccolo quickly penned an urgent dispatch to Florence. The presence of Vitellozzo, disguised as a messenger could mean only one thing—the duke was on the verge of a secret reconciliation with his wayward captains. And reunited, their armies represented a serious threat to the Romagna, to all of central Italy, and of course, most especially, to Florence.

Niccolo was sick at the thought. It was possible that Borgia had been planning this all along. It was possible that he meant to strike against Florence from the beginning. All along, it was he, Borgia, not Florence, who had been buying time.

25

The Third Marriage of the Whore of Babylon

It was a game of cat and mouse. The rebellion among Caesar's officers had temporarily paralyzed his armies. Florence felt secure. Borgia needed Florentine assistance to overcome the rebels, or to pursue his conquests in spite of their defection. Florence played, for time, a cat and mouse game. But who was the cat?

Niccolo had little time to dwell on the consternation produced in him by the sight of Vitellozzo in Borgia's camp. The implications were all too clear, and the Signoria was screaming for answers. But in dealing with Borgia, there were no answers, only more questions.

The game was wearing Niccolo down. He longed for Florence and an end to this nervous, unsettled life, tramping from city to city in the rain and snow, awaiting the pleasure of an unpredictable, inscrutable despot. But no matter how much he bridled, no matter how much he wanted to be quit of the whole business, when Caesar sent for him, he went.

"And what does Florence offer me today? Or should I ask, what does she deny me?" The duke was making a joke. He seemed to be in high spirits.

"Your Excellency should know," said Niccolo. "You read my letters and dispatches before I do."

Borgia laughed. He had indeed taken the precaution of monitoring the Florentine envoy's correspondence. "And from those letters, I learn nothing or next to nothing, about the intentions of your republic. From *your* letters, on the other hand, I learn a great deal—especially about how you've been spending your nights in drunkenness and debauchery. And the company you've been keeping!"

A guilty smile stole across Niccolo's face. In addition to his official dispatches, he had kept up a lively and regular correspondence with

Biagio in the chancery. The substance of that correspondence was, as often as not, the two young men's lewd nocturnal conduct described in great and graphic detail. The letters were downright filthy. And every word was a lie. What Borgia did not suspect was that these salacious epistles were actually ciphers, written using an elaborate system of code names and double meanings worked out in advance, that effectively allowed Niccolo to pass certain vital information on to his superiors without Borgia's knowledge or interference.

Niccolo allowed the duke to enjoy himself for a few minutes more before returning to the same, inevitable questions. "As for Vitellozzo and the others, Florence is concerned. We think they may be preparing some action against us."

"You need not trouble yourselves about them," said Borgia with a dismissive wave of the hand. "Where there are men, there are ways of managing them."

"Yes," thought Niccolo, "but who will do the managing, and when?" Borgia continued, "Men like Vitellozzo are easily managed. Most men are. They're compounded of equal parts lust and greed. They're shortsighted and their own narrow interests are their only guide."

"Unlike your Excellency," hazarded Niccolo.

"Unlike myself," confirmed Borgia. "And unlike the Florentine secretary, unless I miss my guess." He eyed Niccolo shrewdly. "If I offered you money to pass certain misleading information on to your government, would you do it?"

The disdainful expression on Niccolo's face was his silent response.

"If I offered you money, a great deal of money, to join me, would you do it? Think of your future and that of Italy. What would you rather be—secretary to a floundering republic or chancellor to a triumphant emperor?"

Again Niccolo was silent. Cat and mouse.

Borgia went on, "I used to think that you and I were alike. We sparred. We feinted. We kept our cards hidden. You played well. But we're not playing the same game, are we?

"I play to conquer, I play for power and for glory. My objective is nothing less than smashing the system of trivial dukedoms and principalities that you have here in Italy. I want to take these squabbling city-states and weld them into a mighty empire."

"One body and of course, one head—yourself." observed Niccolo without emotion.

"Precisely! A glorious new order! A new empire! My fame will be celebrated in poems and song. My name will live forever. All of this is inevitable, Secretary. It's inevitable. I can make it happen, and I shall! A Holy Roman Empire with the new Caesar as emperor! Don't you want to be part of that?

"No, you don't, do you?" the willful man answered his own question. "I know you, Secretary. I know what drives you, what motivates your odd allegiance to that womanish republic. I'm sure you love your country as all small men love the places of their birth. But with you it's more than that, isn't it? It's not Florence you love, is it? It's the republic!

"You don't think it creeps into your conversation when you're not even aware of it? Your admiration for your republic. The way you despise us 'tyrants.' Even the way the word rolls off your lips like dirty spittle—'tyrant.' As though you were any better. As though what you're fighting for is something far superior. It's not the people or the land you're fighting for. It's not your city or your family. It's an idea!"

Borgia was shaking slightly, but only slightly, when he stopped. For the first time, almost imperceptibly, the iron grip of self-control loosened for a second. But then it was back, as firm as ever. He spoke in his usual low, level tones: "The man who fights for an idea, for an abstraction, may be the most truly dangerous one of all," He was staring intently at Niccolo now. "Or the most foolish."

It was Borgia who finally broke the spell. "Anyway, for the time being, you've been assigned to me as ambassador. Where I go, you go, so prepare to leave."

Niccolo groaned inwardly. He was sick to death of travelling, of following the peripatetic duke back and forth across Italy. "Where are we going this time?" he sighed.

"To Ferrara. And for a while you can forget about politics. We're going to a wedding. My sister Lucrezia is getting married!"

The air was full of rumors, hostile armies were encamped at every crossroads, alliances were being made and broken overnight, Florence was desperate, Niccolo Machiavelli was on the verge of nervous exhaustion, everything was up in the air, and Caesar Borgia was taking time out to attend a wedding, the wedding of his sister, Lucrezia, styled by one and all, the biggest whore in Rome.

The wedding was no ordinary wedding. Nor did it offer, as Caesar had suggested to Niccolo, an occasion to forget about politics for a while. When the pope's daughter marries into one of the oldest and most influential dynasties in northern Italy, it is difficult to forget about politics.

The bridegroom was Alphonso d'Este, son of the formidable Duke Ercole d'Este. The Este of Ferrara, we will remember as the family served by generations of cheerful physicians named Savonarola. For Lucrezia Borgia, it was her third marriage. Her two previous attempts had ended in annulment and death, in that order.

The wedding proper had already been celebrated by proxy, but it remained for the bride and groom to actually meet one another and, God willing, consummate the marriage. The haggling leading up to this momentous union took over a year. The pope wanted it badly, but old Duke Ercole—Hercules—was stubborn. Ercole, the man who still pronounced his own name with bated breath, was reluctant to stain the honor of his glorious ancestry and pollute his fine, rich blood with a tainted Spanish strain. The unsavory activities of the Borgia and the crimes against God and nature attributed to them also played a part in Ercole's deliberations. What finally convinced him was money. The tainted bride's dowry in gold and jewels was worth the equivalent of over four million dollars. And although it was never really brought up in the negotiations, never really put on the table in so many words, if the monetary inducements were not enough, there was always the threat of Caesar and his armies.

Ercole eventually succumbed and agreed to welcome the girl into his family. Being a clever man and well aware of what the Borgias's promises were worth, however, he wisely refused to take delivery of his daughter-in-law until he received an advance on the dowry, 100,000 ducats, cash down.

With this final hurdle cleared, the way was open for the strategic matrimonial alliance between the state of Ferrara and the Borgia papacy. Notwithstanding the rumors of jealousy and the possessiveness with which Caesar was said to customarily treat his sister, he too wanted the wedding badly. Ercole d'Este was famous for his ironworks, which produced some of the most coveted artillery in Europe.

The possibility of Caesar suddenly having access to more cannon weighed heavily on Niccolo as he urged his weary mount through the mud to Ferrara. In places, the mud was so deep that the poor horse sank in over his fetlocks, up to the bottom of his belly. The animal's legs made sucking sounds as he pulled them out of the muck and freed them, only to set them down a few feet forward and sink in again. Niccolo had to admit to himself that his negotiations with Borgia were moving forward about as successfully as his horse was advancing, plunging and plodding, on Ferrara.

Eventually, though, he did reach the city. Ferrara had the reputation of a sober, industrious, orderly kind of place, due in large part to the exertions of her chief of police, Giorgio Zampante. But the Ferrara that greeted Niccolo that day was anything but orderly and well-policed. The first thing that caught his eye was a man suspended in midair. Then another. Ropes had been stretched across a piazza, between two tall towers, and rope-walkers were entertaining the populace. They stood on their heads; they juggled; they threw confetti and coins into the outstretched hands of the cheering mob below. Clowns were everywhere. Men dressed as satyrs were chasing half-clothed shepherd girls through the streets, both groups escapees from some staged pastoral spectacle or other.

It took him a long time to break free from the pandemonium, and it was midafternoon before Niccolo secured a room for himself and stabling for his horse. As he had expected, due to the nuptials and the great influx of foreigners expected in the city, prices were wildly inflated. Utterly drained, he finally sank into a soft, if less than immaculate, bed and slept soundly, in spite of the bedbugs and other vermin with which the place was infested.

He was awakened by a booming of cannons that wouldn't stop. Then the trumpets and the shouting started, and sleep was impossible. Judging from the intensity of the din, the biggest whore in Christendom would soon be making her triumphant entry into the city. Curiosity got the better of Niccolo, and he dressed quickly to go have a look.

This time there was no need to ask directions. Niccolo jumped into the surging crowd, and let its current carry him to the appointed place.

Someone clapped a pint of dark, bitter beer into his hand on the way. The exuberant revelers streamed out of the city proper toward a place on the banks of the Po where many dignitaries were gathered. At least Niccolo assumed they were dignitaries. His diplomatic experience taught him that extravagantly dressed men and women on horseback surrounded by archers and trumpeters were generally dignitaries. It varied little. Today the archers were red and white.

Niccolo could not get close enough to see all the details or, thank God, to hear the speeches. The ornate bulk swathed in silver armor and brilliant green and discernible even at a distance, must be Duke Ercole, who rode at the head of the welcoming party. The bride arrived by barge. Craning his neck, Niccolo saw the craft land amid cheers and drum rolls and trumpet flourishes, and a magnificent coach drawn by four white horses rolled off it. Stretched out along the river were twenty more barges with similar coaches.

The coach drew up in front of the duke, the door opened, and Lucrezia Borgia stepped down. Niccolo could only see the top of her blond head. The duke plopped from his horse, heavily, and, approaching her, offered his hand. She kissed it, and Ercole embraced his daughter-in-law, kissing her on the cheek. A roar went up from the crowd. Another figure dropped from his horse, approached the lady, and fervently embraced her. Even at this distance, Niccolo could tell by his quick, graceful movements, by his arrogant stride, that it was not her husband. It was her brother, Caesar.

Lucrezia was boosted up onto a huge, white charger, and for the first time Niccolo could see that the pope's only daughter was dressed in scarlet and that her golden hair flowed down in great waves past her waist, out across her horse's back. Standing, it would have come down at least to her knees. A cleft opened in the crowd to allow the procession to pass, and Lucrezia Borgia entered Ferrara to the thunderous applause of the people. But the pounding of hands and feet, the redoubled cries of joy that greeted her were not all provoked by love and admiration. Many of the Ferrarrese were celebrating more than a wedding that day. They were celebrating their own salvation. Through this marriage, their city was saved from destruction and saved from the advances of this woman's marauding brother and his armies.

While all eyes were on the blond beauty with the magnificent coiffure,

Niccolo was paying closer attention to the dark figure at her side. It was not Lucrezia but Caesar who rode into Ferrara that day with the sneer of a conqueror entering a vanquished city. Albeit quietly and without a shot being fired, another Italian city had fallen to the Borgia. Niccolo had to keep reminding himself that this was a wedding, that this was not politics.

In the days ahead, there was no shortage of diversions and entertainments, and even Niccolo occasionally found solace or at least some distraction from the nagging problems that beset him and his republic. Flags and banners hung everywhere, and the carnival atmosphere continued, unabated late into the night. Every sort of profligate behavior was tolerated. Music filled the air. There were cycles of plays staged continuously, including elaborate allegories that were impossible to decipher. Did the lion represent Ercole d'Este? Or the king of France? Who was the fox? And the black knights with white doves on their helmets, were they good or bad?

Pageant wagons hauled by horses and mules and oxen filled the streets and squares with every conceivable type of spectacle from the obscene to the sublime, from fire eating and sword swallowing to reenactments of stories from the Old Testament. Were Adam and Eve meant to stand for Alphonso and Lucrezia? Inside the court, where more-sophisticated tastes prevailed, the plays of Plautus were produced in Latin and their lascivious, farcical material rendered unintelligible by the language in which they were staged, a language that almost nobody there understood.

There was a tournament that was more a display of sartorial splendor than a show of manly arms. Exotic plumes and feathered capes were more in evidence than swords and lances and chain mail. There were endless processions in which notables and would-be notables advertised their presence by bearing extravagant gifts to the newlyweds. Nothing in the way of pomp and circumstance was overlooked, no stone left unturned in the pursuit of exciting, exaggerated, ostentatious public display. Wealth was on parade.

Niccolo, ever the astute observer, looked past the glitter and heard the whispers and the sniping that buzzed just below the outer shell of all that finery.

"The Spanish are so vulgar! Duke Ercole's daughters are much more richly dressed. And more tastefully."

"If they take so much time with their dress, it's because they're so plain."

"They may be plain, but their pearls are twice the size of hers!"

So it went. Money and monetary worth were never far from the surface. "Those are scales of beaten gold all down the front of Alphonso's suit. It cost over six thousand ducats!"

A grand reception had been arranged in the Ducal Palace, in the great Hall of Mirrors where the bride and groom were to be presented to one another for the first time. As the ranking Florentine ambassador, Niccolo had been invited. Actually, he had received a curt note from Caesar Borgia. It was more of a summons than an invitation. He had had no contact with Borgia since his arrival in Ferrara, but the unsolicited note made it clear that Caesar was well aware of his whereabouts. Caesar seemed to be aware of everything.

On the way to the reception, Niccolo could not resist stopping one more time to view his favorite diversion. It was the scene in which a knight was fighting a dragon. A naked virgin quivered in the background, anxiously awaiting rescue. She'd been quivering and waiting there for three days while her dauntless knight fought on. To Niccolo, the knight and the virgin were nothing special, but the dragon was a marvel to behold. It was a mechanical construction, a hulking green serpent over ten feet tall. It could reel, thrust, and plunge thanks to a clever combination of ropes, pulleys, winches, and levers. Hot steam and fire shot from its mouth. It made frightening, screeching noises. The interesting thing about the little play—Niccolo had seen it already a number of times—was that, according to the whim of the actors and the response of the crowd, there were two different endings. Sometimes the knight won. Sometimes, it was the dragon. That night, it was the dragon. Walking away, Niccolo found himself wondering, who was the knight? And who was the dragon?

When he entered the Great Hall, Niccolo was greeted by the same rush of light and noise that met the timid, young Girolamo Savonarola many years ago in that very hall. The dwarves were gone, but the fires burned just as brightly, the music and laughter echoed just as loudly. There was just as much blond hair and silk and satin as ever before. Although many of those present might look on him as a social inferior, it meant little to Niccolo. He had a confidence born of matching wits with the likes of the formidable countess of Forli and then with the admittedly witless king of France, witless but a powerful head of state. Niccolo had no fear of the court or its courtiers. In fact, they amused him.

Checkered patterns seemed to be the particular passion of the gentlemen in attendance. Brightly colored squares of the shiniest silk hung from many shoulders and encased many a leg. "How gay," thought Niccolo Machiavelli, who was clad in the dependable respectability of his usual Florentine *lucco*. From the look of it, he was the only Florentine in attendance and, oddly enough, he was conspicuous by the very plainness and sobriety of his dress. In that flowery sea of green and pink harlequin, the stubborn Florentine secretary considered himself one of the few guests who maintained some shred of dignity. His one concession to court life was the mask.

The mask had been a gift from Caesar. It had arrived with the invitation, along with instructions for its use. Masks were all the rage in Rome, and the fashion had taken such a hold in the Eternal City that it was not unusual to see men and women going about masked in broad daylight. Nearly every social affair had evolved into a masquerade.

Needless to say, all the guests at the Este palace that evening were appropriately masked. Niccolo, like many others, rather enjoyed the anonymity it gave him. He mixed easily with the crowd, drifting in and out of anonymous conversations on frivolous subjects. He could identify his interlocutors only by the ring of their accents in his ears, the sing-song Romagnouli, the guttural Lombards, the brutish, sputtering Romans, the Neapolitans, more Spanish than Italian, and then the Spanish themselves. Nowhere did he encounter the clear, sweet tones of his own superior Florentine dialect.

Niccolo moved over to a table on which refreshments were laid out and helped himself to the excellent wine that had been provided. He helped himself to the sweetmeats and the marzipan. On a raised table nearby, however, was one treat to which no one dared help himself. The entire city of Ferrara had been meticulously reproduced in molded sugar! From the top of the miniature Ducal Palace flew the twin flags of the Este and the Borgia families. Niccolo suppressed a sarcastic snort when it occurred to him that at some point in the evening Caesar might swoop down and devour the whole thing. "No," he told himself, laughing, he had to remember that "this is not politics, this is a wedding."

But thoughts of politics were never far from Niccolo's mind, and he had been painfully aware of Caesar's presence throughout the evening. Although he had not spoken to him, it was easy enough to pick the man out in the crowd. Even masked and disguised, his movements and his imperious bearing gave him away. Added to that was the fact that Caesar shared the dais with the portly Duke Ercole. Perhaps "shared" is too strong a word, for it was Caesar and not Ercole who presided over the festivities; it was the guest and not the host who was the center of attention and who dominated the proceedings. As the evening dragged on, a steady stream of masked men and women passed in review to pay him their respects. Hands were kissed and embraces exchanged. Whispered conversations were held. One and all went to prostrate themselves before the new Caesar, to pay him homage. Niccolo finally understood why he had been invited. It was to bear witness to this spectacle of servility, this simple little allegory of power.

His gloomy ruminations were interrupted by deafening trumpet blasts that rattled the plate and silver and shook the walls. Suddenly, from nowhere, smoke engulfed the raised dais. When it cleared away a minute later, a lone young man stood at the center of the platform. The heavy scales of beaten gold on his chest identified him as the bridegroom, Alphonso d'Este. He was wearing the much-discussed 6,000-ducat suit.

The sweet music of viols and flutes then filled the hall, and an immense gold ball appeared in clouds of incense over Alphonso's head. It descended ponderously, wobbling a little, and came to rest at his feet. Imperceptibly at first, the ball began to melt. Niccolo rubbed his eyes, already stung by smoke and incense, to make sure. It was indeed melting. He had no idea how it was done. As the gold covering disintegrated into thin air, the image of the bride inside it emerged. Her dark-red velvet gown was the first visual detail to leak through the rapidly disappearing screen. There were little gasps from the crowd. In a moment, Lucrezia's long, luxurious hair was visible, and, offering her hand to her new husband, she stepped gracefully from her celestial bubble. Wild cheering greeted the couple, who held their joined hands aloft in recognition. But underneath the cheering were the insistent whispers—"A red dress!" An Italian bride would have worn white! *"Che vergogna!"*

The couple danced. Niccolo idly wondered if she were beautiful, if he were handsome, if they would take the masks off later so he could see. After the bride and groom had begun it, the dancing became general. Lucrezia danced the second dance with her brother Caesar. By this time, Niccolo had had quite a bit to drink, and he was finally succeeding in forgetting about politics for a while. He was looking around for a way to rid himself of a fat Venetian companion who had inexplicably latched on to him. The Venetian was hideously turned out in a coat, a fur coat that seemed to be his pride and joy. "Do you know how many?" he was saying. "One thousand three hundred and thirty four! One thousand three hundred and thirty four squirrel pelts in this coat! And I picked every one myself. Don't imagine for a minute either that I only had to buy one thousand three hundred and thirty four. Oh no! I had to buy well over two thousand! Do you have any idea how much . . ."

Someone clamped a hand on Niccolo, so hard that it sent a sharp burst of pain up his arm. He did not have to turn around to know who it was. "Is the Florentine secretary enjoying himself?" asked the silky voice.

"Very much so, Excellency," replied Niccolo nonplussed. Caesar circled around him. He was wearing a black mask with his gleaming white teeth visible through the aperture.

"And how do you find the bride, lovely?"

"Exquisite, to judge by her hair. I haven't seen her face."

"Later she'll remove the mask for the edification of all our friends. And we have so many friends here tonight. Don't you agree?"

"An incredible number of friends," Niccolo sourly acknowledged.

Borgia was pleased that his demonstration had gone well. Florence would soon know that he had many friends among the duchies of the Romagna. "Our friends here have treated us extremely well. They've spared no expense, as you can see. And they've been so generous. Ercole has given Lucrezia a husband and me a brother. His daughter Isabella, who is married to the lord of Mantova, has sent me a gift of a hundred masks. Can you imagine a more thoughtful gift? It seems everyone wants to be Caesar's friend." Leaving Niccolo to draw his own conclusions, Borgia moved off. He moved silently—like a cat.

Niccolo followed him as he moved unctuously through the crowd, again kissing and embracing. Everyone wants to be Caesar's friend.

Ferrara gives him a brother. Mantova sends masks—a hundred masks. And Florence? Poor Florence. Florence sends him Niccolo Machiavelli.

Determined to drive the politics from his mind at any cost, Niccolo continued to drink the wine that went down so smoothly. He stood for a while, watching an incredible display of manual dexterity. A musician was playing three lutes at a time. His fingers moved almost faster than the eye could follow, at least faster than Niccolo's sluggish and drunken gaze was capable of moving. Three lutes at once! He applauded. In a blur of arms and fingers, the man played on, picking up the tempo. He corded and strummed and plucked with both hands. Shouts of "*Ole!*" went up among the Spanish, who were dancing to the frenzied tune, or rather stamping their feet in uncouth but lusty exuberance.

Niccolo's attention turned from the musician to the dancers. Among them were several of the ladies in waiting who had accompanied Lucrezia Borgia. They were all dark and mysterious, all the more dark and mysterious in their masks. All the more inviting. He watched as they abandoned themselves to the music, as small feet and well-turned ankles flashed out from under their long gowns in the heat of the dance.

In a touching little ceremony earlier in the evening, the Spanish ladies were formally, but tenderly, released from service by Lucrezia. They were replaced by Ferrarrese attendants, deemed more suitable to a woman who was now, after all, a daughter of the house of Este. The Spanish maids, like Lucrezia, were dressed in gowns of the deepest red velvet. The newly engaged Ferrarrese maids were dressed more appropriately, in white. But the Spanish girls had gold and strands of tiny pearls woven into their dark, luxurious hair, and they danced recklessly, and they threw their heads back in shameless laughter as they danced, and Niccolo could not take his eyes off of them.

The ambidextrous lutenist almost collapsed from his exertions, but not before bringing the dancers to a feverish, uninhibited climax.

The girls, some gasping for breath, took advantage of the lull in the music to refresh themselves. An embroidered handkerchief was unfurled to mop a graceful neck. Cups were raised to full, thirsty lips. Fans appeared in delicate, jeweled hands to stir the thick air and waft an intoxicating perfume in Niccolo's direction.

While waiting for the music to start up again, the girls became aware of Niccolo's attentions. They were whispering among themselves and giggling. They engaged in a silent dialogue with him, in which their coquettish gestures alternated between the inviting and the demure, the naughty and the modest, the coy and brazen. They beckoned to him and then dissolved into little gales of flirtatious laughter among themselves.

It was not long before the lutenist, fortified by several deep and satisfying draughts of cool wine, was joined by a Spaniard with a kithara and another with a tambourine. The three musicians, pounding on their instruments, had the dancers back on their feet in no time, and Niccolo, a slightly clumsy but enthusiastic devotee of the dance, was drawn into the swirl of black hair and red velvet.

They played on and on. They played like demons. Niccolo danced and danced, passing from one provocative partner to another in the general melee. As the evening flew by, the staccato rhythms seemed to pick up speed, the tambourine rang and crashed, and the applause was more thunderous after every number. Niccolo had finally managed to forget Caesar Borgia and Florence and politics, and he was having so much fun he was not even aware of his achievement. What he was slowly becoming aware of, though, was one girl in the mad, whirling cloud of girls around him whose laugh was more alluring, whose mouth more sensuous, whose breasts a little higher and a little rounder.

And was he imagining it, or was she more responsive? When his hand strayed, as it was occasionally inclined to do, did she let it linger a little longer? Did she chide him less severely? Did she throw herself into his arms more willingly, more impulsively?

As the number of dancers dwindled, Niccolo found himself more and more often paired with her. They sought each other out. Dizzy and breathing hard, they clung to each other for support after each mad, sweaty foray onto the dance floor. They toasted each other. They toasted the musicians and the wine. Her throaty, heavily accented Italian thrilled him.

He felt drawn to her in a visceral way, and the way she pressed herself against him, languidly, unashamedly, told him she too was feeling this thing—and surrendering to it. The rush of desire welling up in Niccolo might well have proved embarrassing, but for the generous lucco he was wearing, which concealed all things in its loose and ample folds. Other gay blades, in short doublets and tight hose had a considerably more difficult time hiding their excitement.

He steered her away from her companions, toward an isolated corner of the great colonnaded and curtained hall. Willingly, she let herself be led. They touched each other, tentatively. He traced the outline of her lips, visible below the black satin mask, with his finger. She planted a tiny kiss on his fingertip. When Niccolo drew her to himself, she offered no resistance. He kissed her on the shoulder and on up the neck and felt the goose bumps his kisses raised. She kissed him lightly on the ear, teasing him with her tongue, and whispered, "You are the Florentine envoy, aren't you?"

Niccolo started at the question. How did she know? "What!" was all he could manage to say.

"I have to talk to you. About the Sforza children in Florence. It's urgent, please. Half an hour. Outside, across the piazza. In the park." And she was gone.

Dumbfounded, Niccolo stood rooted to the spot. He watched as his lover, his momentary lover, gaily rejoined her companions. The magic intoxication of the night's touches and smells melted suddenly away, and the cold, hard edge of anger was left in its place. "*Puttana!*" Niccolo spit the curse through his barred teeth. "Who gives a fuck, who gives a shit, who gives a goddamn about the Sforza children!" But even before he asked the question, he already knew the answer, and it only served to fuel his anger. Only one man was overly concerned at the moment about the Sforza children—Caesar Borgia.

One of the sticking points in the Florentine negotiations with Borgia, and there were innumerable sticking points, was the fate of the Sforza children. Committed by their mother Caterina, they were safe in Florence under Florentine protection. But Niccolo's instructions had been explicit. He was to deny all knowledge of the Sforza children; he was never to admit that they were on Florentine soil.

Borgia had coaxed and wheedled, trying to tease an admission out of him. He had offered huge sums of money to have the boys turned over to him. His intentions, of course, were innocent, humanitarian—he wanted to reunite them with their mother. But everyone knew better.

The only reason Caterina was still alive is that the pope hoped to entice her children to Rome as well, using her as bait. To the Borgias, the Sforzas were a dangerous symbol of defiance in the Romagna. They represented unwillingness to submit to the yoke of the papacy. They were the spirit of independence and rebellion incarnate. As long as the Sforzas were alive, their name would be a rallying cry for the forces of sedition and a threat to Borgia hegemony. So the pope wanted them. He had more than once referred to the Sforza family as a diabolical brood of vipers, and it was an open secret that, when he got his hands on them, he had every intention of killing them, every last one.

The realization that he was being played came crashing down on Niccolo, and he stalked furiously out of the Hall of Mirrors. "Borgia! Borgia! Borgia!" he fumed under his breath. He had eaten and slept Borgia for months, waited on Borgia's pleasure, played Borgia's games. And now for the space of a few brief hours, he had found relief from the overwhelming, demonical presence of Borgia in his life. And what happens? The little pleasure he had hoped to take, the small consolation—where did it come from? Who was his sultry, distracting would-be lover? A whore! A Spanish whore, paid by Borgia! A Spanish whore sent by Borgia to do Borgia's work!

A light rain was falling outside as Niccolo stomped across the piazza. He was filled with outrage. The fact that he was also quite drunk only added to his hostility and his inability to reason. Entering the little park in front of the palace, he tore the stupid satin mask from his face and threw it angrily in the dirt. He crushed it underfoot. Borgia's mask.

For about twenty minutes, Niccolo pounded up and down the gravel pathways, his hot anger gradually giving way to cold contempt. The air and the rain, too, served to cool him down and bring him back to himself. So much the better. He wanted a modicum of sangfroid to deal with this whore Borgia had sent to do his dirty work.

Finally, he saw her coming across the deserted piazza. "She still looks good, the way she moves . . ." He shook the thought out of his head. It was the drink talking. He had resolved to deal with her brutally if need be. After all, "this is no game," he told himself. "This is politics."

Stepping out from behind a tree, Niccolo blocked her path, and the shock of his sudden appearance caused her to utter a stifled cry. She recovered in an instant. He started up the path, and she followed.

He rudely rebuffed her attempt to latch onto his arm. When he spoke, there was an icy viciousness in his voice: "Now tell me about your concern for the Sforza children. Or should I tell you?"

He had stopped to face her in the torchlight. He was aware of sneering his most disdainful sneer, of radiating bitterness and scorn from every pore in his body. As he began his harangue, his posturing had its desired effect, for she stood speechless before him, paralyzed. There was not a sentence in Niccolo's scathing verbal assault that did not contain the word, "whore." She staggered under the weight of his unexpected indictment and stumbled back against a tree, clinging to it for support.

She gasped and seemed to be having trouble breathing, but Niccolo did not relent. With a trembling hand, she grabbed at the mask she was wearing and pulled it down around her neck. Niccolo saw for the first time that her eyes were full of fierce emotion. Then with a dawning sense of horror, he realized why. The face staring up at him, wild-eyed with disbelief, was the dark face of his dreams, of a thousand dreams and a thousand sleepless nights. It was Giuditta.

26

A Honeymoon of Sorts

Caviar and Conspiracy

"You!"

"You!"

"Jesus Christ!"

"Holy Father Abraham!"

"By the blessed saints in heaven!"

"By all the Patriarchs and Prophets!"

"You!"

"You!"

The conversation was at an impasse. Both stood stock still, seeking in each other's thirty-year-old faces the outlines and ghosts of younger features. Hers had softened; his had hardened. Yet Giuditta was able to discern in the narrow face, the long, sharp nose and chin, the high cheekbones and tight mouth, an image of the boy who had once saved her life. Niccolo recognized in her the large, round eyes, full lips, and jet-black hair of the girl he knew only briefly as a child, but who had come to represent so much more to him in his lonely imagination. Only now she was an ally of Borgia. Now she was his enemy.

That knowledge brought him no consolation, nor did it bring any ready words to the lips of the usually clever diplomat. She, too, seemed to be in the throes of utter consternation, and they might have stood there staring for a long time if the rain, which had been falling steadily and with increasing violence, had not started turning to hail. The immediate and urgent necessity of finding shelter from the storm put off, in Niccolo's mind, at least, the decision as to whether he would conduct himself as an old friend or as a new enemy.

The park itself was devoid of buildings, and the leafless winter trees afforded little cover. The hailstones were growing alarmingly in size and their impact on Niccolo's hatless, recently shorn skull was beginning to prove painful. The fugitive couple had reached the extreme end of the low-walled enclosure and found not even a gate by which they might escape into the city streets beyond. It was Giuditta who first spotted the shelter, really only a roof and two walls leaning against the outer stone wall of the enclosed park. They stumbled in, tripping and picking their way over the dark objects that littered the floor of the shed, as the storm outside seemed to redouble its fury. The place was small and seemed to be almost entirely occupied by some sort of low, open cart or wagon.

They could not see each other in the darkness, nor hear each other's labored breathing, since the air around them was filled with the crashing of thunder and the rattling of the hard, stinging balls of ice on the clay-tile roof. A remarkably bright bolt of lightning gave Niccolo an instantaneous glimpse of her, hugging her bare shoulders and shivering in the cold blue light. Instinctively, he moved toward her and gathered her into his arms. She offered no resistance, and suddenly Niccolo forgot about treachery and the implications of politics. In his mind, in the anonymity of the darkness that surrounded them, they were the two people back at the dance again, two masked strangers willing to trust each other—if only for a little while.

She clung to him and they both stared outside, speechless, hypnotized by the awesome spectacle of natural fury that was being unleashed. God's wrath. Even Caesar Borgia seemed puny by comparison.

As the warmth they generated between them rose through the wetness of their clothes, Giuditta's shivering subsided. As her perfume reached Niccolo's nostrils, mixed now with the smell of her hair and skin and sweat, he was aware that the storm outside had abated as quickly as it had blown up. They could go back out now. But they didn't move. They only tightened the grip they had on each other and stood there for a long time, welded together in the darkness by the loneliness and the uncertainty of the night.

Niccolo remembered the last time he had been this close to her, close enough to feel her breath on his face. He could almost smell the thick, sweet vinegar with which the barrel had been impregnated and feel the way he wrapped his legs around her in the cold water to keep her from drowning. When their lips met, it was not in the spirit of playfulness, like the pecking and teasing of earlier, at the dance. They were trembling the way men and women tremble in the face of something momentous and incomprehensible. Every doubt, every caution, was swept away in the wave of blind and desperate passion that engulfed them both.

The morning brought the cold grey light of dawn, as well as the memory of ecstasy, to Niccolo Machiavelli. Like a man who has died and discovered himself in heaven, he felt no particular compulsion to stir, to open his eyes, to awake, or ever to move again. But shortly after sunrise, chased out by an irate groundskeeper, he found himself evicted from Eden and wandering listlessly through the still-shuttered streets of Ferrara. Wrapped half around him, as he was around her, and appearing to be sharing in his feelings of boundless goodwill was a tousled Giuditta.

Niccolo found himself buoyed by a lightness, a giddiness that left him completely untroubled by the conflicts that had tormented him only the night before. All was calm, beautiful, and voluptuous. The ill effects of the alcohol he had consumed could not touch him. The stiffness of the joints that should have been troubling him after a damp night in the open were banished beyond the threshold of consciousness. In the back of his mind, though, a little alarm bell was going off. He ignored it, but he knew it was there. He knew that, sooner or later, reality was going to impinge on this dream and the nagging question would have to be asked—and answered: What will you tell Borgia?

But for the time being, they strolled aimlessly through the still-deserted city. They ducked into doorways and kissed with rapturous, greedy abandon. When the shops began to open, they bought sweets and popped them into each other's mouths—in public! Following nothing but the tug of their mutual passion, they took a tiny room and surrendered once again to each other in sweet delirium. They vowed never to leave that room until the end of time and sent out for food and wine. It was an embarrassing moment for Niccolo when the boy arrived. He had no money, and Giuditta, laughing at him, was forced to pay.

"They keep their envoys hungry in Florence, don't they?" she said, digging into the covered basket and extracting a mound of rich decaying, blue-veined cheese.

"And thirsty," said Niccolo, grabbing at the flask of wine. There were meat pies and crisp apples among the provender that had been delivered, but before discovering them, Niccolo and Giuditta's lips and tongues met, and all thought of food was forgotten as they melted into each other's arms to make love yet another time. It was dark when Niccolo awoke. He lay still and breathed in the intoxicating smells that were the product, not of the perfumer's art, but of their own desires. He wound his fingers idly in the confusion of her hair. He knew the taste of her tongue, the smell of her breath. He knew the way her back curved down into her buttocks; he knew the soft weight of her breasts and her dark, swollen nipples. But what else?

He knew she was a Jewish girl who had fled Florence many years ago and gone to Spain. And now she was in the service of the antichrist and his children. Niccolo lit a small lamp and watched her sleeping. He stared at her for a long time and he wondered to himself—"Who is she?" The flesh and blood were real, but other than that, he was sleeping with a fantasy, one that he had constructed all by himself, over the years. It occurred to him for the first time that perhaps she was doing the same. At the risk of losing all the magic and the happiness they had stumbled into, Niccolo knew it was time to talk.

He was the first to bring the conversation down from the lofty realms of happy lovers' babble, with its cooing and purring and pet names—*tesoro, picconcina*. It was a precipitous drop from, "little treasure," or "little pigeon," to "What business did you have with the Florentine envoy the other night? You never said." They were seated at the table, partially clothed, eating cheese and apples.

Giuditta did not appear to be flustered by the abruptness of the question. She went on eating cheese, crunching on an apple. "I said it was about the Sforza children," she managed between bites.

"But you never finished."

"I didn't get a chance to. You carried me off and ravished me," she pointed out, licking the soft cheese from her fingers in an undeniably provocative way.

"Finish now," he said bluntly. "What about the Sforza children?"

"I have a message for them."

"And for that, you apply to the Florentines. I don't understand." It was the Florentine envoy talking now, not the demon-lover.

"Well, to whom should I apply? The children are in Florence, aren't they?"

"No."

"You're lying to me, Niccolo. How can I ever learn to trust you if you lie to me?" She said it almost impishly. "Anyway, it doesn't matter whether you admit the children are there or not. I have a message for them. You're the envoy. You deliver the message. It's your duty, isn't it? It's as simple as that."

"Is that what Caesar told you?"

"Oh, Caesar!"

"Did he tell you to seduce me too? So the message would be more convincing?" Anger edged into Niccolo's voice.

Giuditta was amused by his remark, and she showed it. "You're jumping to conclusions, aren't you, Niccolo? At any rate, Florentine envoy, will you deliver the message? Tell them their mother wants to see them."

Niccolo's eyes narrowed. "For two months, I've been hearing that she wants to see them. Caesar tells me almost daily how she pines for them and how everything would be so beautiful if only they would join her in Rome. They could be one big happy family again." Flushed, Niccolo concluded, "One big happy family in the clutches of a satanical pope!"

Giuditta laughed at him, "You don't speak very highly of the head of your religion."

The remark only served to further infuriate Niccolo. "How did Caesar think you could help?" he said disdainfully. "What trap were you supposed to spring that he couldn't? What bait were you supposed to use?" Again the word "whore" was on his lips, and he might have used it if Giuditta hadn't interrupted him.

"Niccolo, the message is from Caterina," she said with a beguiling smile.

"So that's the new angle? A brilliant ploy! Caesar didn't send you. She's the one who sent you to plead personally with the Florentines! What else did Caterina say?"

"That you were an enthusiastic, but nervous lover."

Niccolo's jaw dropped.

"I really did come from Caterina, *brontolone!* Not Caesar. Do you believe me now?"

"I want to, but it doesn't make any sense. Why does Caterina want the children to come to Rome? She knows as well as anyone, they'll all be killed once they get there. She knows Borgia wants to wipe out her whole line."

Giuditta shook her head. "Niccolo, I told you you were jumping to conclusions. I didn't say anything about trundling the children off to Rome. She wants to see them in Florence!"

"But how . . . ?" Recognition finally dawned in Niccolo, and so it was that over the next few days, between reckless bouts of lovemaking, they began to plot the escape of Caterina Sforza from the pope's fortress in Rome.

As they talked and the intimacy and trust between them grew, Giuditta's story also emerged. She had indeed gone to Toledo in Spain after her escape from Florence and had been quite happy there. She picked up the rudiments of medicine and the apothecary's trade, skills for which her people were rightfully famous, and was expanding her knowledge by delving into the mysteries of Arabic medicine when the edict was issued.

"The Edict of Expulsion," she said bitterly. "A whole people, a whole race, uprooted. Cast out."

"And so you decided to return to Italy."

"I didn't really decide. It just happened. A girl without family, without too much money. I found myself in Rome. It's as good a place as any for us. Or as bad."

"What did you do when you got there?"

"You remember the little book I showed you—my father's book? I went to one of his friends, one of the people listed in the book, and he took me in. They were kind, but it wasn't long before they began pressing their eldest son on me, telling me that I should marry, that I was getting old."

"Why didn't you?"

"I was saving myself for you," she said brightly, but with a trace of sarcasm. Niccolo looked unconvinced.

"That was when I met Caterina. She was married to one of the pope's sons at the time, and living in Rome part of the year. Even back then, she was dabbling in philters and potions. She was intrigued by what I knew, my 'Moorish science,' so she took me in.

"I was with her until her husband died. Then a new pope came in, and she was no longer welcome in Rome. She left. I stayed on. Even then, the Borgias were already powerful in the city and what could be more natural than for a 'Spanish girl' to find employment among them? They have a huge entourage—servants, cooks, maids, musicians, astrologers—all from Spain. I spoke the language. I understood their customs. I was one of them."

Niccolo pointed out that her thick Spanish accent, the one she was using the night before, had completely disappeared. She laughed, "It was part of the masquerade. You know what they say, *Paese che ve, usanza che trovi*—When in Rome . . ."

"But the Borgias knew you were a Jew?"

"Jews. Christians. Turks. The Borgias don't care. They use whoever is at hand, whoever suits their purposes."

"And how do you suit their purposes?

Giuditta gave him a coy smile. "I serve Monna Lucrezia. Or served. Now that she's a lady of Ferrara and the house of Este, she no longer needs her Spanish retinue."

"You were discharged?"

"Duke Ercole let it be known that he was less than enthusiastic about having a lot of 'those people' around. In private, he says the Spaniards are all spies."

"Are they? Are you?"

"A spy? I suppose in some ways I am."

"And whom do you spy for?"

Again, the coquettish smile. Giuditta made no reply.

"So, do you feel any sort of loyalty to the Borgias?"

"To the Borgias, no. But to Monna Lucrezia, yes."

"And if you had to choose between Lucrezia and Caterina Sforza, which side would you choose?

"I don't have to choose, and I won't have to choose. Lucrezia's interests and Caterina's won't come into conflict, not anymore. Even if it isn't the greatest love match of the century, at least this marriage gets Lucrezia away from Rome and away from her father and her brother."

Niccolo's eyes lit up. "Then it's true what they say about the Borgias?"

"What do they say?" she shot back defensively.

"That the brother loves the sister with a criminal passion, that the father does likewise, that they killed the other brother out of jealousy, to get him out of the way. Don't tell me you haven't heard?"

"Niccolo, Niccolo," she said, scolding him. "Do you believe everything you hear?"

"No, but I don't disbelieve it either, and I don't dismiss any rumor out of hand, no matter how preposterous, until I can learn otherwise. It's the nature of my business."

"Oh, and what business is that?"

"The business of lies and half-truths, denials and equivocation, innuendo."

"Charming business."

Afterward, with Niccolo's head in her lap, Giuditta told him what she knew about the secrets of the strange Spanish family into whose service she had fallen. "The pope is a huge man, as big as a bear. In the household he has a reputation for moderation, especially at the table."

"Borgia! Moderation!" interrupted Niccolo incredulously. "I've heard about the kinds of feasts they give at the papal court. On a fast day, they limit the fare to a mere one hundred and forty-four varieties of fish. That's their idea of moderation!"

Giuditta rapped him on the head with her knuckles. "Do you want to hear what I have to say or not? They do stage extravagant feasts, but Papa Alexander never eats more than a little lean meat and some vegetables. And fruit—he worries about his regularity.

"But if he's moderate at table," she continued, "he gives himself full reign in the bedroom. He's apparently insatiable, and he's constantly surrounded by beautiful women. He has a new mistress now less than half his age, Giulia Farnese. Do you know what they call her in Rome? The Bride of Christ!"

Niccolo laughed. "The Bride of Christ! A sexually insatiable pope! And does the papal insatiability extend to his own daughter?"

"No, it does not," said Giuditta firmly. "Alexander dotes on his daughter, on all his children. He's like any other father. He wants what's best for them. He really loves Lucrezia dearly, and he wept for days before she left him to come here. It was actually very sad, very moving."

"Then it's Lucrezia who's the she-devil?" asked Niccolo.

"Nothing could be further from the truth. She doesn't have a sinister bone in her body. Lucrezia is modest and lovable; she's discreet, pleasant; she's even a very religious person, a fervent Catholic. She used to read the Bible to me, out loud, in Spanish. She has a beautiful voice."

"Did she try to convert you?" teased Niccolo.

"No, but I did learn a few things about your religion from her. Lucrezia is a beautiful woman. Did you see her at the wedding?"

"Not her face. She was masked. I only saw her hair."

"Her hair! It's so long and heavy, it gives her atrocious headaches. That's part of what I did for her. I would brew her a sleeping draft, when the headaches got bad."

"Why didn't she just cut her hair, if it was such a problem?"

"Her father wanted it that way. He liked it long. Everything she did, she did to please him."

"Like going through three husbands by, what, age twenty-two?"

"Exactly. Alexander arranged the marriages. She gave her consent. She did what was required of her. She was only thirteen the first time. When she wasn't happy with her husband, Giovanni, the pope annulled the marriage, even though there were political risks involved."

"I bet he got her dowry back, though," smirked Niccolo.

"Of course he did. That's why they got the annulment. They wanted it to be legal. And apparently the only real legal ground for such a thing is impotence. When Giovanni screamed that he wasn't impotent, the pope set up a commission—two of his cardinals—to investigate. Giovanni was supposed to "perform" in front of them to prove his manhood."

"Did he do it?"

"Of course not. He howled at the indignity of such a trial and refused to submit, so the annulment went through."

"And was he impotent?"

"He's remarried now for the third time and has four children. But Giovanni is the one who started the rumors of incest between Lucrezia and her father. Out of spite."

"Then the pope's family isn't as hideous and unnatural as some would have us believe," said Niccolo thoughtfully.

"You should understand that better than anyone," said Giuditta, taunting him. "Didn't you say it was your business—lies and half-truths, equivocation and innuendo?"

Rebuked, Niccolo remained silent a moment. "What's the matter," said Giuditta breaking in on his thoughts. "Are you disappointed the Borgias aren't the monsters you thought they were?"

"Just because they're not all tangled up in a web of incest doesn't make them necessarily blameless," observed Niccolo.

"True," admitted Giuditta. "They can be fairly unscrupulous, at times. For example, there's always talk of poisonings at court."

"Is it true?"

"Who can say? Someone comes to dinner. He gets sick and dies a few days later. It could have been poison. It could have been bad shellfish."

"But when that 'someone' is conveniently a very wealthy cardinal who collapses after dinner with the pope, who dies, and whose entire wealth and property are then immediately confiscated by the church," said Niccolo, "and when that someone just happens to die and that wealth just happens to reach the papal coffers as Caesar's army is running low on ammunition and supplies, and when that happens several times in the period of a few months . . ."

"No!" said Giuditta in a tone of mock incredulity. "You're implying more than coincidence here!" She laughed before continuing, "To tell you the truth though, the pope is a little obsessed with the idea of poisons. He's asked my opinion on these things once or twice."

"You! What did he want to know?"

"I was with Lucrezia one day when he received a letter that really flustered him. He was arguing with the messenger who delivered it, and he wouldn't touch the thing. Since I was close at hand, he asked me what I thought. He said the letter came from a venomous snake, and that he feared it was impregnated with poison that would seep into his fingers if he tried to read it and eventually kill him. He asked me if there was such a poison, to my knowledge."

"And what was your learned opinion?"

"I said I didn't think such a thing was possible."

"So he went ahead and read the letter?"

"Only after he had the messenger lick the thing all over, inside and out!"

"What a rare and cautious man! What a pope!"

"That's not even the best part. When he did read the letter, it drove him to distraction, and he almost had some kind of fit. He was sputtering and shouting curses. He had to drink a whole cup of brandy before he calmed down again. And do you know who the letter was from? Caterina! Apparently she was writing to tell him to get out of Italy and leave the Italians alone. She signed the letter, 'Death to the Barbarian.'"

After four uninterrupted days in the privacy of their love nest, Niccolo and Giuditta finally decided to venture forth into the outside world again. Ferrara was still in the throes of the wedding celebration, and her streets were thronged with unlikely beings—satyrs and nymphs, ancient Roman gods and goddesses, legendary heroes. Apollo passed by under a huge gold-foil sun. He was accompanied by Neptune with his trident, hung with seaweed and gnawing on a leg of mutton. Giuditta and Niccolo, too, were masked. They thought it was better that way.

As they strolled into a slightly quieter and safer street, Giuditta said, "This celebration is nothing compared to what they do in Rome. Did you hear about the Ballet of the Chestnuts?"

"No."

"Caesar gave a supper at the Apostolic Palace with his usual prodigality. The food was perfumed and some of the dishes sprinkled with gold dust." Niccolo winced at the thought, and Giuditta continued. "After the meal, fifty prostitutes came in—courtesans rather, respectable prostitutes, not common girls. They danced for a while first, with their gowns on, then off. Then the whole room was flooded with chestnuts."

Niccolo looked at her blankly, "Chestnuts?"

"When the girls tried to dance, they lost their footing. Soon they were all on their hands and knees or rolling around on the floor in the chestnuts. Then the guests started to crawl in among the girls and the orgy started. There were quite a few cardinals there, bishops, and even a French ambassador."

"But no Florentines," said Niccolo with conviction.

Giuditta was amused at his self-righteousness. "Oh there was one of your high-minded Florentines there, the cardinal, the flabby one, Giovanni." Niccolo tensed at the mention of his name. Exiled from Florence, he had fled to Rome, and now Cardinal Giovanni de' Medici, the son of Lorenzo de' Medici, was consorting with the Borgias.

"When things began heating up between the prostitutes and the churchmen, the pope suddenly called everyone to attention. Attendants brought in a silk mantle encrusted with gold and jewels, a pair of shoes of the finest Corinthian leather and some caps. Alexander promised these as prizes to the man who could "perform" the greatest number of times with the prostitutes."

"And who won?" asked Niccolo.

"Caesar, of course."

Niccolo was too curious not to ask, "How many times?"

"Six."

They walked on in silence for a while, unconsciously retracing their footsteps back to the small, red-walled park where they had spent their first night together. A brooding expression had replaced the look of dumb beatitude that had been on Niccolo's face for the past several days. "What's wrong?" said Giuditta, brushing his face with both her hands as though she were trying to remove the worry that was starting to settle in there.

"Caesar," said Niccolo.

"The inscrutable Caesar," echoed Giuditta. "You know what they say in Rome? The pope never does what he says, and Caesar never says what he does."

"That's just the problem," said Niccolo. "I've spent the last two months with the man and I'm as ignorant of his intentions as I was on the first day I met him."

"Caesar is dangerous," said Giuditta.

"You don't have to tell me that."

"No," she said, real concern showing in her voice. "I mean it. I've been watching him for years now, and something's happening to him. Even Lucrezia is concerned."

"Does she speak to you about him? Has she told you anything? Do you know anything that might help me?" said Niccolo, hopefully.

"I told you, they're very close. In fact, she may be the only person in the world he really talks to. And lately, she worries. She says there is something gnawing at him. She says there's madness in him."

"He's far from mad," said Niccolo. "He always knows exactly what he's doing. The control he exerts over himself, the way he moves."

"Just the same, be careful with him, Niccolo. Something is happening to him. His behavior is getting more unpredictable."

More unpredictable, indeed. A shiver ran through Niccolo. This was the man upon whose whim the survival of Florence depended. This was man to whom, very shortly, the Florentine envoy would have to report for another round of cat and mouse.

The idyll was almost over. They both felt it. Giuditta knew that soon she would have to leave for Rome, and Niccolo would shortly be caught up once again in the web of intrigue being spun by the diabolical Caesar. Already they had stayed too long.

"Niccolo," she said softly. "Do you ever think of the day we met, the first time?"

"I think about it all the time."

"And if I told you I thought about it all the time, and that I also thought about something else—about revenge—what would you think of me?"

"You can call it revenge. Or you can call it justice."

"And if I call it justice, would you help me, if I needed it?"

"Giuditta," he said taking her in his arms. "I know who killed your father and brother. I found out years ago.

"You knew!" she spit at him. "And you didn't tell me?"

He tried to put an arm around her but she brushed it off. "Listen," he said. "I'm sorry. I should have said something, but I didn't want to open old wounds. Besides, there's nothing you can do about it now. You've long since had your revenge."

"What do you mean?"

Niccolo explained: "You remember the dagger I found, the one I gave to you? It had a small symbol cut in the handle. That symbol was the mark of the Medici family. Lorenzo de' Medici is dead, and the rest of his clan was driven from Florence. Florence has purged herself of the vermin that did that to your father and in the same process, given you the revenge you wanted."

"Has she?" said Giuditta in a voice that left Niccolo wondering. "Has she really?"

The next morning, Niccolo complained of small things to keep his mind off larger concerns. He complained about his chronic lack of money and the impossibility of ever getting enough from his government to even cover his expenses. Giuditta smiled and teased him, "You should go to work for the Borgia. They're profligate, and they pay on time."

"I've already had an offer," he said.

"And you turned it down?"

"What else could I do?"

"You remain loyal to your stingy republic, no matter what. Is that how it is?"

"Loyalty is a virtue. I've never betrayed anyone," asserted Niccolo.

"Did you ever stop to consider that the republic that claims such a large share of your loyalty once tried to kill me?"

Niccolo was instantly on the defensive. "It wasn't the republic then. Those were different times. There was a tyrant in Florence, and I tried to tell you, the tyrant has been consigned to oblivion. It's over. You've had your revenge."

"And something like that could never happen now, under your government."

"Never," affirmed Niccolo.

"But if it did, where would your loyalties lie, Niccolo?"

"You know you don't even have to ask."

"Don't I?" Giuditta laughed at him. "You're an odd duck, Niccolo Machiavelli. This queer allegiance you have to your republic. And to justice. I really think that if you had to choose between me and the idea of justice, you'd pick the idea."

He thought it would be useless to pursue the subject and lapsed into a moody silence. Still, it bothered him that she had reproached him for his loyalty to his republic and the idea of justice. What was wrong with loyalty to an idea, especially a high and noble one?

"Come on," said Giuditta making an effort to dissipate the gloom that had settled around them. "I'm going to do you a big favor." As they made their way through the streets of Ferrara, the ebb and flow of masked partygoers had begun to recede, and normally clad individuals going about everyday errands were beginning to take their places. Giuditta led Niccolo into a street of small shops and entered one of the more modest establishments there.

"Daniele," she called. An old Jew materialized from a back room. He was clad in black, with the yellow symbol emblazoned prominently on his gown by order of the indefatigable forces of law and order under the leadership Giorgio Zampante, the police chief. Giuditta talked quietly with the man for a few minutes. They conversed in their incomprehensible language that came from low in the throat. When Giuditta spoke, her voice was husky and mysterious. To Niccolo, it was thrilling.

Daniele disappeared and Giuditta turned to Niccolo. "Sit down," she said, indicating a small table. "He'll be right back." When Daniele returned, he was carrying paper, pens, and ink, as well as a small, full purse. Giuditta took the writing materials. The purse was deposited heavily in front of Niccolo. "Go on," she said. "Take it. Its fifty ducats. I hope it's enough. I've arranged a loan for you."

Niccolo did not even bother to protest. He needed the money. "And the terms?"

Giuditta replied in a businesslike fashion: "I've given security, so you don't have to worry about that. Daniele will give you the name and address of an associate of his in Florence where you can repay the loan, if and when your republic sees fit to reimburse you. The interest is thirty-two percent.

"Thirty-two percent!" objected Niccolo. "That's usu . . ."

"You were going to say, 'banking'? Anyway, it could have been forty percent. I got you the preferred rate. Besides, the coffers of the republic are full, aren't they? It won't hurt them." She gave him a broad smile. In the meantime, Daniele had brought food and a sweet liquor to refresh them. Having confided the address in Florence where Niccolo could go to discharge his obligation, the old man tacitly withdrew.

"What's this?" said Niccolo, poking his finger in a mound of black paste or jelly that was heaped on a plate set in front of him.

"Eat it. It's good," said Giuditta.

"How?"

"Spread a little on the bread, like this." Giuditta took a thin square of dried bread and covered it with the mysterious substance. Niccolo did likewise. "Well?" she said, waiting for his reaction.

"Salty," said Niccolo dubiously. "Now, what is it?"

"*Caviale*, I think they call it in Italian."

"Never heard of it."

"It's sturgeon, sort of," said Giuditta. "It's actually the eggs."

"Fish eggs? Fish eggs," said Niccolo philosophically. "How do you know about this stuff?"

"The Jews of Ferrara know about it, but the Italians are still ignorant. The Jewish fishermen take the sturgeon in the river here. When the time is right, and the females are full of eggs, you get *caviale*. It's good, don't you think?"

Niccolo was not convinced. He took another tentative bite of the fishy substance to be polite and then sat back and sipped at his drink. He watched while Giuditta began to write. Her delicate hand raced rapidly across the surface of the paper from right to left, again and again until the whole page was covered with indecipherable symbols. She was writing to an associate in Rome.

"Hebrew?" said Niccolo.

"Not really," said Giuditta.

"Well, it's certainly not Italian."

"It is if you know how to read it," she said. "Look." Giuditta took a fresh sheet of the coarse paper and jotted a few words on it. At least they looked like a few words. "Now," she said, taking on the admonitory tones of a schoolmaster, "You know enough about codes and ciphers to appreciate the fact that most often the symbols stand for letters or sounds. The Hebrew characters are just like the letters of your alphabets. You can use them to write Hebrew words, or you can use them to spell out Italian words as well. See here. This character represents the sound 'N,' this one 'C,' this one 'L.' Put them together—and you've written 'Niccolo.'"

"Amazing."

"Well, at least it can be useful. Because the message isn't obviously written in code, or something that would be easily recognizable as a code, like a page covered with squiggly things and exotic little drawings, I can send a message like this, and it will seem perfectly innocent. Mix it in with a batch of commercial dispatches and no one suspects anything. Daniele can send this letter to Rome for me, along with some of his business correspondence."

"Is it difficult to learn?" asked Niccolo.

"Child's play. It may take some time to learn how to write the characters, but with a good eye, you can decode a message quite easily, in no time. Here, let me show you." Giuditta took another piece of paper and ruled it into two columns. Down one side, she put the letters of the Latin alphabet. Alongside them, she inscribed the corresponding Hebrew characters. When she was finished, she wrote a short message at the bottom. "Read it," she said.

Niccolo struggled with the unfamiliar symbols, running his finger up and down the columns and tracing the Latin equivalents as he went. Finished, he inspected his work—"*Non ti voglio lasciare.* I don't want to leave you," she had written. Their hands met among the sheets of paper covered with mysterious writing, and Niccolo squeezed. She squeezed back like someone holding onto something she didn't want to lose.

The next morning, after taking her leave of Lucrezia, Giuditta would return to Rome. With her she would carry a dispatch from the Florentine envoy to his ambassador there. The letter contained instructions to the Florentine embassy in Rome to aid and assist the bearer in the execution of Caterina Sforza's escape from the Belvedere fortress and her subsequent safe passage to Florence, where asylum would be waiting for her.

When she was gone, Niccolo dressed lethargically. He could still smell her like a ghost in the sheets, on the pillows, on his hands. He trudged back to the dirty room he had taken upon his arrival in Ferrara. The innkeeper greeted him with a storm of abuse and from under a counter pulled an enormous stack of letters and dispatches, all doubly and triply urgent.

Niccolo went up to his shabby room and sorted idly through the correspondence. All of it was from the Signoria, and as he read, he was drawn slowly back into the business at hand. Nothing had changed, though, and it all seemed so endless now, so tiresome. The Signoria renewed their demands for information on Borgia's moves, they cautioned him to commit them to nothing specific, and, of course, they promised to send money—soon. It took him the better part of the morning to read through it all, and he was just beginning to write his well-crafted responses when there was a rough pounding at the door, and the insolent innkeeper barged in. He threw a letter on the bed and snarled "Another one" before skulking out.

Niccolo reached for the new missive and his heart leapt. It was from her. He recognized the hand and eagerly, he ripped open the envelope. It was in the Hebrew code! So eager was he to read it that he cursed. He knew it would take a long time for him to decipher the thing and tease its meaning out.

Taking out the sheet Giuditta had given him, with the two columns of symbols, he went to work. He struggled valiantly against the mysterious, recalcitrant text, letter by letter, impatient for the stubborn page to yield its secrets. It was slow and frustrating work.

Finally, he was finished, but to his great dismay, he had produced only gibberish. Laboriously, he went back over everything, every character, and still the thing made no sense. Where could he be going wrong? There must be some other level of code. He searched his memory for some clue, carefully going over their conversation of the day before. But to no avail. What was the matter? He stared at the words he had written down. Utter nonsense. Then it came to him. Of course! He had read the thing the way he always read—left to right. But Giuditta had written the Hebrew letters in the order she was accustomed to reading them—right to left!

Line by line, Niccolo went back over the text, his excitement growing with each new word, each new revelation. He would have been happy with a love letter, ecstatic even. That was all he wanted—a small avowal, a tender word. But this was something altogether different. With a growing sense of disbelief, Niccolo read on. Giuditta had gone to see her former mistress, Lucrezia. Although content with her new husband, and very much in love with him, she was disconsolate over something she had learned only recently from her brother. When Niccolo was done reading, he knew Caesar Borgia's terrible secret.

❧ 27 ❧

Niccolo Meets a Famous Artist and Caesar Arranges a Peace Conference

In the middle of the piazza and attracting quite a bit of attention was a gentleman richly dressed in a red velvet mantle trimmed with silver. His hands and forearms were sheathed in spotless, white kid gloves, and he wore boots to match. A lush, black beard and long, curly, black hair framed his handsome features, although he wore a look of surprise and consternation at being the object of so much gawking and scrutiny.

Niccolo had followed Caesar Borgia south from Ferrara, through Imola and Forli, back here to Cesena. As he prodded his weary mount toward yet another overpriced inn, the commotion in the piazza attracted his attention, and he nudged the horse in its direction to see for himself what it was all about. It took Niccolo a few seconds to actually assemble the confusing visual evidence in front of him. The "gentleman" around whom the crowd was seething had been cut into two pieces. Neatly, cleanly, rather surgically, his legs had been separated from his torso. His trunk was planted upright on the paving stones from where he stared at the onlookers in frozen disbelief.

When he was over his initial shock, Niccolo was able to identify the body in the square as that of Ramiro de Lorca, a Spaniard Caesar had left to govern Romagna in his absence. Apparently Ramiro had not done a satisfactory job. Abruptly and grimly, Niccolo was transported back into the mysterious, violent world of Caesar Borgia and his machinations.

Niccolo was sick, but he had been sick before. He was tired, but he had been tired for months, and so he went about his business, which by now had become routine. He secured lodgings, stabled his horse, and settled in to write dispatches. And to wait. Sooner or later the great man would send for him. There was no need to advise Caesar of his whereabouts. Caesar would already know.

Toward midafternoon, after a heavy meal and a brief nap, Niccolo went out to see what he could learn. He avoided the main square, where the bug-eyed corpse was still attracting curiosity seekers and a great many flies as well. Apart from the crowds milling around the grisly spectacle, Cesena was a veritable beehive of activity. Troops moved in and out of town, and from what Niccolo could tell, they were moving in all directions at once. A contingent of Swiss mercenaries entered from the south. At the same time, a troop of seasoned Romagnouli left the city by the same gate. What was it Giuditta had said? "The pope never does what he says and Caesar never says what he does."

Niccolo smiled. It was not the first time he had found himself using that phrase, "What was it Giuditta had said?" In his dreary life of waiting and anticipation, she was the only bright spot. At night, instead of lying awake and wrestling with demons who all looked suspiciously like Caesar Borgia, he found a little solace in thoughts of her and in his memories of their brief, sweet time together. "Someday," he told himself, "when this business is finished, I'll go to Rome and . . ."

But this business was far from being finished. He knew it, and he tramped off through the cold, wet streets of Cesena to see what he could do about it. An entire section of the city had been taken over by several divisions of Caesar's troops who were making their winter headquarters in Cesena, and it was into that quarter that Niccolo directed himself. He was getting to know Cesena pretty well—and Forli and Faenza and Imola—all Borgia's cities. But Niccolo was growing weary of these Romagnouli cities. He wanted to go home. He wanted to sleep in Florence and eat Florentine food. He wanted to be among family and friends. To make matters even worse for him, in two weeks' time, it would be Christmas. As Niccolo looked at the troops around him sharpening and grinding weapons, cleaning armor, attending to animals and siege machines, his heart sank. They were preparing for something, and it was not a joyous celebration of the birth of the baby Jesus.

Lost in his thoughts and torn between twin longings—for Giuditta and for his native land—Niccolo heard something that he at first mistook for a part of his lazy dream. At first he thought it was only his imagination, but when he cocked his ear and listened attentively, it was unmistakable. Someone was speaking with a Florentine accent. Niccolo's ears, too long tortured by the hard, foreign accents of unfamiliar dialects, leapt with excitement at the clear, bright sounds of his beloved Florentine. A little audible piece of home! Like food for a starving man! Like manna in the desert!

Glancing around, he quickly spotted the Florentine. He was a large, imperious man barking orders at a few laborers. And he was not dressed like a respectable Florentine. His rose-colored satin cape barely descended to his buttocks and did nothing to hide the immodest bulge in his skintight hose. Lace was visible at his wrists and neck. His great plumed hat was downright Spanish!

The man paid no attention to the unassuming Florentine envoy and went about his business of berating the laborers. His voice was high and unpleasant and rushed out of him like air under pressure being squeezed out of a bladder. When he moved, he moved with the easy grace of an athlete entering the arena and with the extreme self-consciousness of one who is always sure he is being watched—and admired. Niccolo followed, shuffling along behind him.

The man seated himself on the edge of a fountain and opened a large notebook he was carrying. Immediately, he was absorbed in it. Niccolo settled next to him and tried to get a look at what he was doing. When the man became aware of Niccolo's presence, he looked up from his work and eyed him suspiciously. "What do you want?" His voice was sharp, but it was Florentine.

"To talk to a fellow Florentine. That's all," said Niccolo. "To ease the burden of my exile a little by sharing it."

"Go talk to someone else then," said the stranger. "You call me a Florentine. I call myself a citizen of the world." With that dismissal, he turned back to his work.

He pulled out a piece of red chalk and began to work on a drawing, throwing a hostile glance over his shoulder from time to time in Niccolo's direction. Finally exasperated by the fact that Niccolo was refusing to go away, he shoved the notebook in his face: "There, ignoramus, have a good look. Now, what did you see?"

"Enough to recognize a siege machine," said Niccolo. "And an antiquated siege machine at that. A trebuchet."

"If I want to design a trebuchet, I will, whether its antiquated or not," said the stranger gruffly.

"Do you know how Germans use them now?" asked Niccolo shrewdly. "Since the arm in one of those contraptions is useless against anything much stronger than a wooden stockade, they use it to lob things up over the walls, not directly at them. They hurl terrible things into besieged towns, noxious things. They'll sling a rotting sheep's carcass over the walls and hope that sooner or later the smell will cause the inhabitants to surrender. Or the disease."

The sharp-tongued man turned to Niccolo. "So you think you know about siege machinery?" he asked guardedly.

"I should," said Niccolo. "Florence has been in the process of besieging Pisa for the better part of a century now."

"That only shows the Pisans know more about defensive fortifications than the Florentines know about siege warfare."

Niccolo had to concede the point.

"Here, Florentine, take a look at these," said the man, moving closer to Niccolo and showing him his notebook. As he flipped through page after page of sketches, Niccolo saw designs for advanced fortifications as well as wheeled penthouses and movable ladders for scaling those fortifications. He saw mortars for showering an advancing enemy with stones or jagged bits of metal and assault wagons for protecting men and horses against just such a barrage. There were innumerable sketches of cannon—light, medium, and heavy. Many of them were decorated with fanciful ornaments—a head of Mars, dragons.

Still, Niccolo could not conceal his admiration for the man's work. Although much of it was distilled from earlier designs with which Niccolo was familiar, much was provocative and new. And the diversity! The eccentric engineer puffed up a little, sensing Niccolo's approval and interest. He was suddenly eager to show off his work and explain it. "You see here," he said, talking rapidly and indicating an odd device with pipes and levers, "a suction pump. It can be used to drain a moat in no time, run the water right out."

"Impressive," said Niccolo. "All these machines are impressive. But what are you going to do with them? Who's going to use them?"

"I am engaged, sir, as military engineer to Caesar Borgia, by the grace of God, duke of Romagna, Valentinois, and Urbino, standard-bearer and captain general of the church," replied the stranger with a flourish.

"Pompous ass," thought Niccolo, but he said, "So you work for Borgia? Let me ask you something. You're a Florentine. Suppose Borgia chooses to attack Florence. Will you make your wonderful engines available to him for that?"

"What do I care where he strikes, whom he attacks?" replied the man. "He pays me. In exchange, I design fortifications and the means for destroying them."

Niccolo eyed the engineer, not without a certain disdain. "Your allegiance is only to money, then?"

"Fool! Money I need to live, but my allegiance is to my designs, to my inspiration, to my own genius!"

Niccolo did not appreciate being called a fool, but he let it pass. He contemplated the self-declared genius as the latter once again applied himself to his sketches. With a mild shock, Niccolo realized that the man was drawing with his left hand. "Sinister implications," he thought, "the devil's work is in the left hand."

He watched that left hand fly across the pages of the sketchbook. The strokes it made were bold and sure, never tentative. "Whatever else he is," thought Niccolo, "he has talent." As if to confirm this observation, a mangy, half-starved dog limped across the piazza in front of the two Florentines. In a heartbeat, the "genius" flipped to a fresh page of his notebook and in less than a dozen strokes, reproduced the dog. The accuracy of the depiction was uncanny. The speed with which he did it, astounding.

Then, without looking up, he went back to the sketch of the catapult on which he had been working. He was drawing in dotted lines to indicate the trajectory the missiles would follow when launched. From time to time, he scribbled something along the lines or at the base of his machine. Niccolo assumed that these were indications of distance and the corresponding angles of fire, but he couldn't exactly read them. There was something odd about this man's handwriting. Niccolo had noticed it when he was reviewing the sketches of the war machines. At first, he dismissed it as an eccentricity, an odd, cramped hand with a funny slant—probably the result of writing left-handed.

But as he looked at sketch after annotated sketch and sometimes entire pages of notes written in the book, Niccolo began to realize that the hand was not just difficult to read, it was completely illegible. Moreover, he began to suspect that it was deliberately so. When he saw the man actually jotting in the numbers and figures on his drawing, Niccolo's suspicions were confirmed. Not only was he writing with his left hand, he was writing backward, from right to left!

"Hebrew!" was the first thought that entered Niccolo's mind. He remembered the way Giuditta had written and how her message had eluded him until he read it in the proper direction. As he was pondering these mysteries, a ragged beggar approached them, pitiful and deformed. He held out an emaciated hand for alms. The genius took one look at him, muttered, "*Dio, che faccia*"—"God what a face," and flipped back to the page where he had drawn the mangy dog.

He sketched the sunken eyes, the toothless leer, the ratty hair, and dirty beard. The portrait was startling in its immediacy, and Niccolo watched spellbound as it emerged line by line on the page. When the brash artist was finished, however, he turned immediately back to his work on the siege machine, leaving the pathetic beggar standing in front of him perplexed and disappointed. It was Niccolo who finally extracted a few coins from his pocket and pressed them into the artist's model's quivering hand.

"Amazing," thought Niccolo, "simply amazing." He had in mind not only the man's extraordinary talent, but his callousness as well. For the better part of an hour, Niccolo watched him. Whenever anyone of interest, anyone physically arresting or bizarre entered the piazza, the genius quickly found a fresh page in his notebook, recorded the image in chalk, then returned to his engines of war. He went at it with a dispassionate objectivity, flipping the big pages back and forth, but he worked at a feverish and unrelenting pace. He drew boys and prostitutes, soldiers and grandmothers. He sketched cannons and mortars and battlements and fortifications. And all the while, he scribbled notes to himself, scribbled from right to left.

Niccolo was intrigued as much by this odd writing habit as he was by the prodigious graphic output of the genius. He watched him carefully and examined the letters as well as he could but could find no resemblance between these odd characters and the Hebrew characters Giuditta had shown him.

"I see you're not just an engineer but an artist as well?" observed Niccolo at one point.

Annoyed at being interrupted, the man glared up at him. "I can do anything," he said matter-of-factly. "Anything in the realms of science and art."

"Anything?" said Niccolo, by now no longer surprised at the man's arrogance, "Do you paint?"

"Exquisitely."

"Fresco?"

"Better than any man alive."

"Sculpture?"

"Don't be silly," he replied imperiously. "That's a laborer's art. Let the dust-caked and dirt-smeared work at it. It does nothing but dirty the hands and the clothes."

"And your writing?" said Niccolo. "I was wondering about that."

"What about it?"

"Is that a special art form too?"

"Do you think I'm going to write plainly like other men?" he scoffed. "So that any fool can come along and read it and steal my ideas?"

"Still, your system isn't as foolproof as you think," said Niccolo.

"What do you mean?" The man's eyes flashed, then narrowed.

"I mean this," said Niccolo. "Give me the notebook." Reluctantly, he handed it over. Niccolo tore out a page covered with indecipherable scrawl, turned it over and held it up to the light. Without hesitation he read, "The art of perspective is of such a nature as to make what is flat appear in relief and what is in relief flat . . . Should I continue?"

The man was dumbstruck, but he instantly realized how Niccolo had discovered the key to his secret code. For years he had been writing this way, keeping all his notes safe from prying, thieving eyes. He wrote backwards, but not just backwards. He rotated each letter on its vertical axis, 180 degrees. The result looked fantastic and improbable. It could be read easily in a mirror, of course, but who would ever think of holding a mirror up to a written page. And now, now . . . He was infuriated.

"As you flipped back and forth, I caught the trick," said Niccolo. "When the light shone through the sheet of paper, the writing was perfectly clear. It can be read '*contraluce*,' held up to the light from the back of the page."

The engineer-artist fumed and made an angry show of clapping the notebook shut, thrusting it under his arm, and taking his leave with an icy, "Good day, sir." Niccolo was still standing there grinning when the renegade genius turned and shook his fist at him. "Savor this moment, sir!" shouted the genius. "Not many men have gotten the better of Leonardo da Vinci!"

Niccolo did not, however, have much time to savor the moment as he had been instructed to do by the irate Leonardo, for later that day, he was summoned into the august and imperial presence of Caesar Borgia. He went with all the confidence of Daniel going into the lion's den.

Usually Borgia received him alone, but this time there were several others in the room. There was a small, retiring man, there was a feathered creature strumming a lute, and there were the dogs. The dogs were big, black Neapolitan mastiffs. When Caesar sat, they sat at his feet. When he moved, they moved alongside him. They had short heads, powerful jaws, and a certain indolence that disguised the fact that, like Caesar, they were deadly.

"My father sent them," said Caesar. "And he sent me Serafino." He indicated the canary in the corner. "Play something for us, Serafino." Your songs will sweeten the air between us while we talk." Caesar beamed, the picture of cordiality, and the muted strains of a lute came softly from Serafino's direction.

"My father begged me to return to Rome. He says my place now is with him for the holidays. But we both know that's impossible, don't we? There are so many things to be done here.

"Finally, the old bear relented. To show his affection, he sent me the hounds and Serafino. He says they'll help to ease the pain of being away from the bosom of the family at Christmas time."

"Oh, and he sent me Don Micheletto," added Caesar, indicating the other gentleman in the room. The little man bowed deeply. His thin, grey hair, beatific smile, and unassuming manner gave him an otherworldly air. He looked more like Saint Francis than someone in the dubious retinue surrounding Caesar Borgia.

"And now, to business," said Caesar. "How is Florence disposed toward me these days?"

"Much as before, Excellency," said Niccolo.

"Splendid, splendid, because I've called you here to tell you that I intend to do Florence a favor, a very great favor, and in the very near future."

"And what might that be?" asked Niccolo. "Would you care to enlighten us?"

"Not just yet," said Caesar. "Not just yet."

It was the old routine. Caesar never says what he does. He hints. He threatens. Now he was hinting at a great favor he intended to do for Florence. Niccolo could only imagine what Caesar's idea of a favor was. If you complained of a headache, Caesar would cut your head off, do you a favor.

"Blind!" someone shrieked, "And begging bread you go!" Niccolo jumped at the intrusion. But it was only Serafino. He was singing.

"He sings splendidly, doesn't he?" said Caesar, the connoisseur. Niccolo looked at the singer. Serafino was wearing a feathered cape and hat to match. His voice was high, unnaturally high for a man his age, which Niccolo put at thirty-five or forty. That piping voice led Niccolo to some dire conclusions as to the status of Serafino's manhood. To make matters worse, he sang in the dull, thick-tongued accent of an unashamed Roman.

"Tonight, we leave for Sinigallia," declared Caesar abruptly.

"Sinigallia?" asked Niccolo. "What for?"

"Why, to add it to my domains," said Caesar.

While not particularly excited about the prospect of more travel, Niccolo was relieved. Sinigallia was to the south; Florence was to the north. For the time being, Caesar would not move against her. But like his namesake, Julius Caesar, this Caesar was capable of moving with blinding speed and striking where you least expected it.

"My lady holds a fan made of Cupid's wings . . ." Serafino again.

"I expect to encounter little resistance, but I don't want to take any chances. I've patched things up with my unruly lieutenants—Vitellozzo and the rest. They'll join us with their armies at Sinigallia. We'll be a united fighting force again." Caesar watched Niccolo's face for his reaction to this information. He was pleased to see shock and consternation there.

But Niccolo recovered quickly. He was getting better at this. "Florence is pleased that your Excellency has taken them under your wing again.

With your guidance, with your wise leadership, they should no longer represent a threat to us." He was lying and Caesar knew it.

As Niccolo left the room, Serafino was singing of a lady's missing tooth and how the gap left by that tooth was a window through which Cupid could shoot his arrows and love could enter . . . It was all very delicate, very tasteful. If your tastes were Spanish.

After hastily packing, Niccolo dashed off several letters to the Signoria and sent them through several different messengers along different routes. That Caesar had reconciled himself with his rebellious subalterns was alarming news, since it swelled the ranks of his army by at least nine thousand foot soldiers, seven hundred horse, and four hundred crossbows. But even more ominous was the "favor" he had promised Florence, the unspecified favor, the veiled threat. Sinigallia was next, but afterward? And who was the kindly old Don Micheletto? Niccolo's dispatches were more full of questions than answers.

Sinigallia was an unlikely target on the Adriatic coast, between Rimini and Ancona. It stood among marshes, between the River Misa and the sea, to which it was connected by a canal. It was, among other things, a difficult place to get into and out of.

The city was taken quickly and without serious bloodshed by Vitellozzo and Oliverotto da Fermo, another of his ilk. The operation was entrusted to them by Caesar as a test of loyalty to him. Both acquitted themselves admirably on the field of battle. With their mission accomplished, Oliverotto informed Caesar that the city was taken. With a light snow swirling around him, Caesar entered the city in triumph, accepted its surrender, and set himself up in the Bernardino Palace, the most sumptuous residence in town. In his wake, the rest of his retinue trailed into town, among them the itinerant Florentine envoy.

Niccolo crossed the bridge into Sinigallia feeling cold and stiff. A damp wind, heavy with the fetid odor of salt marshes, blew from the sea and chilled him to the bone. He immediately sought warmth and restoration in a tavern. As the numbness in his limbs yielded to the heat of the fire and as the empty cold in his stomach yielded to that of the wine, he heard a familiar, if not altogether pleasant sound. It was a plaintive melody about a girl with a fan of Cupid's wings and a gap in the armature of her teeth through which love might enter. Serafino was there.

Niccolo made his way over to the poet and set a pint of wine in front of him, hoping thus to occupy his mouth and hands to keep them from singing and playing, in that order. Serafino was ecstatic, or at least he acted that way. Niccolo was soon to learn that he always acted that way.

"The pleasure is mine, all mine," he kept repeating in his delicate, tripping voice. At least he seemed genuinely grateful for the wine.

"You're not attending the great man today," said Niccolo idly.

"Oh, not today," he said. "The great man is busy today. Extremely busy. Affairs of state. He has no use for his minstrel today."

Niccolo's ears pricked up at the mention of "affairs of state." He wanted to know more, but he thought it a good idea not to press the sensitive soul too soon and too obviously. "Wait 'til he finishes the wine," he thought. "It will lubricate his tongue." And lubricate his tongue, it did. He spilled over with anecdotes of court life in Rome. His accounts were punctuated with little cries of delight—How marvelous! How rich! How novel! At one point, he was in danger of picking up his lute again to celebrate the discreet charms of a certain lady in song, but, fearing the worst, Niccolo forestalled him with another draft of wine.

In his cups, Serafino waxed philosophical. He said, "The theologian argues how many angels can fit on the head of a pin. But the poet, do you know what the poet asks? The poet asks how many angels can dance on the head of a pin!"

"Bravo Serafino!" Niccolo clapped him on the back. "I envy your master. I don't understand how Caesar can do without the services of a capital fellow like yourself, even for one day."

Niccolo's flattery was interrupted by shouts of acclamation from the streets. "Let us fly!" chirped the poet. "The festivities begin without us." Both Niccolo and Serafino managed to push outside in time to see the object of the crowd's attentions—the vile Vitellozzo Vitelli.

The butcher of Tuscany, the rabid dog, the madman sat serenely astride a white mule, looking for all the world like a pilgrim on his way to the holy land. He wore a black cloak lined with green and made generous, gracious gestures to the cheering crowds. The first among Caesar's captains rode through the streets as far as the Bernardino Palace, where he was met at the gate by a nimble, obsequious Don Micheletto.

Niccolo was forced to apply to the poet once again for information. "Who is that Don Micheletto? What does he do for your master?"

"Oh, Don Micheletto has the soul of a poet," replied Serafino.

"Great," thought Niccolo. He asked, "Is he a Spaniard?"

"Spaniard? Italian? What's the difference where the soul is concerned? He appreciates beauty. He's a connoisseur of it."

"And Caesar brought him all the way from Rome to help him appreciate beauty?"

"No, silly man!" replied Serafino reproachfully. "Don Micheletto helps my master with his practical problems. They plan battles, they talk of war. Don Micheletto has seen a hundred wars and a thousand campaigns in Spain, in France and Germany, in the south."

Niccolo understood. A council of war had been convened. He was wondering if he should shoot a dispatch off to Florence immediately when Serafino did an odd thing. Pointing to Don Micheletto, he made a gesture with his thumb, akin to drawing it across his Adam's apple in a quick jerk to indicate the slitting of the throat. His eyes twinkled mischievously. The oddity of the gesture, though, lay in the fact that Serafino did not draw the thumb / knife across his throat but across his waist. Niccolo regarded him for a moment and was on the verge of dismissing his eccentric behavior as that of a fool when the truth suddenly hit him. He remembered the grisly sight of Ramiro de Lorca lying in the piazza of Cesena, severed in two. When Niccolo looked up at Don Micheletto again, a shudder ran through him.

As the morning wore on, Niccolo watched them ride into the city, one by one—the rest of Caesar's captains.

There was Oliverotto. Raised as an orphan, he learned his trade at the side of the cruel Vitelli. When he came of age, he returned to his native city of Fermo, embraced his uncles and cousins, and offered them a splendid feast. When the meal was over, he rose, saying that these were subjects better discussed in private and, with winks and broad hints, promised to bring his relatives into his confidence. When they repaired to an adjoining room for these secret discussions, soldiers fell upon them and slew them all. Proclaiming himself prince and last of his line, Oliverotto rode through the streets, swinging the head of a dead uncle in slow circles above him.

Giovanpagolo Baglione was little better. After a similar disposal of rival kinsmen, he was seen eating the heart of one of his cousins.

All the others as well distinguished themselves in fearful butchery, this one gaining renown by sticking pins in his victims, that one by biting them. One chopped his enemies into little pieces and shared the morsels out among his men as souvenirs. Another kept his vanquished foe hanging in a cage, where he could be taunted and tormented at the whim of anyone who had an inclination to indulge him or herself.

Niccolo watched them file into the city, one by one. Each was greeted in his turn with warmth and affection by the fawning Don Micheletto before disappearing into the confines of the Bernardino Palace. When all had arrived, the gates were shut and thus began the conclave of tyrants convened by Caesar Borgia in Sinigallia on the last day of December in the year 1502.

In 49 BC, Julius Caesar fortified himself with it at Forli, then Forum Livii, before making his momentous decision to cross a tiny stream called the Rubicon. A thousand years before that, according to Homer, the Greek warriors Achilles and Agamemnon consumed it beneath the walls of Troy. Reaching even further back, beyond the bounds of antiquity to the realms of legend, Venus is said to have fed it to her husband, Vulcan, to induce sleep on the nights she waited for her lover Mars.

Now on the eve of the new year, Niccolo Machiavelli sat before a steaming bowl of the venerable *brodetto*. Like his fellow Florentine, the poet Dante Alighieri, who sang its praises and often drowned the sorrows of his exile in it, Niccolo found some small solace in the rich fish chowder. Spread throughout the Mediterranean by the Greeks, and going by a hundred different names—*bouillabaisse* in France, *ghiotto* in Sicily, *ziminu* in Sardinia—*brodetto* was more than just food. It was a source of endless controversy. On the Adriatic coast alone, no fewer than six cities—Sinigallia among them—claimed to make the only real brodetto.

Niccolo had consumed a considerable quantity of the soup since he had been in the Romagna, and the only thing he had come to expect of it was that each time the recipe would be entirely different. Squid or shellfish or lobster might be included, or rigorously excluded. One cook laced his broth with saffron; another considered it anathema. Onions? Garlic? White wine? Each had its defenders and detractors. There are cases of blows having been exchanged on these questions.

Niccolo sat staring into his bowl, stirring the thick broth with its flaky, succulent chunks of white fish, waiting for it to cool a little. His first mouthful had a vague, briny bite to it, evidence of the fact, as the cook had boasted, that the fish was cleaned and washed in seawater only. The cook had gone on to say that that was the only correct way to do it, which is why it was impossible to make a real brodetto in the inland cities.

"Controversy . . . strife . . . local differences," Niccolo thought to himself. Even in something as simple as food. But it wasn't all that simple. Everyone had the one and only correct recipe, but in reality, only chance determined the kinds of fish that went into the soup, whatever the fisherman netted on that particular day. "Why, then," he thought, "the steaming concoction wasn't all that different from the political situation in Italy, was it? On any given day, a half-dozen fish—allies—might be in the soup together. The next day, everything changed. Some were still in; others were out."

He had to stop himself. *"Madonna, Madonna,"* he muttered. "I'm getting obsessed. I'm seeing Caesar Borgia in my soup, political intrigue in a bowl of fish." He took a long swallow of white wine to banish such thoughts, but he wondered at the same time, half-consciously, whether this particular version of the brodetto called for white wine in the stock.

Whether it was the wine or the soup with its purported soporific effect that had been so useful to Venus and her conspiring lover, Niccolo felt drowsy when he finished his meal and decided to retire early. He drifted off to sleep with yet another controversy raging in his head—Was it the saffron that produced the drowsiness? Or was it the *scorpena* fish, said to have a mild dose of venom in its spines . . . ?

He was rudely awakened some time later. After rattling the door nearly off its hinges with resounding blows, someone burst into is room. "Caesar wishes an audience with the Florentine envoy. Now!"

"*Miseria,* what time is it?" mumbled Niccolo.

"An hour past midnight. Now hurry." The blustering messenger waited while Niccolo dressed and then escorted him to the Bernardino Palace, which was, even at this hour, ablaze with light. Still half asleep, half in his murky, fishy dream world, Niccolo wondered what sort of soup Caesar and his confederates had managed to concoct. What fish were in and which ones were out? And were the spines really a little venomous?

Caesar himself greeted Niccolo at the door. "Ah, the Florentine envoy!" he said brightly. "Please excuse us for the lateness of the hour, but matters touching your city have come up, matters of the utmost importance."

Niccolo mumbled something about how it was no trouble, really, and trudged dutifully behind the ebullient Caesar up a broad staircase. The duke was especially elegant this evening in a subdued velvet doublet of black and dark green stripes. Caesar talked as he led the way. "What we wish to discuss with you now is the favor we told you we were planning to do for Florence." Niccolo could not be sure if the "we" referred to the whole council of blackguards gathered here or just to Caesar.

"Please, this way," said Caesar, stepping gallantly aside and ushering Niccolo into the conference room. Niccolo thought to make an aggressive entrance so as not to display any fear or hesitation before this singular band of brigands. All the former conspirators were still there, seated along one wall beneath a row of windows. They were sitting bolt upright in their straight-backed chairs. None of them moved when Niccolo entered the room. Their severed heads were arranged neatly on the table in front of them.

28

Into the Sink of Iniquity

Caesar Borgia was not a man who did things by half measures. Years later, writing of the startling stroke at Sinigallia, Niccolo Machiavelli would compare Caesar to the basilisk, a mythical beast who, with soft whistling, entices its victims into its den and then destroys them. But on the first day of the New Year in 1503, at one in the morning, poetic conceits and elaborate comparisons to mythological creatures were far from his mind. Niccolo had to stifle the urge to vomit. He could already taste the acid in the back of his throat. He swallowed hard and sent it back down.

The only sound in the room was made by the blood dripping slowly over the edges of the table onto the cool, green marble below. From a darkened recess, Don Micheletto surveyed the ghoulish scene, a look of utter contentment on his face.

"It would have cost Florence two hundred thousand ducats to get rid of them," observed Caesar nonchalantly. He stopped to consider the figure for a moment and continued, "At least 200,000 to raise an army to defeat them, maybe even more to buy them all off." Niccolo just stood staring at him in disbelief. The cold man smiled.

"So what do I get from Florence in exchange for my . . ." Caesar paused, looking for the right word, "my . . . gesture of solidarity?"

When Niccolo did not reply, Caesar indicated a vacant chair at the conference table. "Sit and we can discuss terms."

Were it not for the macabre setting, the discussion that followed would have been a perfectly ordinary discussion, touching on all the now-familiar points of the give and take between Caesar Borgia and the republic of Florence. But Niccolo had to keep turning his head so as not to look into the unnaturally still faces of the silent congregation that bore witness to their colloquium. And he had to take his arms off of the table to avoid the advancing pool of dark, black blood that was spreading out across its surface.

Vitellozzo was the worst. The others evoked varying degrees of terror and pity, but Vitellozzo looked as though some mad demon were caught twisting in him and was frozen at the moment of death.

"You look as though you want to interrogate our friend Vitellozzo," said Caesar, seeing that Niccolo was staring at him. "But I'm afraid he would have very little to say in his present condition. You know, Vitellozzo was the most cowardly of them all. He groveled at the end. He actually begged to see a priest."

"Which, of course, you refused him?"

"It wouldn't have done him any good. But Don Micheletto saved him for last—to give him time to say his prayers, eh, Micheletto?" The little man nodded in silent agreement from his post in the shadows.

"But enough of them," said Caesar abruptly. "They did not want to be Caesar's friends, so they became his enemies. And you can see for yourself the fate that awaits Caesar's enemies. Now Florence must finally decide whether she will have me for a friend or an enemy."

"Florence has always held the duke to be a friend and an ally," stammered Niccolo, mechanically repeating a sentence he had used so often before.

"Friends and allies," mused Caesar distractedly. "Still, I've learned something important from my friends here, from Paolo and Vitellozzo and the rest—that the love of friendship is fickle and can be easily withdrawn. I've learned that, even among friends, it is better to be feared than loved. So Florence will be my friend and remain my friend, not because of the excessive love she bears me, but because she fears me! That's why Don Micheletto and I arranged this little demonstration for you—so that what you lack in love toward us, you can make up in fear."

Niccolo left in a hurry. He took one last look at the gruesome row of heads and the dark stains congealing around them. Once outside, he saw that it was snowing, as he retched and vomited uncontrollably. Fat flakes of snow settled softly and peacefully to the ground. Shaking and sweating, he stood heaving for a long time after his stomach had yielded up the last of its fishy contents.

For nearly two months after that hellish night, Niccolo trailed along in Borgia's wake. It was business as usual. Caesar had no trouble securing the services of the now-leaderless troops of his defunct lieutenants, and, with his new and enlarged army, he set about consolidating his gains. He struck off quickly into the heart of the peninsula, securing Perugia and Assisi. From there, he turned north to Siena and halted. He was encamped only thirty miles from Florence. But then suddenly, incredibly, instead of pursuing a fatal northern course for Florence, he turned abruptly and marched south, toward Rome. His father, the pope, required his services.

While Caesar was disposing of the conspirators at Sinigallia, Alexander had been mopping up on their relatives in Rome. Cardinal Orsini, an uncle to Paolo Orsini and one of the richest and most influential men in Holy City, had been the pope's first victim. But the cardinal's murder stirred up more trouble than Pope Alexander had anticipated, and sporadic revolts led by disaffected members of the powerful and far-flung Orsini clan began to break out. Caesar was called to put down these revolts, dispose of the seditious Orsini, and thus render secure the papal grip on central Italy. He made an example of the Orsini stronghold of Cere, near Rome. Using the siege machinery designed for him by Leonardo da Vinci, he took the town in less than a week and slaughtered everyone in it. From there, Caesar proceeded against the other rebellious towns at his leisure. As an observer pointed out, he was "eating the artichoke leaf by leaf."

When Borgia turned south at Siena, heading away from Florence, the possibility of imminent attack receded with him, and the Florentine envoy was recalled, his embassy terminated. Niccolo was finally being sent back to Florence for the first time in over six months.

Not that the Borgia threat had vanished. Far from it. Everyone knew this was only a lull in the contest. However, based on the information Niccolo had been able to supply, and in particular on the secret he had stumbled upon, thanks to the good offices of Giuditta, Florence now had a firm and well-defined policy for dealing with Borgia's threats—they would wait and do nothing, trying to buy time.

Niccolo, meanwhile, immersed himself in the day-to-day affairs of the chancery, the more mundane, the better. Anything was better than going up against the dragon every day. He wrote a speech for Soderini on the necessity of raising taxes. He lost himself in the labyrinth of byzantine regulations and petty, often-dishonest regulators who administered the city's finances.

And he gained weight. The effects of the sedentary life and the gusto with which he threw himself into his native Florentine cuisine began to make themselves felt. In fact, Niccolo found himself spending an immoderate amount of time in the rituals of eating and drinking. He was always at the market, always snooping in pots, offering advice, laying down rules and caveats—what could be eaten with what, whether the ravioli should be boiled, then fried, whether the cheese should be added before or after frying . . . There were so many details to organize to ensure not only the quality of the meals but the safe and regular conduct of the family's digestion. Simple, healthful food for an austere republican family—that was the right way, the Florentine way.

It was early afternoon and Niccolo's thoughts were already straying in the direction of a hearty white bean soup, heavily flavored with garlic and spooned over slabs of bread soaked in newly pressed olive oil. "After that, let's see . . ." And then he lackadaisically forced himself back to the pile letters that awaited his attentions.

Sorting through the stack of routine correspondence from the Florentine ambassadors in Rome, Niccolo kept abreast of Caesar's latest moves as he thrashed around the countryside, reducing enemy strongholds to rubble. Mercifully, he was doing it far, far from Florence.

Niccolo had to smile when he came upon yet another letter bemoaning the shortage of funds to run the embassy in Rome. The Florentine ambassadors in Rome repeatedly besieged him with urgent requests for more money. Now back in Florence, it was Niccolo in the chancery who had the task of writing to say that funds would be on their way—very shortly. Be patient.

As he was wrapping up the day's business with the idea in mind of retiring early—he had hoped to be able to investigate the rumor that the tiny, still-blind eels taken in the Arno at this time of year had started to arrive and were for sale. Flash fried in very hot oil—he came upon an item that drove all thought of food from his mind.

It was only a note appended to the urgent pleas and fanciful budget projections of the Roman ambassador. The papal chancellor had registered a complaint with the Florentine embassy regarding a small band of people thought to be Florentines or in the pay of the republic who had been involved in "some unpleasant business." Said Florentines, after having helped a prisoner of the pope escape from the Belvedere fortress, fled the city. Apparently, the entire party was apprehended outside of Rome on their way to Florence. A struggle ensued when they offered resistance, and they were all unfortunately killed. The note went on to say that His Holiness regrets this business and trusts that the Florentines' conduct toward him in the future will be nothing short of honorable and respectful of his holy office, but Niccolo was no longer reading. The incident could only mean the escape of Caterina Sforza had been aborted. And Giuditta was involved, Giuditta, to whom he had written several times and received no reply. Panic seized him as he reread the dispatch and his eyes fell on the phrase, "all unfortunately killed."

Niccolo's first impulse was to send an urgent letter to their people in Rome to get more information, but he checked it. Thinking back, he remembered how he had written in good faith to the trusted Florentine ambassadors there instructing them to assist Giuditta in getting the countess out of Rome. If the escape party was taken and killed outside Rome, they must not have gotten clean away, they must have been followed. Or there was another possibility. They had been betrayed, and the traitor was someone in the Florentine embassy. The pen was twitching in Niccolo's fingers, but he didn't know what to do. He didn't know whom to trust.

A gnomelike head popped into the preoccupied secretary's otherwise-empty study. It was one of the errand boys. "There's a priest here to see you," he said in a voice heavily laden with sarcasm.

Niccolo looked up. "A priest?" A moment later, he found himself thinking, "That's not a priest, that's Pagolo." The two had been keeping fairly regular company since Niccolo's return from the Borgia wars, and Pagolo was a frequent and appreciative dinner guest at the Machiavelli household. Niccolo barely paid him any attention and returned to the pointless, nervous shuffling of the papers strewn about on his desk. He said, "Pagolo, maybe you should come round tonight. Something just came up here, and it could mean trouble."

"If you don't have time, just a few minutes, for an old friend, then I'll go away," said Pagolo mournfully.

Niccolo looked up at him and saw an unaccustomed look of worry on the little priest's face. "Well, what is it?" he said. "How much do you need?" When Pagolo had problems, they were usually monetary in nature and lent themselves to simple, direct solutions.

"I seem to have fallen in love."

"Not again," sighed Niccolo. "Well, you'll get over it."

"Not this time. This is different."

"It's always different with you, Pagolo. But you always get over it. You know that."

"Niccolo, I know I've made a habit of, shall we say, associating with fallen women. And I've suffered for it, I admit that. But now I've taken up with a different sort of woman."

"And your vow of chastity is preventing you from realizing your love for her, right?" said Niccolo derisively.

"You can laugh," said the pitiful Pagolo, "but it's no joke to me."

"And who is the lucky woman this time?" asked Niccolo, who was well aware of his friend's habit of discharging his excess passions in the company of professional and semi-professional lovers with whom he then fell hopelessly in love for periods often extending up to a week or two.

"Marietta."

"Marietta Corsini!" said Niccolo in disbelief. "No!"

"Yes. I'm afraid."

"Pagolo, how could you?"

"It was destiny. It was God's will."

"Pagolo, anyone but Marietta. She'll eat you alive." Marietta Corsini was a girl from the same neighborhood where Niccolo and Pagolo had grown up. They had known her most of their lives as a sharp-tongued, hellion of a woman. It was not without reason that, although beautiful and from a good family, at thirty-two, she was still unmarried.

Niccolo laughed, "Go back to your prostitutes, Pagolo. They'll treat you better than Marietta ever will."

"I can't."

"Give yourself a week. It'll pass."

"No, it won't. She's pregnant."

Niccolo was stunned, then he burst out laughing. "You got Marietta pregnant!"

"I think she got herself pregnant. She just used me as the instrument."

"And what are you going to do now?"

"I don't know. She says I've destroyed her honor and that when her father finds out, he'll kill me." Pagolo was not exaggerating in his use of the word "kill." Corso Corsini had a reputation for the ferocious and often-violent defense of his honor.

"He won't just kill you. He'll cut your balls off," observed Niccolo. Glumly, Pagolo acknowledged that that probably would be the case.

"What does Monna Marietta want?" asked Niccolo.

"I'm not sure. She said everything is in my hands. She's seems rather unconcerned about the whole thing."

"Can you get her to induce a miscarriage?"

"I've suggested it. She refused. Vehemently. She wants the child."

"How long before it starts to show?"

"Couple of weeks. Then I'm a dead man. A dead man with no balls."

"A dead priest with no balls," corrected Niccolo.

Before Pagolo left, Niccolo assured him he would speak to the formidable Marietta on his behalf and try to come to some sort of an agreement with her. After all, he assured his friend, he was a professional diplomat, a negotiator, and, if he had dealt with the likes of Caesar Borgia, who was the devil incarnate, he could manage things easily enough with Marietta Corsini. Maybe.

Shortly after Pagolo took his leave, a courier arrived with another batch of dispatches from Rome, and Niccolo tore recklessly into them, hoping for more news of the fatal escape attempt. He continued to work throughout the afternoon. He penned half a dozen letters and tore them all up. Messengers and colleagues came and went through his office in a steady stream, but he paid them little heed, absorbed as he was in the problem at hand.

He heard the letter fall on the writing table and was dimly aware that the messenger for some reason had not gone away. Irritable now and without even looking up, Niccolo said testily, "Well, what are you waiting for? If you want a receipt, one of the clerks outside can give you one."

When there was no response he reiterated, lifting his head in anger, "I said, one of the clerks . . ." The words stuck in his throat. Standing before him, disheveled but very much alive, was Countess Caterina Sforza.

"You were saying, 'one of the clerks'?"

"I thought you were dead," stammered Niccolo.

"In spirit perhaps," said the countess. "But in the flesh, as you can see, I'm very much alive."

"There was an ambush and the whole party was killed. How did you get away?"

"Simple enough. I wasn't in the party. I went by sea to Livorno instead."

"*Miracolo,*" muttered Niccolo.

"It wasn't my idea. I would have fought every inch of the way from Rome to here, if I had my way. Right through the heart of Caesar's army too. It was your beloved . . ."

"And she's . . ."

"Fine." confirmed Caterina, to his great relief. "She went with me as far as Ostia, put me on a merchant vessel, and returned discreetly to Rome. But is that all you think about? Don't you even have time to greet an old friend?"

In his surprise and anxiety, Niccolo had been remiss. Now, he rose and kissed her on both cheeks. "Such kisses!" she said, teasing him. "So cold and formal. I see the fire has gone out of the secretary." Niccolo looked embarrassed. "Oh well, to hell with you," she said, laughing. "I want to see my children."

As Caterina was leaving, she turned, "Don't forget the letter I brought you," she said with a knowing smile. "It's from your beloved."

Niccolo ripped the envelope open. As he did so, Caterina's words echoed in his ears, "From your beloved." Giuditta must have talked to Caterina about him. Maybe even referred to him as her "beloved." His breast swelled with pride.

He groaned to see that the letter was written, of course, in code. He couldn't just pick it up and read it the way he wanted to do, but would have to sit down and decipher the thing, coax and cajole its meaning out a letter at a time. But as soon as he had read the completed message, Niccolo was scurrying off to seek an emergency audience with Gonfaloniere Soderini. The gist of what Giuditta had said was that, while Caesar's army was ravishing central Italy, Caesar himself had returned secretly to Rome to meet with his father. Something was afoot. Within three days, Niccolo was on his way to Rome.

As usual, he traveled alone. Niccolo was burning with excitement, not the least cause of which was his anticipated reunion with Giuditta, and he made the trip from Florence to Rome in less than two days. It was mid-July, and he began to feel the sultry, wet heat of the south as he rode down, out of the Umbrian hills onto the low central Italian plain. He followed the course of the Tiber through rich farmlands, and he thought of the renewed distress Caesar Borgia was likely to cause him. But most of all, he thought of Rome.

Roma! Ever since his childhood, when Niccolo had begun his reading of the exploits of the ancient Romans, Rome had come to represent an ideal for him. He pictured her broad, straight avenues and boulevards, lined with temples and palaces that were the epitome of beauty and grace, of simplicity and classical elegance. The city was a living monument built to the clear, sober spirit of the ancient, ardent republicans.

As Niccolo grew older, and his understanding of the accomplishments of the early Romans increased, his admiration for these stalwart people and the great, shining city they built turned slowly to awe and amazement. He was not an overly religious man, and his ideals were not always consistent with the teachings of the church, yet it could be said that sentiments of a spiritual nature stirred in him, and as in others of his age, those sentiments lay in his profound reverence for things of the past, for things Roman. For the pilgrims who flocked to the city, Rome was the center of Christianity, the church. For Niccolo, who had no illusions about papal power and politics, it was the seat of the greatest civilization that humankind had ever produced.

The splendors of ancient Rome danced in his head as he rode past peasants working in the fields. In Niccolo's imagination, they were cultivating wheat to feed the Roman legions, that mighty machine that once went forth to unify all of Italy, the world even, and imposed a benevolent order upon her. As he drew closer to the city, he picked up his pace, passing little knots of pilgrims drawn to the Eternal City for the salvation of their souls. Many were ragged and on foot and had come from unimaginably far away. What little money they carried would in due time be deposited in the pockets of dishonest churchmen selling indulgences and other sacred offices, as well as forged documents and false relics. If, by some miracle, they were not entirely fleeced by these good gentlemen operating in an official capacity, a thriving army of cutthroats, thieves, charlatans, and beggars would finish the job.

Niccolo's first view of the city took him by surprise as he rounded the top of a little hill. There, spread out below him was not the Rome through which he had imagined walking with his beloved on his arm, explaining to her the glories of Cincinnatus and Scipio, retracing their very footsteps. What he saw from his hilltop perch looked more like a pile of rubble, a great, cramped, deformed pile of rubble. And sticking out of this rubbish heap of broken masonry everywhere, there were stiff, protruding towers.

He had expected an impressive skyline, but low and noble. Instead, everywhere broken remnants of nobility were punctuated by the towers, like hundreds of mocking, obscene gestures, defying and denigrating whatever spirit, whatever philosophy had once reigned in this place. Niccolo could see plainly, even at this distance, that many of these offending towers had been grafted onto magnificent older buildings, destroying their clean classical lines. And he knew from experience why these kinds of towers were built. For defense. With a sinking feeling, Niccolo guided his horse down, not into the ancient, classical city of his dreams, but into a rats' nest of contemporary viciousness.

If the sight of Rome was bewildering, the smell of her was all the more daunting, and Niccolo was not noted for his strong stomach. The wet smells of decay rose from every fetid corner, relieved only by an occasional breeze that blew from the dirty brown water of the flaccid, muddy Tiber. Instead of cleansing the city, this once-majestic river now sat in her heart like a stagnant, open sewer. The bloated and decaying bodies of dogs and goats and rats floated lazily by. The eddies and backwaters near the river's banks teemed with malaria-carrying mosquitoes. The excretions of forty thousand citizens usually found their way to her, and, thanks to the river's frequent flooding, were just as often redeposited in the streets and houses from which they came, along with a dank, disease-breeding coat of Tiber mud.

Fighting his way through crowds of vermin-infested beggars who grabbed at his legs and saddle bag, Niccolo pushed on through the filth. He saw a struggling, sweaty man dragging the carcass of a dead calf through the muck of the unpaved street. Was he going to eventually eat that thing? He shuddered. And he remembered the advice Biagio had given him—never eat the rabbit in Rome. It's cat.

Niccolo did not doubt his friend's word, for cats were everywhere in this city. As were cows and pigs and sheep. They were not, as in Florence, being driven to market. They were not tended, but roamed free, rooting in the slime. There were vast tracts of land within the city walls, hopelessly overgrown with vines and trees and choked with weeds and dense underbrush. Once they had been magnificent public squares and buildings, exquisitely laid out, lovingly tended. Now they were abandoned to the advances of the wilderness. What man had built could no longer hold out against the ceaseless insinuation of ruin and decay. In one of these urban forests, Niccolo thought he glimpsed a deer. If he had felt an inclination to go exploring, he would have found much more—foxes and wolves and the corpses on which they often fed, dumped there to rot.

What had once been a Roman forum was now an urban swamp. The collapse of the ancient Roman sewage system, through centuries of neglect, had produced these cesspools in low-lying areas throughout the city. As Niccolo rode past one of them, he saw the arm and hand of some ancient statue sticking up out of the green surface of the polluted mire, and he thought bitterly, "Better to remain down there than to emerge into the light of day in this pestiferous city. *Requiescat in pace.*"

Most of the streets through which Niccolo passed were lined with abandoned buildings, once splendid, but now dark and empty, like grinning, toothless mouths from which wafted the dank, unclean breath of disease and decay. When Niccolo rode under a laurel tree, he reached up and grabbed a handful of leaves. Crushing one in his fingers, he held it up to his nose to get some respite from the overpowering stench.

His eyes stung from the smoke and dust that blackened the late-afternoon air. Noxious effluvia from dozens of recognizable industries reached his nostrils, harsh sulfuric fumes and the burning smells of foundries and forges. Although the acrid smell of urine penetrated all of Rome, unusually intense concentrations of it told Niccolo that even tanners were allowed to operate within the circle of this city's dirt-smeared walls.

What Niccolo had at first mistaken for a tremendous amount of building activity turned out to be, on closer inspection, just the opposite. Everywhere he went, buildings were being torn apart. It was as if these devils were wreaking a bloody revenge on the very body of

Rome herself, tearing her limb from limb in a frenzy of destructive activity. Some of the ancient pieces of marble were being carted away to adorn the houses of the wealthy in better parts of Rome and all over Italy. A lively market in antiquities had developed, and Rome was still considered a shopper's paradise for priceless statuary and other decorative pieces.

Through clouds of gnats and flies, Niccolo advanced from the city's more deserted periphery to her more densely populated center. There were occasional signs of elegance, of care in the buildings here, but more often than not, even those were ringed with a motley jumble of squalid huts and sheds. Mysteriously, laundry hung from open windows, even though Niccolo had seen no evidence thus far that the Romans had any predilection for clean clothing. Butchers threw guts out into the muddy streets, where filthy children fought with mangy dogs over them. A group of shrieking urchins, armed with sticks, came hurtling from a building in pursuit of a huge rat. The bloodied thing was wounded and lumbering, and Niccolo had to pull up short to avoid crushing it beneath his horse's hooves. Close up, he saw it was not a rat at all, but a porcupine. It didn't matter. The beastly children were on it just the same with their merciless sticks.

"*Roma caput mundi,*" sighed Niccolo in despair. "Rome, the head of the world." With bitter irony, Niccolo reflected that this squalid, fallen city was indeed a fitting setting for the moral turpitude and the stinking corruption of the Borgia papacy. No wonder Savonarola had chosen Florence and not Rome as the place from which to launch his crusade to cleanse the peninsula.

Niccolo had been in Rome for less than half an hour, and already he missed Florence. His dreams of past Roman nobility of spirit had evaporated before his eyes—and nose—and he was left with nothing but the unbearable stench of the present. Several times, he had to ask for directions, and the blustering, guttural Roman accents in which they were delivered amounted to yet another blow to his sensibilities. He was literally reeling when he reached a small corner of the Ponte section and stopped in dismay. Was he hallucinating? Had the fumes gotten to him? Overwhelmed him?

Before Niccolo's eyes, the grim world of Rome had been transformed magically into a picture of his beloved Florence. Clean streets, houses with stern, well-kept Tuscan facades, orderly rows of market carts and stalls, the smell of meat being grilled and not rotting in the afternoon sun.

"Where am I?" he babbled in confusion to a man bent under a sack of grain.

"Little Florence," the man snapped back in crisp Florentine tones. "We've built our own houses and walls to keep the filthy Romans out. Here we can live like men instead of beasts." Waves of relief washed over Niccolo as he looked around him in disbelief and slowly crawled down from his horse.

After washing and scrubbing himself more vigorously than he had in years, Niccolo was received by his old friend, the cardinal. Following his brother Piero's rise to preeminence in Florence's civilian government, Bishop Soderini had become Cardinal Soderini. He embraced Niccolo with genuine affection and invited him to make himself comfortable in the cool, simply furnished Florentine sitting room. *Berlingozzo,* a sweet cake—a sweet Florentine cake—taken before meals were served.

"I suppose you've discovered why Rome has more perfumers than any other city on earth," said the cardinal. Both Florentines laughed.

Later, when they sat down to dinner, the cardinal explained the genesis of the Florentine colony to Niccolo and pointed out that everything on the table from the flour to make the tortellini to the grilled beef had been imported from Florence. "And we're not the only ones to isolate ourselves like that here. Every nationality, every city in Italy, maintains a colony in Rome, and it's generally a tight-knit, closed colony."

"And what do the Romans think of all these colonies of foreigners?"

"It doesn't much matter what they think. We outnumber them! I think that Romans, real Romans, make up only about one-fourth of the population here."

"And the rest?" asked Niccolo.

"God, everything under the sun," replied the cardinal. "The French and Germans and English all have substantial delegations here. There are wild Irish monks and even a whole quarter of taciturn Slavs and mysterious Albanians. Venice, Milan, Naples—they all send their people to deal with the pope—and with each other. Even the Turk has an embassy in Rome, and Jews come and go as they please—as long as they pay their taxes, which are much heavier than what the Christians pay."

"And the Spanish have a presence here, unless I'm mistaken," added Niccolo.

"Ah, the troublesome Spanish," said the cardinal, falling silent.

When they had finished eating, Niccolo expressed a wish to go out, which alarmed the cardinal. "At night! In Rome! By yourself?" He seemed incredulous. Finally, when he saw that the stubborn Niccolo would not be denied, the cardinal forced him to accept a compromise. "Let me send someone with you, at least until you learn your way around. It's safer that way."

Cardinal Soderini chose an embassy employee, a Florentine named Michelozzi, to guide the newly arrived Niccolo around the dangers of nocturnal Rome. Michelozzi was a high-spirited young man with bright eyes and a ready smile, although Niccolo thought he was dressed rather abominably for a Florentine. His tight jacket was worked in a harlequin pattern of loud red and yellow, and under it he wore a shirt with billowing slashed sleeves. He must have seen Niccolo's arched eyebrows, for he quickly explained, "Protective covering. Dressed like this, I'm just another luckless gigolo among hundreds. If you want to take a chance going out as a respectable Florentine citizen, I won't argue with you, but I suggest we requisition a contingent of armed guards to keep the thieves at bay."

Michelozzi's wisdom prevailed, and before they left the Florentine colony, Niccolo was disguised as a counterfeit Roman in suitably rakish attire. They crossed the Tiber into the Trastevere section, Rome's oldest and most popular quarter. The density with which people and animals were packed into this neighborhood made the rest of Rome seem spacious and airy by comparison. The smells, only slightly less nauseating at night, were still overpowering. The big difference seemed to be that the smoke of industry that filled the daytime air had given way in the evening to the heavy odor of cooking fat.

Michelozzi proved to be a delightful and informative companion as he steered Niccolo through the damp, crowded, twisting streets. He talked incessantly and provided a running commentary on the people and things they encountered, in much the same way the poet Virgil was said to have guided Dante through the seven circles of hell.

"Look at that one over there," said Niccolo, pointing in the direction of a small, compact man who, sweaty and shirtless, was making obscene overtures to a fat fishwife of a woman stooped over an open cooking pot in the street. "Fifteen hundred years ago, he would have been a Roman legionnaire—rugged, stalwart, indestructible. Now look at him, grinning his drunken, toothless grin, smacking his lips like that for the benefit of that swollen, greasy hag."

Michelozzi agreed. "SPQR," he intoned solemnly. "It no longer stands for *Senatus populusque Romanus*—the Senate and People of Rome. Today it's *Sono porci questi Romani*—These Romans are pigs!" Both Florentines agreed that it was sad, but true, that the Romans had squandered their birthright. And of course both agreed that the real heirs to the glories of ancient Rome were the Florentines. Who could doubt it?

As they continued their nocturnal prowl through this morass of human degradation, Michelozzi, with fierce Florentine superiority, announced, "They eat in the streets." Niccolo shook his head.

"And what they eat!" fumed Michelozzi. "It's a wonder the Borgia need poison to dispatch their rivals!" Then, turning to Niccolo, he confided to him in a whisper, "Never eat the rabbit."

When Michelozzi had demonstrated the inferiority of the Romans to a sufficient extent, the two arch Florentines, their confidence in their own superiority fully confirmed, turned back across the river and strolled north toward the Vatican.

It was in a relatively open space along the way that they were treated to a spectacle that, even by the bizarre standards of the phantasmagoric Roman night, was singular and arresting. Six blindfolded men were lined up and tied to posts. Except for the incongruous miters on their heads, they were naked. And by the hellish glow of the red torchlight, they were being mercilessly flogged.

To put more force behind each stroke of the lash, the sadistic executioner walked back a few steps and then took a running, flying leap at his victims. The welts on their bleeding backs and their inhuman howling were proof enough that the cruel whip was doing its job.

Niccolo asked, "What's this?"

"Compared to what usually goes on here, this is a mere diversion," said Michelozzi, looking on at the ghastly scene. "This is the *Campo de' Fiori*—such a pretty name, don't you think—the Field of Flowers? Anyway, this is where the public executions take place. It's one of the busiest places in Rome."

"And these fellows?" inquired Niccolo.

"A celebrated case, but nothing really serious. They're peasants who came to town with a couple barrels of olive oil to sell. They were approached by some gentlemen who apparently wanted to bathe in the oil."

"I'll never understand Roman customs," said Niccolo.

"Bathing in olive oil is supposed to be a cure for the French disease. And from what I heard, these gentlemen were pretty far gone with the infection. Anyway, the peasants protested; they haggled a little and finally agreed to let the gentlemen take their bath, for a price. Afterward, of course, they sold the oil."

"And the gentlemen with the disease, did the bath help? Were they cured?"

"You know as well as I do, there is no cure for the French disease. Death is the only way out."

Niccolo shuddered and wondered what happened to the oil. Probably some of the authorities confiscated it and sold it later, so that it eventually found its way into the already-unhealthy diet of some poor Roman. The screams of the men being flogged followed Niccolo and Michelozzi as they moved off into the night, picking their way through the jumble of odd Roman monuments jammed in among hovels and huts. Gradually, as they got closer to the Vatican, Niccolo began to notice a better class of buildings. In some areas, entire blocks had been cleared and palaces were going up.

"Well, you've seen enough horrors for one night," said Michelozzi. "Let me show you something pleasant for a change. Let me take you to a little pleasure palace I know that caters to a better class of people. Nothing fancy, but the girls there take an occasional bath, not like the ones you find in the streets."

"No," said Niccolo, declining the proffered treat. "I've really got somewhere else I should go. But I'd appreciate it if you could show me the way, or at least point me in the right direction."

Disappointed, Michelozzi was nevertheless courteous. "Fine, where is it you'd like to go?"

"To the *Convento Degli Angeli Caduti*."

It was hard for Michelozzi to conceal his surprise, "You want to go to a convent?"

The Convent of the Fallen Angels was no ordinary convent, as Niccolo was soon to discover. His new friend, Michelozzi, left him at the door and promised to call back for him in a few hours. After knocking for several minutes, the door opened and Niccolo was admitted by an ancient nun. As he had been instructed, he asked to see the mother superior. From within the folds of her habit, the venerable sister clucked, "Follow me," and set off down a dimly lit corridor. Crucifixes and portraits of the saints, variously transfixed, adorned the walls at regular intervals.

They passed through a tidy chapel, where candles burned and several kneeling sisters applied themselves to their devotions. Behind the chapel was a courtyard. Before proceeding, his guide stopped and said, "Here, you'll be wanting this." She handed Niccolo a mask.

Puzzled, he took it and followed the little nun across the courtyard. He thought he heard music, then it was unmistakable—lutes and tambourines. At the far end of the courtyard, the evening air stirred a wall of nearly transparent curtains, and behind them Niccolo thought he could see glowing balls of light bobbing and weaving in the air like giant fireflies.

When they stepped through the curtains, Niccolo saw the source of this mysterious phenomenon. Negroes, naked and glistening, both men and women, were dancing with lighted candles in their mouths. They ducked and swooped gracefully in some sort of exotic ballet. The air was thick with incense. All over the vast room, strewn about on couches and cushions, some wallowing in shallow bathing pools, were men and women in various stages of undress. Niccolo had just stepped into one of the most exclusive brothels in Rome.

"The mother superior's up there," said the nun who had conducted him to this unlikely place. With a jerk of her head, she indicated a low balcony that looked out over the sprawling, squirming minions of Eros. Seated there above it all in apparent tranquility, surveying the scene below her with serene detachment, was his beloved.

She rose when she spotted him, and Niccolo saw several guards stationed discreetly around the room snap to attention simultaneously. But Giuditta only beckoned, and the guards settled back. Niccolo hastened across the room, treading his way between the dancers and the heaps of exquisite, discarded clerical vestments. He even spied a red cardinal's cap thrown nonchalantly on the floor.

A short staircase led him up to his beloved, who had by this time drawn a curtain across her little balcony. For a moment, Niccolo debated making some wry observation like, "I see you've found yourself an employment." But only for a moment. Without saying a word, they rushed into each other's arms.

An hour or so later, Niccolo was lured out of a light sleep by a nagging, whining sort of singing. As he came to his senses, he thought he recognized the voice. "Serafino?" he asked incredulously, turning to Giuditta.

"None other," she confirmed.

"Does he still do the song about the missing tooth and the window of love?"

"Oh no, he's gone on to something much better. He has a new one called '*La formica*.'"

"The ant?" said Niccolo. "I didn't know the good poet was interested in insect life."

"This particular ant has a rather unique erotic experience. He manages to crawl up Venus's leg while she's asleep and penetrate the goddesses' pudenda!"

"I bet he uses the word *honey* more than once in that one."

"Five times."

"And how is it that Serafino found his way into this bordello?

"He works for the Borgia. I work for the Borgia. Borgia owns this bordello."

"Amazing," said Niccolo. "What an enterprising spirit Our Holy Father has. Not content with the sale of offices and benefices, he takes in revenues on a bordello as well."

"Oh, on several," corrected Giuditta. "And each one offers the customer something different. There's even one that specializes in boys. They say a lot of Florentines frequent that one, Niccolo."

Niccolo poo-pooed the notion. "Lies. Attempts to discredit us."

"Then why do they call sodomy 'the Florentine vice'?"

"How should I know? Let's drop it. Why don't you tell me what this particular establishment has to offer its clients?"

"In a word, discretion," replied Giuditta. "That's why we have the convent for a front. It seems a lot of your northern churchmen are not used to Roman ways and are uneasy about flaunting their appetites. Here, we let them slip through the back door."

"With their reputations and their hypocrisy intact."

"Exactly," said Giuditta, and in the shimmering light they kissed. She kissed him on the forehead and on the mouth and chin. She took Niccolo's hands in her own and gently kissed his fingertips. Then, suddenly, her grip on them tightened and Niccolo felt a stab of pain. He let out a sharp cry.

"What's this," said Giuditta, flushed with anger, her hands trembling.

Niccolo realized it would be best not to lie. "A wedding ring," he said.

29
The Hospital for Incurable Diseases

It was thus that the matter of Marietta Corsini came up, or to be more precise, the matter of Marietta Corsini Machiavelli. Giuditta was furious. Niccolo's explanations were not terribly convincing, and he sounded for all the world like an adulterous husband trying to reassure an irate mistress that he cares little for his wife and that she is the only real love of his life.

With cold eyes fixed on him, Giuditta said, "You're asking me to believe that you married a girl to save her honor because a friend of yours got her pregnant. Why didn't your friend marry her himself?"

"He can't," said Niccolo sheepishly. "He's a priest."

"And he can't just keep her?"

"Her father would kill him. Besides, you don't know Marietta."

"No," she said icily. "I don't know Monna Marietta, or should I call her Signora Machiavelli?"

"Call her whatever you want. Listen, *piccioncina* . . ."

"Do you call her *piccioncina* too?"

"Of course not. I told you I left Florence on our wedding night. I've never even slept with her. I never intend to."

"You Christians have an odd conception of marriage. But then you have an odd conception of a lot of things, from what I see around here—Christian charity, vows of chastity, celibacy, should I go on?"

"No need. Listen, Giuditta. I promised Pagolo I would speak to her. For him. To try to work out some sort of compromise."

"And you wound up marrying her. That's a compromise? I thought you were supposed to be a skilled negotiator?"

"I am. When I asked her what she wanted, she was perfectly blunt.

She said she wanted children. As for a husband, she said she could do without one but . . ."

"But they occasionally come in handy when one wants to have children."

Niccolo ignored the remark. "I begged her to consider Pagolo's fate. She said he had served his purpose, and if her father chose to kill him, well that was Pagolo's problem. He could always leave town. There were a number of solutions. Then she came up with the idea. 'Why don't you marry me?' she said."

"How did she know you weren't already promised in marriage, or God forbid, even in love?" asked Giuditta sarcastically.

"She accused me of being a sodomite," said Niccolo. "You know, the Florentine vice?"

"Then?"

"Then we all sat down together—Marietta, Pagolo and I—and she laid down her terms. If I married her, Pagolo's neck would be saved, her honor preserved, and her father kept from doing anything rash."

"And what were you supposed to get out of the bargain?"

"According to Marietta—respectability, a screen for my shameless homosexual activities."

Giuditta laughed.

"Then, of course, there was the dowry, the not-inconsiderable dowry."

"Who gets the dowry?"

"I get part of it."

"You married her for her money. That's disgusting."

"I don't get much. This is the arrangement. She comes to live with the Machiavelli family as any wife should. But since my family owns a house in the city and a smaller one in the country, she stipulated that she occupy one house and I the other. When I come out to the country, she goes into the city. And vice versa. In return, she'll pay me at a fixed annual rate, what amounts to the upkeep on one of the houses."

"You didn't get that good of a deal."

"With my salary and with the problems in the Florentine treasury right now, I didn't get such a bad deal."

"And what does the priest get?"

"Nothing. His skin. But I think she has a perverse affection for him."

"Who gets the rest of your 'not-inconsiderable' dowry?"

"Marietta keeps it for herself. And her children."

"Some diplomat."

"I do derive one additional advantage from the arrangement," said Niccolo.

"Oh?"

"Suppose I do have some hidden love to cover, not the Florentine vice, but an unlawful, some would say unnatural appetite, just the same? Wouldn't a sham marriage be a perfect way to conceal such a dangerous thing?"

"And what would that unlawful, unnatural appetite be?" said Giuditta, relenting finally and yielding to Niccolo's embrace. Neither had to speak, but both were aware of the precariousness of their situation. There was scarcely a city in Europe that did not have laws on the books for dealing with the illicit union of Christians and Jews. In times of indulgence, like the present, those laws were not enforced. But in times of persecution, they could be applied with maniacal severity. And times of persecution were never far away. With the Inquisition gaining in strength and fanaticism in Spain, the tolerance or indifference toward Jews that characterized the Borgia papacy was coming to an end.

In Germany, a spirit of rebellion was brewing that would soon erupt into the full-blown revolution known as the Protestant Reformation. The church was about to be squeezed—very hard. And when the church was squeezed, she struck back. She lashed out at enemies—real and imagined, internal and external—with the full arsenal of weapons at her disposal, weapons like rarely enforced statutes, like the laws that prescribe the death penalty for any Christian found guilty of consorting sexually with a Jew. That the Jew was beheaded as well goes without saying. In fact, the offending couple was usually beheaded together on the scaffold. According to the penal code, such a twin beheading was the lawful punishment for all acts of bestiality.

"Your friend's here," whispered Giuditta. Niccolo had completely forgotten about Michelozzi. Looking down, he saw that his fellow Florentine, masked, was cavorting with three nymphs, dancing with a candle in his mouth. Niccolo recognized him by the loud harlequin doublet, although his friend's equally garish hose done in the same pattern were nowhere to be seen.

"Look at him there! With that candle. *Che spiritoso!*"

"That fool in the red-and-yellow checkered outfit? You know him?"

"That's my new friend. He works at the Florentine embassy here in Rome. Isn't that who you meant?"

"No, I meant your old friend. Look there."

Following the line of her gaze, Niccolo saw the old friend she meant—a dark figure, poised in the shadows. Caesar Borgia.

"Well, I suppose I should go down and greet him," said Niccolo, pulling on the slightly ridiculous clothes Michelozzi had lent him. He would never have chosen blue for himself, not powder blue at any rate.

"So the diplomat is going back to work," said Giuditta with a wicked smile. "I hope you manage negotiations for your city better than you did your marriage contract."

Niccolo did not appreciate the humor and skulked out of the room to meet his nemesis. He put on the mask.

The usually taciturn man was talking freely, boasting of his military exploits. Niccolo joined the small group gathered around him and listened patiently to Caesar's account of the taking of one of the Orsini fortresses in the hills outside Rome. He described with verve and apparent pleasure the execution of the leaders of the rebellious stronghold.

When he had finished, Caesar paused for a drink, then continued, "But the Orsini," he mused. "Fighting the Orsini is beneath our dignity, like swatting flies. We've left our subordinates in charge of the campaign against the contumacious Orsini. Don Micheletto can deliver their heads to us here in Rome by the cartload if he wants to. We have better things to do."

"And what might those better things be, Excellency?" said Niccolo, removing his mask.

Caesar's head snapped around at the sound of his voice. A malicious grin spread slowly across his face. "So the Florentine envoy has followed us here all the way to Rome. What an unexpected pleasure. It would be remiss of us not to show him every courtesy." He called for wine, and, with a nonchalant wave of his hand, dismissed the little circle gathered around him like a man dispersing a cloud of gnats.

When they were alone, he turned his masked face to the Florentine envoy. Only the evil smile buried in the thick black beard was visible beneath the mask. "Shall we talk?"

"We've done little else since our first meeting," observed Niccolo.

"Then perhaps the time for talk is over, don't you agree? Let us be blunt. Our ears have grown long listening to the Florentines. Since they've repeatedly rejected our offers of friendship, we intend to destroy them."

Niccolo was taken aback but didn't show it. "And how do you propose to do that?"

"With money and bread and men and iron! First by taking Pisa and cutting off your access to the sea. Then by marching directly against Florence and tearing her walls apart stone by stone." A certain uncharacteristic rage had crept into Caesar's voice as he outlined his brief program. The village strongman was losing control.

Niccolo countered, "And if your designs should incur the displeasure of the king of France?"

"Then the king of France will have to learn to live with that displeasure, won't he?" Caesar shot back vehemently. "We will no longer be denied." The velvet glove had come off the iron fist.

Niccolo leaned close to Caesar in the dim candlelight and said matter-of-factly, "I think, Excellency, that if you go against Florence you will find far stiffer resistance than you've ever encountered before."

Caesar roared with laughter. "Does the Florentine envoy threaten us then?"

"Consider it what you will."

Caesar was smiling now. The dark cloud had passed. "I know the Florentines," he said. "Stiff necked and uncircumcised of heart, but grasping, grasping. When the time comes, we'll know how to deal with you. We'll see which you value more—your vaunted liberties or your pocketbooks. Do you want to wager we can take Florence without firing a single shot? By buying her off?"

Niccolo winced. That was always a distinct possibility. There were more than enough Florentines willing to sell the city and her government for thirty pieces of silver—to Caesar, to the Medici in exile, to the highest bidder.

"But this is wearisome," said Caesar. "We didn't come here to argue politics. We came to worship Venus and her son Cupid! Pasiphae! Pasiphae!"

"Pasiphae?" inquired Niccolo.

"Pasiphae is my personal favorite among the ladies here—for the time being. Do you know the origin of the name? Do you know who Pasiphae was?"

Niccolo knew all the old legends. He recited by rote: "Pasiphae was the wife of Minos who was cursed by Poseidon and conceived a mad, destructive passion for a bull, with whom she eventually coupled."

"And do you know who the bull is?" said Caesar with smug satisfaction.

Borgia's gloating was interrupted by a strange sound, by the indescribable tinkling of a thousand tiny bells like the far-away voices of a thousand happy children. A woman appeared in front of them clad in a long, heavy dress, covered with shimmering silver bells like a coat of living, singing armor.

She bowed to Caesar, but it was not a bow of submission. It was a simple acknowledgement. "My Pasiphae," said Caesar, presenting her to the Florentine envoy.

Another bow sent out another wave of tintinnabulation. Niccolo was stunned by the singing dress. He had never seen such a thing before. The light played on its lustrous, undulating surface, and every small movement or shift in position produced another chorus of tiny, ringing voices. When he was finally able to take his dazzled eyes off of the thing long enough to look Caesar's dark beauty in the face, he was all the more stunned. It was not the razor-sharp features or the high shaved forehead or the arrogant lips in themselves that startled Niccolo. It was the shock of recognition.

The dress was new, but the face was one he had seen before, only the last time she had gone by the name of Faustina, and he had been charged by Piero Capponi to deliver her over to Charles VIII, monster-king of France.

As the bull collected his prize and turned to go, Pasiphae whispered discreetly in Niccolo's ear. "You were right. Six toes."

Niccolo quickly got over his surprise, reasoning, correctly, that nothing could be more natural than to find a whore in a whorehouse. And Pasiphae did not concern him nearly so much as her lover, the Borgia Bull. Caesar had changed, and Niccolo had anticipated that change. His iron-willed self-control was slipping. Caesar the tight-lipped had become a boaster. And an incautious one at that. He could have had no way of knowing who his audience was in that circle of strange, masked creatures that surrounded him. The fat man with no ass and a generous belly who seemed to approve Caesar's discourse—who was he? And the girls—eyes and ears of God knows what king or duke or archbishop in this den of iniquity.

And as far as his plans for Florence were concerned, Caesar seemed to have abandoned the cat-and-mouse approach. Indeed, he was throwing all caution to the four winds—bragging, swaggering. Where was the Caesar who never says what he does? And his insistent invocation of the royal prerogative—"we" and "us" had replaced "I" and "me." Already an emperor in his own mind, he was losing control over his ambition. The question was, did that make him less dangerous? Or more?

It was near the end of their conversation when Niccolo had leaned close to him, very close, that his suspicions were confirmed. In the subdued light of the brothel, they had been barely discernible, obscured and hidden among the curly growth of beard that wreathed Borgia's mouth. But the yellow pustules were there. The disease had taken root. It's inevitable, destructive rush to madness and death was underway.

The Italians generally referred to it as the French Disease. The French preferred to call it the Neapolitan Disease. The Neapolitans, for their part, were inclined to label it the Spanish Disease. No one, it seems, wanted to accept responsibility. It went by many other names as well—*bolle*, the pox, even plague—but its effects were the same for all, no matter what it was called. It was a rapid, degenerative, and mortal illness.

The first cases of syphilis in Europe were diagnosed in Barcelona in 1493. An outbreak of the disease was discovered among the crew of the recently returned ships of the Genovese navigator Cristoforo Colombo, who, sailing under the flag of Spain, claimed to have discovered a new world.

From the sailors who had contracted it from the inhabitants of this new world, the disease quickly spread to prostitutes, and from them it entered the general population. Transmitted by sexual intercourse, the new disease spread like wildfire through all of Europe. The primary agency of that spread were the incessantly warring armies full of itinerant mercenary soldiers. In the wake of these ubiquitous armies, the new pestilence burned its way from one end of the continent to the other. Within the space of only four years, no small corner had been left untouched, unravaged by its onslaught.

In the rapid spread of this scourge, there were many who saw the hand of God at work, many who said that immoral sexual behavior was being punished and that the moral turpitude of the times was being made manifest in the rotting bodies of the infected. To be sure, the disease was denounced from the pulpit, although, curiously enough, many of the very prelates who raised the hue and cry most vociferously were themselves both victims and transmitters of the curse.

Treatments, of course, had been devised, the most extreme of which was the cauterization of the lesions with red-hot irons, but nothing had proven even remotely effective. To make matters worse, it was impossible to chart the course of the disease with any accuracy. Some died rapidly within a year after being infected. Others succumbed several years later. Still others seemed to recover but lived in constant fear of a relapse. How long could the disease remain virulent in the body? No one could say. At the time of our story, it had only been known in Europe for a period of nine years. Many could be infected without even knowing it, and an entire continent was in the grip of the indescribable terror of uncertainty.

Like the madness and death it engendered, the epidemic struck impartially among rich and poor alike, prince and pauper, man and woman. The fact that he was the pope's son did not exempt Caesar Borgia from its ravages.

As Niccolo climbed the stairs to his beloved, one image tormented him—Vitellozzo Vitelli. In Caesar Borgia's chamber of horrors, among those hideous rows of severed heads, only Vitellozzo displayed no anger, no fear. Even in its ashen, bloodless mask of death, his face was twisted into a mad, demented smile. His skin was covered with scabs and ugly, running sores. Only a few pus-clotted strands of scraggly hair remained on his scalp, and his nose had been almost completely eaten away. Yet he was grinning, grinning even in death. His toothless mouth was pulled back and frozen in the grinning rictus of the utterly, impossibly mad.

Giuditta was waiting for him. Immediately sensing Niccolo's bewilderment, she refrained from needling him again and simply asked how things had gone. "Miserably," said Niccolo. "You were right about the disease—I saw the evidence, the chancres around his mouth. And from the way he talked and acted, it's beginning to affect his mind, his judgment."

"Then all you have to do is wait him out."

"That's just the problem. How long do we have to wait? Caesar mad may be even more unpredictable, more volatile. His moves may be even more rash and destructive. You have medicine, science, you tell me how long it will take for him to succumb to the disease."

"It could be a week. It could be years."

"It could be years," said Niccolo, throwing up his hands. "And in a year's time, Caesar could be insane and still be emperor of all of Italy. In a year's time, he could be hopelessly demented and still be pope!"

"Or he could be dead," said Giuditta. "Caesar's been infected for almost eight years now. Time is on your side."

"And there is no cure, you're certain of that?"

"There are ways of treating the lesions to ease the pain. Sometimes they even go away, but they come back."

"What sort of treatment would you use?"

"A balm made of mercury mixed in pork fat. That seems to work best. Sometimes it slows the progress of the disease. But it has one disadvantage."

"What's that?"

"It makes the hair fall out."

Niccolo thought again of Vitellozzo, hairless in death. He had obviously been using the balm, the best remedy available against the disease. It had done him precious little good.

"Here, take a glass of this, to get your mind off of disease," Giuditta presented a small cup of delicately scented liquor to the troubled diplomat.

"This is delicious. What is it?"

"Something I made myself—Rossoli."

"What's in it?"

"A few pounds of rose petals, orange blossoms, cinnamon, and cloves. They have to soak in plenty of alcohol. Then I distill it."

"It's probably good for the digestion," said Niccolo absentmindedly, contemplating his cup.

"Oh, no doubt."

"What about the woman who went with Caesar?" said Niccolo suddenly. "Isn't she afraid of getting the disease from him?"

"Pasiphae? She isn't afraid of anything. And how can anyone refuse the Bull? Besides, she likes to boast that she's immune to the disease, that it can't touch her."

"Is it true?"

"She doesn't have it. And she's not always discreet about the company she keeps. Some of her companions are downright ulcerous, in fact."

"And she doesn't get the disease. What's her secret?"

"Maybe it's because she's Florentine and her blood is too proud and fierce and too pristine to get infected."

Niccolo sulked.

"There is one other possibility," said Giuditta.

"What's that?"

"It only works for Christians though," she said wickedly. "Holy water and prayer."

Niccolo stayed the night, and the next morning, he collected his exhausted friend Michelozzi on his way out of the brothel. They passed once again through the small chapel where the nuns still maintained their vigil. Niccolo looked at them with renewed interest. Giuditta had told him they were armed guards.

The stench that greeted them in the streets was as overpowering as it had been the night before, but the noise level had died down somewhat. It was Sunday morning—the day of rest. "I've got an idea," said Michelozzi gaily. "Since it's the Lord 's Day, why don't we attend mass?"

Niccolo begged off, but Michelozzi was insistent. "Not just any mass, a papal mass! Don't tell me you wouldn't like to get a look at the supreme pontiff."

Niccolo jumped at the idea—Alexander VI! The Borgia pope! The antichrist! Caesar's father! And so, at Michelozzi's suggestion, the two of them took up positions at the far end of St. Peter's Square to await the arrival of the Vicar of Christ. Across from them, the massive, but unfinished church looked mournful and neglected.

"That's St. Peter's," said Niccolo. "It's a shambles."

"You're not implying the Holy Father's been remiss in the execution his ecclesiastical responsibilities, are you?" said Michelozzi.

"There have been certain rumors to that effect," said Niccolo. "Not a single saint canonized during his pontificate, and he's been pope now for eleven years."

"The saints are dead and they can wait! Alexander reserves his energies for the living."

"And for his mistresses." added Niccolo. "But seriously, has he done anything for the church at all, aside from trying to pass it on to his son as a hereditary kingdom?"

Michelozzi searched his memory. "He has sent missionaries to convert Greenland to Christianity."

"Where's that?"

"North. To the far, far north. But he's sent them to the south as well, to Africa, to the Congo."

"I suppose that's his way of getting rid of the overzealous priests."

"Don't be so cynical," said Michelozzi. "It was Alexander who divided up the New World between the Spanish and the Portuguese with his famous line of demarcation. And the only stipulation he put on the conquests of both nations was that they contrive to introduce the Catholic faith into their new territories."

"Bravo!" said Niccolo. "One day, all the world will be Catholic and have only Alexander to thank for it." As he spoke, a shrill blast of heralds' trumpets filled the air, announcing the arrival of Pope Alexander VI.

Preceding him into the piazza was a double line of about thirty cardinals, all dressed in the most exquisite red satin. Behind him were as many courtiers, mostly Spanish, attired from head to foot in purple. The pope himself was clad in white—immaculate, stunning white—and mounted on a snow-white charger. From the ends of his soft, white leather shoes to the tip of his gold-and-white triple crown, he was the very picture of angelic brilliance. Floating in a cloud of blinding light above the stained and sodden city, he dispensed blessings freely as he went, and flung handfuls of coins into the ragged crowds at his feet.

"So this is Caesar's father," Niccolo thought to himself. There was no real family resemblance. While Caesar was dark and swarthy, the pope's complexion was a cheerful, rosy color. Alexander was a big man, bigger than his son. Not fat, but portly, he wore his seventy-some-odd years well. His smile was radiant, his countenance kind and indulgent. He carried himself in a manner that was grand, altogether papal—some might say, imperial.

Alexander stepped lightly from his horse, for such a large man, and proceeded on foot into the church. His movements were easy, generous, and like those of his son, confident. Following the procession into the church, Niccolo noticed signs of stonework and plastering that had apparently been suspended and left unfinished. There was rubble and debris piled everywhere.

Alexander intoned the mass in a strong, sonorous voice that filled the cavernous basilica—"*In nomine Patris et Filii et Spiritus Sancti. Amen. Introibo ad altare Dei.*"

A chorus of high-ranking prelates responded, "*Ad deum qui laetificat juventutem meam.*" And the mass was underway. Niccolo did not notice it at first, through the initial prayers and readings, but it became apparent by the time the pope reached the Credo, the solemn profession of faith that occurs about half way through the mass. The Holy Father had forgotten the words! He skipped over certain passages, substituted Spanish phrases for Latin, and occasionally had to be prompted by one of his cocelebrants. Through it all, his munificent smile never deserted him, and his buoyant, confident tone never faltered. If nothing else, the pope was a consummate showman.

For the rest of July and the beginning of August, Niccolo made himself comfortable in Rome, dividing his time between days in the Florentine colony, attending to chancery business, and nights in the Convent of the Fallen Angels. If the stifling heat and humidity grew steadily worse as summer wore on, Niccolo's over-sensitive nose and his delicate stomach adapted little by little to the smells and tastes of Rome. He got to the point where would even take an occasional meal outside the safety of the Florentine colony and its imported Tuscan fare. Of course, most of these meals were prepared for him by his beloved. He was still not courageous enough to entrust his digestive apparatus to a Roman trattoria.

"What's that?" said Niccolo, pointing doubtfully to a contraption that Giuditta was assembling over the fire. She was making a lamb stew, and, as usual, Niccolo insisted on supervising in the kitchen, as much from curiosity as caution.

"It's a *bagno-Maria*, Mary's bath," she replied going about her work. The "bath" consisted of two parts, a pot suspended in a pan of water. "It's the best way to stew meat."

"You can't fry it?"

"This way the meat cooks gently, over steam. It stays moist."

"Hmmmph," said Niccolo. "It looks more like a piece of alchemist's equipment than a cooking utensil."

"You're very observant," said Giuditta. "That's exactly what it is. Or was. Alchemy and cooking are two branches of the same science, you know. I read about this device in a treatise on distillation that covered all three of the related arts—cooking, medicine, and magic!"

Niccolo rolled his eyes. "And who wrote this dark treatise? Some Moorish sage?"

"A woman, as a matter of fact. Maria di Cleofa. That's why it's called a *bagno-Maria*. She invented it."

"Never heard of her," said Niccolo dismissively.

"No? Are you sure? And I thought you were such a historian! Always trailing around with those books by your sacred Livy on the ancient Romans."

"Your Maria was no Roman."

"Wasn't she? Perhaps not by birth, but she was involved in governing a small, far-flung corner of their empire for them. Egypt, to be exact, where she ruled under the name of Cleopatra the Wise."

Niccolo groaned. He was going to have to eat a meal prepared by a sorceress with the aid of a treatise written by a witch. However, his apprehension vanished when that meal was finally served. Giuditta put before him thick, succulent chunks of lamb as big as his fist and swimming in a sauce perfumed with sage. On the plate beside the stew, grilled artichokes lay like fat, black flowers. At the first bite, all Niccolo's doubts were dispelled, and he believed that Cleopatra the Wise had indeed discovered something valuable—the marriage of cooking and magic.

When they had finished eating, Niccolo washed down his superb repast with several doses of Giuditta's Rossoli, the exquisite liquor that represented the marriage of drinking and magic.

"Would you like to accompany me on an errand?" asked Giuditta. "I think it's something that might interest you."

"What's that?" said a groggy, sated Niccolo.

"I heard about a man who has a cure for the French disease."

Niccolo sat up at attention.

Giuditta continued, "It's only a rumor. One of the girls heard it from somebody who heard it from somebody else. But it's worth checking it out—for professional reasons."

Alert now, Niccolo agreed to accompany her. "And where are we going?"

"To the hospital of *San Giacomo degli Incurabili*—Saint James of Incurable Diseases."

Giuditta walked with ease and confidence through the treacherous, teeming streets of Rome like an angel walking blithely through the fires of hell. Just as nonchalantly, she explained to Niccolo the infinite variety and the specialization of thieves and thievery in Rome.

"A cutpurse would never stoop to stealing bread or fruit or stores from a shop. The men who steal livestock pride themselves on hustling the living animals and would never consider stealing a side of dead meat. There's a whole professional guild system of thievery. Pride in one's craft. Specialization. Some specialize in robbing foreigners. Others boast that they touch only Frenchmen. There are thieves who steal clothes while they're drying on a line. Others who tear them from the backs of clerics alone. Some thieves will not move out of a particular neighborhood; others range over the whole city. There are women and children who lure strangers into dark places with the promise of sex and have them set upon. It goes on and on."

"And the law?" asked Niccolo.

"What law? The pope is the only real power here, and he's busy with his own projects. Otherwise, there are *maestri di strada*, neighborhood strongmen, who are better at extortion than keeping the peace. That's how things are done in Rome."

Niccolo had another flash of Florentine chauvinism, which he kept to himself since he was tired of Giuditta teasing him about his feelings of superiority. But he could not help drawing a comparison between this stinking Roman corruption and anarchy and the way things were done in Florence, where citizens were protected by the rule of law and a constitution. And where the streets were clean and the food safe to eat.

They passed through the Borgo district in the shadows of the Papal palace, where printers and booksellers had set up their shops and stands. Niccolo insisted on stopping and browsing through the piles of books and manuscripts available there. There were bargains to be found, as much of the merchandise was stolen and the thieves, being for the most part illiterate, had no idea what they were selling.

In triumph, Niccolo extracted a dusty tome from a heap of similar volumes and eagerly began examining it to determine if it was complete with all the gatherings in place.

"What are you so excited about?" asked Giuditta.

"Plutarch's *Parallel Lives!*" said Niccolo. "Lives of illustrious Greek statesmen alongside biographies of illustrious Romans—so comparisons can be drawn. It's fascinating."

"You and your Romans," sighed Giuditta. "You better get ready to meet one now—a live one. Here comes the proprietor."

Niccolo looked up at the dirty man who was approaching. He was covered with black printer's ink, dirt, but a more noble kind of dirt than the common dirt in which most of the Roman populace wallowed. And the bookseller was no thief or fool, either. He knew what the book was worth and drove a hard bargain, forcing Niccolo to pay a fair price.

"You want to buy something else," he grinned.

"Not today," said Niccolo.

"Then make it soon," said the bookseller. "These may not be available in the future."

"Why?"

"The edict," said the man with bitter resentment. "The pope, the most Christian pope is concerned about the spread of error—doctrinal error. The edict declares that no book can be printed from now on without the permission of the church. Violators subject to excommunication, fines, possibly imprisonment and death."

The city was in utter moral chaos, and yet the Holy Father was concerned about the spread of false doctrines! Romans were menaced every day in the streets by assassins, and the pope was worried about purity of dogma and the danger represented by books. But Niccolo thought he saw the logic behind this papal decision. It was the logic of absolute power. With the printing press and the dissemination of ideas that it made possible, another phenomenon was born—censorship.

As the bookseller wrapped his purchase in a dirty cloth, he looked at Niccolo and said, "Did you hear about the monster?

"They found it this morning on the banks of the river," said the ink-stained little man with relish. "It had an ass's head with long, long ears and a woman's body covered with scales. The face of a man, a bearded man, was growing out of its stomach!"

"Did you see it?" asked Giuditta skeptically.

"Didn't have to," said the man unruffled. "Didn't have to consult an astrologer either to know that something's going to happen. Something evil."

"Come on," said Giuditta, dragging Niccolo away from the book-stall. "You've got what you wanted. We don't have to stand around and listen to superstitious nonsense all day."

"I wasn't . . ."

"Have you ever seen some of the things that wash up on the banks of the Tiber? His 'monster' is benign by comparison. They're in the habit here of throwing men and animals—cocks, rats—into the river—sewn up in leather sacks together. The animals eat into the men, or vice versa. They drown or gnaw each other to death. Then, a week later, the bloated, stinking sack washes ashore. By that time, it's usually burst and the whole rotted, swollen, decomposing mess, full of hungry little fishes, is exposed. That's probably what someone saw." Niccolo thought that, on balance, he would have preferred the monster.

From the bookseller's, it was not far to the Hospital for Incurable Diseases, and Niccolo and Giuditta made their way there, pestered all the time by swarms of ragged, rabid children, begging and clawing at their clothes.

The hospital, like everything else in Rome, was run down and in deplorable condition. They entered through the main door and immediately found themselves in a huge, cavernlike room. Large, high, open windows admitted light and air, but the sights and smells that greeted them were still overpowering. An odor of putrefaction and decay struggled with the sharp, astringent tang of alcohol and acid and lime.

The patients were scattered about in confusion on cots and mats spread on the floor. They looked less like human beings and more like a hapless jumble of broken, discarded dolls. While Niccolo stood paralyzed, taking in this horrific scene, two men pushed past them from the street door behind. In a mason's wheelbarrow, they were transporting a third man. Making their way into the hospital, they found an empty space and, without ceremony, dumped their charge onto the floor.

The hospital was quiet, unnaturally quiet. Most of its inmates were too sick, too weak, and too close to death to cry out. As they walked among the incurably ill, Niccolo scarcely had the courage to look at them. The French disease and leprosy and a host of revolting ailments had rendered them far more pitiful than anything he had ever seen before. The aftermath of the Battle of Mordano was civilized by comparison. Only the description of Giuditta's "monster" seemed equal to the horror of this place. It was a room full of bloated, rotting carcasses, a room full of bones stripped of their meat, a room full of monsters.

The only figure who seemed to be stirring in the late-afternoon heat was a man bending over one of the incurables. Giuditta called out to him, *"Senta, Dottore!"*

The man straightened up and looked at the two intruders from across a sea of broken bodies. He was an odd sight. His hair was long, much too long, even for an anarchical Roman. When he started toward them, Niccolo saw to his disbelief that the man wore his long hair parted down the middle of his skull and gathered in two thick plaits on either side of his head. *Che fantasia!* What fantasy! What a fantastic!

As the man in charge of the incurables made his way across his domain, he stopped several times to examine or inspect a patient, including the new arrival. He seemed to be in no hurry. When he got closer, Niccolo could see that his strangeness was not limited to his eccentric hairstyle but extended to his clothing as well. He was wearing what appeared to be a doublet decorated with some sort of beadwork, but of a design that even in the licentious circles of the Borgias would have seemed exotic. In bold colors—reds, blues, yellows, and whites—there were birds, fantastic, angular birds depicted on the garment. Feathers hung from the sides of the thing, and it seemed to be decorated with—Niccolo could scarcely believe his eyes—bones!

"This is the man who has the cure for the French disease," he thought. "It must be an unusual cure, indeed." Skeptical as always, Niccolo hung back. This was not his affair. He was only here to accom-

✣ 30 ✣

A Voyage to the New World and Last Respects to a Departed Pontiff

This month is deadly for fat people.

—Pope Alexander VI

Niccolo tasted it and grimaced. It was the sulfurous white wine that came from the hills outside of Rome, not nearly as good as the Trebbiano he took in Tuscany, but it was cool. By the second or third swallow, his pallet had become accustomed to the acrid aftertaste, but he could not dissociate it from the legendary brimstone native to the one place that was even hotter than Rome in summertime.

Callimaco had ushered the little group through the back of the hospital and up a worn staircase to the garret that served as his living quarters. Looking around, Niccolo noticed that he had managed to assemble for himself the same devil's workshop he had had in Florence, complete with the penned animals and walls lined with vials and jars and smudge pots. Giuditta took in the laboratory, but with a more educated, professional eye.

Callimaco, meanwhile, was recounting his adventures to his fascinated guest, who could only speculate as to who this bizarre creature was and where he had been. "Pirates!" she said in disbelief.

"Pirates," he affirmed. "If I hadn't been kidnapped by pirates, I probably wouldn't be here. Well, they weren't really pirates so much as Spaniards, but Spaniards at sea all tend to piracy." Suddenly aware of Giuditta's dark coloring and the Moorish cast of her clothes, Callimaco stopped short and blushed, "The lady isn't Spanish . . . ?"

"Not strictly speaking," said Giuditta.

Turning to Niccolo, he said, "After I left you, I followed Charles's glorious descent to Naples, patching up some of the wreckage the army left in its wake. But when the king turned north again with the intention of marching all the way back to France, I gave up. My old teacher, Maître Albert, assured me I could set myself up in Paris and practice in peace, even turn a modest profit, so I booked passage on a merchantman out of Naples bound for France. That's when my troubles began.

"I quarreled with the captain, who was an overbearing Frenchman, before we were even out of port. He was shorthanded and wanted me to pull ropes and trim sails and generally assist in all this sailorly work. Stand watch. Of course, I refused. I told him I was a physician and a man of science.

"When we sailed past Gibraltar out into the open ocean, we were accosted by a Spanish ship of the line. It was a touchy situation, and the captain feared for his cargo. Finally, he struck a deal with the Spaniards. He bartered several barrels of stores and me for his safe passage! Without having any say in the matter, I was on my way to the New World.

"The Spanish captain, the crew, all of them were the worst sort of brutes. Prisoners pressed into service for a long, doubtful, and dangerous voyage. Pigs. I can still see those black-bearded sons of bitches, sitting on deck, gnawing on moldy jerked beef while the fish were almost jumping out of the water into the ship. When we were out two months, they all got scurvy, which did nothing to improve their dispositions. The ordinarily surly and mean became sadistic. They blamed me for not being able to cure them. I can't even describe the humiliation I was subjected to, not in front of a lady." Callimaco paused for breath.

"We made land after two and a half months at sea. A beautiful, tropical place, lush vegetation, plenty of fruit and game, friendly inhabitants. The first thing the Spanish wretches did was to rush out and look for gold. When they didn't find any, they were furious. At that point, the seasons were beginning to change, and the ship left to go back to Spain. They were supposed to return in the spring with livestock for the fledgling settlement.

"I was left behind with the 'colonists' who were among the most nasty and brutish members of the party. At first things went well enough. We had a good relationship with the inhabitants, who showed us where to find food and water. The native men were friendly. The women were even friendlier . . ." Callimaco's eyes twinkled knowingly, but he flushed when he saw Giuditta looking at him.

She laughed at his embarrassment. "You don't have to feel ashamed in front of me," she said. "I run a brothel."

A surprised "Oh," was all Callimaco could muster in response, and then recovering, he continued with his tale: "When it came time to start building some sort of shelter, the Spaniards agreed the best way to do this was to enslave some of the locals, whom they referred to as savages, since they weren't Christians."

"Didn't you try to convert them?" asked Giuditta.

"Oh, efforts were made, but they didn't seem the least bit interested. Nor were they much more interested in applying themselves to slave labor. The Spaniards had to beat them to make them work, and even then, they weren't much good. Most simply ran off. The ones who stayed caught the grippe from the Spaniards and died. It's odd from a medical point of view: None of the Spaniards died of the grippe, but the savages succumbed."

"Well I suppose we struck a good-enough bargain with them then," said Niccolo. "Our grippe in exchange for their French disease, or whatever you want to call it."

"Ah, the pox," said Callimaco. "Of course, all the nasty Spaniards came down with the pox, although most had already left the island before they discovered it."

"And you?" asked Niccolo.

"I told you, I'm a man of science," said Callimaco proudly. "Before the voyage, I was already seeing the devastation of the pox in Italy. When six-toed Charles brought his army down into Italy, he brought more than just new kinds of cannon and bad French ideas about Charlemagne and empire. He brought the pox. That army was the poxiest army ever assembled—mercenaries from all over, the worst kind of men, worse than Spaniards. And everywhere they went, they left a lasting legacy."

"True," said Niccolo. "When the great Charles left Italy, everyone promptly forgot about him. The only permanent thing he left behind was his cursed French disease."

Giuditta interrupted. "You were saying, you didn't contact it because . . .?"

"Because he kept himself chaste," injected Niccolo.

Callimaco ignored his remark. "The lady has a professional interest in these matters, I presume?"

"Of course. Anything that can cut down on the spread of the disease is good for my business. Besides, I dabble in medicine."

"Ah," said Callimaco, drawing closer to her in a spirit of collegiality. "Well, from my observation of the spread of the disease, I started to draw some conclusions about how it was transmitted. What I was able to learn from the inhabitants of the Indies confirmed my guess. If someone is infected with the pox, he—or she—can only pass the disease along when the ulcers and pustules are visible. No ulcers, no contagion."

Giuditta spoke, "So in the early stages of the disease, before the pustules appear, there's no danger of passing it along."

"Exactly," said Callimaco. "But in the later stages, when the pustules and sores get worse and worse, it's almost inevitable that the disease will be passed on. Of course, by that time, it hurts so much, at least for the man, that it tends to dampen the desire."

Giuditta looked thoughtfully at him. "So as long as there's no contact with the sores themselves, the disease won't spread. That must be Pasiphae's secret."

"Pasiphae," said Callimaco, puzzled.

"A girl who works for me who claims to be immune to the disease," explained Giuditta. "If she were very careful, very expert in her craft, she could avoid contact with the infected areas and preserve herself from the disease."

"She doesn't even have to be that careful," said Callimaco.

"What do you mean?"

Callimaco was on his feet and moved quickly across the room to a trunk. "She doesn't have to be that careful if she uses one of these," he said triumphantly, producing an object that looked like a transparent, flabby, deflated penis.

"No contact, no contagion," said Callimaco proudly. "This is nothing but a piece of sheep gut, tied securely at the end with a fine thread, but it works."

"And it would offer the added advantage of preventing pregnancy," observed Giuditta.

"This woman grasps the most fundamental implications of my science immediately! Where did you find her, Niccolo? Where did you find such a gem?"

"It's a long story."

"I wonder what else your science tells you about the French disease," said Giuditta tactfully. "I heard a rumor that there was a man here who had a cure for the disease."

"If I had a cure, would I be at the Hospital for Incurable Diseases?" said Callimaco sadly, all the enthusiasm draining out of him. He was left as deflated as the thing he held in his hand.

Sensing his friend's chagrin, Niccolo sought to change the subject. "Enough medical talk," he said. "Callimaco, I want to know how you got back from the New World."

"The ship with the livestock and the seed returned the next year, only there was no livestock and no seed. The crossing had been longer than expected, and the crew had eaten everything on the way over. There was no reasonable way to start a proper settlement, and besides, the would-be settlers were disgruntled and ready to go home. We poked around a few more islands, looking for gold, found none, and then sailed for Spain.

"Since there is a steady flow of Spaniards into Rome, I had no trouble getting passage back here. And since I know as much, if not more, about the French disease as anyone, what more logical place for me than a hospital full of its victims?" Callimaco shrugged his shoulders in a gesture of helplessness. "What else can I do?"

"Ah, Callimaco, there's something else I've been meaning to ask you," said Niccolo. "Your clothing, your hair—it's a little extravagant, even for Rome."

"You like it?" said Callimaco, brightening. "I brought it back from the New World. This is how the men wear their hair there. And this shirt was given to me by a very special lady."

"It's different," said Niccolo skeptically.

"It's lovely, Callimaco," said Giuditta, shooting a sidelong glance at her beloved.

"I have several more, if you'd like one," he said eagerly.

"I wouldn't dream of taking such a valuable thing away from you," said Giuditta. "You keep them. They have a special meaning for you."

"I do have something I can share with you, though," said Callimaco. "Food from the New World!"

Niccolo groaned, but Giuditta expressed interest, and Callimaco was soon racing around his room, setting the table and preparing something to eat.

"I don't have much in the house, just some cheese and bruschetta—and the little golden apples," he apologized. The bruschetta was one of the Roman staples that Niccolo had found acceptable, if unexciting. It was a dry, circular, flat piece of bread made of coarse flour. To reanimate the desiccated bread, it was soaked in olive oil and rubbed with garlic and salt for seasoning. The resulting flavors were simple, but bold. And bruschetta was filling and cheap.

Callimaco put the various ingredients on the table, along with a serious lump of cacciacavallo cheese. He then went to a window where a few pots of soil held several leafy, climbing plants that Niccolo had idly taken for some sort of lemon trees. Harvesting the yellow fruit, Callimaco returned to the table with a handful of it.

Niccolo examined the fruit suspiciously. It was round and yellow, about the size of a walnut. He sniffed. Acidic. "You brought these back from the New World?" he inquired.

"The seeds," corrected Callimaco. "If I had tried to take the fruit, the Spanish sailors would have eaten them. Go ahead, taste one."

Giuditta did so first and frowned. "It's piquant," she acknowledged.

Against his better judgment, Niccolo bit into one next. "Bitter," he said. "Too bitter. Maybe if you cooked them?"

"Nonsense," said Callimaco. "Rub it on the bruschetta. The flavor's excellent mixed with the garlic and oil."

And so, reluctantly, Niccolo did as his friend advised. Although the result was palatable, he did not think he would go out of his way in the future to obtain any of Callimaco's precious little golden apples. From inauspicious beginnings like these, it would be another full two centuries before the tomato would assume its rightful place in the Italian diet and in the pantheon of Italian culinary culture.

As they ate, the talk and the wine flowed freely. Niccolo filled Callimaco in on the events of his life and even supplied a few sketchy details about his relationship with Giuditta. Since he had never discussed these things openly with her, he thought it prudent not to go into the minutiae of feelings and emotions, to say nothing of future plans and commitments.

Callimaco, meanwhile, had begun what looked like a curious ritual, and he was fully aware that Niccolo and Giuditta were watching him with curiosity. He had fetched, from his endless store of odds and ends, several broad, wrinkled, heart-shaped leaves. Rolling them tightly together, he made a small tube and trimmed the ends with a knife. Going over to the fire, he held the tube in the embers until it caught. When he returned to the table, the brand was burning slowly, a lazy, sweet-smelling smoke curling up from its tip. Then Callimaco did a remarkable thing. He put the other end of the tube in his mouth and drew the smoke in. With a hiss, he let it out like a dragon or a fire-eater.

Both Niccolo and Giuditta were stupefied. "The pleasures of the New World," said Callimaco, greatly amused at their consternation. "Care to try?"

Callimaco had finally prevailed upon his guests to sample the tobacco he had brought back with him. In answer to Niccolo's strident objections, he had informed him that the natives of the New World customarily indulged their habit of smoking tobacco after eating because they believed it produced a beneficial effect on the digestion. And although Niccolo had agreed to try it for the sake of his digestion, afterward he wished he hadn't.

When he left Callimaco later that evening, he was feeling a little nauseous, his stomach a little queasy. After accompanying Giuditta to the convent, Niccolo pleaded illness and returned to the Florentine colony.

Once back in the colony, Niccolo went directly to bed. As he drifted off to sleep, the envoy of the Florentine mercantile republic unconsciously began toting up in his imagination the fantastic balance of trade, as he understood it, between the New and Old Worlds—the one side offered tobacco, the golden apples, and the French disease. The other side took these goods in exchange for the grippe and the benefits of civilization, which included slavery, plunder, and, of course, conversion to Christianity.

As he drifted further off, visions of Callimaco filled Niccolo's head.

He saw his friend on some far shore with a strange, exotic woman. Both were dressed in unlikely beaded attire. Both were puffing on long tubes of tightly rolled tobacco leaves, blowing the smoke in each other's faces and laughing, laughing, laughing . . .

Abruptly the laughing became shouting and the noise seemed to be reaching an urgent, hysterical pitch. Niccolo sat up with a start and realized that the noise was not coming from his dream. The house in which he was sleeping was filled with shouting, and cries rose up from the streets outside. He ran to the door and threw it open just in time to see a half-dressed Michelozzi come bounding down the staircase.

"Michelozzi, what is it?"

"The pope! The pope's dead!"

Rumors poured into the Florentine embassy. There was wild talk—a devil in the form of a monkey had been seen crawling into the dying pope's bedchamber, a gigantic black sow prowled the square of Saint Peter's, another devil waiting to drag his soul down to hell. Just before expiring, Alexander was said to have muttered, "I'm coming, Satan, I'm coming." And when his black spirit was finally released, his body began to swell hideously. Blood and rabid foam boiled from his mouth.

Gradually, more credible information began leaking in, although details were sketchy. The pope had entertained Cardinal Adriano di Corneto at a dinner the evening before. Both had fallen ill afterward. The cardinal was now hovering between life and death. The pope, burning with fever, had succumbed after a series of violent paroxysms. Inevitably, there was talk of poison. Toward morning, another piece of news reached the embassy that set off a whole new round of speculation and diplomatic scurrying: Caesar too had been at that fatal dinner.

By the next day, the forces of violence and retribution had been set in motion. Those who had been denied during the eleven long years of Alexander's pontificate, the exiled, the proscribed, the wronged, came galloping furiously toward Rome from all over Italy.

In the city itself, looting had already begun. The Orsini and the Colonna, Rome's two most powerful families, emptied the prisons to get the manpower they needed. They sacked the Spanish quarter, burning over a hundred shops and houses. Fabio Orsini, son of Paolo Orsini, who had been decapitated by Caesar at Sinigallia, satisfied his lust for revenge by washing his face and hands in the blood of a Borgia relative he had beheaded.

And where was Caesar? No one knew. That he was alive seemed probable. Immediately upon the pontiff's death, Caesar's lieutenant Don Micheletto had sealed off the Vatican and systematically removed over 500,000 ducats worth of coin, plate, and jewels. What Don Micheletto left behind was quickly snatched up by the servants, so that when the common looters finally gained access to the palace, there was nothing left. Their howls of protest and indignation filled the empty, ransacked papal apartments.

Niccolo, the cardinal, and the entire embassy staff had worked feverishly throughout the night, and it was not until midmorning of the following day, with the first batch of urgent dispatches well on their way to Florence, that the frenetic pace slackened a little. It was Michelozzi's casual remark that they should perhaps go out and join some of the looting that caused Niccolo to take an abrupt leave of his colleagues and sent him hurtling into the streets.

He was in the grip of panic. It was inevitable that the pope's death would trigger the decimation of the Borgia properties. No one expected any better or worse from the Romans. What had not occurred to Niccolo until that moment was that Giuditta might be affected! She presided over one of the pope's properties! How could he have been so stupid? So remiss?

To his great relief, the Convent of the Fallen Angels was still intact. Inside, it was business as usual, as a few stragglers moped about, gathering together clothing discarded in the heat of last night's revels, groaning and nursing their headaches. Giuditta looked a little worn, but pleased to see her lover so suddenly appear.

"You're safe," said the out-of-breath Niccolo.

"You came to rescue me?"

"I was terrified," he said with emotion.

"It took you long enough."

He had to bite his lip in silent shame, but Giuditta seemed untroubled by his lapse. "I told you we offer discretion here," she said. "Not many people know about this place. And certainly no Orsini or Colonna has ever set foot in my establishment. We'll be fine here. Besides, what's there to steal? The girls?"

Giuditta called for warm milk and made Niccolo drink it to settle his stomach and calm him down. The brothel, like the Florentine embassy, had been a beehive of activity all night long, with contradictory rumors arriving faster than they could be digested and coordinated.

"It's been quite a night," said Giuditta.

"What have you heard?" asked Niccolo wiping the white moustache from his upper lip with the back of his hand.

"Everything. We've heard just about everything you could care to imagine here."

"Was it poison?"

"That's only the first question! And if it was poison, who poisoned whom? And was the poison in the wine or in the peaches? Or was it in the sweets? There are a lot of different versions of the story going around."

"What do you think?" asked Niccolo.

"I don't think it was poison."

"Why?"

"There are two possibilities: either the cardinal was trying to poison Caesar and the pope or they were trying to poison him. Since all three are sick and possibly dead, somebody made a serious mistake."

Giuditta continued, "You've eaten with Caesar. You've seen how careful and suspicious he is. The pope is even worse. Now, does it seem likely they would inadvertently poison themselves while trying to kill someone else?"

"I see your point."

"As for the cardinal, would he be foolish enough to try to poison the pope and Caesar in their own lair? Do you know how many tasters and guards there are in the Borgia kitchen? The security there is tighter than at the papal treasury."

"What about the wine butlers? They could have made a mistake."

"They've been with the Borgias since the old days in Spain. They don't make mistakes. And anyone who's a guest of theirs brings their own wine and wine butler. It's not even considered offensive anymore."

"So if it wasn't poison, what was it?"

"Bad pork? Disease? Who knows what malevolent things breed in the air and water of this city?" Then she added, "You know, if you really want to know, there's an easy way to find out."

"How?"

"By taking a look at the body. Don't you Christians have some barbarian funeral custom of exposing dead bodies to the public?"

"It's not called exposing dead bodies to the public; it's called lying in state," said Niccolo. "It's supposed to be dignified."

"If I can get a look at Alexander 'lying in state,'" she said sarcastically, "I can probably tell whether he was poisoned or not."

"You can tell just by looking at the body?"

"Most of the time. Or by smelling it," she said dispassionately.

"Alright," said Niccolo. "Tomorrow, we'll go see the body. Right now, I have to get back to the embassy. It's extremely busy there."

"You're leaving me already? You've just arrived," she said with an inviting smile.

"I have to go. There's so much . . ."

"I'll tell you about Caesar if you stay another hour," said Giuditta coyly.

"What about Caesar?" said Niccolo. "What have you heard about him?"

"Stay an hour?"

"Alright."

"I heard he's been taken to the Castel Sant'Angelo."

"Dead or alive?"

"Somewhere in between. He has his Spanish physician, Terella, with him."

"What do you know about this Terella?"

"Not much. But they say that, like the master he serves, he's a man of extremes."

Extreme was indeed an apt characterization of the methods of Don Terella, and nothing less than extreme measures were required, for Caesar was on the point of death. Racked by violent chills and delirious from fever, he was carried to the Castel Sant'Angelo under heavy guard. The Castel Sant'Angelo was as safe a place for him as any in Rome could be. It was a massive, thick-walled fortress, built for defense. Manned by Caesar's men, it was impregnable—at least for the time being. Inside, Don Terella was left to work his magic. With all the resources of the arcane sciences at his disposal, he set about his task with industry and imagination.

Later commentaries, no doubt inspired by literary evocations of the Borgia family emblem, insist that a live bull was slit open and eviscerated and Caesar was placed naked inside its still-warm body. In fact, it was a mule. Shivering uncontrollably, Caesar was wrapped in the disemboweled carcass in order to draw into himself its lifeblood and precious animal spirits.

In a burst of scientific, or perhaps poetic inspiration, Terella then had his illustrious patient plunged into a large jar of freezing water. Caesar emerged with his skin blistered and peeling, his face livid. When he lost consciousness and his seizures became all the more violent, another mule was brought in and the procedure repeated. Outside, Rome waited. The impassive castle walls gave no hint of the desperate medical measures being taken within.

The dead pope, meanwhile, was receiving little better treatment than his son. His corpse had been washed and dressed, placed between two lighted candles, and left alone. The cardinals had been summoned to pray over him, but no one came. Choristers were called to sing the offices of the dead, but they too declined. Burchardi, an intimate of the pope and the Borgia master of ceremonies was the only one to attend the body that evening. He brought with him a pair of crimson velvet slippers and put them, lovingly, but not without difficulty, on the swollen feet of the dead prelate. He attached two gold crosses to the slippers with pins and secured them with string tied around the pope's ankles. Then he sat and wept.

The body was finally removed to a small chapel and secured behind a locked grating with its feet sticking out through the grillwork. By the time Giuditta and Niccolo arrived to pay their respects, the shoes with the gold crosses were already missing. The first thing Niccolo saw were the hastily penned epitaphs stuck to the grating. "A mass of cruelty, trickery, rage, fury, excess, lechery; a fearsome sponge soaked with blood and gold—I, Alexander VI, lie here."

The body was so hideously swollen that it was on the point of bursting through the loose maniple in which it was wrapped. The dead man's feet were bloated, his face bloated and black. His fuzzy, purple tongue was so large that it filled his whole mouth and kept it agape. From beneath the ceremonial vestments, a stink arose that even by Roman standards was unbearable.

"It wasn't poison," declared Giuditta flatly.

"But the body's decomposing," said Niccolo. "He's only been dead about thirty-six hours, and he's already rotting away. Doesn't that indicate the working of poison?

"Just the opposite. Most poisons, like the cantarella, which is the one used in the Borgia household, contain arsenic. And arsenic prevents decomposition. Didn't you know a thoroughly poisoned body will last days longer than one that succumbed to sickness or old age?"

"Then what did he die of?"

"I'd say a fever of some sort. The decomposition has been too rapid. Something must have been eating away at him even before he died."

"And what are Caesar's chances of survival, if he has the same fever?"

"Who can say?"

As they were leaving, Niccolo spied another one of the epitaphs that had been posted on the protective grating: "Here lies the carcass of a serpent who has filled the world with his venom."

Shortly afterward, the faithful Burchardi came to pay his last respects to his master. Aghast at the disgusting and rapidly disintegrating state of the corpse, he covered it with a cloth and knelt to keep his vigil. At midnight, the gravediggers came for the body. A place had been prepared for it in one of the Vatican's small chapels—Santa Maria delle Febbre, Saint Mary of the Fevers.

Burchardi watched in silence as six surly workmen went about their task, growling and joking. They freely insulted the pope as they finished the excavations for his grave. When the carpenters arrived with the coffin—a plain wooden one—it was found to be too small. Burchardi said nothing as they ripped the miter from the dead pope's head and crushed it down into the coffin. He said nothing as they pummeled and punched the swollen body with their fists, beating it, forcing it into the too short, too narrow coffin.

31

Two More Popes, Another Famous Artist, and a Recumbent Caesar

The days following the little-mourned passing of Pope Alexander VI were busy, frantic days, and the machinations leading to the election of a new pope had already begun in earnest. The Florentine cardinal Soderini was an extraordinarily busy man during this interregnum, as was his special assistant, Niccolo Machiavelli. Negotiations continued around the clock. Votes among the Italians and French were bought and sold and bartered for future favors. Still there was an enormous question mark—the Spaniards. They were awaiting word from Caesar, but from the Castel Sant'Angelo, no word was forthcoming. It was a full ten days before doubts were dispelled. On August 27, Caesar sent for the Spanish cardinals. He was alive and ready to play the game. Whether he had survived because of the bizarre ministrations of his physician, Terella, or in spite of them was never decided.

The contest for the papacy centered on the efforts of the French cardinal d'Amboise and those of the vitriolic Italian cardinal, Giuliano della Rovere. Caesar supported the Frenchman and had instructed his Spaniards to vote for him as a block. If the Italians had lined up solidly behind the contender, della Rovere, the election would have been his, but as so often happens they could agree to nothing among themselves and so, splitting their votes, the conclave reached an impasse.

When the white smoke finally rose from the chimney and the chamberlain stepped out on his balcony to announce, "*Papam habemus*—We have a pope," he was referring to neither of the two principal aspirants, but to a compromise candidate instead, a sixty-four-year old invalid who took the name Pius III. His primary qualifications seemed to be that he was weak and he was inoffensive to all sides.

The coronation ceremony took place on October 8, and Niccolo attended as part of the official Florentine delegation. With him in the knot of soberly dressed Florentines was his friend and colleague Michelozzi. The city was in a festive mood, as willing to celebrate the accession of the new pope as the death of the former. Cheers greeted the papal caravan as it approached Saint Peter's. "Papa, Papa, Papa, Papa!"

"Look at him," said Michelozzi. "He's more ancient and decrepit than I imagined."

"You're right," replied Niccolo. "He can barely lift an arm to wave to the crowd. The weight of that gold brocaded cape is too much for the old man."

"I give him a year," said Michelozzi, and then, "Look there!"

Niccolo turned to see the captain general of the Papal Armies bringing up the rear of the procession. With the ascension of Pius III to the chair of Saint Peter, Caesar had reentered Rome, as in the old days, triumphantly. The pope had placed Caesar under his protection and strictly forbidden anyone, especially the angry Orsini, to harm his dear and beloved son, Caesar Borgia, duke of Romagna and Valentinois, standard-bearer of the church . . .

In this coronation procession, Niccolo noted that Caesar rode at the head of two hundred horsemen and three hundred foot soldiers and looked for all the world like an emperor. "But which mad emperor," he thought, "Nero or Caligula?"

Today, it was Caesar who was making a show of strength, Caesar, mounted on a huge, black warhorse, with his two hunting dogs at his side. It was Caesar who intended to be the power behind the throne, Caesar, dressed in flaming scarlet and white, with gilded armor shining underneath. It was Caesar who was going to set the direction for papal policy, Caesar grinning devilishly from beneath his mask.

When they filed into the church, Caesar, still accompanied by his dogs, took a prominent position in the front rows. He smiled once during the sermon, when Pius declared himself to be the "Pope of Peace." At several points during the coronation mass, Caesar could barely conceal his delight. The new pope was so feeble that he had to celebrate the mass sitting down.

With the installation of Pius III and the establishment of an uneasy truce between the various warring factions in Rome, Niccolo was recalled to Florence. He stayed on a week in Rome because Cardinal Soderini could not bear parting with him, but finally he could put off his departure no longer. On the eve of that departure, Giuditta had arranged a simple farewell dinner for him and his friends.

Callimaco, who had long since been initiated into the rites of the Convent of the Fallen Angels, was already there when Niccolo and Michelozzi arrived. Wreathed in a blue cloud of tobacco smoke, he and Giuditta were deep in conversation. When he spied Niccolo, an excited Callimaco leapt to his feet. "Niccolo, your lover here has just made me an astonishing proposition!"

Both Niccolo and Giuditta blushed. It was the first time that anyone had ever referred to them as "lovers" in public. Niccolo quickly moved to cover his embarrassment: "What proposition is that? A lifetime subscription to the convent with access to the services of the little sisters at half-price?"

"That too, I hope. But even better. She found my hospital squalid. That was the word she used, *squalid*. I told her she should see it after an outbreak of the plague. I said I did what I could but funds were low. I rely almost completely on charity, and this is not a charitable town. I had to point out that inevitably my patients die and it's difficult to collect a fee from a dead man, especially a destitute dead man from a poor family."

"It seems you should either go after a better class of patient or learn how to treat the ones you have so they recover," scoffed Niccolo.

"At any rate, Sister Giuditta, in her capacity as mother superior and treasurer, pharmacist and physician of the Convent of the Fallen Angels has proposed that in exchange for my medical advice on combating the spread of the pox, she will turn over to me, a certain portion of the revenues of this fine establishment. What do you think?"

"Can you do that?" asked Niccolo incredulously, looking at Giuditta.

"In all the confusion after the late pope's demise," she said, "I seem to have been completely forgotten. No one has come to collect; no one has come to take over. It would appear that I'm now sole proprietress."

"And of an extraordinarily profitable enterprise," Callimaco hastened to add.

"Bravo," said Niccolo. "Now the wages of sin can be used for the greater honor and glory of God and the relief and succor of the least of His little children! A more worthy use than buying cloth of gold for the pope's sons and daughters and mistresses!"

When Giuditta went to supervise the serving of the meal, Niccolo's eyes narrowed and he fixed them on Callimaco, "You didn't bring any delicacies from the New World, did you?"

"I'm sorry, old friend. Not this time, but if you come back with me later, I can let you have some of a starchy tuber that's better than a turnip or even a parsnip, for that matter . . ."

Niccolo was not even listening when a plate heaped with crisp-fried sardines was put in the center of the table. When he bit into one with a crunch, he discovered it was stuffed with spinach. Later, eels roasted with oil, wine, garlic, and laurel were served, and then little ringlets of squid smothered in scallions and peas.

Despite the growing boisterousness of Callimaco and Michelozzi, melancholy began to suffuse the little group. It was the sadness that comes with the inevitability of departure. Sensing this swing in Niccolo's mood, and in that of their hostess as well, Callimaco and Michelozzi diplomatically withdrew to disport themselves in the convent below.

Left alone, Niccolo and Giuditta endured a long, embarrassed silence. Then both spoke at once. Then both stopped.

"What were you going to say?"

"No, go ahead, what were you going to say?

Neither could sleep, and sometime after midnight, Giuditta rose to prepare an infusion of chamomile flowers. Then, thinking the better of it, she took down a flask of the potent Rossoli liquor instead. As a matter of course, on her way back to bed, she peeked through the curtain to survey her rowdy domains below. Everything seemed to be in order.

"Psssst, Niccolo, come here," she said. "There's something that should amuse you."

"Not Caesar?" groaned Niccolo.

"No, he hasn't been here at all lately. This is one of your countrymen, one of your noble Florentines."

Intrigued, Niccolo came up behind her and peeked through the opening in the curtains. Out of the corner of his eye, he saw a staggering but happy Callimaco, who had given his odd, beaded mantle to one of the girls and was apparently trying to teach her some exotic dance step.

"Do you see him?" asked Giuditta.

Niccolo focused on an overgrown cherub who would have made the plumpish Pagolo look lean and haggard by comparison. Sitting with his feet up, he was perhaps the only one in the place still fully clothed. Some sort of dance was being performed for his benefit.

Eight men dressed as hermits were dancing in a lugubrious circle around the beaming, congenial spectator. They led a little figure in chains who appeared to be Cupid. Then Cupid began to charm the hermits and escaped. As he danced provocatively, the hermits threw off their robes and became armed young men who fought with one another. The victor, then claiming Cupid, sang a song about love in a bell-clear contralto voice.

"Don't you recognize him?" asked Giuditta.

"Of course I recognize him," said Niccolo. "It's just that I was caught up in the charming little spectacle." As he spoke, both Cupid and the victor retired to places on either side of the chubby man they were entertaining. His fat, bejeweled hands caressed them both as he chatted animatedly with the dancers.

"Does he come here often?" asked Niccolo.

"Only occasionally."

"And he likes the little boys?"

"Not really. He likes to watch. He's fond of saying he loves beauty in all her manifestations."

"Especially in the castrated honey-tongued youth of Rome," said Niccolo sarcastically.

"He's not a bad sort. He's extremely generous."

Niccolo cut her off. "Generous with the money his ancestors sweated and bled out of Florence!"

"Oh, don't be so censorious," said Giuditta, trying to dispel Niccolo's gathering anger. "He's harmless enough."

Niccolo had to admit that the precious, flaccid, youth fondling the two castrati seemed harmless enough. The Florentines had been keeping a close watch on him, and although he dabbled in intrigue, it was almost always aimed at the illegal procurement of some antiquity or art treasure.

"You know about his problem?" asked Giuditta.

Niccolo grunted. He knew. Flatulence.

"They say that's what makes him so generous. He's terribly concerned about being unpleasant to those around him, about being offensive."

"He should check himself into the Hospital for Incurable Diseases if he's so concerned," said Niccolo bluntly.

By now, the fleshy, happily babbling prelate had taken off his cardinal's hat and crowned the cooing Cupid with it, to the great delight of the other entertainers. Giovanni de' Medici, son of Lorenzo the Magnificent, seemed to be enjoying his exile. But his innocuous pleasures were suddenly interrupted by a man who rushed into the brothel, shouting. Niccolo and Giuditta could not at first make out what he was saying, but they could see that he was creating quite a stir.

Many of those in the brothel began hastily snatching up clothing and preparing to leave. As the panic spread, Giuditta became alarmed and feared that some sort of a raid or attack might be in the offing. Then they managed to hear what all the consternation was about:

"The pope! The pope's dead!"

The pontificate of Pope Pius III, the self-styled Pope of Peace had lasted exactly eleven days.

Niccolo's eyes lit up and his mouth curled into a salacious grin. He reached for Giuditta and pulled her to him.

"Does the death of a pope always have this effect on you," she said, not displeased.

"Not always, but this time it does. There will be another conclave. It could take weeks. Months. And I suppose I'll have to stay in Rome until it's over."

As they kissed, Giuditta cast one last watchful glance over her little empire, now rapidly emptying out as prelates and church officials scrambled back to their posts to begin deliberations. In the hubbub, she thought she saw Michelozzi leaving in the company of the Cardinal de' Medici, but as Niccolo half-carried, half-pushed her back into the bedroom, she abandoned herself to him and all thoughts gave way to the rush of passion that swept them both away.

The impetuous but not stupid Italian cardinal Giuliano della Rovere had learned his lesson. Seeing that the Italians were still deeply divided among themselves, he applied instead for support from another quarter—the Spaniards. Making the same promises to Caesar Borgia that his predecessor had made, namely the supreme command of the Papal Armies, he secured the Spanish vote, and, after the shortest conclave on record, which lasted less than twenty-four hours, he was elected pope.

Smug in the obsequious assurances offered him by the new pontiff, Caesar's arrogance grew daily. But one telling detail escaped his notice. Caesar was always fond of boasting that, like his namesake, Julius Caesar, he was destined to conquer and rule an empire. If he had not been so blinded by his own ambition, he might have attributed more significance to the name this new pope adopted, he might have wondered what this man had in mind when he chose to call himself Pope Julius II.

Cardinal Soderini finished giving Niccolo his instructions, which consisted, naturally, of making no firm commitments to the new pope on behalf of Florence. He was to attempt to determine where Pope Julius stood with respect to Caesar, to the Papal States in Romagna, and to Venice. If possible, he was supposed to stir up as much animosity between the different parties as possible.

"Oh, and Machiavelli," added the cardinal. "There's somebody waiting for you in your study. Why don't you see him before you go?"

Distracted, and going over in his mind the arguments and phrases he would use in his audience with the pope, Niccolo returned to the study to find a gnomelike creature with matted hair and huge, wild eyes waiting for him. "A ragged Roman beggar" was his first thought, "a ragged Roman madman," his second. So Niccolo was startled when the gnome greeted him in a perfect Florentine accent.

"Messer Machiavelli, I've come from the Signoria," he said. "I have something for you."

"And what might that be?" inquired Niccolo, intrigued by the appearance of the unlikely messenger. He was shuffling his sandaled feet, not nervously, but restlessly, impatiently, as though some tremendous force were building inside him. "He's wearing sandals," thought Niccolo. "In November, in the rain . . ."

The messenger reached under his cloak, pulled out a dusty purse, and threw it on the table. "Money," he stated flatly.

"Money?" said Niccolo incredulously. "Money from the Signoria? Is such a thing possible? I'd given up hope. I can't remember the last time I wrote asking for money. And now they're actually sending it!"

"I know what you mean," said the gnome, grinning from ear to ear.

"How do you know?"

"I have trouble too, getting any money out of them."

Niccolo shook his head. Had things come to such an impasse in the Florentine republic that they begrudged a common messenger a few florins? Was the treasury that strapped?

"That's why I've come to Rome," said the odd little man. "For the money."

Niccolo wondered if messengers were better paid in Rome than in Florence. "So you hope to find work here, in Rome?"

"Oh, it's not just a hope. I have work. I just hope this time I'll get paid for it. I'm going now to see the pope."

"The pope!" said Niccolo. "You're going to go ask the pope for work? I think maybe you better reconsider. I'm sure we could find something for you here around the embassy."

"Thank you, sir, but the pope sent for me, and I don't want to antagonize him."

"He sent for you? The pope? Just what kind of work is it you do?"

"Mostly sculpture, sir. In marble."

"Ah, another artist," said Niccolo skeptically. "I suppose you also paint, do fresco, cast bronze, carve wood, write poetry."

"Yes, sir, I can do all that, but I prefer the marble."

"And tell me," said Niccolo, probing. "Are you also an engineer? And a scientist? Do you design siege machines?"

"No, sir, Leonardo does that," he said with a hint of rancor in his voice.

"You know Leonardo?" asked Niccolo.

"Yes," the little man replied laconically.

"And what is your opinion of him?"

"May I speak freely?"

"Please."

"Leonardo is a pompous, perfumed prick," said the sculptor, barring his teeth. "A genius but a prick. And a whore."

"Well at least we agree on that," said Niccolo. "But aren't you something of a whore, too? You said you were going to work for the pope, for the money."

"It's different."

"How so?"

"I carve marble, and I'll do it for anyone who pays me and gives free reign to my imagination. But you don't see me trailing along behind a tyrant, building engines of war, do you? Engines of war that can be used against my native city?"

"And if the pope asked you to construct such a device?"

"I'd spit in his eye!"

"Bravo!"

"And then I'd ride as fast as my poor horse could carry me to Florence and fortify her walls so that no engine designed and built by man could breach them."

Niccolo clapped the spirited little man on the back and in so doing raised a cloud of dust that set them both coughing for a minute. When it subsided, Niccolo said, "Come along, sir. I too have business at the Vatican. Since it seems that we are of one mind on a number of things, important things, why don't we keep each other company? What do you say?"

"Lead the way, Messer Machiavelli," said the dusty, ill-kempt gnome.

"Since we are going to be friends, call me Niccolo. And your name?"

"Buonarotti, sir. Michelangelo Buonarotti."

As they passed through the gates of the Florentine embassy, Niccolo could be heard saying, "Tell me Michelangelo, you say you know something about fortifications. Now I saw a bombardment once that in the space of a few hours breached a solid stone wall. What puzzled me is why the stones fell . . ." And as they went, the animated little man, hopping more than walking at Niccolo's side, began to pour out his ideas on the strengthening of the city walls of Florence.

When they reached the Vatican, Niccolo saw immediately that

everywhere, changes were underway. Workmen came and went, and the sounds of hammering and sawing filled the air. It looked as though Pope Julius was taking energetic steps to repair the damage done during the funeral rioting and reverse the course of neglect and decay that had characterized the Borgia years. For over an hour, he and Michelangelo waited in a large, airy antechamber amid hordes of foreign ambassadors and cardinals and bishops, all biding their time, waiting to see the pope. Most were richly and stiffly dressed, as befits a papal audience, and Niccolo could only marvel that his fellow Florentine, the sculptor Michelangelo, had come in his work clothes, covered with the dirt and dust of his art. He watched the little man scamper around the antechamber, oblivious of the dignitaries that it contained, intent only on examining the paintings and the sculpture that adorned the place. This he did with a critical and unforgiving eye, with frequent frowns, erratic hand gestures, and violent shaking of the head, as though he were conducting a contentious dialogue with the works of art themselves. It was the first time Niccolo could remember meeting an artist he actually liked.

When they passed into the main reception hall, Niccolo got his first look at the new pope. He had none of the radiant, imperial serenity of Alexander, nor was he a cringing hermit like the poor Pius. He was leaning forward in his papal throne, haranguing a group of cowed ambassadors who stood before him. His strong, gravelly voice carried well in the hollow marble hall and boomed off the walls. His tonsured head was wreathed with a ring of thick grey hair, and his chiseled face framed with a beard the color of steel. He was bareheaded—no tiara, no miter, not even a skullcap. As he talked—or lectured or scolded or declaimed—he punctuated his sentences with short, menacing thrusts of his head. It was a head at odds with the soft crimson velvet stole and the flowing white silk robes underneath. It was a head that belonged in a suit of armor, rising out of a shining breastplate and clapped in a helmet of polished steel.

When Pope Julius had finished, he sat back in his throne the way a lion settles back after having eaten its fill. A buzz of supplications, explanations, and gestures of protest immediately arose from the ambassadors crowded at his feet. The pope eyed them for a minute, reached out with his right hand for a small silver bell at his side, and rang it. He looked idly away, out over their heads. Two obliging, obsequious cardinals jumped to hustle them out of the papal presence. The audience was over. As the befuddled, protesting ambassadors were quickly ushered away, the pope called out to one of them, "And Giustiniani, the next time you must come to see me, send someone else!"

When the Florentine envoy was announced, Niccolo approached the dais with the requisite humility, but with a hint of a half-cocked smile of detached amusement on his face. He was by now accustomed to the tantrums of princes and kings. He doubted that a papal tantrum could be much worse.

He kissed the pope's ring and noted that there was nothing soft or fleshy about the calloused hand. Julius examined him with hard eyes, the way a man might look at a lobster before eating it, trying to decide what was the best approach, trying to decide where to crack it open first. "You're the Florentine envoy who has been on an extended legation to Caesar Borgia, the captain general of our armies?"

Niccolo nodded in acknowledgement.

"Then you should know that the captain general has asked our permission to march through Tuscany on his way to reclaim our territories in the Romagna."

Unmoved, Niccolo said nothing.

"He has also asked that if Florence should deny him that right of passage, he be permitted to attack and subdue her and bring her under the yoke of the church."

"Florence already submits to the authority of the church, Your Holiness," said Niccolo diplomatically.

"And will she let Caesar's armies pass?"

"That decision would not be mine to make," said Niccolo, hedging. He saw the pope already reaching for his dismissal bell and knew he had only one more chance. "If Your Holiness chooses to wage war on Florence, who is no enemy of the church and who poses no threat to her territories, you may do so. But if you follow that course, you will soon be no more than a Venetian chaplain."

"What?" said the pope angrily, moving his hand away from the bell.

"I mean that Florence in no way threatens the realms of the church, but Venice does. Florence is not expansionary in her ambitions, but Venice is. It is not Florence who has captured Imola and is even now besieging Faenza, but Venice! Venice! Venice is waging war on you, taking the Romagna away from you piece by piece while you sit here and dangle idle threats before the Florentines."

The pope was furious. "Imola? Faenza? When did you hear these things?"

"We had the news only this morning. Imola has fallen. Faenza is hard-pressed. Will Your Holiness send his captain general against Venice, then? Or will he allow him to threaten Florence and lose the Romagna?"

Julius tugged on his beard and eyed Niccolo warily. "I have no intentions of losing the Romagna or of becoming a Venetian chaplain, as you put it." He grunted. It could have been a laugh. "As for our captain general, perhaps there are others to lead our armies, others more qualified, neh?" As he said these last words, Niccolo saw a dark smile crawl across his face. As the Florentine envoy withdrew, the pontiff was staring hard at his own powerful right hand, flexing and unflexing the muscles, stretching the taunt sinews.

Niccolo passed Michelangelo on his way out of the pontifical presence and wished him good luck. When the little man was announced, he heard the pope roar something about another impertinent Florentine. As Niccolo left the reception room, he heard an uninterrupted stream of talk from the direction of the papal throne, but it was not the rasping harangue of Julius II. It was the excited, nervous Florentine patter of the irrepressible sculptor, Michelangelo. Pope Julius had his hands full with Florentines that day.

Niccolo's work was only half done as well. He had another stop to make before returning to the embassy to report to Soderini. When he climbed the steps to the San Clemente palace and stated his name and business, he was asked to wait. In a moment, the guard returned and, after saying something incomprehensible in Spanish, showed him into the presence of Caesar Borgia.

Whether or not Borgia was pleased to see Niccolo was difficult to ascertain at a glance. He wore a mask, a kind of black veil that completely covered his head and face. His features were only dimly discernible inside. In the fingers of one gloved hand, he rolled a small gold ball, which Niccolo took to be perfumed, since Caesar frequently passed it in front of his nose. The hand that was not thus engaged was busy scratching and rubbing, incessantly picking and digging.

Sphinxlike, the hooded figure regarded Niccolo for several minutes.

Then he sat up slowly in the bed, drew one indolent leg across the other and spoke, "So the Florentine envoy returns."

"Excellency," replied Niccolo curtly.

"And what does Florence offer me today?" said Caesar, beginning the conversation as he had begun so many in the past, when he had played deftly at cat and mouse with the Florentine envoy.

"Only news, Excellency," said Niccolo.

"News?"

"The Venetians have made a proposition to Florence. They want to divide the Romagna with us."

The duke of Romagna sat up suddenly. The great shaggy hunting dogs in the bed with him whipped their heads around at the shock, but seeing that nothing was amiss, nuzzled back into the satin cushions and covers. "Romagna is mine!" he shouted, throwing the perfumed ball across the room at Niccolo. He missed.

"There is no need to be angry at me, Excellency," said Niccolo in a soothing voice. "No need to hang the messenger. At any rate, you'll be pleased to know we refused the Venetians' deal."

"Then you did well," snarled Caesar. "I'll crush anyone who tries to steal the Romagna from me. Florence is no exception."

"Oh, but the Venetians have already begun on their own. They said they didn't need the Florentines. Apparently they don't. They've taken Imola, and Faenza is about to fall. Rimini has gone over to them voluntarily."

"What!"

"You didn't know?"

"You're lying!"

"I've just come from the pope, and he seems concerned about it, concerned enough to send his troops against Venice."

Borgia crossed his arms and sat back. "Then I had better prepare to move. His Holiness will want me to start immediately."

"I'm not so sure."

"You've always been the uncertain type, you and all the other Florentines. What is it that you're not sure about now?" Caesar seemed amused.

"I'm not so sure the pope intends you to lead his armies. In fact, I think he rather fancies leading them himself."

"*Sangre de Toro!* I will be the one to lead the armies! I have his word!"

"And you think he intends to keep it?"

"Why wouldn't he?"

"Did you always keep yours?"

"The pope loves me like a son!"

"You always said it was better to be feared than loved."

Caesar was speechless with rage, and Niccolo continued in a dispassionate voice, "Who fears you now, Caesar?"

"I'll smash Florence. I'll go to Pisa and put myself at the service of your mortal enemies. Then I'll march across Tuscany and devastate it, burn the countryside to the ground on my way to Romagna, where I'll teach the Venetians a lesson."

"And if the pope's in Romagna with an army?"

"To hell with him! I'll join the Venetians and wrest the papacy from his filthy, lying hands. It's mine! The papacy! The Romagna! Mine! Mine! All mine!" In the access of fury that accompanied these last words, Caesar shrieked something in Spanish, and the deadly dogs snapped to attention.

Niccolo had remained on his feet during the entire interview and was quick to grasp the danger of the situation. He stepped nimbly through the half-opened door and slammed it shut behind him just as another command sent the bloodthirsty dogs hurtling for his throat. They crashed violently, but harmlessly, against the solid oak panels, and their ferocious howling mixed with Caesar's empty Spanish curses followed him down the corridor.

Niccolo had not been able to see anything of Caesar's face during the colloquy, but he suspected that the French disease had left its grisly signature there and that that was the reason for the mask. Once again, he thought of the mad, grinning Vitellozzo, so hideous in life, more so in death. He imagined the same pustules and scabs, the same rot and disfigurement on the face of the once-handsome Caesar. One thing he did not have to imagine. On the big, square, white silk pillows where Caesar rested his head, he had seen it plainly enough—long black hairs and clotted tufts of short wiry hair. Caesar's hair and beard were falling out.

"So that's how David slew Goliath," said Giuditta when Niccolo had finished recounting the details of his last meeting with the fallen Borgia. "And now that you've saved the republic, will you be returning to Florence?"

"Not right away," said Niccolo.

"More business? Who is it this time, the pope? Venice?"

"Personal business," he said.

Niccolo had written to his superiors in Florence to the effect that wise men in Rome entertained "gloomy" ideas about Caesar's future and that the once-forceful man had been reduced to the most vile and contemptible state that he was wavering and suspicious, bullying, irresolute, and quite mad. In the end, instead of defending what he had taken with the sword, he had reverted to the most servile and humiliating behavior, courting the pope's favor with flattery and trusting in his obviously empty promises.

Niccolo also advised the Signoria that, if any of Caesar's armies should pass through Florentine territory on their way to aid their master in Rome, they could be disarmed, plundered, and imprisoned without fear of consequences. Caesar's power was definitively broken. In that same dispatch, Niccolo informed the Signoria that even though matters with Caesar appeared to be concluded, he would have to stay on in Rome for a few weeks. He said that he was unable to travel. He had a cough.

The city at this time of year was enjoying what is called Saint Martin's summer because the feast of Saint Martin falls on November 11. In this brief season, a resurgence of mild summer weather grants a temporary reprieve from the cold rains of autumn and the advance of winter. Now that the burden of Caesar had been lifted from his shoulders, Niccolo felt secure and worry free for the first time in several years. On top of that feeling of relief, he was enjoying the company of the woman he loved. They passed their days in dalliance and long walks. They took little trips to the idyllic hills outside Rome. But Niccolo knew that, like Saint Martin's summer, this period of uncomplicated happiness was destined to be brief. Already the Signoria was clamoring for his return. There was urgent business to be attended to. There was always urgent business.

"Come to Florence," he said to her.

"You're a married man," she said evasively.

"I told you it's an arrangement."

"Look over there," said Giuditta, changing the subject abruptly. "That's where you'll find the most beautiful people in Rome." Their divagations had taken them into the area of the Trinita dei Monti.

"And why is that?" said Niccolo, irked that she refused to discuss, not for the first time, following him to Florence.

"Artists come here looking for models—painters and sculptors. So every woman in Rome who thinks she looks like a Madonna and every man who thinks he looks like a hero or a saint and every angelic little child comes here too. They pick up a few pennies, and the work isn't very difficult."

"I've always heard that all the Madonnas and saints are actually modeled on the artist's favorite prostitutes and that the *putti*, those adorable little angelic creatures, are their favorite boys."

"True enough. A lot of the girls at my place have posed. Even the formidable Pasiphae or Faustina or whatever you want to call her was once in a painting."

"And who was she, Saint Lucy or one of the virgin martyrs of the early church?"

"No, she kept saying that the subject matter was rather pagan. It was a painting of Perseus. She was Medusa."

Niccolo laughed, then he turned wistful again, "Why won't you come?"

"Let me think about it for a while," she said.

"Can't you just come?"

"If I asked you to drop everything and stay here with me, would you do it?"

"Are you asking?"

"No, because I know you wouldn't stay. You have your work and your precious republic."

"And what do you have here, your work?" said Niccolo with a scornful accent on the word *work*.

"I'm sure it's not as noble and exalted as your work, but I have my independence and freedom from persecution. Can you guarantee me that in Florence?"

Niccolo was silent.

"Besides," said Giuditta. "There's probably still an outstanding warrant for my arrest in Florence. The last time I was there, they didn't treat me very well."

"And that's why you won't go back?"

"There is that dimension. And the thought of what they did to my father and brother. There's always the thought of the unavenged murders of my father and brother."

"And I told you that the people responsible are all dead by now. They've all met similar or worse fates."

"Maybe," she said. "Maybe." And once again they lapsed into a frosty silence.

"Hey, bookworm!" somebody hailed Niccolo. He was grateful for the distraction. It was the bookseller who had by now become Niccolo's fast friend, ferreting out for him copies of hard-to-find works and saving things he thought might be of interest to the studious Florentine.

"What have you got me today?" asked Niccolo. "Did you find the Tacitus?"

"Not yet. Still searching for that one. But look here." He indicated a handcart full and brimming over with elegantly bound red volumes. Niccolo picked one up and examined it. The rich leather binding was as soft and supple as baby's skin. It was stamped with an intricate design that was outlined and highlighted in strands of gold. The book had a small gilded clasp and a velvet ribbon sticking out the bottom to mark the reader's place. When Niccolo opened it, he saw the milky-white paper was of the highest quality. This was no ordinary reading matter.

Flipping to the title page, he saw that it was a poem in Latin by someone named Fausto Evangelisti. The title was printed in red letters: *Borgiad*. It was an epic—hundreds of pages of stiff Latin verse on the splendors and accomplishments of the family Borgia.

"Cheap," said the bookseller. "I'll let you have it dirt cheap. Two for the price of one."

No longer able to postpone the inevitable, Niccolo finally left for Florence in early December. Giuditta stayed behind in Rome, for the time being, she said. Pope Julius II lost no time in putting aside the crucifix and taking up the sword, and, true to his namesake, rode at the head of his own armies into the Romagna to secure for himself the states previously conquered by Caesar Borgia.

On his deathbed, Pope Alexander VI was supposed to have expressed concern over the fate of his son. "What will become of him when I am gone?" he asked. His worries were not misplaced, for, after his father's death, Caesar's decline was precipitous and irreversible.

His armies disintegrated, opting to sell their services to captains and commanders whose prospects were far brighter than those of Caesar. The French disease ate away at his sanity bit by bit, so that his threats grew wilder, his posturing more extravagant, his behavior more reckless. He was imprisoned by the pope, and rumors circulated for a time that his body had been found floating in the Tiber.

The rumors proved to be untrue; Caesar was released on good behavior and made his way to Naples, which was under Spanish rule. In Naples, he began to make loud noises about raising an army to attack Florence, to punish the pope, to retake the Romagna.

He was on the verge of slipping out of Naples to make good on his threats when he was betrayed by his own officers and imprisoned once more. At the pope's insistence, Ferdinand and Isabella, the Most Catholic monarchs, finally ordered Caesar back to Spain.

Once there, he spent the last of his mad days as a hired soldier in the service of a petty king. Riddled with syphilis and disfigured beyond recognition, he perished in an obscure skirmish that was more an act of paid brigandage than a battle. His body was found stripped of its armor and clothes and bearing the imprint of twenty-three lance and dagger wounds. The former cardinal of Valencia, duke of Romagna and Valentinois, gonfaloniere, and captain general of the church was thirty-one years old when he died.

Vitellozzo Vitelli, Oliverotto da Fermo, and the others killed by Caesar at Sinigallia have all but vanished in the mists of history. The professional historian, the archivist, the researcher can still read of their exploits and misdeeds because their names have survived in the records. We are a civilization adept at keeping records, if nothing more.

Of the countless tyrants who strutted and crowed across the stage of sixteenth-century Italy, only Caesar Borgia's name still lives, not because his actions were more memorable than the others or his perfidy greater. The mighty Caesar was rescued from oblivion not on the strength of his own accomplishments, but because he was destined to appear larger than life on the pages of a handbook for rulers written by an unassuming Florentine diplomat. That book would be called *The Prince*.

Part 4

Lessons in Civil Government

32

The War with Pisa 1

Scientific Advances

In the hour after the midday meal, the streets of Florence were nearly deserted and the shops closed. Citizens and shopkeepers lingered at their tables, consuming a last cup of wine, or took to their beds and couches for a brief respite. Among the young and the ardent, there were a few who braved the exertions of lovemaking on a full stomach in the afternoon heat, but they were the exceptions, and Niccolo Machiavelli, perhaps more concerned than the average man with the workings of his digestive apparatus, was certainly not one of them. With the bite of sharp *taleggio* cheese still alive in his mouth, Niccolo strolled along the river.

He was content, and why shouldn't he be? Florence was independent and secure. Under the prudent administration of Piero Soderini, gonfaloniere for life, the republic was prospering, and Niccolo's fortunes were rising. In the six years since he had gone to work in the chancery, he had attained a premiere position. His lengthy and difficult legation to Borgia had earned him the respect and admiration of all and a much-deserved appointment at the right hand of the gonfaloniere himself.

So Niccolo's thoughts were not unpleasant ones as he lolled along the riverbank, fingering the effigy of Saint John the Baptist that he carried in his pocket. Idly, his fingers traced the reassuring outlines of the saint's image that was stamped into the cool, solid, gold coin. And there were over a hundred more just like it at home. One hundred broad florins! Everything seemed to be going his way. For once, he had even been paid on time.

As Niccolo tripped up the stairs to the Signoria, the hot sun on his face gave way to the luscious shade of the interior of that thick-walled, stone building. The smooth green-and-white marble floors still held enough of the chill of the night air to keep the immense, high-ceilinged rooms cool through the afternoon, even in the dead of summer. Passing into his darkened study and sitting down at his writing table, with nothing more pressing to do, Niccolo could once again turn his full attention and energy to that abiding, if somewhat less than urgent, Florentine problem—the prosecution of the sempiternal war with Pisa.

Three galleys were hired to harass Pisan shipping and cut off the enemy's supplies from the sea. Pondering the problem, Niccolo realized that Pisa would have to be cut off from her allies on land as well, and, since the city of Lucca insisted on supplying the contumacious Pisans, something would have to be done about that. Penning a letter to the Florentine commissaries at the camp before Pisa, he admonished them to make it understood to the Lucchese in the most vigorous terms possible, that they could no longer offer, "so much as a glass of water" to the Pisans without incurring the wrath of the Florentine mercenary forces. He rewrote the dispatch several times, trying to make up with his threats and the harshness of his language for the sad lack of resolve in the troops and their commanders. Niccolo found himself shaking his head and muttering that this was no way to fight a war, when an excited Gonfaloniere Soderini burst in upon him.

"Niccolo, come quickly," shouted the big blond, abandoning his characteristic reserve that some confused with detachment and others construed as incompetence. "Pisa is ours!"

Niccolo looked up. "Don't tell me the illustrious armies have finally made a breakthrough," he said sardonically.

"No, nothing like that, not yet, but it doesn't matter. I've got a plan! A marvelous plan! A plan that will bring Pisa to her knees!"

Niccolo had learned to be wary of the gonfaloniere's "plans." Although Soderini was a more than competent administrator, noted for his honesty, fairness, and attention to detail, he exhibited a marked tendency to get carried away from time to time with big, extravagant "plans," which he devised and elaborated with the help of "experts" whom he consulted and by whom he was easily swayed. The present situation proved to be a case in point.

The two experts in question were ruminating and nodding gravely over piles of papers and charts when Niccolo entered the room. With a triumphant grin, Soderini introduced them as Signor Bruno and Signor Buffalmacco, military engineers.

Recalling his other recent encounters with "military engineers," Niccolo asked if they also sculpted, painted, and wrote poetry. Their silent, grave, faces said that they did not.

The enthusiastic Soderini shook his great blond head and fluttered excitedly around them and their diagrams, in as much as a big man can be said to flutter. "This is Niccolo Machiavelli, my trusted secretary, my confidant, my right arm. Tell him about the plan."

Bruno, or perhaps it was Buffalmacco, unrolled and spread a large sheet of paper before Niccolo for his inspection. In what looked at first like a child's drawing of a snake, Niccolo gradually discerned the course of the river Arno winding its way through the Tuscan countryside.

A bony finger came down on the site of Pisa near the river's mouth about ten miles from the sea. "This is the objective," announced Signor Bruno, or perhaps Buffalmacco, pompously. Niccolo settled in for a long presentation. Bruno and Buffalmacco took turns pedantically describing the strategic problems involved in the siege of Pisa, none of which was news to Niccolo.

"In conclusion," said one of the engineers, "we cannot effectively surround and cut the city off because of her position on the river. No matter what we do, she manages to slip in and out of our hands down that river."

Niccolo interrupted, "I've said before, with a bigger fleet, we can cut her off. But we need more ships to run an effective blockade, and ships cost money."

"These gentlemen have a more elegant solution," said the gonfaloniere, with his eyes shining.

"Precisely," said Bruno and Buffalmacco, producing another chart and laying it out for inspection. "What you propose, Messer Secretary, is tiresome, simpleminded, and expensive. What we propose is much more direct, more logical."

"And cheaper!" piped in the exuberant Soderini.

"Alright," said Niccolo. "What do the gentlemen propose?"

"Your untrained mind, Messer Secretary, unaccustomed to looking at all sides of the problem from an informed and rigorously scientific point of view, naturally seizes upon the most dismal and pedestrian solution to the problem. The two engineers exchanged smirks.

"What you overlook is that the Pisans need not only ships to get to the sea; they need something else as well. The river!" What we propose is denying them access to the river."

Niccolo objected, "The river runs right through the walls into the heart of the city. How can you keep them from the river?"

"By changing its course!" said the engineer triumphantly, stabbing at the map with his finger. Niccolo looked down in disbelief. The new map, an exercise in fantastic geography, showed a different Arno suddenly swerving south around Pisa and flowing into a large and previously nonexistent lake near Livorno.

"Imagine the consternation of the Pisans when they see their precious river suddenly disappear, suddenly turn into a deep and muddy ditch!" said Soderini. "Imagine!"

Niccolo ignored the effusions of the gonfaloniere and turned his attention on the two demigods of engineering who would alter the course of a river that had flowed undisturbed in her bed since the dawn of creation.

In a flurry of scientific enthusiasm, the engineers produced drawing after drawing of dams, earthworks, counterscarps, trenches, and systems of canals with sluice gates for taming and redirecting the flow of the mighty Arno. Undaunted, they brought out tables of calculations relating to every aspect of the unlikely project—elevations, rate of water flow, time tables, along with budget and manpower projections.

In the face of all this expertise, Niccolo was overwhelmed, but not convinced. His objections were dismissed as they were raised. The engineers finally procured Soderini's fervent endorsement by declaring that beyond the shadow of a doubt, the entire project could be successfully completed with a maximum of thirty or forty thousand man-hours of work. In other words, two thousand men might accomplish the task in fifteen days!

"Two thousand laborers will do in fifteen days what three thousand men-at-arms could not accomplish in several years!" said Soderini, already savoring the victory of science over nature and brute force. "Fifteen days! A miracle!"

Niccolo grunted. He did not believe in miracles. But belief is no prerequisite for carrying on with one's job, and so in the days that followed, Niccolo was charged with organizing the details of the mighty endeavor. The engineers, Bruno and Buffalmacco, left immediately for Pisa, eager to get a look at the actual lay of the land, since neither had ever been there before.

The work began on August 20. On September 3, fifteen days after the commencement, Niccolo received a report from Giacomini, the Florentine commissary who was coordinating things at the Pisan end. The miracle had not been accomplished in the allotted time. Giacomini, while declaring his continued readiness to do his duty and carry out the instructions he received from his superiors, expressed grave reservations as to the feasibility of the enormous project. Using no more sophisticated mathematical instruments than multiplication and long division, he showed in a simple series of calculations that in order to dig the two main canals five feet deep and twenty feet wide, approximately five hundred thousand square feet of soil would need to be excavated and removed. Almost apologetically, he concluded that it would take two thousand men not fifteen but at least two hundred days to get the job done. Bruno and Buffalmacco had miscalculated the length of the canals.

Undaunted, the two engineers redoubled their efforts, calling for more sappers to dig the trenches. In a frantic rush of enthusiasm, they began working around the clock, with shifts of men toiling on the excavations at night by torchlight. But as the days stretched out into weeks, nothing flowed into the trenches and canals but sweat and more money. In mid-September, Giacomini resigned in disgust. In his final letter to the Signoria, commenting on the hopelessness of the project, he said, "You will find that fresh difficulties arise each day."

The disillusioned Giacomini was quickly replaced by Tommaso Tosinghi, and the Ten of War, the official governmental body charged with the conduct of the works at Pisa, sent their trusted secretary, Niccolo Machiavelli, along with the new commissary to inspect the gigantic project and report back.

Niccolo and Tosinghi rode into the Florentine camp under the ramparts and walls of Pisa and, much to their surprise, found it deserted. There were supposed to be over three thousand armed men here, and the city was supposed to be surrounded and sealed off.

Niccolo accosted a passing belligerent and demanded to know what was going on. Where were the troops? The man stared up at him for a minute, a look of profound incomprehension on his swarthy, unshaven face. When Niccolo repeated his demand, the man let fly at him with a volley of curses—in Spanish.

Determined to get to the bottom of the mystery, Niccolo and Tosinghi pressed on until they located the commander's tent in the center of the camp. Inside, a card game was being conducted amid rude and blasphemous exchanges and slurred threats.

"Who's in charge here?" asked the irate secretary.

"Fuck you, Cap'n," was the insolent reply he received from a pasty-faced lieutenant in a language he could not even begin to fathom. The disheveled men returned to their game and paid him no attention.

"Where's your commander? Where's Colonna?" Niccolo demanded.

"Colon est la-bas avec touts les soldats aupres du fleuve."

At last, here someone who was willing to communicate, even if it was in French. Questioning the man, Niccolo discovered that Marcoantonio Colonna, a Roman and commander in chief of the Florentine troops, had removed almost the entire garrison to the site of the massive earth-moving operations, some ten miles to the north of the city.

"And he's abandoned the siege?" asked the incredulous Tosinghi, as he and Niccolo hurried off in that direction.

"Not exactly," said Niccolo. "According to the Frenchman, the Pisans began to mount sporadic attacks on the laborers up there. They were utterly defenseless, and so some of the troops had to be sent to stand guard over them. As the Pisan forays against the construction workers became more frequent, Colonna kept diverting more troops."

"And the siege?"

"See for yourself," said Niccolo, pointing to a spot on the far side of the river. Both Florentines watched as a large flat barge anchored there hoisted live sheep, wooden cages packed with squawking chickens, and sacks of grain up over the walls and into the eager arms of the defenders of the hungry city.

A little over an hour later, they rode furiously into the construction site past a half-dozen sleeping sentries. The commander in chief was in bed with a woman when they arrived and did not wish to be disturbed.

Barging in on the general's postprandial pleasure anyway, Niccolo elicited a groggy response to the effect that the engineers had demanded the protection of the soldiers so that the great work could go forward. Colonna said not to worry, because once the dam was complete Pisa would be finished anyway. And it would only take another week.

Niccolo was beside himself. Storming out of Colonna's tent, he saw the two experts responsible for the debacle. They were waving their arms excitedly and flapping their academic gowns like big, black crows perched on opposite ends of the rising breastworks behind their surveying equipment. Niccolo sent for them immediately and demanded an accounting. He did not even bother to give them good day. "You've spent over 14,000 florins already, and what have you got to show for it!"

The two men of learning shook their heads in disbelief at Niccolo's scientific naiveté. "We've run into unanticipated difficulties of a geological and hydrographical nature, or was it a geographical and hydrological nature? Ahem, at any rate, problems arose in the construction of the dam."

"And?"

"And we were forced to defer to the opinions of a colleague of ours as to the nature of these problems and their most expeditious solution." As if on cue, another black-clad expert appeared from behind the two principles. "This is Dottor Balonzon, of Bologna."

"What's the problem, Balonzon," said Niccolo irritably.

"Dottor Balonzon," corrected the pedant, raising his eyebrows in a dramatic gesture. "It seems that the silting behind the dam did not take place as projected . . ." The man prattled on. In spite of his anger, Niccolo had to stifle a laugh, for the grave doctor's face was all lumpy and swollen with red mosquito bites.

Here is what Niccolo was given to understand: Bruno and Buffalmacco had projected that, as the breastworks extended from the sides of the riverbanks toward a meeting place in the center, the river would begin to deposit large quantities of mud and silt against the rising walls, in effect building the dam herself against the bulwark as it went up. Just the opposite had happened. As the space between the two walls narrowed, the river was forced to flow into an ever-narrowing channel. The resultant increase in the rate of flow and the force of the water carved an even deeper channel. Instead of clogging herself up, the Arno was rapidly digging a canyon for herself and beginning to undermine the work already completed. Niccolo threw up his hands in despair, "What about the trenches and canals?" asked Niccolo. "Are they at least on schedule?"

"Ahem," said one of the sages through his welts. "The men have been recalcitrant and refuse to work."

"Why? Aren't they being paid?"

"Oh, yes, they're being paid and paid handsomely."

"Then what's the problem?"

"Well, it's a trifle really. You see they claim to have . . ."

"Have what? Speak up!"

"They claim to have contracted . . . ah, malaria, which is perfectly ridiculous . . ."

Niccolo clenched his fists and rolled his eyes heavenward. *"Putta del cielo!* What in God's name is going on here!" As he turned angrily to go and ascertain the condition of the laborers, the worthy Balonzon caught him by the sleeve. "Messer, my colleagues told me that I should take up with you the little matter of my stipend . . ." He never finished the sentence as Niccolo sent him sprawling to the ground in an undignified tangle of skinny limbs and professorial gowns.

As it turned out, malaria was rampant in the low-lying swampy areas where the canals were being carved out, and many of the workers had in fact succumbed. Many of those remaining were thinking of leaving. Niccolo stayed in the camp and, with Tosinghi, the new commissary, moved energetically to whip the workers and troops into some sort of order, but their efforts were too little, too late. By the end of the week, the rains began to fall and brought with them what Niccolo, writing back to the Signoria, could only call "fresh disasters."

The three ships hired to guard the coast were all lost in a storm. Money began to run short, and there was grumbling on the part of the mercenaries when the deathblow came. The onset of the rainy season produced a flash flood in which the foundation and breastworks of the dam were completely washed away. Niccolo stood under a dripping canopy and watched the scaffolding crack like matchsticks in the rush of the foaming water. The heavy boulders hauled and pushed and rolled into place with manpower and oxpower and horsepower tumbled over one another like papier-mâché stage props before the boiling fury of the river.

Over two months had elapsed since the beginning of the colossal labors. Extraordinary sums of money had been disbursed, and the republic, no longer able to pay her soldiers and condottieri, was forced to disband the army and lift the siege entirely. In late October, the works were finally abandoned. The trenches so laboriously eked out of the marshy ground at such great expense of both money and lives were gleefully filled in by the triumphant Pisans in a matter of days.

In the wake of the disastrous and costly Pisan experiment, Piero Soderini suffered his first serious loss of prestige, and his reputation as a cautious and prudent administrator was being called into question. Wearily, he set about raising more money to hire more troops to besiege the proud city at the mouth of the Arno. The solution to Florence's military problems and the successful resolution of the "Pisan affairs," however, was not to come from Soderini's fund-raising efforts but from a new and bold plan being formulated by his astute secretary.

Money Bread Men Iron

Niccolo wrote the four words across the top of a blank sheet of paper. That's what an army was. He understood that men and iron should be able to get money and bread, provided the men were properly trained and motivated. But Florence had taken the opposite approach, trusting that money could get bread, iron, and all the men she needed. It was all but an article of faith that wars were waged by hired captains and paid professional soldiers, by mercenary armies—and that was precisely where the problem lay.

The Florentine encampment before Pisa was a case in point. The men were insubordinate and surly. They were adventurers eager for loot but cautious in risking anything in actual battle. And who could blame them? They drew their pay regardless of whether or not they fought. Why take chances? If no results were achieved, why, their contracts would be renewed!

And if the enlisted men were less than enthusiastic partisans of Mars, the captains were even worse, even more addicted to bad faith and personal enrichment. "*Il pesce puzza da capo*—the fish stinks from the head down," thought Niccolo.

He stared at the four words he had written and drew a thick black circle around the key term in the equation:

Money Bread (Men) Iron

Niccolo recalled the motley appearance of the troops before Pisa. Each man had a different uniform in a different state of ragged disrepair. No identifiably human tongue was spoken among them. Animal grunts and shouts served to communicate most of their need and wants. Cursing was the only other lingua franca, and the curses rose in their belligerent throats in a half dozen different languages—Spanish and French and German—even Arabic. And every dialect of Italian was well represented, the most disreputable being the most frequently heard. What interest could these men possibly have in fighting for Florence? If the Pisans offered them more money—which often did happen—they were quick to change sides and do their gambling and grumbling and drinking on the other side of the lines of fire.

As long as the men fighting for the Florentine cause were nothing more than a collection of outcasts and profiteers, nothing would be accomplished. In the past few years, Niccolo had been slowly putting together ideas for an alternative kind of army. For inspiration and examples, he first looked to the north, to the loosely confederated German states and to the Swiss. The small German states were independent and defended their own interests, Germans fought for themselves. They were well armed, and as a consequence, free. The Swiss were very well armed and very free. Even the Pisans, constrained by necessity, had taken up arms in their own defense which, Niccolo had to admit, explained to a great extent, their stubborn refusal to surrender.

And then, of course, there were the Romans—*I miei Romani*, My Romans—as Niccolo had come to refer to them. They were stalwart models of everything that was good and honest and worthy of imitation in civic and military virtue. And in the Roman republic, only Romans fought in the army, Romans defending Rome and her interests, ordinary citizens, like Cinncinatus, leaving their farms in times of trouble to come to the defense of the republic. Why couldn't the Florentines do as much? And Niccolo's mind drifted into visions of disciplined Florentine troops, drawn up in smart and orderly formations, speaking, not Spanish or French, but the sweet Florentine dialect of Italian. He reached for his pen and began work on his proposal, writing slowly at first, but then with mounting speed and excitement. As his hand flew across the page, and as his ideas and arguments took shape, the Florentine militia was born.

It was an odd match of talent and ability to the task at hand. Niccolo was a secretary in the chancery, a man of letters, and had never received any formal military training. On the other hand, he was shrewd, was an avid reader and student, was something of a visionary, and was a zealot who pursued his ideas with an ardor and passion to which few men in the republic of Florence could lay claim. It was Niccolo's unique mix of qualifications and lack of experience that would lead to the subsequent triumphs and disasters of the Florentine militia.

He had little trouble persuading Soderini to allow him to begin incorporating an army of native-born Florentines. He presented the idea to the gonfaloniere as a big, new "plan," a novel approach to the ruinous and taxing problems of war and peace. For the next three years, Niccolo's prodigious energies would be dedicated almost exclusively to the formation and training of his army of honest patriots.

His work was divided primarily into two parts—working out the rules for the incorporation and governance of the militia, and actually recruiting and training the new citizen-soldiers. In this latter capacity, he was indefatigable, traveling tirelessly throughout Tuscany, enrolling infantry, distributing arms, studying camps and garrisons and fortifications, and supervising training exercises.

It was at one of the these early training exercises, under the hot noonday sun outside the walls of Florence that Niccolo had his first opportunity to put his military science into practice. He began by making a short inspirational speech to the assembled recruits.

"The infantry is the backbone of the army," he said proudly. "Through discipline and drill you will learn to be an infantry such as no other since the times of the Roman republic. Using the enlightened strategies of these very Romans, you will become an invincible bulwark to your republic, a shield against her enemies and the defenders of her sacrosanct liberty."

Having said this, Niccolo gathered the heads of the various companies and battalions around him and, using charts and drawings that he had made himself from descriptions and designs found in the old Roman historians, explained the first order of battle to them. They were going to practice a simple maneuver in which an army marching forward closes ranks and turns to meet an enemy approaching from the left flank. He spoke clearly and concisely, using the drawings to great advantage so that the essence of the maneuver was immediately clear to his subalterns. They returned to their companies and relayed his instructions to the men.

When the recruits were brought up in marching order, Niccolo gave the command to turn and close ranks. But instead of the *x*'s and *o*'s pivoting and drawing together in an orderly fashion into a solid block, and allowing the little *v*'s—the pikemen—to move from the head of the column to the left flank, chaos ensued.

Niccolo called the commanders together for another conference, and the maneuver was repeated with similar results. For over two hours, he kept the company there under the blazing sun, repeating the same maneuver, but the stalwart, patriotic butchers, bakers, and candlestick makers recently turned militiamen could not seem to master the thing.

Niccolo darted in and out of their ranks, explaining what the men were doing wrong and exhorting them to try harder, to try again. He emphasized the need for coordinated action, for precise timing, but still the men missed their cues and blundered into one another. When they had repeated the maneuver for perhaps the tenth time, it was clear that they had all finally mastered the difference between right and left and were moving in the desired direction, but their movements were anything but precise and coordinated. Beginning to feel the frustration and the heat, Niccolo nevertheless called upon the sweaty recruits to line up yet another time. He was determined to make a go of it. As he raised his arm in anticipation of giving the command, a loud peal of laughter rang out from behind him.

"Generalissimo! Buon di'," It was a lusty woman's voice that called out to him, and, spinning around, Niccolo saw the countess, Caterina Sforza.

"You don't mind if we watch?" she said. With the statuesque blond was her oldest son, Giovanni.

"You can watch, but I'm afraid there isn't much to see. This is their first day. They're a little inexperienced."

"They're inexperienced?"

As the bewildered troops milled about, awaiting the next order from their commander, Caterina came up alongside Niccolo. "Call it a day, Niccolo. It's hot. Let the poor dears go. Come on, we'll have lunch."

"I can't," he said stubbornly.

"Very well," she said. "You want to see them do it right? Giovanni, will you?"

The boy looked at Niccolo, and, receiving a begrudging nod, leapt to execute his mother's wish. He was a dashing black-clad lad of seventeen or eighteen years of age.

Caterina watched as her first-born strode confidently over to the rag-tag ranks and began issuing orders. "He's been in Milan with my first husband's family," she said. "Soldiering."

When Giovanni had the troops aligned to his satisfaction, he gave the signal and a great roar of drums exploded. As the drummers beat out their staccato rhythms, the young man barked his orders in time, and the men moved smartly. He put them through their paces, and with the thrill of drumbeats pounding in their hearts and limbs, they had no trouble marking time. When the maneuver was complete, the drums stopped and the men stood stiffly at attention. Giovanni beamed.

"He takes after his mother," acknowledged Niccolo.

"Lunch?"

33

Clogs

The Florentine peasant has clumsy shoes and a delicate mind.

—Proverb

On Niccolo's recommendation, the Signoria instituted a search for a professional military commander who would be able to instill discipline and the other martial virtues in the neophyte militia. Although he relinquished his active role in the hands-on training of the men, the secretary was still very much involved in other aspects of the militia, in particular, recruiting. He excelled at speaking to groups of skeptical farmers in the countryside, lauding the virtues and advantages of Florentine freedom and independence. It was seldom that after one of these stump speeches Niccolo was not surrounded by crowds of men, eager to enroll in the new people's army.

On one such occasion, however, speaking in a small farming village a few miles south of Florence, Niccolo had not succeeded in adding any names to his militia's roll. Frustrated and tired, he was wrapping up the heavy enrollment ledgers along with his writing materials and putting them into his saddlebags when he saw a man approaching him. He was a small, grizzled fellow whom Niccolo had remarked in the crowd, leaning against a barn, arms crossed defiantly on his chest. Niccolo was accustomed to these cynics—he saw them in every village—and paid him little mind.

"You make a great speech, sir, but it didn't do much good, did it?" said the man sarcastically.

"I'm sure," said Niccolo testily, stuffing the last of his belongings into the bags and pulling the straps tight. He was eager to be on his way and did not envision spending precious time arguing with a contentious bumpkin.

"Won't you stop for a drink to wash the dust out of your mouth? All those high-sounding words must have left you dry."

From the other side of his horse, Niccolo declined: "I have two more stops to make today, and it's already late. If you have some business you'd like to take up with me, please be brief."

"Business indeed! Brief indeed! You must be a very important gentleman," said the other, with exaggerated deference.

Ignoring him, Niccolo mounted his horse, took the reins, and prepared to ride off, but the man was standing in his way, blocking his path. He was standing there just grinning like a pernicious elf. "You weren't such an important gentleman the last time we met, Machiavelli," he said.

Niccolo took a long, hard look at his antagonist and, through the thick grey beard and hair and the wild, bushy eyebrows, he discerned the deep, crooked scar that cut across his forehead, through the blind eye and down his cheek like the number 7.

"*Madre di Dio!*" exclaimed Niccolo, nearly falling off his horse. "The Archbishop of Outlaws!"

Niccolo did accept the proffered drink after all, to renew his acquaintance with an old friend. After that fateful day many years ago, Niccolo had seen Michele several times, making the trip out into the countryside to enjoy his company. But his visits became less and less frequent as other interests and pursuits and friendships claimed more and more of his time. Finally, as two people living in different worlds are wont to do, they simply lost touch.

Now, almost twenty-five years later, comfortably ensconced in the shade of a grape arbor at the rear of a rural tavern, the two men talked. Michele seemed pleased with the progress Niccolo had made in the world, shaking his head judiciously as the younger man recounted how he had come to be on his present errand.

"And you, Michele?" said Niccolo. "Are you still the terror of the Tuscan countryside?"

"No," said the wizened little bandit, "too old for that kind of work. I keep to myself these days, tend my vines and my garden."

"And Cesca? Is she still the most lovely lady in the *contado*?"

"Dead," said Michele, staring into his wine cup. "It was a long time ago, almost ten years, in '95, when the armies came. The soldiers killed her."

"The French?" asked Niccolo.

"Maybe the French," said Michele bitterly. "Or our own. Italy was full of armies in '95, and soldiers are all the same."

Michele sighed. "I live with one of my sons now. I'm not much good for anything except telling stories of the old days to entertain my grandchildren."

"Nonsense," said Niccolo in an attempt to cheer his gloomy friend. "I bet you can still use a bow with the best of them! Why not join my militia! We can always use a good archer to train the recruits."

"My son, my idiot son," said Michele, shaking his head. "He'll probably want to run off and join your militia when he hears about it, but not me. Never."

"Why not?" asked Niccolo. "We'll enroll the two of you! Father and son!"

"Why not, indeed! What's there to fight for? What's there to defend?"

"Freedom!"

"Whose freedom?"

"Yours, mine, everyone's! The freedom and independence of the republic, of the Florentine people!" Niccolo was unconsciously slipping into his recruiting speech.

Michele noticed the escalation in rhetoric: "Save the oratory, Niccolo. I don't need a lesson in Florentine liberty."

"Maybe you do."

"No, maybe you do, my young friend," the outlaw fired back. "Maybe you can learn a thing or two from an old man."

"About what?" asked Niccolo suspiciously.

"About freedom and liberty and your republic!" said Michele. "And about betrayal."

Niccolo consented to listen and sat back. He was more than a little miffed that his old friend presumed to lecture him on what was, after all, his area of expertise. But he would let him have his say. For old time's sake.

Michele was grinning like a man holding all the cards as he began: "It happened a long time ago. Nobody knows how it started. Was there a single incident that sparked things? Or was it thousands of incidents, in thousands of places happening to generations of us, year in and year out, decade after decade? Nobody knows, but one day it exploded.

"It started with secret meetings, late at night. Speakers, not nearly as polished as you, but burning with anger, excited the crowds. Then one morning, the seething cauldron boiled over and sent a scalding torrent through the streets—the *Ciompi*. It was the beginning of the clothworkers' revolt.

"I know about the revolt of the Ciompi," said Niccolo. "A popular uprising that happened over a hundred years ago."

"That's right, a popular uprising!" said Michele. "Combers and carders, beaters, dyers, fullers, spinners, and menders. Out of the washhouses and stretching sheds they came and headed north across the river to the Signoria to demand their rights. Their ranks swelling as they went, they were joined by carters, boatmen, laborers, peddlers, and all the other wretched and dispossessed.

"They called them Ciompi because of the heavy clogs they wore in the washhouses." He eyed his young friend, "Have you ever worn a pair of clogs, or tried to walk in them?"

"Not I," said Niccolo, eyeing his smart, pointed, black boots.

"Clogs aren't made for moving around; they're made for standing still, or for moving one step in this direction, then one step back. They wear them in the washing houses to keep their feet dry. Not that anything keeps dry for long in the washing houses. You stand there for fourteen, sixteen hours a day, from sunup till sundown. As long as there's light to work. You stand in water up to your ankles, sometimes up to your knees. It's not terribly bad in the summer, the water will keep you cool, but your feet hurt from standing for so long, and the water swells them and makes it worse. But the winter is a killer, because the water is freezing and it seeps into your bones and makes them ache beyond what a man can endure. The rough wood of the clogs chafes at your wet, frozen feet, so that walking home is so painful you can't stand it and you're lucky to have a few lumps of coal to throw in the brazier to bring a little warm blood back into your blue, lifeless feet at the end of the day.

"Anyway, the Ciompi finally rose up. In their battered clogs, they went marching, clomping through the streets, not on their way to another man's war, but to their own. And do you know what standard they chose to march under, what banner they took as their own?

Niccolo said he didn't.

"The *gonfalone di giustizia*."

"Under the standard of justice, they marched to the Signoria and surrounded it. The Signori, the rulers, were terrified. One at a time, in various disguises, the cowards slipped out of the besieged building and vanished. The next morning, the people stormed the palazzo. Lowborn, dirty workers poured into the hallowed marble halls to claim what was rightfully theirs—Florence, and justice!

Michele paused and fixed his eye on Niccolo: 'The reason I know these things, Niccolo, is because I've heard them told again and again ever since I was a child. I've heard them told by people who were there. I've heard them told by men and women with fierce tears streaming down their faces. These were the things my people remembered. I don't think you'll find them written down in books. So listen.

"When the people took the palazzo, the standard of justice was in the rough hands of a common wool carder. That was my grandfather—Michele di Lando."

"Michele di Lando was your grandfather!" Niccolo was shocked. "The man who led the revolt of the Ciompi was your grandfather!"

"None other. The old outlaw continued his tale, "There he was, waving the banner of justice for everybody to see. Barefoot and dressed in rags, but with the symbol of justice clamped in his hands! How cool the marble steps must have felt under his bare feet! How good that banner must have felt in his hands!"

Michele, the grandson, stopped and was staring at his own hands. Not for the first time, he was imagining his grandfather holding the banner aloft on the steps of the Signoria. Justice for all within reach, its symbol in his hands.

"Barefoot?" asked Niccolo. "Where were his clogs?"

"Where were his clogs?" said Michele, coming back to attention. "Why, if he was at the head of the crowd, he must have kicked them off to keep moving faster. Or maybe he felt the need to throw the cursed things away, to rid himself of them forever.

"When the people took the Signoria, my grandfather turned to the shabby armies of the hopeless and abused and called for silence. 'You see,' he shouted, 'this palace is yours! And this city is in your hands!' Roars of triumph greeted his declaration.

"The multitude cried out spontaneously that Michele should

take the title of gonfaloniere and rule the city in their name. Can you believe it? In a few minutes, my grandfather went from a position of near slavery to the highest office in the city. Why him and not someone else? Perhaps his determination was greater. Or his indignation. A man with some modest talent for leadership, with some initiative, suddenly finds himself issuing orders. Who knows?

"Bowing to the will of the crowd, he accepted. A new hope was in the air, a promise of something better for those who had nothing, a promise that someone would finally listen to them. Michele moved quickly to consolidate the gains of their violent seizure of power. Reforms were instituted. He brought in good men, wise and experienced men known to be friends of the people. He summoned Salvestro de' Medici to help him rule. In those days, the Medici had a reputation as staunch defenders of the people."

"In those days," said Niccolo.

"My grandfather wasn't greedy or ambitious. He realized he couldn't manipulate the machinery of Florence's government and economy by himself. He couldn't even read! He had to have a secretary with him at all times. But he did everything he could to distribute honors and distinctions and power evenly, because he knew that envy and greed were the engines that drove the blacker hearts of Florence, and he would have to defend his fragile new order against them."

Niccolo knew the end was near, but not how near. "How long did he stay in power?" he inquired.

"About three years. But it started almost immediately. Some of the people felt cheated that Michele had agreed to share power with their former oppressors. They broke away and set up another government seat. Emboldened by the open struggles between factions, the guildsmen and the nobility filtered back into the city. They brought in mercenaries.

"Michele's government began to disintegrate. No matter what concessions he made, someone on another side was offended and took up arms. Representatives of the old ruling families and the guilds began to make their way back into the government, charging Michele's men with fraud and corruption. By treachery and force of arms, Florence's old masters recaptured the city. The experiment was over. And it failed."

"And what happened to your grandfather?"

"Gone, disappeared. Nobody ever knew. But you can guess.

"They say that the night before he was last seen, someone presented him with a silver goblet at dinner. It was full of dainty, delicate, sweet-smelling treats, but when he reached into the cup to take a handful and distribute them to the other guests, he felt something rough and cold. He pulled it out and held it up for all to see—a heavy, black iron nail. My grandfather sighed wearily, and said to his assembled company, 'I see someone is trying to tell me something. Either my enemies are making a threat, or some dear friend is giving me a fair warning. I want to believe it's the latter.' With that, he rose, left the table, and was never seen again.

"After his disappearance, only Salvestro de' Medici, himself in disgrace for having sided with the common people, had the courage to stand up and do my grandfather the honor he deserved. He praised his courage and his vision, and he heaped scorn on the heads of those who had used him so badly. But his words of praise were lost in the rush to discredit Michele di Lando, the wool carder, and to destroy his dangerous vision of a better city built under the sign of justice for all."

Having come to the end of his tale, Michele took a long drink and stared off into the red ball of the setting sun. Niccolo spoke, "I understand now why you're less than enthusiastic about my militia and the defense of Florence," said Niccolo, breaking the silence that had settled between them. "But you can't hold a grudge against the city forever."

"It's not a grudge but a realization of the way things are," said Michele. "An admission of the futility of things—not just the futility of serving in your militia, but of all your grand schemes for the republic, for freedom and justice for the people. What will it all come to in the end? Oppression and injustice. The people are fools to think it can be any other way."

"Didn't Jesus say, 'Blessed are those who hunger and thirst for justice, for they shall be satisfied'?"

"Blessed they may be, but they won't be satisfied until His second coming. They won't find their justice in this world, and they certainly won't find it in the republic of Florence."

"And you think there's a lesson in all this for me?"

Michele smiled a weary, understanding kind of smile. "*Chi ha orecchie, intenda*—He who has ears, let him hear."

"But Michele," pleaded Niccolo. "What the city did to your grandfather was over a hundred years ago. The republic we've built this time is different—stronger, based on laws and a constitution, on the consent and goodwill of the people—all the people. Nobody can overturn that now, reverse the progress we've made. And with the militia to defend us, Florence won't have to fear anyone, inside or outside the city. There's a new spirit, a new age. Things are different now! Things change!"

"Do they?"

Riding back into Florence through the Porta Romana and north toward the Signoria, Niccolo was tracing what he imagined to be the route taken by the rebellious clothworkers so many years ago. He could almost hear the low rumble from deep down in the stinking bowels of the city as it turned to a growl and rose in her throat. Finally, it issued from her mouth in a mad, anguished roar. He could hear the distant echoes of the heavy wooden clogs on the cobblestones. Thousands of feet battering the pavement, clattering, clamoring, clomping, a frenzied storm of wooden shoes with cleats and iron studs beating on the pavement. The heart of the city, worn out and long overburdened with too many cares, was throbbing violently, and suddenly it burst, and in a howl of liberation, sent a river of cleansing blood into the filthy streets.

Then the reign of justice was announced. The wheel of fortune was spinning madly then, wildly out of control. And in that madness, she had plucked a wool carder from the crowd and placed him at the top of the world. But Fortune was quick to recover the regular motions of her ever-spinning wheel, her endless circles. And if she catapulted the obscure Michele di Lando to the very summit, it was only to begin again her long, inexorable spin, downward, to the bottom.

The wheel spun on in Niccolo's imagination. On it, he saw a tiny representation of Michele di Lando, bearded and bristling with thick dark hair, not unlike his grandson. And as Michele's image spun laboriously up and then precipitously downward, other faces appeared on the wheel. Niccolo saw the rise and inevitable fall of Caesar Borgia and Charles VIII of France. He saw emperors and kings and popes, all spinning round and round, up and down. Then he tried to shake the image from his mind.

It was absurd, fatalistic, childish. It was an outmoded notion, based on the superstitions of the past and the poets' lore, based on the cringing inevitability and fatalism of the Dark Ages. His was an era of light, of striving and human achievement, of progress.

Still, he could not ignore the lesson of what happened to Michele di Lando. But that was just the point! He wasn't ignoring it. He was thinking about it, trying to understand where Michele had gone wrong, what he should have done to hold onto the power that was thrust upon him. If his old friend the outlaw had told him the story as a cautionary tale, to warn him off, to convince him of the futility of his endeavors, then he had failed! The tale only served as a prick and a goad to Niccolo. If one reformer failed, then the next one would learn from his mistakes and not repeat them. Wasn't that what the study of history was for? And wasn't that what the present republic was doing? Consolidating its power? Strengthening its institutions? Providing for its defense with the militia? Learning from the mistakes of the past?

Niccolo felt relieved that he had worked through the dilemma posed by Michele's story. He felt sorry, though, that there was nothing he could do about his old friend's resignation and his pessimism. But as he rode across the Piazza della Signoria, another thought jolted him. It was the thought of the rise and fall of another republican reformer, another champion of justice, one who had ended his career right here in this very piazza. And in the back of Niccolo's mind, the creaky wheel began to spin slowly again. The face on it this time was Savonarola's.

Niccolo stopped by the Signoria to deposit the ledgers and make a quick report to Soderini on the progress of his recruiting efforts. Bone-tired and with much on his mind, he made a hasty deposition for the benefit of the implacable gonfaloniere and then, promising to do the requisite paperwork the next day, begged to be excused.

"Fine, fine," the tall blond waved him away. "Get some sleep. Take a day off, if you wish."

But as Niccolo was turning to go, Soderini called him back. "I almost forgot. We found somebody for your militia."

Forgetting his fatigue, Niccolo quickly brightened. "For the training?"

"Yes, for the training. He's a consummate military man. Comes highly recommended. Has a reputation for being able to turn raw recruits into fighting machines in no time. The Council of Eighty has already approved the appointment. Gave him the title, captain of the guard."

"Who is it?"

"Gentleman by the name of Coriglia."

"Florentine?"

"Claims to be. At any rate, several members of the council vouch for him. They say they've worked with him before."

"When do I meet him?"

"Right now, if you want. I gave him the office next to yours, since you two will be working so closely together on this thing. I think he's still there. Why don't you drop in on him before you go home?"

"Excellent idea," said Niccolo briskly. "Well, good night, sir."

With a peremptory knock, Niccolo opened the door without waiting for a response and announced himself, "Coriglia, Machiavelli here. I wanted to catch you before you left for the day."

The little man behind the desk in the unprepossessing black gown stared up at him, somewhat surprised by the abrupt entrance.

Niccolo gasped audibly. "You!" The new captain of the guard, Coriglia, was none other than Don Micheletto, Caesar Borgia's former second-in-command. Caesar Borgia's former hangman.

Michele Coriglia, Don Micheletto, waited patiently for the initial shock of recognition to pass. The indulgent smile never left his kind, wrinkled old face.

"Well, we've met before, haven't we," said Niccolo, managing to recover a little.

Don Micheletto smiled his angelic smile, "Yessssss, we have, haven't we?" he hissed. "Many timessssssss."

34

The Black Death Spawns a Family Fortune; Niccolo Goes to Germany and Suffers Abdominal Pains

This pestilence was so powerful that it was transmitted to the healthy by contact with the sick, the way a fire close to dry or oily things will set them aflame. . . . The plague was of such virulence in spreading from one person to another that not only did it pass from one man to the next, but, what's more, it was often transmitted from the garments of a sick or dead man to animals that not only became contaminated by the disease but also died within a brief period of time. My own eyes were witness to such a thing one day: when the rags of a poor man who died of this disease were thrown into the public street, two pigs came upon them, and as they are wont to do, first with their snouts and then with their teeth they took the rags and shook them around and within a short time, after a number of convulsions, both pigs fell dead upon the ill-fated rags, as if they had been poisoned.

—Boccaccio, *The Decameron*

Whether we believe Boccaccio's eyewitness account of the vehemence of the plague, and the hideous speed with which it could spread and kill, his views must be taken into account if we are to understand the terror that this disease inspired in the men of his times. Boccaccio was not alone in his exaggerated fears of contamination, and the tales he propagated were representative of the very real fears of a population held hostage by a dreaded, inexplicable disease, for which there was no cure and from which there was no escape. The Black Death, so called, some said, for a black comet that appeared in the sky to announce its arrival, engendered many tales, many explanations. In Sicily, a black dog bearing a sword in his paws and gnashing his teeth attacked a sacred procession to herald the impending doom of the island. In Germany, it was a man on a black horse, in France, a black giant striding through the countryside at night.

Others, of a more scientific bent, called it the Black Death because of the livid black patches that discolored the skin of the victims, shortly prior to their inevitable demise. The first signs of infection were the swellings or buboes—hence the designation bubonic plague—that appeared in the groin and armpits. These painful excrescences quickly grew to the size of an egg or an apple and spread indiscriminately over every part of the body. Secondary symptoms include fever and the coughing up of copious amounts of blood. Everything that exudes from the body of a victim of the plague from that point onward gives off an unbearable stench—sweat, excrement, spittle, even the breath is fetid and overpowering. The urine turns black and red. Within three to five excruciating days, death follows.

Because everything about the disease was so disgusting, its victims became objects of revulsion more than pity. Those suffering the most hideously often found themselves abandoned by family and friends alike. The bodies of the dead either lay in their houses and rotted, or thanks to the offices of a terrified relative or servant, were thrown into the streets and piled up there to rot.

How did the disease spread? How did it manage to engulf all of Europe in so short a time? Many blamed it on a miasmic cloud, a corruption of the very air with putrid fumes. These fumes were said to have arisen from the bowels of the earth itself, set free by a gigantic, shattering earthquake. Others attributed the original poisoning of the atmosphere to a peculiar and deadly alignment of the planets. It is a curious tribute to the eternal, nefarious ingenuity of man that, acting quickly to take advantage of the deadly properties of this supposedly infected air, many enterprising individuals went so far as to risk filling flasks and bladders with the vapors. Later they would attempt to sell this lethal concoction or use it to visit destruction on their enemies. Such is the boundless, never-failing capacity of the human race to harness and turn to their own advantage or profit the malevolent forces that nature provides and our own genius exploits.

Not that this horrible contagion brought out only the worst in man. Brutality, selfishness, and the ruthless desertion of the dying were only one side of the story, and many chroniclers have overlooked the selfless devotion of doctors and nuns and priests in seeking to comfort the sick and alleviate their suffering. And perhaps nowhere in Europe were their efforts more outstanding and more worthy of commendation than in Florence. Here, the civic administration was nothing short of heroic in its early attempts to stem the tide of the noxious disease. Provisions were made for public hospitals and infirmaries to receive the sick at the first sign of infection, in the hope of containing the spread of the disease and further, rampant contamination.

Despite all her protective and humanitarian efforts, however, Florence was destined to fall beneath the scythe of grim reaper. The density of her population and her position as the preeminent trading city of southern Europe virtually assured it, for, although it was not remarked at the time, the progress of the plague raging through Europe followed a very specific path—the path of trade.

The bacterium that we now know caused the Black Death came from Asia or the Mideast in the stomach of a flea. From there it passed into the bloodstream of an animal—the black rat. For reasons of drought or flood, these rats were forced to migrate from the hills where they lived, and some turned up in seacoast towns, where eventually they found their way on board Genoese and Venetian trading vessels bound for Europe. Sailors were contaminated en route. As the sailors signed on board other ships bound for other ports, they took the plague with them. As cargo was crated and transferred to barges and vehicles for overland conveyance, the rats with their fleas nestled between the crates, in the barrels and bales and boxes. And Florence, whose merchants imported enormous quantities of goods from all over the world, began to import this tainted cargo as well. Death streamed into the city.

As the disease spread and it became clear that it was out of control, those who were able to do so left the city. More and more administrators and leaders fled; of those who refused to do so, many died. Everywhere there were dead rats, thousands of rats, but nobody noticed them, because everything was dead and dying—horses, pigs, chickens, dogs, and cats, and of course, men, women, and children. Before it was over, sixty-five thousand people would die. The plague spared no one. Order began to break down, and putrid corpses piled up in the streets. Chaos ensued, and the sinister *becchini* made their first appearance.

These *becchini*, or gravediggers, were engaged to remove the stinking bodies to the mass graves that were prepared for them in the cemeteries and other open spaces in the city. In general, they were depraved and brutal men who had long since resigned themselves to their own inevitable, grisly deaths. But in the meantime, they had decided to enjoy themselves in drunken, heedless orgies of debauchery and depravity, until that fateful day arrived. At first they were content with the exorbitant fees they extracted from the commune and from private households to cart the infected dead away. But they quickly turned to robbery, looting, and extortion as ways of increasing their short, doomed pleasures. Rape and the threat of rape added to their enjoyment, as did murder and a host of other unspeakable crimes.

These events involving the devastation of Florence took place many years before the time of our story, but are not without relevance to it, for it is in the vile, stinking sink of the plague that Don Micheletto has his roots. Among the most notorious and feared of the infamous *becchini* was one named Coriglia, Don Micheletto's grandfather.

Coriglia was a gravedigger by profession and managed to make a mean, but adequate, living by selling the bodies and parts of bodies turned over to him for disposal. His customers were artists and scientists who were eager to conduct clandestine anatomical investigations to further their knowledge of their respective disciplines. When the plague struck, Coriglia sensed a windfall and was one of the first to volunteer for the gruesome detail of removing the bodies of the dead. He was also one of the most blasphemous, reckless, and defiant in the execution of his duties, and it came as no surprise that he was one of the first to succumb to the disease. But in the case of the gravedigger Coriglia, something rare, something almost miraculous happened. He did not die. He recovered. At the end of five days, he was still alive, and the boils and buboes began to burst. The noxious pus leaked out of him, and with it the virulence of the disease. At the end of a week, he was on his feet, disfigured, scarred for life, but very much alive, and more important, immune to the disease. The fortunes of the Coriglia family had just taken a dramatic swing upward.

Grandfather Coriglia's criminal instincts were still at the early stages of development, so he began modestly, by breaking into the houses of those not yet sick and threatening to drag them out into the streets and infect them. When they paid for his protection, he left them alone. Then, he quickly moved on to more-profitable undertakings. He seized a fine deserted house and made it his own. He organized marauding bands to find and appropriate what wealth was still left in the city.

When he had thus accumulated enough capital, he went into legitimate business. If he noticed that linen for shrouds was in short supply, and it always was, he bought up all the linen he could find—or stole it—and charged outrageous prices for it. Likewise, he managed to grab and accumulate food and medicine, which he also sold at grotesquely inflated prices. By the time the danger of the plague was past and Florentines in exile began to filter back into the city, Coriglia was one of the wealthiest men in Florence. Although his ill-gotten gains did not serve to advance him socially, his reputation for unscrupulousness soon made him an intimate of a number of powerful and notable families. When there was work to be done of an unpleasant or dubious nature, the services of Coriglia were eagerly sought out and, indeed, were often deemed indispensable.

As in respectable families of honest tradesmen, Coriglia trained his son in the crafts that had brought him so much success, and that son in turn passed on the family secrets to his son—Michele.

Michele Coriglia became Don Micheletto when he took up service with Caesar Borgia. Before that, he was attached in various unsavory capacities, as we have seen, to one of Florence's leading families—the Medici. When they were driven into exile, Don Micheletto went with them, eventually gravitating to the Borgia as the kind of family who could use his peculiar talents and who were able and willing to pay for them.

When Caesar Borgia left Italy in disgrace, Don Micheletto was briefly detained and imprisoned by Pope Julius II, but then released at the insistence of ten cardinals who interceded on his behalf. Unwilling to tempt fate and remain too long in the hands of the mercurial new pope, Don Micheletto headed north, back to his native Tuscany, back to Florence. His sudden reappearance after a ten-year absence went largely unremarked by Florentine officials preoccupied with their long, drawn-out struggle with neighboring Pisa, but in certain quarters Don Micheletto was well received, very well received. His friendship was cultivated, his interests looked after, and, when the position of captain of the guard of the new militia was created, the wheels of intrigue, long rusty, began to turn again, and his name was advanced.

Mild opposition to Don Micheletto's appointment in the Council of Eighty, based on his association with the Borgia and his reputation for atrocity was overruled. It was pointed out that, after all, he had been found guilty of no crime and been made a free man by no less an infallible judge than the pope himself, who had the power to bind and loose on earth as well as in heaven.

On the occasion of that traumatic initial meeting, Niccolo had virtually fled Don Michele's presence in confusion and disarray, muttering a feeble and incoherent excuse. Even for the seasoned diplomat and confident dissembler, the double emotional shock had been too much to absorb all at once. Niccolo needed time to sort out the conflicts and the implications.

As Soderini had suggested, Niccolo took the next day off. Not anxious to begin working hand-in-glove with the grim reaper himself, he was nevertheless not idle. He made discreet inquiries and pieced together much of the above related history of the Coriglia clan. These fresh discoveries brought him little consolation.

How could such a man, steeped in the ignominy of three generations of evil, how could such a black-hearted, reprobate, such a vile and bloodthirsty creature, hateful in the eyes of God and man alike, be selected to train the virgin militia? Niccolo's militia! Whose idea was it?

Wheedling what information he could out of carefully selected colleagues in the chancery, Niccolo learned that Don Micheletto's name had originally been put forward by a loose affiliation of young and relatively unknown representatives from obscure quarters and neighborhoods, who were loosely associated with families loosely attached to some of the more ancient and honorable interests and names in Florence. "Well, that explains exactly nothing," he thought.

Wherever Don Micheletto's nomination originated, however, one thing was clear—that it had rapidly gained general acceptance. Everywhere Niccolo went, he received the same bland assurances. When his record was examined from a strictly military point of view, almost everyone was willing to admit, however grudgingly, that Don Micheletto was the right man for the job. In his heart, Niccolo knew it too, despite the waves of revulsion that rolled over him every time he thought about the bloody mark this man had left upon the world.

In Romagna, when Niccolo was engaged in the endless, maddening negotiations with Borgia, he had many times been witness to Don Micheletto's military prowess. He had seen him drill units that moved in solid, fearless, confident blocks. He had seen him take towns and villages with half the number of men an ordinary commander might have employed. And he had remarked Borgia's near total confidence in him.

Caesar often bragged that his most elite corps were made up of men picked up in the countryside, neither mercenaries nor professional soldiers. But once subjected to the rigorous and demanding discipline of Don Micheletto, they were the equal of any fighting force on the continent. Niccolo had to acknowledge the truth of these allegations. Despite his other shortcoming and miscalculations, Caesar Borgia, with Don Micheletto as his second-in-command, had never been dealt a defeat on the field of battle.

But Niccolo still had doubts. Would Don Micheletto contaminate the troops he was assigned to train? How could a man so tainted and corrupt not infect everything he came into contact with? Was it safe to commit the militia and the future of Florentine liberty into the hands of a moral monster?

Eventually, Niccolo reached a conclusion, a tentative conclusion. His wavering and intermittent attacks of conscience gave way to a kind of grim determination. Ultimately, there was only one really important question, only one overriding priority—the survival of the republic. If Don Micheletto could train its militia to become half as effective a fighting force as Borgia's army, then so be it. The Lord moves in mysterious ways. Don Micheletto would be given his chance. But Niccolo knew that he would bear careful watching and constant scrutiny. "One false step," he told himself, "and the axe falls on Michele Coriglia." Niccolo preferred not to think of it as nourishing a viper in his breast. He preferred to think of it as rendering a service to the republic and keeping the dangerous man close at hand where he could be watched.

But having resolved his dilemma, Niccolo realized he had resolved nothing at all, for one burning question remained. If he had been able, for the time being, to reconcile the interests of the republic with those of Don Micheletto, he could perform no such feat of prestidigitation when it came to Giuditta. He could not escape the fact that he was harboring her father's murderer.

What would happen if he told her? Would she insist on taking her revenge? No one could argue that Don Micheletto did not deserve it. But would she be able to do it? And what would happen to her if she did? Her act of vengeance could very well prove to be one of self-annihilation.

Niccolo rationalized that he would say nothing to Giuditta—not yet, anyway. He was doing it for her own good, both to avoid the pain it would cause her to know her father's assassin was still alive and to avoid the possible harm she could bring down upon herself if she attempted to get to him. He was protecting her. It was the only responsible thing to do. He was doing it for her own good. Still, for all his good intentions, in his heart of hearts, he knew one thing, and that knowledge would not go away. He knew that he was wrong. He knew that it was not his decision to make.

He also tried to shake off the memory of something she once said to him, "If you had to choose between me and that republic of yours, which one would you choose?" He had to keep reminding himself that he had not chosen, that he had betrayed no one. Not yet.

Although Niccolo shrank from actual physical contact with Don Micheletto, the captain of the guards was never far from his thoughts and never far out of his sight. Whatever Niccolo's feelings toward the man he regarded as a blight and a moral monster, one thing was clear beyond the shadow of a doubt—the militia under his supervision was shaping up rapidly into a formidable armed force.

As Niccolo was going over a series of letters to the podestas and mayors of the outlying villages instructing them to forward muster rolls of all able-bodied men in their districts, he was distracted by a tentative sort of shuffling in front of his desk. A boy of about eighteen, looking slightly out of place and ill at ease in a rustic cloak, was standing in front of him, twisting his cloth cap nervously in his hands. He looked vaguely familiar, but Niccolo could not place him immediately.

"What can I do for you?" said the secretary in a tone calculated to put the boy at ease.

"I have a letter for you." And so saying, he handed it over.

Niccolo looked at the rather large, inelegant script on the letter addressed to him. It was not a hand with which he was familiar. Opening it, he read the short injunction:

> Maybe times do change. I don't know. This is my boy. I'm sending him to you. Teach him to fight. And Machiavelli, teach him what it is he's fighting for.
>
> Michele di Lando

Niccolo looked up. "What's your name?"

"Salvestro, sir."

Piero Soderini was waiting for him when he got back. The gonfaloniere was pacing with his hands clenched behind his back. "There's trouble, Niccolo, I need you."

"To do what?"

"To go to Germany."

"Germany! No! We're not going to go through all that again, are we?"

"It's already settled and cleared with the Great Council."

"Oh, now the Great Council approves of me, does it?" said Niccolo sarcastically. "When you wanted to send me to Germany two months ago, I remember they called me your 'little puppet' and 'the gonfaloniere's personal errand boy.'"

Soderini winced. "Some are still grumbling and calling you my puppet and personal errand boy, but you're going to Germany anyway."

The grumblings referred to by Soderini had been going on for quite some time, but of late they had grown appreciably louder. There were those who were jealous of the gonfaloniere and grumbled that he was usurping too much power, even though his every move had to be studied, deliberated over, and approved by a bewildering array of committees, councils, and legislative bodies. There were those of Florence's finest and most ancient families who grumbled that too many "new men" had made their way into the government and that men of less than exalted birth had managed to acquire undue influence over the gonfaloniere. They grumbled that Soderini deliberately ignored the citizens of higher standing and courted the more vulgar elements in the population as a way of maintaining his position of power. Still others, of a more imaginative bent, grumbled that Soderini was training the militia to act as his own private army and that he intended to use it to set himself up as tyrant and absolute ruler. Needless to say, in the course of these dissatisfied and jealous grumblings, the name of Soderini's most trusted secretary, Niccolo Machiavelli, came up frequently.

Two months previously, when the German emperor Maximillian had demanded an ambassador be sent to him from Florence, Soderini had naturally turned to Niccolo as his obvious choice. But the grumblings ensued, grew quite raucous, and finally Francesco Vettori, a man of impeccable background and lineage, was elected to the post.

"And what has the illustrious Vettori been up to in Germany? Is he having trouble handling the republic's affairs?" asked Niccolo.

"Vettori's made a balls of everything," sighed the gonfaloniere.

"What's he done?" said Niccolo, amused now.

"You know about Maximillian's fantasy. Even though nobody pays him much attention, even in his own realm, he now styles himself Holy Roman Emperor."

"*Dio ci guardi!*" said Niccolo. "God save us! Not another one."

"Yes, another emperor," said Soderini. "He intends to take Constantinople back from the Turks and establish universal Christian rule over all of Europe."

"The usual imperial agenda," said Niccolo, thinking of Charles VIII of France and of Borgia. "So what does he want from us?"

"Money."

"How much?"

"Five hundred thousand ducats."

Niccolo burst out laughing. Soderini too, smiled at the absurdly high figure. The gonfaloniere continued, "Since he's going to be Holy Roman Emperor, he insists on coming to Rome to be crowned. He's asking us for the five hundred thousand ducats to help defer some of the costs of his coronation. He says it would be a sign of good faith for us to cooperate."

"And what does Vettori advise?"

"He thinks we should pay and wants me to send the money."

Again, Niccolo burst into laughter. But within the week, he was on his way to Germany.

The Germany of the time was not a strong and unified nation state, like France, but a loose confederation of staunchly individualistic and independent states. The Emperor Maximillian, although he dreamed large dreams, was scarcely capable of controlling the rambunctious cities and towns in his own reputed territory, let alone extending his domains. He was in constant need of money and troops and yet was already at war with France and Venice, and doing poorly on both fronts. Undaunted by reality, he fancied himself the last of the knights errant and the true heir of Charlemagne. And he did not stop there. So far-fetched and fantastic were his dreams that he even harbored a secret desire, once he was crowned emperor, to make himself pope as well! It was to this man, imbued with medieval dreams of empire, but described by his contemporaries as, "on board ship with a scant store of biscuits," that Niccolo was now sent.

The details of the actual legation were all too familiar. The emperor demanded 500,000 ducats. Florence was prepared to pay, but would need time to raise such an enormous sum. The emperor would accept a down payment of 50,000. Niccolo assured him that 20,000 were already on their way. . . . So it went. Compared to dealing with Caesar Borgia, it was child's play.

Niccolo followed the itinerant emperor throughout his far-flung domains. In his dispatches, he complained bitterly of the cold, the snow, and the despicable condition of the inns where the travelers were lodged under one roof with the animals and where they slept in great, stuffy overheated rooms smelling of straw and horse shit. He complained too, of the lack of decent wine and food and the insufferable quantities of beer and greasy sausages he was therefore compelled to consume. He even complained that the Germans were poorly dressed. But despite the many faults he found with his northern neighbors, Niccolo was also aware of their genius for military organization. As he traveled from town to town in Germany and then through the cantons of Switzerland, he was impressed with the discipline of the fighting units and the thoroughness of their military training. His letters were filled with the most minute observations, and in studying these small, but sturdy, republics maintained by their own strength, Niccolo derived many a fruitful lesson and many a prescription for the fledgling Florentine militia. All this, he duly set down in writing and forwarded to his superiors.

After several months of back-and-forth travel across Germany and give-and-take at the bargaining table, Niccolo had followed Maximillian to Cadore where he was facing the hostile forces of Venice. When the emperor realized he was out of money, he impulsively flew back to Innsbruck to pawn what jewels he had left in order to continue the war. He foolishly left his armies waiting for him at Cadore, and it was not long before the leaderless troops, left to fend for themselves, were slaughtered by the Venetians. The threat posed by Maximillian, always feeble, now simply evaporated, and the glorious emperor himself went into hiding. Niccolo's legation came to an end, but he did not leave Innsbruck for quite some time. He was gravely ill.

From his first days in Germany, he had feared that the diet that was forced upon him would do him some serious harm. His well-regulated digestion was not prepared for it. The food was too heavy. He was rarely able to get wine to stimulate his digestive juices. His sweat and urine smelled different. His stools looked funny, and the consistency was all wrong. He ate less and less.

One night in Innsbruck, shortly after the emperor's disappearance, he was feeling slightly sick to his stomach. Going to bed, he dismissed it as the usual bloated discomfort caused by the beer and the sausages that always sat like lead in his belly. In the middle of the night, however, he was awakened by shooting, stabbing pains. He found himself too weak and too delirious to move, and as his stomach contracted and convulsed, he vomited over the side of the bed. Afterward, he lay back, shivering and feverish, clutching the dirty, sweat-soaked sheets around his neck, and staring vacantly, only half-conscious at the ceiling.

Morning found him little better, although a maid did clean up the mess he made on the floor during the night. For several days, he did not leave his bed, and even after the fever broke, Niccolo remained incapacitated by the dreadful, sharp pains in his stomach. He could hold nothing down save a little weak, lukewarm broth.

In a shaky hand, he informed Soderini and the Signoria of his predicament, and for over two weeks, they heard nothing further from him. Convinced that the dismal climate and diet were responsible for his illness, Niccolo was determined to leave Innsbruck as soon as possible. Feeling somewhat better, but still unable to ride, he decided to make the journey home by hired coach. Undertaken prematurely, the trip through cold, narrow mountain passes along bumpy roads did his failing health little good and further depleted his already low resistance. When Niccolo arrived at Bologna, he was feverish again. He was only dimly aware of the last, jostling leg of the trip and was unconscious by the time he reached Florence.

For several days, he slipped in and out of a tortured, uneasy sleep. He was troubled by blinding headaches, the light hurt his eyes, and his back ached. Haunted by nightmares, he thrashed in his sleep. Awake, he was too weak to move. When he finally came to himself and looked around, it took him awhile to realize that he was back home and in his own bedroom. He became aware of the fact that someone was in the room with him. Someone was humming.

Propping himself up on one elbow and making a mighty effort to bring his bleary eyes into focus, he discerned the outlines of a woman—his one and only domestic servant, bequeathed him by his father. Weakly, he called out to her, "Emilia."

"*Eh, finalmente!* At last!" The bright, almost-musical voice was not that of the ancient serving woman, who was in the habit of gasping and cackling when constrained to communicate verbally.

"Who's that?" asked Niccolo, although he was too debilitated to really care.

"Don't you recognize me?"

"Giuditta?" stammered Niccolo in disbelief.

She touched his forehead with a soft hand. It was so cool to the touch. Gently but firmly, she pushed him pack into the pillows. "Yes, it's me."

"But how . . . why? . . . when?" Niccolo was confused.

"Don't try to talk. Just rest now," she said soothingly.

Collecting himself for another sally at understanding, Niccolo asked feebly, "How long have you been here?"

"A couple of days."

"How did you know I was . . ."

"Caterina told me. Ssssshhhhh, now."

"I can't believe you came . . . I . . . Was it that serious?"

"Niccolo, someone tried to poison you."

35

The War with Pisa 2

Corruption in High Places

Niccolo was sitting up in bed now, sipping a broth with eggs swirled into it. The pangs in his stomach had subsided, and the muscular aches in his back and neck were easing up. "What makes you so sure it was poison?"

"When we administered the antidote, you responded."

"It could have been coincidental. Maybe I would have pulled out of it on my own."

"Maybe not. When Caterina sent for me, you were *in extremis*. She tried a few concoctions but nothing seemed to work."

"And you . . . ?"

"Saved your life," affirmed Giuditta.

"You're absolutely sure it was poison?" said Niccolo, not wanting to believe he was the object of an attempted assassination.

"Tell me again what happened."

Niccolo described his symptoms.

"And where was that?"

"At Innsbruck."

"How long were you there before the night you got sick?"

"About two weeks."

"And you weren't eating anything except sausages and drinking beer?"

Niccolo thought for a minute. "Wait, as a matter of fact, I was. At Innsbruck they seemed to have plenty of eggs. I was glad for the change. I ate a lot of eggs."

"Eggs! I knew it!" said Giuditta triumphantly. "Eggs are the base for making *venenum atterminatum*."

"Which is?"

"A slow-acting poison that takes effect over a period of time—usually about two weeks. It's more difficult to pinpoint when and where it was administered that way. And the symptoms are the same as those of a bad fever."

"*Affogaggine!*" whistled Niccolo.

"What probably happened was that you didn't quite get a lethal dose the first time. You got sick but recovered. They must have slipped you another dose just before you left. You say you started getting sick again on your way back?"

"Crossing the mountains. Yes, it was the cold and the damp. But you just said the symptoms of poisoning were the same as those of a bad fever. Couldn't I just have had a bad fever?"

Giuditta smiled and took Niccolo's hand. "You want proof? Look," she said, running a finger across his fingernails.

He looked at his fingernails. They were a little longer than usual and needed paring.

"Do you see anything different?"

Niccolo moved his hand closer to the lamp burning at the bedside. On each nail, about half an inch up from the cuticle, he could see a thin purple line that had never been there before. "The line?" he said. "What is it?"

"The signature of the poison."

Giuditta's hypothesis that two attempts had been made on Niccolo's life was confirmed by the emergence of another thin, telltale purple line etched across his fingernails. At her insistence, he began to dine almost exclusively at home. When he went out, he took his own wine in sealed flasks.

One spring afternoon, he returned home in particularly high spirits, toting a cumbersome sack on his shoulder. Giuditta was waiting for him, as she had been for the past month or so. No one had said anything about the length of her stay, but then, no one had broached the topic of her leaving, either. Thoughts of her going back to Rome troubled Niccolo, but he didn't dare ask her what she was thinking, for fear she might announce her imminent departure.

"What's in the sack? You look like an itinerant peddler."

Niccolo's eyes glowed. "It's spring and in the spring, a young man's fancy turns to . . ." He upended the sack as he spoke—"Artichokes!" He shook it, and the tender, young, green-and-purple chokes tumbled out onto the table.

"I'll fry them whole," said Giuditta, delighted. "I'll make them for you the way the Jews do in Rome. You'll love it."

Niccolo did indeed love it, and that evening he managed to eat three of the crisp, blackened, deep-fried artichokes. After demolishing the better part of a roasted rack of spring lamb, he sat back, almost too full to move. He drank, perhaps a little more than usual, because he was nervous. He had to speak to Giuditta. It was not a big matter, but anything that might disturb the delicate equilibrium of the present and alter the unspoken agreements between them was cause for concern.

"I have to go to Pisa," he said abruptly.

Giuditta eyed him curiously. "With your militia?"

"It's the first time they're going to be tested in the field. After all the drilling and training, we're finally going to see them in action. Don . . . , ah, ah, the captain of the guard has already left with two companies of men to take up positions. They won't go into action until I get there." He stumbled on the name of Don Micheletto, unwilling to even pronounce it aloud in Giuditta's presence.

"I always knew you'd leave me for the militia," she said noncommittally.

"It'll only be for a few days, and I really do have to be there. I was wondering . . ."

"If I'll be here when you get back?" She finished the sentence for him.

"Well?"

"Well . . ." she hesitated. "Since you may go and get yourself poisoned again, I suppose I could stay around until you got back. Just in case."

Relief washed over Niccolo. All the tension went out of his body. Now he could have a drink, just to enjoy it, not to bolster his courage. He sipped his wine.

"Of course, I'm sure if I weren't here, your wife would take care of you. How is the Signora Machiavelli these days?"

"Oh she prospers. She's in the country. Already she has two children and she's pregnant again."

"Prolific."

"It would seem that in the prolonged absences of her husband, she's been enjoying the regular consolations of a little priest."

"Your fat friend, Pagolo?"

"The very man. He claims she has an iron grip on him, and you know what they say—when you have them by the balls, their hearts and minds will follow. I think that, in a strange and curious way, he's fallen in love with her. She scolds him constantly, badgers him, and occasionally batters him, but he takes it all in stride. I think he feels something for her. And I know he likes the children."

"There's no accounting for taste," said Giuditta wistfully. "Some of the most unlikely people wind up together."

"Like a mysterious Jewess . . ." said Niccolo.

"And a headstrong, incorrigible gentile who's in love with freedom and justice and a militia, and who virtually ignores the flesh-and-blood people around him."

"*Mea culpa, mea culpa, mea maxima culpa,*" confessed Niccolo. "I have sinned exceedingly in thought, word, and deed."

"Maybe I should start administering some of that medicine your wife doles out to her lover," said Giuditta. As she spoke she cuffed him playfully on the side of the head. Niccolo was leaning back in his chair, and, overreacting to the blow—he was also a little tipsy and off-balance—he fell. From where he was sprawled out on the kitchen floor in the clean straw and spring flowers that were strewn about, he looked up at Giuditta and laughed. Then, tugging sharply on the leg of her chair, he upset it and pulled her down on top of himself. After a few moments of mock-heroic struggling, their lips came together and they kissed. In the fragrant mix of sweet hay and flowers that covered the floor, they made love and fell asleep in each other's arms.

Riding into the camp, Niccolo immediately saw a difference. To be sure, the shabby, sullen, and drunken mercenaries were still in evidence, and they still made up the bulk of the Florentine force arrayed against Pisa. But in their midst were the signs of change—the red, yellow, and white tents drawn up in orderly rows of the new militia. Gradually, as more men were equipped and trained, the militiamen would entirely replace the undependable hired soldiers.

Niccolo asked after Don Micheletto and was pleased to learn he was in camp. Having eschewed more sumptuous lodgings in a nearby village, he was staying in his tent among the men. It was a good sign. As Niccolo rode through the rows of new tents, he heard the usual cursing that was so much a part of camp life, but the curses rang like music in his ears. They were all in his native Florentine dialect.

When Niccolo found Don Micheletto, the captain of the guard was deep in conversation with another odd-looking man. Waiting at a polite distance for the audience to come to a conclusion, Niccolo nevertheless could not ignore the fact that the stranger was holding, and occasionally petting, Don Micheletto's hand and talking earnestly, even intensely, to the captain. He was about to conclude that Don Micheletto, among his other pernicious habits, was also a practitioner of the "Florentine vice," when he realized the little man was not making love to the captain. He was reading his palm.

As the chiromancer glided out of the tent, Niccolo stepped in. "What do the signs say, Captain?"

"The ssigns are propituousssss," whispered Don Micheletto. "An engagement is imminent."

"And did he tell you how the engagement would turn out?"

"I believe we will be victoriousssss."

As Niccolo settled into a portable camp chair to discuss details of strategy and tactics with the captain, he stared hard at his colleague and enemy. He never ceased to be amazed at that peaceful, composed, kindly face, a face he knew to be so at odds with the black heart that beat in his breast. As he always did in Don Micheletto's presence, Niccolo suppressed a shiver.

The sun rose higher in the sky as they talked of military matters, and the day began to heat up. Don Micheletto called for refreshment, and Niccolo instructed the same servant to bring him wine from his own saddlebags.

When the wine was served, Don Micheletto helped himself and watched Niccolo pour and drink from his own bottle. "Of course," he said gleefully. "You drink yourssss. I'll drink mine. It'sss better. SSSSSSSafer," he trailed off, hissing and smiling. "That way there'ssssss no danger of poisssson."

Don Micheletto's bluntness in bringing the topic of poison out into the open shook Niccolo. Then he had to remind himself, that, after all, the man had been in service with the Borgias for over ten years. If there was any substance to rumors, he would have acquired some familiarity with and caution about the art of poisoning. Suddenly, Niccolo felt a little silly, insisting on drinking from his own stores.

A young soldier ducked breathlessly into the tent. "Sir, the enemy is met!" Both Don Micheletto and Niccolo rushed outside.

Don Micheletto explained the situation. For several days, parties of Pisan soldiers had been sallying outside the walls to meet small supply vessels coming up the river. They managed to unload quickly and escape back to the cover of the walls before they could be challenged.

"They've become quite brazen over the past week," said Don Micheletto. "But today will be different. Watch."

From their hilltop perch, Niccolo saw a column of Florentine militiamen hustling into position between the Pisan raiders and the ship waiting on the riverbank. He watched with great satisfaction as his men drew themselves up into fighting formations, moving quickly and flawlessly.

When the Pisans turned, preferring to flee to the safety of their walls, rather than face the enemy, another column of Florentines moved in on them from behind, cutting them off. Left with no other choice, the Pisans fought hard. Although outnumbered, they seemed to be getting the better of their Florentine adversaries in the hand-to-hand confrontation. The little party repulsed three Florentine advances and was on the point of breaking through to safety when a contingent of Florentine archers moved in and began to whittle away at their ranks. Completely surrounded, and too far from the walls to take advantage of any protective cover that the Pisan archers might have been able to provide, the leader of the little force signaled for a surrender. Cheers went up in the Florentine camp.

"They're raw," said Don Micheletto. "They haven't got the ssssmell of blood in their nostrilsssss."

As the victors straggled into camp with their prisoners, Niccolo went out to meet them, congratulating them and offering encouragement. Some of the men he remembered having enrolled in the militia, but most were strangers to him. He was a little shocked to realize how young they all were.

As he moved through the ranks of the archers, he spotted a familiar face. It was Michele di Lando's son. "*Salve,* Salvestro!" said Niccolo, eagerly grasping the boy's hand. "Well done, there. Your archers acquitted themselves in a manly fashion."

"Thank you, Captain, uh, I mean Secretary, uh, Chancellor? Well, thank you, sir." The boy was still a little awkward. "It wasn't that hard, sir. All we do is stand at a distance and shoot. It's the men down at the line with pikes and swords who do the real fighting."

"Don't belittle yourself," said Niccolo. "Without your help, they might well have lost out to the Pisans."

"Yes, sir."

"Shall I send a message to your father about this first, splendid victory and the part you played in it? He'd be proud of you."

"If you say so, sir."

"But I'm surprised to see you up here, at the front. You weren't in one of the first units trained. I would have expected the older, more experienced hands to get the first shot at the fighting. You must be pretty good with that bow, Salvestro. You must have made a very favorable impression on the captain."

"I do my best."

Niccolo was about to take his leave of his friend's son when he saw that Salvestro was looking at him with a queer expression on his face, part consternation, part indecision. "Is there something wrong, Salvestro?"

"You're a friend of my father's, sir, and he told me I could always trust you."

"Well?"

"Can we," he hesitated. "Can we go over this way a little?" As they moved off, Salvestro cast a furtive glance over his shoulder at Don Micheletto, who was listening gravely to the report of the two victorious commanders.

When they were off by themselves, the young archer said, "I don't want to appear mutinous . . ."

"Mutiny! What are you talking about?"

"It's the captain, sir."

"So the captain's been hard on you, has he? I'm afraid that's part of the military life, Salvestro. There's not much I can do about that."

"It's nothing like that, sir. Look." Salvestro was pointing to a line of stretchers moving into the camp. The sight of the dead and wounded momentarily brought a halt to their exchange.

"Do you see how young they are, sir?"

"Young and brave."

"They shouldn't be here."

"They volunteered," said Niccolo, trying not to sound callous.

"I know they did, but they're not ready. Some of those men have only had two or three weeks of training."

"Nonsense," said Niccolo. "Don Micheletto has been drilling them for close to a year now. Since long before you joined the militia."

"Not those men, sir."

"What do you mean?"

"The older men, the more experienced men, they're gone."

"Gone? Where to?"

"They've gone off to join the mercenary companies."

"What! They've deserted!"

"Not exactly. I know it's not my place, sir, . . ."

"Speak up boy!" said Niccolo, visibly agitated.

"Don Micheletto has been selling them off."

"Selling them!" said Niccolo, astounded.

"Yes, sir. He's been meeting with agents of the free companies. They've offered to hire all the men he can provide. He trains them and then sells them off for a bounty to the mercenary captains who are always looking for armed men."

"And the men go along with this?"

"Not all of them, but some do. They're poor men, sir, and the free companies pay an awful lot of money. It's a temptation."

"Why didn't anyone come to me?"

"Don Micheletto said it was your idea, sir. He said you were in on it, and it was best we all just kept our mouths shut. It wasn't any of our business."

Niccolo was incensed. "He said I was in on it! When did all this start?"

"About six months ago, sir, right after I joined."

"And right after I was sent to Germany," thought Niccolo. To the boy he said, "You've done the republic of Florence a great favor today, Salvestro, a very great favor indeed."

"Thank you, sir. My father told me to come to you. He said he knew you couldn't be involved. He said you'd know what to do."

"Oh, I know what to do about traitors," said Niccolo. "You can depend on it."

Riding back to Florence, Niccolo reviewed the situation. "So Don Micheletto is in business for himself. Florence pays for the training and equipment, and Don Micheletto sells the finished product to the highest bidder at a handsome profit. Very pretty. A very nice scheme."

And then he thought of Paolo Vitelli. Only five years ago, Paolo Vitelli had double-crossed the republic. He was in command of the Florentine troops at Pisa and was taking money from the Pisans at the same time. The war dragged on and Vitelli got rich. But then he got caught. And once Niccolo had prepared the indictment, without delay, with little ceremony, Vitelli was relieved of the burden of his traitorous head. Such was the fate of traitors, and such would be the fate of Don Micheletto.

And Niccolo knew that that decapitation would also resolve the biggest contradiction in his life. Giuditta would finally have her revenge. He smiled to himself as he rode on toward Florence. Revenge is a plate best eaten cold.

"The last thing I want to do is see a horserace," said Giuditta firmly.

"It's not just a horserace," objected Niccolo.

"Grown men flailing at the flanks of excited animals and at each other—you call that entertainment?"

"Yes, besides they're not grown men," countered Niccolo. "They're little stunted men or slim boys who weigh less, so the horses have less weight to carry."

"Dwarves on horseback. That makes it all the more appealing."

"Giuditta, the palio is a tradition. The whole city turns out for it. And the militia will pass in review before the race."

"Oh, the militia! Why didn't you say something before? I didn't realize the militia was going to pass in review. Now that's real entertainment."

"Come on," pleaded an exasperated Niccolo. "I have to go. I have to be there, because our horse is set to win the race this year."

"What do you mean 'set to win the race'? Are you telling me it's not just a stupid horserace, but a stupid, fixed horserace?"

"It's not exactly fixed. It's negotiated."

"*Bella differenza!*"

"I told you it's not just a horserace, and it isn't. The race is just the last step. We've been working on this thing for months, working out the details."

"What details? Who's been working on what?"

Niccolo explained, "The palio is like a war. Each neighborhood is represented by one horse. Before the race is run, pacts and alliances are concluded. We work out deals. We make agreements among ourselves not to obstruct this horse, to promote that one. We exchange information. We pass on rumors. Sometimes we start them. Sometimes misleading information gets out—like the rumor that our horse came up lame last week."

"Your horse isn't lame?"

"How could we win if the horse were lame? I told you, it's all worked out."

Giuditta eyed her lover curiously. "Does everything you do have to be like that? Deals and negotiations? Secrets and promises? Can't you ever get away from it?"

"I get away from it with you," he said even though he knew it wasn't entirely true. He did have a secret; he was keeping something from her. But all that would be over in a few days. The wheels were turning, and the end was in sight for the perfidious Don Micheletto. When he was brought to justice and sentenced, Niccolo would tell Giuditta everything. Her revenge and that of the republic would be consummated together.

Reluctantly, Giuditta finally agreed to accompany him to what she considered an idiotic horserace, the results of which, apparently, everyone knew in advance. When they arrived in the piazza where the race was held, they saw the shoulder-high wooden barriers that had been erected to keep the crowds from spilling onto the racecourse and to keep the horses and riders from careening into the pressing crowds. In the center of the course, a group of children was dancing in a ring and singing. Niccolo bought watermelon and wine at a booth and presented the offerings to his beloved. They climbed up into the makeshift scaffolding and made themselves comfortable.

A blaring of trumpets put an end to the children's ring-dance and cleared the center of the piazza. Another blast, accompanied by the roll of drums, signaled the arrival of the militia. They marched in lockstep. The sun glanced off their polished breastplates. Most of the militiamen carried long lances, although companies of archers marched that day as well.

They were all dressed in white waistcoats emblazoned with the crimson cross of the republic and smart, white caps. Their stockings were half-red, half-white, so that when a company was viewed from the left side their legs appeared uniformly white, from the right, uniformly red. When they turned sharply as a group, the sea of legs abruptly seemed to change color. This effect along with the crisp manner in which the men went through their paces drew murmurs of respect and admiration form the crowd.

"*Amappolo!*" Giuditta blurted out.

"What!" said Niccolo. Several other people turned and directed disapproving stares at Giuditta. "*Amappolo*" was not an acceptable Florentine expression. It was Roman, and it sounded vulgar.

"It's him!" said Giuditta.

"Who are you talking about?"

"Don Micheletto!"

"You know him?" It was Niccolo's turn to be surprised.

"Of course I know him. I've known him for years. He was one of my customers. He used to come to the convent all the time with his master, Caesar, before the Bull was put out to pasture."

"He used to come to your place with Caesar Borgia? For years?"

"That's not all. When Caesar disappeared, Don Micheletto continued to come around. He came courting then. He came for Pasiphae or Imperia—whatever you want to call her. She seemed very fond of him."

"So the second-in-command inherited the master's concubine?"

"Apparently. She disappeared too, shortly after Don Micheletto stopped coming. I always thought she might have run off with him. And now he's here in Florence. How odd."

"Odder than you think," said Niccolo, aware of the heavy irony. Giuditta had been acquainted with her father's murderer for years! He wanted to shout it at her. That's the man who killed your father! But he had to bide his time. He had to wait, and when he finally told her, he would also be able to offer her the assassin's head on a silver platter—in a manner of speaking.

"What's he doing with your militia?" Her question cut in on Niccolo's thoughts.

"Training them."

"I don't understand?"

"Whatever his faults, he's a good soldier and a good disciplinarian."

"No, not that. I mean, didn't you always tell me that the Medici were the sworn enemies of your republic, and that they'd do anything to get back into power in Florence?"

"That's true, but what does that have to do with anything?"

"You remember the time at the brothel I showed you the fat cardinal, Giovanni de' Medici?"

"The one who just likes to watch?"

"Well, the cardinal was also one of my regular customers, and that man down there commanding your militia was one of his most constant companions."

"Don Micheletto and the Cardinal de' Medici!" said Niccolo in alarm.

"After Caesar's disgrace, they were inseparable."

36

Politics, Compromise, and Revenge

Niccolo was too numbed by this latest revelation to realize that his horse, although comfortably in the lead, slipped going into the final turn and went crashing into the wooden barricades, badly injuring his rider. When the horse managed to right itself, it was whinnying in pain. The animal was dragging its left rear leg pathetically, limply, behind it. A grotesque splinter of bare white bone was sticking out mawkishly from the broken leg, and blood was gushing from the wound. The horse would have to be destroyed.

The race, a three-hundred-year-old tradition of local rivalry and political wrangling, did not turn out as expected. The deals had been made, the bargains struck, sides had been chosen, but in the end, fortune intervened. With the implications of Don Micheletto's treachery whirling in his head, however, Niccolo was oblivious to the outcome. He did not even notice the triumphant winner, strutting alone around the track, bearing high the blue-cloth standard of the Virgin, which was the day's prize. After the festivities, the rider would carry the banner back to his neighborhood, where it would remain until next year's race. In this case, the unexpected beneficiary of the favorite's fatal stumble was the representative of San Lorenzo, the quarter where the Medici Palace now stood empty and boarded up, abandoned by its inhabitants.

"I have to go. I have to see Soderini."

"Niccolo!"

"Can you make it home by yourself?"

"Niccolo! Please! It's a holiday." protested Giuditta.

"This won't wait," he said, giving her an absentminded kiss on the cheek. He disappeared into the crowd.

Everything seemed to fall into place. Don Micheletto was once an agent of the Medici. What could be more natural than that he return to his former employers? And there was no doubt in Niccolo's mind that Don Micheletto's coming to Florence was no accident. His insinuation into the militia was likewise carefully planned. And not only was he enriching himself, and probably his employers, by selling off the best soldiers to the free companies—at the same time he was deliberately weakening the militia and undermining the defenses of the republic. Don Micheletto and the Medici! Who knows what "lessssonssss" they had in store for Florence?

Niccolo, sweaty, out of breath, and looking a little mad, took the stairs leading into the Soderini Palace two at a time. The place was bustling with servants. He collared a liveried footman and demanded to see the gonfaloniere.

"The gonfaloniere has not yet returned from the festivities," the footman informed him. "Would the gentleman care to wait?"

"I'll be in his study," said Niccolo, rudely pushing past the startled servant. "Send him in to me as soon as he gets back."

The gonfaloniere arrived, accompanied by his familiars, several other dignitaries, and visiting members of a trade delegation from France. Upon being informed that an "excited gentleman" was awaiting him in his study, Piero Soderini excused himself and proceeded there with his usual unruffled aplomb.

"Niccolo, this is unexpected," said the gonfaloniere.

"I've come on business."

"Business on a holiday? You never let up, do you?"

"I wouldn't be here if it weren't urgent."

"Well, what is it, Chancellor?" said Soderini, resigning himself to the conference and sinking into a soft leather chair.

Niccolo continued to pace back and forth, too agitated to sit still. "It's Don Micheletto."

"I thought we had that all under control. Would you like a drink to calm you down?"

"No, I don't need anything. Thank you. Listen, Piero, there's more to Don Micheletto's treason than just his making a handsome profit on the men he trains and sells. He's working for the Medici."

At the mention of the Medici, Soderini came to attention. "What are you saying?"

"He's been seen in Rome with Cardinal Giovanni."

Soderini was a little skeptical: "Being seen with the cardinal hardly constitutes working for the Medici."

"He was with him all the time. Constantly. And that was right before he turned up here. You draw your own conclusions. He used to work for them before, you know."

"You think he came here at the behest of the Cardinal de' Medici, and that he's working for him." Soderini looked thoughtful. "I don't know, Niccolo. You may be jumping to conclusions. But the charge is serious. I'll have to look into it."

"Look into what! I'm telling you he's up to his neck in some kind of conspiracy with the Medici. And the first step is to undermine the effectiveness of the militia!"

"Niccolo, I'm not questioning the credibility of your information, but really, if Don Micheletto had been conspiring with the Cardinal de' Medici, don't you think our people in Rome would have been aware of it? Why do you think we pay all that money to spies? They keep an eye on the cardinal. Don't you think they would have let me know?"

"Maybe we should start asking some questions about our people in Rome, then!" Niccolo was angry.

"I resent that!" The gonfaloniere stood up. "My own brother is in charge of our embassy in Rome!"

"Then maybe you better ask your brother what's been going on down there!"

"Niccolo, Niccolo, you don't mean that. You know Francesco is above suspicion. You've worked with him so many times." The gonfaloniere attempted to sooth his overwrought secretary. "I promise you I'll look into things. If there's anything to your story, I'll find out soon enough. In the meantime . . ."

"In the meantime, have him arrested! Have Don Micheletto arrested!" Niccolo was adamant.

"On what charge?"

"Treason!"

"I just said, I'll have to look into things first."

"You already have enough evidence on his tampering with the militia to put him in prison, to take his head off if you want. Go ahead and arrest him. You saw the indictment I prepared."

"Yes, it was very impressive. The allegations were certainly serious."

"Allegations!" Niccolo exploded. "You call those charges allegations! I've gotten the names of over a hundred men whom he sold, outright sold, to the free companies. I've gotten the names of the mercenary commanders he dealt with. I've got witnesses in the ranks who are willing to give evidence against him. And you call those allegations! I say arrest him and hang him! Now!"

Again the gonfaloniere assumed a paternal tone and posture: "Niccolo, Niccolo, you're letting yourself get carried away. If it were only that simple."

"It is that simple!" said the younger man. "We had less on Vitelli when he betrayed us, and we sent him to the gallows!"

"Yes, but things were different then. The Council of Eighty appointed Vitelli. Who do you think appointed Don Micheletto?"

"Ultimately, you were responsible."

"That's correct. As the gonfaloniere for life, I am ultimately responsible. And if the extent of Don Micheletto's perfidy is exposed, who do you think will have to take the blame?"

"They can't blame you. It wasn't your idea to engage him."

"It wasn't my idea, but I'll be held responsible. I'll be made to look ridiculous or incompetent, at best, culpable at worst. The whole government will suffer. The republic will suffer."

"Not if we move quickly."

"Niccolo, you know we have enemies. You know there are men on the council who resent me, who resent the type of government we've built and nurtured. You know that there are men who would rather see a return to the old ways of autocracy and even a restoration of the Medici. If I falter, what do you think will happen? If the people lose confidence in me, how long can this government last?"

"The people won't lose confidence in you if you deliver Don Micheletto over to his punishment. And his fate will serve as an example to the other traitors."

"You think our enemies won't raise a hue and cry and say that I'm just getting rid of my accomplice because he became too greedy? You know sometimes I think the whole thing with Don Micheletto may have been a plot to embarrass me from the very beginning."

"I still say, arrest him."

"I have a better idea," said the gonfaloniere. "We'll have a talk with Don Micheletto. We can confront him with the information we have. If he knows what's good for him, he'll agree to give up the game. In a month or two, he'll decide to resign his commission and leave the city to seek honest employment elsewhere. The cloud will pass without incident. We'll appoint a new captain of the guard."

"A month or two! Do you know what sort of damage he can do in a month or two? He could have the Cardinal de' Medici sitting in your office in a month or two!"

"Niccolo, you're exaggerating."

"Exaggerating! Don Micheletto is destroying the militia, he's conspiring with the Medici, and you want to wait a month or two to do anything about it! He even tried to poison me!"

"He what?"

"He tried to poison me when I was in Germany!"

"Niccolo, you've been working too hard lately. Why don't you let me handle Don Micheletto. Why don't you take a few days off and go to the country to relax."

"Relax! Piero, they're undermining the republic, and you want me to relax!"

"Take a few days. When you get back, the republic and the militia will still be here. Then we'll take care of Don Micheletto."

"Piero, now is the time for action! I'm convinced of it!"

"Of course you are, Niccolo. Of course you are. But now my guests are waiting. I really should attend to them. Would you care to stay for supper?"

"He thinks I'm mad," thought Niccolo, stalking out of the Soderini Palace. "He thinks I'm overworked!" But Niccolo was convinced that Don Micheletto was a Medici agent. And he was convinced that Don Micheletto and whoever was supporting him were responsible for his being sent on the long and tiresome legation to Germany—to get him out of the way. The timing was just too pat. As soon as Niccolo was out of the way, Don Micheletto had begun his selling off of militiamen. And when his return from the worthless legation was imminent, Niccolo was convinced they tried to poison him.

Although much of Niccolo's reasoning was based on conjecture and instinct, and although his head was swimming with the details of it, he was convinced that he had put the pieces together correctly and that he had uncovered a dangerous plot.

Yet Soderini had no immediate plans to do anything about it. Soderini was cautious. It was his strong point—and his weakness. Yet they were living in impetuous times and fortune favored the bold. He had only to think of Caesar Borgia's early success. And the new pope, Julius, was taking cities and provinces because he had the resolve to act. If Soderini delayed, his enemies would gain in strength. Something had to be done. Don Micheletto had to be stopped. And then there was the matter of justice. Niccolo felt strongly about justice.

It was already dark when Niccolo returned home, and he could tell from the lights in the windows that Giuditta was waiting for him. The realization cheered him. It cheered him immensely. For the first time in his life, he was experiencing the joys of a woman's constant companionship, a lover's companionship. At the end of the day—and the days were always long and difficult—he knew she would be waiting for him. He knew there was comfort and sympathy waiting for him. He knew there was love and warmth in that old, cold Florentine stone house for the first time in so many years.

"*Piccioncina*," he called out. No answer.

"*Tesoro?*" Hmmph, where could she be? Mounting the stairs, he passed through the empty kitchen and found her on the *lettuccio*, the little day bed in the alcove where he took his afternoon naps. She was asleep, but the noise he made—quite deliberately—soon woke her. When she sat up on the edge of the bed, Niccolo was at her side. After a few attempted kisses, which Giuditta, still in the thrall of sleep, shook off irritably, Niccolo began to talk. Slowly regaining consciousness, Giuditta watched him as the steady stream of words poured out—another episode in the never-ending adventures of Soderini and the council and the militia. Don Micheletto seemed to figure prominently in this one as well.

"Niccolo, I'm leaving."

"Wait a minute, let me finish, because this time . . ."

"I said I'm leaving. I'm leaving Florence," she said with finality.

"What?" He was stunned into silence.

Giuditta looked down at her hands folded in her lap. "I'm going back to Rome. For a while at least."

"You can't leave now. I need you! I need all the support I can get."

"Oh, you need me!" she said defiantly. "What about what I need, what I want?"

"Giuditta, please, this isn't the time. Bear with me for just a little longer."

"Bear with you? And then what? When this crisis is past, another one will come up and you'll be off and running again."

"I thought you were happy here," said Niccolo sheepishly.

"I am happy, but . . . but . . . what kind of a life am I leading here? What do I have here? When you're done playing with the militia, you come back here exhausted, you prattle on about some problem at the chancery for an hour, you take a little something for your digestion, and you fall asleep on the balcony. Niccolo, you don't have time for me!"

"I'll make time."

"When?"

"As soon as I get this thing with Don Micheletto straightened . . ."

"See what I mean? There's always something, isn't there?"

"But women are supposed to . . ." He thought the better of what he was going to say and held his tongue.

"Women are supposed to what?" said Giuditta sharply.

"Never mind," said Niccolo. He realized that many an honest Florentine citizen in his position would simply beat his woman into submission. He also realized that wouldn't work with Giuditta.

"Niccolo, don't you see? I'm not a woman like other Florentine women. I'm an outsider. I don't go to church and gossip. I don't have any friends but you and the people you bring to the house. We have to be careful about being seen too much in public, because it might cause a scandal. What kind of a life is that?"

For the first time, it occurred to Niccolo that Giuditta did not consider being cooped up in his house all day, waiting for him, the equivalent of paradisiacal bliss. "I didn't know . . . I didn't realize . . ." He didn't know what to say. Suddenly the possibility that she might actually leave became very real to him, and a sense of empty hopelessness began to steal into his thoughts.

"Giuditta, don't go. I love you."

"What did you say?"

"I said, I love you."

"Niccolo, how long have I been here with you?"

"Six months, seven months?"

"In all that time, you never said that before. You never said you loved me."

"I thought you knew."

"Niccolo, Niccolo, sometimes you're so stupid," she said, shaking her head. "I love you too, but, but . . ." Sobbing, they rushed into each other's arms and whispered more things they never said to one another before.

"It's no good, Niccolo, I can't," she said, suddenly breaking the embrace and sitting down on the edge of the bed. "I have to get away. It's not just you."

"What do you mean?"

"This afternoon, when you abandoned me at that imbecilic horserace, I did something I've been afraid to do ever since I got here. I went down to the ghetto to see the house where I used to live with my father."

"And?"

"It was empty. The whole street was empty, except for some squatters. I walked through the rooms that I grew up in. I sat in the little courtyard. Niccolo I sat there all day, and, at first, I wept and was sad. But then, I started to get angry." She stopped for a moment, steeling herself.

"That house was the only place I ever felt secure in my life. I know I was just too young to know any better, but I had my father, and my father would protect me. Then they killed him, and they took all that away from me. They took my father and my childhood and my happiness. They took my innocence, and they chased me into exile. Florence did that to me, Niccolo! Florence murdered my family! Florence ruined my life!" She was sobbing when she finished.

Getting control of her emotion-choked voice, Giuditta continued, "I know you've told me that that was all in the past, that it was a different Florence then, that the men who did it are all dead and gone, but it doesn't matter, Niccolo. It's the horror of it all that's still alive. I can almost feel it here. And as long as I stay in Florence, I know I'm going to keep feeling it. It's going to haunt me. It's going to drive me insane."

"Giuditta, I can help you."

"What can you do, Niccolo? Can you bring my father back? My

little brother? Can you clear the Florentine air of the memories that it holds for me, of the evil that I feel in this place?"

"I can try."

"Oh, Niccolo, I don't doubt your good intentions, but I've made up my mind. I want to go back to Rome."

"Giuditta, listen. What if I tell you that I can clear the Florentine air of the memories it holds for you?"

"Niccolo, this isn't a matter of diplomacy. This isn't one of your negotiating sessions where you can buy time with extravagant promises. This is real life, real pain. This is me."

"I'm not buying time. I'm perfectly serious," he said flatly. And he was. Niccolo had figured out a way to solve both of his problems: what to do with Don Micheletto and how to keep Giuditta in Florence.

"Giuditta, I want you to help me poison someone."

"Niccolo, I watched that man kill my father, my brother, and my uncle. I stood there and watched."

"So did I."

"How long have you known," she said icily.

"About a year."

"And you never said anything? You never told me?"

Niccolo was contrite. "I wanted to take care of it myself—when the time was right."

"And why, now, all of a sudden, is the time right?"

"Because Don Micheletto represents a danger to the republic. He has to be stopped and Soderini refuses to act."

"And you decided to take matters into your own hands?"

"What other choice do I have? I'm not doing this for personal glory or because I'm reckless or bloodthirsty or ambitious. It's to preserve the republic. What other choice did Brutus have with Caesar?"

"Who were they?"

"Let me put it this way—what other choice did Judith have with Holofernes?"

"And you want my help?"

"You have your reasons for wanting Don Micheletto dead. I have mine. Will you do it?"

"What other choice did Judith have with Holofernes?"

37

A Dinner Party

The days following Niccolo's decision were difficult ones, and more than once he wanted to back out of the task he had set for himself. But the continued irresolution on the part of the Gonfaloniere Soderini, coupled with Giuditta's firm resolve, stiffened his will. He had to remind himself that there was no other way. He had to keep thinking of Brutus.

Paolo Vitelli had been dealt with swiftly by the republic for his crimes, and he had been dealt with justly. He had been beheaded on the basis of Niccolo's indictment and vigorous prosecution. Don Micheletto's crimes were infinitely worse. Because the mechanisms of justice had stalled for one reason or another, was that any reason for him to be let off? Niccolo kept telling himself, no. "The charges were the same as those against Vitelli. Vitelli was guilty. Vitelli was dead. The republic was served. Don Micheletto was guilty. Don Micheletto would be dead. The republic would be served again," Niccolo kept telling himself.

Giuditta had no such compunction about the man who had killed her father and brother, and she busied herself with the details. All the ingredients and equipment were already at hand. She had brought them with her to mix the antidote for Niccolo when he had been poisoned. The same chemicals and procedures could be used for salvation or destruction, for life or death.

For this occasion, she decided to use the deadly cantarella, an arsenic compound with a slightly bitter taste. The snow-white powder could be dissolved and mixed with either food or drink. It was generally better to use it in something strong tasting and sweet in order to disguise the faint, but to the educated pallet, perceptible, trace of bitterness.

Rossoli, the rose-petal liqueur that Giuditta had once prepared for Niccolo was the perfect vehicle. Aside from its heavy, cloying taste, the Rossoli was perfectly suited to the undoing of Don Micheletto. Giuditta knew from experience that it was one of his favorite concoctions. He could not resist it.

When she was finished, she poured the deadly substance into an exquisite decanter. The deep ruby redness of the Rossoli showed through the smooth glass. Glass was rare, and the small decanter had been expensive, but it allowed the rich liquor to be displayed to advantage—at its most tempting.

Giuditta laid the table, although she would not be at the meal itself. Don Micheletto would recognize her, and needless questions would arise. It was better this way. On a sideboard, she arranged the wines, a white, a red—a Spanish red, the kind Don Micheletto liked. And she placed the polished, deadly bottle of Rossoli among them in a conspicuous position, where it would catch Don Micheletto's eye. Even if he brought his own wine, which was a possibility, he would not be able to resist the lure of the Rossoli.

Niccolo was nervous. This was no ordinary dinner party. The thought of dining with Don Micheletto, even under normal circumstances, was enough to make him uncomfortable and vaguely ill. The thought of having to poison him, to sit and watch while he drank the poison . . . He shivered. When his guest finally rang at the door, Niccolo's stomach was a churning, acidic, knotted mess. Giuditta squeezed his hand one last time—for courage—and disappeared upstairs. He was on his own.

It had not been difficult to lure Don Micheletto into the trap. He and Niccolo were, after all, colleagues, and colleagues were required to observe certain norms of polite social behavior between themselves. Dining together was a perfectly normal activity, and though Niccolo had always kept his distance when it came to Don Micheletto, the latter seemed to find nothing amiss in a dinner invitation. In fact, he received it rather enthusiastically.

"Buona Sssssera," hissed the little man, when his host threw open the door. Niccolo froze. Trouble!

Don Micheletto was smiling as usual. A few strands of stiff grey hair peeked out from under his ordinary black *beretto*. In his unremarkable, almost-clerical cloak, he looked for all the world like a kindly old country priest or a groundskeeper or a man who loved animals. All these usual, incongruous details, so at odds with the nefarious nature of the man, Niccolo took in at a glance. But it was not Don Micheletto's appearance that sent a shock through him. It was an entirely unanticipated complication. Don Micheletto was not alone.

"I took the liberty of bringing a companion," he said. "I hope you don't mind. She will make the evening all the more fesssstive, don't you agree?"

And what a companion! There was no mistaking the black eyes, the bladelike nose, the preposterously high shaven forehead, and the mouth like a blood-red smear. The enterprising young prostitute who went by the name of Faustina—the devil's plaything—and who later turned up at the side of Caesar Borgia in Rome, had now come home to Florence on the arm of Don Micheletto. She seemed to make it a point of attaching herself to the ambitious and the ruthless. "Like a crow," thought Niccolo, "she hurls herself more willingly and voraciously on rotten carrion than on fresh, wholesome meat."

As Don Micheletto shrugged out of his worn cloak and removed his hat, he introduced his consort, "Maria Madalena, Niccolo Machiavelli, Ssssecretary in the Ssssecond Chanccccery."

"I believe the secretary and I have met before." She graced Niccolo with an indulgent smile.

"Now she's styling herself Maria Madalena," thought Niccolo. "Mary Magdalena, the repentant whore!" Despite the name, Madalena showed no outward signs of repentance. She was dressed in something bright blue and shimmering and provocative. When she walked, it rustled, and she gave off a heavy, musky, perfumed smell. Niccolo noticed that her long fingernails were painted black. But he was letting all these details distract him. Already in his mind he was backing away from the deed, looking for a way out.

Now he had an added problem—what to do about the girl. Was she to be sacrificed in the destruction of Don Micheletto? Was that fair? Could it be avoided? In his head, Niccolo began to evolve schemes for getting Don Micheletto to drink the poisoned draft while keeping his concubine from doing so. Although he was sure that she was far from innocent, her name—whatever it was—was not on the indictment against Don Micheletto.

As they sat down to dinner, Niccolo thought he had found a way. He could pour most of the liquid into his own cup, he could give Don Micheletto his dose, and then accidentally drop and break the delicate glass vessel. He might even be able to spill his own portion in the process, if he acted clumsy enough. But what if she . . .

"Excccellent," said Don Micheletto after chewing on a mouthful of the Spanish red wine and swallowing it. He regarded Niccolo, then the cup of wine. "You see I didn't bring my own wine along, as some people are in the habit of doing." He let the barb sink in, and Niccolo suddenly remembered the afternoon in Pisa when he had refused Don Micheletto's wine in favor of his own. "God, he's on to me," he thought. "He suspects something."

But Don Micheletto kept on smiling. "After all, if I can't trust my new partner, whom can I trust?"

"New partner?" Niccolo started.

"Come, come, Machiavelli. Let's get right to the point. Don't play the fox with me. My subordinates tell me you've been looking into my affairsssss. Then I receive a dinner invitation. I'm not stupid. How big of a cut do you want? How muccccch? How many broad gold florinssssss?"

Niccolo was taken aback. Don Micheletto thought he wanted in on the militia scheme! He was offering him a bribe! Niccolo thought hard for a minute. He had to play the game, but he wasn't sure how much to ask for, how big a bribe was appropriate. Finally he spoke. "Shall we say ten percent?"

"Such modest ambitionssss."

"Make it retroactive." Niccolo did not want to seem faint of heart in the bribery scheme with his new partner.

"Done!" declared Don Micheletto. "Now let's drink to our new partnership." The three raised and clinked cups, and then something happened to further disconcert Niccolo and throw his plans into disarray: Don Micheletto and his concubine intertwined arms and drank from each other's cups!

This unforeseen action set off another feverish round of plotting and counterplotting in the thoughts of the amateur poisoner. Now Niccolo would have to figure out a way to induce Madalena to leave the table for at least a few minutes. That was the only way. Of course, he breathed easier. Eventually, she would get up to attend to her needs or her toilette. Then he could get the Rossoli into Don Micheletto's cup and spill the rest before she came back. Although he was almost afraid to look, he shot an occasional glance at the sideboard where the fatal vial seemed to glow bright red and burn with a frightening, evil intensity. In Niccolo's imagination, it seemed much more conspicuous than it actually was.

These considerations aside, the meal was a tremendous success, at least for the two guests who seemed not to notice Niccolo's acute discomfort. Don Micheletto ate with a sound appetite, asked for seconds, and lavished praise on each course. Madalena slurped her oysters with a lascivious delicacy, licked the brine from her black fingertips, and made comments about the aphrodisiac qualities of the succulent shellfish. Both drank heavily, and Niccolo half hoped that the woman might pass out from the alcohol or ask to lie down after the meal. But no such thing happened, and, as the evening wound down and the fatal hour approached, Niccolo's nervousness increased. He could scarcely bring his cup to his mouth without betraying the shakiness of his hand. When he poured wine for his guests, half went into the cups, half onto the tablecloth. "Well," he thought, "it would serve him well if he was going to go through with his plan to spill the liqueur later. They would think him merely drunk."

She called him "*Capitanone*," my big captain, and treated Don Micheletto with all the solicitude of an infatuated lover, popping bits of food playfully into his mouth, mussing his hair, even dabbing at his lips and chin with her napkin. Don Micheletto reveled in the attention. He was lolling in his chair, drunk and happy, telling old war stories. He seemed to be genuinely enjoying himself. Niccolo was not sure at what point he had decided, but he was aware of his decision long before his conscious mind fully acknowledged it. He knew he couldn't do it. Giuditta would be furious, but he just couldn't. He couldn't go through with it.

Breathing a tremendous sigh of relief, Niccolo drained his cup and set it down hard on the table. Already he was thinking of options. Already he was getting another idea: If he went to Soderini and told him that Don Micheletto had tried to bribe him, that he was that brazen, then maybe the gonfaloniere could be persuaded to take action . . .

"Your cup is empty. You're not thinking of stopping the festivities now and cutting us all off, are you?" It was Madalena who spoke to Niccolo.

"No, of course not," he said, coming back to the reality of his guests, although all he wanted now was for them to leave.

"Don't get up. Let me," she sang out, swirling out of her chair and over to the sideboard. Too late, Niccolo realized he had made a critical mistake.

"What's this?" she said, returning to the table with a devilish grin on her face. "You weren't planning on holding out on us, were you?" In her hands was the deadly decanter of Rossoli.

"It's nothing," stammered Niccolo. "It's just a tonic I take for my digestion. I have a stomach problem."

"*Bugiardone!*" she said, removing the glass stopper and smelling the fragrant liquid. "*Capitanuccio*, do you know what we have here—Rossoli! Your favorite!"

"Rosssssoli," said Don Micheletto, his drunken, watery eyes lighting up. "Rosssssssssoli."

"Here let me do that," said Niccolo, reaching for the decanter.

Madalena snatched it away from him. "You're so drunk, you can't even find the cups," she teased. "Let me do the honors."

Niccolo tried again. "It's really not very good. I keep it for my own use. I'm the only one who drinks it here. Why don't you let me get you some hazelnut liquor. It's much better."

"Nonsense," said Madalena cavalierly. "I'm sure it's exquisite. The Florentines make the best Rossoli."

Niccolo didn't know what to do as he watched her pour out three large measures of the drink. Don Micheletto and Madalena raised their glasses and with a sinking, sickening feeling in his stomach, Niccolo followed suit. This was, after all, what he wanted. This was what he had planned to do.

"To the milittttiia," hissed the jubilant Don Micheletto.

"To the militia," confirmed his consort.

"Amen," said Niccolo.

Their goblets met. Niccolo pretended to drink while he watched over the top of his upturned cup. His guests once again wound their arms around each other and raised cups to one another's lips. As

Madalena's wicked red lips closed around the rim of the silver chalice, and the first drops of the liquid touched them, she started suddenly and pulled back. Don Micheletto had the cup wrenched abruptly from his open and waiting mouth.

"*Caspita!*" she said. "That's strong!"

"It'sssssssuposed to be," laughed the don. "It's Rossssoli."

"I don't think you need to drink any of this, *Capitanuccio*," said the woman, taking the cup from her lover's hand. "At your age you have to be careful. And on top of what you've already had, it might give you a brain hemorrhage."

Don Micheletto protested and was pawing at her in an attempt to recover his cup. "You don't need it!" She shot him a fierce look, and her lips pulled back from her teeth. Don Micheletto acquiesced.

Niccolo was so amazed at this unexpected turn of events that he found himself muttering a long-forgotten prayer of thanksgiving under his breath. He reached for the bottle, hoping to whisk it away out of sight before any more damage could be done, but as he was lifting it from the table, a cold hand closed over his wrist. Her grip was surprisingly strong for a woman's, and the black fingernails dug into his flesh, almost breaking the skin.

"Maybe I need it." Her voice was almost a whisper.

Niccolo watched as she poured herself another drink. She set the bottle down well out of his reach and drained her cup. It was almost an act of defiance. When she had finished, she refilled the silver goblet and again, drank deeply.

"It is strong," she said. "But good, wickedly, sinfully good." By the time she had filled her glass for the third time, the little decanter was empty.

"Do you have any more?" she asked. Niccolo wanted to make the sign of the cross.

"What happened?" Giuditta was downstairs as soon as she heard the heavy door slam shut.

"I botched it," said Niccolo. "I botched it horribly."

"You couldn't go through with it, could you? I knew you couldn't. Not for all your talk about justice and the republic and Brutus."

"It's worse than that. I'm afraid we managed to murder a prostitute."

"What!"

Niccolo explained that Don Micheletto was not alone, and he recounted what had happened and how things had gone awry.

"Pasiphae was with him!"

"She calls herself Maria Madalena now."

"And she drank the poison, but he didn't?"

"She drank three cups. Three full cups."

"Niccolo, that's impossible! I put enough cantarella in the Rossoli to kill a whole army of Don Michelettos. Two or three sips would have been enough. And the effects are almost instantaneous!"

"She drank three cups."

"She would never have walked out of here alive if she took that much."

"I'm telling you what happened," said Niccolo. "You must have done something wrong when you mixed the stuff."

Giuditta snorted. "I don't make those sorts of mistakes." With that, she marched off into the candlelit dining room where the fateful supper had taken place.

"Niccolo, come here," she called. "Is this the cup you poured for yourself?"

"I was so distraught, I almost drank from it at one point. I guess it wouldn't have made any difference if I had, would it?"

Without saying a word, Giuditta swirled the liquor in the cup and raised it to her nose to smell the bouquet. She poured a thin stream of the Rossoli out onto the white tablecloth. Several flies buzzing around the cherry pits left over from desert were attracted by the intense, pungent aroma. They converged, circling, and then quickly alighted on the rivulet of sweet, sticky, blood-red liquor. Within a few minutes, they were dead.

The dinner at which Niccolo and Giuditta's aborted attempts to poison Don Micheletto had produced such unsatisfactory and ultimately enigmatic results took place on a Friday evening. Stifling the urge to rush to Soderini's house at dawn on Saturday morning, Niccolo spent the rest of the weekend carefully going over the case against Don Micheletto, marshaling his evidence and honing his arguments. He intended to make a fresh assault on the gonfaloniere first thing Monday morning and plead for the arrest of his and Florence's enemy.

Soderini listened patiently to the already-familiar arguments of his rambunctious chancellor. He raised an eyebrow when Niccolo told him about Don Micheletto's attempt to corrupt him by cutting him in on the militia scheme.

"How much did you ask for?" said the gonfaloniere, amused at the idea that someone would offer a bribe to the famously incorruptible Niccolo Machiavelli.

"Ten percent," said Niccolo.

"Not very substantial," mused the gonfaloniere. "You should have asked for more."

"Maybe you can enlighten me as to what would have been the appropriate amount," said Niccolo irritably. The gonfaloniere smiled amiably, and Niccolo continued. When he finished, the statuesque blond leader was still smiling imperturbably.

"Well, what are you going to do?" Niccolo demanded.

"Absolutely nothing," said the gonfaloniere serenely.

Niccolo was incensed but managed to bottle up his rage. Still, it was obvious that it was bubbling beneath the surface and ready to explode. Making a great effort to control himself, he spoke in measured tones. He had to talk through his clenched teeth. "Piero, you cannot stand idly by while that man hands over the militia and our security and our independence to our enemies!"

"There's not a thing we can do about Don Micheletto. He's vanished! Disappeared!"

"What! Why didn't you tell me?"

"You didn't give me a chance."

"When did it happen?"

"Sometime Saturday or Sunday. When his adjutant went to collect him this morning to escort him here, he found the don's apartments empty. Cleaned out."

"Did he make off with any money?"

"Some, I think, but not enough to really embarrass us. I'm looking into it now."

"Anybody else missing?"

"Two of his lieutenants—the ones you said were in on it with him. You were right about that."

"They didn't find any evidence of foul play, did they? Dead bodies? Anything like that?" Niccolo had thought fit to conceal from the gonfaloniere the details of the disastrous dinner party and the prostitute who had imbibed a lethal dose of poison. He thought perhaps her body would have been discovered in Don Micheletto's apartments.

"No, nothing like that."

"How is this going to affect us?"

"Not too badly, I think. By fleeing, Don Micheletto has taken the burden of guilt upon himself. There are grumblings that we should have done something sooner, but they'll die down. In time."

"Are you going to send somebody after him?"

"As far as I'm concerned, the matter is closed. As long as he doesn't try to come back to Florence."

Niccolo knew better than to argue with the gonfaloniere on this point. If Soderini had been reluctant to act against Don Micheletto when Florence was nourishing the serpent in her very bosom, it was entirely unlikely that he would pursue the villain outside Florentine jurisdiction. The matter was indeed closed.

But not for Niccolo. All day he turned over one question in his mind: Why did Don Micheletto flee just when he did? There were only two possibilities: The first was that Don Micheletto realized he had been the target of an attempted assassination by poison. If the dead body of his concubine turned up, that would confirm that the don indeed knew he was in serious danger. If the body didn't turn up, it would prove nothing, but would make the second explanation much more likely, and the second explanation was that Don Micheletto had friends who were looking out for his interests, and they had warned him away. These friends would have to be highly placed in the Florentine government—very highly placed.

The other question occasioned by Don Micheletto's sudden flight was considerably less troubling. Where did he go? Of that, there was no doubt in Niccolo's mind. The don had fled to Rome, that great cesspool of treachery, intrigue, and ambition. Where else would he go but back into the arms of his Medici masters? An old proverb had it right: Man returns to his sin and filth like a dog to his own vomit.

"You can't stop me," she said with bitter determination.

Niccolo had foreseen this. "I'm not even going to try. All I ask are two things."

"Well?"

"Don Micheletto is an extremely dangerous man."

"Not to me. Even if his concubine died and he's figured out you tried to poison him, there's no way he can link me to you. I'm someone he knows in Rome. To him, I'll still be the proprietor of a brothel that he frequented with his old master, Borgia, and his friend the Cardinal de' Medici. And don't you think it's probable he'll turn up there again?

"Like a dog to his own vomit. But you can't try the poison again. It's too risky. He may be on the alert for it. Besides, I've thought of a better way. You need help."

"I can get all the help I need, Niccolo."

"I want you to go to Michelozzi in our embassy in Rome. I'll give you a letter for him explaining everything. You know Don Micheletto has enemies in Rome, especially among the Orsini, since he and Caesar Borgia murdered one of their own at Sinigallia—poor Paolo Orsini."

Niccolo continued: "We have contacts with the Orsini, good contacts. With Michelozzi's help, I know the Orsini can be stirred up against Don Micheletto. Let them do your dirty work for you. Let them be the instruments of your revenge."

"That's a very clean solution."

"It's a diplomatic solution," said Niccolo. "A political solution."

"And you're a diplomat and a politician," said Giuditta. "But not a poisoner?"

"Not that," he acknowledged. "You're right."

"Are you worried that Don Micheletto's blood might be on my hands?"

"The scriptures say, Thou shalt not kill. Even your people observe the Ten Commandments, the law of Moses."

"Oh, look who's quoting the scriptures to me now!" said Giuditta. "The heathen has become a biblical scholar all of a sudden! Then you should also know that the same scriptures advise us to take an eye for an eye and a tooth for a tooth."

"Oh, Giuditta, you know I'm not questioning your right to revenge on Don Micheletto. After what he did to you, you have every right in the world. And he does deserve to die. I'm just worried about you, that's all. I don't want you to take any unnecessary risks. I don't want you to get hurt—or worse."

"Alright," she said. "I'll do things your way. I'll go to see Michelozzi and enlist the help of the Orsini. But I want to be there when it happens. I want to make sure he doesn't get away this time."

"Good, and you and Michelozzi will keep me informed?"

"Yes, dear."

"Good."

"You said two things?"

Niccolo coughed.

"What's the other one? What's the second thing?"

"I want you to promise to come back to me when it's over."

Two days after Niccolo told her about Don Micheletto's disappearance, Giuditta left for Rome. Consumed by guilt at not being able to go with her, Niccolo stayed behind in Florence and buried himself in matters concerning the militia, which had been left in a state of frightful disarray by the former captain of the guard's abrupt departure.

In the wake of Don Micheletto's flight and the scandals that came to light after his disappearance, Soderini did come under fire, and the criticism was stronger and more vicious than he had anticipated. He was blamed and attacked from all sides in the council. Members of Florence's old and powerful families openly questioned his ability to lead. They held him responsible for having brought Don Micheletto into the militia in the first place. When Soderini protested that it hadn't been his idea, they held him responsible for not having secretly put Don Micheletto to death when his treachery was discovered. They said that, in allowing the don to escape, Soderini had made a powerful and dangerous enemy for Florence. The gonfaloniere was caught in the middle, and for three weeks the storm raged about his mishandling of the affair. Then he got lucky. The first reports began to arrive from Rome. Don Micheletto had been murdered.

Although the circumstances of his death were obscure, the gonfaloniere and his government were quick to claim responsibility. They had been on his trail all the time. They had no intention of letting him escape. They were only keeping quiet so as not to expose their plans and their agents. Now that the villain had been justly punished for his crimes, they could speak openly in their own defense. Criticism was quickly silenced and the gonfaloniere's grip on the reins of power once again tightened. A political and diplomatic solution had fallen into Soderini's lap. Florence had brought Don Micheletto to justice. But there was more to it than that—much more.

38

Confusing News from Rome

The days after Don Micheletto's assassination were anxious days for Niccolo. Since Giuditta left for Rome, he had received only one brief, coded, communication from Michelozzi—"Everything under control." And then silence.

A week passed. Ten days. She promised she would come back. With Don Micheletto dead, the veil of evil had been lifted from Florence, and city absolved of her guilt. The real culprit had been made to pay for his crimes. Giuditta could come back now. But in the back of his mind, other arguments echoed, her other objections sounded: *What kind of a life do I have here? I'm not a woman like other Florentine women. I'm an outsider . . .*

Niccolo vowed to change all that. He would make time for her—a lot of time. They would get away to the country, just the two of them, for a month or two at a time, every year. He would use his contacts to see that she could practice medicine in Florence, if she wanted to. If she wanted to open a brothel, he wouldn't stand in her way. If she wanted to sell poisons, he wouldn't stop her! If she would just come back . . .

His work suffered. He ate less and his stomach bothered him. He slept poorly, and every noise in the street below—every horse that stopped, every rider that dismounted, every carriage door that banged open—sent him scurrying to the windows. She promised she would come back. Two weeks passed.

Niccolo had written several times to Michelozzi, but he had gotten no reply. That morning, as he walked up the steps to the Signoria, he was grimly determined to write again and dispatch a special messenger within the hour. He passed two of the young men who worked under him in the chancery without acknowledging their cordial greetings. "What are they so happy about," he thought. "What do they have to laugh about?"

"Messer Niccolo," someone called out to him. It was one of the *bidelli* who did odd jobs around the Signoria. Niccolo answered him with a grunt.

"Messer Niccolo, I just showed someone down to your study. Come all the way from Rome to see you." Niccolo bolted and ran. She was back!

"Giudi . . ." He stopped short. It was Michelozzi.

"Is that any way to greet an old friend? Stand there and gape? Come, Niccolo!" Michelozzi moved to embrace his companion, and the crestfallen Niccolo submitted. But in a moment he was all over him with questions: "What happened? Who killed Don Micheletto? Where? When? How?" But most persistently: "Where's Giuditta?"

"Slow down," said Michelozzi. "Slow down. I'll tell you everything."

"Then what are you waiting for? Tell me!"

"When Giuditta came to me with your letter, I set up a meeting with the Orsini. They weren't just happy to have a shot at Don Micheletto, they were ecstatic. They're really rather horrible people to deal with. They're all crazy. And bloodthirsty. Anyway, they agreed to do it, and we worked out the details.

"Since Don Micheletto had taken to frequenting the Convent of the Fallen Angels again, they were going to wait for him outside one night. Giuditta was going to see to it that he was extremely well entertained that evening, so that he wouldn't be on his guard. Not that it really mattered that much, since the Orsini were going to bring at least fifty men on the ambush. The whole family wanted a piece of Don Micheletto!"

"They brought it off then?" said Niccolo.

"Not exactly," said Michelozzi uneasily.

"Don Micheletto's dead, isn't he?"

"But the Orsini didn't do it."

"Who did?"

"I'm coming to that."

"Then come to it," urged the impatient Niccolo.

"There was a problem."

"What!"

"The night before the ambush, Don Micheletto took the brothel."

"What do you mean, 'took it'?"

"Like it was a military objective. He surrounded it with armed men and stormed it."

"And?"

"He ordered all the men—the customers—out."

"And?"

"He killed the girls. Every last one of them."

"But Giuditta got away?" Niccolo was almost pleading for it to be true.

"Nobody got away, Niccolo. I'm sorry."

"But she had to get away! She killed Don Micheletto! He's dead, isn't he? She got to him, didn't she? She got her revenge, didn't she? Well, didn't she!" He was shaking Michelozzi, screaming his questions in his face. "Where is she! Michelozzi! Where is she!"

"I'm sorry, Niccolo."

Niccolo sank back into his chair, numb and inert. Blind grief crowded out the hundreds of questions he would have asked. Michelozzi left quietly. There would be time later for details.

Niccolo was not aware of how long he sat there frozen, that one horrible thought vibrating and ringing in his mind. The gonfaloniere actually had to slap him to draw him out of his stupor and get his attention.

"I thought you had an attack of apoplexy. Are you alright?" Soderini wore a look of paternal concern on his face.

"No, I'm fine," said Niccolo.

"I came to apologize—and congratulate you."

"For what?" said Niccolo.

"I came to apologize for not believing you and to congratulate you on your intelligence and astute analysis."

"I'm sorry, Piero. I'm not myself today. What are you talking about?"

"You told me Don Micheletto was working with the Medici, and I didn't believe you. I thought you were being an alarmist. But you were right."

"What difference does it make now? He's dead, isn't he?"

"That's right. Dead at the hands of his Medici masters. Apparently, they were unhappy with the job he did here in Florence and with his untimely departure. They killed him."

"Oh, really?" Niccolo was not even interested. "Why is he telling me these things?" he thought to himself. He was wondering if there was a way to raise Don Micheletto from the dead, so he could cut his throat with his own hands.

"After you came to me with your accusations, which I thought were quite fantastical at the time, I told my brother, the cardinal, in Rome to look into Don Micheletto's doings. It seems he had been in contact with the Cardinal de' Medici. But when he fled Florence and returned to Rome, things must have soured between them, because my brother learned that Don Micheletto was meeting secretly with the French Cardinal Chaumont. Apparently he was contemplating going over to the French. But the Medici got him first. They waited for him outside the Frenchman's house with their daggers, and that was the end of Don Micheletto."

"How does your brother know it was the Medici?"

"The pope. The pope seems to be taking more of an interest in our affairs lately. When Don Micheletto's body was found, the pope called my brother, Francesco, in to discuss it. The pope wanted him to know that the Medici were busy, that something was going on with them. Naturally, he said, a good Florentine like the Cardinal Soderini would be interested to know that the Medici were up to something and that they might bear watching."

"That's good, Piero," said Niccolo impatiently. "I guess everything's settled?"

"Things couldn't be better," said the optimistic gonfaloniere. "Now I want you to get that militia in shape. As soon as you can, Niccolo. I want Pisa before the year is out!"

"Of course, Pisa," said Niccolo from a distance. Again, the normally astute Niccolo would have peppered the gonfaloniere with a thousand questions on these revelations, but he was already sinking back into his lethargic, desperate, panicky world of private pain and grief.

"Oh, I almost forgot," said Piero Soderini. "I've got a memento for you. Since you're the one who first exposed Don Micheletto, I thought you should have it. It seems the Medici left their calling card when they came for him." Something clattered on the hardwood table in front of Niccolo, and from a dim place very, very far within himself, Niccolo thanked the gonfaloniere. Soderini left shaking his head.

"Messer Niccolo, Messer Niccolo! Wake up!" It was the *bidello* shaking him. "Why don't you go home now, Messer Niccolo? Everyone else is already gone. It's late."

"Yes, thank you, I will. Thank you." Slowly Niccolo collected himself and stood up.

"Here, take this lamp, Messer Niccolo. It's getting dark. You'll have trouble finding your way out." The ever-helpful *bidello* placed the oil lamp on Niccolo's desk.

"Thanks again," said the catatonic secretary. Bending down to retrieve the lamp, Niccolo caught a glimpse of something lying on the desk. "What the . . ." He grabbed it, but before he could hold it up to the light for closer inspection, it fell from his shaking hand onto the floor. Going down on his knees, he clutched in the dark and dust under the desk until he found it again.

"Where did this thing come from?" he thought. Searching his memory, he realized it must have been the thing Soderini left behind. "The memento. Something to do with Don Micheletto? What was it Soderini had said? The Medici calling card?"

Holding it in the circle of light given off by the lamp, Niccolo gasped. It was a small dagger with a little design carved in its smooth black handle. That little design, as Niccolo had learned many years ago, was the Medici calling card.

"Call him away from his dinner!" The Soderini servants were beginning to take a dim view of Messer Niccolo Machiavelli, who seemed to be in the habit of barging into their domains and making strident, extraordinary demands on the gonfaloniere's time. Finally, to keep him from crashing into the dining room itself, they were obliged to disturb the gonfaloniere.

"Niccolo," he said magnanimously. "I should have guessed it was you. You're looking more alive than you were this afternoon."

"Where did you get this?" said Niccolo, breathing heavily.

"That? From my brother."

"And where did he get it?"

"The pope's men found it when they found Don Micheletto, if you must know. That's how they concluded that the Medici were behind the murder. You see that little design there . . ."

"I know what the design is. But are you saying that this is what killed Don Micheletto?"

"Well, not exactly. Apparently the don was torn open with about twenty-five wounds all over the place and most of them were much larger than this little dagger could have inflicted."

"Then they found this on the body?"

"In it, I should say. It's funny. The blow from that dagger was perfectly gratuitous. It couldn't have done him much harm and was probably even administered after he was already dead. That's why the pope thought somebody was trying to send a message, that the Medici were marking their victim—as a warning."

"Where was the dagger? Where was it found?"

"In his back, between the shoulder blades."

Involuntarily, Niccolo clutched the knife so tightly in his hand that he cut himself.

"Be careful, Niccolo. Here! Look, you're bleeding? Are you sure you're alright?" The gonfaloniere was a little alarmed. "Let me have someone dress that cut for you."

But Niccolo was already gone. He could scarcely believe it. This was the knife that he had pulled out of a little boy's body twenty-five years ago. Out of his back, from between the shoulder blades. Don Micheletto's dagger had come home to rest. And only one person would have put it there in that exact spot between the shoulder blades. Not the Medici! Only one other person knew.

He had to talk to Michelozzi again. He dashed out of the Soderini house and into the street. It was late, but no matter. This couldn't wait. But by the time he had gotten to the Piazza della Signoria, however, Niccolo realized, to his chagrin, that he did not know where Michelozzi was staying in Florence. It would have to wait until morning.

On the way home, the questions began to coalesce: Why did Don Micheletto "take" the brothel? Was he after Giuditta? If he was, then that meant he had to know! Nothing made any sense, unless Don Micheletto knew about the plot against him. None of his actions from leaving Florence to the murders in the brothel made any sense unless he knew. But if he knew, how did he know? Who was telling him? If he had obtained information about moves against him both while in Florence and while in Rome, he had to have sources at both ends. Going over it all, the conclusion was inescapable. There was only one way he could have found out everything he had found out, one conduit with two outlets, one in Rome, one in Florence. Two men, brothers, with identical interests, with the same name—Soderini.

But it didn't make any sense! Why would the Soderini be protecting Don Micheletto when Don Micheletto was working for the Medici? Piero Soderini was gonfaloniere for life, the most prestigious position in the republic. His brother Francesco was a cardinal who represented Florentine interests in Rome. The Medici were in exile. They were the sworn enemies of the republic, of everything it stood for, and of its standard-bearer, Soderini. It was inconceivable that the Soderini could be involved with them. The Soderini were above reproach. They were selfless in the pursuit of the interests of the republic. Unless, Niccolo began to speculate, unless they knew something, something . . .

But all these questions and considerations were only incidental or preliminary to the great question—was Giuditta alive? Of course, she was, he told himself. The fact that the dagger was found in Don Micheletto's body was proof of it! But his confidence in his own wild, unsubstantiated conclusions was eroding, and the more he thought about it, the more cause for fear he saw he had. Niccolo knew that there were probably hundreds of daggers like that. Lots of Medici retainers and employees and henchmen had daggers marked with that sign. Maybe it was just what Soderini said it was—a Medici act of vindication against Don Micheletto. Maybe Giuditta hadn't been involved. Maybe she really was dead, as Michelozzi said. Michelozzi! He had to talk to Michelozzi! He was the key. Did he just assume she was dead? Or did he know? Could he be sure? Had he seen the body?

The prostitutes calling to him did not draw Niccolo out of his self-absorption. Recently they had moved into several streets near his house to ply their trade. Ordinarily, he found their presence, while not alluring, at least interesting. Their taunting and laughter made the walk home at night more lively. But this evening he was oblivious to their solicitations. He plowed through their ranks, running the gauntlet of lewd invitations and impossible promises without even acknowledging their presence.

At the door, he fumbled with his heavy keys before finally getting it open and stepping wearily inside. Exhausted from the emotional ups and downs of the day, Niccolo skipped his supper, took several large swallows of a rough, searing brandy, and threw himself into bed. Thanks to the brandy, which now stood on his bedside table, he knew he would be able to induce sleep for a few hours at least, before waking again in the dark and wondering and worrying. But he craved those few hours of oblivion.

His dreams that night were not particularly pleasant ones, and the slumber induced by the brandy was not particularly profound. He heaved and tossed and squirmed, so that he might as well have been stretched on the torturer's rack until a heaven-sent vision of Giuditta came to soothe him. She took him in her arms. She pushed the sweaty hair back from his forehead and kissed his burning brow and at her insistence, safe in her care, he allowed himself finally to be lulled into a deep and restful sleep.

The next morning, Niccolo awoke in a panic. The hateful dreams had come back to torture him. Sitting up abruptly made him aware of the intense throbbing in his head, and he sank down into the pillows again with a groan. The questions raced back into his mind, all the more confusing, all the more unanswerable. They rushed into his consciousness, competing with each other, vying for his attention, overwhelming him. It was all he could do to summon up the blissful dream of Giuditta to drive them off for a minute's peace.

Lying perfectly still, he assessed the degree of pain in his head. It was not incapacitating, but, coupled with the knot in his stomach and the dryness in his mouth and throat, it was not encouraging. It was not the best way to start a day. For a moment, he considered taking another dose of brandy and trying to buy a few more hours' sleep, but he decided against it. He had to see Michelozzi, but he dreaded the interview. He was afraid his friend might tell him something he didn't want to hear, something he couldn't bear to hear.

With a supreme effort of the will, Niccolo hoisted himself up and swung his feet out. He closed his eyes to deaden the pain in his head. From his sitting position on the side of the bed, he slowly stood up. The headache was worse than he thought. He looked at the flask of brandy on the table. It was on its side—empty. "*Che miseria,*" he muttered.

Holding his head and directing himself toward the enclosure where the chamber pot awaited him, Niccolo tripped and went sprawling onto the floor. The thick carpet prevented the fall from doing him any serious injury, but he swore mightily nonetheless. In frustration, he kicked and flailed at the cursed tangle of clothing beside the bed that had gotten wrapped around his feet and caused him to stumble. In the ensuing fracas, he managed to scatter the offending garments all over the room in his anger until there was nothing left within reach but a single woman's shoe.

"*Amappolo!*" He clutched the thing, almost unwilling to believe the evidence of his eyes. "It wasn't a dream!"

All thoughts of headaches and stomachs that required nursing suddenly vanished as Niccolo threw open the door and bolted for the stairs. He used his hands on the walls and rails to catapult himself down six and seven steps at a time. His feet barely touched the ground. There were sounds coming from the kitchen and as he rushed in, he saw the long, dark hair swirl as she spun around to face him.

"*Cara! Tesoro!*" he shouted throwing himself at her. Then he saw the beard.

"Well, I'm pleased to see you too, *tesoro*," said Callimaco, by now in Niccolo's arms.

"Where's . . ."

"Over here, Niccolo," said Giuditta. "I'm over here."

He must have held her and squeezed her to himself for some time before Callimaco interrupted the happy reunion. "Why don't you go back up and put some clothes on, *tesoro*. Then we can all have something to eat."

When Niccolo's initial astonishment and subsequent euphoria had given way to a feeling of peace and infinite serenity, they talked. Giuditta explained that everything had been going fine, and she had made plans with the Orsini for the mutually beneficial dispatch of Don Micheletto.

"I was at the convent late in the evening the day before the ambush was supposed to take place. Callimaco here was with me. In fact, he'd been staying there for several days."

"What were you doing there for several days?" asked Niccolo.

"Hiding."

"Hiding from what?"

"The wrath of a jealous husband, what else?"

Giuditta continued, "All of a sudden, there was noise and screaming. I looked out and saw Don Micheletto waving a sword and shouting. The house was in chaos, with people running all over the place. He was ordering all the men out. 'I just want the girlssss,' he kept saying, 'Just the girlsssss.'"

"What was he up to?" asked Niccolo.

"He came for me," Giuditta answered.

"Are you sure?"

"When most of the men had been evacuated, he began asking the girls, 'Where's the *padrona*? Where's the bosssss? The Jewessssss?'"

"One of the girls said I was out, that I was gone. He didn't believe her and said he was going to start killing them one by one, until they told him what he wanted to know. Finally, someone told him I was in my perch, in my balcony on the mezzanine."

"They betrayed you!" Niccolo was full of furious indignation.

"Not exactly. They knew I would be gone by the time he got up there."

"What do you have? A secret passage?"

"Nothing as complicated as that," said Callimaco. "My quick thinking saved her life. When we saw how badly things were going, I knew we had to get out. When I saw they were letting all the men go, I figured out the way."

"What was the point in letting the men go?" asked Niccolo.

Giuditta answered: "If Don Micheletto were planning a massacre—which he was—he had to let them go first. A house full of dead whores is scarcely remarkable in Rome, but a whorehouse full of dead clergymen is something altogether different. I told you we were highly selective about our clientele. There were a lot of very distinguished people there. If they all turned up dead, eyebrows would be raised and questions would be asked. Don Micheletto didn't need that kind of attention."

"Go on," said Niccolo. "How did you get away?"

Callimaco gave me his clothes, and in the melee of half-dressed cardinals and bishops running every which way, I managed to slip out."

"Dressed as a man!"

"Dressed as a bishop."

"And Callimaco?"

"I was forced to make my exit in somewhat less than distinguished guise," he said, pulling on his beard. "Having ceded my clothing in that last heroic act, I went running out into the streets as naked as the day God made me."

"Then what?" asked Niccolo.

"When I was on the way out, I caught one of the girl's eyes," said Giuditta. "She recognized me, saw that I was getting away, and that was when they sent Don Micheletto upstairs after me. What happened after we left, I'm not sure. But I'm sure of the results. He killed them all. Whether he thought I was still hiding somewhere and he wanted to get it out of them or whether he was incensed that I got away—I don't know."

"And who killed Don Micheletto?"

Giuditta smiled a grim smile of satisfaction.

"Then the dagger *was* yours!"

"The Orsini lived up to their part of the bargain. I was there, but they did the job. I put the dagger in his back when it was over—in the same place where he put it in my brother's back. The whole scene was revolting, Niccolo. But now it's done."

The affair of Don Micheletto had raised a number of disturbing questions, and none of them could be definitively resolved. Discreet inquiries in Rome seemed to confirm that Don Micheletto needed money, and he saw the brothel as a golden opportunity. He must have known from his associations with Borgia that it was one of the family properties. If he found out that it was in Giuditta's hands, and that she had no powerful protectors, then the whole enterprise—which was one of the most profitable in Rome—was there for the taking. There were reports that he had fallen out with the Medici, and it seemed reasonable to conclude that he had moved on the brothel solely for the income.

Michelozzi had spent the better part of the month of July with Niccolo at the Machiavelli country house in San Casciano, and the two of them had talked. Closeted together all day long, they discussed the changing situations in Rome and in Florence and all the possible permutations of their positions, past, present, and to come with regard to the republic, the pope, the Medici, and the defunct renegade, Don Micheletto. They carefully traced the countless threads of intrigue and mutual and conflicting interests that bound all these parties together, often tied their hands, and sometimes strangled them.

While these questions and problems occupied the better part of Niccolo's mornings and afternoons, he made a point of setting the evenings aside for recreation, entertainments, and Giuditta. Frequently joined by Callimaco and occasionally by the rotund Fra Pagolo, the little company amused themselves at cards and charades late into the night. They played a game in which each of them wrote a sentence of a story, one after the other, without seeing what the other players had written. At the end, after the story-in-the-making had gone around several times and reached an appropriate length, the result was read aloud. It was frequently obscene and always hilarious. Callimaco's contributions in particular reflected a talent and genius for the salacious, what has since been labeled the *Gallic* element, although in truth, this fascination with the risqué was always more congenial to the Italian spirit than the French.

When Michelozzi was finally due to return to his post in Rome, an elaborate dinner party was planned. Before dinner that evening, the men amused themselves in much the same way they had done as boys. Niccolo set up a heavy table in the courtyard and erected a low barrier across its middle, and they proceeded to smash a hard leather ball back and forth across the table at each other with wooden paddles. The ball gave out a sharp "thwack" with each blow as the tennislike game progressed and the score mounted. It was considered by most bad sportsmanship to deliberately aim the hard little ball at your opponents face or head. Of course there were others who made this shot an integral part of their overall approach to the game, maintaining that the loss of the point was more than compensated by the intimidating edge it gave the player. It was all a matter of philosophy and strategy.

More than once Giuditta had sat and watched this little ritual combat and she never ceased to be amazed at the way ostensibly grown men could hurl themselves into something so silly and, ultimately, so boring. "Strange are the ways of these sons of Ishmael," she thought. "They spend their days in endless plotting and counterplotting and their evenings playing childish games."

"Thwack!"

"Thwack!"

"Thwack!"

"Did you see that shot!" shouted a winded Niccolo.

"Great shot," said Giuditta, bestowing the necessary accolade of approval.

When the sweaty competitors had finally concluded their game and washed their hands and combed their hair, they came to the table.

They were still flushed from their valiant exertions and full of talk about how the game could have gone, and, in fact, would have gone if Pagolo hadn't gotten extremely lucky and Niccolo hadn't tripped and banged up his knee . . .

"They're still boys," thought Giuditta, looking around the table at her four dinner companions. Niccolo was forty years old, she knew. And the others must all be about that age to judge from the grey hair around their temples and the white bristles among the stubble on their cheeks and chins. "Just boys."

"The soup is over seasoned, don't you think so?" asked Niccolo of no one in particular. "Too much cinnamon. It makes it a little cloying."

"Onion soup is supposed to be cloying. It's supposed to have a lot of cinnamon," responded Pagolo between noisy slurps. "I think it's fine."

"Excellent," chimed in Michelozzi.

Niccolo rolled it around in his mouth and made faces. "Maybe there's too much pepper. I don't know."

"When did you become so particular about the way your food is seasoned?" asked Pagolo.

"He's been that way ever since I've known him," said Giuditta.

"He wasn't always so bad," said Pagolo. "In fact, I remember him eating some pretty dreadful things once upon a time. Remember the *puls*, Niccolo."

Niccolo shot his old friend a wicked glance.

"Remember, Niccolo?"

"You're not going to bring that up again, are you?"

But there was a chorus of "do tells" from the others at the table, and, by popular demand, Pagolo was forced to bring it up. "Anyone who knows Niccolo knows that he always exhibited an immoderate interest in the doings of the ancient Romans. 'His Romans,' as he calls them."

"Once when we were boys, he hit upon a wonderful idea after reading about the exploits of his Romans. The Roman legions, those fierce, stalwart Roman legions had gone out and conquered the world. And how did they do it? What was the fuel that fed this invincible war machine? *Pulmentum! Puls* for short."

Niccolo scowled. Pagolo smirked. "Niccolo reasoned that if the Roman soldiers could get that way from eating nothing but *puls,* he could do it too. And once he makes up his mind, you know there's no arguing with him. So, in imitation of his ancient and noble Romans, he started with the *puls*. First he made a kind of a mushy gruel by boiling the grains in water. What did you use, Niccolo? Was it barley or rye? I don't remember. Then he diversified. Sometimes he had the mush baked into hard, flat little cakes. Of course, all this was strictly consistent with the example of the Romans. For weeks it was nothing but *puls*. His mother tried to tempt him with his favorite dishes, but he refused. His father tried to lure him with sweets, but he stuck to his *puls*." Pagolo beamed. "Now here sits the very same man, turning up his nose at the seasoning in the soup, when earlier in his life, he spent months—months!—eating nothing but mush!"

"Did it make you stronger, Niccolo?" teased Giuditta.

Pagolo answered the question: "The only thing it made him was sick. It gave him a bad case of diarrhea!"

Everyone laughed at Niccolo's expense, but the laughter was good-natured, and soon the conversation passed on to other subjects. Chastised, however, Niccolo did not complain about the food or offer comments on its relative merits for the rest of the evening. When the heavy eating was done, slices of cool melon were brought out to soothe the overheated pallets and calm the churning digestions of one and all.

Niccolo pushed himself up stiffly out of his chair, announcing that he wanted to walk off a bit of the evening's indulgence, and Michelozzi volunteered to accompany him. As they wandered out of earshot of the merry company in the courtyard, they could hear Callimaco launching into another one of his scabrous stories: "Now her old and jealous husband, Cocco, never let her out of the house, and the only way I could get in to see her was to disguise myself as a woman. She told her husband I was one of her girlfriends, and pretty soon I could come and go as I pleased. Then one day, Cocco, the husband, saw me leaving and thought the way I walked was so alluring and so provocative that he conceived a lust in his heart for me. The trouble started one day when the old man followed me home . . ."

"Where does he get that stuff?" asked Michelozzi. "Does he make it up?"

"Worse, I think things like that really do happen to him," said Niccolo.

"They certainly don't happen to us."

"Stranger things happen to us."

"Indeed." For a while they walked on in silence.

For a month Niccolo and Michelozzi had gone over the evidence and the possibilities and the conjectures again and again. In an attempt to get at the truth, they had analyzed the situation from every conceivable angle, but in the end, they were like two men peeling away the layers of an onion. Layer after layer of lies and falsehoods were exposed and discarded, and as they probed deeper and deeper, they finally arrived at the heart of the onion. But when all the layers had been peeled away, there was nothing there.

39

The War with Pisa 3

Conclusion

After the Byzantine intrigues of the past months, life in the camp at Pisa came as a blessed relief to Niccolo. He was working with his militia, their aims and objectives were straightforward, and the enemy was known. For the time being, he was able to escape the insoluble dilemmas of betrayal and double-dealing, of feinting and deception, that had dominated his life since his discovery of the treachery of Don Micheletto.

Because of the stubborn resistance of the Pisan defenders, Niccolo had decided that the most effective way of ensuring their surrender was a siege, not a porous and half-hearted siege, but a total blockade. Since the mercenary armies had been replaced almost entirely by Florentine militiamen, the dangers of bribery and corruption that had, in the past, always defeated the Florentine efforts to impose an effective blockade were no longer a problem. The militia companies acquitted themselves well and gave their commanders no trouble whatsoever. In an age where armies were characterized by disruptive mutinies and desertions, constant demands for more money, and a lust for looting and plunder, the Florentine militia was a model of discipline and military decorum.

To interdict the efforts of enterprising private individuals and other war profiteers, the army was divided into three camps. One was stationed on the Arno, one in the Serchio valley, the main means of communication between Lucca and Pisa, and the third at Mezzanna, from where the numerous mountain paths and passes that led down into the city could be watched and controlled. The circle was complete. Moving constantly between the three camps, Niccolo attended to everything, every detail, with feverish energy, and by February, Pisa was completely cut off.

The Pisans, in spite of themselves, were beginning to feel a certain grudging respect for the capabilities of the Florentine militia. Nor were they alone. In other quarters too, the apparent success of the upstart militia was being carefully monitored, and it would be safe to say, viewed with some alarm.

Niccolo almost split his sides laughing as he read the latest dispatch from Soderini. Niccolo Capponi, an unimaginative man and the official commissary of the Florentine garrisons at Pisa, eyed him with suspicion. Although Capponi was the nominal director of the Florentine war effort, he yielded in all things to the secretary of the Ten of War.

"What's so funny?" he asked.

"Listen to this—France is indignant," said Niccolo.

"Why should she be indignant? For once we haven't gone running to her for troops and materiel to fight our war."

"That's just it," said Niccolo. "Our loyal ally is outraged that we haven't gone to her for assistance! When we ask for her help, she procrastinates. When we don't ask, she demands that we do!"

"What does she want?"

"The right to send troops immediately and a payment of one hundred fifty thousand ducats toward their support. And that's not all—Spain is begging for money too! Spain claims to have shown incredible forbearance in not coming to the aid of the beleaguered Pisans who daily beg her for help. Spain feels that Florence should recompense her for the loss of the Pisan revenues!"

"And what will Soderini do?"

"Oh, he'll accept their offer immediately."

"And then the camp is going to be full of French mercenaries," said Capponi, a little uneasy at the prospect.

"Not a chance," said Niccolo. "Soderini will agree with the French and apologize for slighting them. He'll dispatch ambassadors on the spot. And then the fun begins. They'll haggle about the one hundred fifty thousand ducats, offer to pay some now, some later. They'll demand more or fewer troops, depending on what the French are prepared—or unprepared—to offer. They'll have to send back to Florence for instructions and, eventually, permission to conclude terms. Communications are slow, messages will get lost. Negotiations of this sort can be a very protracted kind of thing. You see?"

"And in the meantime, within a month, two at the most, Pisa will have surrendered."

"Exactly," said Niccolo, relishing the victory already. "And for the first time in recent memory, an Italian state will have settled her affairs with another Italian state without outside interference. That's what all the concern is about, Capponi. What will they do when they no longer have an excuse to send their armies down into Italy? Who will pay for all their hired soldiers if we won't? They can't stand to see us succeed! They can't stand to see us standing strong and alone, fighting our own battles and winning them!" And as Niccolo spoke, visions danced in his head—visions of a larger militia, an Italian national militia capable of defending the entire peninsula, capable of sustaining a united and independent Italy, and capable of throwing the barbarians out forever!

This glorious march to Italian independence was rudely interrupted by the appearance of a messenger. "Sir, I was sent to tell you that Bardella's been withdrawn."

"What!" screamed Niccolo. "Who withdrew him? Who gave the order?"

Bardella was a Genovese corsair who had been hired, with three of his ships, for 600 florins a month to blockade the mouth of the Arno and prevent supply ships from sailing up the river.

"The Genovese, sir," replied the messenger. "Here, here are the details." He handed Niccolo a dispatch. The incensed Florentine secretary tore the heavy official seals from the letter and read, to his chagrin, that, ". . . due to the extraordinary pressures from Genovese merchants who complained daily of their lost trade with Pisa, the Government of Genova was unfortunately no longer in a position to make available the services of Captain Bardella."

"Damn!" said Niccolo. Then, thinking quickly, he turned to Capponi. "Where's the narrowest part of the river?"

"San Piero in Grado. Why?"

"Get eight hundred troops down there as fast as you can. And as many light cannon as you can spare. Hurry."

The effort was successful, but only partially so. Later that day, two Genovese ships loaded with grain tried to run the blockade. The cannon fire frightened them off, but Niccolo knew they would try again. And he knew that a fast-moving ship was not an easy target for the Florentine artillery, accustomed to hitting a fixed spot in a stationary wall. It was only a matter of time before some of them would break through. But what could be done? Florence had no ships, no navy. If supplies started to get through, all the work of the past seven months would be undone, the siege would stretch on into eternity, political problems would arise with France and Spain. Niccolo clenched his fists and looked out over the river. For a moment he thought of the massive efforts of a few years ago to change the course of the river. If they had succeeded, there would be no problem today. But he knew all along that the plan had been utter folly. The river was there to stay. Then he had an idea.

"How deep is the river here?" he asked Capponi.

"I don't know. Fifteen feet? Twenty feet?"

"Find out," ordered Niccolo. "And send someone to Florence right this minute. Tell them I want an architect. Tell them to send me the best architect they can find."

Antonio da Sangallo was perhaps not the best architect in Florence, but neither was he the worst. He had been accused of being timid and old-fashioned in his designs, of lacking imagination, and, indeed, later in life he would be replaced on many an important project for just those defects. But for Niccolo's present purposes, he was more than adequate.

The architect himself was intrigued to be sent to the camp at Pisa. Like most of those in his profession, he was aware of the recent attempts to divert the course of the Arno and was a little afraid that he was going to be engaged in a similar effort. He was more than a little afraid that his reputation and his commissions would suffer as a result.

When the lanky architect walked into his tent, Niccolo came right to the point. "Have you ever built a bridge?"

Sangallo hesitated, not wanting to commit himself. At the mention of a bridge, he thought he smelled folly. He began to hedge: "I am familiar with the principles underlying the construction of bridges and have, upon occasion, acquired some familiarity with their implementation. But you will have to understand that there are many kinds of bridges. There are, for instance, arched stone bridges, which are suitable for spanning a narrow stretch of water and then, of course, for longer distances there are suspension bridges and wooded bridges built . . .

"*Basta,*" said Niccolo.

"You asked me . . ."

"I said that's enough. Have you worked on a bridge project or not?"

"Yes," said Sangallo submissively. A picture of a fantastic and impossible bridge rising from the banks of the Arno at its widest point began forming in his mind, and along with it, he envisioned the utter demolition of his career.

But Niccolo had an entirely different project in mind. "Then you know how to drive piles into a riverbed?"

"Why of course. Nothing could be simpler. Why?"

The ambitious architect sagged in relief when Niccolo explained what he had in mind. "And if you begin immediately, how long will it take?"

"Two weeks?"

"Go to it then," said Niccolo confidently. "And make sure you have it finished in two weeks." When he was alone, Niccolo fell prey to his own doubts. Two weeks. If the work was indeed completed in two weeks, the siege would hold. "Two weeks," he thought. That was the same amount of time that two military engineers had once said it would take two thousand men to change the course of the river.

The Pisans could scarcely conceal their delight when they saw the brigades of sawyers and axmen coming to work on the side of the river. The large quantity of timber that was quickly moved into position did even more to bolster their spirits, as they looked forward to another Florentine folly on a gigantic scale. But what Niccolo had in mind was neither foolish nor out of scale, and, true to Sangallo's assurances, it was finished in two weeks.

Across the river, between its mouth and the city of Pisa, three rows of sturdy wooden piles capped with iron jutted up out of the water. The stubby black fingers, spaced at intervals of about a foot and a half did nothing to arrest or change, or even slow down, the flow of water, but they made the passage of shipping an utter impossibility. A fast-moving vessel that tried got hung up on the barricade and was taken apart piece by piece by the Florentine gunners. The circle around Pisa had finally closed.

"Antonio di Filicaia," the smart young man introduced himself.

"Alammano Salviati," his equally smart companion did likewise.

"We have orders."

"Let me see," said Niccolo resignedly. They carried a letter from the

Signoria. They were to be instated as commissioners and assume direction of the campaign. Niccolo swore to himself. "This is my project!" He had directed it all along, and, now that the end was in sight, they wanted to rob him of the victory! He looked up at the two would-be commissioners for a minute. They looked perfectly capable of ruining everything he had worked for. Looking back down at document he held in his hand, he saw that there was a note attached.

> Niccolo,
>
> The Council finds it very strange that you, a diplomat with no military training, should have assumed the entire burden of running the war. Over my objections, they have appointed Filicaia and Salviati as commissioners to assist you. You've done a splendid job so far, and I have every confidence you will continue to do so, but please, it would be in our best interest to humor the new commissioners and to employ them in some capacity or other. I leave it to your discretion.

The note was signed, "Piero Soderini."

Even the arrival of the new commissioners, however, could do little to slow the momentum of events as the Florentine siege reached its climax and the Pisans reached their breaking point. Niccolo shuttled his commissioners, now three in number, counting Capponi, back and forth between the three camps and kept them fully occupied. When the Pisans asked for a meeting in Piombino to discuss terms, it was Niccolo who went to meet them. When it became clear that they were only trying to buy time, he walked out, telling them that an unconditional surrender was the only possible solution acceptable to Florence.

On the twenty-fourth of May, a delegation of Pisans—five citizens and four representatives of the countryside—rode into the Florentine camp and said they were prepared and empowered to arrange terms of complete capitulation. By sunset, after riding hard all day, they followed Niccolo Machiavelli through the gates of Florence and into the chambers of the Ten of War. The conflict of a generation was over.

The siege of Pisa had been conducted in a deliberate and methodical way. A strategy had been decided upon and then executed, down to the last detail, until the desired results were achieved. In the process, the Florentines had learned the inestimable value of keeping supply lines open, provisioning the troops adequately, meeting payrolls on time, and maintaining good communications. The order with which the entire operation had been carried out would not have been possible were it not for the disciplined, well-organized companies of militiamen who made up the army.

The aftermath of the siege was a further demonstration of the discipline and restraint of these most excellent troops. On the day of the surrender, there was no sack of the defeated city. In fact, just the opposite occurred. When three hundred starving Pisans, the last of the valiant defenders, straggled out of the city and into the Florentine camp, they were given bread. Stores of provisions were soon on their way to the suffering city.

The terms of capitulation, although dictated by Florence, were unusually lenient for the times. All real property that had been confiscated was restored. Damages were paid for the devastations inflicted on the countryside, and interest was even calculated on the loss of revenues. The Pisans were allowed to retain their old administrative magistracies, most of their rights to self-government, and freedom of commerce. In some matters they were subject to Florentine jurisdiction, but they received the same guarantees and rights under the law as the inhabitants of Florence.

These terms, arranged primarily by Soderini and his secretary, Machiavelli, brought nothing but honor to the gonfaloniere's government. Niccolo's prestige was greatly enhanced, although his success piqued old jealousies and instigated new ones against him as well, but such is the nature of all bureaucracies and all administrations.

In the days that followed the formal surrender, Niccolo was allowed to savor his victory. He passed the smart red-and-white-clad troops in review. He rode in parades with the victorious militiamen and generally enjoyed the happy outcome of his labors come to fruition. But in the heady rush to celebration that followed the long, drawn-out war, Niccolo and the rest of Florence lost sight of one factor, one critical factor. The citizen's militia had indeed acquitted themselves well and were worthy of all the praise heaped upon them. They had indeed taken Pisa at last. They had surrounded her, cut her off, and starved her into surrender. They had ravaged the countryside and beaten back or run off convoys of would-be suppliers. They had demonstrated the value of competent administration in a war. They had done all these things in a professional and commendable fashion, but they did not fight. There had been no enemy army to face in the field, no seasoned soldiers on the other side, no pitched battles. Niccolo and everyone else in Florence now placed unbounded faith in their citizen's militia, an army that had tasted victory, but without the stench in their nostrils of either gunpowder or blood.

The days and months after the capitulation of Pisa were the happiest in Niccolo's life. Professionally, he was at the peak of his powers. He traveled frequently on government business, but the trips were not long and the embassies not difficult. A free and independent Florence was secure and at peace. Commerce flourished with the opening of the port at Pisa. And Niccolo was in love—gloriously, unabashedly, shamelessly in love.

What is more, he had, by dint of almost having lost the object of his affections, become an altogether more dutiful and ardent lover. He and Giuditta did spend long weeks together in the country. He did take time off from his work to be with her.

For her part, Giuditta was no longer prey to idleness and isolation. Thanks to Niccolo's intercession, Callimaco had been licensed to practice medicine in Florence and was even looking forward to eventual admission into the physicians' guild. Although it was unthinkable that Giuditta, as a woman and a Jew, could enjoy the same legal status as Callimaco, she worked closely with him, and in many areas, particularly the concoction of medicines, her knowledge far exceeded his.

In the afternoons, Niccolo and Giuditta would often take long walks through the city. Giuditta particularly enjoyed strolling through the dyers' quarter, where yards and yards of brightly colored cloth hanging out to dry gave the whole neighborhood a fantastic and dreamlike character. The cloth was suspended on poles hung from hooks sunken into the fronts of the buildings, and every street was a billowing corridor of royal purples and deep reds and bright yellows—a permanent festival, an uninterrupted celebration of color and life.

"I've never understood those things," said Giuditta, stopping in front of a chapel and pointing to a bewildering array of different objects hanging from the walls and scattered on the floor in front of the small shrine. Most of "those things" seemed to be crutches.

"*Ex votos*," declared Niccolo. "Someone prays to a saint for a favor or protection, and, if his prayers are answered, he leaves a memento in front of the shrine as a sign of gratitude."

"Aren't those crutches?"

"The lame pray to walk again, and when they do, the crutches get deposited here."

"And the bandages and the bloody dressings, too, I see. It looks so untidy, like a refuse heap. What about those."

"Those are watermelons."

"I know what they are. What are they doing here?"

"A farmer probably put them there in thanksgiving for a good harvest."

"And does the saint come down at night and eat the watermelons?" asked Giuditta perniciously.

"Probably not," said Niccolo. "The beggars will come and collect them later on, so the offering does serve a purpose."

"What about that barrel?"

"Ah, that's Monna Lapa's famous keg of wax!"

"Famous for what?"

"Mona Lapa had a lover, a monk, according to the story, and every day when he came to her, she offered him a cup of wine. To keep her husband from noticing that the level of wine in the barrel was going down, she would pour wax into it. After many visits, all the wine was gone and the barrel was full of wax. She brought it here to thank the saints for their protection."

"Such devotion! And such an odd religion!"

"You think this is odd? This is nothing!" said Niccolo gaily, and that afternoon he took her on a whirlwind tour of some of Florence's more egregious religious oddities. There was the little finger of Saint John the Baptist, the patron saint of Florence, and the arm of Santa Reparata, which everybody acknowledged was made of wood and plaster, but it was the idea that counted, and besides, the arm had been around for a long time. It was a disrespectful afternoon full of dismembered corpses and moldy clothes, and it culminated in a little convent, where the body of a holy nun was kept and shown to the public, usually for a small donation.

"It's ghastly," said Giuditta, staring at the mummified corpse. "Her fingernails are almost a foot long and her hair's down below her waist."

"That's because they've kept on growing after her death!"

"Ugh! You believe that?"

"You never know," said Niccolo, smiling an impish smile. "You never know what to believe."

Once out in the street again, though, Niccolo was recognized and confronted by an armed band. They were a half dozen little boys in the red and white of the republican militia, waving little wooden swords. "Aren't you the man who's in charge of the militia?" demanded their leader.

"My, you're becoming quite a celebrity," observed Giuditta.

"We want to join," declared the little soldier resolutely.

Niccolo squatted, so as to speak to them face-to-face and eye to eye. "Someday you will," he said seriously. "But for now, you've got to learn to march in a regular column like regular soldiers. Are you in charge here?" He addressed the purported leader of the band, and in a few minutes he had them all smartly drawn up in a straight line. "Now, Captain, give the order to march."

The intrepid little captain barked out something in a fairly credible imitation of a drill instructor, and the column went marching off proudly across the piazza, garnering the respectful, if exaggerated, salutes of amused adults as they went. Niccolo stared wistfully after them as they receded from view. Giuditta caught the look in his eye.

"What are you thinking, Niccolo?"

"About how some day they may be called upon to put on real uniforms and take up real weapons."

"You weren't perhaps, thinking about children?"

"No," he replied in a sad voce, "I wasn't thinking about children. Maybe. Don't you ever want to have children?"

And Giuditta sighed. She knew. She knew they weren't like any other couple. Their love had no legal status, no social recognition. Nor could it ever. There were laws against what they were doing, laws laid down by his odd religion that kept little bits and pieces of its saints and martyrs in glass cases so people could go and stare at them. He was a Christian and she was a Jew. Even an enlightened city like Florence had statutes on the books dealing with the union of Christians and

Jews. They were not likely to be enforced in this day and age, in a republic that cherished freedom and the rights of its citizens, but they were there.

Giuditta tried to think of happier things. And there were many happy things to think about. She had never been happier in her life. If the future was unwritten or written in a code no one could decipher, it should in no way diminish her present happiness. She had to keep reminding herself of that. At least for the time being, they were safe. After all, the saint had not started gurgling or waving her arms in the air. No impending disasters were on the horizon.

"*Picconcina*, I have something to tell you." Niccolo said it in the tentative, apologetic voice he used to convey bad news.

"Get it over," she said.

"I have to go to France."

"Will you be gone long?"

"It's another one of those missions with no object but to temporize and delay. The longer I'm gone, the more successful I'll be."

Giuditta sighed, but Niccolo started grinning as if he had not told the whole truth. "I want you to come along," he said.

"When do we leave?"

They left two days later, and traveled slowly, not to say languidly, or even voluptuously at times, enjoying themselves very much along the way. They were gone for over four months. And it was during their absence that the trouble started.

40

An Anonymous Denunciation, a Pope Rampant, and a Rat King

Niccolo's mission to France proved to be neither as unimportant nor as pointless as he had anticipated. Shortly after his arrival, His Holiness, Pope Julius II, declared war on France, and Florence was caught in the middle. As the traditional ally of France, she was bound to side with King Louis against the pope. As a dutiful daughter of the church, however, and as an Italian state not wishing to incur the wrath of a fellow Italian state—a neighboring Italian state, a powerful Italian state—she might also be inclined to side with the pope against outside French interference. A guarded neutrality seemed to be the only reasonable course of action open to the republic, but neutrality became more and more difficult to maintain as the crisis escalated and both sides prepared for battle.

Niccolo was instructed to protest friendship for the French crown, but, as usual, not to make any firm commitments. But this time, King Louis wanted actions, not words. He wanted nothing more or less than for Florence to attack Rome.

After a particularly heated session with the French minister Rubertet and the cardinal de Chaumont, Niccolo returned to his lodgings more exhausted and exasperated than usual. To make matters worse, the innkeeper accosted him and presented him with a handful of bills for food, drink, and lodging that had not been paid for a month and a half. As discreetly as possible, that stout gentleman suggested that he would like to have his money, and on that issue too, Niccolo was forced to make vague promises in order to buy time.

Giuditta was waiting for him. The holiday in France had not

turned out to be what she had expected, either. The weather was atrocious; the French, rude; Niccolo, a nervous wreck; and they were out of money. To top things off, they never even got to Paris as promised but were stuck in the dreary environs of the castle of Blois, awaiting the pleasure of the French court. During her time in Blois, Giuditta had become accustomed to hearing rather long and detailed rehearsals of each day's proceedings and their attendant difficulties. That she found it all a little tedious, she did not intimate to Niccolo. So as he came in, she resigned herself to yet another session of, "the cardinal insisted and the minister demanded and I absolutely refused . . ."

The scowl on his face told her that things had not gone smoothly that day. "*Che cazzo vogliono!* What the hell do they want from me!" It was not a good sign when he came in cursing.

"Something came today while you were gone," said Giuditta. "Maybe it's good news."

"Maybe its money. Or maybe they're finally going to send someone up here to replace me in this thankless job and this God-forsaken country."

Niccolo recognized his friend Biagio's hand on the letter. It wasn't money. And it wasn't good news. Giuditta watched his face cloud over as he read.

"What is it?" she asked.

"Trouble."

Giuditta was also accustomed to this kind of trouble by now. Nearly every letter from Florence brought more news of trouble—trouble for Soderini, trouble for the militia, trouble for the blessed republican way of life. Always trouble. Without too much genuine interest, and with a faint trace of amusement, she asked the obligatory question, "Who's in trouble this time?"

"I am," said Niccolo. There was no amusement in the way he said it. "Listen to this: A week ago today, a certain unidentified person introduced himself, masked, to the notary of the courts and presented a deposition declaring that you, Niccolo Machiavelli, son of Bernardo, are not qualified to hold the post of secretary to the Ten of War and chancellor in the Second Chancery."

Putting down the letter, Niccolo looked hard at Giuditta. "Somebody is trying to have me removed from office."

"Who? Why?"

"Biagio doesn't know. The denunciation was anonymous. But he says a complete investigation of my financial affairs is underway. Can you imagine that! My financial affairs! What financial affairs? I don't even have any financial affairs!"

"Are you going to go back to Florence?"

"Biagio thinks it would be better for me to stay away for the time being. He says there's a lot of talk going around, a lot of things being said about me, and I should stay away until some of the furor dies down."

"Is it serious?"

"Biagio says no. He says he can handle it for me. He knows which strings to pull. So I guess we wait."

Niccolo did not have long to wait. Quite unexpectedly, quite unannounced, Roberto Acciaiuoli, one of his colleagues in the chancery, turned up in France to relieve him of his duties as ambassador. Acciaiuoli also carried a message from Soderini. The message was written in code and marked urgent. Niccolo Machiavelli was ordered to return at once to Florence and report without delay to the gonfaloniere. There was trouble.

Before presenting himself to the gonfaloniere, Niccolo thought it prudent to call on Biagio in order to find out what exactly the case against him entailed. His friend was surprised to see him.

"Returned from France so soon?"

"Soderini sent for me. He says there's trouble. Tell me what's going on, Biagio. What have they got against me?"

"You're in debt."

"I've always been in debt. What's new about that?"

"It's worse than you probably think. Your brother, Totto, signed over all your father's inheritance to you, isn't that right?"

"All my father's inheritance. Don't make me laugh."

"But your father left considerable obligations, and in the ten years since his death, your brother Totto did nothing to clear them up. In fact, Messer Totto added considerably to the amount of the debt. When he had made such a tangled mess of the affairs that not even an army of notaries and lawyers could straighten things out, he signed everything over to you."

"That was two years ago. He said he was weary of the whole business and wanted me to take care of things for him."

"Have you looked into those affairs carefully, Niccolo?"

"I keep meaning to, but something always comes up. You know how busy I've been."

"Niccolo, no taxes were paid for ten years and interest was allowed to accumulate on a number of outstanding obligations, some of them involving fairly substantial amounts. You're up to your eyeballs in debt."

"Is that all?" Niccolo was relieved. What was a little debt?

"No, that's not all. Whoever denounced you claims that you should be forced to resign your position. You know there's a prohibition on holding or exercising public office for anyone who's in debt."

"That's absurd! That goes for elected officials! I'm a functionary! I don't have any real power, especially budgetary power. And anyone can see I'm so broke all the time that I couldn't possibly have my fingers in the till." Niccolo was indignant.

"It may be absurd, but it caused quite a stir in the Signoria."

"Where do I stand now?"

"Everything is in the gonfaloniere's hands. He's supposed to make a decision."

"And what do you think he'll decide?"

"Niccolo, there is talk of dismissal in the council."

Niccolo lost no time in going to see the gonfaloniere. Debt! Debt indeed! If he had neglected his personal business and slipped into debt, it was because he was minding the republic's business instead. And they never even paid him half the time! Now they had the nerve to reproach him for being a little in debt! His level of righteous indignation was high when he entered the gonfaloniere's chambers, but he stopped short when Soderini rose to greet him. The gonfaloniere had aged visibly in the last three months. His face was drawn and haggard. There were cracks in the statue. His resplendent blond locks, always meticulously combed and curled, were plastered to the sides of his head like stiff, dirty straw.

"Niccolo," he said wearily. "Welcome back."

Notwithstanding the twinge of sympathy the man's appearance evoked in him, Niccolo came right to the point. "I understand you're considering dismissing me from my post?" He said it bluntly.

"Where did you ever get that idea?"

"Biagio said there've been calls for my head!"

"There have indeed."

"And?"

"I've quieted them down as best I could. I think I've settled matters satisfactorily for all parties concerned."

"Then if everything is settled, why did you call me back so quickly from France?"

"There are other problems, Niccolo. Bigger problems. I need you here now."

"Has something happened I don't know about?"

"Yes," said the gonfaloniere gravely. "Something has happened. There's been an assassination attempt on me."

Niccolo's eyes narrowed. All thought of his personal debt crisis vanished as duty called him once again to attend to matters concerning the survival of the republic.

"Prinzivalle della Stufa," said Soderini. "You know him?"

"Not really."

"He's a minor character in the plot. Somebody else put him up to it."

"Do you know who?"

"The usual enemies—the powerful and the resentful—the Albizzi, the Ridolfi, the Salviati, the Gianfigliazzi." Soderini reeled off a list of several of Florence's most prestigious families, ones who, ever since his administration had taken power, had been grumbling. They grumbled about the loss of the privileges they had become accustomed to, about the unfair share of taxes they said they had to pay, about the "new men" who had insinuated themselves into the government and were usurping all manner of power at their expense. They had always, by the sheer weight of their money, been assured positions of preeminence in Florentine life. They had always run the city as they saw fit, but now this upstart republic had taken it away from them—this republic that seemed to actually be taking the idea of equality seriously!—and so they grumbled. Lately, though, their grumblings had been gathering force and had already reached the pitch of a dull, but insistent, roar.

"How did you find out?" said Niccolo.

"Filippo Strozzi came to me when Prinzivalle asked him to join the plot."

"Then Strozzi is on our side?"

"Not exactly. He told Prinzivalle first that he was coming to me. Prinzivalle escaped. Strozzi claims he wants to remain aloof from politics."

"In other words, he doesn't want to choose sides until after the battle's over?" observed Niccolo.

"He's not the only one."

"What else has been going on here?"

"A lot of things aimed at discrediting me. These are complaints." He held up a thick sheaf of papers of various sizes. "Complaints that there are too many prostitutes in the streets at night, complaints about security, about sanitation, about the water level in the river! Complaints about everything, and they all imply that everything is somehow my fault! And this whole business about your indebtedness. That was part of the plot to discredit me! Albizzi had the nerve to offer me some advice about exalting men of low degree. He said that, while I no doubt found you useful as an instrument for the execution of my personal agenda, it was certainly not in the interests of the republic that she be served by such debt-ridden scoundrels."

Niccolo Machiavelli, the debt-ridden secretary of low—at least relatively low—degree brooded in silence.

"It's not just what's going on here that worries me, Niccolo. It's what's going on in Rome."

Niccolo snapped to attention: "The Medici?"

"Cardinal Giovanni's influence is growing daily. Suddenly the pope is very much his friend. The pope showers him with favors."

Niccolo was aware, through reports from Michelozzi, that the Cardinal de' Medici was up to something. He had begun to court Florentine merchants and bankers in Rome and other exiles like himself. He was generous to all and, having the pope's ear, was able to get things done for Florentines who needed to have things done. His influence was growing at an alarming rate, and it was growing at the expense of the Cardinal Soderini, Florence's official ambassador in Rome. For several months now, it was apparent that Florentines in need of a favor applied more readily, and often with better results, to the Cardinal de' Medici.

Knowing all this, and very much dubious of the cardinal's honorable intentions, Niccolo asked Soderini whether the cardinal had made a move.

"Not overtly. But Prinzivalle told Strozzi that the pope had approved of his plot. He says the Pope is interested in reinstating the Medici as the rightful rulers of Florence."

"'Rightful' my ass! We have to do something, Piero!"

"I know, but what?" said the gonfaloniere.

"Arrest them. Arrest every one of the bastards, Albizzi and all the rest."

"On what charge? That I don't like them?"

"Arrest them on charges of treason."

"We can't prove anything, and besides, there'd be an outcry. The point they keep trying to make against me is that I've become too powerful and that I want to set myself up as a tyrant. The arrests will seem arbitrary, and their charges against me will be vindicated. In the long run, it will do more harm than good."

"Then what do you suggest?" asked Niccolo.

"I'll go before the council and explain things. I'll appeal to them, Niccolo. I'll appeal to the people."

Niccolo threw his hands up in the air, "Oooofa, Piero," he said in frustration. Then he acquiesced, "Fine, go to the council, and explain. If that doesn't work, we'll try something else." And he knew it wouldn't work. This was what maddened him about Soderini—his timidity! His enemies were closing in around him, and it was time to act. So what does he propose? To make a speech and explain everything! As he was getting up to leave, Niccolo found himself thinking, "Caesar Borgia would not have made a speech."

The gonfaloniere called out to him as he was leaving the room, "Niccolo, about your debts. I've arranged to have your salary garnished until the taxes and the larger creditors are paid off."

"Thanks. Thanks a lot."

Before the assembled Great Council of over one thousand members, in the great, ornate Council Chamber enlarged by Savonarola, Soderini gave a minute accounting of his administration. He held up the heavy account books and declared them open for all to inspect, challenging any man to find fault with them. When he had exhibited the ledgers, he put them in an iron box and slammed its heavy lid shut. The ringing sound had a finality about it that greatly enhanced the image of authority the gonfaloniere was trying to project.

When he finished, unanimous roars of approval rose from the crowded council room, and before the day was ended, several measures were passed strengthening the gonfaloniere's position and giving his administration the full backing of the council and the law.

As Niccolo watched the performance, he was moved, and he was happy for Soderini. The gonfaloniere had been right. The majority was still with him. He still had the support of the people. But would that be enough? Niccolo noticed that there were those in the Council Chamber who did not participate in the rousing chorus of acclamations. He watched the fat, sleek faces of some of the better citizens. They remained unruffled, impassive, and unmoved by the gonfaloniere's words. They looked peeved or bored or slightly embarrassed. They busied themselves with papers in their laps or fell to adjusting sashes and doublets. They were in the minority, to be sure, but they were a powerful minority not without resources and full of ruthless ambitions. They were not particularly impressed by anything as flimsy and ephemeral as the will of the people. They had their own plans, and they were not giving up. Mindful of this, Niccolo returned to his study and began drawing up plans of his own—plans for the defense of Florence, plans to augment and strengthen the militia. He did not want Soderini to meet the fate of Savonarola, the fate of the unarmed prophet.

Niccolo worked on the hasty formation of a new mounted militia, armed with lances, crossbows, and matchlocks. He increased the size of the infantry, once again taking upon himself the task of recruiting men and light horse throughout the region. He worked tirelessly, inspecting the outer perimeters of the Florentine defenses.

While Florence watched and prepared herself, Julius II, the warrior pope, was not idle. With an army composed mostly of Spanish mercenaries, he took Bologna, to the north of Florence. So hot for war and conquest was the old pope that he insisted on entering the city as soon as the walls were breached. Unable to climb because of his age and unsteady legs, he was hoisted up through the breach in a wooden box. One of his first actions on taking possession of the city was to commission a bronze statue of himself to be placed in the main square. "And put a sword in my hand, not a book or a cross," were his instructions to the sculptor.

These papal incursions set off new rounds of frantic diplomacy and Niccolo, on behalf of Soderini and the republic, flew back and forth across northern Italy. Like Caesar Borgia before him, the pope now occupied Bologna and the rest of the Romagna, as well as the lands of the Papal States in the south. Once again, Florence was, for all practical intents and purposes, surrounded by forces hostile to her continued independence. The number of malcontents in the city increased, or at least the voices of the existing malcontents were raised to new and more strident levels, giving the impression of an increase in the forces and will of the opposition. It was at this critical juncture that France finally decided to intervene militarily.

Bologna rebelled against the papal occupation forces and drove them from the city, preferring to join with the French. The statue of Julius II was pulled down, smashed to pieces, and the pieces of bronze were melted down and recast as a canon. While the Bolognese were thus occupied beating their ploughshares into swords, the French army began to pour into the Romagna, and the stage was set for the decisive Battle of Ravenna, which took place on Easter Sunday in April 1512.

By the time the battle was decided, over twenty thousand men had lost their lives. By anyone's reckoning, the French were the victors. The rout of the pope's armies was received with wild enthusiasm in Florence. Bonfires burned in the streets.

Florence celebrated her deliverance, and for a few days the French too enjoyed the fruits of victory, pillaging Ravenna. But the victory was short-lived. On another front, France found herself being harassed by her eternal enemy, England. Overextended, exhausted, and increasingly unable to defend her conquests, France was forced to begin pulling back, inexorably ceding her Italian possessions as she went.

In all this Florence played little part. When it was over, the pope found himself once again lord of Romagna. When he sat down with the French to work out terms, they had difficulty agreeing to much of anything, but on one point they were perfectly in accord: Both felt betrayed by the Florentines. Surrounded on all sides and abandoned by her purported protector, France, Florence was now at the mercy of the rapacious Pope Julius II.

When Niccolo stepped out into the open air, it had a cooling, almost-bracing effect on him, despite the fact that the afternoon temperature was over ninety degrees. He had just emerged from one of many establishments in the Via dei Castellani, where the heat was all but unbearable, one of the infernal workshops where vats and pots of molten metal were poured to make cannons and guns for the militia. The gunnery smiths were working around the clock now. All night, their workshops lining the banks of the Arno glowed blood-red, and the flames reflected off the dark, shining surface of the water.

Niccolo was glad to be out of there. It was so hot that the men worked almost naked, wrapped only in grimy loincloths that looked like a baby's diaper. Most were stretched to the limits of their endurance, and yet they continued to pull on their bellows and pound on their anvils with what little strength remained. The city was preparing for war.

Niccolo wiped his brow with a soiled handkerchief and felt a slight breeze of blessed relief stir in his sweaty hair. His wet shirt clung to his back. He was exhausted, having little time to eat and getting by on only four or five hours of sleep a night, but he had to speak to the gonfaloniere, and so he set out, half dragging his feet, for the Signoria.

Some sort of disturbance was taking place in the piazza, and Niccolo mixed with the curious crowd to have a look. An itinerant vendor was attempting to solicit money from the people gathered around him, but he was having a difficult time making himself understood, since he was speaking German. What ware he was peddling was entirely undetermined at this point.

Having some acquaintance of the German language as a result of his mission to the emperor, Niccolo worked his way toward the peddler. He was a vile man, dirty, stocky, suspicious looking. In his hand he held a pole about the height of a man. Whatever was on the end of the pole—his capital no doubt—was wrapped up in a thick, coarse greasy piece of cloth. And he kept repeating, *"Rattenkönig . . . Rattenkönig . . . Rattenkönig."*

"Christ," thought Niccolo. "I don't believe this. *Rattenkönig!"*

"What's he saying? What's he got under there?" The crowd pressed. Niccolo translated: "He's saying 'Rat King'!"

Upon being apprised of the nature of the showman's burden, many of the faint-of-heart drifted away. Niccolo turned to go, but one of the more interested and strong-stomached of the Florentines grabbed him by the sleeve. "Tell him to show it to us! Tell him we want to see it. Tell him we want to see his Rat King."

Niccolo repeated the man's imperative to the little German, who coolly demanded three lire, in advance, before he was willing to unveil his prodigy. The thought of a giant rodent made Niccolo a little sick, but he seemed to be stuck now as translator and negotiator between the depraved crowd and the bizarre showman. The crowd was willing to put up two lire. The German was adamant in his demand for three.

Finally, several of the more eager spectators ran to fetch other citizens of an inquiring bent like themselves and managed to raise the requisite three lire. The little German began to unwrap his burden, slowly, almost lovingly. When he pulled the dirty cloth completely off, there were ooohhhs and aaaaahhhs. There were gasps and imprecations. Niccolo had already turned away when the inquisitive citizens pulled him back, pressed him into service again and prevailed upon him to translate.

Not wanting to look, he nevertheless caught a glimpse of the thing out of the corner of his eye. It wasn't just a single large rat at the end of the pole. It was several. Fourteen! The German was gleefully mouthing the number fourteen.

Niccolo forced himself to confront the grisly exhibition. The rats were all dead, long dead to judge from the stiffness of their furry little bodies. And they were joined at the tails. When the man spun the pole, which he did to the great delight of the crowd, the rats opened up and fanned out in the shape of a wheel. Applause.

Niccolo listened, revolted and intrigued, to the German's explanation. He did not, he said, fasten the rats together this way. He found them like that! And they were still alive. After a flood that inundated the plain where he lived and came up around the very foundations of his house, the German said he heard squeaking under the floorboards. When it didn't go away, he pried up one of the boards, saw a rat, and killed it. When he tried to pull the slain creature out from under his floor, the dead rat would not come free. After pulling up several more floorboards, he discovered the *Rattenkönig*! Fourteen of them!

He explained how the rats must have been forced up there and trapped by the rising waters. In their panic, the slippery creatures crawling all over each other, switching their long terrified tails, managed to tie themselves up tightly like that in a knot. He said he removed his precious find to a field and then just watched. Pulling against each other in every conceivable direction, the rats began to starve to death. They were easy prey to other predators, but the would-be exhibitor, sensing the value of his discovery, beat the outsiders off. And he watched. In the last hours of their desperation, the frenzied rats turned on each other, attacking with bloodied tooth and claw until they were all dead.

The German was still spinning his pole and eliciting gasps of wonder and disbelief from his enthralled spectators when Niccolo finally managed to break free. He was late, and he hurried off to the Signoria. The grotesque image of the *Rattenkönig* stuck in his mind. Unable to work together, pulling in a dozen different directions, the rats had assured and even actively brought about their mutual annihilation. "There could be a lesson in that," thought Niccolo. "The next thing you'll be thinking is that it was an omen." "Baaah," he said aloud. Niccolo dismissed the thought. Only the superstitious think that way. Or poets. And he was neither.

Soderini was pale when Niccolo entered his chambers. With him was a man dressed in muddy riding clothes, slumped over a table. The noise of Niccolo's entry brought the man to attention. It was Michelozzi.

"Tell him what you just told me, Michelozzi," said the gonfaloniere.

"Hello, Niccolo," said his friend. "Give me a minute though. I've just ridden all the way from Rome without stopping."

"Without stopping! What happened?"

Michelozzi spoke slowly: "There was a meeting. The Cardinal Soderini was requested to attend, and I went along. The pope was there, a representative of the French king, and Giuliano de' Medici."

"Cardinal de' Medici's little brother?"

"Yes, him. Without wasting any time, Giuliano, speaking on his own behalf and that of his brother, the cardinal, offered the pope twenty thousand ducats for the use of his Spanish infantry encamped near Mantova."

"Twenty thousand ducats! To do what?"

"To return the Medici to Florence. As private citizens, of course. The pope agreed on one condition."

"Which was?" Niccolo was extremely agitated.

"That the first order of business, when the troops enter Florence, be to depose the Gonfaloniere Soderini."

"And what did Cardinal Francesco say? Surely he protested!"

"The pope wouldn't hear him. Wouldn't listen to a word he said. As far as he was concerned, Cardinal Soderini no longer had any official status in Florence. He turned to Giuliano de' Medici and began discussing the future of Florence and the kind of government she should have with him! As though *he* were the constituted representative of the republic!"

Niccolo turned to the gonfaloniere, "Well, Piero?"

Early that evening, the *vacca* began to toll. The great bronze bell, the largest and the heaviest ever cast in Italy, was referred to as "the cow" because her tones were so deep, they resembled the resonant mooing of that animal. The *vacca* was only used in times of civil crisis, in case of an emergency to summon the citizens of the republic—all the citizens—into the piazza for consultation.

Soderini put the case to them in as few words as possible. Florence would presently be under attack from Spanish forces led by the Cardinal de' Medici and his brother Giuliano. The express purpose of this expedition was to depose the gonfaloniere and set up a new government in Florence. The Florentines could fight if they chose to do so. But Soderini offered them another option, a bloodless one. He offered to step down as gonfaloniere and go into exile. He asked the people of Florence to decide.

When he finished speaking, isolated shouts of "*Popolo e libertá!*" filled the air. They grew in volume until there was nothing but one unanimous, deafening roar: *Popolo e libertá! Popolo e libertá! Popolo e libertá*!

Stepping down from the podium, the gonfaloniere turned to his secretary, Niccolo Machiavelli. "Prepare to deploy the militia," was all he said.

41

The Gonfaloniere Abdicates, Eggs and Pudding Are Consumed

The Swiss were feared for their efficiency and their skill with weapons. The Germans were feared for, if for nothing else, their size. The French, while not exactly feared, were respected enough to be taken seriously on the battlefield. But the Spanish infantry in the sixteenth century, above all others, struck an abject terror into the hearts of their enemies. They were notorious for their absolute, unflinching cruelty, their delight in bloodshed for its own sake, and a kind of rabid, fanatical ferocity in battle. Their reputation for unbridled fury in the field was exceeded only by their reputation for depravity and ferociousness in the enjoyment of their victories.

The force that was marching on Florence under Raimondo de Cardona had already been tested in the battle of Ravenna. There were men in this army who, only seven years later with Hernando Cortes, would assist in the ruthless destruction of the Aztec Empire and the near-complete annihilation of its people. There were other conquistadors who, along with Pizarro, would blaze a trail of blood through the jungles of Peru and delight in the indiscriminate slaughter of the Incas. And some of the youngest among the men marching toward Florence would survive long enough to accompany De Soto on his mad, destructive dash through what is today the southern United States. The coming battle, which would decide the fate of the Florentine republic, was only practice for these men. Greater glories and greater horrors awaited them.

The first lines of the Florentine defense were drawn at Prato, where the forward assault of the Spanish troops was expected. Four thousand infantrymen of the militia were entrusted with her defense. But Prato, with her ancient and crumbling walls, was ill suited to withstand the brunt of the Spanish attack. And she did not withstand it for long.

Cardona, the Spanish commander, deliberately withheld pay and food from the men, "to sharpen their edge," he said, "to give them more of a taste for battle, more of a hunger." The companies of militia inside Prato were hungry too, for supplies, artillery, and ammunition were all inadequate for the hastily mounted defense. The matchlock men had to strip the lead from the roof and gutters of a church to make bullets. And the disarray of the Florentine body politic, some siding with Soderini, some against him, was also reflected in the ranks of the militia. Treason was afoot. There were reports of gunpowder, already in short supply, being deliberately scattered on the ground. As the Spanish army approached, the rats, joined firmly together by the tail, tugged furiously in opposite directions.

The first attack failed because the Spanish lacked artillery, but the papal legate, most eager for a Spanish victory, supplied the solution. Cardinal Giovanni de' Medici trundled along in the army's wake, borne on a litter like some fat, decadent Roman emperor because his inordinate bulk and his various anal and abdominal afflictions made going on horseback an extremely distasteful experience. The obese cardinal's progress was further retarded by the fact that he had brought along with him two cannons purchased at his own expense for the expedition. These he gladly delivered over to his Spanish allies upon reaching Prato.

Although one of the guns burst when it was fired and the other was by no means a formidable and up-to-date weapon, it was sufficient to open a small breach in the deteriorating walls of the ancient town. When the assault was given, the rabid Spanish army poured fearlessly and furiously into that breach. The inexperienced militiamen were no match for them, and the first line of defenders was hacked to pieces. The appalling brutality of the assault gave the second line of militiamen pause, and that was all the time the Spanish needed to take control of the gates, throw them open, and invite their starving, bloodthirsty cohorts to join the fray.

The militia gave way. Many threw down their arms. They would have fled, but fleeing from a walled town whose gates are controlled by the enemy is a difficult proposition, and so they chose surrender. Estimates vary, but the death toll from the ensuing slaughter can be placed at approximately five thousand, including four thousand Florentine militiamen in smart red-and-white uniforms, who were exterminated to a man.

Two days of sacrilege and slaughter followed, as the Spanish furor raged unopposed through the city. Even by the standards of the times, the brutality of the Spanish was judged to be extreme. Women, young and old alike, flung themselves from towers and windows to avoid falling into their hands. Their broken bodies littered the streets. Consecrated places were defiled, churches, monasteries, and convents invaded, and priests and nuns choked, stabbed, decapitated, and dismembered. People were tortured until they revealed the hiding places of their valuables. Ditches and sewers ran red with blood and were clogged with naked bodies and severed limbs.

Having witnessed, and indeed contributed to, this stupendous triumph, the Cardinal de' Medici addressed a letter to the pope. Sitting unconcerned at the vortex of this swirling spectacle of horrors, he wrote,

> Today at four o'clock in the afternoon, the town of Prato was taken, not without some bloodshed, but then these things are unavoidable in war. However, the speedy capture of Prato will, I am sure, have the good effect of serving as an example and a deterrent to others who may think to oppose us.

News of the defeat at Prato reached Niccolo while he was supervising a second line of defenses in the Mugello. After the first shock, reports of the appallingly barbarous conduct of the victorious Spaniards began to pour in, and the secretary hastened back to Florence. He arrived in the city at the same time as the arrogant demands from Cardona—demands for surrender, demands for an extravagant amount of money to be paid to his troops, and, last but not least, demands to welcome the Medici back into Florence.

The city was in a state of utter chaos. Citizens were fleeing to the country, and rural people were fleeing to the city for protection. As order broke down further, many of those entrusted with its maintenance, sensing opportunity, turned to looting. Doors were locked and barred. Rioting erupted. And for the first time in eighteen years, the cry of *Palle! Palle! Palle!* was heard openly in the streets.

Niccolo went immediately to the Signoria, but was barred entrance to the building by armed men. When he insisted on speaking to the gonfaloniere, he was informed that the gonfaloniere was being held incommunicado. He had been taken prisoner in his own chambers.

He rushed to the houses of several of Soderini's relatives and his trusted supporters in the Signoria, but at one after another, he was greeted by stony silence or told to go away. This bitter recognition of the depth of their loyalty—to Soderini and to the crumbling republic—finally drove Niccolo back to the refuge of his own home. Numbed by the speed with which everything had taken place, he accepted the ministrations of Giuditta in silence. His thoughts were far away, his plans in total confusion, and his future uncertain. And the wheel of fortune was spinning, spinning, spinning. New faces appeared on the wheel now—the haggard visage of Soderini among them, and, for the first time, Niccolo saw his own face teetering at the very top of the wheel as it spun. And inevitably, ineluctably, inexorably, it kept right on spinning.

Niccolo was awakened from a fitful and haunted sleep by loud pounding at the door. Peering through the wine window, he saw three diffident men lounging outside his door. They were armed.

"Machiavelli?"

"What do you want?"

"Are you the Machiavelli that's secretary in the chancery?"

"I am."

"Then get dressed. You're coming with us." The man's voice was gruff, but not threatening. If anything, he was sleepy and desirous only of discharging his nocturnal duties as quickly as possible.

"Where do you intend to take me?"

"To the Signoria. There's a meeting in progress, and your presence has been requested. Now hurry." He yawned.

Although Niccolo was wary of these men, they made no attempt to restrain, intimidate, or otherwise harass him en route to the Signoria. Along the way, they encountered bands of looters scurrying to safety with their ill-gotten gains, and small bonfires of destruction burned in the windows and courtyards of some of the more prominent partisans of Soderini and the republic, the usual price of political change.

This time Niccolo was not stopped at the gates of the Signoria but was allowed to pass with his escort. They led him straight to the gonfaloniere's apartments. "In there," said the weary guard.

As Niccolo stepped into the familiar chamber, the gonfaloniere rose anxiously to greet him but was pushed rudely down into his chair again by one of the angry young men at his side. The room was full of similar young men, similarly angry. They strutted and preened around the enormous, ornate chamber. They were all red hose and flash, gold and silver brocade, rustling flamboyant silk capes cut impudently above the buttocks. Even their daggers and short swords were pretentiously wrought, lavish, showy. Niccolo recognized several of them—scions of notable and noble families like the Ridolfi and the Salviati. They were cousins of the Medici.

"In the interests of the city of Florence, the gonfaloniere for life here has decided to step down." His voice was dripping with sarcasm when he pronounced the title, "gonfaloniere for life." The one who made this announcement was an Albizzi, and he seemed to be the leader of this arrogant band of interlopers. He was wearing a big, crushed-velvet, purple hat and a yellow-and-purple-checked doublet. He seemed to be inordinately proud of his fine patrician profile and kept cocking his head at different angles and striking manly poses so as to display it to advantage.

By contrast, the gonfaloniere looked disheveled and unkempt. His clothing had been torn, and there were bruises on his face. He looked defeated. Niccolo took in all these details without saying a word. When he spoke, it was to Soderini and not his arrogant captor. "Gonfaloniere," he said in a deep and reverential voice, bowing, removing his hat. "How may I be of service?"

"Ah, Niccolo," sighed Soderini. "Faithful, selfless Niccolo. My fate is to be decided this evening. And I wanted someone here I could trust."

Niccolo eyed the strutting, fatted calves. "Your fate is to be decided, and these peacocks are to serve as judge and jury?" he said, almost amused.

The objects of his scorn, however, were not amused, and many a soft hand went clutching after a jeweled dagger in a demonstration of fierce, aristocratic outrage.

"Shut up, Secretary." It was the young Albizzi who spoke. "The gonfaloniere—or should I say 'the ex-gonfaloniere'—has asked that you be present. You may confer with him until we're ready to begin." So declaring, he ambled off, making a great show of his disdainful airs and his superiority.

"Piero," said Niccolo urgently when they were alone. "What happened?"

"They broke in on me. They were very resolute."

"I told you to strengthen the guard," said Niccolo angrily.

"But I never thought there was any danger here, in my own office."

"Never mind that now, Piero. What do they want?"

"They demanded that I release all the prisoners we took the other day, the Medici partisans."

"And you've ordered the release?"

"I have."

"Do the guards still obey you then?"

"They look to the young firebrand before executing my orders. They're caught in the middle. They don't know whom to obey."

"And what else does the young firebrand want?"

"He wants me dead," said Soderini.

As Niccolo and the gonfaloniere talked, there was a ruckus at the door as a group of corpulent, officious gentlemen bustled into the room in a great cloud of scarlet and dark-blue robes. They were the recently imprisoned leaders of the resurgent Medici party and the fathers of the gilded pups who were holding the gonfaloniere prisoner.

Anton Francesco degli Albizzi was the first to speak. "Piero, you've been ill-treated," he said solicitously to the fallen gonfaloniere. "Please, I'm terribly sorry. This should never have happened."

The son of the prudent old politician, emboldened by his successful seizure of the gonfaloniere, and perhaps by the splendor of his dashing yellow-and-purple equipage as well, spoke up. "Father, this is no time for pity. This is the time for action, rash action if need be. You lack the nerve! You lack the will, you and your generation. Step aside now, and let us bring things to a fitting conclusion. The gonfaloniere is no longer of any use to Florence. Let us dispatch him. Don't stand in our way!"

"Is that a threat?" said the older Albizzi, glaring at his impetuous offspring.

"*Chi ha orecchie, intenda,*" said the young man smugly. "But if Soderini lives, sedition lives. We'll never be free of his plotting and scheming."

The elder Albizzi regarded the broken gonfaloniere. Then he took in his son and the fidgeting crowd of high-strung champions he had gathered around him. He spoke to the hot-headed young tribe: "I counsel prudence. After all, Piero, for all his republican sympathies, is one of us. He merits some consideration, some mercy on that account."

"He's betrayed us all by siding with the vulgar and the low born! He's dragged the name of Florence in the muck. He deserves death." Young Albizzi was not to be denied. His band of intrepid civil warriors eagerly seconded his sentiments, and a fierce round of inter-generational conflict was set off. To all this, Niccolo and the gonfaloniere remained mute witnesses.

As the battle of words over Soderini's destiny raged between the peacocks and patriarchs, Niccolo noticed that there was another silent observer, who also remained at a distance. Young, but not dandified, he was dressed plainly, in a simple brown lucco. And he wore a beard, which was unheard of for any self-respecting Florentine of the day.

The vociferous argument had reached an impasse, and the hot-blooded youths were on the point of driving their sires from the room with their stiff little daggers, when the bearded stranger rose. He approached the front lines of the battle, where the two Albizzi squared off as respective champions of their generations. The shock of recognition registered first on the face of the older Albizzi, who ceased arguing and assumed a posture of respect. "Ser Giuliano," he muttered. One by one, the older men fell silent until only the screeching voices of their angry offspring filled the air.

The purple-and-yellow Albizzi had worked himself up to a pitch approaching rabidity when his father suddenly turned on him, put his heavy, sagging but still authoritative, face within an inch of his son's and shouted, "Shut up, you fool!" A loud slap that sounded like a thunderclap brought the message home and stunned the boy into silence. "Now show some deference in the presence of my lord, Medici."

Turning to the bearded man, he said, "I apologize for my son, Mio Signore, please forgive his impetuosity."

"No apologies are necessary," said the man in an even voice.

"Unless they're addressed to the gonfaloniere. He seems to have been badly used."

In a matter of seconds, the blustering army of youth was reduced to a pack of groveling courtiers, fawning, pawing for favors at the feet of Giuliano de' Medici. Respects were paid and repaid and paid again for insurance. All this, Giuliano received graciously, not arrogantly, and when the little pageant of obeisance had played itself out, he turned to the problem of the gonfaloniere.

"Piero," Giuliano called him by his first name. "I have no grudge against you, but as you can see, it would be awkward to allow you to stay on here in an official capacity. You have—*ahem*—made enemies," he indicated the pack of would-be lions, chaffing in the corner.

Then, approaching them, he said, "And you, do you think that you can win the backing of the people by murdering their gonfaloniere? Who among you is going to replace him in their affection? You? You?" Heads bowed. Rakishly shod feet shuffled uncomfortably.

To Soderini, Giuliano de' Medici continued, "You've given much to Florence in the past, and perhaps you deserve more from her now than I or anyone else can offer. But we're on opposite sides in this quarrel, and now my party is in the ascendancy. If we struggle with one another, if our supporters fight, it will tear the city apart. More blood will be spilled, Piero."

Soderini stood up. He shot a fierce glance at his young tormentors. Then he spoke. There was a tremendous amount of dignity in his voice, in his bearing. He spoke to Giuliano de' Medici not as a defeated man but as an equal: "For the good of the city, I yield. The reins of government are in your hands now. Use them wisely. Listen to the voice of the people."

"I promise you that much, Gonfaloniere," said the younger man solemnly. "And I promise you my protection, if you accept a sentence of exile." There was grumbling from the revolutionaries at the offer of exile. Soderini only smiled in response. He knew he had no other choice.

"This man is someone you trust?" asked Giuliano, indicating Niccolo.

"Above all others," acknowledged the gonfaloniere.

"Then let him act in your behalf to arrange for your departure."

Two days later, escorted by a troop of forty horsemen, still clad in the colors of the republican militia, the Gonfaloniere Soderini rode out of Florence and into exile.

In the wake of Soderini's abdication, a Ridolfi, one of the innumerable Medici cousins, was chosen as gonfaloniere. The Great Council was well stocked with Medici supporters long excluded from the government, and, of course, their salaries were raised. But aside from these changes in personnel, little else was altered. The institutions of Soderini's government and the old republican forms were maintained. Giuliano de' Medici seemed determined to remain, as he had promised, a private citizen among other citizens in Florence. He eschewed inhabiting the sumptuous Medici Palace and, instead, set up temporary quarters in the house of the elder Albizzi. He even shaved his beard to accommodate Florentine tastes.

At first, it was with an understandable degree of trepidation that Niccolo returned to the chancery after Soderini's departure, but it soon became apparent that the massive and intricate bureaucracy that actually ran the day-to-day affairs of the city would remain in place. Letters still needed to be written, and thousands of petty foreign and domestic matters had still to be settled daily. For the most part, chancery business proceeded as usual, and if Niccolo had yielded some of the enormous influence he enjoyed under Soderini, he was nevertheless consulted frequently on the many routine administrative matters that fell within his jurisdiction. In addition, his work at the chancery was rendered easier and more enjoyable by the presence of his friend Michelozzi, who now worked alongside Niccolo. But in mid-October, about two months after Soderini's downfall, something happened to upset the delicate balance that had been struck between the new regime and the old. The Cardinal de' Medici came to Florence.

He entered the city in triumph, reclining on his litter and looking for all the world like an enormous roast pig on a giant platter. He was swathed in yards of dazzling, loose white silk and crowned with his red cardinal's hat. He was accompanied by four hundred arrogant Spanish lances and one thousand Spanish foot soldiers—those who had most distinguished themselves in the carnage at Prato. The undisputed head of the Medici family had arrived. The experiments in civic reconciliation were about to come to an end.

A *balia* was a sort of emergency government proclaimed in times of great crisis or civil strife. The *balia* was given extraordinary powers, for a short period of time, so as to be able to meet the crisis without submitting to the normal, and often-cantankerous, workings of parliamentary government. Only the assembled people had a right to call for a *balia* and demand the convocation of one of these short-term provisional governments.

A rather tawdry and mercenary assemblage of drunks and paid hangers-on in the Piazza della Signoria was represented as just such a spontaneous public outcry. It was called a tumultuous, explosive outburst, a unanimous expression of the popular will, a *cri de coeur*, a groan from the belly of the people, a rousing call to arms, a plea for change. . . . The cynical exploitation of this staged event knew no bounds.

In response to this clamoring from below, the Cardinal Giovanni de' Medici—what choice did he have?—dissolved the Great Council and proclaimed the appointment of an interim *balia* to superintend the formation of a new government. The list of those who made up the *balia*, they were forty-five in all, read like an excerpt from the Medici family album. How could it be otherwise? They were all chosen personally by the cardinal.

"Reforms," for so they were designated, followed rapidly. The militia was abolished. Citizens were denied the right to bear arms. All powers—legislative, executive, and judicial—were concentrated in the hands of the narrow forty-five-member *balia*, and the *balia* answered only to the Cardinal de' Medici. This entire process took less than two weeks.

Niccolo, along with his colleagues in the chancery, watched these developments with a growing sense of hopelessness and impotence. Just like that, it was over. The republic had evaporated before their very eyes. And there was nothing they could do to stop it. Their reactions to this remarkable chain of events varied, ranging from outright collaboration and slavish prostration before their new masters to bitter denunciation and self-imposed exile.

And Niccolo? He did what was required of him, rendering accounts to the new council members when requested to do so. He burrowed into his work and wrote his letters. And he waited and hoped. He was determined to come to some sort of working relationship with the Medici, to hang on, and eventually, he thought, some form of republican government might be established under their protection. The younger brother, Giuliano, especially was open to the idea.

"Besides," Niccolo said to himself, "what else can I do?" In fact, he had never had any other sort of employment except in the chancery. He hardly fancied the idea of becoming a wool merchant or a money changer or a locksmith or a stonemason or a barrel maker . . . The chancery and the Signoria were in his blood, and he would stay on and do what he could. He would bide his time and watch for an opening. And then Niccolo recalled a promise he had made long ago. He heard in his mind once again, the soft voice of the dying prophet—"Carry on my work. You will carry on my work? Won't you?" Savonarola had been right. For people like himself and Niccolo, there was no other way. He would carry on the prophet's work. Somehow.

While Niccolo was thus engaged in thought, a messenger darted into his study and off-handedly flung a letter on the table. The paper was of a rich, creamy vellum, hardly the stuff of routine diplomatic correspondence. Turning it over idly, Niccolo saw the red wax seals and the impression left in them by the signet—the balls. The wax was still warm and soft to the touch. It was only a brief note in an elegant hand, requesting his presence in the Via Larga, at the newly restored Medici Palace.

The austerity of the building's exterior gave no clue whatsoever as to the sumptuousness that lay within. Although many of the art treasures from the days of Lorenzo de' Medici had been lost to looters, his son the Cardinal Giovanni had been more than energetic in his efforts to restore the glories of the past. While in Rome, the cardinal had been an astute dealer in stolen antiquities and objets d'art, and now the palace was filled with his purchases. Niccolo was led through gleaming, gilded corridors, past fountains, past statues carved a thousand years ago by some unknown Greek hand, past paintings, and under ornate arches inscribed with the Medici balls.

Niccolo was told that the cardinal would receive him in the dining room, as he and his familiars were just concluding their midday meal. As they neared that room, roars of laughter could be heard. Niccolo thought he heard a great hoarse chorus shout, "Thirty-four!" Then "Thirty-five!" accompanied by another rousing burst of merriment. "Thirty-six!" What was going on?

Nobody paid the least bit of attention to Niccolo Machiavelli as he was ushered into the hall. "Thirty-seven!" "Thirty-eight!" The excitement was mounting. The spectacle that had the gay company enthralled was that being provided by a rotund man seated at a table behind a huge pile of eggshells. Next to the shells on the table were two hard-boiled eggs. As he popped one of them into his mouth, whole, the diners roared, "Thirty-nine!" And when the last egg disappeared a moment later, a resounding, delirious chorus of "Forty!" filled the air. There was wild applause. Apparently the man had just eaten forty eggs.

The bleary-eyed champion sat back in his chair and ran two small hands over a massive, distended belly. He was being showered with confetti. His triumph was complete. As Niccolo watched with a sort of detached amusement, the cardinal rose, banged repeatedly on a silver goblet, and called for silence. Gradually the delirium diminished to a point where he could make himself heard. "Mariano Fetti," he proclaimed. "The undisputed king of jesters!" More cheers. The cardinal continued, "Who doubted my word? Who said he couldn't eat forty eggs? Pay up! I've won the wager!"

Several of his fellow diners reached into pockets and purses and grudgingly extracted gold coins. These were passed down to the cardinal, who counted them carefully, looked around the table, and, with a burst of laughter, flung the handful of money recklessly over his shoulder. The entire company joined him in another round of laughter. Banging again for silence, the cardinal called for the prize to be awarded to the irrepressible Fetti, consumer of forty eggs. Two servants went scuttling off and returned a minute later with a large pie, which was placed in front of the champion. "Go ahead, Mariano," said the cardinal with a mischievous grin. "Cut it open. It's yours."

With a long silver knife, Mariano Fetti bisected the pie, and, to the delight and amazement of all, two live nightingales flew out. As they circled the cavernous dining hall, the lusty cheers and cries of assembled diners rose and mixed with their joyful song. Breathless and red-faced from laughter, the jolly cardinal sank back into his ornately carved and gilded chair.

The chamberlain who had kept Niccolo waiting, not wanting to interrupt these capital festivities, now approached the cardinal and whispered something in his ear. The cardinal was wagging his great, flabby face up and down as he listened. He looked over at Niccolo and squinted in his direction with his one good eye. He stuck his pink tongue out between his teeth in the effort. Still squinting, he reached under the table and extracted something, a long tube that he raised to that blue, watery eye. It was a spyglass, and he trained it on his newly arrived guest. Thus he conducted a leisurely examination of Niccolo from a distance of about twenty feet. The cardinal was almost blind.

Satisfying his curiosity, the cardinal rose abruptly, excused himself, and disappeared through a doorway behind the table. The chamberlain motioned for Niccolo to follow. When he reached the antechamber, the cardinal was already reclining on a day bed in the little room.

"Come in, come in, Machiavelli," he said effusively. "Did you see Fetti? Isn't he superb? Did you see he ate forty eggs?"

"Quite remarkable, Your Excellency," said Niccolo.

"He can also eat twenty chickens in a sitting. Twenty chickens! And he has the most vile, outrageous sense of humor. He can keep you laughing for days." The chubby cardinal chuckled at the mere thought of his superb jester. Niccolo said nothing. He watched the cardinal's hands. For the moment, Florence was in those hands. His swollen, stubby fingers looked like sausages with gold rings on them.

The next time the cardinal spoke, he was holding several sheets of paper in those pink hands. "Did you write this?" he asked, handing the sheets to Niccolo.

"These are the letters I addressed to Your Excellency's brother, Giuliano."

"And they contain advice? That's your word, 'advice' about how to reorder the city government?"

"That's correct."

"Some of this is really very astute, quite astute," said the cardinal, chuckling again. "You warn us against confiscating a man's property. He'll feel more grief at the loss of his farm than at the loss of his father or brother, you say. Quite amusing. You don't have a very high opinion of your fellow man, do you Machiavelli?"

"On the contrary, Your Excellency," said Niccolo respectfully. "I have a tremendous amount of confidence in the people."

"Yes, that comes through in these letters too," said the cardinal thoughtfully. "You advise us to seek the people's support. And Giuliano agrees with you. He thinks the support of the people is vital, if we are to remain in power here."

As the cardinal spoke, Niccolo became uncomfortably aware of the odor seeping up out of his bowels and intestines through the rich cloth and gradually filling the tiny room. It was true what they said about his uncontrollable flatulence. The odor of sanctity. Niccolo wondered if it embarrassed him or if he was even aware of it—or if he used it consciously as a weapon to disconcert his interlocutors.

As the fetid gas rose, the cardinal talked on, unconcerned. "Tell me, Machiavelli, do you think the people put us back in power?"

"Not exactly, Your Excellency," said Niccolo, trying to be as discreet as possible.

The cardinal smiled at his candor. "Of course you're aware that only a very small number of the people, and the better people at that, arranged for us to return to Florence."

Niccolo hazarded, "The people didn't put you where you are today, but they might easily remove you one day."

"Perhaps," said the cardinal. "So what would you advise?"

"Gaining their support, as I wrote to Giuliano."

"I don't agree with you. I think the will of the people can be, how shall I put it, managed?"

"Giuliano seemed to agree with me," countered Niccolo.

"But Giuliano's gone to Rome," said the cardinal through his gas cloud. "I sent him there on some urgent business."

Just as he finished speaking, a small dark woman in diaphanous green veils—one of the merry diners—came running into the room shrieking, "The pudding! The pudding!"

"Ah, the pudding!" The cardinal's face lit up. "I must go and attend to the serving of the pudding." Turning to Niccolo, he said, "Well, I've enjoyed our little chat. I appreciate your advice and the work you're doing in the chancery. Feel free to call on us anytime." With that, he swept out of the room, leaving Niccolo more than a little puzzled at the reason for this interview.

As he passed through the dining room, Niccolo saw the pudding being carried out in a giant bowl, a tub really, and placed before the cardinal. Something appeared to be bubbling beneath the surface of the thick, sweet desert. Suddenly emerging from the murky depths of the pudding, two naked children stood up in the bowl! The cardinal threw back his head in exaltation, and the hall erupted in another orgy of laughter.

As Niccolo stalked out of the Medici palace, ruminating on the apparently pointless exchange that had taken place between himself and the cardinal, he saw flocks of people lining up at tables in the Via Larga. Free wine was being dispensed. And sweets. The people were being, how did the cardinal put it, "managed."

After Niccolo was gone and the diners, stupefied with food and drink and entertainment, began to disperse, the cardinal rose and repaired once more to his day bed. A woman entered the small chamber from another door.

"Well?" said the sleepy cleric.

"He's the one," she said as her hand closed on the cardinal's pudgy wrist. "He's the one who tried to poison me and Don Micheletto. Her long black fingernails sank into the soft pink flesh.

42

Boiling Lead

"Messer Niccolo!" The *bidello* popped his head into Niccolo's study. "The council wants you again."

Again. For the past several weeks, Niccolo was continuously summoned before the council to explain this, to account for that, to offer his opinion on such and such an option. He had never realized before how indispensable he was. No matter who ruled the city, they needed to know where the funds were deposited, what couriers were reliable, which allies could be trusted, which could be used. A thousand details.

"What will it be this time?" he wondered, as he made his way to the Council Chamber past the rows of portraits of the illustrious ancestors of the Medici. It was never without a twinge of nostalgia now that Niccolo entered the vast hall where the council sat. The room had been given its present form by Savonarola. It was enormous, intended to accommodate an enormous council. Under the republic, one thousand representatives were seated on the council. All around the perimeter of the great hall, benches had been built. From these rows of benches, the people were allowed to witness the debates and hear the speeches of their representatives.

Now armed guards stood at the doors. Admission was by invitation only. Now the benches were gone. And the tables at which one thousand elected representatives once sat had been removed. Only two tables were needed to seat all the members of the new council. They were placed against the far wall, under the windows. From where you entered, you could barely make out the features of the men who occupied those tables now, across that big, empty room. It took forever to reach them. And as you crossed, the only sound was the clicking of your own heels on the marble floor in that great, abandoned, lonely hall. Saddened as always by this state of affairs, Niccolo went nevertheless, with his ledgers tucked under his arms, to do what he could for the good of Florence.

That evening when he returned home, his face was a white mask of shock and disbelief. He lowered himself uneasily into a chair and sat, just staring into space.

"*Tesoro*, what's wrong?" asked Giuditta.

He looked at her for a minute without saying anything, then tears welled up in his eyes and the words tumbled out: dismissed . . . stripped of all offices . . . barred from the Signoria . . . and banished!

The next morning, Niccolo trudged up the stairs of the Palazzo della Signoria for the last time. He would render up a final account of his administration, and then he would be forbidden to cross the threshold of this building ever again. He was also to be exiled from the city of Florence for a period of one year and made to pay a surety of 1,000 lire to guarantee his submission to the sentence.

Although many of the other clerks had already begun to distance themselves from him—the proscribed, the disgraced, the exiled, the tainted—Michelozzi had been very helpful that last day. Niccolo was grateful for this small kindness.

"You'll be back, Niccolo," he said, trying to sound encouraging.

Niccolo just shook his head.

"I bet within the week they'll have to send someone out to consult you on something or other. You wait and see."

"How did it happen, Michelozzi? How did all of this happen? How did the republic just disappear?"

"Try not to think about it, Niccolo."

"What else am I going to think about?"

"Think about the future."

Niccolo grunted. "The future," he said bitterly. "What future?"

"Come on, the sentence is only for a year. You'll be back, I tell you. Sooner or later, they'll realize they can use you. They can't ignore your experience or your talent. In the meantime . . ."

"In the meantime, I can take up beekeeping or some sort of animal husbandry. Great."

"It could be worse," said Michelozzi.

"You're right," said Niccolo. "It could be a lot worse. Look what happened to Boscoli and Capponi."

"What did happen to them exactly?"

"They just disappeared. I heard they'd been arrested, but there doesn't seem to be any confirmation of that. The council denies it."

Michelozzi shook his head. Boscoli and Capponi were two younger men who held minor positions in the chancery. A week ago, they stopped coming to work, their desks were cleared out, and they were replaced by two new men. Their families were worried. Nobody seemed to know what happened to them, but Niccolo was about to find out. As he and Michelozzi speculated on the fate of their two young colleagues, Niccolo's door flew open, and a dozen rough and bearded Spaniards with drawn swords burst into the little room.

"Which one of you is Machiavelli?" said the captain.

"What's the meaning of this?" said Niccolo, jumping to his feet, indignant at the intrusion.

"You Machiavelli?"

"Yes, and who are you?"

"You're under arrest," said the captain. And before Niccolo could even open his mouth to protest, he was in the grasp of two soldiers. Their vicelike grips pressed his arms to his body, and a sharp-pointed sword held at his throat ensured his cooperation.

Helpless thus pinned, Niccolo was led from the room. He cast one furtive glance over his shoulder, and caught Michelozzi's eye. "Giu-dit-ta," he mouthed the word silently with his lips. Michelozzi indicated that he understood.

Niccolo's warders had escorted him in silence, not to a magistrate for arraignment, not to the *podesta* to hear charges read against him, but directly to the *stinche,* a dank subterranean system of prison cells in the bowels of the city, along the banks of the Arno. The only communication he received at all from his captors were the last words of the jailer as he banged the heavy door shut behind him: "I'll make you shit as small as a rat shits."

There was water on the floor of Niccolo's cell, about an inch of it. It squeezed in through the cracks in the damp, glistening walls and trickled down endlessly, day and night. He had heard rumors that when the level of the river rose, these cells were allowed to flood and that prisoners sometimes found themselves waist deep, neck deep, in icy water. It was part of the punishment.

The moldy wooden bench that served him as chair and bed was the only relatively dry place in the underground cell, and it was crawling with vermin swollen to a magnificent size on God knew what offal. For days, Niccolo was left with nothing to do but shiver in the cold and flick the cursed, hungry vermin from his bench and clothes. He lost track of how long he was there. The only interruption in this routine was the daily arrival of the taciturn jailor with his food. And then there were the screams in the night—at least he thought it was night. They seemed to come from far away. They were faint, muffled, but they were long and drawn-out. As indistinct as they were when they reached him, they still made Niccolo's flesh crawl and his hair stand on end.

At first he was furious. He hadn't done anything! Why were they holding him? He was aflame with righteous indignation at not being told what were the charges against him, at being held incommunicado, at not being given a proper hearing. . . . But all these abstractions were beginning to appear insignificant compared to the unbearable immediacy of the numbing cold and the dark and the terror of not knowing what was in store for him. His spirit was sagging, breaking down, and his shit, true to the jailer's predictions, was as small as rat shit. He wanted out.

Finally, keys rattled in the lock, the bolt was lifted, and Niccolo's name was called. He jumped up and sloshed through the water on his cell floor. He felt it seep into his boots as he crossed to the door. Two brawny jailors fixed to his legs fetters that must have weighed forty pounds. Did they think he was going to run away? As he clanked between his captors down the corridor, their torches threw ghostly, moving shadows on the prison walls. To Niccolo's repeated questions as to where they were taking him, they answered only, "For questioning."

He was led into a large, infernal subterranean chamber, domed and ringed nearly all around with blazing hearths and chimneys. The air was filled with the clanking of iron and the rattling of chains. A quick glance around told Niccolo all he needed to know about the nature of the "questioning" to which he was about to be subjected.

In the sixteenth century, the guilds of Florence covered nearly every aspect of economic life. They were not workers' organizations, but rather cartels composed of owners, producers, professionals, and skilled craftsmen. Enjoying a virtual monopoly in their particular spheres of activity, they were thus able to fix prices, dominate markets, eliminate unwanted competition, pool resources to lobby, and, if need be, bribe public officials. However, they also provided comprehensive systems of training, licensing, and quality control over the products and services they offered. They were highly specialized organizations, these guilds, and among themselves they divided and subdivided the spectrum of commerce and industry into minute and very particularized segments so that, for example, there was not merely a butcher's guild, but a hog butcher's guild, a goat butcher's guild, a sheep butcher's guild, a poultry butcher's guild, and so on.

There was scarcely a skill known in Florence whose practitioners had not banded together into one of these corporate entities. But there was no guild for torturers. There was no organized system of apprenticeships and journeymen and masters. One who wished to practice the art or craft or trade did not have to pass an examination or present any "masterpiece" before his colleagues as proof of his skill and attainments.

Although there were undisputed masters of torture, they came from diverse sources. Butchers of large mammals were ideal recruits because their long and thorough study of the disarticulation of animals made them readily adept at the systematic dismemberment of the human system of muscles and nerves and sinews and bones. They knew how to kill painlessly, which meant, by implication, that they also knew how to kill by inflicting a great deal of pain. Other practitioners of the ancient art were often recruited from the ranks of the blacksmiths and ironmongers. Their familiarity with heat and fire and molten metal made them qualified candidates.

In the Florentine republic under Soderini, this fine art of torture had been allowed to fall into a state of woeful neglect. Institutions and a system designed to protect the individual from rash and arbitrary victimization had eliminated torture from the legal arsenal of the day. Trial by ordeal had been replaced by courtroom proceedings. But these legalistic methods could often be cantankerous in their execution and inconclusive in their findings. In the new autocratic regime under the tight control of the Medici, torture as a method of speedy, simple, straightforward, and cost effective inquiry was enjoying something of a renaissance. Because native Florentines with the requisite experience and will to assume these demanding positions as state torturers were in short supply, it had been necessary to seek outside help. And who but the formidable Spanish were so well suited to the task? The Inquisition, now in its twelfth year, had trained an entire generation of men whose credentials were above reproach and whose reputation for results was legendary. Their experience, along with the stunning variety of hardware at their disposal, had enabled them to attain a dazzling new level of technical achievement that was the envy of all Europe.

The first evidence of their handiwork to greet Niccolo was the heavy, sick odor of roasting flesh and scorched hair that hung in the air. He stared around in disbelief—fires and furnaces, bubbling pots, chains and ropes, and horrific engines . . .

"Bring the new one over here," barked one of the Spanish denizens of this little private hell. "He can say hello to his friend Capponi."

The slim, naked body of Agostino Capponi, formerly of the Second Chancery and barely twenty-five years old, was slumped over in a chair. He was prevented from falling out by thick leather straps around his waist, arms, and legs. His body was covered with welts and yellow blisters and, in places where his torturers had been more insistent, burned, blackened skin. Blood was running from his mouth.

"Is he . . ." Niccolo hesitated before the revolting tableau.

"Dead? Oh no, there's plenty of life left in Messer Capponi. We won't let him die until he tells us what we want to know." Several of the Spaniards grunted in agreement. While they waited for Capponi to come around, Niccolo was fastened to a pair of irons embedded in the wall.

Capponi was screaming when he came to. He was spitting and spraying blood from his mouth. The Spaniard who seemed to be in charge turned to Niccolo. "He bit off the tip of his tongue! He thought maybe he would bleed to death that way." Then, walking over to what appeared to be a forge of some sort, he extracted an iron bar about a foot and a half long. The tip was white hot.

"Can't let him bleed to death, can we? We'll have to cauterize the wound." The matter-of-fact way this man went about his grisly business made Niccolo shudder. As two other men held Capponi's writhing head, now slippery with blood, the torturer thrust the iron bar deep into his mouth. There was a searing sound as the hot iron touched flesh and blood. Niccolo saw the intense, momentary explosion of wild panic in young Capponi's bulging eyes and then once again the tormented boy descended into darkness. Steam and smoke escaped from his mouth as the bar was withdrawn. When this hellish spectacle was over, Niccolo was returned to his cell to think about what he had seen. That was all for the first day.

On the second day, Niccolo was shown Pietro Paolo Boscoli, who had disappeared from the chancery at the same time as Capponi. Boscoli was stretched out spread-eagle on the floor, his four limbs tied securely. On his chest was an iron plate, and on the plate were heavy iron weights, upward of three hundred pounds. Boscoli was literally being pressed for a confession. The prostrate Boscoli did not seem to recognize Niccolo. His once-rosy cheeks were ashen pale. He scarcely had the strength left to groan. He was gulping and gasping painfully for air, but the weight on his chest made breathing almost impossible.

As Niccolo watched, horrified, some of the weights were removed and Boscoli was allowed to speak. When all he said was, "I've already told you everything," the crushing weights were replaced and ten extra pounds were added.

"He's been like that for a week," said the torturer. "It's surprising he's held up that long. He looks soft. At the beginning, they scream. He screamed bloody murder, this one. But then they learn to save their breath. They can't stop breathing. They want to, but they can't," he chortled. "You know what this one did? He begged me to jump up and down on his chest to get it over with!"

Niccolo was led from the chamber with the memory of Boscoli's weak, labored wheezing in his ears. That was the second day. He knew they were softening him up. He knew that it would be his turn soon. He did not know how he would hold up under torture. And he did not know what they wanted from him.

On the third day, there was no evidence of Boscoli or Capponi in the torture chamber, but there was a prim young man who seemed out of place in this dungeon, in his fine clothes among these oily Spanish inquisitors. He cut quite a figure in velvet slippers and slashed sleeves. He threw his long, thick, black hair around grandly when he talked.

He seemed to be issuing orders to the torturers, and they seemed to be listening to him with the patient acquiescence of men who need no instructions and who know how to go about their business.

When Niccolo was brought into the room, the prim one looked up and said, "This is him?" He had a reedy voice and an annoying, overly precise, way of articulating each individual syllable.

"Leave us," he said with a wave of the hand. It was a dismissive, but not assertive, gesture. "I'll question him." The Spaniards, unconcerned, went about their business of stoking fires and hammering and banging pieces of iron in preparation for the day's work.

"You're Niccolo Machiavelli?" The slightly weary, disdainful note that crept into his voice piqued Niccolo and stirred old resentments. This was exactly the kind of exalted courtier and dandified ass that he had had to deal with on so many occasions in the past. Against his better judgment, but unable to resist, he said in a firm but defiant tone, "Whom might I have the honor of addressing?" It was clear that he did not consider it an altogether tremendous honor.

"Lorenzo di Piero de' Medici."

"Christ," thought Niccolo. "Another one." They were coming out of the walls, these Medici. They were descending on the carcass of the republic like a pack of vultures. And this one was still talking, dragging out his lineage and his titles: ". . . grandson of Lorenzo, called the Magnificent and by declaration of the Cardinal Giovanni de' Medici, captain general of the Florentine republic." He stopped to let it all sink in. Niccolo waited and said nothing.

"You have had an opportunity to witness the sad conditions of the unfortunate Messers Boscoli and Capponi, have you not?"

No answer was required. Little Lorenzo continued: "Messers Boscoli and Capponi were involved in some nasty business. We have reason to believe that you were also involved, and we would like to ascertain the extent of your involvement. Now, what was your relationship with Boscoli and Capponi?"

Niccolo answered truthfully. "They worked in the chancery, but I barely knew them. There are over a hundred clerks in the Second Chancery."

"I see," said the young inquisitor, pausing for effect. "Then you have no idea how your name got on a piece of paper that was in Messer Boscoli's possession?"

Niccolo was a little relieved. He had no idea, and he said so, but his response did not seem to satisfy the inquiring mind of the young Medici lion.

"Let me speak plainly, Machiavelli. A certain Bernardino Coccio of Siena was at the house of a certain Jacopo Lenzi, who is a kinsman of the ex-gonfaloniere Soderini, and found a certain piece of paper that had fallen from the pocket of your Messer Boscoli. Do I make myself clear?"

"Clear," thought Niccolo. He had heard diplomats and politicians express themselves more clearly than that! Tactfully, he said, "I'm not sure what Your Excellency is getting at."

"Your name was on that slip of paper!"

"Ah, well there. You should have said so earlier!" Niccolo had no idea what this was all about, but he was beginning to see that the charges against him, whatever they were, were absolutely groundless. He was beginning to take heart.

"You should not make light of this, Machiavelli," cautioned the young Medici, with his precise, severe articulation. "That list contained the names of eighteen men. Eighteen conspirators! We want to know what your role was in the conspiracy."

Niccolo protested, half-laughing, "A conspiracy? With poor Boscoli and Capponi? A list of names on a slip of paper that fell out of someone's pocket! That's preposterous! You must be joking. You can ask your uncle Giuliano about me. You can even ask the cardinal. We're on good terms. A slip of paper!"

Young Lorenzo was not amused, however. Sensing an affront to his authority, he said "Uncle Giovanni has put me in charge of this affair, and I'll handle it as I see fit. Now tell me what you know about the conspiracy."

"I can't tell you anything because I don't know anything. Ask Boscoli. Ask Capponi."

"Messers Boscoli and Capponi have confessed to being traitors and they've been dealt with. They were decapitated this morning." He said it dryly. "I suggest you reconsider your position." With that, Lorenzo pivoted in his delicate slippers, gave a signal to the Spaniards, and strode out of the chamber. The Spaniards were grinning.

Niccolo could not believe this was happening to him. He was being tied down on the rack. The rack! He was going to be questioned on something he knew nothing about. What was he going to say? He didn't have any secrets to guard, anyone to protect. And he had no information to give up, nothing to offer when the pain became unbearable, nothing to say to make it stop. He thought of poor Boscoli and Capponi. What lies had they admitted to? What crimes had they confessed?

The Spaniard was almost apologetic as he fastened the straps around Niccolo's ankles and wrists. Almost. He was saying, "It's nothing against you personally. But I've got a job to do like anyone else."

This detachment, this professionalism, made it all the more maddening. He went on, "Like I said, it's nothing personal. If I saw you on the street tomorrow, I'd probably buy you a drink." Then the man smiled a cold, evil smile, "But I probably won't see you on the street tomorrow, will I?" Niccolo saw the tinge of madness in his eyes. There was no detachment in his eyes, only a fierce anticipation of pleasure.

The ropes extended from Niccolo's outstretched limbs and wound around two drums, one at his head and one at his feet. The drums had a system of levers and ratchets that allowed the ropes to be pulled an inch or so at a time without sliding back. By the second turn, Niccolo's body was stretched taunt.

He had decided to make a manly show of fortitude and not cry out. He repeated that he knew nothing about the conspiracy. He summoned up thoughts of the ancient Romans to give him courage. He bit his lip so hard that the skin broke. Tears streamed down his face. He would not cry out. On the third turn, he shrieked.

The questions were repeated, and he could barely enunciate his denials. His body was being torn—literally torn—apart. It was the worst in his hips and shoulders. He wondered how long it would take for his joints to be ripped apart, for the bones to pop out of their sockets and the tendons and sinews to snap. He wondered how far they would go. At the fourth turn, he felt something snap, and the pain shot to new and excruciating levels. Again, the Spaniard with the gleam in his eye repeated the same questions. Niccolo's denials now were almost inaudible, squeezed out through clenched teeth. The last thing he saw before losing consciousness was the single broken tooth of the Spaniard set in the middle of that grin, that sublimely evil, but somehow tender, even erotic grin.

When Niccolo came to, he was in his cell again. His body was a sheet of fire. He became dimly aware of something crawling up his leg, but when he tried to move his arm to brush it off, a blinding burst of pain sent him down into the blackness again. It was a full twelve hours before he regained consciousness. Someone had entered his cell with a lamp. "Here. Here's a lamp and writing materials," said the voice with the thick Spanish accent. "Messer Lorenzo wants you to write out your confession. If you can't think of everything, we'll go six turns tomorrow to jog your memory." With that injunction cheerfully delivered, he retreated, whistling.

Niccolo lolled on his bench. The light in the cell added a new dimension to his horror. Before he had only heard them scurrying around underneath him. Now he could see their little rat's eyes, huddled in the corner and shining. He could move his neck, but little else without invoking the pain. Six turns! He had not been able to bear four! Then he wondered if one got used to it, inured to it. He wondered if, after a while, one just lost all sensation and the pain didn't matter anymore. He thought of the pathetic Boscoli and Capponi. He still had a long way to go.

He was trapped. The only way out was to confess to something he didn't do. And if he confessed, he would, in all likelihood, be put to death, just like Boscoli and Capponi. For Niccolo, tyranny had ceased to be an abstract enemy, an unacceptable concept of government. He was afraid, but he was also full of bitterness and resentment. He thought of the arrogant young Medici playing at ruler of the city. For a long time he sat, composing the words in his head. He fed on his defiance, and it gave him courage. It was a courage born of recklessness, and there was a certain desperation about it, but what choice did he have? He was doomed if he cooperated or if he didn't. Eventually, he was sure they'd break him. He winced at the thought of six turns. But he wasn't broken yet. With a supreme effort, he wedged himself up into a sitting position, took the paper and pen, and began to write. It took him over an hour, and when he was done, he reread his work. If nothing else, it had lifted his spirits. He had written an obscene sonnet and addressed it to Lorenzo di Piero de' Medici, grandson of Lorenzo, called the Magnificent and nephew to the farting cardinal . . . etc., etc. The next day, Niccolo was not subjected to another session on the rack. Rather, all the bones in his right hand—the hand with which he wrote—were broken.

When they came to get him the next time, Niccolo still could not walk unassisted. He was helped, rudely enough, by his captors and tormentors, and, to his amazement, they led him limping through the torture chamber without stopping. He was thrust into a small room and told to wait. There was a window in the room. For the first time since he had been arrested, he saw the natural light of day and it heartened him a little. How long had he been here? Niccolo rubbed his chin. To judge from the growth of beard on his face—ten days? Two weeks? And now what? The fact that he had not been put back on the rack was a good sign. The fact that he was in this anteroom instead of the torture chamber was a good sign. Something might happen. There was hope. The Spaniard stuck his head in the door. "A lady to see you." Niccolo's heart leaped. It pounded in his chest. Giuditta! But how! Why! He was dizzy. And it was not Giuditta.

She stared hard at him. He was dirty and unshaven. His clothes were in tatters. His face and arms were covered with rat bites, some of which were infected and beginning to fester. "Are they treating you well?" she asked nonchalantly, amused.

"What are you doing here?" stammered Niccolo, the hope draining out of him.

"You mean, what am I doing alive when I'm supposed to be dead? Poisoned!" She drew a black fingernail over the red smear of her mouth.

"What do you want with me?" Niccolo was utterly confounded.

"Revenge. You and the Jewess plotted to kill Don Micheletto. You intended to poison him at that cozy supper you arranged, but I foiled the plan, didn't I?"

"That's absurd." It was a weak bluff.

"You think I didn't detect the poison then? In the Rossoli? You think I didn't warn Don Micheletto not to touch it."

"If the Rossoli were poisoned, you would be dead," countered Niccolo, not knowing what else to say.

"You don't know what went wrong, do you?"

Niccolo was silent. She regarded him with the same sort of detachment as his torturers. But the same evil glint was in her eyes. "Do you know who Mithradates was?" she asked casually.

Niccolo racked his memory. The name was familiar. He remembered reading something about Mithradates in Livy. He was a king who had stood in the way of the Romans in the early days. Somewhere in the Mediterranean. In the east. His interrogator waited patiently, enjoying his perplexity.

Finally, she explained herself: "Mithradates was defeated and sentenced to death by the Romans. The usual way to carry out the sentence against an enemy honorably defeated in battle was to allow him to poison himself. It was considered a concession. But when the poison was administered to Mithradates, nothing happened. And do you know why?"

She drew her sharp face closer to Niccolo, so close he could feel her damp, sweet breath on his cheek. "Nothing happened because Mithradates had fortified himself ahead of time. He poisoned himself, a little at a time over a period of years. At first it makes you ill, but then you become accustomed to the small doses. And you increase them. After a while, there's no limit to the amount you can ingest because the poison is a part of you. It's in your blood and every fiber of your body."

Realizing what she was saying, Niccolo jerked back, away from her face, away from her poison breath. She looked down her long, thin nose at him. Her nostrils flared a little. "You and the Jewess wanted to dabble in poison, but you didn't know who you were up against, did you? It's too bad, really. You missed your chance, and now I have you both." She said it casually.

Niccolo jumped up, but the pain in his joints forced him back onto his bench. Wild-eyed, he asked, "What do you mean you have us both?"

"The Jewess is in the Immurate. And they have a special treatment for Jews there. You can depend on that. It will be far worse than what you're being served up here."

"You're lying!" Niccolo was blind with anger.

"I hear they tie the Jews up by their feet so that they're hanging a few feet from the floor. Then they bring in the dogs. The dogs are hungry when they bring them in, but not starving yet . . ."

"Stop it! You're lying! This is part of somebody's plan to break me. Giuditta has nothing to do with this. I'm in here for political reasons."

"Are you? Boscoli and Capponi confessed, but they cleared you and the others. They were conspirators, but inept ones. They wrote things down. The names on their list were of people they thought of contacting but never did. All your fellow conspirators who were arrested have already been set free. But you're still here, aren't you?"

"You're lying! How could you know all that?"

"I'm under the protection of the Medici," she said with finality. "And they owe me a favor. That's why you're still here and the Jewess is in the Immurate. Because I wanted you. I wanted my revenge."

"But that doesn't make any sense," pleaded Niccolo. "How could you . . . why would you . . ." He was desperate.

"You don't understand my desire for revenge? I didn't think you would. That's why I've come to see you before the end. So you would know who did this to you. I wanted you to know what will happen to the Jewess, as well. And now you do. Now you know everything."

"But why?"

"You haven't figured it out yet, have you?" she said, glaring down at him like some savage Medusa bent on hideous revenge. "It's not for me. It's for him. Because you killed him. Don Micheletto was my father."

If Niccolo had one source of solace during his captivity, it was the thought of Giuditta. She was safe. She had nothing to do with his present difficulties. This was chancery business, and she was not involved. This was politics. And now the awful truth was that she was in the Immurate, the women's prison, and they were both at the mercy of a woman who knew no mercy, who knew no forgiveness, and who thirsted only for revenge, a woman with an inheritance of terror, a pedigree.

If he could only get out, do something! But he could barely walk, let alone escape. He had no way of communicating with anyone on the outside, and besides, she said it was all going to be over the next day. She said there was going to be a trial—for him, not the Jewess. Jews don't need trials, but somebody might ask questions about him, so they would go through the motions of a trial. The trial would be short, however, and the result would be well known even before the proceedings began, just as they were for Boscoli and Capponi. In fact, the sentence of death had already been drawn up.

Still—a trial. A chance to get out of this stinking, filthy place, if only for a few hours. A chance to get a message to someone, anyone. A chance to reach a friend—he still had friends, didn't he? A chance to get someone to do something, to intervene on Giuditta's behalf, if nothing more. A tiny ray of hope began to shine in Niccolo's dark and fetid cell. He still had paper and a pen. A slip of paper dropped on the floor? Who could say who might find it? Into what hands it might fall? A slip of paper had gotten him into this mess. Perhaps it could redeem him as well? And Niccolo began to write.

The next morning, Niccolo's hopes were dashed. He was not led out of the prison as he had anticipated, but conducted directly to the torture chamber. His "trial" was to be a trial by ordeal. Lorenzo, grandson of Lorenzo, was there to supervise the proceedings. With him were several of the young rogues who now formed his entourage. They basked in the glow of Medici favor. They were the new lords of Florence, in their short capes laden with brocade and covered with fanciful designs of flowers and butterflies and parrots and dragons.

The young Medici addressed Niccolo in the most supercilious voice imaginable. He was putting on a show for his retainers. "I have here two documents, two pieces of paper. They were given to me by the cardinal, who incidentally cannot be with us today. He apologizes for his absence, but he was called to Rome on urgent business. The pope, it appears, is gravely ill." He paused dramatically.

"Two pieces of paper. Two flimsy pieces of paper." He held them up. "One is an order to release you from prison. The other is your death warrant."

Niccolo was defiant. It was the defiance of a man *in extremis*, a man with absolutely nothing to lose. "And you've been constituted judge and jury to decide which one is to be implemented."

"Oh, glory be, no," said Lorenzo, feigning surprise and indignation. "This matter is far too grave to leave the decision in the hands of one such as myself. No, this is a matter of life and death. We feel that an appeal to a higher authority is the only way to dispose of things in accordance with our concerns that justice be done."

Justice. He had the effrontery to use that word. Niccolo wanted to spit, but his mouth was too dry.

"Gentlemen, shall we begin?"

"Take off your shirt." It was one of the Spaniards. Niccolo was led across the room to an open hearth, where a grimy man was working an enormous pair of bellows. Above the superheated fire that he was feeding there was a crucible. And in the crucible, bubbling as merrily as any stew or soup ever had, was molten lead. Niccolo was placed in front of that fire.

Now Lorenzo spoke again. He was punctilious in explaining the procedure. "Your fate is in the hands of the Lord God Almighty. He will be your judge and jury. You should feel flattered that so exalted a judge has been appointed to hear your case. The legal thinking is simplicity itself. The tradition goes back thousands of years. You will place your hand in the cauldron of molten lead. If when you withdraw it, you haven't been burned, then it is a clear sign that God has taken you under his protection. Your innocence will be proclaimed, and you will be released." He paused here, savoring every moment, every word of his facetious legal discourse. Then, gravely, he continued, "If, on the other hand, you should happen to burn yourself, then that is a clear sign of the Lord's disfavor. That, unfortunately for you, would be an indication of your guilt. We would have no other choice than to enforce the sentence of execution."

Lorenzo smiled. His confreres smiled. The Spanish torturers smiled. Only Niccolo was not smiling. He fidgeted before the fire, his eyes riveted on the surface of that boiling metal. He cowered.

Although it was hot, Niccolo was shivering. He clutched his clenched fists under his arms in what looked like an attempt to keep warm. His tormentors leered.

Niccolo inched closer to the fire, mesmerized by it.

"Whenever you're ready," said young Lorenzo. "And remember, if you're innocent, you have nothing to fear."

Niccolo's agitation appeared to increase as he eyed the pot of boiling, molten metal. He began to gnaw on his left hand. His torturers saw him shaking and biting at his hand, but they were unmoved. They were chortling. The Spaniards were already arguing over who would get his cloak, his boots . . . when the final indignity occurred.

Niccolo was wearing a pair of light-brown woolen hose, and as he stood staring into that hideous fire, a dark stain began to spread in the area of his groin. One of the Spaniards saw it first. "He's pissing himself!" There were roars of cruel laughter as Niccolo clutched the offending organ in a desperate attempt to stem the humiliating flow. His debasement was complete.

"Well, what are you waiting for?" said Lorenzo. "Get it over with. Here. Let me make it more interesting." He pulled a small, jeweled dagger from his belt, examined it for a moment, and then tossed it into the boiling pot. "Go ahead. Retrieve it."

After what seemed like an eternity, Niccolo made his move. With a tremendous effort, he plunged his hand into the bubbling metal. There was a hiss and sizzle. Then he withdrew it. It was done quickly. He turned slowly to face his accusers. There was rage in his eyes. Clutched in his fist was the dagger.

He threw the flimsy weapon on the floor, and it shattered. There were audible gasps from the little circle around him. The young hellions shrank back. The impious torturers crossed themselves. Now he held his bare hand, the hand that he had just withdrawn from the cauldron, in Lorenzo's awe-struck face. With a sneer, Niccolo flexed his fingers, once, twice, to show that they moved, that they were unharmed, and that the hand had not become a charred, blistered mass of pulp. Slowly he curled that hand into a fist.

"Is the verdict satisfactory? Has God spoken? Did you hear Him?"

Niccolo stood there, glaring at the effeminate, terrified Lorenzo for a long time. When he looked around at the others, they averted their eyes. He laughed a howling, joyous, triumphant laugh. And they were sore afraid.

He had won his release. He had saved himself. But for Giuditta, it was too late. Michelozzi was the only one who had tried, but his efforts brought only the tale of a corpse dangling from the ceiling of a prison cell, its long black hair almost brushing the floor, its face and throat already torn out, and starving dogs jumping higher, ever higher, in search of more succulent pieces of flesh.

Alone and virtually friendless, broken in body and soul, Niccolo Machiavelli went into exile two days later. As he rode through the gates of Florence, he heard a final great resounding metallic crash. He was too numbed and too drained to feel any curiosity. It could have been the end of the world for all he cared.

It was the *vacca*, that ponderous, mooing bell, that deep voice of freedom that could be heard at a distance of thirteen miles, that stentorian call that, for over three hundred years, had summoned the people of Florence into the piazza for consultation in times of great crisis. Such consultations were no longer deemed necessary in the new Florence. The ancient bronze bell had groaned her last, as she struck the hard ground at the foot of her tower. Now she lay shattered on the stones of the Piazza Maggiore.

Part 5

Wheel of Fortune

43

A Lean Christmas and a Fat New Pope

Nessun maggior dolore
che ricordarsi del tempo felice
ne la miseria

There is no greater pain
than to remember, in our present grief,
past happiness

—Dante

The goose was cold. The fire had died in the fireplace. Outside it was drizzling, and a damp chill had penetrated the small house and the very bones of its sole inhabitant. He sat alone at the table, cold and stiff, wrapped in a blanket. It was getting dark, but there was no point in lighting a lamp because there was nobody and nothing to see. He wanted to rekindle the fire, but walking still caused him a great deal of pain, and so, for the time being, he pulled the blanket more tightly around himself.

A woman from the nearby village of San Casciano came in three or four times a week to prepare his meals. It was she who had prepared the goose for him—out of pity, no doubt—before rushing off about noon to spend the rest of the day with her own family. Since that time he had picked at the bird, but for want of appetite he left it largely untouched and undamaged. His right hand, which had been crushed with the screws, was still bandaged and useless. The scars on his wrists and ankles had healed, but they still bothered him. His joints, which had almost been torn asunder, ached when he moved, and they ached when he sat still. Alone with his pain and his memories and his resentments in the dying grey light, Niccolo lifted his goblet of wine to his sole companion, his dumb, mute goose of a companion. "*Buon Natale,*" he said bitterly. "Merry Christmas."

In an hour or so, he would put some embers in the warming pan, drag himself, with the aid of his cane, into the frigid bedchamber and warm the cold sheets. And then he would lie all night on that bed, scarcely more comfortable than he had been on the torturer's rack, his mind lacerated by visions and nightmares. This was what he had to look forward to. Tonight. And tomorrow. And the day after. This was his life.

These somber ruminations were interrupted by a rattling at the outer door. If Niccolo had been paying attention, he would have heard the plodding approach of the mule and the heavy "plop" with which its rider dismounted and landed in the mud. Although he started when he first heard the noise, he soon settled back into his chair and blanket unconcerned. Maybe they were coming to take him back to prison? Maybe they were going to put him out of his misery?

But it was a friendly voice that hailed him from the entry hall and bid him good cheer. It was Pagolo: "*Che miseria!* Why is it so dark in here? Niccolo, are you home?"

Niccolo could see his generous bulk outlined in the doorway against the dim light of the fading day. "In here," he grunted. "In the kitchen."

"And it's freezing," said the rotund friar, bumbling his way into the house. "I knew I'd find you here stewing in your misery. I came to cheer you up. Besides, it's my duty as a monk to perform the corporal works of mercy, in this case, to visit the sick."

"You mean, to bury the dead," said Niccolo resignedly.

Pagolo squinted in the half-light and tried, not very successfully, to steer a course between the dark hulks of furniture that littered the hallway and kitchen. He had stubbed toes and a skinned shin by the time he finally reached the fireplace. "Why is the furniture all over the place like this?"

"It's easier for me to get around if I have things to lean on," said Niccolo glumly. "I'll have it moved back against the walls when I can walk again. If I ever walk again."

"*Castrone! Buffalone!* Such talk!"

In no time, Pagolo had the fire going. He found a lamp and lit it. He helped his embittered friend into a chair near the hearth and helped himself to the abandoned goose. When he had "sampled" it to his satisfaction and sampled the dressing and the pudding as well—it was there on the table and would otherwise go to waste—he reached into his satchel and said, "Look what I've brought you. Chestnuts!"

Niccolo smiled weakly. Pagolo was surprised at how thin he had grown and how haggard he looked. Even in the rosy glow of the fire, Niccolo's complexion was ashen and ghastly. His eyes were sunken. Pagolo put a cast-iron griddle on the fire to roast the chestnuts. While it heated up, he busied himself puncturing each of the nuts, so they wouldn't explode. All the while, Niccolo stared into the fire, uncommunicative and sullen. The last time Pagolo had seen Niccolo was in Florence the day after his release. In the torrent of words and anguish that had poured out of him, Pagolo found little that was coherent or substantive or informative. There was only an overwhelming, urgent, blind, desperate pain.

Pagolo went over to the griddle and spit on it to see if it was hot enough. The little ball of spittle beaded up. It jumped and sizzled on the hot iron surface. The griddle was ready. Inexplicably, Niccolo burst into laughter.

Pagolo shot him a questioning glance. "What's so funny?"

"What you just did reminded me of something. Do you want to see a trick, Pagolo?"

"What kind of a trick?"

"Bring me that pail of water." Edging closer to the fire, Niccolo dipped his hand in the water and, before Pagolo could react or stop him, he placed it squarely on the hot iron grill.

"*Porco Giuda!*" In that moment, Pagolo sincerely believed that his friend had gone utterly, irredeemably mad. But Niccolo was laughing at him. And obviously, miraculously, his hand appeared to be unhurt.

"How did you . . . Why did you do that?" stammered Pagolo.

"That's how I got out of prison. I had to dip my hand in a bucket of molten lead."

"What!"

"They subjected me to an ordeal," explained Niccolo. "If I didn't get burned, I was considered innocent."

"And you didn't get burned?" said Pagolo incredulously.

"The same way I didn't get burned just now. It was something I learned when we were casting guns and cannon for the militia. In the forges, Pagolo, I used to actually see ironworkers wash their hands in streams of molten metal as it poured from the crucible. I saw a man skim the surface of a ladle of melted copper with his bare hand. Do you know what the secret is?"

Pagolo was aghast. "No."

"The hands have to be wet. The water turns to vapor and cushions the skin. The hot metal never really touches the skin—just the layer of water and vapor. It's almost like wearing a protective glove."

"And you stuck your hand in a bucket of molten lead on the basis of this . . . this theory?"

"I didn't have much of a choice, did I? I didn't know whether or not it would work, and I had a real problem getting my hand wet enough. First I put it in my armpit, but I wasn't sweating enough. Then I tried my mouth. They thought I was gnawing my hand in agony but I was really trying to moisten it with saliva. That didn't work either, though, because I was so scared my mouth was bone dry."

"So what did you do?"

"The final ignominious solution: I pissed myself!"

"Good God Almighty!"

"You should have seen the young Medici pup's expression when I pulled my hand out of the molten lead and shook it in his face! He cringed like I was the devil himself!" Recounting his moment of triumph brought a tinge of color into Niccolo's face and a hint of animation into his voice, but almost as soon as these signs of life appeared, they were gone, and he lapsed back into his chair and his blanket and his all-consuming despair. When they were ready, he ate one or two chestnuts almost without knowing what he was doing.

Little news of the outside world reached the former secretary in his isolated family villa. What did reach him made little impression on his ever-brooding mind. Political problems in Florence, who was allied with France, who with Spain, what the emperor was planning—all these things that had so consumed his energy in the past meant little to him now. They were far away, even though he was only seven miles from Florence. The terms of his banishment stipulated that he was to remain outside the city but within a fifty-mile radius. They wanted to keep an eye on him, but even those assigned to watch him soon lost interest.

As Niccolo recovered his ability to walk and the use of his right hand over the months that followed, he slowly began to emerge from his torpor. But it was a daily struggle and not without frequent setbacks. Then something happened that did jolt him out of his complacency. A piece of news arrived that even the ignorant rustics around him could not ignore. Julius II, the warrior pope, had died. As the College of Cardinals convened and began their machinations and plotting and counterplotting, Niccolo found himself starting to take an interest in the proceedings. Every day he used to hobble into the little village of San Casciano to hear the latest news and round of rumors from Rome. And then disaster struck.

The new pope took the name of Leo X. Tonsured at seven, made an abbot at eight and a cardinal at fourteen, now at the age of thirty-seven, Giovanni de' Medici had been elected supreme pontiff. His fleshly, immense, leaky bottom, with its anal fistula, now sat on the throne of Saint Peter.

The Cardinal de' Medici was not considered a likely candidate for the papacy in the early going, but as the conclave dragged on and as vehemently competing powers like France and Spain effectively neutralized one another, his name was put forward. With the resources of the entire Florentine treasury behind him, he had eventually been able to buy enough votes in the consistory to carry the day. Always scrupulously attentive to matters of ecclesiastical detail, Giovanni was solemnly ordained a priest on the day prior to his coronation. Although he had been a cardinal for over twenty-five years, he had never before taken the time to receive holy orders.

The news hit Niccolo like a thunderbolt. With the papacy in those pudgy Medici hands, the family's grip on power was near absolute. They ruled in Rome now, as well as in Florence. It was not long after Giovanni's elevation that rumors began to circulate about his plans for Florence. The new pope was talking about making his nephew, the dandified, despotic Lorenzo, king of central Italy. Niccolo crawled back into his shell of torpor and despair.

The thread on which he finally climbed out of those black depths of self-absorption and back into the sentient world was his correspondence with Francesco Vettori. Vettori was an old friend of Niccolo's. They had been together on many a diplomatic mission in France and Germany. They understood each other.

Vettori had survived the Medici housecleaning, in part because of his aristocratic origins, in part because his reputation for probity had made him an acceptable go-between when power was being transferred from Soderini's regime to the new masters. Along with Niccolo, it was Vettori who had taken an active hand in arranging Soderini's abdication and exile. While he was not a member of the Medici inner circle, he was tolerated, and even given a post in the new government, although the position itself was something of a joke. He was named Florentine ambassador to Rome, and as such he had absolutely nothing to do. Pope Leo X and a horde of Medici cousins personally saw to all Florentine business conducted in the Holy City. Despite the fact that he was infinitely better off than the disgraced secretary, Vettori too was prey to a kind of lonely isolation. Like Niccolo, he too had been at the center of things, and now he was a mere observer.

The letters that went back and forth between these two intellects represented some of the most astute analyses of the tangled Italian political problems of the day, but nobody listened to either of them. Nobody asked either of them for his advice. Nobody cared. And it was this impotence that goaded Niccolo. He had all the answers, but how could he make himself heard? It was maddening, all the more so when he learned from Vettori of a letter that the pope had addressed to his coxcomb of a nephew on governing Florence: "Introduce your own men into all the principal offices of the state," he wrote. "And whatever you do, make sure that you surround yourself with unremarkable men of little courage and talent . . ."

For his part, the flatulent Leo's civil methods consisted primarily of lying, cheating, and lavish expenditure. From Vettori, Niccolo learned that he ruled by whimsy when he ruled at all. But he had little taste for government, and his energies were directed into other channels. He hosted lavish dinners, and his table was always thick with dwarves and fools and jesters. He wrote verse, but it was doggerel, and he sang, although poorly. He surrounded himself with poets and musicians, although most were of a mediocre quality and none ever achieved lasting fame or recognition. In a year, he bankrupted the papal treasury and was borrowing money, sometimes at interest rates as high as 40 percent. In all things, he was faithful to the kind of excess that he had enjoyed all his life. The day he was crowned with the great, jeweled tiara, the triple crown of the head of the one, holy, Catholic and Apostolic Church, Pope Leo had turned to his cousin and was heard to have quipped, "God has given us the papacy. Let us enjoy it!"

And enjoy it he did. One of the few childless popes in recent memory —Niccolo remembered he liked to watch—Leo nevertheless took care of family. The Medici and their relatives flocked to Rome, where the payoff for graft and corruption was on a scale unheard of in Florence. Meanwhile, in Germany, an obscure Augustinian friar of severe bent and reformist tendencies named Martin Luther was looking with a jaundiced eye on the excesses of the Papal Court and was working on a tract titled, *On the Babylonian Captivity of the Catholic Church.*

San Casciano
10 December 1513

To Francesco Vettori at the Seat of the Supreme Pontiff, Rome:

Magnificent Ambassador. It had been quite a while since your last letter, and I was worried that I had lost favor with even you—I have few enough friends as it is in these difficult days. I wasn't sure why you stopped writing, although I feared it was because you didn't want to be associated with as disgraced and as unwholesome a person as myself or, worse, because you didn't trust me. But your latest of the 23rd of the past month put these fears out of my mind.

I'm happy to see how regularly, calmly, and discreetly you carry on with your public duties, and I urge you to continue in this way. We both know that a man who sacrifices his own interests for those of others is left with precious little to show for his efforts. We both learned that we live in a thankless world. It is Fortune who controls everything and we know that, for now, she wishes us to leave her alone, to be quiet, and not to give her any trouble. We must wait until she allows us to act again. In the meantime, you do well to go about your business quietly and observe things closely and carefully. If things go according to plan, I might soon be able to leave my idyllic country home here and come to see you in Rome. Idyllic indeed! Since you asked and since you treated me to an engrossing and amusing account of your life among the peacocks and courtesans and clerics and cardinals there, I might as well tell you what my life is like here.

If you think you would like to exchange yours for mine, I would be very happy to do so.

I live in the country in a villa in a state of dreadful disrepair. Since my misadventures in Florence, I have not spent a total of ten days there. Until recently, I have devoted a great deal of time and energy to snaring thrushes with my own hands. Rising before daybreak, I prepare the bird lines and go out with such a bundle of bird cages and traps on my back that I look like a Spanish soldier loaded with booty after the sack of Prato. I usually catch at least two, at most six, thrushes. I spent all September doing this, and then suddenly it ended. The thrushes vanished. I have no idea where they went, but they're gone. So this strange little pastime, rather lowly and certainly not in keeping with my august attainments and abilities, came to an end. And, oddly enough, I miss it. It was something I enjoyed.

Let me tell you what I do now instead. I get up at dawn and go down to a wood I am having cut. I stay there for two hours or so, in order to check on the work that was supposed to have been done the day before and to supervise the ongoing labors. I pass time with the woodcutters who are a vile, dishonest, lazy, and contemptible lot. I could tell you a thousand amusing and outrageous things about them and their machinations and arguments with each other and with the neighbors. Yesterday, they let Frosino da Panzano, a neighbor, take away several cords of wood without paying for it, and when I finally got him to agree to payment, he wanted to hold back ten lire, which he said I owed him from four years ago when he beat me at a game of cards. And we argued and bickered about those ten lire, I and a fat bumpkin with a big, round head and rotting teeth. The discussion was heated. Others joined in—a carter, the woodcutters, an old uncle of mine. I had to use all my skill and wit to negotiate an honorable settlement. And for a moment, Francesco, I thought of how you and I once stood before the king of France and his ministers and with them argued the fate of armies and cities and kingdoms. . . . Now I use my talents, my experience, to debate the fate of ten lire with workmen and peasants. But enough of that.

Three good citizens whom you know—Batista Guicciardini, Fillipo Ginori, and Tommaso del Bene—each bought a cord of wood from me when the north wind was blowing. I think they did it more out of pity than need, but I'm grateful for any help I can get. Old friends and colleagues are not exactly flocking to my door with protestations of friendship and offers of assistance.

At any rate, leaving my wood and my woodcutters, I go to a spring, and on the way I check my bird snares, which I still leave out but with little hope of catching anything anymore. I bring a book—Dante or Petrarch or one of the Latin love poets like Tibullus or Ovid. Can you believe I'm reading poetry now? And love poetry at that! I read about these poets' amorous passions and about their loves, and I remember my own, and for a few moments I revel in this thought. Then, with a sigh, always with a sigh, I move on up the road to an inn and speak with those who are passing by. I ask them for news of the area and the world beyond, and I learn a few things. Lunchtime comes and I return home to eat what little food my poor farm and slender patrimony permit me.

After eating, I return to the inn. There I usually find the innkeeper, a butcher, a miller, and two bakers—gruff and hardy company. With these men, I waste the afternoon playing cards, and a thousand disagreements and countless offensive words arise between us. Most of the time our arguments are over a few cents, but that doesn't make them any the less vehement, and we can be heard yelling all the way to San Casciano. And I yell loudest of all, but not at them, Francesco. Caught this way among these men with lice crawling in their hair, I wipe the mold from my brain, and I raise my voice and give vent to my indignation and my resentment. I release all my feelings of being ill-treated by Fortune. I am biding my time with Fortune, Francesco, and letting her drive me along this road of humiliation. I am waiting for the day when she will be ashamed to continue doing so.

All day I play cards and scream with this bunch, but when evening comes, I return home to my study. On the threshold, I take off my everyday clothes, which are covered with muck and mire, and I put on splendid and curial robes. Dressed in this more appropriate manner, I enter into the ancient courts of ancient men and am welcomed by them kindly, as one of their own. There, among these sages long dead, I taste the food of wisdom that is mine and mine alone, the food for which I was born. There, I am not ashamed to speak to them, to ask them questions. And they, in their humanity, answer me, and for hours I feel no boredom, no distress. I dismiss every affliction, I no longer fear poverty, and I do not tremble at the thought of death. I become completely a part of them, a part of their world, of their ideas. And as Dante says, that knowledge does not exist without the retention of it in memory, I have noted down what I have learned from their conversation, and I have composed a little work about principalities, where I delve as deeply as I can into thoughts on this subject, discussing what a principality is, what kinds there are, how they are acquired, how they are maintained, and, of course, why they are lost.

If any of my fantasies has ever pleased you, I think this little book will not displease you now. But more important, for one who rules, especially for a new ruler, it should be most welcomed. Therefore I thought of dedicating it to Giuliano de' Medici, whom we both know to be the best of the family—indeed the only good Medici. I would appreciate your advice in this matter and any help you could give me. Do you think I should take the book myself to Rome or send it to you and have you present it to him in my name? Do you think he will be interested in it? Will he even read it? All these questions! But what else can I do? Necessity constrains me. I am wearing myself away, consuming what little I have left, and I cannot remain in this state for long without being despised for, and ultimately defeated by, my poverty.

But there is also a larger constraint, Francesco, something else that drives me. Fortune has decreed that I must talk about the state—not knowing how to discuss either the silk trade or the wool business, either profits or losses. I have to vow to either speak of these things or remain silent. If I could win Giuliano's favor with this little book, it would be an opening. It is my desire to be useful, to do something, anything, with myself for the good of Florence, even if it means working with the Medici. Even if they start me off by rolling stones up a hill! Francesco, you know I have been at the study of statecraft for fifteen years, and I have not slept or played about during that time. Giuliano should be happy to obtain the services of one who is so full of experience and experience acquired at another man's expense. Can he, can anybody, doubt my loyalty to Florence? I have always kept my word and do not intend to break it now. Anyone who has been faithful and honest for forty-three years, as I have been, cannot change his character. And my present poverty is witness to my faith and honesty.

I should like you, therefore, to write me what you think concerning these things. I am still polishing and enlarging the little book, but will send you a few chapters as soon as possible for your comments. In the meantime, I commend myself to you. *Sis felix*.

Niccolo Machiavelli
formerly secretary in the Second Chancery

The "little book" that Niccolo mentioned in his letter to Vettori, of course, was *The Prince*, destined to be one of the most widely read and controversial books ever written on the subject of politics. It was a slim volume, scarcely ninety pages long, but its influence and the furors it would create would be out of all proportion to its modest size. Called a work of genius, it was eventually hailed as the beginning of a whole new era. It was declared to be the first real instance of modern political thought. It was an achievement without precedent in the annals of history and politics and even literature. But because of the blunt and practical way of Niccolo's little book, it had its detractors as well. It was denounced from the pulpits and the lecture halls as cynical and downright wicked. Misconceptions grew up about the book, promulgated to a great extent, as is usually the case, by those who had never read it. Legends grew up about its author, and his name became synonymous in a dozen languages with treachery, deceit, murder, and bad faith.

Niccolo Machiavelli would have smiled at the irony—the hot debates, the furious denunciations, the occasional book burnings, the outbursts of censorship, and on the other hand, the impassioned defenses, the flood of books and articles and university dissertations, the translations into hundreds of languages, the thousands of editions, and even the book's recent availability on such unlikely instruments of the devil as e-readers, personal digital assistants, and the Satanic smartphone. The veritable maelstrom of trouble and attention that has been swirling around his little book for four centuries would indeed have drawn Niccolo's lips back into their characteristic, sardonic, pursing half smile–half sneer. Despite his excitement about the work and the great plans he had predicated on its favorable reception, in Niccolo's own lifetime *The Prince* went unpublished, unremarked, and virtually unread.

44

A Perfumed Progress and the Garden of Earthly Delights

> **And if, as I said, it was necessary that the people of Israel be slaves to recognize Moses' ability and it was necessary that the Persians be oppressed by the Medes to recognize the greatness of spirit in Cyrus, and it was necessary that the Athenians be dispersed to realize the excellence of Theseus, then, likewise, at the present time, in order to recognize the ability of an Italian spirit, it was necessary that Italy be reduced to her present condition and that she be more enslaved than the Hebrews, more servile than the Persians, more scattered than the Athenians; without a leader, without organization, beaten, despoiled, ripped apart, overrun, and prey to every sort of catastrophe. . . . This opportunity, therefore, must not be permitted to pass by, so that Italy, after so long a time, may behold its redeemer. . . . What Italian would deny him homage? This barbarian dominion stinks to everyone! Therefore, may your illustrious house take up this mission with that spirit and with that hope in which just undertakings are begun; so that under your banner this country may be ennobled and, under your guidance, those words of Petrarch may come true:**
>
> **Discipline over rage**
> **Will take up arms; and the battle will be short**
> **For ancient valor**
> **In Italian hearts is not yet dead.**
>
> —Machiavelli, *The Prince*

Niccolo saw an opening, a moment in Italian history that was ripe for consolidating the peninsula under native Italian rule. Like many others, he had taken up the old battle cry of Caterina Sforza—*Fuori i barbari!* Out with the barbarians! His little book, *The Prince,* was written in a rush of inspiration, and it ended with an impassioned plea addressed to Giuliano de' Medici to liberate Italy from the stench of barbarian dominion. If the methods for taking and wielding power that he outlined in the book were extreme, that was due to the extreme nature of the times in which the book was written.

In these turbulent times, Niccolo saw something in the ascension of the Medici, even though he loathed their autocratic methods. For the first time in many years, Florence and Rome were united. There was an axis of power in central Italy that, if properly exploited, could be extended both north and south to drive out the French and the Spanish. And Giuliano de' Medici, whose reputation for probity and whose republican sympathies were no secret, was the man to do it. Niccolo's hopes for a united Italy were fanned when Giuliano was named captain general of the Papal Armies, the position once held by Caesar Borgia, and it was under these circumstances that he wrote, in a fever of excitement, *The Prince*. Giuliano would be the redeemer, the liberator.

When Niccolo sent the first three chapters to Vettori in Rome, the latter declared them brilliant and was eager to read more. Niccolo sent the rest and waited. He had already envisioned being called to Rome by Giuliano to advise him in his great work of unification. His book, he felt, virtually assured him of a position of responsibility. So he waited.

When a letter from Vettori arrived from Rome, he would tear it open so anxiously that he was often in danger of accidentally destroying it. And he would read voraciously, scanning the letter the first time through and then going back and rereading it carefully, one, two, three times. But the news he was waiting for never came.

Vettori's letters were full of promises and vague hopes. More and more, they limited themselves to ribald accounts of his adventures among the Roman courtesans. To Niccolo's pleas, Vettori responded with assurances, with admonitions to be patient, and with more promises. In fact, while Niccolo teetered on the verge of nervous exhaustion, Vettori dithered, wondering about the advisability of presenting the book to Giuliano, wondering how it would be received, and, of course, wondering how it would affect his own precarious position at court and his own ambitions. He was finally rescued from these bouts of indecision by the intervention of external circumstances. Giuliano de' Medici died of tuberculosis.

To Niccolo, the news was a crushing defeat. The wave of enthusiasm he had been riding suddenly crashed and slammed him hard into the unyielding rocky shore. With the death of Giuliano, his hopes for advancement, for employment, and, above all, for a united Italy died as well. The moment had passed, the opening for him and for Italy was closed. The cycle that had begun with his despair after being tortured and exiled and that had seen him through a period of rising hopes and expectations had come around to despair again. He slipped back into listlessness and discouragement. It was a pattern that would repeat itself, with little variation, for the next twelve years of his life, that is, for the last twelve years of his life.

Niccolo's debts continued to accumulate. He could not pay the taxes that were assessed on his small estate. He considered teaching. But the impossibility of reconciling himself to such a mundane pursuit and the company of children slowly drove him back to his study and his conversations with the ancients. Gradually, he was drawn again to the questions and problems that had fascinated him all his life, and he began work on a new, more comprehensive analysis of states and statecraft, couched in the form of a commentary on Livy's monumental *History of Rome*.

"I don't see why you concern yourself with these things anymore, Niccolo," said Pagolo. "A united Italy? Who cares about a united Italy? Do you think that fellow there cares?" He indicated the only other man in the tavern besides the two of them. It was one of the bakers with whom Niccolo still sometimes played cards. He was hunched over a leg of mutton like a dog ready to snarl or snap at anyone who got too near to him or showed an unwarranted interest in his joint of meat.

Niccolo shrugged off the question with his usual mumbled apologies about it being the only thing he knew how to do. Pagolo said, "Do you want to know why Italy can never be united?"

"What do you think Pagolo?" said Niccolo indulgently. Even though Pagolo was not much of an authority on politics, he was just about the only friend he had left, and so Niccolo let him ramble on.

"The reason for all this disunity and strife, in a word, is fat."

Niccolo cocked his head. "What's that supposed to mean?"

"Fat!" said Pagolo. "How can you unite a country that is so sharply divided and so violently insistent on the question of cooking fats? Here's what I mean: If you want to divide Italy up into her three great regions, you can do so along the 'fat lines.' Here in central Italy, from Florence to Rome we prefer . . ." He left it hanging.

"Olive oil," Niccolo supplied the obvious answer.

"But to the north, it's butter. They fry everything in butter, they smear butter on everything they put in the oven. They smear butter on everything they put in their mouths." Pagolo was waxing eloquent. "And in the South?" His voice took on menacing overtones. "In the South, its lard!"

Niccolo shook his head sagely, "I see the problem. What do you propose we do about it?"

"That's obvious. When you can get your Neapolitans to try a little butter and your Milanese to use a little lard, all the hostilities will vanish."

"You're brilliant, Pagolo, brilliant! I'm going to compose a letter to the pope and lay it all out to him." He added sardonically: "The pope hangs on my every word these days. There's scarcely a matter of importance that he doesn't consult me on." And then, as he did so often in these days, he lapsed into a stony silence.

Pagolo looked at his friend. What did he want? Pagolo knew the answer. He only wanted two things. He wanted to bring the dead back to life, and he wanted a united and independent Italy. It was really very simple, very straightforward.

Pagolo was thinking of taking his leave when the door flew open and four men entered the tavern. They were dressed like woodsmen and had the papal insignia on their leather jerkins. Since the little tavern in San Casciano was on the main road between Florence and Rome, it was not unusual to see papal retainers stopping over there to refresh themselves. There was a lot of traffic between Florence and Rome these days, and all the more so because the pope himself was preparing to visit his native Florence.

Watching them guzzling and snorting between guzzles in their uncouth Roman speech, Niccolo was forced to summon up some of his deep Florentine disdain for the peoples of the south. However, when they began buying rounds of drink for all present, he revised his opinion and condescended to commend their generosity. They were, after all, only woodsmen and could be forgiven a little roughness around the edges. It was Pagolo who first began joking with them, but Niccolo, always eager for news and gossip of papal doings, soon joined in the conversation.

"His Holiness, he likes to hunt now. He's got a great passion for hunting," said the man who seemed to be the leader of the group. "And we're going on ahead to arrange things to his satisfaction, so he can hunt up here."

"Whereabouts?" asked Niccolo.

"In the Bugello? Mugello? Some land his family's got outside of town."

"What's there to arrange for a hunt?" asked Pagolo.

The Romans all guffawed and exchanged knowing looks, and the leader said, "His Holiness don't hunt like other men. Special arrangements have to be made to accommodate his, ah, his unique tastes."

"What do you mean?" said Niccolo.

"Well, His Holiness has got some trouble riding, especially for any length of time." Some of the men made blatting, farting sounds to the great amusement of all, then the explanation resumed, "And his little bow-legs, they don't carry his big body far without collapsing under him. It's these, ah, disadvantages, that need to be taken into account when His Holiness goes hunting. Since His Holiness has trouble getting to the game, it's our job to bring the game to him."

"And how do you do that?"

"First we gotta pick a site that can be enclosed—a valley, a depression between some hills, a piece of land that borders on a river or marsh. We fence it round as good as we can, and usually, if we have the manpower, we'll put soldiers or peasants or beaters all along the fence to keep the animals from getting out."

"Where do the animals come from in the first place?"

"Oh, we bring 'em in. We stock it. Everything you can imagine: little stuff like rabbits and hares, but the pope mostly likes the bigger game best—deer, boars, rams, goats. You name it. Wolves."

"Then what?"

"Then we're ready to go. The pope goes into the enclosure first to a platform we've built up in the middle, and he gets up there with his spyglass ready and drops a white handkerchief. Then all hell breaks loose. The trumpets and horns go off. We release the animals and drive 'em into the big pen. They're screaming and braying and howling. The dogs get all excited and start to bark. The horses are snorting and whinnying. The hunters are yelling and whooping. The pope is jumping up and down with excitement on his platform with his spyglass."

"I understand he likes to watch," said Niccolo.

"Yeah," the man acknowledged the characterization with a leer. "He likes to watch all right. And when the hunters hit the field, there's plenty to see. The enclosure isn't that big, and you've got hundreds of panicked, half-crazy animals running around, with no way to get out, nowhere to go. And when the hunters start hacking and gouging, and the beasts smell blood it gets a whole lot worse. Swords are flying all over the place. The pope, he whoops and hollers. He loves it—all the confusion, all the slaughter. And because there's so much confusion, there's always a lot of accidents."

"Yeah," interjected one of the other gamekeepers. "Especially with the dwarves."

"Yeah, God the dwarves! Those little bastards are the most crazy of the lot. And they're always getting gored by a boar or gouged by mistake trying to make the pope laugh. Anyway, we'll set up snares and nets near where the pope is, and when something gets caught and it's safe, His Holiness'll come down with a long spear and run the animal through. Then everybody'll cheer and applaud at that point."

"So Pope Leo doesn't just watch. He participates in the manly exercise of the hunt," said Niccolo.

"Yeah, some, but mostly he watches. His favorite thing is to plant charges of powder in certain spots and then have the animals driven over them when they explode. Then he's up there with that spyglass following a boar carcass sailing through the air. He loves it. They all love it. Christ, these Florentines. Strange tastes. You know what I mean?"

"Yeah," said Niccolo, imitating the man's speech. "I know what you mean."

The next day was the day set for the arrival of the supreme pontiff. Since he was traveling from the south along the main road from Rome, it was inevitable that he pass through the little village of San Casciano on his way to Florence, and the villagers, seldom treated to so rare a spectacle as the passage of a reigning pontiff—one of local origin no less—had already lined the road for miles in both directions, eager for a glimpse of him, perhaps a blessing. Niccolo had sworn that he didn't care a fig for the pope, that he had already seen him and that he certainly wasn't going to go out of his way to do so again. But curiosity got the better of him, and when the cheering started, he stepped out of the tavern for a look. The first thing he saw was the elephant. Vettori had written about him. He was a gift from the king of Portugal. The pope's favorite elephant. Did he have others, less favored?

As the procession passed in review, nothing escaped Niccolo's sardonic eye and cynical evaluation. He counted eighteen cardinals in the train—all Leo's men, all newly created, no doubt, and not a one had had the purple for a ducat under 100,000. He saw the lavishly equipped troops and the exquisite corps of hangers-on and the carts full of enthusiastically waving dwarves and jesters and fools.

At first Niccolo thought it was the woman in front of him. It was that heavy, cloying smell of cheap perfume that you get when standing downwind of a less than savory prostitute. He moved a little, but the smell stayed with him. He took a couple of steps, and it still didn't go away. It was then that he realized that it wasn't coming from the crowd. It was coming from the procession. They were all perfumed—cardinals, courtiers, soldiers, dwarves. The elephant was probably perfumed! The entire procession was exuding the sweet smell of a cheap whore.

And then came the pope. He was in some sort of vehicle drawn by two white Arabian stallions. Propped upright and a little flushed from his exertions, he was lazily waving his hands in that uniquely papal wave. It was as though he were languidly gathering in the praise and admiration that rose up from the crowd and wafting it into his face, all the better to smell it, to appreciate it. That slow wave. That chubby, placid, cherubic face ending in a succession of chins too numerous to count. That bobbing red skullcap. Reaching down into the folds of his white silk robes, Leo pontifically drew out hands full of coins and flung them into the crowds, showering them with his largess. Niccolo stooped to retrieve one of the coins that landed at his feet. "*Spiccoli*," he thought, small change. Upon examination, he saw that it was coined by the Florentine mint, and he knew that the money supply of Florence was flowing slowly out of the Florentine treasury and into the papal coffers. Before pocketing the coin, he held it up to his face for one last look. It, too, was perfumed.

The procession swept by and left Niccolo standing there, just the way life was sweeping past him. History was a parade, and he wasn't marching in it anymore. It was a river, and he was standing on the banks, just watching. Once he had been in a boat, a fragile boat, risking the rapids swirling and raging around him. Once he had been knee deep in the water, laboring to build containment walls, dikes, and channels to control the crushing, rushing torrents. Now he was perched on a hilltop far away, and the river flowed on—sometimes placidly, sometimes boiling, but always indifferent to the presence of this lonely observer.

Unaware of Niccolo's dilemma, the country people cheered the procession lustily. Their beaming pontiff serenely took up his spyglass to survey these faithful, grateful sons and daughters of the church, his church. He swung the optical instrument in a slow arc and everywhere he saw happy upturned faces. Everywhere except over there near that tavern. He stopped his sweep of the crowd for a minute, because he thought he might have recognized someone. It was a gawky middle-aged man in a threadbare cloak and a cloth cap scowling in the way only Florentines can scowl. For a moment, Leo searched that high forehead and long, straight nose. No, he finally said to himself, just another one of those flinty, defiant self-righteous Florentines. Really! And with that, the happy pontiff moved on, drinking in the adulation of the crowd, bestowing his blessings upon them along with the money he had appropriated from their own treasury.

When he entered Florence several days later—the pope had to delay his triumphal entry to give the city time to complete the lavish decorations erected in his behalf by two thousand workmen at a price of over 70,000 florins—Leo did so through a breach in the city wall that had been opened especially in his honor, to allow his magnificent train and his beloved elephant to pass in state. After remaining there several weeks, allowing himself to be pampered and feted around the clock and putting the affairs of his relatives in order, however, he proceeded on to his real destination, the real object of his northward journey—Bologna. There he was received with little ceremony, and as he made his way through the empty streets, he was greeted only by occasional shouts of derision. He had come to meet with Francis I, the energetic new king of France. Put more bluntly, he had come to grovel at the feet of Francis I, to cede territory, to make monetary concessions, and to implore the goodwill of the French sovereign. The armies of France, after having dealt a humiliating blow to a shilly-shallying Papal Army of hastily assembled mercenary forces at Marignano, were now lords of Milan and most of northern Italy. Even all the perfume of Leo's court could not hide the stench of the barbarian dominion that had reasserted itself so forcefully on Italian soil.

Niccolo suffered through several more years of Leo's mismanagement of the Holy See. His hopes were raised and dashed by circumstances more than once. There was word of a plot to assassinate Leo by poisoning the bandages that were applied to his anal fistula, but the plot failed and the conspirators—all cardinals—were rounded up and executed. The entire episode worked to Leo's advantage by opening up several positions in the College of Cardinals, lucrative positions that could be sold at a handsome profit to the papacy. Fortune seemed to be smiling on Pope Leo X. Everything seemed to fall his way.

When the pope decided to begin selling indulgences in Germany to replenish the papal coffers and the choleric, idiot monk Luther began to shriek again, Leo could not be less concerned. "Another voice crying in the desert," he sighed, another grating, tiresome voice that he wished would just go away. And so, while Luther raved, the pope spent his days playing chess and cards and improvising little Latin melodies with his poets and fellow literati.

In Florence, the young snippet Lorenzo had been steadily incurring the wrath of his fellow citizens with his arrogant ways. Surrounded only by a court of like-minded dandies, he attempted to rule the city from the secret recesses of the Medici Palace. When he sought the advice of the council—which was seldom—he convened it at his home, not in the public chambers of the Signoria. When he succumbed to a deadly combination of tuberculosis and syphilis at the age of twenty-eight, he was not mourned. Another Medici drawn from the endless supply of Medici was quickly sent to replace him.

Through all this, Niccolo had only his work in which to find solace. Outside of his conversations and disquisitions with the ancients, there were only the intervals of idleness and tedium and restless despair that filled his days. Since the term of his exile had expired, he was free to return to Florence once more, but he rarely did so. When he was in need of a book he did not own, he would occasionally venture into the city, but he found few friends there. Most of his former colleagues, especially those who had managed to retain their positions in the chancery and curry some favor with their Medici overlords, were loath to appear over-friendly with the former secretary. When he moved among them, he was like a ghost, an embarrassing apparition that everyone could see but nobody wanted to acknowledge. So he would consult the records he wanted to consult and borrow the books he needed for his research and lug them back to the lonely little villa and lose himself in scholarship and speculation.

Niccolo's visits to Florence only aggravated the sense of sadness and loss with which his life was now imbued. When he saw men hurrying out of the Signoria and brush past him, he thought of them as men on errands, bustling men with someplace to go, something important to do. Once he himself had come hurtling out of that building on his way to the camp at Pisa, to Caesar Borgia, to Rome, to France and now? Now he felt inconspicuous, almost invisible. His clothes were shabby and neglected, but it didn't matter. Who could see him? Who was looking? He felt diminished. He had lost hair. He had lost weight. Had he grown shorter too? Was he old enough to start shrinking? Actually? Physically?

On one such visit to Florence, he had stopped to rest in the Piazza della Signoria. He had sought the shade of the Loggia della Signoria, the old, porticoed structure that offered shelter from sun and rain and in years past, a lively market in ideas and opinions. Here so many times in the past he had debated and discussed the great issues of his day, from Savonarola to Soderini, and the debates had been heated and the discussions contentious. Now the Loggia was nearly deserted. Isolated groups of old men with nothing to do straggled here and there. They knew each other so well and had so little to communicate that nods and arched eyebrows sufficed in the place of words. Much to his annoyance, an idiot had seated himself next to Niccolo and engaged him in an animated conversation. The idiot spoke eloquently in a deep baritone voice. He used his graceful hands to advantage to emphasize his points and draw attention to his conclusions, but the words that issued from his mouth were utter nonsense. He kept up a steady stream of gibberish, most beguiling, most thoughtfully nuanced and cadenced, but still incomprehensible gibberish. From a distance, one would have mistaken him for a consummate speaker, a philosopher. One would have believed Niccolo deep in thought, reflecting on the words of this street-corner sage.

And he was deep in thought. The idiot, he realized, did not require any response or stimulation to keep on talking. He just did it. Niccolo was convinced that when he got up and walked off, the animated little man would still be jabbering away, cajoling his imaginary audience, patiently going over this or that difficult concept and explaining it as often as need be. It was not pity that crept into his heart for the man's dilemma, but a sad sense of recognition. He, too, was like the idiot speaking a language that nobody else understood, addressing his imaginary audience, day in and day out, writing this immense, comprehensive analysis of history and politics that no one would ever read.

Someone clapped him on the back and gave him good day. Niccolo was aware that the comprehensible syllables in plain Florentine did not come from the idiot, and he looked up.

"Messer Machiavelli!"

"Michelozzi. *Salve.*"

"Such enthusiasm. I didn't know you were in town. Why didn't you come to see me?"

"Oh, you know . . ." said Niccolo weakly. He didn't want to say that he was embarrassed to see anyone he knew anymore. "I feel like a leper when I come to town. I feel like I should be wearing a bell around my neck to warn people off."

"I've never shunned you, oh leprous one. Look, I'm even willing to touch you and risk infection." He put an arm around Niccolo's shoulder. It was true that Michelozzi had been a good friend, but in the days and weeks after Niccolo's banishment, as the former secretary became more sullen and difficult to be with, and as Michelozzi's fortunes began to rise, the two of them had gradually drifted apart.

"Thanks, Michelozzi. Would you like to meet my friend here?" He jerked his head in the direction of the idiot. "I'm finding we have quite a bit in common."

Michelozzi settled in on the other side of Niccolo. "So, what's new with you?"

"New? Let me see." Niccolo paused to think. "Well, I saw the pope."

"You were in Rome?"

"No, when he passed through here."

"Niccolo, that was three years ago!"

"Well, that's the last thing I can remember that was new or out of the ordinary."

"No women?" Michelozzi hoped to turn the conversation in another, less morose, direction.

"Women."

"Niccolo, a woman would cheer you up. I myself am . . . well, let's say I'm watering two gardens, have one foot in two shoes. You know what I mean. And I'm enormously cheerful. Look at me!"

"Women! You sound like an old friend in San Casciano. She's intent on finding me a woman, and she claims to be some kind of a witch. She says if I give her a few little pieces of my hair and nails she can boil them in holy oil that she stole from a church lamp and make a potion for me. Any young woman, upon being administered this potion, will fall madly in love with me."

"You should give it a try! What have you got to lose?"

"Nothing. Absolutely nothing at all." Niccolo said it with conviction.

Ever friendly, ever buoyant, Michelozzi pressed on: "If you're not chasing women, then what are you doing these days?"

"I sit at a table. I write. When I can't think of anything to write, I stare at the walls. When I'm finished for the day, I get drunk. It's a fascinating life. You should try it."

"Are you still working on the Livy commentary?"

"Yes, I'm still working on the Livy commentary."

"Niccolo, it wasn't an accusation."

"I'm sorry. I'm not in a very good mood today. What have you been up to lately? Are you still in the chancery?"

Michelozzi hesitated and then decided to tell his friend the news: "Not only that, but I've gotten a promotion. They gave me your old job."

Niccolo's ears burned with envy. "That's great, Michelozzi. I suppose I should congratulate you."

"I suppose you should, but it's not like when you were chancellor, Niccolo. There's nothing to do in the Signoria these days—no militia to superintend and all the real government business is done at the Medici Palace. I write a few letters. That's all."

"A few letters." Although Niccolo was glad for Michelozzi—he told himself he should be at any rate—he could not suppress his jealousy. Michelozzi! He was a nice guy and even a decent friend. But secretary! His old job! He could never do it! He wasn't up to it! And he tried to imagine Michelozzi—the sincere but mediocre Michelozzi, a man who was guided by his cock instead of his brains, a man with one foot in two shoes even as they spoke—he tried to imagine poor Michelozzi face-to-face with Caesar Borgia.

"Niccolo, if you were there today, you'd be dying of boredom. I mean it. It's not the same job anymore."

"Dying of boredom, right."

"Look, the only reason I told you is that if something ever does come up, I want to be able to come to you for advice. Is that alright?"

"Pathetic," thought Niccolo. "He's trying to cheer me up. Come to me for advice. Indeed!" He said, "Oh, feel free, I've got plenty of advice these days, more than enough advice to give out."

Suddenly Michelozzi stood up. "Come on. I've got an idea. Something to draw you out of this torpor."

"Forget it, Michelozzi. I don't want to go to any whorehouse," said Niccolo irritably.

"This isn't a whorehouse. It's something different. There are some people I want you to meet."

"People? Shall I wear my leper's bell so they don't get too close?"

"Niccolo, please. Trust me."

"Where are you taking me?"

"It's a kind of . . . association."

"What kind of association?"

"You'll see." With that, Michelozzi skipped down the tiered benches and landed lightly on the ground. Morosely, Niccolo followed. "No wonder he's so happy," he thought, "he's got my old job. Messer Michelozzi, secretary in the Second Chancery! And a gay blade of a secretary in that outfit! Smart grey hose, smart satin pumps, smart black velvet doublet, smart white linen shirt rakishly open at the neck . . ." Niccolo knew he was being unkind. He couldn't help it. His own heavy riding boots still had mud on them—the mud of the country, where he dawdled and doodled while the world ignored him and elevated smartly turned-out fellows like Michelozzi in his place. . . . Under the vast, now-empty portico, oblivious to Michelozzi's gaiety and Niccolo's jealousy, oblivious to their departure and lost in the world of his own nonsense, the idiot prattled on.

"Here, this way." Michelozzi steered Niccolo to the left, into the Via della Scala. They marched past the forbidding faces of several buildings and along a high, severe stone wall—more monuments and expressions of the stony Florentine temperament and, at the moment, ample reflection of the temperament of the brooding Niccolo Machiavelli. There was a discreet door in a hole punched in the silent mask of a wall, and when Michelozzi knocked and identified himself, they were admitted. From the street, they stepped through the grim, unforgiving facade and into another world.

The clatter of the crowds of people and animals was shut out abruptly as the door closed behind them. There was a rush and a whisper of fountains, of trees being gently stirred in the early-evening breezes. There was an intense scent of cypress and pine and laurel that suffused this secret place. They had entered an immense garden of delights, an unlikely earthly paradise, here in the heart of the cramped city. Lush vegetation was everywhere. Cascades of cooling water spilled and tumbled from rocks in little grottos where benches were arranged around clear, sparkling pools. Paths and walkways wound through the luxuriant, abundant greenery and lost themselves. But most of all, there were the trees—conical trees and scrubby trees that smelled of the sea, huge fan-shaped trees and towering maritime pines, drooping willows and mighty oaks and chestnuts and olive trees, pear trees and apple trees and fig trees and cherry trees, some so heavily laden with fruit that their branches almost touched the ground.

Momentarily overpowered by the charms of the garden, even Niccolo surrendered to the cool, soothing, perfumed breezes. Whatever was going on in the world, this place was not part of it. This place was insulated. Eden before the fall of man.

"What do you think?" asked Michelozzi.

"It's astounding, another world."

"I thought you might enjoy it," said Michelozzi with satisfaction.

"Who created it?" asked Niccolo. "Who's God in this little, private world?"

"Would you like to meet our host then? Come on." Michelozzi guided Niccolo through the verdant maze. They encountered little groups of men who chatted unconcernedly, like philosophers of days gone by. Everywhere there were statues and pieces of statues, some apparently of great antiquity. Greek and Roman. In fact, the whole place had a Roman air to Niccolo—not contemporary cesspool Roman, but lofty, ancient republican Roman, Rome before the fall of man.

"Where's Cosimino?" asked Michelozzi of one of the intimates of the garden.

"He hasn't come down yet, but he sent word that he'll be here shortly," came the reply.

Niccolo looked around while Michelozzi drifted from group to group, exchanging greetings, kissing and shaking hands. He seemed to be on intimate terms with these people. Most of them were a generation younger than Niccolo. Here and there, he read in the eager young faces around him the unmistakable features of some ancient Florentine family—a Strozzi or a Nardi or a Nerli—but he didn't know any of them personally. They were, he surmised, the flower of Florentine youth. Like Michelozzi, they were well turned-out, smartly clad. Unconsciously, he shuffled in his heavy boots. Uncomfortably, he shoved an errant strand of uncombed hair up under his cap and pulled it down firmly on the back of his head.

Michelozzi had said this was some kind of association, and looking around him, Niccolo began to suspect just what kind. Preciosity was in the air. He greatly feared that before the night was out, poetry would be read aloud.

45

A Person on His Way Up

Niccolo Gathers Disciples

> **To everything there is a season and a time to every purpose under heaven. . . . A time to kill, and a time to heal; a time to break down and a time to build up.**
> **—Ecclesiastes 3:1–3**

It wasn't long before their host appeared. He was carried out in a box. It was gilded and carved and inlaid with ivory and lined with plush velvet, but it was undeniably a box. His arrival was greeted with effusions from the others present as they crowded around him. Niccolo kept his distance and examined the contents of the box. The little man reposing therein was grotesque, but not ugly. His head seemed huge, but it was no larger than Niccolo's own. It was the deplorable, shriveled condition of the rest of his body that made the head seem out of all proportion, Still, he held it erect.

He was simply dressed in a *lucco,* and the ends of little useless legs projected from the bottom of the gown. His chest was sunken and his arms mere spindles. His skin was pale, but he was very much alive. His teeth flashed as he joked and smiled. He did expressive things with his eyes and mouth. Occasionally his handsome features were distorted in a fierce, momentary grimace of pain, but then it would pass and he would return to his animated exchanges and disputes.

While Niccolo watched, Michelozzi finally engaged their host. When they both turned in his direction, he was obliged to shuffle over and submit to the polite, obligatory introduction.

"Niccolo, this is Bernardo Rucellai, Messer Rucellai, Niccolo Machiavelli."

"It's my pleasure, Messer Rucellai," said Niccolo with the requisite degree of deference.

"And mine as well. But call me Cosimino. Everyone here knows me as Cosimino. We're a very informal society."

"Cosimino, then," said Niccolo. "Although that's an odd nickname for Bernardo."

"Ah," sighed the little man, "Cosimo was my father's name. He built this place, and I inherited it. To his friends I was never Bernardo, just Cosimino—Little Cosimo. I've always lived in his shadow, but I can't complain. It's been a pleasant life here, in the gardens. By the way, how do you find them?"

"Utterly disarming, a miracle." Niccolo was on his best behavior.

"Do you know the *Aeneid*, Niccolo?" asked Cosimino.

"I've read around in it from time to time." It was a decided understatement. Niccolo had nearly memorized the entire heroic epic.

"Then you'll be pleased to know that here in the Orti Orcellari, my gardens, I have had planted at least one specimen of every tree mentioned in the *Aeneid*. Every one."

Niccolo coughed. "That's . . . that's remarkable," he said. "You must have a tremendous admiration for Virgil."

"For Virgil and for all the classics! For all things Roman!" said the little host. "And your tastes too, run in that direction?"

"Of course."

"Then later, let me show you some of the statuary I've managed to collect. It's genuine. Of Roman origin. You've probably seen it strewn about here and there. Some magnificent pieces . . . Oh but look, here's Luigi. Luigi's going to read tonight. Shall we listen?" With a gracious smile for Niccolo, Cosimino turned his attention to a callow youth who had mounted a dais and assumed a position behind a lectern. The thick sheaf of papers in his hands announced that the evening's reading was going to be a protracted one.

Niccolo took up a position as far from the center of the crowd as he could, vowing all the while to himself to wring Michelozzi's neck for getting him into this. A poetry reading! And among people who planted their gardens with all the trees named in Virgil's *Aeneid*! Such scholarship! Such an understanding of the Romans! Oh, how they were to be commended on their intellectual attainments, these lovers of antiquity! These collectors of fragments of old statues! Virgil worshipers! The superstitious who, because they were too ignorant to understand anything about Virgil, made lists of all the trees he mentioned in his epic!

Niccolo knew only too well this brand of pedantic reverence for antiquity. They had all their lists together. Lists of all the rivers and all the bodies of water, lists of all the animals, all the birds, all the ancient cities, and on and on. These flaccid flowery fluffy Florentines! What did they really know about the Romans? What could they understand! What did they know about virtue and commitment and courage and self-sacrifice? What did they know about the struggle for liberty? What could they ever feel when they read the line, "*Tantae molis erat Romanam condere gentem*—How tremendous an effort it was to found the Roman race!" What could they know about that effort? Did their breasts ever heave with such an effort? With the effort to establish a race of new Romans? Did they know how hard it was? Did they have any idea how hard it was? How many turns of the rack could they stand? What did they care about the struggle for freedom and justice—these pampered slaves in their artificial paradise? They knew the names of all the trees in the *Aeneid*.

Once again embittered—it didn't take much—Niccolo settled into an obscure spot in the groves of Virgiliana and tried to make himself comfortable. It was going to be a long night.

"*Sed parva licet,* to use the words of the master, if I might compare small things to great, I'd like to read from a poem I've been working on patterned after Virgil's *Georgics*. I call it, 'On Cultivation,' and it's a celebration of the country life." And with that introduction, Luigi began to read. His voice was a little nervous at first, but by the time he got to the simple rustic pleasures of shepherds and shepherdesses, he was reading with more confidence. He read through the planting and tending and harvesting of crops and described in minute detail the changes of season that accompanied each of these farmerly activities. He waxed poetic on heroic feats of animal husbandry and was fairly glowing when he forged into the section on cheese making.

Through it all, Niccolo regarded the youthful poet with a practiced and cynical eye. The joys of country life indeed! The golden age indeed! What this poetaster didn't seem to know was that out there in the golden age, the streets were paved with mud and manure. Niccolo fancied the young man out in the fields with his simple but elegantly cut and exquisitely tailored clothes. In Florence they might pass for "country attire," faux rustic, or whatever, but out there they would peg him for an urban dandy a mile away. The thought of those brilliant lacquered boots caked with horseshit brought a smile to Niccolo's lips. Ah, youth! Ah, Florence! He sighed inwardly. These young Florentines took up the example of the ancients, they read the classics, not to learn about valor and liberty and justice, not to learn how to organize a government and an army, but to learn how to make cheese and herd sheep! For that they applied to the Romans, when any illiterate peasant in San Casciano could give them an infinitely better lesson in the muddy pursuits of the pastoral ideal.

When the reading was over, Niccolo thought only of escape, but Cosimino caught his eye and beckoned him. He would have to say something nice about Luigi's poem.

"Well, you're new to our little circle, what did you think?"

Niccolo, to whom flattery never came easy and who was incapable of an outright lie, gave a neutral reply: "Imitation of the ancients is always a laudable undertaking."

Cosimino smiled, eyed him with curiosity, and said nothing. He chuckled softly to himself. "Ah, Machiavelli, you damn by faint praise. Imitation? Don't you think Luigi is a competent imitator of the classics?"

"I think our young friend should walk in mud up to his ankles for a few days and share a shed with the pigs and cows at night, if he wants to learn about the country life."

"Is that all you think?"

"I think that there are a number of different ways of imitating the ancients. Young Luigi is certainly a competent stylist."

"But you apparently don't think much of that sort of competence?"

"May I speak freely?"

"And if I said you couldn't?" There was a crafty expression on Cosimino's face. His dark eyes gleamed.

"Very well. Since you asked, we all know how much honor is attributed to antiquity these days. Your little circle here is proof enough of that. But what are we honoring? Luigi is writing about shepherds. You yourself spend enormous sums of money to acquire pieces of statues, statues with no arms or legs. And our artists and sculptors, if they can produce a slavish copy of one of these statues, they can get a good price for it. That's the value we place on antiquity. That's the use we put it to."

"But you know better? You think we dabble in the effete and the useless."

"We honor these empty forms, but we do nothing but degrade the men and the culture that inspired them—the captains and the citizens and the legislators and judges whose example we ignore. Not the slightest trace of their ancient nobility of spirit remains alive today. And there's nobody trying to revive that, to imitate that."

"Except you, of course?"

Niccolo looked down. He thought he had gone far enough. Memories of the rack told him not to go any farther. He knew where his opinions could land him these days.

Cosimino continued, "I came across a little pamphlet of yours, a pernicious little pamphlet about princes and principalities. I had it from Lorenzo Strozzi, who got it from his brother Filippo in Rome, who got it from your old friend Vettori. It's quite provocative." He waited. Niccolo said nothing.

"I seem to recall that you ended your tract with a call to arms and a citation from Petrarch: '*Che antico valore / nelli italici cor non è ancora morto.*' That's a rousing ending and an optimistic one: Ancient valor in Italian hearts is not yet dead."

"That was six years ago, when I wrote that."

"And it doesn't hold any longer? Our ancient valor has expired in the meantime?"

"If it's not dead, it's sleeping soundly."

"And who will awaken it?"

"I doubt it can be awakened. The moment is passed."

"And the struggle is over?"

"You can see for yourself the times we live in."

"Perhaps you underestimate the times? Perhaps you underestimate these young ones like Luigi. Perhaps you underestimate me." Cosimino paused. "Perhaps you underestimate yourself?" He left the question hanging.

"Perhaps."

"I'd like to make you a proposition. Why don't you read us something of yours some time?"

"Nobody's interested in the sort of writing I do," said Niccolo. "There's no meter and no rhyme and no happy shepherds."

"Ah! How you resemble our patron Saint John the Baptist," said Cosimino facetiously. "*Vox clamantis in deserto!* The voice crying in the wilderness! And no one is listening. How sad. You feel sorry for yourself, don't you, Machiavelli?"

Niccolo glared at him. He did not like being made the butt of jokes.

"Do you think I was always like this?" Cosimino swept a frail hand across his collapsed chest and down in the direction of his crippled legs. "No, I was a whole man once, but the excesses of youth, the ravages of disease, and the incompetence of doctors has reduced me to an atrophied shell, a cripple who has to be carried around in a box. Do you think I don't know self-pity when I see it? I can spot self-pity at a distance from here to Fiesole!" Again he paused and fixed Niccolo with his unflinching gaze: "Stop feeling sorry for yourself, Machiavelli. And come in out of the wilderness. There's work to be done."

The spell was broken by the arrival of Luigi, the flushed, triumphant poet. Cosimino congratulated him and then said, "Luigi, there's somebody here I'd like you to meet. Luigi Alamanni, may I present Messer Niccolo Machiavelli."

Luigi's mouth dropped open. "Machiavelli? Machiavelli of the militia?"

"The same," said Cosimino.

"I thought you were dead, I mean, I hadn't heard anything about you for such a long time."

"He hasn't been dead, Luigi," interjected Cosimino, "only sleeping. And I think I've managed to convince him to read something to us in the near future."

But Luigi had already taken Niccolo by the arm and was leading him away. "Come with me. I want the others to meet you, Messer Machiavelli."

"Of course," said Niccolo, still a little shaken by Cosimino's rebukes.

"You don't remember me, but we've met before," said Luigi, talking excitedly. "It was in the days of the war with Pisa, and I wasn't more than ten years old, but, oh, how I wanted to run away and join the militia. I even had a little uniform and a toy sword and we used to go on expeditions around the city. One day I saw you and I recognized you, because my father had pointed you out to me in a parade. I went right up to you, bold as brass, and demanded to join the militia. You were amused and told us we'd have to wait until we were old enough. Then you formed us up in a column and marched us across the piazza. And for weeks we talked about nothing else—Machiavelli of the militia had taught us how to march!"

"That was a long time ago," said Niccolo.

"I'll never forget that day," said Luigi. "Machiavelli of the militia taught us how to march! It was in front of the church where they keep the old nun with the hair and nails that keep on growing, even though she'd been dead a hundred years. We spotted you coming out of the church. You were with a beautiful lady."

And then the memory turned bitter and stung. "With a beautiful lady." At the mention of it, Niccolo reeled back into the black pit of emptiness and loss. There was no militia anymore. And there was no beautiful lady.

"Is something the matter, sir?"

"No, I was just thinking about something you reminded me of," said Niccolo, coming to himself.

"Good. Now here are my friends. They had approached a little knot of young men, all Luigi's age, about twenty years old. "*Compagnacci*, here, here's somebody you have to meet," announced Luigi.

They all turned and looked at their friend, the excited young poet who had an older and decidedly unfashionable man in tow. Their appraisals were quickly made; their expressions were dubious. They were waiting.

Luigi made his introduction: "Friends, may I present to you Messer Niccolo Machiavelli!"

Jaws dropped. There were incredulous whispers. Machiavelli of the militia! And then, one by one, they stepped forward and introduced themselves.

"Zanobi Buondelmonte."

"Giovan Batista della Palla."

"Jacopo da Diacceto."

"Francesco da Diacceto."

"Francesco da Diacceto."

Luigi interrupted: "They're cousins, and they both have the same name. We call him Nero because he's always dressed in black and the other we call Pagonazzo because he's always dressed like a peacock!"

Niccolo listened to the explanation and verified the truth of it, but his attention was almost wholly fixed on something else. It was something he had read in the faces of these solemn young men who had stepped forward and gravely presented themselves to him. It was the first time in a while that anyone had looked at him like that. If he was not mistaken, they were regarding him with a mixture of awe and reverence in their eyes. To them, he was Machiavelli of the militia once more.

"Cosimino says Messer Machiavelli's agreed to share some of his work with us!" announced the delighted Luigi. And almost immediately the whole eager crowd closed in on him. Niccolo was overwhelmed at his sudden notoriety. "One at a time," he protested. "And please, let me sit down."

He took a seat on a bench and they gathered around, some standing, some at his feet. In response to their clamoring inquiries, Niccolo explained, "I suppose, in the broadest sense possible, what I'm working on is what we Florentines can learn from our ancient, ancestors, the Romans." Suddenly he was Plato, and they were the Academy. He was Jesus, and they were the Disciples.

"Now, suppose we begin where the history of Rome and the history of Florence intersect. Who founded Florence?"

"It was a Roman colony," volunteered one of the Francescos.

"Ah, but what sort of a Roman colony?" said Niccolo, raising a finger of warning. "Or rather a colony of which Rome?" He let the question sink in, then continued. "There are two stories about the founding of Florence. Sometimes one of them holds currency, sometimes the other. In one version of the story, Florence was founded by Julius Caesar, and so she was a product of the empire and the emperor. In the other version, she was older than that, founded by soldiers of the old Roman republic—free citizen soldiers.

"Now I don't have to tell you which version is being bruited about today, do I, when the glory of empires and the glory of royal houses and dynasties is held in such high esteem?"

"But which is the true story?" said Luigi.

Niccolo smiled. "It's not all that important which is the true story, and I doubt if we could ever really find out. What is important is that we have a choice to make about our past, about which version of the past we want to accept. Were we born as subjects of a decadent and corrupt empire, or were the first Florentines virtuous citizens of a free republic? It's not a matter of what happened, it's a matter of what you believe."

"And what do you believe, Messer Machiavelli?" Several of them asked at once.

Niccolo sat back, and a broad grin stole over his face. In a moment, there were broad grins all around. There was no need for words. They had found common ground. And after years of neglect, Niccolo had found someone who was willing to listen—and learn. They put questions to him, a thousand questions that night, and he answered. And his words fell on their young minds like sparks on gunpowder.

In a very short time, Niccolo became not only a regular and an intimate of the little circle that met in the Orti Orcellari, but its leading luminary. Readings from his "Discourses on Livy" never failed to excite the imaginations of his youthful companions. His ideas were eagerly embraced, and the questions they raised, hotly debated. Talk of shepherds and wood sprites soon gave way to ardent discussions of republics and tyrants, of militias and mercenaries, of Florence and Rome, and of freedom and slavery.

And as Niccolo's esteem grew in the eyes of his zealous young compatriots, his self-esteem also began to revive. Bitterness and reticence yielded to an easy acceptance of, and even enthusiasm for, his new life and friends. He began dressing better. He began visiting a barber again on a regular basis. He had his long, scraggly hair trimmed close, the way he used to wear it, and although his hairline had receded a little, the thick hair still covered his skull like a cap of black-and-silver velvet.

He began staying in town again and getting accustomed to the rhythms of urban life. He would make it a practice to spend a week, sometimes two, in Florence, during which time he would join Cosimino and his circle in the Orti, those luxurious gardens, almost every night. Then, with their questions and objections and suggestions in mind, he would return to the little villa near San Casciano to rework, expand, and clarify his ideas.

All of this had little effect on Niccolo's purse, which was as empty as ever, but his poverty was more bearable now. He had found a new role for himself. Excluded from the councils of those who ruled, he had set his sights on preparing a new generation to someday take their place. When the time was right, these young men, imbued with republican ideals, would step forward and assume their rightful places in a free Florence. Niccolo's teaching and his writings would provide them with the background they needed. He was passing something on, something important. In a sense, he was doing what Savonarola had done—passing on the torch. Niccolo seemed to realize and accept the fact that his time was over, just as Savonarola's time had come to an end. But his stubborn commitment to the same ideals that had animated the fiery preacher refused to die, and so, in his way, true to his promise, he was keeping the flame alive. One important lesson he had learned from Savonarola was that the times change and that men must adapt their actions to those changes. For Savonarola, the times had changed, but he had not changed with them—or not rapidly enough. And he had paid the price. Niccolo, perhaps by mere chance, had managed to survive and, after a period of adjustment, was looking again toward the future and preparing, if not himself, then his young charges, who would one day, when the time was right, carry on his work.

But if Niccolo's spirits were on the rise, all was not well with Cosimino. The weakness of his shrunken body, which seemed to diminish in size a little every day, was becoming more and more apparent, and when the discussions went late into the night, Cosimino often drifted off into sleep and dozed in his box. He was usually carried up to bed without reawakening. But, after one particularly boisterous and longwinded evening, and after having slept through the more detailed discussions of power and corruption, he was lively and awake. As the little company was breaking up and preparing to go, he signaled to Niccolo.

"Niccolo, I may have something for you if you're interested, something in the way of a commission."

"I'm interested," replied Niccolo flatly and quickly.

"And it will even entail an honorarium, if I'm not mistaken."

"I'm very interested."

"The Cardinal is soliciting ideas."

"Ideas about what?" Niccolo cocked his head. "The Cardinal," for so he was known to all, was the de facto ruler of Florence. When the former Florentine cardinal, the corpulent Giovanni de' Medici, was elevated to the papacy, one of his illegitimate cousins, Giulio, quickly materialized to take his place and assume the cardinalate. Of course, he had to be hastily legitimized in order to aspire legally to the purple, but then Caesar Borgia, too, had gone through the same process before his father had made him a cardinal. There were many precedents, and the procedures were well established. Although a bastard, Cardinal Giulio de' Medici had acquired a reputation for caution and prudence in managing the affairs of the city. After the disastrous reign of his haughty cousin, Lorenzo, anyone would appear cautious and prudent.

Cosimino said, "The Cardinal is soliciting ideas on how best to govern Florence, now and in the future. He's applied to several men who have had experience in these matters in order to get the widest range of opinions possible, in order to be able to consider all the options. Anyway, your name came up."

"Just came up?"

Cosimino eyes twinkled, "Let's say it was put forward by a friend with your interests at heart. It was mentioned in the right circles and passed along through the right people . . . You know we're all cousins here in Florence, Niccolo, all of us members of the old families."

"What would I have to do?"

"Just get together a little tract on the details, all those things you know about—the constitution of councils and committees, the appointment of magistrates, all that. Do you want the commission?"

Niccolo could barely conceal his emotion, "Cosimino, I don't know how to thank you. You've done so much for me." He kissed the sick little man on both cheeks to show his profound gratitude. As he turned to go, Cosimino shouted to him, "And Niccolo, Remember whom you're writing it for! No fiery talk about tyrannicide and radical republics, you understand?"

"I understand, Cosimino, I understand." It was the opening he'd been waiting for.

"You understand what?" said Luigi, coming up alongside Niccolo.

"That there are times that favor impetuous men, and that the present time is not one of them," replied Niccolo.

"Eh?" said Luigi, puzzled. "What are you talking about?"

"Never mind. I'll explain later. I've just been given a commission to contribute to the reordering of the Florentine government."

"Bravo, magister! Then we have to celebrate! Zanobi has invited everyone over to his house. Will you come?"

"*Volentiere!*" declared the ebullient Niccolo, and then, arm in arm with young Luigi Alamanni, he strode out of the isolated Garden of Eden and back into the crowded streets of Florence.

When they arrived, the others were already there: Zanobi, the Francescos—Nero and Pagonazzo—their cousin Jacopo, and Giovan Battista della Palla, recently returned from Rome. Giovan Battista was regaling them all with tales of papal misdoings at the ever-incredible court of Pope Leo X:

"Chigi, the banker, has this competition going with the pope. They try to outdo each other in extravagance. First the pope hosted a dinner and invited the entire College of Cardinals. When the food was served, every cardinal was given dishes and specialties from his native region or country. And wine too!

"But Chigi, not to be outdone, invited the pope to his palace and gave him an excellent meal in a brand-new and lavishly appointed dining hall. When they were done eating, Chigi invites the pope to inspect the hall. And Leo pulls out his spyglass and starts looking around and nodding his big head, 'very nice . . . hmmmm . . . exquisite indeed.' The room is all hung with tapestries and curtains an inch thick. When the pope's done, Chigi asks him what he thinks. Of course, the pope tells him how beautiful everything is, how impeccable his taste is. Chigi is already beginning to laugh. Then he springs his joke. The tapestries are rolled up, and behind them are stalls full of animals! Chigi is whopping, tears running down his cheeks, and he says, 'But Your Holiness, this isn't my dining room, these are only my stables!'"

Gales of laughter erupted as Niccolo and Luigi made their way to the places set for them at table. "*Salve,* magister!" They all greeted Niccolo as he passed. "Don't let me interrupt," he said to the spirited company. "Go on, Giovan, finish your story."

"Well, the pope invited Chigi to dinner, this time out in the country at one of his villas up in the hills. They set the tables up on platforms on the banks of the Tiber to catch the cool evening breezes. The first course was served, something really prodigal, like a perfumed soup with rose petals floating in it. Now all the table service is silver—the plates too. When they finished the soup, everyone was waiting for the pope to give the signal for the servants to clear and serve the second course. Instead, Leo took his soup bowl, said 'I like it but it's only silver,' and flung it into the river! Chigi howled and followed suit, and then after every course, all the silver was thrown into the river."

"But that's not all," said Giovan. "When Chigi left, the pope sent his servants scuttling down to the river. They started heaving, and pretty soon all the silver was back up on the banks. There were nets in the water to catch it!"

Again the company dissolved in laughter, and Zanobi called for food and wine. He apologized that his fare was not as exquisite as that offered by the pope, but said he trusted it would be sufficient for sterner republican spirits like themselves. They all drank to his health. And to that of their magister! And to each other!

As the evening wore on, they coaxed old war stories out of Niccolo, who was not entirely reluctant to tell them of his encounters with Charles VIII and his six toes and the mad syphilitic Caesar Borgia. He told about the time the Medici were driven from Florence in '94 and how he personally knocked Piero in the head with a stone. He told them about his five—or was it six?—turns on the rack. And they listened, spellbound.

Niccolo sat back and watched them for a minute. He looked around the table from face to face. They were like sons to him. And what more could he want? A circle of bright young men who hung on his every word, like-minded spirits, earnest partisans who shared his views on the future of Florence. When he explained to them about the commission from the Cardinal, they were elated, and one and all declared him, *una persona da sorgere*! A person on his way up!

"Again." He thought to himself, irresistibly. "Again." And he thought of Fortune's wheel. He had spent his time at the bottom and survived. If the wheel kept spinning, as it must, there was no place for him to go but up.

"So Guinigi said, 'I'll give you anything I have if you let me deal you a good, sound whack on the head. Just name it. What do you want?'"

"Castruccio thought about it for a minute and said, 'A helmet.'"

Luigi and Zanobi burst out laughing. "What else did this wise man have to say?" asked Zanobi.

Niccolo pursed his lips and said judiciously: "He used to say, that is, he is credited by everyone in Lucca, with having said, 'I've never understood why, when a man is about to buy an earthenware vase or a jug, he thumps it on the bottom to see if it is sound, yet in choosing a wife, why, he's content with just a look.'"

"What's his name again, Niccolo?" asked Luigi.

"Castruccio Castracani."

"Superb name! Castruccio the Dog Castrator! How did you find out about him?"

"He's a legend in Lucca. There are all sorts of stories circulating about him. They say once, he went to the house of a Messer Taddo Bernardi for dinner. Taddo showed him into a room full of tapestries and exquisite furniture. The floor was marble and inlaid with gold and precious stones of a dozen different colors arranged in the shape of flowers and plants and trees. After dinner, Castruccio started to feel a good deal of saliva building up in his mouth and looked around for a spittoon. Nothing of the kind in the room. He looks around—everywhere there is nothing but all sorts of rich embroidery, beautiful designs, everything perfect. So he spits right in Messer Taddo's face! The man was outraged and demanded an explanation. Castruccio shrugged and said, 'I was only looking to spit in the place where it would offend you least.'"

"*Che palle! Che coglioni!*" Both Luigi and Zanobi expressed their admiration for the cheek of the irrepressible folk hero, Castruccio Castracani of Lucca. Niccolo had just returned to Florence and was full of tales and stories about this man who had risen from obscurity to prominence in Lucca over two hundred years ago. Through a combination of valor and political acumen, he had made himself ruler of that city and even waged a war—a successful war—on powerful neighboring Florence.

Niccolo was saying, "The legend has it that he was found in a cabbage patch and that, from such villainous beginnings, he trained himself in the exercise of arms and eventually went on to throw the tyrants out of Lucca."

These subjects—arms and tyrants and oppression and revolt—now formed the mainstay of the discussions between Niccolo and his little circle of adherents. Zanobi and Luigi, eager to hear of the exploits of another paradigm, another secular saint in the irregular pantheon of political activists whom master Niccolo had unearthed, clamored for more and pressed him for details.

Niccolo begged off, "Please, I want to eat. I want to eat. I've been riding all day. I'm starved." So saying, he shoveled another generous portion of zucchini and lamb's brains onto the plate in front of him and set upon it. His appetite had returned. Through mouthfuls, though he made them a promise, "I'll tell you what I'm going to do. I'll write the whole story down and I'll even dedicate it to you two. How's that?"

"*Salute!*" Luigi lifted his glass. Zanobi joined in, and Niccolo followed. "Hear! Hear!"

When Niccolo had finished eating, he made a hasty swipe at his mouth with his napkin and rose to leave.

"Magister, you're not going already?" Both were disappointed. "You've only just arrived and we have a lot to catch up on."

"This evening at the Orti," said Niccolo. "Now I have business to attend to. I have to file my report, but more important—and this is something you pampered young gentlemen will probably never understand the urgency of—I have to collect my salary!"

"Oh, his salary!" howled Zanobi. "Then Magister Niccolo will be buying the drinks tonight! For everybody!"

"I don't make enough in a month to keep you thirsty pups in wine for one night," objected Niccolo. "*A stasera!*"

"*Fatti con Dio.*"

Niccolo hurried out of the *osteria* and into the Piazza Maggiore. He had just returned from a month-long legation to Lucca on behalf of the Signoria. It was a minor legation, as legations go, more in the line of a civil suit than a real affair of state, but it was a beginning. And it paid.

The irony of it all was that he would have to report to Michelozzi—in his own old office! But he had long since ceased to feel any animosity toward the new secretary, and the rise in his own fortunes had gone a long way to dampen the fires of jealousy that once tormented him. In fact, on more than one occasion, Michelozzi had come to consult him on matters of procedure and on matters of judgment as well.

"Niccolo, you're back!" Michelozzi rose and they embraced. "Everything in order? Everything concluded?"

"Concluded to the satisfaction of all parties involved. The Lucchese are happy, the offended Florentine merchants are happy, and I'll be happy when you pay me."

"In a minute. In a minute. But I've got something else for you. It could be something big."

"What?" said Niccolo, feigning indignation. "The Luccan affair wasn't something big? Collecting gambling debts and settling commercial obligations for our guildsmen wasn't something big?"

"I mean it. Something big. The Cardinal wants to see you."

"The Cardinal!"

"The Cardinal. I'm not kidding. He said to send you to him as soon as you arrive."

"What's it about?"

"I don't have the faintest idea."

"Well," said Niccolo impatiently, "Shall we go find out or just sit here? Where does the Cardinal hold court these days? The Medici Palace?"

"Oh no," said Michelozzi. "Right here in the Signoria. The Cardinal's very wary about stirring up public opinion against himself. He does everything by the rules. No secret councils late at night in the Medici Palace."

"I guess that makes him a regular partisan of republican government," said Niccolo. They both laughed.

Michelozzi accompanied Niccolo as far as the apartments that used to belong to the Gonfaloniere Soderini and left him there. The Cardinal was sitting behind a huge desk with his hands folded precisely in front of him. He was clad in purple as befit his office, but there was nothing ostentatious about his appearance—no ermine, no velvet, no gold.

Niccolo had gotten used to the idea that the Medici came in all shapes and sizes, but this one was so utterly different from his ebullient first cousin the pope that it was difficult to believe the same blood flowed in his veins. In fact, Cardinal Giulio de' Medici was so stiff and cold and rigid, it was difficult to believe that any blood flowed in his veins at all. Leo was over three hundred pounds of perpetual motion, all belly and bluster and blubber and head wagging, while Giulio was devoid of anything that looked like human or animal spirits. Leo was pink and Giulio was grey. Leo was round and Giulio was razor-sharp edges and angles. Leo was all jowls and chins; Giulio had only one, very prominent, very pointed chin, with a very deep cleft, very high cheekbones, and a very long nose. A thick black fringe of hair was chopped straight across his forehead. His eyes betrayed neither kindness nor amusement, nor was his gaze penetrating or cruel or pitiless or even inquisitive. If, as the poets tell us, the eyes are windows to the soul, Giulio had long ago drawn the curtains and closed the shutters. There was no trace of a soul peeking or peeping or leaking out.

Niccolo bowed. "Your Excellency."

"Machiavelli. Thank you for coming." The voice was toneless.

"How may I be of service, Excellency?" Niccolo was always polite with tyrants these days.

"I've finally had the opportunity to pursue your little discourse on what sort of governmental arrangements are best suited to Florence. There was much in it that I found interesting."

"I'm honored."

"Of course, there was also much that was, shall we say, impracticable, at least for the present, but overall it was an astute analysis. And a discreet one. You have learned something about discretion in the past few years, haven't you, Machiavelli?" He remained utterly motionless. He didn't blink, his lips didn't move when he spoke.

"I believe so, Excellency."

"I've been privileged to read a number of things from your pen lately. You think clearly, Machiavelli, and you write well. Therefore, I'd like to make you a proposition. I'm prepared to offer you a salary of 100 florins a year for two years."

"For what, Excellency?"

"For you to employ yourself in writing a history of Florence. Do you accept?"

Niccolo did not want to appear too eager. "A history of Florence," he said, "beginning?"

"Anywhere you want."

"And ending?"

"Wherever you see fit."

"In Latin?"

"Or in Florentine, the choice is yours."

"100 florins a year for two years?"

"Longer, if the project demands it. Are you satisfied?"

"Why, yes, I . . ."

"Good. I'll have the necessary papers drawn up. Good day, Machiavelli." The Cardinal did not waste words or time.

And the interview was over. Niccolo was astounded at his good fortune. It wasn't until later that evening that he cursed himself for forgetting. In his excitement about the new appointment, he had neglected to collect the salary due to him from his mission to Lucca.

The Cardinal rested his unblinking, expressionless eyes on him until Niccolo turned and walked off across the big, still room. When the newly commissioned communal historian was gone, a side door opened noiselessly and someone else slipped into the chambers.

"Well? You heard?" said the cold Cardinal.

"I told you he'd accept," said the other man.

"And so he has."

"It will keep him busy for years, digging around in the dusty archives, reading old moldy books. And he's utterly content to do it for 100 florins a year. And you wanted to offer him 200."

"What about the young pups?"

"You don't have anything to fear from them. He keeps their heads full of all that Roman nonsense and his high-minded ideas about the militia and his grand old republic." There was a snort of derisive laughter. "They used to write poems about herding sheep and making cheese. Now they're busy scribbling about Numa Pompilius and Sulla and whether the infantry is more effective than the cavalry."

"You're sure they're harmless?"

"Utterly so."

"Just the same, I want you to keep an eye on them. His ideas are dangerous and they could be inflammatory."

"Don't worry, the history will keep him busy."

"It's amazing how throwing a sop to a barking dog will quiet him down," observed the Cardinal without emotion.

"But what if the dog starts up barking again, Your Excellency?"

"I suppose we'd have to take the stick to him in that event. What other choice would we have?"

"I understand castrating a dog takes the spirit out of him?"

"I suppose you're right. At any rate, keep me informed, and I'll decide if and when we have to take further action on his account."

"Excellency."

"Good day, Michelozzi."

❧ 46 ❧

Enthroned in a Privy, Niccolo Receives Important Messages; A Dutchman Is Elected Pope

Concerning the discovery of conspiracies, it is impossible to protect oneself from malice, imprudence, or carelessness so that the plot will not be revealed whenever the participants in it exceed the number of three or four . . . and everyone should guard himself from ever writing anything down, for there is nothing that can convict you more easily than your own handwriting.

—Machiavelli, *The Discourses*

Since his history required frequent access to records and books kept in the Signoria, Niccolo began spending a great deal more time in the city. One night, when he was working later than usual, he thought he heard something at the door. Putting down his pen, he listened. Nothing. It was his imagination. He was jumpy. It was late, and, bleary-eyed, he decided to retire for the evening, although he thought to check the front door before going off to bed. The bar was in place. He tugged to make sure the latch was engaged. All secure. But, pivoting to go, something scraped under his foot on the floor. Looking down in the dim light, he saw a letter.

He brought it over to his writing table, where a small but bright candle still burned, the only circle of light in the otherwise dark and empty house. In the yellow light, he could see that there was no name on the it. No address. A letter slipped under the door at night. He was intrigued. Niccolo unfolded the single sheet. He spread it out atop the mountains of papers and documents with which he was working. A cursory glance at the missive was enough. He was astonished to see that it was written in some kind of code!

It had been years—almost ten years—since Niccolo had received or sent a coded message. He stared uncomprehendingly as the odd symbols danced in the flickering candlelight. He didn't know where to begin. He couldn't read it. His eyes darted back and forth over the mysterious symbols, looking for something familiar, something to latch onto. Then he spotted it. A single character. He recognized the S-shaped figure that had always reminded him of a snake. It was part of an old chancery code. It was the unique symbol they had used, quite appropriately, he always thought, for the pope, and by extension, for Rome. As he examined the document, letter by letter, other symbols emerged from the general clutter. He remembered the *A*, the *R*, and the *N*, then the *S*, but try as he may, he could not summon up any more of the old cipher.

Working with the few letters he had, Niccolo scribbled out a hasty transcription, leaving blank spaces where his memory failed him and hoped to be able to fill in some of the vowels and other consonants with guesswork. It wasn't enough. He had too little to go on. Most of the words were nothing but four or five blanks. But as he concentrated on the fragmented signature at the very end of the document, something clicked. Suddenly he saw it:

- - - r - s- - - r - n -

The letter was from Piero Soderini.

Hastily, Niccolo went back and filled in the new letters—the *I*, *E*, *O*, and *D*—but it was still not enough to make much sense emerge from the maddening and intractable letter. He would have to wait until the next day. He would have to go to the chancery and hope that the old code books were still around somewhere.

As he tried to sleep that night, he could make no sense of it. Why would Soderini be writing to him? Why now, after nine years? And why in an outmoded code? What was afoot? Since the fall of the republic and the gonfaloniere's abdication, he and Niccolo had, not just carefully, but scrupulously avoided contact with one another. They had employed enormous precautions on both sides in order to avert dangerous suspicions. Even the hint of a conspiracy, the whiff of a plot to return the gonfaloniere to Florence would be taken deadly seriously and acted upon without hesitation. They both knew that Soderini's every move was under close scrutiny and that the assassin's dagger was never far from his breast.

The next day, Niccolo browsed seemingly casually through stacks of forgotten books and documents that were even dustier and moldier than his usual obscure reading material. He felt fortunate to be working on the history, since his research provided him with the perfect excuse to rummage around old chancery files without arousing suspicion. Finally, he found the old collection of ciphers that he was looking for, the ones they had used in 1502, when he was on legation to Caesar Borgia and the pope was a snake. He didn't dare take the papers home. He waited until he was alone and copied the code out quickly on a scrap of paper, which he thrust deep in his pocket. He replaced the cipher where he had found it.

Luigi and Zanobi were waiting for him when he came out of the chancery and compelled him to accompany them to the Orti, as usual, to read. The evening dragged on. It seemed endless, and all the while, Niccolo was itching to get away, to go home and transliterate Soderini's mysterious, unexpected letter. It was dark before he was finally able to beg off.

He slammed the door shut and locked it behind him like a man who has something to hide. He stumbled around in the dark until he found a candle, lit it, and sat down. Shoveling the mounds of historical documents aside, he cleared his table and took out Soderini's letter. Alongside it, he spread the scrap that contained the key to the code, and alongside that, his sheet of paper with the blanks and the seven letters he had already deciphered. He worked quickly, coaxing and wheedling the document's secrets out of her gradually, one letter at a time.

Finally, he sat back and read:

Niccolo,

I have sent you several letters, which may or may not have reached you. I have no way of knowing. While I can't go into any great detail, I've found employment for you here in Rome, and I want

> you to come. I want you to set out at once and not say a word to anyone. The work that I have in mind here will most assuredly be of interest to you. At any rate, it seems to me decidedly preferable to writing miserable histories at 100 florins a year, which is how I understand you now occupy your time. *Valete!*
>
> Piero Soderini

The letter left Niccolo profoundly perplexed. The obscure, but tantalizing, reference to "work" in Rome could mean only one thing—that Soderini was plotting something against the Medici, plotting to return to Florence. Could it work? Who else was with him? Who was behind him? The French? A million questions sprang instantly to mind. And a million nagging doubts.

Why now? Why after all these years, when he had finally managed to haul himself out of despair and dejection? When things were going his way for a change? Five years ago, he would have jumped at the opportunity. A conspiracy! In his desperation, he would have taken any chance, tried anything. But now, things were different. Now he was getting on. Now he had a new role to play.

Soderini's contemptuous reference to his "miserable histories" bothered him. Was he miserable? Was he a groveler? Or was it true that he was working quietly, in his own way for the Florence he loved? Preparing for her future, educating her youth, and writing to inflame the Florentine hearts of tomorrow? Should he throw it away and rush off to join Soderini in a conspiracy that had one chance in a million of succeeding?

Niccolo knew that if he left for Rome, he could never come back unless a successful coup were mounted and carried out. And a successful coup meant, just for starters, disposing of the pope! As long as Leo controlled the papacy, the Medici would rule Florence. How were they going to get rid of him? And then there was the Cardinal. The list of obstacles was too long even to go over, too insane even to contemplate. Soderini was mad. The times were all wrong for this sort of thing. The gonfaloniere had been timid when he should have shown some resolve, and now when he should be proceeding with caution, he was about to strike out on some mad, adventurous enterprise.

But then there was the dream, through the haze of difficulties, the dream of a resurgent republic! And the obstacles melted away, as if by magic. For many hours, Niccolo vacillated between the objections, which were countless, and the pull of the dream, which was irresistible. One minute, he was ready to ball up Soderini's letter and hurl it into the fire; the next, he was on the verge of dashing out the front door, saddling a horse, and galloping wildly off to Rome.

He cursed the despicable letter that had brought such an impossible choice into his life. He slammed it with his fist, hard, repeatedly. He picked it up and shook it the way one would shake some naughty child or some offensive wag by the shirtfront. He held it up and stared grimly at its fanciful, seemingly innocent, characters. They were like the squiggles a child might make before learning to write. He focused his eyes on them so intently that he thought he might almost burn a hole in the paper. Then his focus faded and the characters began to blur. They swam far away and became meaningless and . . . then . . . No! Then he saw something that gave him pause.

Niccolo sat bolt upright, at first incredulous. A bigger character had suddenly and miraculously superimposed itself over the smaller squiggles. Holding the letter up in front of the candle had brought it out. For a moment, Niccolo could not believe his eyes. It was as if the finger of God had traced an answer for him in the paper.

When Niccolo had the time to shake these visions of divine intervention from his mind, he realized that what he was staring at was the watermark. He knew enough about making paper to know that pulp is boiled and then left to dry on a screened rack. The fineness of that screen mesh, among other things, will determine the quality of the paper. Any defects in the regularity of the screen will show up, etched in the very fiber of the paper. Long ago, papermakers began the practice of marking their products by twisting a rogue wire in the screen in the shape of an initial or a trademark. Over time, these designs, left when the water dries out of the pulp and hence called watermarks, became more elaborate. Wealthy clients often commissioned special signature marks for the batches of paper they ordered. There was already a whole history and a science of identifying the origin of a sheet of paper by its watermark. But Niccolo needed to consult no code book to decipher this one. He did not have to return to the archives and pore over dusty volumes to know what it meant. A crooked, cunning smile crossed his face as he stared down at it, and he began to laugh. It was so clear, so obvious, when the paper was backlit against the candle:

The letter had not come from Soderini at all. It had come from the Medici!

Having successfully avoided the trap set for him, and in so doing, having earned a certain grudging measure of confidence from his Medici masters, Niccolo was employed more frequently on official business. His latest mission, however, was causing him to have second thoughts about serving his city as a minor official. He sucked in a mouthful of soup and looked around him. Arranged in orderly rows up and down long tables on uncomfortable backless benches, the monks were all sucking and slurping almost in unison. The only other sound in the refectory was the drone that issued from the pulpit placed high up in the wall. Talking at meals was forbidden, and edifying readings from the Scriptures and the Church Fathers took its place. No conversation, no conviviality! They called this a meal! And the food! The broth was so thin, so colorless, so tasteless and weak that had one chicken been boiled in all the water in the Mediterranean Sea, the result would have been more hearty and flavorful. And it wasn't even warm.

Niccolo took another mouthful and swallowed. Looking to the head of the first table—he wasn't even seated at the first table—he saw the suave minister general of the order working his plump, shaven jaws up and down with great determination. He was chewing! He actually had something real to eat. Whatever was in his dish, it was definitely not the unappetizing, watery gruel that Niccolo had been served. There was nothing substantial enough in his sorry bowl to require the intervention of teeth before swallowing. He only hoped the second course would include more robust fare.

Niccolo had been sent to Carpi, to attend a general assembly meeting of the Friars Minor, the Franciscan order, and to conduct a number of affairs on behalf of Florentine interests, among them the recruiting of a preacher for the wool guild to preach the Lenten sermons in the cathedral the following year. He had arrived that morning and been told that his business could not be transacted until after the chapter elections were held and new officials were chosen. This, he was told, could take some time, and so he was shown to a cell that could only be described as monastic and told to make himself comfortable. Was that a joke? The cell reminded him of nothing so much as his cell in the infernal *stinche*. It was a little cleaner, but the furnishing were approximately the same, consisting of a rough wooden slab that he supposed was to serve as a bed. There was a window and, for comfort, a crucifix on the wall. He had passed the day hunched up in there, reading, looking forward to dinner. He knew from Pagolo that the prodigality of monastic hospitality was often boundless, but he was beginning to suspect that this house at Carpi was not one of those lavish establishments. He quickly drained the half cup of wine that had been served him and waited in vain for another. There was no pitcher on the table, and nobody was coming around with one. His spirits were sinking.

Finally, the bowls were cleared. At last, something to eat! The monks all bowed their heads in mumbled prayer. Did they pray before every course? Was there going to be another ration of watered-down wine with the meat? Such were the questions that preoccupied Niccolo. Such were his concerns. Then the praying stopped, and the monks did an unexpected thing. They rose, as one man, and began to file out of the refectory. Dinner was over!

When Niccolo returned to his cell, hungry and unrefreshed, there was a letter waiting for him, containing further instructions relating to his mission. It was from the papal governor of Modena, within whose jurisdiction Carpi fell. In the future, Niccolo was to address all correspondence to him, for as long as he was at Carpi, etc., etc. The letter made clear that the entire mission to the monks was something of a farce and that Niccolo should simply enjoy himself, if possible. It was signed, "*Franciscus de Guicciardinis,*" and under the name, pompously in Latin, "*Gubernator*—Governor."

But a postscript was appended to the letter: "Early in my career, while I served as Florentine ambassador to the court of Spain, I used to receive instructions from the Ten over the signature of a Niccolo Machiavelli. Are you related to him? Was he perhaps your grandfather?"

Niccolo let the letter slip to the floor. Once again, he was confronted with the painful recognition of how far he had fallen. He remembered sending off dispatches to this Guicciardini, an insignificant ambassador at the time. Now Guicciardini had risen to the rank of governor, and he assumed that Niccolo was the grandson of that Niccolo

Machiavelli, chancellor and secretary to the Ten of War. Formerly chancellor and now? Now he was ambassador to the Sandaled Republic of Parsimonious Friars Minor. An insignificant man on an unimportant assignment.

In the days that followed, having nothing better to do while the monks quibbled in their chapter meetings, Niccolo penned a letter to the governor, apprising him as to his actual identity and reduced circumstances. He was almost apologetic. To his surprise, he received an immediate response from this Guicciardini. It was a letter that brought tears to his eyes when he read it, for it was full of genuine affection, the utmost respect, and a tragic meditation on the course of history and fate. From that moment on, Niccolo and Francesco Guicciardini were fast friends. The friendship led first to a lively exchange of very candid letters in which Niccolo complained of the treatment he was receiving at the hands of the stingy monks, and soon, between the two of them, they worked out a way to remedy the situation.

It was midmorning and Niccolo was alone in the vast communal toilet, meditating as he later wrote to Guicciardini, on the vanity of the world. The toilet was a spacious, airy place that could accommodate up to twenty-four monks at a sitting. Two rows of low, hollow cement benches, punctuated at regular intervals by holes, had been constructed down the length of the walls. The monks, who did everything together at regular intervals, occupied the toilet en masse after breakfast, if you wanted to call a hard crust of black bread breakfast, for about twenty minutes. Niccolo had no desire to share this intimate moment with twenty-three other men, and so, at the cost of considerable violence to his own digestive system, he contrived to have the place to himself from about half past nine to ten o'clock.

The rider arrived with such a show of haste and importance that the monks were at first cowed when he clattered into the small courtyard on a giant, black, lathered steed. Leaping from his horse, the man, an armed and liveried crossbowman, demanded to see the Florentine ambassador. From a pouch, he produced a most magnificent and impressively sealed letter. One of the friars babbled that the Florentine ambassador was "occupied." "He, *ahem*, doesn't like to be disturbed at this time of day. You may leave the message with us." The messenger balked at the suggestion like a man asked to leave his only daughter in the hands of a known child molester. "I insist on seeing him personally. Now!"

With no other recourse, the monks meekly indicated the closed door of the toilet, and in clamored the obstreperous messenger, without so much as a knock. When Niccolo emerged a few minutes later, cinching himself with one hand, holding the letter in the other with the other, and nodding gravely, he looked up to see the entire chapter gathered around him in a circle with inquisitive looks on their faces. "I need a table. Quickly! And bring me writing materials!"

He was shown into the library and was barely seated when the second messenger arrived. This one bowed so low to the ground in front of Niccolo that it brought an audible mummer from the curious assembled monks. When he spoke, it was in a harsh and guttural German. Astonishing! The next mud-splattered messenger spoke French, the one after that, Spanish. Arriving almost on each other's heels, their displays of haste and obsequiousness threw the entire monastery into a tumult. Perhaps they had underestimated this Florentine?

For his part, Niccolo was engaged in a flurry of letter writing, saying out loud for all to hear, "The emperor is expected at Trent . . . The Swiss are on the march again . . . The king of France wishes an urgent interview with the Florentines . . ." The monks meanwhile, gathered around this prestigious person in open-mouthed awe and hung on his every word and gesture. The messengers continued to arrive. Niccolo would write like one possessed for a few minutes, then pause. He would knit his brows and puff out his cheeks, and their astonishment would only increase. At the end of the day, the minister general approached Niccolo, who was making a great show of his exhaustion. "Perhaps you would care to dine with me this evening? In private?" A big smile lit up Niccolo's face.

And from then on, it was fat ravioli swimming in butter and garlic, roasts and fowl and sausages and generous drafts of inky red wine that exploded with taste on the tongue. Niccolo was given a more commodious room—one only recently vacated, he was assured, by a most important member of the order. As the chapter meetings dragged on, he was able to pass his days reading, lost in the depths of a massive, exquisitely soft feather bed.

Finally, the mission came to an end, or rather, Niccolo was unable to prolong it any further for fear the monks were beginning to discern that he was making fun of them. Indeed, his letters to Guicciardini were full of scandalous observations, which, if they had come to the attention of the good friars, would have been the cause of much consternation, not to say a severe beating for the Florentine ambassador. Since the exchange of these letters had been such a source of delight to Niccolo, he was determined to stop over in Modena on his way back to Florence for the express purpose of making the personal acquaintance of Messer Francesco Guicciardini. It was just as well, because a few miles outside of Modena, he was subjected to a severe attack of the stone and would have been unable to continue in any case, because of the pain.

Francesco Guicciardini was a thick and placid man. His head was large and his face, fleshy. It disappeared into his neck without coming to any point that could properly be called a chin. He wore a look of bland and regal insouciance that some men acquire after years of cruel experience and bitter observation. Francesco Guicciardini was born with that look on his face.

When he moved, which he did as little as possible, he moved ponderously and deliberately. He had a pair of delicate and lazy white hands, which rested on his ample stomach in an affectionate, complacent, paternal way when he talked. He could make the most clever and astute and ready observation or deliver the most stinging barb with a detachment that was uncanny. He was also capable of absorbing the news of the death of his wife, the fall of the Roman empire, or the end of the world and the second coming of Christ with an equal and magnanimous indifference.

Sitting across the table from Niccolo at breakfast, he puttered with his boiled egg in its little silver eggcup. He cracked the shell cautiously and explored the interior with a dainty, silver spoon. He was wearing a deep-purple morning coat with massive, bushy, white fur trim that hung down to his waist, both in front and back. He looked like a successful hunter with a large fur-bearing animal slung over each shoulder.

In the days since Niccolo had recovered from the sporadic shooting pains in his side, he and Guicciardini had done little else but debate the stormy course of recent Italian history. On the vicissitudes, on the deplorable condition of the present, and on the causes for all the disasters that had befallen Italy, they were in complete agreement. When it came to solutions to the problem, however, they differed markedly. In a spirit of collegiality and intellectual equality, they had taken to addressing each other by their last names.

Still toying with his egg, Guicciardini was saying, "Your problem, Machiavelli, is that the story of your life isn't the story of your life at all. It's the story of the ups and downs of your damned republic."

"To a certain extent," admitted Niccolo. "But lately I've been learning how to get along."

"Lately?" sniffed Guicciardini. "How old are you now Machiavelli?"

"Fifty-two this month."

"Fifty-two and you're finally learning how to get on in the world? A remarkable achievement for one as bright as yourself."

"I've always tried to put the good of the republic before my own personal ambitions."

"That's where you're wrong, Machiavelli, don't you see? Anyway, your dreary republic seems to have been put out of business for a while. You won't have that choice to make any time in the near future."

"Perhaps not," said Niccolo noncommitally.

"Oh, you still have that cricket in your head, don't you? *Chirp! Chirp! Chirp!* It never stops, does it? The resurgent republic! The example of the ancient Romans! By the way, I think you make far too much of your ancient Romans."

Niccolo shook his head, "Guicciardini, you'll never understand about passion and commitment and valor and virtue."

"I should hope not! It would put me at a distinct disadvantage in the world if I did. There's certainly not much valor or virtue in His Holiness, is there? And I can't for the life of me think of more than a handful of valiant men in Florence in this day and age. No, Machiavelli, I'm afraid the age of valor has long since passed. I'm afraid valor is quite dead."

"Or maybe just sleeping?" said Niccolo mischievously.

"You'll never give it up, will you? Machiavelli, learn to live with it. Look at you! Fifty-two years old and you're still dreaming the romantic dreams of a boy of fifteen! You're really quite a marvelous study in obstinacy and stubbornness. Even the clothes you wear. You still insist on wearing that old *lucco*, your solemn citizen's gown, your toga, your badge of membership in the new Roman republic!"

Niccolo stiffened, "The *lucco* is a respected and dignified garment, apart from any associations you may choose to attribute to it."

"You should get something nice to wear like this." Guicciardini lovingly stroked the magnificent wooly beasts who adorned his shoulders.

"I couldn't afford it," said Niccolo diffidently.

"Whose fault is that?"

"You were born rich, Guicciardini."

"And I intend to remain so. But what about you? You certainly had more than enough chance in your years of service to put a little something aside for a rainy day?"

"I was honest."

"Honesty has nothing to do with it. I'm not talking about outright plundering the treasury or even accepting bribes, necessarily. Let me give you an example—the way you bungled the Soderini abdication."

"Bungled!"

"Bungled. What did you advise Soderini to do when the first signs of trouble started to show themselves?"

"I told him to throw his enemies in prison and stand and fight."

"Which he didn't do until it was too late. Piero was never very assertive. Now, I would have counseled a more conciliatory approach. I would have made deals with the Bigi, because there were deals to be made in those days. Soderini could have gone gracefully, early on, without a struggle, his wealth intact. You could have gone with him into exile and lived happily ever after."

"I could never live far from Florence."

"Not that! Maudlin sentimentality."

Niccolo huffed, "I love the city, Guicciardini, and I'm not ashamed of it. And I was faithful to Soderini—to the last."

"So was I, faithful to Soderini, but up to a point. I saw what was coming, and I made my arrangements. When the republic flourished, I worked for the republic. When the republic, unfortunately or otherwise, fell, I made my peace with the Medici. Now, I work for them."

"And so, finally, do I," said Niccolo.

"But I have a much better job," said Guicciardini, laughing. "And besides, Machiavelli, you can't fool me. You don't really work for them, do you? You're working for your imaginary republic, your fantasy vision of Florence. Because the real Florence happens to be in their hands, you've called a temporary truce. Isn't that right?"

"Whatever you say, Guicciardini. Whatever you say." And Niccolo thought of that moment in which he had been so perilously close to dropping everything, dropping the facade and rushing off to conspire with Soderini in Rome.

"Let me give you some advice before you do something stupid. Forget about your dreams of a republic. If it happens, if it comes about, then by all means, offer your services. In the meantime, watch out for your own particular interests. I can assure you nobody else will. Be discreet. When you've provided for your own security, which you are on the way to doing, finally, then you can do what I'm doing."

"Which is?"

"Sit back and watch."

"Is that all?"

"You might want to take some notes, so that you can write about it later."

"Francesco Guicciardini, you're a man without a soul," said Niccolo, regarding him with amused disbelief.

"Thank you," said the portly aristocrat, dabbing at the bits of egg yolk on his slack upper lip. "I'll take that as a compliment to my dispassionate and analytical side. Now this history, you're writing. Let's talk about that. You know, I once began a history of Florence?"

"And you didn't finish?"

"God no! It was just too messy. But here's what I want to know. It seems to me you might have a little problem with historical objectivity."

"There's no such thing as objectivity."

"Well, I'm glad we agree on that, but I had a much more concrete kind of problem in mind. You are writing this thing under the patronage of the Medici, whom you consider to be 'the enemies of freedom,' I think the phrase is yours?"

"And?"

"How are you going to reconcile your rabid republican sympathies with the interests of your patrons? I mean, I hardly think they expect to be vilified in a work they're paying you to write?" Guicciardini was delighted by the conundrum he had exposed.

"Oh, that's simple," said Niccolo slyly. "I have complete freedom to begin and end the history wherever I want. I choose to end it just when Lorenzo the Magnificent comes to power."

"Splendid, Machiavelli! You are learning something! Finally!" And the talk turned to the broad outlines of Niccolo's work. While the two of them were thus parsing the history of Florence into manageable and meaningful units, a messenger entered with the morning's dispatches."

"Ah, duty beckons," said the unflappable Guicciardini, sorting through the pile of mail.

"Anything for me?" asked Niccolo.

"Doesn't look like it." He began opening letters, giving each a cursory examination and arranging them in piles on the table. Niccolo was carving a pear.

"Oh, dear," said Guicciardini, stifling a yawn.

"What is it?"

"It seems good Pope Leo has expired."

"*Cazzus!*" Niccolo leapt to his feet, and in his head, thirty thousand demons leapt to life. With the pope dead, the calculus of power in Florence and Italy and all of Europe was suddenly changed! And the relative positions of the kings of France and Spain and the emperor, and—yes!—the Medici—everything was thrown into disarray! Anything was possible! "This changes everything, Guicciardini, don't you see," he said excitedly.

"Yes, I suppose it does," said the suddenly thoughtful papal governor, stroking his fur collar. "I suppose I might have to find a new job."

"Adrian Dedel!" said Giovan Battista della Palla, just back from Rome. Luigi Alamanni and Zanobi Buondelmonte chorused in, "Dedel! Dedel! Dedel!" making comic gobbling sounds in the backs of their throats. Cosimino and Niccolo, the elder statesmen in the group, maintained a degree of reserve, but were obviously enjoying the amusement of their younger compatriots.

"And he's decided to keep his own name as pope! Pope Adrian VI!"

"Hopeless Pope Adrian!" said Luigi. "Pope Leo wanted to be a lion. Pope Julius and Pope Alexander fashioned themselves conquerors and emperors. What does Pope Adrian fashion himself?"

"A man of God, a humble servant of the church, and a devotee of religious reform." Everyone howled with laughter. What kind of a pope could this be? They were all talking at once:

"How many children does he have?"

"Not a one!"

"And he's from Utrecht?" Zanobi pronounced it Oooooothrecht, mimicking what he considered to be a Dutch pronunciation.

"A Dutchman as pope! Who ever heard of such a thing?"

"Someone said the Englishman, Wolsey, wanted to be pope."

"A Dutchman! An Englishman! Don't they know the pope is supposed to be Italian? What will they think of next, a Pope from Poland?"

"Pope Leo should have been more mindful of his duty and left a son to succeed him!"

"It's a sad day when there isn't even one Italian left with enough money to buy the papacy!"

"And the Dutchman can't speak a word of Italian!"

"His Latin is so bad you can't understand that either!"

"What do the Romans say?"

"They're incensed. They hate him. No more parades, no more festivities, circuses, processions. The pope wants to be frugal!"

"A frugal, childless pope! Is this a sign the end is drawing near?"

"All the poets and musicians and jesters and dwarves who were living in the Vatican apartments have been evicted. He drove them out of there like Jesus driving the money changers out of the temple!"

"And the whores as well! What a black day for the Holy See!"

"His advisers have preposterous and unpronounceable names like Vincl and Trinkvoort and Kurtius. All Dutchmen!"

As the young men fell to composing disrespectful couplets on the outlandish new personalities with whom the pope chose to surround himself, Niccolo edged closer to Cosimino. The little cripple's breathing was labored, but his eyes were still alive. "And what about our cardinal here, Cosimino? What does he do now that the pope is gone?"

"I think he's doing the prudent thing, Niccolo. I think he's preparing for a gradual transfer of power and the reconstitution of some sort of republican government."

"You really think so?"

"Without the power of the papacy behind him, he has to give

ground. You know he's been here to the gardens several times since you were gone?"

"I know, Luigi told me."

"And he listens with great interest to what we have to say. He asks the boys questions, solicits their advice. He applauds their judgments. He commends what he calls their youthful ardor."

"So you think he really intends to make changes?"

"Let's face it, Niccolo, he was never as bad as most of his family. He's been prudent and done the city a lot of good. Instead of lavishing his money—our money—on fantastic palazzi and extravagant architects, he dug that canal to control the Arno in flood times. I think he has the city's best interests at heart."

"And them," said Niccolo, indicating the cavorting young scholars. "What do they think?"

"They're enthusiastic. Luigi, at the cardinal's request, has submitted a treatise on the restoration of popular and elective government." Cosimino chuckled, "Although I must say that it bears a strong resemblance, a very strong resemblance, to your work."

Cosimino continued, "They want to do great things, Niccolo. They've found direction and meaning. They want to accomplish something, build something. And they have you to thank. You're the one who started them off down that road. You're the one who pointed the way."

Niccolo felt deeply gratified by Cosimino's observation. He was passing his torch along. They were taking it up. His sons. His spiritual descendants. Dancing and laughing, full of the brash disrespect of youth, but full of passion too, full of commitment and hope. He wished the staid, world-weary Francesco Guicciardini could see them. But would he understand? Could he ever understand?

Niccolo had gone back to the country for the summer to work on his monumental history of Florence. The weather was mild, and he passed his days easily enough in research and writing. The evenings were cool, and he used to sit outside his little villa to take advantage of the occasional breezes and enjoy the moist, perfumed night air that descended upon the place when the hot sun went down.

Between the past, which was often painful but stirring too, and the future, which he increasingly regarded as hopeful, he had made a rough peace with the world. Immersed in the cycles of Florentine history that he was charting and explaining, Niccolo had little time to dwell on his own personal losses and tragedies—at least not in his waking hours.

He liked to sit facing the road, dressed only in light hose and a loose, open, linen shirt, feet propped up magisterially. He often amused himself in trying to guess the origin and destination of travelers who passed. From their muffled, overheard conversations, he could usually identify the language they were speaking or the dialect they were condemned to use if they happened not to be Florentine. From the dark shapes they cut against the moonlit night sky, he could pick out a cleric or a peasant or a dandy or a soldier. Or a Dutchman. The road was full of Dutchmen making their way to Rome to fete the new pope, who was one of their own. Most were humble pilgrims who would be robbed and fleeced and sent home again when they had been relieved of their money; others were more astute souls—office seekers who were looking to make their fortunes from the happy and unexpected election of Pope Adrian VI.

One night he heard a heavy tread coming fast from the direction of Florence. Before he could see anything, he could tell that it was someone on foot, which was odd. People in a hurry were always on horseback. Nobody ever ran down the Roman road. Especially at night. He heard whoever it was lose his footing on the dusty road, roll over several times, then regain his feet and start running again. The dark figure was on him almost before he knew it, hurtling straight at him, and if Niccolo had not jumped out of the way, he would have been sent sprawling in the dust.

"*Gesu Cristo!* What the hell! What is this? What do you want! *Potta del cielo!*" and a stream of similar indignities escaped Niccolo's lips.

"Magister, it's me, Zanobi!" the man said between gasps, seemingly having a great deal of trouble getting enough air. Niccolo relaxed when he realized who his unexpected visitor was.

"I . . . can't . . . I can't . . ." he heaved.

"I know," said Niccolo indulgently. "Take a minute to catch your breath."

Zanobi's lungs were burning, and his stomach was twisted in a tight knot. He made his way to the corner of the house, and, leaning on it for support, vomited. Niccolo waited while his heaving and riotous breathing quieted down.

"Zanobi, what are you, crazy?"

"I just barely got away. I ran all the way from Florence."

"That's seven miles! Why did you run seven miles? And what did you just barely get away from?"

"Soldiers. They came to arrest me!" He was still breathing with difficulty. "They got Luigi . . . and Jacopo."

"Arrest you? What on earth for?" In the moonlight, Niccolo could see that Zanobi's boyish face, streaked with sweat and dust, was contorted in a grimace of real terror.

"Niccolo, we . . . we . . ." he hesitated.

"You what!" Niccolo was alarmed now.

"We were plotting to kill the Cardinal."

"Oh God."

❧ 47 ❧

Amid the Clamor of Lutherans, Niccolo Visits the Little Sparrow in Florence and Sees a Startling Cartoon in Rome

Luigi Alamanni endured seven turns of the rack before he confessed to the conspiracy. By that time, both of his arms had pulled free of their sockets. He and Jacopo da Diacceto were both beheaded before daybreak on the seventh of June 1522. In an isolated courtyard, with nobody but their executioner to hear them, the two idealistic young men both affirmed that they had acted, not out of any malice toward the Cardinal, but like Brutus, out of a love of liberty and a hatred of tyranny.

The coup that they were preparing was discovered when a courier from Giovan Battista della Palla in Rome was intercepted on his way to Luigi Alamanni. The papers he carried included the names of all the coconspirators, who were fourteen in number, all young, all members of the circle that gathered at the Orti Orcellari under the patronage of Cosimino Rucellai and the tutelage of Niccolo Machiavelli.

In the wake of the arrests, the society that met at the Orti was dispersed. Most of its members were forced into exile. Cosimino Rucellai languished for a few months, his health growing steadily worse, until, robbed of the one delight that had kept him alive for so many years, he died, a broken-hearted man. In Rome, Piero Soderini, who was in touch with the hot-blooded young republicans through

Giovan Battista della Palla and who was behind the conspiracy, also died. Zanobi Buondelmonte, with Niccolo's help, made it to Venice, and from there to France. Talk of instituting republican reforms was no longer heard in Florence. The idea of restoring liberty was abandoned, and the Cardinal de' Medici, having smoked out his potential enemies, tightened his grip on the city.

Disillusioned, Niccolo buried himself in the isolation of the country once again, with the full knowledge of his own guilt weighing heavily, impossibly, upon him. He was the one who had inflamed them. He was the one who had fired their imaginations with stories of great and bold deeds, of Brutus and Cassius, of swift strokes of the dagger in defense of liberty. Now two of them were dead—tortured and mutilated before being decapitated; the others had all left the country. This had been the upshot of his preaching and his proselytizing—martyrdom and murder and exile and the destruction of innocent young lives. With that bitter knowledge, it was to his ancients, to the long dead, that he now returned for company.

In the two years it took Niccolo to complete his history of Florence, he virtually ignored the outside world, although events there did not stand still for lack of his supervision. Only nine months after his assumption of the papal tiara, the well-intentioned but moribund Dutchman, Adrian VI, died. The Romans were so grateful for his demise that they decked the house of his physician with banners and garlands and danced joyously in the street in front of it for many nights.

After a fiercely contested election and the longest conclave on record, a new pope emerged whose reign was to prove disastrous to himself, to Florence, to Italy, and to the Catholic Church. That pope was none other than Cardinal Giulio de' Medici, first cousin of the late Pope Leo and ruler of Florence on his behalf. Was it with an ironic smile that the merciless Cardinal de' Medici chose for himself the name Pope Clement VII?

Beyond Rome, the great powers that hovered over Italy like vultures waiting for the right moment to descend and devour her took heart. In Germany, a new emperor had been elected. The former emperor, Maximilian, had been a weakling with a head full of unlikely dreams. The new emperor was cut from a different bolt of cloth. Charles V was an Austrian grand duke of tremendous ambition who managed to impose some sort of unity on the loosely confederated German states.

Through the skillful manipulation of marriage bonds, he added the Netherlands to his dominion and—fatally for Italy—Spain and the kingdom of Naples as well. No longer would the Italian peninsula be menaced by Spain from the south and Germany from the north, no longer could these two powers be played against one another. They were one kingdom now, or rather one empire, one claw with two iron pincers. When Charles V assumed the title Holy Roman emperor, for the first time since Charlemagne, it was not a hollow dream or wishful thinking.

Only France stood in his way, and Pope Clement eagerly applied to her to protect him from this precocious, threatening, would-be emperor. At the Battle of Pavia in northern Italy, the French army was routed and the French King, Francis I, taken prisoner. Nothing now stood between the Emperor Charles and Rome.

Had the situation been uncomplicated by other factors, and had Clement been more resolute, he could no doubt have arranged matters with the emperor. He could have bought him off. But there were other factors. There was in Charles's army a faction that would not be appeased. They were vocal, and they were implacable. And under the leadership of the redoubtable and ferocious Georg von Fundesberg, they were deadly serious.

Who were these implacable elements? The followers of the seditious monk Martin Luther. Pope Leo had finally excommunicated the tiresome Luther and dismissed him entirely from his mind. But Luther did not go away. He continued to preach and denounce the deplorable conditions to which the church in Rome had been reduced under a long line of unworthy and demented and wicked popes. The church, he claimed, with some reason, was in the hands of the antichrist. And who would liberate her?

Early in the year 1525, an immense army of *Landsknechte,* the most feared and respected troops of the German army, were poised to strike that liberating blow. They were sharpening their lances, as von Fundesberg said, "to teach the pope a lesson he would never forget."

As the Lutheran grinding wheels shrieked in Germany, Niccolo put the finishing touches on his history of Florence. It was the most complete and provocative work of its kind to date. The spirit of inquiry and analysis that informed it was something entirely new in European historiography. But despite all its merits, Niccolo was having a devil of a time collecting the stipend he was promised for it upon completion. His letters of inquiry to the Signoria went unanswered. The Cardinal, who had commissioned the work, was now pope and in Rome, being threatened from every conceivable quarter. So, wearily, Niccolo dug up his old contract and made the trip into Florence, hoping the Medici might see fit to make good on one small promise.

On his way across town, Niccolo stopped at a public fountain, scooped up a handful of cold water, and used it to swallow two of the large, blue pills his doctor had prescribed for his increasingly rebellious digestive system. In addition to the not-infrequent attacks of the stone to which his aging body was now subject, Niccolo's stomach, always over-sensitive, had become irascible and undependable. He feared for his liver and kidneys as well. Gulping down the pills, which were almost as large as pigeons' eggs, brought him instant relief. He had an unbounded faith in medical science.

Even the ranks of a family as prolific as the Medici sometimes wear thin, and even loins as active as theirs sometimes fail to produce a sufficient supply of offspring to run the universal Catholic church, Florence, and the better part of northern Italy as well. Such was the case in 1525, when the only two available Medici—Ippolito and Alessandro, both bastards—were both underage and, even by Medici standards, not yet up to running the city. The cardinal of Cortona, Silvio Passerini, a staunch supporter of Pope Clement, had been made a kind of regent and empowered to act on their behalf. Passerini had been left in Florence by the Medici pope to execute his instructions, and it was with him that Niccolo sought audience in order to discuss his commission.

He was kept waiting a long time. Not that the time did not pass quickly. There was no dearth of entertainment in the corridors of the Signoria these days. Animated, exciting people in impressive and even outlandish outfits came and went. Niccolo sat on a bench next to his hefty manuscript—eight books, over a thousand pages—and watched. Two boys, both with red hose, both with yellow codpieces, were engaged in a lively round of *civettino*—little owl. The game required good reflexes, a quick eye, and the ability to feint and parry blows. The object was to slap one's opponent silly. The movements of the players were limited by the fact that they had to keep within an arm's length of one another. The loser of the previous round planted his right foot on the ground, his opponent planted his left foot on top of it, and the feinting and the slapping began. Long arms were a distinct advantage in the sport.

Of the two combatants before Niccolo, one was administering a sound thrashing about the face and ears of his opponent. The smaller boy, whose head was surmounted by a terrific bush of black hair, however, did not seem to mind, and he threw himself with abandon into the idiotic pastime. Slaps and little owl-hoots of pain and triumph rang off the walls of the venerable government building. "It was nice," thought Niccolo sardonically. "Like a circus."

Finally, Niccolo was admitted to the suite of offices where he was so often welcomed in the past. "Well?" said Passerini.

Never had a man been more aptly named. Passerini—the little sparrow—was indeed a birdlike specimen. He had a tiny, narrow head that came to a point in a small, sharp, beak, and thin, pursed lips. No chin, no forehead. He was a small man, but an extraordinarily plump and rotund body swelled the space beneath his purple cassock.

"Who are you?" he chirped. "And what do you want?"

Niccolo explained the nature of his errand, depositing the heavy manuscript on Passerini's polished desk.

"What do you want me to do with that thing?" He looked at it with obvious repugnance, as though it were the carcass of some dead animal.

"I would like to be paid for it, Your Excellency, according to the terms of this agreement." Niccolo handed over the contract, and the cardinal examined it.

"This isn't my signature."

Niccolo bit his ready tongue and choked off the stream of obscenities that was about to escape. He remembered that, when asking for money, it paid to be polite. "The former cardinal de' Medici, on behalf of the city of Florence, concluded this arrangement with me. I am applying to you as his legally—the word almost stuck in Niccolo's throat—constituted representative to carry out the terms of the agreement."

"Why bother me? Why don't you take this thing to Rome and present it to the pope? He's the one who ordered it. If he wants it, let him pay for it."

"Your Excellency, I was hoping to avoid a trip to Rome. I'd very much like to settle this matter in Florence. I'm getting old and I don't travel well anymore."

"I'm sure that's not my problem. I'm simply not empowered to honor this thing. I don't see any way around it. You'll have to go to Rome."

Niccolo realized he was being evasive, whether for financial reasons or political concerns was not entirely clear. "I'm sure there's some way we can work this out here. If you'll just write to the pope . . ."

"The pope has enough on his mind."

"Is there anyone else Your Excellency can consult?"

What passed for a tight little smile broke out on his face. "Very well, if you insist." Then, turning toward the back of his chambers, he hollered, "Secretary! Secretary!"

A door opened and closed, and Michelozzi bustled into the room. He was surprised to see Niccolo, but shot him a warm smile. "Excellency?" Michelozzi bowed low, and, for a minute, Niccolo thought he was going to kneel at the cardinal's feet.

"This gentleman has an old contract from the Cardinal de' Medici and insists on us honoring it. I told him I'm simply not empowered to do so, but he insists. Would you please go and find my lords Ippolito and Alessandro. I'm sure they can satisfy the gentleman."

Michelozzi hastened out of the room, but as he was going, the cardinal stopped him, "And secretary, bring us a little rose water. It's frightfully close in here today, and we would like to refresh ourselves."

When he returned with the rose water in a few minutes, Michelozzi also had in tow the two youthful combatants from the *civettino* match Niccolo had witnessed in the corridor. So these were the Medici bastards! Red hose and yellow codpieces!

"Alessandro," said the cardinal. The smaller one with the frizzy hair stepped forward. He had enormous, thick lips and skin that was much darker than even a Spaniard would feel comfortable with. "Alessandro, look at this." He handed the boy Niccolo's contract. "Did your father ever give you any instructions regarding this?"

Niccolo watched while Pope Clement's illegitimate son examined the document. So the rumors were true. When he was Giulio de' Medici, the present pope had been keeping an African slave who also served as his concubine.

"Well?" said the boy a little stupidly.

The cardinal said, "Are you inclined to authorize the disbursement of 100 florins for this rather, *ahem*, lugubrious tome on the history of Florence?"

"One hundred florins! I should think not! Father told us to be frugal."

The cardinal turned to the older boy, "You, Ippolito?"

"I stand behind Alessandro's decision."

"There," tweeted the cardinal, turning to Niccolo. "I told you there was nothing to be done for you here. The young lords of the house of Medici have denied your request. You are free to go to Rome to present your petition to the pope. In the meantime, good day, sir."

Petition! Niccolo was furious as he stalked out of the room. He didn't have a petition, he had a contract. He wasn't a beggar! He was a historian! And two fifteen-year-old bastards had refused to pay him the money that was rightfully his!

Michelozzi hurried out after him. Putting a hand on his shoulder, he said, "Niccolo, I'm sorry. Things have changed around here. The Signoria is not what it used to be."

"Those two children are running the city?"

"No, the cardinal is in control. He uses them, the authority of the Medici name, to add a little weight to his decisions."

"And you? The chancery?"

"He uses me to fetch rosewater and write letters to his mistress."

"You've fallen on hard times, Michelozzi. The whole city has fallen on hard times."

They both nodded sadly in agreement. "What will you do now, Niccolo?"

"Go to Rome, I guess. What else does an old man like me have to do with his time?" As he spoke, the boisterous new generation of Medici clattered out of the cardinal's chambers.

"Secretary!" sang Alessandro.

"Secretary, we require your services," chimed in Ippolito. "The cardinal has lent you out to us for the afternoon. We're giving a banquet, and we need someone to write the invitations!" The last Niccolo saw of Michelozzi, secretary in the Second Chancery, Alessandro de' Medici, the pope's son, was leading him down the hallway, affectionately, playfully, by the ear.

Before undertaking the journey, Niccolo had written several times to his old friend Francesco Vettori in Rome, seeking advice. Vettori wrote Niccolo advising him to come to Rome. Vettori wrote Niccolo advising him not to come to Rome. Niccolo wondered about the extent of Vettori's friendship, and about his judgment, but in the end, spurred on by poverty and restlessness, he decided to make the trip. He had nothing to lose and everything to gain.

Riding distances proved to be a more painful proposition than Niccolo had anticipated, and his kidneys soon ached from long days in the saddle. The blue pills helped somewhat, but, by the time he arrived, he was feeling discouraged and tired and constipated and old. Rome, as he entered it, was much the same sad, squalid, sorry mess he remembered from years before. But as he progressed toward the Vatican, he began to see evidence of ambition and the flood of money that had poured into the city from all over Christendom. Both Pope Julius II and Leo X had spent lavishly on building and construction projects. Many cardinals and other churchmen, fattened by graft and corruption, had done likewise. Through the jumble and clutter of huts, they had cut, or caused to be cut wide, open avenues and lined them with lofty and exquisitely classical palaces.

Niccolo took note of these changes, but only in a detached and uninterested way. As he had feared, the ghosts in this city seemed more real to him than its present inhabitants. As he rode along familiar streets, he could remember the echo of her laughter, the way she smiled, the way she tossed her long hair back out of her face. He could almost see her making her way confidently, nonchalantly, through these teeming, vibrant streets. This was her city, Giuditta's city, and, even though he had spent time with her in Florence and in the country and even in Ferrara, it was in Rome that her image rose up to haunt him. It was here that she was more maddeningly real than in any other place. Here the memories were stronger, more visceral, more tangible, more inescapable. More than once, Niccolo had to shake himself, to force himself to realize that the fleeting glimpse of a beautiful dark-haired woman was nothing more than an optical illusion or a case of mistaken identity or a bad case of wishful thinking.

It took him a day of wrangling at the Florentine embassy to secure an audience with the pope. He passed through gallery after gallery, antechamber after antechamber. He had plenty of time to examine what seemed like hundreds of miles of frescoes and friezes and hundreds of statues of the living and the long dead. He would wait, then a door would open and someone would beckon. He would pick up his heavy volumes, lug them through another lavish and ornate doorway and wait again. This went on all morning.

"Machiavelli?"

Niccolo jumped up.

"His Holiness is pleased that you have come," said the chamberlain. At least he had a Florentine accent.

"Good," said Niccolo, a little tired, a little irate, but grateful nonetheless that he had finally reached the end of his quest. "Can I be shown in now? I've been here all day."

"His Holiness is also pleased that you've completed the history, and instructs that you leave it in my care."

"What! I came all the way from Florence! I want to see him!"

"In due time, I'm certain you will. But for the time being, you'll have to be content to leave your opus with me. When the Holy Father has had time to peruse it, you will be notified."

"Notified! How long will that take?"

"If I were you, and I didn't have any other urgent business in Rome, I wouldn't bother to tarry here. Not on account of this. It could take a while. I'm sure His Holiness will know where to reach you in Florence."

Niccolo was outraged and in his anger could scarcely find words to express his feelings. "Two years of sweat and blood . . . all the way from Florence . . ." he sputtered.

The chamberlain regarded him with a bored, slightly pained, expression. "Do you want to leave the book or not?"

Niccolo stifled another outburst. He handed the volume over. Abruptly, the chamberlain turned in a smart, military fashion, walked crisply to a bench set in a niche in the wall and deposited Niccolo's enormous volume there—on top of a great pile of enormous volumes. There must have been over two hundred of them.

Niccolo was limp when he turned to go, but his descent into chagrin was barely underway when a loud clap brought him out of it. Through the great carved portals behind which the papal presence presumably reposed, a gnome had been forcibly ejected. He hit the marble floor hard but was on his feet in an instant. He was hopping in his anger and pounding on the great, closed doors. Bald, shabby, and choleric, he had a long, cleft beard that made him look like a goat or the devil. He was saying uncomplimentary things about the supreme pontiff. He was casting aspersions on the pope's origins, which were, in fact, dubious, and on his mother, who was either unknown or long forgotten. He did, however, have the good taste to deliver his tirade in Florentine. Niccolo noted that Rome seemed to be full of Florentines these days. Disappointed Florentines.

Gradually, some of the anger bubbled out of the small man, and his hopping became less incessant. Still red-faced, with fists balled at his sides, he delivered one final kick to the doors with such violence that his sandal flew from his foot. "What are you gaping at?" he said to Niccolo, his face twisted in a tight scowl.

"Buonarotti? Michelangelo?"

The artist glared at him, squinted, and then his features softened: "Machiavelli, Niccolo! Well met!" They exchanged a hearty embrace. In the years since their first meeting, the secretary and the sculptor had had intermittent contact, since Michelangelo had been charged with several commissions by Soderini in the name of the republic of Florence and Niccolo had arranged the details.

"You've been in audience with His Holiness?" Niccolo asked the obvious question.

"The bastard!" fumed Michelangelo. "The ungrateful bastard! They treat you like servants. Do you have any idea what it's like to work for these Medici overlords?"

"As a matter of fact, I do," said Niccolo.

"They hold us hostage!"

"We're nothing but slaves!" A hail of similar denunciations and imprecations followed. They were entirely in agreement on the subject, and so, linking arms, the two poverty-stricken Florentine geniuses made their way out of the Vatican into a sunlit Saint Peter's Square. They spoke at length of the injustices that had been thrust upon them. They spoke vehemently of ingratitude.

"The point is, now, you either work for the Medici or not at all," Michelangelo was saying.

"And you're working?"

"Oh, first they had me working as quarry master, because I was the only one who knew how to recognize the good marble and cut it without damaging it. When we found it though, it was in such a remote place that we couldn't get it out, so the pope said, 'Build a road.' Then I was a road builder! And when I finally got the blocks I wanted out, perfect blocks, mind you, they used them to pave the floors! Can you imagine! It's a sacrilege! They might as well pave their floors with the body and blood of Christ!"

And on and on he went. Niccolo marveled at the seemingly endless reserve of temperamental outrage in this little man. He had finally met his equal in righteous indignation.

"And the pope?" asked Niccolo when there was a break in Michelangelo's tirade.

"Oh, he's the worst one yet. Lorenzo was the best—Lorenzo the Magnificent, not little Lorenzo. Little Lorenzo was a beast. But the Medici strain seems to be getting diluted as the years pass, they get worse and worse, they live shorter and shorter lives."

"Have you seen the latest generation?" asked Niccolo. "The pope's son?"

"The mulatto? I'm sure we have great things to expect from him!" said Michelangelo. "Great things for Florence, eh Machiavelli? Great things for old hands like you and me!"

"*Non vedo l'ora*—I can hardly wait," confirmed Niccolo.

Enjoying the rounds of mutual spleen-venting in which they were engaged, Michelangelo invited Niccolo back to his studio. The passed through an open courtyard littered with giant, half-carved blocks of stone. There was something mysterious and almost holy about the way the silent statues were beginning to emerge from the marble and come to life—here a sinewy arm, a muscled leg, there a rippling torso just starting to take shape, something alive struggling to be born, twisting in agony to disengage itself from the cold, inert matter.

Inside, Niccolo was overwhelmed by the sweet, piney smell of turpentine. And the visual clutter. Tools and brushes and pots of paint. Pieces of statuary—dismembered stone limbs, severed stone heads. There were huge drawing tables covered a foot thick with piles of paper. From the walls and ceiling beams hung the immense, thin sheets of paper, the cartoons, on which designs for frescoes were sketched before being painted. They were covered with life-size and larger-than-life figures—vibrant, living figures bending and straining, some tormented, some in ecstasy. Everywhere he looked, Niccolo saw this great, intimidating surge of life, the raw energy and emotion of the human body captured in charcoal or paint or stone. It was exhilarating—and haunting. It was like being in a room with thirty thousand ghosts or silent, raving demons.

"I'll get wine," said Michelangelo. "Sit down."

"So what will you do now?" said Niccolo when he had made himself comfortable.

"Go back to Florence and carve Medici statues, I guess. There are still a number of Medici who need to be immortalized. Like little Lorenzo."

"You're going to carve him?" said Niccolo with obvious distaste. He remembered having been tortured by little Lorenzo.

"You either work for the Medici or you don't work at all. And you should see the design the pope's approved. If I do it and if the statue survives, posterity is going to think little Lorenzo was some kind of a Greek god, because that's exactly what they ordered, a Greek god. You knew him, didn't you?"

"Skinny, phlegmatic, crooked teeth, sunken chest . . ."

"The same. Only the statue is going to have massive and powerful limbs, a torso like a tree trunk! The strength of Hercules! And with such a pensive expression! The wisdom of Solomon!"

"You're kidding?"

"Do you think they're going to pay me to carve a statue of a scrawny consumptive coughing up blood into a silk handkerchief?"

"Such is the nature of patronage," sighed Niccolo.

"Look, I can't seem to find anything to drink. I'm going to run out and get something. I'll be right back."

Michelangelo was not gone for more than thirty seconds before he returned, looking a little embarrassed. "You don't have any money, do you? I . . . I . . ."

Niccolo grinned and tossed him a coin.

"Be right back!"

With the master of this bizarre household gone, Niccolo was left with the ghosts. They were alive. Not like the bloodless saints you see painted on the walls in dark churches. They had a depth and an energy, a fury about them. Idly, Niccolo wandered through this human menagerie, marveling at its inhabitants. There were figures from the Bible and from Roman history. Niccolo smiled to himself—his ancients.

He stopped in front of one of the cartoons tacked to the wall. Even with nothing more than a few bold strokes of charcoal on this thin, yellowish paper, Michelangelo could breathe life into his figures. Here was a sketch of the rape of Lucretia. She was twisting to get out of the grasp of the brutish Tarquin, but to no avail. He was bearing down on her with beastly delight in his eyes, the sinews in his neck and arms visible. Lucretia's face had been barely sketched in, but even in those few lines, you could already read the terror—and something else? What was it? Niccolo shrugged off the odd feeling. There was something frightening about this man's work.

Niccolo continued his inspection. Arranged in a row next to the Lucretia was a series of studies for a *Pieta*—the Madonna holding the broken body of Christ after it had been taken down from the cross. Michelangelo was just as skillful in depicting a limp and lifeless body as he was a robust, breathing one. He was a master of life and death.

It couldn't be!

Niccolo gaped at the Madonna, then the next one, then the one after that. He began to shake. It was at once obvious and unintelligible—completely obvious and absolutely unintelligible. Niccolo was stunned speechless. He was stricken. He was spellbound. Was he hallucinating? Was he taking a plunge into madness? He could hardly catch his breath. His eyes flew back and forth from Lucretia to the Madonna, from Madonna to Madonna, from Madonna to Lucretia. The faces were all the same. And it was not the face of any imaginary Lucretia or any imaginary Madonna. It was a face he recognized. Tears were streaming down his face.

His unbelieving eyes told him who it was at the same time as his mind was breaking apart on that impossible knowledge. Giuditta.

✦ 48 ✦

AN ARTIST'S MODEL, A LOTTERY TICKET, AND BIG, BLUE PILLS

Michelangelo returned a few minutes later with a large clay jug of wine to find his guest oddly rooted to a spot in front of some old cartoons, his head jerking wildly from drawing to drawing, his mouth moving, but no words coming out.

"When you're done admiring my work, we can have a drink over here," he said, busying himself clearing a small space on the tabletop and setting out two cups.

"Machiavelli?"

Niccolo persisted in his bizarre pantomime without showing any sign that he was aware of Michelangelo's return. The latter, curious now, picked his way across the cluttered studio and tapped his guest on the shoulder. Niccolo spun around with unexpected violence and grabbed the little artist by his stained shirtfront. "Who is that?" he said, shaking him.

Taken aback, Michelangelo blurted, "A Madonna. It's supposed to be a Madonna."

"No," screamed Niccolo, "I mean the model!"

"How should I know who the model was? You think I ask their names? You think I'd remember if I did? And Jesus Christ, Machiavelli, Put me down."

Coming to himself for a moment, Niccolo released his startled host. "When did you do these drawings?" he demanded in an emotional voice that, to Michelangelo, seemed out of all proportion to the question.

"A long time ago, I don't remember exactly."

"How long ago," roared Niccolo. "Think back! How long?"

"A year, maybe?" Michelangelo took a step back to avoid being collared and shaken again.

"A year!" The wildness in Niccolo's eyes seemed to grow with this revelation. "Where did you find her? Where? I have to know."

"At the Trinita dei Monti. On the steps going up to the church. There's always a crowd of prostitutes and pretty boys there who are willing to pose for artists. Why?"

But Michelangelo's question and his observation went unanswered and unremarked. Niccolo was already gone. He was running, and he was aware of a sharp pain in his side. He held it with his left hand and kept running. With his right, he clutched the folds of his dignified citizen's gown up around his waist to give his legs clearance. He made his way running up the Via del Corso, where horse races were often held and where, during Carnival, the Jewish community was required to provide old men to run naked in an antic footrace all the way to the foot of the Testaccio. Niccolo, at fifty-six years old, was running as desperately and as painfully as any one of these unwilling racers ever did. His insides rebelled; his lungs screamed, but his legs kept churning. Sweat was pouring from his forehead when he was finally forced to stop for a minute. He plunged his head into the tepid waters of a fountain, and, as soon as he was able, when his riotous breathing had calmed down, he drank deeply. Determined, he set off again, this time limping, dragging himself at a half run.

The wide-open piazza in front of the church was full of people utterly indifferent to his frantic concerns. They lounged on the steps in the sun; they loitered in clusters, talking and laughing. Niccolo dashed about like a madman, but Rome was full of madmen, and no one bothered to take any special notice of him.

Here were the beautiful people who earned a few pennies a day posing for the legions of Rome's painters and sculptors. The men were vigorous and handsome, the women, fetching. Nearly all were studied in their nonchalance, cool and indifferent, waiting for something better to come along. Niccolo went madly from group to group. The sight of a mane of long dark hair was enough to send him scurrying across the piazza to investigate. More than once, he came up breathlessly behind some raven-haired beauty and spun her around in his excitement.

More annoyed than shocked by these intrusions, they would give him an odd look, shake their heads, and return to their loitering.

He had crossed and recrossed the piazza to no avail. He had looked into the faces of nearly everyone there before collapsing on the steps. Overheated in body and spirit, he needed a rest. He calmed himself as much as was humanly possible under the circumstances and took up his vigil. From his vantage point, he ran his eyes ceaselessly over the little knots of people and the stragglers, keeping track of their comings and goings, noting new arrivals. Still nothing. He was formulating a plan in the back of his head. It consisted of staying in the piazza on those steps until the trumpets sounded on the Last Day—or until she came—whichever came first.

Someone touched him on the shoulder, and Niccolo, utterly absorbed in his feverish search, jumped at the unexpected contact. "You want to make a few lire?" A gap-toothed, paint-spattered individual was grinning down at him. "I'm doing a big scene of the damned cast down into hell. I need desperate-looking men." He was laughing at his own joke. Niccolo fixed him with a look of such intensity that the man backed away, carefully, apologetically—the way one backs away from a man with a dangerous weapon or from a mad dog.

People came and went. His desperate hopes were raised and dashed, raised and dashed, raised and dashed. Slowly, he began to question the sanity of his enterprise. The light of reason began to break through, here and there. How many times since he had been in Rome had his heart thrilled because he thought he saw her? And every time it had been an illusion. A wish. Because she was dead and had been for twelve years. But Michelangelo's drawings!

The he began to doubt himself, doubt the evidence of his own overworked, overwrought senses. He was suffering a severe disappointment, he was breaking down, he was falling prey to the dementia of old age. Wearily, resignedly, he decided to make his way back to Michelangelo's studio. He would have another look at the drawings—maybe he was wrong. He would have a talk with Michelangelo (after apologizing for his rudeness), see what he could remember about the model . . . He put his head in his hands, put his thumbs against his aching eyeballs and pressed hard. And then she was just there.

There was something wistful about her. Age had softened her, but not robbed her of her beauty. She was standing with a small group of women and talking. She stood erect, not with the haughtiness of youth, or the cocked-hip defiance of an ageless prostitute, but with the dignity of a woman, the dignity and sorrow of . . . of . . . a Madonna—just like Michelangelo had drawn her.

Then she turned, and the turn was graceful. She smiled to herself, a sad little smile, but to Niccolo the smile was beatific. Someone called to her and she looked up. She began walking toward that someone when something about a crumpled, disheveled figure sitting on the steps caught the corner of her eye.

Her astonishment was no less overwhelming, the shock no less severe, than was Niccolo's at the discovery of the cartoons. He watched as waves of contradictory emotions washed over her face. And then there were the tears and the rush of choked-off, incoherent phrases and the halting, stammering protestations of incredulity. And then the rest of the world disappeared, as if by magic, and they were the only two people in all of Rome, on all of God's earth. Without even knowing they were moving, they moved toward each other and they reached out for one another, seeking in the solidity of touch, some confirmation of this mad and impossible dream.

Who can say what they talked about that day? Who can say if they talked at all? Who can say where their footsteps led them? Were they aware of the path they traced through the streets of the Eternal City? Were the aware of following in the footsteps of Dante, on a journey to some spot high above the Empyrean, to some sphere where they could look down upon the tiny sun and the fixed stars. They were caught up in a rapture, blinded by the light, not of those heavenly bodies that were already far away and receding, but by the power that turns them all and binds them in their orbits, by the love that moves the sun and other stars. And as the poet was forced to admit, conceding defeat, *"A l'alta fantasia qui manco possa"*—there is no way to describe that lofty fantasy.

When the realms of bliss finally released them and they fell to earth again, or rather drifted back languorously through the haze of delirium that had engulfed them, Niccolo found himself tracing the lines of her radiant face, lingering lovingly over each feature—her long nose, her full lips—touching them, assuring himself that they were real. "I thought you were dead," he kept muttering over and over again to himself. "I thought you were dead."

"Shhhsshhhh," She put her finger to his lips, and he stopped talking, and the magic swallowed them up again.

It wasn't until the next morning that the time for explanations came. "Why did you leave?" asked Niccolo.

"I thought you were dead."

"Who told you I was dead?"

"Michelozzi."

"I thought you were in prison?"

"I was."

"Then how did you get out?"

"Michelozzi."

And so it continued. At every critical juncture of their overlapping stories, at every unlikely twist and turn of the plot, one name cropped up again and again—that of Michelozzi. As Niccolo and Giuditta talked, as they tried to untangle events, it became clear that it was Michelozzi who had engineered, for whatever reason, their separation.

"But then he saved your life?" asked Niccolo, puzzled. "He got you out of prison?"

"And he hid me," confirmed Giuditta.

"Why would he do that and tell me you were dead?"

"Because I ran away from him."

"And why did you run? If he saved you?"

Giuditta hesitated for a minute, then steeling herself, she said, "Because he tried to rape me."

They were going to have to have a long talk with Messer Michelozzi, secretary in the Second Chancery. But not now, because as soon as something dark or unpleasant came up, they could both feel themselves withdrawing from it, back into their cocoon, back into a heedless love and each other and ecstasy, back after so many years . . .

It would be cruel to interrupt our lovers' bliss, but Fortune does not wait on the preparedness of any two individuals before dealing out her indiscriminate blows. Her wheel turns unrelentingly. One morning, perhaps a week after they had been reunited, Niccolo and Giuditta were awakened by a distant, piercing wail. Although incomprehensible, it was unnerving in its high-pitched, hysterical insistence. Soon enough, though, the cry was taken up by others, and, in a matter of minutes, it reached their ears. There was no mistaking the frenzied message that suddenly reverberated throughout the city, passing frantically from household to panicky household: "'*A pistolenza! 'A pistolenza*! The Plague!"

There was only one way to successfully avoid the ravages of the plague, and that was to flee before them. Niccolo and Giuditta, like thousands of others, therefore, made hasty preparations to leave Rome. Out of an impulse to protect himself, either medical or magical or a little of both, Niccolo gulped down two of the big blue pills before stepping out into the dangerous streets. It couldn't hurt. Already people were going about with bouquets of flowers and bundles of herbs shoved in their faces, breathing through these aromatic talismans, hoping to sweeten the air they took in and stop the stench of infection from entering.

Niccolo retrieved his horse, and Giuditta climbed up behind him. They had been unable to find a horse for her. The price of horses in Rome had suddenly risen to the stars. They joined the plodding stream of traffic that was flowing in one direction only—out of the city. Already the corpses were piling up in the streets.

"Niccolo, look," said Giuditta. She pointed across the little piazza in front of the hospital for incurable diseases. The square was crowded with the unwanted dying. Brought there by relatives and friends to assuage their own consciences—we can't do anything for them at home, the hospital's the place for them—the infected were dumped unceremoniously and left to their final agonies out there in the open, alone. Alone except for one bizarre, solitary figure that moved among them. It looked not so much like a man as a giant bird, a black bird with black gloves and a black hood and a big yellow beak.

Niccolo and Giuditta pulled out of the stream for a minute and stopped to watch. The bird was doing what he could to alleviate the hellish suffering of the condemned—mopping feverish brows, applying compresses, lancing painful buboes. It was not enough. It could never be enough, but it was all he could do. When he saw his two old friends on horseback, Callimaco stopped and straightened up. He stood erect and forlorn in that sea of writhing bodies amid the cries of the damned. Without removing his great prophylactic mask, he waved to them, a solemn wave, a final good-bye. And then he bent once more to his endless, futile labors.

"I'll miss him," said Giuditta as Niccolo turned the horse to go. "I owe him a lot."

"Oh?" There was a hint of jealously in Niccolo's voice.

"When you were in jail and I thought you were dead, Callimaco hid me until we could get out of the city."

"Not in the bottega where you were both working?"

"No, that would have been stupid, and that was the first place Michelozzi looked."

"You never told me how you got away from Michelozzi of evil intent in the first place."

"Michelozzi came and got me out of prison. I was grateful."

"Then the whole story he told me about you having been torn apart by dogs in your cell was a complete fabrication."

"Not complete! Someone was torn apart, but it wasn't me; it was his accomplice, Pasiphae."

"His accomplice! Faustina!"

"Whatever. The two of them came to see me in my cell, and she was gloating, telling me how you were having your arms and legs wrenched from your body on the rack and telling me what was in store for me—the dogs. She laid everything out. This was her revenge for our having tried to poison her and for Don Micheletto."

"Then she told you that he was her father?"

"She told me everything. She couldn't stop talking. She was starting to go into the details of how Michelozzi had helped her all along, how he had been with the Medici and Don Micheletto from the very beginning. It was Michelozzi who warned Don Micheletto that I was setting a trap for him in Rome."

Niccolo cursed under his breath, "Michelozzi."

"She was bragging and enjoying herself. She was getting shrill, taunting me. Then Michelozzi did the unexpected. He knocked on the door to signal the guards that they wanted to leave. When the door opened, he grabbed me by the arm, thrust me out into the corridor, pushed her back into the cell, and slammed the door shut."

"The guards didn't do anything?"

"They were in on it with him, I suppose. I was stunned. Michelozzi told me to be quiet, he'd explain later. And he led me out of the prison, just like that."

"Why?"

"You may find this hard to believe, Niccolo, but I think he did it because he was in love with me. He was gentle with me—at first. He took me to his house and said he was doing everything in his power to get you out of prison. He said that Pasiphae was only a pawn, and that he had been playing her along all the time, pretending to be on her side, gathering information, fraternizing with the enemy."

"What did he say would happen to her?"

"He said the Signoria wanted her imprisoned. They would hold her for a while, question her, and then probably release and banish her. He thought it would be best for me to stay with him for a few days, keeping out of sight, until he got word that she was safely out of town."

"Was she released then?"

"That's when I started to have my doubts about my savior, Messer Michelozzi. One night someone came, and they were closeted in his study. Michelozzi had a lot of late-night visitors. I just happened to be in the next room—I thought it might be news of you—and I overheard them talking. The stranger said, 'You won't have any more trouble with her and the money's all yours.' Michelozzi said, 'Are you sure?' 'I saw it myself,' said the other man, 'she was hanging by one ankle and the dogs had torn her to shreds. Funny thing though, both of the dogs were dead too, just lying there all bug-eyed and swollen and dead.'"

Niccolo let out a long, low whistle—the final revenge of the poison-woman.

Giuditta continued, "A few days later, we were eating, and a messenger arrived with the news of your death. He was out of breath, he made a very dramatic delivery, for my benefit, and there were tears in Michelozzi's eyes."

"And in yours?"

"I've seen too much to cry," she said unconvincingly.

"Michelozzi took to comforting me in my desperation. After a day or two, I told him I wanted to leave, and I would take my chances with Pasiphae, but he insisted I stay a little longer. He said I needed a friend. Then he started to get friendly, edging closer to me at the table, breathing on me, finding too many opportunities to touch me on the hand or the shoulder."

"Making love to you."

"He was a bashful lover—until I outright refused his advances."

"Then what?"

"Then he locked me in a room. When I still refused him, he started to get nasty. He started threatening to put me back in jail. He started to belittle you. 'Our Machiavelli of blessed memory' he called you. He said a lot of things that were true."

"Like what?"

"Like you always went around with your head in the clouds and dreamed big, preposterous dreams."

Niccolo made a face.

"He also said a lot that wasn't true. He said he was twice the man you were, and that you had had all the breaks, but he had had to scheme and work for everything he got. He even went so far as to imply that you were sleeping with Soderini to hold onto your position."

"The bastard!"

"Messer Michelozzi was a very bitter man. But he said he could wait, because now he had it all within his grasp—everything that you had."

"Meaning?"

"That he had already been promised your job by the Cardinal de' Medici, and now he had your woman too, whom he said he loved from the first time he laid eyes on me."

"And you believed him!"

"It was obvious. He was insanely jealous of you. He said you were a fool and didn't know how to treat a woman, and it drove him crazy to see you ignoring me and going off on your fantastic exploits with the militia."

"And what did you think of that?"

Giuditta ignored the question, "He said he could make me happy. That I should give him a chance."

"Why didn't you, if you thought I was dead?"

"Niccolo, he was obviously mad."

"And that's all?"

"What do you want me to say, that I vowed never to love another man as long as I lived and to be faithful to your memory until the day I died?"

"That would have been nice."

"Perhaps there were some residual feelings, hmmmm, *caro?*"

He relaxed. "What happened then?"

"He came to me all on fire one night, and when all his arguments failed, he tried to force himself on me. That's when I managed to get away."

"How?"

"I kicked him in the place where his balls would be if he had any."

"And he doesn't? Have any I mean."

"Not in the sense that you sons of Ishmael use the word, no. Anyway, I grabbed his keys, locked him in his own prison, and was gone."

"Where to?"

"I didn't want to go to your house, so I went to Callimaco and told him everything. He took me to a place called the Burelle.

"Where's that?"

"I found out it's where an old Roman amphitheatre used to be. There are all these caves, deep underground, and tunnels. They used to keep the wild animals and the gladiators down there."

"How did Callimaco know about this place?" asked Niccolo. "I never even heard of it."

"Callimaco knew about it because the old tunnels and caves are full of prostitutes. You know he made a point of finding out those kinds of things. He hid me there and went back to the bottega, so as not to arouse suspicion. He said guards came and questioned him, asking about me. He said he thought they were watching the place, too. After a few days, when things had calmed down, we escaped."

Giuditta pulled herself closer to Niccolo as their horse plodded up into the foothills outside of Rome. For a while, they rode in silence, these two lovers who had, miraculously, risen from the dead for each other. She squeezed him tightly until they were so close and were moving so much in unison that it was like one person sitting in the saddle.

"Niccolo, where are we going?"

"Back to Florence, I guess."

"I don't want to go back to Florence. Not yet. I want you to myself for a little longer. I'm afraid if we go back, they'll take you from me again."

"I told you I'd never let that happen again. I promised."

"I know. Just the same, let's go somewhere else for a little while. Just the two of us."

"Where do you want to go?"

"Let's go somewhere magic where we can dream some more."

"Constantinople?"

"That's too far. I don't have enough money to get there and I'm sure you don't."

"Where then?"

"Have you ever been to Venice?"

And so they headed north and east, to Venice, even in those days called *"La Serenissima,"*—that most serene city by the sea.

When it came to shipping, Niccolo was accustomed to the flat-bottomed barges and small skiffs that plied the Arno. He had seen larger vessels before, ocean-going vessels, but he had never seen so many in one place. Venice was surrounded by them—galleys and galleons and galleasses, carracks and caravels. Rising from the sea on all sides was a veritable forest of masts. Every banner in Christendom could be seen depending from them, and even the crescent of the Turkish sultan was much in evidence, flapping gaily in the salty sea breezes.

The three-masted ships of the mighty maritime trading empire hovered and buzzed around the island city like bees, coming and going, laden with precious cargoes of saffron and silk. Venice, through much of her history, had turned her back on the Italian peninsula and turned her attention outward, toward the sea. Because of this reaching out to the East across the Adriatic and the Mediterranean, she had become a more exotic place by far than most of the inland Italian city-states. A Turkish or Moorish flare could be seen in her arches and domes, and even the fashion in hats tended toward the turban.

But by far the most exotic of exotic touches was the fact that the city itself was built on the water, on a group of islands linked by bridges and crisscrossed by an intricate network of canals. The only way to reach the exotic wonderland was by boat or ferry from the mainland. From the moment they glided into this watery paradise, Giuditta was taken by the beauty and the strangeness of it all. Niccolo was more skeptical and spent the whole first day after their arrival making fun of Venetian accents—all fricatives and sing-song.

They had settled into a tavern where the smell of fish was overwhelming—fish frying and roasting, steaming and stewing. Platters heaped with crabs and scampi and lobsters floated by. Fish of every size and shape, from huge sturgeon to tiny eels, could be seen adorning the tables of their fellow diners.

"Squid," said Niccolo. "I want to try squid." Giuditta took no exception. The tavern keeper buzzed and hummed at Niccolo's choice. In his silly Venetian accent, he lauded the excellence of his establishment, of his cook, of the catch, and of Venice in general. Finally going away, he left a flask of prosecco on the table for their entertainment while the squid was being prepared.

"A little sweet," was the dour Florentine's verdict.

"And not as good as Tuscan wine," added Giuditta judiciously, before breaking into laughter.

"Certainly not," said Niccolo, failing to get the point of the joke.

"Niccolo, isn't there anything about Venice yet that you like?"

"It's not my fault if the air smells heavy and rotten and wet."

"That's the smell of the sea, the salt."

"I'd rather have my salt on my meat and vegetables than up my nose."

"Don't you think the canals are marvelous, the way they reflect the evening lights, the way they shimmer. It's like being in a magic city, floating out to sea."

"It's like being plopped down in the middle of the world's largest open sewer. Have you seen some of the stuff that's floating around out there? Dead dogs and cats, turds of every description . . ."

"You're such a keen observer."

The conversation was interrupted by the arrival of the tavern keeper who ceremoniously set a large bowl of black sludge on the table squarely in front of them.

Aghast, Niccolo looked up at him. "What's that?"

"The squid," he replied.

"Squid is white, if I'm not mistaken," said Niccolo severely. "This is very black."

"Ah," buzzed the obsequious Venetian, always ready to please and explain, "This squid is cooked in its own ink. That's what gives it such intensity, such a rich flavor. Try it, Messer, you will see." And with that, he ladled rich, steaming mounds of the inky stuff onto Niccolo and Giuditta's plates.

More adventurous than her companion, Giuditta sampled the fare first. Her face lit up. "Delicious! Niccolo, try it."

"He dipped the tip of the spoon in the stew, tentatively, the way an uncertain swimmer dips his foot in ice-cold water before taking a plunge. He dug up the smallest morsel he could find and laid it on his tongue. His face clouded over.

"Well?"

"It's good, but I don't like the way it feels in my mouth. And I don't like the way it looks. Besides, I don't think I'm all that hungry. My stomach's upset."

"*Dai Niccolo, l'apetito viene mangiando*—you'll find out how hungry you are as you eat."

"But it doesn't look like something you eat! It's grey-black. I don't eat things that are that color. It looks like something you scrape up out of the bottom of . . . of . . . of a . . ."

"That's enough, Niccolo. If you're not going to eat it, don't spoil it for me. I think it's mouthwatering."

Niccolo prodded his squid, fished out a few more pieces of the black flesh, and managed to send them down. On the way out of the tavern, he gulped down two of the big, blue pills, which he knew would be needed if his stomach were to make any headway with the sullen black sludge.

After the meal, they strolled in the direction of the Piazza San Marco, where Giuditta wanted to stop to see the new dolls. The dolls were changed frequently. They were life-size models designed to show the latest in Venetian fashions for women. And Venetian fashions for women were the latest fashions in the world. With a score of other women, she clucked and oooooed and aaaaahed around the exhibit. The colors were bright, the cut daring, and, like everything else in Venice, tinged with exoticism. Niccolo wandered off, having little interest in these womanly affairs. He inspected the great cathedral of San Marco and, in no time, was coming to the conclusion that it lacked the majesty, the sublimity, of the cathedral in Florence.

"Pssssst, you! Hey! *Ecco qua Signore!*" A rather grimy and disheveled collection of beggars seemed to be competing for his attention.

Niccolo ignored them. A clawlike hand reached up, grabbed hold of his cloak, and hung on.

"What do you want? I don't have any money."

"You look like a lucky man. Buy a chance?" It was a crone speaking and waving a book of tickets.

"What?"

"Buy a ticket in the lottery. You could win. You could be rich."

Niccolo laughed out loud at the very idea. The crone pulled him closer. Conspiratorially, she whispered, "This one is the winner, this ticket. Do you want it? You look like a lucky man."

"That one's the winner?" said Niccolo. "How do you know?"

"I know!" she said, her eyes flashing with that secret knowledge.

"Another madwoman," thought Niccolo. Nevertheless, to disengage her iron grip on his cape without violence or unpleasantness, he acquiesced. "How much?"

"Two lire."

Niccolo came up with the coins and handed them to her. She looked at them suspiciously. "Not Venetian money. You have any Venetian money?"

He rooted around in his pockets until he found the correct coinage. "Here."

"Write your name and address here." She handed him the book. He scribbled his name and the name of the inn where they were staying. She tore off half the ticket and gave it to him. "That's your name?" she said, examining what he had written.

"Is there something wrong with it?"

"Not a Venetian name, that's all," she said suspiciously. "A foreign name."

"Florentine," declared Niccolo.

Unimpressed, eyes still sparkling, she said, "Doesn't matter. That ticket is the winner. Mark my word."

"What was that all about?" asked Giuditta coming up behind him.

"I just bought a ticket in the lottery, but not just any ticket. It's the winning ticket and I'll soon be rich."

"And when you are, will you buy me one of those dresses over there?"

"Anything you want, *picconcina*. Anything you want."

"Well, what shall we do now?" said Giuditta. "It's still early in the day."

"I think I'd like to stop and get something to eat. You know, I'm a little hungry."

"What happened to your upset stomach?" she said, prodding his belly. "I thought you were indisposed?"

"Maybe just something light would be good for me, you know, some soup . . ." So they went to another tavern, scrupulously avoided the local squid concoction, and, in the end, Niccolo was satisfied with two "light" helpings of liver smothered in onions with a turnip compote on the side and plenty of red Bardolino to wash it down.

Having little to do but eat and stroll, Giuditta and Niccolo rose late in the morning. To Niccolo, who was not at all taken with the pleasures of Venice, their lingering in bed was the best part of the day, so when he was rudely awakened early the next morning by a rough pounding on the door, he was irate.

"Go away," he moaned sleepily.

The pounding continued. "Open up in there."

When Niccolo did nothing of the sort, they barged in on him. "Machiavelli?"

"What do you want? Get out of here."

"Are you Machiavelli?"

"What if I am, you have no right . . ."

"We have orders to take you to the commune."

"What for? I haven't done anything."

"Oh, yes you have," said one of the two men standing in the room. Both were dressed in some semimilitary, semiofficial kind of uniform. They were beginning to make Niccolo nervous.

"Get dressed and come with us."

"I'm not going anywhere with you," said Niccolo firmly.

"Suit yourself," the man shrugged. "But if I had just won the lottery, I'd be running to collect my prize."

"What!" Niccolo nearly jumped out of bed. Only a last-minute twitch of modesty restrained him. "Are you saying I won the lottery?"

"Only three thousand ducats," said the man, as though the figure were common enough, as though he personally found nothing extraordinary in the sum of 3,000 ducats.

"Three thousand ducats," said Niccolo to himself, letting out a low whistle and sinking, dumbstruck, back into the bed. In his fifteen years of working tirelessly and relentlessly in the chancery office, he had not managed to earn 3,000 ducats!

He turned to Giuditta. "Do you still want one of those dresses you saw yesterday?"

"Yes," she said coyly, "but I still haven't decided which one."

"Forget about it," he said. "Don't trouble yourself. You can have one of each."

The wheel of fortune was spinning so merrily in Niccolo's head that, when they finally returned to San Casciano to spend the rest of the summer, he was in such high spirits that he took up his pen and wrote, of all things, a stage comedy. It was produced in Florence and was such a tremendous success that its fame quickly spread throughout Italy. Niccolo's friend Francesco Guicciardini saw to it that the comedy was staged in the Romagna and then in Venice. Orders and commissions for more plays began to pour in. For the first time in his life, thanks to the Venetian lottery and the revenues from his plays, Niccolo was solvent. He paid his back taxes. He paid off his creditors. And he was deliriously happy. He was content to spend the rest of his life in just this way—with Giuditta and with his Venetian ducats writing comedies. What more could any man ask?

"What are you writing, another play?" asked Giuditta. "Let me see."

"No," said Niccolo, scrambling to cover up the piece of paper on which he was working. "It's just a letter."

"Who's it to," she said. "And why are you trying to hide it from me?"

"It's nothing. I'm not trying to hide it from you. It's only to Guicciardini."

"Are you sure it's not to another woman?"

"That's absurd."

"Then let me see what you're writing."

"I told you it was nothing, don't you believe me?"

"I thought we didn't have any secrets from each other?"

"There's nothing secret about this."

"Then let me see it," she said devilishly.

With a guilty smile, Niccolo uncovered the page and she bent to read it. "I can only send you twenty five now, but I'll send the recipe so you can have a batch made up for yourself. They work really well for me. Start by taking one after dinner. If that does it, fine, if not, take two or three more. You can take as many as five, but I usually don't take more than two. And they're good for headaches as well as the stomach . . ."

"Niccolo, what is this nonsense. You're not sending him those blue pills that your charlatan prescribed for you?"

"He asked for them. He's been having a lot of trouble with indisposition."

"Where's the famous recipe?"

"Here," he said sheepishly.

Giuditta snatched up the little scrap of paper: "Cardamom, 1 dram; saffron . . . What is this? It sounds like a recipe for roast chicken."

"It happens to be very effective," said Niccolo evasively.

"Brettonica, pinpinella, whatever that is," Giuditta continued to read from the treasured recipe, "Ah, here's the active ingredient—Armenian tree bark! So that's the secret! Niccolo, when are you going to learn? I told you those pills weren't good for anything."

"That's your opinion."

"I've studied medicine. I know what I'm talking about!"

"Moorish medicine."

"At least a Moorish physician would never prescribe something like that . . . that placebo you're taking! And make you pay for it!"

"Call it what you want. It works for me."

Giuditta shook her head like a mother with a naughty, headstrong child. "Go ahead, Niccolo. You and your friend Guicciardini take your big, blue pills. I hope they keep you both alive long enough to save the world." Laughing, she trailed out of the room.

Niccolo went back to his letter and copied out the recipe for the questionable pills. He also added an explanation of several words and phrases in his most recent comedy that Guicciardini professed not to understand. It was uncanny that a man so highly educated, so intelligent, and a Florentine from a family as old as the city itself should be mystified by words and phrases that were so common and so vulgar and so ubiquitous in the streets and alleys that an urchin of ten could tell you what they meant, or any prostitute or cutpurse . . . But Francesco Guicciardini was not one to associate with those kinds of people, was he? Not Guicciardini! When he was done, he signed the letter "Niccolo Machiavelli" and added after his name, "Historic and comic author."

His correspondence with Guicciardini would continue throughout the summer, but shortly, it would take on an altogether different character. Shortly, frivolous talk of comedies and digestive remedies would give way to more serious concerns. For even as Niccolo transcribed the prescription for the blue pills, a strange silence suddenly descended on the hills and valleys of Germany. In the Tirol, the Lutheran grinding wheels, their work done at last, finally came to a halt. And the righteous, wrathful, dissenting, Protestant von Fundesberg took his place at the head of the mighty army he had assembled. After vowing to hang the pope and pawn his estates to pay his men, after listening to the cheers of his rabid legions and their undying hatred for the better part of an hour, von Fundesberg gave the order to march.

49

Liqueur for a Lickspittle

It is coming.
—Savonarola

When everything was ready, Giuditta withdrew. The table had been laid and the bottle of Rossoli was placed on the sideboard, much as it had been for Don Micheletto, many years ago, only this time the guest of honor was Michelozzi.

Niccolo waited calmly, almost blithely for his guest to arrive. He showed him in graciously, seated him at the table, and served a light, bittersweet concoction to stimulate his appetite.

"Michelozzi you don't look well. You look a little frazzled."

"It's the work."

"They keep you running over there at the chancery, do they?"

"The chancery? I hardly ever see the place anymore. I'm running back and forth to the Medici Palace most of the day."

"At Passerini's behest?"

"Passerini doesn't do a thing all day. Oh, occasionally he has an idea for some new tax or some novel way to squeeze a little more money out of people. But that's all. I rarely see him anymore."

"Then what keeps you so busy?"

"Our Medici lords. God, Niccolo, they've reduced me to a virtual babysitter for those two little bastards."

"You shouldn't speak of your young charges that way, even if they were born under dubious circumstances. After all, they represent the future of Florence, don't they?"

"Some future," said Michelozzi glumly.

"I should think it a great honor to be in service to so distinguished a family—and Alessandro the pope's son on top of everything else!"

"He's worse than the other one, Ippolito. Because he's the pope's son, he thinks he can do whatever he pleases. Lately he's taken to going out at night and lopping the heads off statues. The next day I have to trail around the city, soothing outraged citizens, paying damages, and setting things right."

"It could be worse."

"It is worse. In the last couple of weeks, the two of them have discovered a mutual interest in dressing up as women and then tearing through the streets on one horse, throwing things at passers-by and shouting insults at them. And do you know what else? I even found out that they're sleeping together now!"

"No?"

"Every night. And I doubt very much if it's innocent, if you know what I mean."

"Ah, the Medici," sighed Niccolo. "Would that God had saddled Florence with a better set of rulers."

"Would to God they could be more discreet in their depravity. They're making my life hell. And if they keep going the way they are, they're going to bring everything down around themselves. There's a lot of grumbling out there, Niccolo."

"They don't have anything to worry about as long as Clement's pope. With daddy on Saint Peter's throne, little Alessandro will have all the backing he needs to stay just where he is. And Clement is a young man, Michelozzi. You've got your work cut out for you for years to come."

"Some work," Michelozzi shrugged. "And I don't even get paid half the time."

"Ha," declared Niccolo, laughing. "Now you're finding out what it really means to be secretary in the Second Chancery."

Niccolo kept up the banter through the soup, through the lamb, through the salad, and through the dessert. "Look at us now," he was saying. "Both old men, and here we are, virtually useless. Who would have ever thought it would turn out this way? Oh well, at least you have a position."

"That brings me nothing but consternation. I'd gladly change places with you, Niccolo."

"You already have," said Niccolo. "You remember I used to be secretary."

"Those were better days," sighed Michelozzi.

Taking his cue, Niccolo steered the conversation around. "You remember when we were all in Rome together?"

"You and me and Callimaco and . . ." He trailed off.

"Yes, and her," said Niccolo sadly.

"Do you still think about her?" said Michelozzi.

"What's done is done," said Niccolo. "I've always tried to be a practical man, take care of the present, look to the future—and learn from the past."

"Still, it's hard not to look back."

Niccolo seemed to be reminiscing: "Do you remember when we were going to save the republic together—just the two of us? You in Rome and me up here?"

Michelozzi shook his head, then changed the subject: "Speaking of Rome, I haven't had a rack of spring lamb like that since I left the Eternal City. How did you ever get it to taste so good?"

"Oh, I brought back a girl from Rome to cook for me."

"That's ironic, isn't it? A quintessential Florentine like you with a Roman cook. I remember when you used to turn up your nose at Roman fare."

Niccolo chuckled to himself. "Would you like to meet her? You might find her, well, interesting, my cook. I certainly do. You know what I mean?" His eyes twinkled mischievously.

Michelozzi caught his innuendo and sly smile. "Well I've never turned down the company of a young lady before. Perhaps I just might find her, interesting, as you say."

Niccolo rang a little bell, and Michelozzi sat back in his chair, grinning in anticipation. What are friends for? An interesting little Roman cook. What better way to cap off a superb meal? What hospitality! What an excellent host this Niccolo was! You had to give him that. Sure, he had been something of a dupe in the past, but when it came to entertaining, he knew how to treat a . . .

Giuditta was not smiling when she appeared. And Michelozzi? He was not stupid and in an instant, he realized that he had stepped into a trap. He bolted for the door.

"It's locked, Michelozzi," said Niccolo casually. "And there are two armed men waiting outside, courtesy of Messer Francesco Guicciardini. They're there to see that everything goes, ah, according to plan."

Michelozzi, stricken with panic, had flattened himself against the unyielding door and seemed unable to move. "Come, come, Michelozzi, come sit down. I promised you an interesting evening, didn't I?"

Michelozzi edged back toward the table, sweeping in a wide arc around Giuditta, keeping his distance as if she were some sort of harpy or fury. When he was seated again, Niccolo said with satisfaction, "Now we can talk, Michelozzi. Now we can be frank with each other."

"Niccolo, I . . ."

"Would you like something to drink? You seem a little out of sorts. Something to calm your nerves?"

Michelozzi babbled in the affirmative. Giuditta reached for the bottle of Rossoli and a single glass, which she placed in front of him and filled with the sticky red liquid.

"Please, help yourself," said Niccolo, ever the ingratiating host.

"You're not going to . . . join me?"

"Me? No. It doesn't agree with me. My stomach, you know."

Michelozzi stared at the glass, his stomach turning, fearing the worst.

Giuditta spoke for the first time: "It doesn't agree with me, either," she said icily. "But you should enjoy it, Michelozzi. Drink up."

Like a rat in a corner, his small eyes darted back and forth between his two tormentors. They couldn't make him drink it, could they? Yes they could. Niccolo went to the door, knocked, giving a prearranged signal, and it opened. A surly, oafish, uniformed man stepped inside. "We need your assistance," said Niccolo. The man already knew what to do. He lowered his lance and placed its gleaming tip so that it was just touching the soft flesh on the back of Michelozzi's neck.

"Bottom's up, Michelozzi?" Michelozzi was trembling so badly that he had to use two hands just to get the glass to his mouth. A good deal of the red liqueur dribbled down his chin.

"Look what you've done, you're spilling it all over yourself," said Niccolo. "Giuditta, pour him another glass. I don't think he's had enough yet."

As she poured with a deadly, steady hand, she said, "Do you like this decanter, Michelozzi? I bought it years ago, for the night Don Micheletto came to dinner." If there was any doubt in Michelozzi's mind, the reference to Don Micheletto erased it and sealed his fate.

When he had finally been forced to gulp down the second glass, Niccolo smiled.

"Now, Michelozzi, I believe you have over an hour, maybe even two. Shall we talk? Let's start at the beginning."

Michelozzi slumped in his chair. Like a man condemned to death, he had nothing left to do but confess.

Niccolo began the questioning. "When we tried to poison Don Micheletto and failed . . ." He paused, "We were so naive about it then, so unpracticed, weren't we? But you see we've come a long way, haven't we, Michelozzi? Well, the good don fled to Rome, and Giuditta followed him, you remember, Michelozzi? And I sent her to the Florentine embassy to get help, didn't I, Michelozzi? I sent her to you."

"It wasn't like you think."

"What was it like, then?" said Giuditta. "Don Micheletto was warned of the plot in advance and would have killed me but for dumb luck. Who warned him, Michelozzi?"

Niccolo proceeded with all the calm and systematic methodology of the dispassionate historian trying to uncover the facts: "First you told me it was Cardinal Soderini, didn't you, Michelozzi? Then you amended your story and said the whole embassy was riddled with spies and the cardinal could have told anybody, but he didn't, did he? You told Don Micheletto. You were the spy, weren't you?"

"I told the Cardinal de' Medici to get Don Micheletto out of town for his own good, that there was a plot against him. That's all."

"And when the cardinal told Don Micheletto, he took matters into his own bloody hands, didn't he? A whole houseful of innocent girls, Michelozzi. Don Micheletto killed them, and the blood is on your hands."

"I didn't mean for anybody to get hurt," said Michelozzi feebly.

"Such nobility of spirit!" commented Niccolo offhandedly. Then abruptly, "How long were you a spy for the Medici?"

"Almost since I was posted to Rome. Cardinal Soderini thought it would be a good idea if I penetrated Medici circles to keep an eye on their activities."

"And so Cardinal Soderini created a monster?"

"At first, I reported back to him faithfully, but when I saw the way things were going, and when the Medici made their overtures . . ."

"Such touching loyalty! You remember how we used to stay up nights back then, arguing, worrying about the survival of the republic? You remember, Michelozzi? You remember how passionate you were? And it was all a lie, wasn't it?"

Michelozzi sneered, "Look where your loyalty to the republic's gotten you, Niccolo. Look at the last ten years of your life!"

"And look at yours, Messer Michelozzi! Look where your loyal service to the Medici has landed you! A lickspittle for two little bastards!"

"I don't work for them, I work only for myself."

"Then I'd say you're soon to be without an employer," taunted Niccolo. "But why all the intrigue, all the betrayal?"

"I told you, I worked only for myself. I didn't have a big protector like you did, Niccolo," said Michelozzi bitterly. "I didn't have the gonfaloniere advancing my interests at every turn for me. I had to do that myself. No one was looking out for me. Your republic, bah! Your Medici, ha! To hell with them all!"

"What about your friends, Michelozzi? What about us?" said Giuditta. "We trusted you and you betrayed us."

"Betrayed you!" he said, turning on her. "You betrayed yourselves! You were both just two fools with your dreams! And you, Giuditta! I tried to save you from him. I could have made it easy for you. You should have stayed with me when you had the chance!"

"What, so that today I could be the mistress of a lickspittle?"

The term infuriated Michelozzi. "I lasted longer than he ever did! I stayed on top for fifteen years longer than he did!"

"Yes, indeed, you did, Michelozzi. You stayed on top for fifteen years longer than I, thanks to your cunning. But what do you have to show for it now? Look where it's gotten you."

Already Michelozzi was beginning to feel the effects of the draught he had been forced to take. His stomach was churning, and his bowels were on fire. Niccolo regarded him with a patient sort of curiosity. "Time is running short, Michelozzi. There's only one more thing I want to know from you. Tell me about the gardens."

"The Cardinal told me to take you there so we could keep an eye on you—you and the other potential troublemakers."

"Some of those troublemakers are dead now, Michelozzi."

"They were plotting to kill the Cardinal. They brought it on themselves."

"And how did the Cardinal find out?"

"You know that very well. They discovered documents on a messenger."

"But how did they know to search that particular messenger? How did they know that on that particular night, he would be carrying the documents? Who tipped them off, Michelozzi?"

Michelozzi hung his head and said nothing. For the first time that evening, a trace of emotion crept into Niccolo's voice: "Luigi Alamanni is dead, Michelozzi. Jacopo da Diacceto is dead, Michelozzi. And the rest are lucky to be in exile! They're lucky they weren't caught in the bloodbath that you arranged."

Niccolo sat back, out of breath. Giuditta nodded to him. "Alright, Michelozzi, get out of here," he said wearily.

Michelozzi looked up. He couldn't believe his ears. "What?"

"I said, leave us. There's no reason you should stay in here and foul up my dining room with your presence. Go out in the streets and die like a dog."

"Good-bye, Michelozzi," said Giuditta in a chilly, unforgiving voice.

The explosion in Michelozzi's bowels hit him almost at the same instant he was thrown out into the street by the two burly guards borrowed from Messer Francesco Guicciardini. The force of it caused him to crumple up right there on the paving stones. He curled himself up into a ball as the liquid shit boiled out of his screaming entrails. The pain stabbed at him from the inside like an erratic madwoman wielding a dagger in his stomach. He pulled up tighter and clenched his teeth to await death, pressing his burning forehead on the cold, wet stones right there in front of the house of his assassins. But death never came that night for Michelozzi. The Rossoli had contained nothing more than a fierce purgative.

"I still think we should have poisoned him, Niccolo."

"He's too pathetic to poison," said Niccolo, crunching down on a large slab of crusty, fried bread.

"So you think we did the right thing?"

"Indubitably. We found out what we wanted to know from him.

And we did get our revenge, even if it was in a sort of burlesque fashion."

"You don't think he'll strike back?"

"What can he do? Michelozzi is impotent, castrated, no balls. Besides, you heard him, he never does anything except for personal gain—and what would he have to gain by coming after us?"

"Revenge. What else? He could have you thrown in prison."

"I don't think so. The days of Michelozzi wielding power and influence have pretty much come to an end. He said himself he's been reduced to an office boy and a babysitter."

"He still has Cardinal Passerini's ear, doesn't he?"

"And Passerini hasn't shown his face in public for a couple of weeks now. He's hiding in the Medici Palace and won't come out."

"What do you think will happen to him?"

"Michelozzi or the cardinal?"

"Michelozzi."

"Well, if the present regime, for some reason, were to falter, I think it would go very badly for Michelozzi. I think if I were him, I would get out of town very fast—if something were to happen."

"Niccolo, do you know something? Have you heard something?"

"You don't have to hear anything; you can see it on people's faces. They hate Passerini because he's a foreigner—from Cortona of all places, and they hate him because he's the pope's hand-picked man. They also hate him because he doesn't have any balls. They've taken to calling him 'the Eunuch.'"

"So what's in the cards for the Eunuch?"

"As long as the pope holds on to power, the Eunuch stays."

"And what's in the cards for the pope?"

"Who knows? The Lutherans are rattling their spears and threatening to cut off his head. Guicciardini says they've already crossed into Italy near Brescia and are heading south."

"And what is the pope doing about it?"

"The usual. Trying to buy them off, but I don't think he has enough money this time."

"Is there going to be a war then?"

"Maybe. Probably."

"And Florence?"

"Who knows? We're right in the middle of the high road to Rome. We're part of the pope's domains. We may be attacked."

"And if it comes to that, what will you do?"

"Me? Absolutely nothing. I told you I'm finished with that business. I intend to keep on scribbling, writing my plays."

"Is that all you've been writing?"

"I swear! Do you want to see the new one? Do you want to see how much I've gotten done on it already?"

"I notice you seem to be writing a lot of letters lately. And they're longer and fatter letters too."

"To Guicciardini. He asks my advice. I'm happy to let a friend benefit from my years of experience with the things of this world."

"What things?"

"Armies and truces, popes and emperors, things like that."

"You still have that cricket in your head, don't you?"

"I told you, not me. I'm an old man and a happy one. Let's just say I look on all this grave business of war and revolution as a kind of hobby. I can't help it. Some men study butterflies or birds or collect old manuscripts or coins. I watch governments and empires rise and fall."

"For the sheer entertainment of it all?"

"What better spectacle is there under the sun? Now let me finish my breakfast."

"Finish your breakfast. Take your stroll down to the river. Then it will be dinnertime. After your nap, we'll take a walk, and by then, of course, it will be time for your supper."

"Isn't it glorious?" said Niccolo, grinning up at her from his bread and fruit. While he finished eating, Giuditta went downstairs to open up the big outside doors for the day. A messenger dropped off several letters for Niccolo, and when she went back up to the kitchen, she deposited them on the table in front of him, just like every day.

"Mmmmm, something from Venice," he said between bites. He opened the letter and scanned it rapidly. "Look at this! The Florentine merchants in Venice are pleading with me to send them another comedy!"

"Bravo, Maestro!"

"I told you, I'm Niccolo Machiavelli, comic author now!"

"I know you are, *caro*," she said, planting a dainty kiss on his forehead. "Niccolo, listen, I'm going to get dressed and go out with you this morning. There are some things I want to get. Will you wait for me?"

"Of course, go on. I'll finish these letters and clean up here. Come get me when you're ready." And the happy man went back to his correspondence and his breakfast.

When Giuditta returned about twenty minutes later, however, Niccolo was still sitting at the table, engrossed in one of his letters. The comic author's face was screwed up in a worried look.

"Something wrong?"

No answer.

"Niccolo, is something wrong?" louder this time.

"What? No. It's from Guicciardini."

"Did he get his pills?"

"Oh . . . yes. . . he got the pills. They're working fine."

"Then there must be some bad news on the movement of armies or the rise and fall of empires and governments?"

"The Germans are getting closer."

"We already know that, don't we?"

"Yes." Niccolo hesitated. "Guicciardini said he convinced the pope that Florence should prepare to defend herself, in case of an attack. And . . ."

"And what?"

"And they need someone to take charge of the preparations. Francesco wants me to take it."

"And what will you tell him?"

"What should I tell him?"

"That you're a comic author now?"

Within an hour, the ex-comic author had packed an old, worn bag with the few things he would need and was riding into a stiff March wind, riding rather briskly for a man his age, on the road to Bologna.

Francesco Guicciardini had survived the death of his patron, Pope Leo X, and the brief pontificate of the Dutchman Dedel, to emerge as governor of all the Papal States in Romagna under the new Medici Pope, Clement VII. When news of the threatened German invasion reached the pope, the supreme pontiff had hastily assembled the usual rag-tag army of mercenaries under the command of the duke of Urbino and sent them off into northern Italy in the event diplomacy failed and they might be needed to stave off the barbarian hordes. This army was encamped at Bologna where the papal governor, Guicciardini, who now also served in a military capacity as pontifical lieutenant, had his headquarters.

The high-sounding name of Pontifical Army had been bestowed upon the undisciplined, multinational rabble encamped around Bologna. To Niccolo, the sights and sounds of the camp, although long unseen and unheard, were depressingly familiar. The snarling and cursing of unruly mercenaries from all over Italy and Europe, the arguments over trivial gambling stakes, the drunken singing.

Niccolo found the pontifical lieutenant comfortably ensconced in a little villa in the middle of the sprawling camp. Notwithstanding the military honors and titles that had lately accrued to him, Francesco Guicciardini would never submit to the discomforts of staying in a common camp tent. When Niccolo was admitted without delay to the chamber where Guicciardini was working, the first thing he saw was a great mound of fur. From between dark fur collar and dark fur cap, the ever-unperturbed, ever-bland face of Francesco Guicciardini peeked out. Although a roaring fire had been built to ward off the evening chill and the room was uncomfortably hot and stuffy, Guicciardini, wishing to take no chances with the malevolent night winds, was sheathed in fur from head to foot.

"*Salve Gubernator!*" said Niccolo in greeting. Then he added wryly, "Or should I call you *Presidente?* Lieutenant?"

The bear sniggered, "'Your Excellency' will do."

"You should have been a cardinal, Francesco. You have the girth for it."

"But not the inclination. I have a reputation for anticlericism, you know."

"Entirely undeserved, I'm sure," said Niccolo, settling into a chair. "Now, tell me what's going on."

"The situation is abysmally complicated, and I'm not that optimistic about our chances for success."

"And by 'our' you mean . . . ?"

"The pope's, Florence's . . . Niccolo, things are at such a dreadful impasse, I may not even be able to salvage my own career."

"That bad?"

"Worse than you can imagine." As Guicciardini spoke, laying out the situation, from time to time his plump white hands crept cautiously out of the fur, like two fat white mice, scurried around among the documents on the table, rearranged them, and then retreated.

"It falls to me to stand between the fulminating Germans on the one hand and on the other, the object of their hatred, the pope. Clement, who, as you know, was a great and respected cardinal, is now a small and shabby pope who commands respect from no one. His indecision and his waffling in the face of this imminent invasion are a scandal and a disgrace. And as things get steadily worse, he seems to become even more craven and cowardly."

"Francesco, do you actually have command of the army?"

"No, I'm only a papal liaison and advisor. I relay information to the pope and advice, and I relay his orders to the duke of Urbino. He's the commander."

"And what sort of a man is he?"

"The duke? A coward and probably a traitor. The usual."

"Will he fight?"

"I doubt it. In any case, the pope refuses to issue the order. He's trying to make a deal with the Germans. So we wait."

"And where are the Germans now?"

"Pretty far north of here. But they're on their way."

"Are they disposed to a truce? Or a payoff?"

"The emperor is. But the emperor isn't with them. Just that loose cannon, von Fundesberg, and his hordes of religious dissenters. There's no telling what he'll do."

Then, Niccolo, who really cared very little about the fate of the pope, asked the question that was on his mind, "What about Florence?"

"If the fate of the pope and the Universal Catholic Church were all I had to worry about, my problems would be complicated enough. But I have to worry about Florence as well. That's why I asked for you."

"What do you want me to do?"

"Prepare for the worst. Assume that this army here will either be defeated or overrun. Assume that the Germans will march on Florence on their way to Rome and attack her. Assume that we won't be able to get any outside help at all."

"Those are pretty dismal assumptions."

"Those assumptions, in all likelihood, represent what is actually going to happen. You know it as well as I."

"Is there any money available for the defenses?"

"There's money being raised, but no one can decide what to do with it. The pope wants to use it to buy a treaty."

"That's madness!"

"Of course it is, but try to talk him out of it. He has every faith in diplomacy and in the honor and good intentions of the emperor, Charles V. So there you have it, Machiavelli. Go back to Florence and prepare for war."

Niccolo shook his head, "With no money, no outside help, no cooperation from the pope . . . It's impossible."

"Why do you think we're calling on you, old man?"

"How much time?"

"A month? Two at the most."

"Jesus Christ, Francesco!"

"Will you do it?"

A look of almost malicious delight spread across the old diplomat's face: "I better ride back tonight. There's no time to waste."

The great furry beast smiled.

Niccolo's undertaking proved to be every bit as gargantuan as he had anticipated, his struggle every bit as uphill. He was given an official title, *provveditore delle mura,* overseer of the walls, but little else in the way of support. He was given a secretary.

With uncommon energy, he threw himself into a thorough examination of all the defense works of the city. He sent for his old friend from the days at Pisa, Antonio di Sangallo, the architect who had gone to Lombardy to study fortifications. He worked tirelessly. Eating and sleeping were only dim memories from the past. Perhaps the only assistance Niccolo did receive that proved to be of any value was from Mother Nature. Torrential rainstorms and late and unseasonable snow squalls were slowing the progress of the German marauders over the Alps and through the narrow mountain passes. The inevitable day of reckoning was postponed for a while due to bad weather.

Niccolo was coughing badly as he hauled himself up the stairs, long after dark. Giuditta was waiting for him with another reprimand that she knew would go unheeded. "Listen to yourself! You sound like you're dying of consumption. Niccolo, you have to stop pushing yourself like this."

"I'm fine, I'm fine," he waved off her concerns. "My lungs are perfectly sound. The only reason I'm coughing so badly is all this dust I've been eating all day long." To prove his point, he slapped at his cloak and a little cloud of dust materialized. "See?"

"You've been out crawling around on those walls again today?"

"They have to be inspected. The work has to be supervised."

"You're going to fall someday."

"Better that than a German lance in my stomach."

"Speaking of your stomach, how do you feel?"

"Better."

"Do you want to eat something?"

"I'm too tired. I want to go to sleep. In the morning, I'll eat a fat, greasy breakfast. Will that make you happy?"

"Did things go badly today?"

"Things go badly every day. Do you know how many letters I've written to the pope, detailing my recommendations and pleading for money to get the works going? And today he sends me not money but his plan, his plan for the fortifications!"

"What does he want to do?"

"Enlarge the circuit of the walls to include all the San Miniato hill! That could take years! Do you know what his argument is? That the value of the land added to the city would be over 80,000 florins! I wrote back and informed him there wasn't even going to be a city if we didn't do something fast! Imagine! He's thinking about real-estate speculation!"

"*Calma, caro,*" she cooed. "Can't Guicciardini do something?"

"He's tried to overcome the pope's obstinacy, but nothing yet."

"What about Passerini?"

"Ah, the Little Sparrow is nesting furtively. He's walled himself up in the Medici Palace. Somehow he found enough money to fortify that!"

"And what about you, my poor, dear man?"

"Giuditta, my head is so full of bastions and towers and fortalices and ditches . . ." Niccolo collapsed in a heap on the table.

"My poor, dear man," she repeated, stroking his head. He was already asleep.

Summer came and went. The pope vacillated, and no work was done on the walls of Florence. Niccolo made a trip to the camp of the Pontifical Army, now at Cremona, near Milan. Guicciardini was vainly attempting to hold the army together, but already what little unity they had was dissolving, and the captains were at each other's throats like snarling dogs.

In November, the Germans crossed into Italy at Brescia. Twice, the pope ordered the Pontifical Army to withdraw before the advancing hordes rather than stand and fight. Twice Guicciardini complied. The pope was still confident that matters could be arranged and wanted to avoid any outright confrontation with the imperial troops.

In Florence, all was chaos. No one seemed to be in charge. The pope was supposed to be making the decisions, but he was ludicrously indecisive. Passerini had burrowed deep into the Medici Palace. There was the Council of Eight and the Council of Eighty, but they were disorganized and incapable of coming to any sort of agreement. The smarter council members had already left town. Nothing was being done for the defense. Twice, once in November, once again in February, the panicky city sent Niccolo Machiavelli to plead with Guicciardini for assistance.

In the mountains and hills north of Florence, it was so cold that the ground, including the roads, had frozen solid. Although the biting winds and occasional snow presented problems for the traveler on horseback, the hard ground made progress a relatively straightforward, relatively rapid thing. Not so when Niccolo descended down and out of the hills, onto the plains—where a sea of mud awaited him. While he was not cut and worried as much by the bitter wind, the mud made any sort of rapid progress impossible. Such were the extremes, such were the trade-offs and discomforts of winter travel. All told, Niccolo preferred the milder temperatures with the incumbent sloshing and slipping in the mud to the piercing cold of the high country—that is, until it started to rain. While the rain did not cut as sharply through several layers of wool as a mountain wind could do, once the icy wetness penetrated, it was there to stay. Niccolo was shivering so violently when he arrived that it took the better part of an hour by the fire and the better part of a cup of brandy before his chills subsided. As the heat penetrated his old bones, Niccolo began to revive, and it was only then that the harried, skinny, hawk-nosed diplomat sat down with the stolid, unflappable aristocrat to discuss what, if anything, could be done to save Florence from impending disaster.

"So the plans for the defensive measures never got off the ground?"

"There was nothing but haggling and indecision. I plotted out exactly what had to be done—what could be done in the shortest time possible with the least possible expense. I wanted only to fortify existing emplacements, not build any fantastic new walls. But I couldn't get any money. When I got a little money, the mayors of each district were supposed to supply laborers, but the laborers never materialized. By the time I finally managed to get a labor force together, the money had run out. On and on like that."

"And what are the good citizens of Florence doing now?"

"Wringing their hands, praying. They're melting down the gold and silver from the churches."

"To do what?"

"Hire mercenaries, if they can find any. Buy weapons if there are any available. Pay ransom if worst comes to worst."

"*Ahi serva Italia,*" quoted Guicciardini.

"If there were only a militia, Francesco, if the citizens were armed and trained and capable of defending themselves, we wouldn't be in this situation."

"Aren't there any arms or soldiers at all in Florence?"

"What little armory there is is inside the Medici Palace with the Eunuch. Same goes for the soldiery."

"And he isn't budging?"

"Absolutely not."

"What do you want to do?" asked Guicciardini.

"The only thing we can hope to do is turn aside the brunt of the storm, divert it around Florence. Where are the Germans now?"

"Oh, hard by. If it were a clear day, you could probably see them from up on the roof. Not that there's much hope for a clear day in this wretched place."

"How many?"

"My estimate? Thirty thousand."

"Thirty thousand!" said Niccolo, astonished. "I thought they were twelve thousand, fifteen thousand at the most."

"They were—when they started out. But they trickled down out of their mountains like a little stream—a little stream of heretics. As they went, they were joined by other little streams of dissenters, and the stream got bigger and more powerful. They're a regular river of cleansing destruction now."

"What sort of shape are they in?"

"Worse shape than you," replied Guicciardini. They're colder, wetter, and sorrier than you were when you arrived. They have no artillery, no money, and no provisions. One of my spies was caught in the camp, and do you know what the first thing they did to him was? They stripped him of his boots! Half of that rabble is barefoot out there. Barefoot and shivering."

"That makes them vulnerable."

"Or more dangerous. A rabid animal, backed into a corner, and hungry on top of that, can be a formidable opponent. The only thing that keeps them going now are the fires of religious zeal—and the more earthly desire to kill the pope and loot the Vatican."

"Can you hit them, now?"

"With what?" sighed Guicciardini. "My army is all over the place. Every captain and lieutenant has gone off in a different direction. At most, I could muster five thousand men. And they'd be in as bad shape as the hungry Lutherans. They haven't got any arms to speak of. Instead of a battle, we'd have a fist fight. Besides which, the pope will never give the order to attack, and even if he did, the duke of Urbino wouldn't carry it out."

"*Cazzus!*" Niccolo swore.

Guicciardini sat back and said philosophically, "And you come to me for help?"

While they both considered the situation in silence, more news arrived. The duke of Ferrara, famed in all of Europe for the high quality of his cannons and guns, had agreed to intervene in the crisis. He had decided to provide all the artillery that was needed—to the Lutherans.

This time it was Niccolo who quoted Dante, "*Ahi serva Italia!*"

The impassive Guicciardini reflected on this new development for a moment. "I suppose there's nothing much we can do now. Shall we have dinner?"

Never a friend of papal interests in the Romagna, the estimable duke of Ferrara thought that, once and for all, the papal stranglehold on northern Italy might be broken. If it took the armies of the barbarians to do it, well, the Lord works in mysterious ways. Within a week, the Lutherans had at their disposal some of the most powerful and advanced artillery in Italy. Within a week, they were on the march.

Like Proteus, Guicciardini's quarreling army twisted itself into a dozen different configurations, one more ineffective than the other, none of them in the least bit threatening. Then word arrived from Rome—the pope had signed a truce with the emperor's representative. War was averted. Terms had been concluded. They were ignominious terms and humiliating for the pope. They would require the cession of considerable territory as well as huge sums of money, but then, the pope was not in a strong bargaining position. As a sign of his good faith, the pope also dismissed over thirty thousand troops whom he had massed in Rome for his defense.

"Do you think it's over?" asked Guicciardini, lapping at a cup of warm milk.

Niccolo laughed softly to himself. He was still laughing when, suddenly, he winced. His face was contorted, and he doubled over with pain. He wrapped both arms around his stomach and squeezed hard, and after a moment the pain passed.

"What is it?"

"I don't know. Nothing. Gas. Revenge of the digestion. It must have been something I ate."

"Are you all right?"

"I'll be fine." Niccolo fumbled in his pocket for his pillbox. It was empty. "Damn!"

"You need one of these?" Beaming, Guicciardini extracted a handful of the blue pills as big as birds' eggs from an intricately wrought silver box on the table, right next to the saltcellar.

"*Grazie*," said Niccolo, gratefully reaching for the proffered remedy. His gullet had to work hard to swallow the big pills—he took four—and his Adam's apple bobbed convulsively with the effort. When he was done, however, he seemed relieved and in a minute was able to resume his debate with Guicciardini on the immediate future of the vengeful legions of Martin Luther, encamped not ten miles away.

Although Pope Clement had ordered his Pontifical Army to withdraw, neither Machiavelli nor Guicciardini thought this to be the most prudent course. They were on the verge of deciding that the wisest decision, for the time being, was to put off making a decision, when a breathless messenger arrived and did not even bother to knock before bursting into the room. Piqued, Guicciardini made his displeasure felt for this breach of etiquette. He fixed the messenger with a glare that stopped him in his tracks and forced him to assume an attitude of humility. "Well?" he finally asked disdainfully of the anxious messenger.

The man was dressed in rags and badly shod. "I just came from the German camp." His chest was still heaving.

Guicciardini was waiting patiently for the man's report, but Niccolo was already up out of his chair.

"Von Fundesberg . . . It's von Fundesberg! He called the men together to read them the terms of the truce. Told them they would get several hundred ducats each. . . . They grumbled. . . . He started to harangue them. . . . They grumbled louder. . . . The next thing he knew, they were thrusting the points of their halberds in his face!"

"I do hope the old Lutheran was able to talk some sense into them," said Guicciardini.

"He was trying to, when he had some sort of a fit. His teeth clamped up tight and he went all stiff and keeled over. They carried him away. He's not dead but . . ."

"But he might as well be," said Guicciardini. "And the men?"

"They're shaking their lances and shouting, 'On to Rome!' 'Down with the antichrist! Hang the pope!' It's like the devil's loose in that camp."

"And they're getting ready to march?" asked Niccolo.

"March or stumble or crawl. Anyway, they're determined to push on to Rome."

"Have they got anybody to lead them?"

"Charles of Bourbon. But they had the lances at his throat, too, and said that he could lead them as long as he led them to Rome. If he tried anything or attempted to make a truce, it was pretty clear what they had in mind for him."

Guicciardini turned to Niccolo, "Isn't that the kind of popular government you've always advocated? Rule by the rabble? The will of the people? All that? Our Lutheran friends seem to be ahead of us on that score."

Niccolo ignored the jibe. "It seems our Lutherans have come this far and will not be denied."

"Well, what shall we do with our Pontifical Army now?"

"Can you get them mobilized to retreat?"

"I'm sure that's the only order they would follow," said Guicciardini.

"And that's what the pope wants, anyway. Isn't it?"

"He has indeed issued orders to that effect."

"Well, send for that scoundrel, Urbino, and have him sound the order to retreat, then."

"I'm surprised at you, Machiavelli. I thought you would opt for some sort of heroic, self-sacrificing last stand."

"It may happen yet, but not here, not to save the pope."

"Meaning?"

"If the army withdraws, as the pope wants it to withdraw, we'd only be following orders, correct?"

"Obviously."

"But the orders don't specify where to withdraw to or what direction to withdraw in, do they?"

"A retreat is a retreat, as long as we get out of the way. The pope has confidence in his truce and doesn't need us to protect him."

"What I propose," said Niccolo, "is that we retreat in the direction of Florence. Why not? It's as good a direction as any other. And we can draw up the army right in front of the city. It's as good a place to stop as any other."

Guicciardini was nodding approval. "Yes, I see what you mean."

Niccolo continued, "If the Lutherans are so intent on hanging the pope, do you think they're going to stop on the way to loot Florence, especially if there's an army there? Even such an army as it is."

"They'd only be asking for trouble."

"And they have more important business to attend to, don't they?"

"Ah, yes," said Guicciardini. "They have their religious problems to work out with His Holiness. I do hope they're not too hard on him. Oh well, you can't say we didn't warn him."

The Pontifical Army, therefore, withdrew, to the south and west. Guicciardini managed to maneuver it in the general direction of Florence. The hydra-headed Lutheran monster advanced toward Rome, to the south and east, the smell of blood already in its thousands of nostrils. They swept through Tuscany, stopping only long enough to pillage for food along the way, barely casting a glance in the direction of Florence.

All but leaderless now, they advanced lurching and careening. All semblance of order had long since broken down in the ranks. But as order and their physical condition deteriorated, their ardor to reach the end of their unholy pilgrimage was only inflamed. Propelled by an almost-mystical vision, their desire for an apocalyptic ending intense and all consuming, they trudged on. Snowdrifts and landslides in the mountains of central Italy did little to impede their progress. On they came. Rains and swollen, roaring mountain streams could not stop them, or even slow them down. They formed themselves into long lines, and, joining hands, they crossed the treacherous terrain, holding onto each other to avoid stumbling on rocks and plunging into the gullies and ravines that lined their dangerous, God-forsaken path.

✦ 50 ✦

The Ragtag Armies of the Apocalypse and the Regeneration of Florence

At a considered distance, after reflection, thoughtful historians have designated the sack of Rome in 1527 by the armies of the new barbarians as the event that marked the end of that great outpouring of artistic and intellectual achievement known as the Italian Renaissance. For those Romans caught up in that cataclysmic event, and perhaps less concerned about the formalized beginnings and ends of historical periods, it seemed more like the end of the world.

The Lutherans descended on the Holy City like the proverbial swarm of locusts, and, like that biblical plague of locusts, they left nothing but devastation in their wake. Ragged and hungry, they reached the walls of Rome on the fifth of May. The irresolute Pope Clement, realizing too late that the Lutheran hordes did not intend to abide by the terms of the agreement he had reached with their nominal overlords, shut himself up, along with a dozen or so cardinals and three thousand other fugitives in the Castel Sant'Angelo. The castle, built in the days of the Roman emperors as a mausoleum and frequently and heavily fortified thereafter, was a walled fortress within a walled city. When the pope and his retainers had obtained the relative safety of those ancient and impregnable walls, they drew up the drawbridge behind them, effectively turning their backs on the rest of the city. The Vicar of Christ, the Good Shepherd, had abandoned his flock to the wolves.

Left to fend for themselves by the pontiff who had virtually handed them over to the enemy and assured their destruction, if not actually invited it, the Romans made what scanty arrangements they could for the coming storm. Those with any foresight fled, abandoning wealth and property. Those who were unable or unwilling to do so had the doors and windows of their houses walled shut and retreated to the upper stories with what weapons they could muster, hoping to wait things out. In the final days before the onslaught, the price of poison rose astronomically. Supply could not keep up with demand.

On the morning of the sixth of May, when the first assault came, the Tiber valley was shrouded in a fog so thick that defenders and attackers were not even aware of each other's movements. By the time it lifted, the Lutherans, using good Italian cannon, had blasted two holes in the city walls, and the rout was on. The first civilian casualties were reported in the Santo Spirito quarter, where a hospital was ransacked and all the patients slain, while across the street, an orphanage suffered the same fate. The unholy work of destruction now begun would last for a week. It would be the seventh day before the invaders, sated with booty and blood, finally rested.

The final, desperate, feeble measures taken by the citizens of Rome to protect themselves, their families, and their property proved to be miserably inadequate, and torture soon yielded up the hiding places of their valuables, their daughters, and their wives. In their impatience, the greedy soldiers thought nothing of dismemberment to obtain the prizes and baubles they sought—they chopped off fingers for rings, arms for bracelets, ears for earrings. Many a young woman—and many an old one, for that matter—was given the choice of an invading Lutheran penis or a sword in the vagina. Many chose the latter. Suicide by defenestration was almost epidemic.

If this bloodlust and common lust raged unabated for a week, and the general population was forced to submit to its depravity, it was nothing compared to the horrors inflicted upon the clergy, for they were the particular target of this wrathful act of Lutheran retribution. Monks, priests, bishops, and nuns were rounded up and subjected to depredations of every sort, most too gruesome even to describe. For the cardinals, those princes of the church, especially atrocious treatment was reserved. The churches were turned into slaughterhouses, the convents and monasteries into brothels. The altars became tables where bloody and outrageous feasts were held and afterward were transformed into gaming tables, where the prize was the chastity of young nuns and monks. Lurid travesties of the mass were represented, and naked priests were forced to participate in these degrading spectacles. One of the most abiding delights of the merry barbarians was to see the Eucharist administered to pigs and asses that were dragged squealing to the communion rail. Sacred vestments were thrown on the backs of murderers and thieves. Sacred vessels were lifted in drunken, blasphemous toasts. Never had sacrilege been practiced on such a programmatic and all-out basis.

Scarcely a corner of Roman life escaped the pikestaffs, the short swords, the daggers, and the torches of the furious *Landsknechte*. Tombs were even ripped open and the dead despoiled. Houses to which the rabid barbarians could not gain admittance were burned, and much sport was made as the sorry inhabitants hurled themselves in flames from the windows. Artists were tortured for having painted the Madonna or the saints. A professor at the university was forced to sit and watch while his recently completed manuscript—a commentary on a commentary on Pliny, a life's work!—was mercilessly burned before his eyes.

By the time the fury began to subside, ten thousand were dead and lay unburied. The streets were like open sewers running with blood and clogged with corpses. Dogs and other scavengers could be seen tugging carcasses and pieces of carcasses through the desolate, wasted ruins of the Eternal City.

Whatever else this most unchristian event signaled, it signaled the definitive end of the unity of the Christian church in Europe. It paved the way for centuries of warfare and bloody persecution both within and between the emerging nation-states and empires, wars and persecutions that could now be carried on, blithely, confidently, under the banner of religious zealotry. In mute testimony to this dissolution, there stood a painting by Raphael in the Stanze in the Vatican. It was titled, *The School of Athens*, and it represented the highest Renaissance ideals of harmony and reconciliation. In it, through the use of allegorical figures, the artist depicts the two great schools of pagan philosophy joined together and reconciled with Christian teaching. Across that spacious scene of consummate harmony, of philosophical synthesis and peace, someone had cut with a lance the name of Martin Luther.

The Pontifical Army, summoned frantically, hysterically, and too late by the pope, had also marched south, always keeping a respectful distance between itself and the infuriated Lutherans. With the danger of fighting definitively past, the duke of Urbino had boldly assumed command and brought the army to a standstill halfway between Rome and Florence. Guicciardini accompanied the shameful march, as did Niccolo, and listened to the idle boasts of the duke, who was loudly waiting for the right moment to strike. Grim bulletins from the front arrived daily. Rome was taken and destroyed. The pope was being held prisoner in the Castel Sant'Angelo. All was lost.

In time, the pope would escape and go into hiding, and, eventually, after the payment of an enormous ransom and the total subjection of himself, the church, and all of Italy to the will of a foreign emperor, he would be allowed to return to the chair of Saint Peter and resume his ignominious pontificate. The ravages of the Lutherans in Rome would eventually abate when summer came on, with its malarial and pestilential heat. The very end product of their depredations—the streets piled high with corpses—would prove to be the source of their own undoing, as a fierce outbreak of the plague would drive them from the city and disperse them. Laden down with their ill-gotten gains, they would go scampering and straggling back over their mountains, back across the Alps, back to Germany.

But in the days following the sack of Rome, none of these things was yet clear, and apprehension was in the air. The most commonly expressed fear was that the Lutheran army, gorged on Roman blood but not sated, would turn its hungry wrath on the other fat cities of central Italy. Few were prepared to resist them, least of all, as we have seen, Florence, which led to a not entirely unforeseen but still quite surprising and momentous circumstance. Niccolo first got wind of the events while still in the camp of the Pontifical Army at Civitavecchia. Since news from Rome, which had gone from grim to unutterable, required a strong stomach, he had all but given up on even trying to keep track of the situation there. When messengers rode into camp from the south, not only were they no longer besieged for news, they were avoided like the plague. Nobody wanted to know. Nobody wanted the details. Then, one day, a messenger rode in from the north. He came on wildly, not plodding and dispirited. He was waving his hat and shouting.

Niccolo was sulking, carving idly at a piece of wood with a small knife, and meditating once more on the vanity of earthly treasures.

The news went through him like a bolt of lightning. He ran after the flagging messenger and pulled him down off his horse. He pressed him for details, and when he was satisfied, he dragged the messenger bodily into Guicciardini's headquarters. Flushed with excitement and exertion, Niccolo stood the man in front of the obviously pained Guicciardini: "Tell him! Go on! Tell him what you told me!"

"There was a riot. In Florence," he said haltingly. "The people were demanding arms to defend themselves. Things got worse. They besieged the Signoria. Passerini panicked and fled with the two Medici bastards."

Guicciardini now abandoned all pretense of passivity and stood up. "And . . ." he demanded excitedly.

"And by general consent, a new government was proclaimed—a republic!"

It took Guicciardini only a minute to fathom the implications of this proclamation. He turned to Niccolo. "Well, what are you standing there staring for? Let's go!"

Niccolo howled a howl of long-suppressed triumph and delight. "*Popolo e libertá!*" he shouted. It felt good to be able to say it again. "*Popolo e libertá!* Saddle the horses!"

Guicciardini only gave him a queer look. They were on the road in less than an hour. Niccolo was jubilant and made no attempt to conceal his joy. He shouted the good news to anyone who passed by and would listen. He sang old republican songs. He forgot about his aching bones and stiff joints and failing digestion. Messer Francesco Guicciardini, although more subdued, seemed equally eager to get on to Florence.

"I'm surprised at you, Francesco. Really, I am. I'm surprised that you're so eager to get back. You of all people—eager to go to work for this new republic."

Guicciardini eyed his companion with his infinite, jaded weariness. "You must be joking, Machiavelli. Work for the new republic? I'm only hoping to get back in time to prevent something disastrous."

"Like a bloodbath?"

"Like the confiscation of my property by a band of unruly plebeians."

They were still dancing in the streets when Niccolo and Messer Francesco Guicciardini reached Florence. Put off by the spectacle, the sententious Guicciardini was mumbling something about mob rule as he hurried off to look into his own affairs. Niccolo let his horse wander aimlessly through the familiar streets and across the piazze, drinking in the sounds and sights of the renascent republic. Bells pealed, banners waved in the warm May breeze, and everywhere the joyous work of revision was already underway. Scaffolds were going up, workmen with hammers were crawling up the sides of buildings, attacking the crests of the Medici family that adorned so many walls and towers. As their masons' hammers smashed through the stone Medici balls and these crumbled and fell away, the red-and-white shield of the republic that had lain hidden beneath them for fifteen years was finally visible again. Each blow was greeted by a roar from the crowds below. Each crimson cross that emerged from hiding was hailed as a sign of triumph and redemption.

Despite his exhilaration, Niccolo was aware of a dull pain in his side and deemed it the better part of wisdom to return home and rest. He would need his strength in the days and weeks ahead. There was much work to be done.

Head bowed, he rode through the doors of his house and into his own courtyard like a weary conquering hero, a little the worse for wear. The past several months had taken their toll on him, emotionally but also physically—the bitter winter, the cold, wet spring, camp life, and bad food. And the last two weeks at Civitavecchia were the worst of all. You could almost smell the malaria on the wind that crept out of the surrounding marshes. Then the long ride home—they had pushed it and covered the distance in two days. All the while, Niccolo had marveled that a man of Guicciardini's girth could sit a horse with such apparent ease and ride at a good clip without sagging and tiring. "There must be at least a few steel rods somewhere in that fat, soft body," he thought.

Giuditta watched from a window as he dismounted, slowly and stiffly, like an old man. She watched him trudge across the courtyard and up the outside stairs. He hadn't even bothered to unsaddle his horse. But when he walked in, covered with dust, she saw that a young man's fire burned in his eyes and lit up his face.

"I'm home," he said. "For the first time in fifteen years, I'm really home. Florence is Florence again."

Giuditta hugged him and could feel his bones through the heavy riding clothes. He seemed smaller to her, weakened and diminished. She made him sit down, pulled off his boots, and brought him a flask of wine. Although she was concerned, the wine seemed to revive his spirits, and in a few minutes, he was hunching over the table and talking excitedly about all the things that could be accomplished now . . . now that the republic was restored.

"The last thing you have to worry about now is the republic," she said. "You look frightful. Have you been taking care of yourself, Niccolo?"

"I take my pills every day."

"You and those pills," she huffed. "Let me get you something to eat."

"Not now, I'm exhausted. Let me sleep for a little while, first. Then we'll eat."

When Giuditta went up to the bedroom several hours later to see if he was up and hungry, she found him on the bed, still clothed and sound asleep. He seemed to be smiling in his sleep. As gently as possible, she undressed him and pulled the linen sheet up over him. He slept right through the night, and it was almost noon the next day before he finally stirred.

She heard him stirring and went up to see how he felt. "Much better," he said from behind the closed door of the *gabinetto*, the little closet where the chamber pot was kept.

"Then get washed and dressed and come on downstairs. The day's almost over already."

It was nearly half an hour, and he still wasn't down when Giuditta went back up to see if everything was alright. She saw Niccolo still in his nightshirt, near the window, bending over, of all things, the chamber pot! And examining its contents! He had always been obsessive about his digestion, but this was carrying it to extremes. Like a little boy!

"Oooo fa! Niccolo," she said in frustration. "What do you think you're doing?

He looked up, surprised to see her. Caught in the act.

"Are you looking for a sign in there? Trying to divine the future in your stools, the way your ancient Romans did? Have you taken up augury now?"

"Something like that," he replied.

"Oh, and what do you see? What do the signs say?"

"The signs aren't good, Giuditta," he said seriously. "There's a lot of black blood in here."

Terrified by the oracle of the blood, Niccolo submitted willingly to the strict regime of diet and rest that Giuditta imposed upon him over the next week. Gradually, he felt his strength returning, and after a few days, even his careful scrutiny and constant vigilance were unable to turn up any more frightening surprises in the chamber pot.

Unable to endure the enforced idleness, especially with the energetic spirit of the new republic bursting forth all around him, Niccolo took it upon himself to return to public life. Strolling through the Piazza della Signoria, he stopped to watch a cheering crowd of revelers burn the pope in effigy. Although the likeness was not particularly exact or flattering, the papier-mâché tiara was unmistakable.

"Such a lack of respect for authority, don't you agree?" said a familiar, bored voice behind him.

"Messer Guicciardini!"

"Messer Machiavelli. I suppose you'll be throwing in your lot with this rabble?"

"How could I do otherwise? And what about you?"

"I'll be going into exile until things cool down. Apparently there's no great affection in the city for those of us who served the Medici."

"And your property?"

"A little damage to the facade of the palazzo, but nothing serious. If I leave town, they'll let me hold onto it."

"Somehow, that doesn't surprise me," said Niccolo good-naturedly. "Where will you go, Francesco?"

"South, to wait until they release the pope."

"And if they hang him?"

"I doubt they will. He's worth more to them alive than dead. But if they do . . ." Guicciardini shrugged, "There will be another pope."

"There will always be another pope. Eh, Francesco?" said Niccolo, laughing.

"I should think so," said Guicciardini matter-of-factly. "At any rate, I'm going now to eat, as they say, the bitter bread of exile."

"Why do I get the impression that it won't be all that bitter to you?"

"I hope not! The least a poor man can do in exile is eat well. Well, good-bye, Niccolo. Until we meet again."

"*Arrivederci*."

"And Niccolo, if you get something from this rabble, depending on how things turn out, you know, you might put in a good word for me, neh?"

"Of course, Francesco. Of course, I'll put in a good word for you."

Niccolo stood and watched the stately aristocrat walk across the piazza still shunning contact with the crowds, still looking down his nose at them, still acting as though he were the rightful lord and master of the city. Guicciardini had disappeared down a side street when Niccolo caught a glimpse of a small, angry man with a bundle darting in and out of the crowd. Michelangelo!

He had to hurry to catch up with him, and when he did, he saw the little artist was red-faced and fuming as usual. "*Salve*, Michelangelo!"

"Eh, Machiavelli. You're here," he said flatly.

"As are you."

"You ran out on me in Rome? What happened?"

"I found something I thought I had lost forever. It's a long story. I'll tell you about it later. But what brings you back to Florence?"

"Work. What else?"

"Still carving the Medici statues?" said Niccolo maliciously.

"Not much of a market for Medici statues anymore, is there?" said Michelangelo slyly.

"No there isn't," said Niccolo. "So what are you doing now?"

"First, this," he said indicating the bundle he was carrying. It was long and cylindrical and wrapped in heavy canvas.

"What's that?"

"An arm!"

"That's revolting."

"Haven't you heard the stories about how all artists are grave robbers?" he said, with his eyes twinkling now. "Let me show you." He started to unwind the cloth in which the arm was wrapped.

Niccolo turned pale and told him it wouldn't be necessary, but it was too late. "See," he said, exhibiting the severed limb.

To Niccolo's great relief, the arm was made of stone, and Michelangelo cackled with delight at his own joke. "The revolution has not been kind to my statue of David. When they started throwing furniture out of the Signoria, a bench or something struck his arm and knocked half of it off. Now I have to repair it."

"Of course, you'll be paid for your efforts," said Niccolo facetiously.

"Of course," said Michelangelo. "Aren't we always?"

"Are you going to stay in Florence now?"

"I have a commission from the new government—and a very important one at that."

Niccolo guessed, "What? A winged victory? Blind justice?"

"Better than that," said Michelangelo. "It's a little out of my line, but I'm going to fortify and rebuild the city walls."

"So you do have a soft spot for the republic under that crusty exterior, don't you?"

"I'm a Florentine, like you."

"So you are, Michelangelo," said Niccolo. "So you are."

When Niccolo finally reached the Signoria, he was set upon almost immediately by a mob of eager and determined young men: "Zanobi! Francesco! Giovan Battista! You're all back!"

"We couldn't ride fast enough, when we heard the news," said Zanobi. "It's good to be back, Magister." And they hugged, the old master and the students. "It's good to be back."

On the way to the tavern, Zanobi and the others talked excitedly, incessantly. They were bursting with news, full of reports—and each piece of information brought another surge of enthusiasm and contentment to the old master: "The government had been reconstituted along the same lines as in Soderini's days. . . . The empty Council Chamber was soon to be full of elected representatives. . . . And for the defense of the infant republic, the militia was to be reestablished!"

Everything that Niccolo had ever wanted. Everything he had hoped for and worked toward all his life. Everything. A free and independent Florence. There was much to celebrate that day when the old circle of the Orti Orcellari was reunited. And it was only toward the end of their long afternoon of reveling and carousing that Zanobi introduced a somber note into the conversation. "You heard about Michelozzi, didn't you?"

Niccolo stopped what he was saying. He had forgotten all about

Michelozzi. "What happened? I assumed he must have flown away long ago with the Little Sparrow and the Medici bastards."

"No, they weren't taking anybody with them. They left in the dead of night without telling a soul. Afraid of being discovered and brought to trial."

"And Michelozzi didn't follow?"

"They found him in the Medici Palace. He was dressed in Medici finery—the most exquisite there was—satin, gold, and jewels. He was dressed like a Medici lord. He hanged himself that way."

That night, Niccolo slept the sleep of the just. After so many years of confusion, dislocation, and disappointment, everything seemed finally to have fallen into place. Even the sad end of Michelozzi was, in the end, an act of justice. He had bargained for his thirty pieces of silver. He had taken them and enjoyed them. Finally, he must have realized at what price.

Niccolo moved closer to the sleeping Giuditta and nestled his nose in the nape of her neck, in her lightly perfumed hair. He kissed the back of her head. He wrapped his arms around her and squeezed. Everything.

The next morning found him in excellent spirits and hungry enough to consume several fat slabs of cured ham to break his diurnal fast. And cheese. And butter. And some sweet cakes. And pears. And a little white wine mixed with water. And a little more. He was about to start in on a black pudding when Giuditta stopped him: "Hey, greedy guts, what are you trying to do? Eat yourself into a stupor?"

Niccolo issued a few words of protest, muffled by food and incomprehensible.

"Will we be going to the country soon, Niccolo?" asked Giuditta. "I'd like to. It's starting to get sticky and uncomfortable here."

"Not just yet," he said wiping his chin with a voluminous cloth napkin. "There's too much going on. There's too much work to be done in the city. Besides . . ."

"Besides, what?"

"Besides, the Ten of War have been reconstituted and the militia. The Ten are going to need a secretary. The militia is going to need someone to superintend the reorganization, someone with experience," he said slyly. "You see what I mean?"

"Hmmm, someone with experience."

"And the chancellorship of the Second Chancery is open now that Michelozzi . . ."

"Maybe we can get away in July, then?"

"Maybe," said Niccolo noncommittally.

Giuditta sighed a sigh of resignation, "Didn't I tell you years ago that you loved your republic more than you loved me?"

"Don't be silly."

They were still at the table arguing the point when Zanobi Buondelmonte came in with the news. He talked excitedly, nervously. His hands were never still. "And the new gonfaloniere is Niccolo Capponi."

"I knew his father." Niccolo smiled to himself. He found it amusing that a man half his age was now gonfaloniere. Ah, youth!

"Everything's going to be the same, Magister. I even saw the documents for the militia ordinance being drawn up, and they're using the ones you drew up twenty years ago as a model. Using—nothing—they're copying them verbatim. I saw the old files. I recognized your handwriting."

Niccolo could scarcely conceal his satisfaction. He was Machiavelli of the militia again! His ideas were going to be given another chance, only this time they wouldn't make the same mistakes. This time they would do things right. No Don Michelettos, no corruption in the officers' ranks, more rigorous training . . . his mind was running on ahead with plans and projects and schemes.

Zanobi was watching his old master. He could almost hear the wheels of thought turning and whirring behind that blissful countenance. "Niccolo, there's something else." He was looking down at his own hands now, folding and unfolding.

"It wouldn't be the matter of a secretary for the Ten, would it?"

"They've already nominated a secretary, Niccolo." Zanobi bit his lip. "They're going to give the post to Francesco Tarugi."

Silence. "Francesco Tarugi?" Niccolo formed the syllables incredulously with his mouth. "Who is Francesco Tarugi?"

"He's a good man. He's young but he's capable—and . . . and committed. You'd like him."

"And I'm too old, is that it?"

Zanobi winced, and the hands worked faster and more furiously. "Magister, your name came up but . . . "

"But what?"

"But several of the new council members pointed out that you were . . . for the last several years . . ." He hesitated, then gulped and went on: ". . . that you were a servant of the . . . of the tyrants they had just expelled."

Niccolo's eyes widened. "Me? A servant of tyrants! I . . ."

Zanobi was quick to intervene with further explanations and rationalizations: "They said that you were tainted by association with the Medici, that you couldn't be trusted. They said you were a potential enemy of freedom and the republic."

Niccolo's mouth was moving, but no words were coming out. The idea was too absurd, too fantastic! Enemy of freedom! Enemy of the republic! When he spent his whole life! His whole life!

"They said that your relationship with Michelozzi was suspect, too, and that you may have even joined the Orti circle as his spy, to spy on us and report back to the Cardinal. . . ." Zanobi looked helpless and infinitely uncomfortable.

A Medici spy! Of all things, a Medici spy! As Niccolo listened to the charges that had been leveled against him, as he slowly came to realize how utterly ridiculous they were, how preposterous, how ludicrous, how farcical, how inane and misplaced and inaccurate . . . those long, thin lips started to curl up into their caustic, slippery, ironic smile. And he began to laugh. Even Niccolo Machiavelli, comic author, could never have contrived a situation so fraught with bitter, delicious irony. And so he laughed—from his belly, from the bottom of his heart.

Zanobi hazarded a grin when he saw the master laughing. At first he thought he might be coming unglued. But no, he recognized that devilish merriment in his eyes. And soon the two of them were laughing together, laughing at the absurdity of it all, tears rolling down their cheeks, choking with hysterical laughter, doubled over with laughter, laughing until it hurt. And then Niccolo suddenly stiffened and collapsed. Before Zanobi could reach him, he tumbled over onto the floor.

Before he even regained full consciousness, he was aware of the shooting pains in his bowels. His teeth were already clenched when his eyes finally opened. He was in bed and Giuditta was there. "What happened?"

"You had an attack. Don't worry. Rest. Here drink this, it will help you sleep."

"My . . . pills."

"You don't need the pills," she said petulantly, but indulgently. "Drink this, and sleep. You'll be alright."

But Niccolo was not alright. The next day he was unable to get out of bed. The day after, he could barely sit up and hold his head erect long enough to drink the draughts and broth Giuditta brought him. He became drowsy and lethargic. The only thing capable of penetrating that lethargy and arousing him was the stabbing in his stomach, the excruciating lightning bolts of pain that even Giuditta's elixirs could not entirely deaden and suppress.

When the pain subsided, he knew it had not gone away. He knew that his senses were being extinguished, that his body was failing. He knew that the pain was still there; he just couldn't feel it anymore. He asked Giuditta to send for a priest.

Niccolo opened his eyes, and a weak smile crossed his face. "I said to send for a priest and you brought Pagolo."

"Enough of your anticlericism," said Pagolo. "I'm as good a priest as any."

"Or as bad as any."

When Giuditta had withdrawn, Niccolo said, "Pagolo, you see that cabinet over there. In the top drawer. Get me my pills."

Pagolo complied.

"Water."

"Do those things do any good?"

"They can't hurt."

"What now, Niccolo?"

"Can't you see, I'm a dying man. I want to make my confession."

"Niccolo, I'm genuinely surprised. You of all people. Why this sudden interest in the sacraments and the consolations of Holy Mother Church?"

"It can't hurt?"

Pagolo raised his right arm. "*In nomine Patris et Filii et Spiritus Sanctus . . .*"

For several hours, he slipped in and out of consciousness. Zanobi and the others came to visit, and when he sent them on their way, he was laughing softly to himself as Savonarola had been laughing when

Niccolo left him on the night before his execution. The work would go on now. The torch had been passed to the next generation. He had done what he'd promised. It was up to them now.

"Giuditta . . ."

"I'm here, Niccolo.

"I . . . with you . . . I never . . ."

"It's alright."

"I thought I would have more time . . . for you. I'm sorry . . . things . . ."

"I know, Niccolo. Things have a way of sweeping us up, carrying us away."

"I wanted to . . . I really wanted to . . . as soon as things were settled . . . I've been so unfair . . ."

"It's alright, Niccolo. It's alright."

"Is it really?"

"Yes, Niccolo. Everything's alright. Everything."

Later that day, Niccolo Machiavelli, who had lived through so many storms and cataclysms, died at peace with himself, with Giuditta, with the world, and with his God. Everything he had worked for had come to pass. Finally. Everything.

Pagolo and Giuditta were sitting in the kitchen, talking fitfully and quietly.

"He never stopped, did he?" said Pagolo.

"Right up to the end, he was still mumbling about his republic and the barbarians and some promise he made."

"Was he happy?"

"I think so. He said that everything he ever wanted had come to pass. 'Everything.' That was his last word."

"The same obsession all the time with Niccolo. He could never get away from it. You'd think he would have taken the time for some tender word for you."

"He did. In his way. He said he was sorry for neglecting me, but things had just spun out of control, and there was never enough time, and there were so many important things to do."

"Did he go so far as to say he would have done it all differently if he had another chance?"

"Who would have believed him?" Giuditta sighed. "Well, he's at peace now. He can take a rest from his obsession."

"Don't be so sure."

"What do you mean?"

Pagolo eyed her warily. "Well, I suppose I can tell you. It wasn't really part of his confession."

"What wasn't?"

"Niccolo told me about a dream he had last night. He said he died, and an angel came for his soul. The angel took him and showed him a crowd of poor people, all shabbily dressed, in rags, hungry-looking, but seemingly very happy and contented. 'Who are these?' Niccolo asked the angel. And the angel replied, 'These are the blessed souls in paradise.' And he showed Niccolo an inscription that said, 'Blessed are the poor in spirit for theirs is the kingdom of heaven.'

"Then these people faded away and another group appeared, a much larger group. And they were arguing and fighting with one another, shouting and yelling. 'And these?' Niccolo asked. The angel said, 'Don't you recognize them? Look. There you can see Plato and Seneca and Plutarch. Tacitus. Livy. All the Greeks and Romans. All the pagan philosophers. These are the souls who are condemned to eternal damnation.'

"'And what are they doing?' Niccolo said in the dream.

"'They're arguing with one another.'

"'What about?'

"'About the things that the pagans were so adept at arguing: philosophy and politics and history.'

"Then both groups appeared at the same time, the sheep and the goats, the blessed on the right hand side, the damned on the left. And the angel said, 'Well, your decision?'" Pagolo stopped.

"And what did he decide?" said Giuditta. "In his dream."

"What do you think? He said he looked one last time at the blessed before he turned to go off to that other place, and he said he saw Fra Girolamo there, among the souls in paradise, waving good-bye to him and smiling like he knew and understood and had already forgiven him. And then Niccolo went down to join his Romans and enter into their infernal debates for all eternity."

Giuditta just smiled and shook her head. It was getting dark outside. After a while, she said, "Pagolo, who was Fra Girolamo?"

"Oh, that was a long time ago. You wouldn't know about that. Niccolo used to be friends with him. He was a heretic. And a madman."